THE WORLD'S CLASSICS

THE COUNTRY OF THE BLIND AND OTHER STORIES

MICHAEL SHERBORNE is Head of the English Department at Luton Sixth Form College. He is the author of *Modern Novelists: H. G. Wells*, written under his previous name, Michael Draper.

PATRICK PARRINDER, General Editor of H. G. Wells in World's Classics, is Professor of English at the University of Reading. He is the author of *H. G. Wells* (1970) and editor of *H. G. Wells: The Critical Heritage* (1972), and he has also written books on science fiction, literary criticism, James Joyce, and on contemporary fiction and literary theory. He is a vice-president of the H. G. Wells Society.

THE WORLD'S CLASSICS

H. G. WELLS

The Country of the Blind
and Other Stories

Edited with an Introduction by
MICHAEL SHERBORNE

New York

OXFORD UNIVERSITY PRESS

1996

Oxford University Press, Walton Street, Oxford OX2 6DP

Oxford New York
Athens Auckland Bangkok Bombay
Calcutta Cape Town Dar es Salaam Delhi
Florence Hong Kong Istanbul Karachi
Kuala Lumpur Madras Madrid Melbourne
Mexico City Nairobi Paris Singapore
Taipei Tokyo Toronto

and associated companies in
Berlin Ibadan

Oxford is a trade mark of Oxford University Press

Introduction, Note on the Text, Explanatory Notes
© Michael Sherborne 1996
Bibliography, Chronology, Preface
© Patrick Parrinder 1995

First published in the USA as a World's Classics paperback 1996

Library of Congress Cataloging-in-Publication Data
Wells, H. G. (Herbert George), 1866–1946.
The country of the blind and other stories / H. G. Wells ; edited
with an introduction by Michael Sherborne.
(The world's classics)
Includes bibliographical references
1. Science fiction, English. I. Sherborne, Michael. II. Title.
III. Series.
PR5772.S48 1996 823'.912—dc20 95-49945
ISBN 0-19-282827-4

1 3 5 7 9 10 8 6 4 2

Typeset by Graphicraft Typesetters Ltd., Hong Kong
Printed in Great Britain by
BPC Paperbacks Ltd.
Aylesbury, Bucks.

CONTENTS

ACKNOWLEDGEMENTS

I am grateful to the many members of the H. G. Wells Society who have assisted my appreciation of Wells's writings over the years and, more specifically, to those who offered information and advice for the present edition: J. R. Hammond, Sylvia Hardy, David Lake, David C. Smith, Leon Stover, and the general editor of the series, Patrick Parrinder. My good friend Iain Zaczek also gave valuable advice and encouragement. Above all, however, for her patience and support, I must thank my wife, Marianne.

MICHAEL SHERBORNE

BIOGRAPHICAL PREFACE

Herbert George Wells's early life was a struggle against social and physical disadvantages. He was born on 21 September 1866 in Bromley, Kent, where his father was an unsuccessful small shopkeeper. Joseph Wells was originally a gardener by trade, and it was while he was working at Uppark, a large country mansion on the Sussex Downs, that he met and courted Sarah Neal, a lady's maid. Joe Wells's one claim to fame lay in his brief career as a professional cricketer; in 1862, bowling for Kent against Sussex, he took four wickets in four balls, a feat that still stands in the record books.

Much of Wells's childhood was spent in the basement kitchen at Atlas House, as the shop was called. At the age of 7, he was laid up for several weeks with a broken leg and became an avid reader. A photograph taken in 1876 shows the smart, well-groomed 10-year-old sitting at a table with a book laid open in front of him. However, the family fortunes declined towards insolvency, and soon his school fees remained unpaid. When he was barely into his teens his mother left home to return to Uppark as resident housekeeper. The young 'Bertie' also left home to become a draper's apprentice, working a thirteen-hour day and sleeping in a dormitory with the other apprentices. Like his heroes Kipps and Mr Polly, he felt he was bound to the drapery trade for the rest of his life.

After two years at Hyde's Drapery Emporium in Southsea, Wells left his situation, using the threat of suicide to force his mother to release him from his apprenticeship. His talents had made an impression on Horace Byatt, the headmaster of Midhurst Grammar School near Uppark, who took him on as a student assistant, and encouraged him to take a series of examinations in elementary science. There was a new scheme for training science teachers, and, thanks to his examination successes, in 1884 Wells was awarded a government scholarship to study biology at the Normal School of Science (now Imperial College) in London. Here, in what was perhaps the most decisive encounter of his life, he became a pupil of T. H. Huxley, the friend of Charles Darwin and champion of Darwin's evolutionary theory.

When he became a science student, Wells had already undergone a strenuous process of self-education. At Uppark, on his infrequent visits, he would steal away from the servants' quarters to the library of the great country house. Arriving in London from the English provinces steeped in the writings of Plato, Swift, Voltaire, and Gibbon, Wells found in post-Darwinian science a continuation of the subversive rationalism of the Enlightenment. The settled Victorian age was cracking up: scientific and technological developments, and the doctrines of socialism to which he soon became committed, would surely determine the future.

Wells took a prominent part in student life, entertaining his contemporaries at the Debating Society and editing the college magazine (where the earliest version of *The Time Machine* was published). His experiences in the biology lab under Huxley fired his imagination for the rest of his life. But Huxley soon fell ill, and Wells chafed at the limitations of the other professors. Moving on to study physics and geology, he became discontented with the utilitarian, teacher-training ethos of the Normal School, and failed his final examination in 1887. Physically he was in bad shape; his grant of one guinea a week was barely enough to live on. After leaving college he spent a few weeks in his first teaching post before suffering an accident on the football field which left him with a lung haemorrhage and a crushed kidney. Thin, undernourished, and suspected of being tubercular, Wells was now fighting for his life.

The next dozen years were punctuated with a series of dangerous relapses. He returned to London as a science teacher, took his B.Sc., and worked as a tutor for the

University Correspondence College. His first book, the *Text-Book of Biology*, is a product of this period. In 1893, when chronic ill-health forced him to give up teaching, he found he could make a living as a journalist, reviewing fiction and drama, writing scientific and educational essays, and—most importantly—producing short stories and comic sketches for the London evening papers. The 1890s, as he later recalled, were a golden age for the writer of short fiction. The magazines which bought his short stories also serialized the longer 'scientific romances'—*The Time Machine, The Island of Doctor Moreau, The Invisible Man, The War of the Worlds*, and *The First Men in the Moon*—which soon flowed from his pen. The impact of these books was immediate. Hailed as a 'man of genius' on the strength of *The Time Machine* in 1895, by the end of the century his books were already being translated into several languages. Soon he was moving in literary circles and making intimate friendships with such fellow-writers as Arnold Bennett, Joseph Conrad, George Gissing, Henry James, and Bernard Shaw.

In 1898, after a final bout of ill-health, Wells moved to Sandgate, where he had a house built suitable for an invalid and overlooking the English Channel. Conrad, James, and Stephen Crane were among his neighbours on the Kent coast. He finished the first of his autobiographical novels, *Love and Mr Lewisham*, and as his health improved his thoughts turned to the social and political themes pursued in a long series of books beginning with *Anticipations, The Discovery of the Future*, and *A Modern Utopia*. To the imaginative depiction of the future in his scientific romances he now added a reputation for serious social prophecy. He first joined and then spectacularly quarrelled with the Fabian Society of Shaw and the Webbs, becoming a leading figure of the intellectual Left. By the end of the Edwardian decade he had written his comic masterpieces *Kipps* and *The History of Mr Polly*, as well as *Tono-Bungay* with its combination of fictive autobiography and a scathing, panoramic view of English society. Wells was coming to rival Hardy and Kipling as one of the most famous and prestigious writers of the English-speaking world. Yet he remained restless and troubled, and his career was soon to take another decisive turn.

After a brief first marriage he had settled down with Amy Catherine Robbins ('Jane'), with whom he had two sons. His marriage remained stable although he soon embarked on the long series of sexual relationships he was to describe in *H. G. Wells in Love*, the posthumous third volume of his autobiography. His brief liaison with a young Fabian led both to his suffrage novel *Ann Veronica* and to the birth of a daughter, Anna Jane. In 1912 Rebecca West, then a young journalist, scoffed at him as the 'old maid among novelists' in a review of his novel *Marriage*; Wells and West became lovers shortly afterwards and, all too soon, Rebecca gave birth to a son. These events not only caused an atmosphere of scandal but—together with his quarrel with the Fabians— suggested an outlet for his crusading instincts. After 1910 his main fictional vehicle was the 'discussion novel' or novel of ideas, a mixture of semi-autobiographical narrative with a series of treatises or dialogues about the state of the world and the changing conditions of male–female relationships.

The New Machiavelli was his first and best novel of this type. Among its successors the most notable was the best-selling *Mr Britling Sees It Through*, published at the height of the First World War. Wells had invented the slogan 'The War That Will End War', and he became increasingly concerned with peace-making and the setting up of a supranational authority to avoid future conflicts. He now returned quite explicitly to the role of an educator, writing a series of encyclopaedic textbooks beginning with the bestselling *Outline of History*. His concern with promoting world citizenship and the idea of a World State were reflected in the *Outline* and in campaigning manuals such as *The Open Conspiracy*. Characteristically, *The Outline of History* ends with a review of humanity's prospects in the twentieth century which includes one of Wells's most memorable sayings: 'Human history becomes more and more a race between education and catastrophe.'

With *The Outline of History* Wells reached the height of his fame. He met Lenin in 1920, and in 1934 he revisited Washington and Moscow for well-publicized conversations with Roosevelt and Stalin. His *Experiment in Autobiography*, which ends with an account of these meetings, sums up his political outlook under the heading 'The Idea of a Planned World'. But, as he entered his seventies, he found in the rise of Fascism a cruel and reactionary parody of his ideal of a new and rational world order. Wells reacted to the age of the dictators by committing himself more explicitly than he had done earlier to the values of liberal democracy and human rights. He became the leading spirit behind the Sankey Declaration of the Rights of Man, which influenced the setting up of the United Nations.

As the Second World War approached, he once again suspected that civilization was on the verge of destroying itself. In some of his later imaginative fables he returned to the haunting pessimism of his early scientific romances. (Following the coinage of the American magazine editor Hugo Gernsback, the romances were now becoming known as 'science fiction'.) In *The Shape of Things to Come*, which was filmed by Wells and Alexander Korda as *Things to Come*, Wells returned to the mode of the future history, portraying humanity's recovery from a devastating mid-twentieth-century war, which he had pioneered twenty years earlier in *The World Set Free* with its forecast of nuclear weapons.

Wells spent the Second World War in London, staying on throughout the bombing in his house overlooking Regent's Park. He compiled and published a D.Sc. thesis for London University, but failed in his lifelong ambition to become a Fellow of the Royal Society. His last book, *Mind at the End of Its Tether*, was black and despairing, though shortly before this he had expressed a far more resilient mood in *The Happy Turning*. In *Mind at the End of Its Tether*, he sums up the 'habitual interest' of his life as 'critical anticipation': 'Of everything he asks: "To what will this lead?"' Here the author of over 120 books and pamphlets was reaffirming the prophetic, speculative outlook that had been most strikingly expressed in his early science fiction, beginning with *The Time Machine* with its journey of thirty million years into the future.

Should Wells be summed up as an artist or a teacher, a journalist or a prophet? He was the first to admit that much of his writing had been careless, hurried, and repetitive, and that all of it had designs upon the reader. He has at least three different literary personalities, as a scientific romancer in the tradition of Swift, Mary Shelley, and Poe, a comic novelist who may be seen as a successor of Dickens, and an educator and social critic like Carlyle, William Morris, and Bernard Shaw. Whatever his weaknesses he was a great intellectual liberator, the prophet of an open rather than a closed society, and one of the most dazzling literary figures of a period when the agency of mass communication was still the printed word (though in later years Wells eagerly turned on occasion to cinema and radio). Describing himself as a 'conscious common man', he wrote tirelessly for ordinary people, and is one of the great exemplars of the democratic man of letters.

PATRICK PARRINDER

INTRODUCTION

Herbert George Wells is best remembered today for science fiction masterpieces like *The Time Machine* and *The War of the Worlds*. His short stories, which were produced during the same period, share the qualities which make those longer works so compelling. Among them are first-rate story-telling, audacious imagination, an even-handed mastery of comedy and horror, and, above all, the power through fantasy to open extraordinary, often subversive, perspectives on everyday human life.

Writing shorter fiction gave Wells the opportunity to experiment with what we might loosely call the 'formula' underlying all of his best work. Typically, some exotic phenomenon punctures everyday reality: a vampire plant, a drug which speeds up the human body, a door which offers access to a heavenly garden. Often the story begins with an apparently mundane situation—a shopping trip, a conversation in a bar, a meeting with a friend—possibly located in a real place, certainly supported by detailed description. By the time we realize where events are taking us, a retreat into incredulity has somehow become impossible. The narrator may tell us that the strange occurrences were not seen by him personally, that he very much doubts whether some of them happened at all, and that the only explanation for them which he has to offer is entirely implausible but, paradoxically, the sober disclaimers only add to the credibility of the tale. We have made our imaginative investment. We are no longer capable of questioning—only of reading on, agog.

For the central characters of Wells's stories, there is an equal chance that the outcome of exposure to the unknown will be comical or fatal. For the reader the result is sure to be entertaining. But its implications may also be disorientating. Images of light and darkness, windows and lenses,

xiii

hallucinations and dreams, suggest a world of competing realities in which an over-confident guide, like Nunez in the title story 'The Country of the Blind', may find his confidence to have been shockingly misplaced. Will the wonder drug tested in 'The New Accelerator' be a blessing to humanity or a curse? Is the out-of-body experience recounted in 'Under the Knife' a religious revelation or a hallucination caused by chloroform? There is no way of telling from the stories—any more, indeed, than there would be if we had lived through the events for ourselves. Although many of Wells's tales seem to imply a 'moral' of some kind, they cannot be resolved into anything as straightforward as fables or allegories. The Russian author Yevgeny Zamyatin concluded that the most satisfactory way of classifying Wells's scientific romances and short stories would be to label them 'urban fairy-tales', modern myths reflecting and calling into question the 'stone, asphalt, iron, petroleum, mechanical country . . . called twentieth-century London'.[1]

That Wells was able to build a breathtaking number of variations on this one, apparently simple, 'ground' shows the fertility of his imagination and the power of the underlying formula itself. One obvious source of that power comes from the time of composition, the turn of the nineteenth and twentieth centuries. A reaction against Victorianism was firmly under way by the 1890s. To enquiring minds, the established order had come to seem pompous and reactionary, ill-equipped to deal with the challenge of the new century. Radio, motor vehicles, aircraft, X-rays, and aspirin were making their first impact on the world while these stories were being written. Many people expected—correctly, as it turned out—that in the coming decades science would transform the world for good and ill, and that the alterations it caused would be linked with equally dramatic social upheavals.

---

[1] 'Herbert Wells', in Patrick Parrinder (ed.), *H. G. Wells: The Critical Heritage* (London and Boston: Routledge & Kegan Paul, 1972), 259.

Introduction

Already, working people were striking for a fairer share of
wealth and power, suffragettes campaigning for votes for
women, revolutionaries proclaiming the class system obsolete
and demanding radical new forms of political organization.
As someone who had risen from the lower ranks of society
and as a creative writer who was also a trained scientist,
Wells was uniquely placed to explore these anxieties. In time
he felt able to deal with such matters explicitly, in non-fictional
books with titles like *New Worlds for Old* (1908)—perhaps
most effectively of all in his best-selling *Outline of History*
(1920)—but in the earlier part of his career the sense of
living through a precarious era, spooked and intoxicated by
what might yet come to pass, already saturated his stories.
The young George Orwell's reaction on discovering Wells
is one which many readers must have shared: 'here was this
wonderful man who could tell you about the inhabitants of
the planets and the bottom of the sea, and who *knew* that the
future was not going to be what respectable people imagined.'[2]

Wells's best stories are more, however, than cultural time-
capsules. Their dramatic conflicts between the realistic and
the fantastic call to mind dichotomies which readers continue to recognize from their own experience: between childhood and adulthood, the inner life of the spirit and the outer
world of public pressures, religion and materialism, art and
science. The Argentinian author Jorge Luis Borges recognized this quality when he described Wells's early fictions
as 'symbolic of processes that are somehow inherent in all
human destinies'.[3] Similarly, one of Wells's most perceptive
critics, Bernard Bergonzi, has suggested that the early writings have an unacknowledged resemblance to the work of

[2] 'Wells, Hitler and the World State', in Sonia Orwell & Ian Angus (eds.),
The Collected Essays, Journalism and Letters of George Orwell, ii (London:
Secker & Warburg, and New York: Harcourt, Brace, 1968), 171.

[3] 'The First Wells', in Parrinder (ed.), *The Critical Heritage,* 331. See also
Valerie Shaw, *The Short Story: A Critical Introduction* (London and New
York: Longman, 1983), 205.

contemporaries from the *fin de siècle* era such as Wilde and Yeats. Wells, in his description, was 'a symbolic and mytho-poeic writer whose work has closer affinities to poetry than to the conventional realistic fiction of his time'.[4] Taken out of its original context, this statement seems excessive, but it does suggest something of the subject-matter and tone of Wells's most powerful work, and is perhaps less surprising when we think of the common ancestry of symbolist poetry and science fiction in the work of that eccentric American genius Edgar Allan Poe, an original from whom Wells was not slow to learn.

Wells's artistic aims in his tales are primarily intuitive. I do not mean by this that he was naïve or ignorant, but that in his earlier writing (all but one of the stories in the present volume date from before his fortieth birthday) he largely follows where his imagination leads:

I found that, taking almost anything as a starting-point and letting my thoughts play about it, there would presently come out of the darkness, in a manner quite inexplicable, some absurd or vivid little incident more or less relevant to that initial nucleus . . . I would discover I was peering into remote and mysterious worlds ruled by an order logical indeed but other than our common sanity.

(The quotation is from the original introduction to *The Country of the Blind, and Other Stories*, reprinted as Appendix 1 of the present volume.) To a large extent, Wells was able to fuse topical entertainment and symbolist parable, the journalistic and the poetic elements of his stories, because his writing was a natural outgrowth of his life. Through the interaction of the 'realistic' and the 'fantastic', he was able to explore a pattern of repression and liberation which he had experienced during his formative years.

Born into the lower middle class, Wells seemed destined

[4] *The Early H. G. Wells* (Manchester: Manchester University Press, and Toronto: Toronto University Press, 1961), 166.

to a life of menial work with limited rewards and prospects. After leaving school at 13, he passed his adolescent years in a series of unappealing jobs, the last and longest of which was as an apprentice in a drapery, or dry goods store. His feelings here are bluntly summed up by the drapery assistant Minton in the novel *Kipps* (1905): 'We're in a blessed drainpipe, and we've got to crawl along it till we die.'

Wells singularly declined to crawl. After a vigorous series of appeals to his parents, he managed to escape from the drapery and become a pupil-teacher at a school. A year later he won a state scholarship to the Normal School of Science in London, where he was able to explore the big city, read widely, and socialize with educated men and women. It was a far cry from working a dull thirteen-hour day, then reporting to the apprentices' dormitory in time for 'lights out' at half past ten. Wells had learned from personal experience that reality was not always as immovable as it seemed. The 'paper walls of everyday circumstance', as he calls them in his comic novel *The History of Mr Polly* (1910), 'those unsubstantial walls that hold so many of us securely prisoned from the cradle to the grave', could be torn apart by the combined power of will, vision, and social change. He especially associated his welcome deliverance with the rise of science, and it became his hope that the rapid development of knowledge and technology in the twentieth century would set everyone free from the chains of the past. It is hardly surprising, then, if many of his short stories depict the staid world of Victorian England being disrupted by shocking events, particularly events consequent upon scientific discoveries.

However, as the stories with their alternate openings-up and closings-in of circumstance might suggest, Wells's personal experience of change also had a strong negative dimension. At university he found himself to be at a disadvantage compared with students from more affluent families. More significantly, the scientific assignments which he was set by his tutors proved less attractive to him than reading literature, stirring up the debating society, and expressing himself in the college magazine. To his dismay, the outcome of his extracurricular adventures was that he failed to get a degree and had to turn for a living to teaching in cheap private schools. At one of them, a rowdy soccer match left him with kidney damage, and this, together with general ill health exacerbated by many years of poor living conditions and diet, made him a periodic invalid for over a decade. At this stage of his career the 'realistic' might seem to have decisively reasserted itself over the 'fantastic', but again Wells refused to accept his unsatisfactory lot in life. After a depressing period of recuperation, he resumed teaching, worked hard to get his degree, married his cousin, and became a successful correspondence course teacher and science journalist. In 1893 there came a further setback, however, which threatened an end to all his ambitions, when he suffered a near-fatal lung haemorrhage. Determined to make the most of whatever remained of his life, Wells made a desperate bid for fulfilment by running off with one of his students (later to become the second Mrs Wells) and launching himself as a professional writer.

The short stories were among the first fruits of this death-defying resolve and were written in what for their author must have been a time of mingled elation and despair. In the majority of them the topic of personal extinction is never far away. 'The Story of the Late Mr Elvesham', for example, conveys with grotesque verve the sense of injustice felt by a young man cut off before his time. 'Under the Knife' makes us feel clearly the apprehension of a patient awaiting surgery. Characteristically, Wells does not report his own experience in the fatalistic spirit of realism or naturalism, but uses it as the raw material for narratives which glory in the unexpected.

'A Slip under the Microscope' is unusual in offering an entirely downbeat account of its author's life as a student. In his later years Wells liked to boast of his scientific training, but this tale of humiliation and failure, at one level a rather self-pitying rewriting of the truth about his exam results, gives vivid expression to the resentment and the fear of rejection which he was normally at pains to conceal. The strains of Wells's social mobility may also be glimpsed in another comparatively realistic piece, 'The Jilting of Jane', where the upstart author, until recently living in sin and still struggling to make a living, boldly impersonates a comfortable member of the upper middle class, commenting patronizingly on the love-life of his servant. The complex ironies of this tale and its satire on social customs are, however, sketched very cautiously. Wells needed a more secure reputation and the length of a comic novel (specifically, *Kipps*) to come to terms fully with this kind of material. 'The Obliterated Man' is a much more imaginative, and by the same token far more successful, expression of Wells's discomfort in taking on new social roles. It is also a dramatization of one of his fundamental beliefs, that social reality is a set of conventions which with sufficient determination (something its hapless narrator entirely lacks) we can revolutionize. Wells thoroughly ridicules conformity in 'Miss Winchelsea's Heart', where snobbery, prejudice, and living by the rules bring their own punishment. In this story Wells makes a point of linking narrow-minded conservatism and the approach to culture which today we label the 'heritage industry', since both are determinedly backward-looking and generally supportive of class privilege.

Science, in contrast, seemed to be opening a door to worlds which had not yet been colonized by the forces of reaction. In 'The Crystal Egg', 'The New Accelerator', and 'The Remarkable Case of Davidson's Eyes' science allows us to see life from startling new perspectives. (It is an intriguing question, incidentally, whether the opium pills that Wells took after his haemorrhage contributed anything to his extraordinary capacity to visualize the fantastic. As his picture on the cover of the Beatles' album *Sgt. Pepper* testifies, some of his fiction might virtually be used as a hallucinogenic substitute.) The vision revealed by science is often a disorientating and threatening one, but this is no bad thing from Wells's point of view, as he relishes the opportunity to inflict imaginary destruction on the society which had caused him so much frustration. 'The Flowering of the Strange Orchid', 'The Sea Raiders', and, above all, 'The Star' combine menace and exhilaration in thrilling proportions.

The threats to the established order presented by Wells's stories are not only physical. 'The Star', first published at Christmas 1897, seems to be intended in part to parody the star of Bethlehem, while parodies of conventional religion feature unmistakably in 'The Lord of the Dynamos', 'Jimmy Goggles the God', and 'A Vision of Judgment'. Wells was fascinated by the cosmic imagery of the Bible and by the idea that this world might one day be swept away and replaced by a better one, but he could see no evidence that the human race had a privileged place in the Creation. Like many of the writers whom he had read and admired in his student days, Dickens and Blake among them, he was deeply influenced by Christian idealism, but was repelled by those authoritarian brands of religion which centre on a repressive father-figure extorting worship by threats of everlasting torture. Wells's fullest response to the nineteenth-century debate between evolutionary science and fundamentalist religion as competing explanations of life is *The Island of Doctor Moreau* (1896). In this uncompromising mixture of horror story and satire, a megalomaniac scientist attempts to turn animals into people by surgical methods, only to produce monsters which, while fearfully worshipping him, regress ever more deeply into sin. The short stories, somewhat less provocatively, make a point of debunking the pretensions of *Homo sapiens*, whether as scientist or priest, to understand and control human behaviour, let alone the universe. 'The Cone', in particular, is a strikingly unpleasant account of what can happen when animal passion breaks through the civilized Victorian façade.

Yet this descent into unrelieved horror is hardly typical of Wells. His temperament is not a tragic one, and in the short stories he has come not as a preacher of despair, but as a mischievous teller of tall tales. The whole world is destroyed by human folly in 'The Man who could Work Miracles', but a twist on the last page puts everything back as it was before. This good-natured exuberance may have been encouraged by Wells's need to please his public, but above all it reflects his joy in existence and, more particularly, in escaping from the draperies and schools in which society had once sought to imprison him. Elsewhere in his work, when he is more self-consciously serious in his intentions, Wells can seem at odds with himself; the artist and the propagandist pull in different directions. In the short stories he is happy to leave the deeper meanings to his intuition and get on with the job of spinning a good yarn. And here, of course, is the final reason for the power of the Wellsian 'formula'. The eruption of the unexpected offers a thousand opportunities for suspense, surprise, and irony. In the first fifteen years of his literary career, Wells was in the mood to make the most of these opportunities.

Consider 'The Story of the Late Mr Elvesham'. The opening phrase ('I set this story down, not expecting it will be believed') signals to us that we are venturing into Edgar Allan Poe territory and must expect a tale of strange, claustrophobic horror. The following lines lure us onwards by hinting at the narrator's 'fate', while the reference to the 'next victim' creates an additional element of suspense which is only resolved, and then in a highly unexpected way, in the very last paragraph.

Having secured our full attention, Wells supplies a biographical sketch of the protagonist, modelled on the opening lines of *Robinson Crusoe* and *Gulliver's Travels*, before revealing the central characters in action. Their personalities are deftly sketched (for example, Eden's embarrassment at his untidy room, and at the state of the shoes he is taking for repair, confirm his poverty and his impatient 'ambition to succeed in the world', a dangerous combination of which Elvesham quickly takes advantage). After two intriguing meetings, the story increases in intensity with the vivid descriptions of 'dissolving views', as two realities compete within Eden's dysfunctional brain. Gradually Eden awakens from the drug, and his slow realization of the truth, always one step behind the horrified reader, is unobtrusively accompanied by the light of dawn entering the room. Finally comes the abrupt change of narrator in the concluding paragraph and the perfectly judged 'punch-line'. At no point does Wells give us the opportunity to reflect critically on the fantastic element of the story, the proposition of 'man's detachability from matter', and in any case the conclusion leaves the credibility of Eden's narrative in dispute, giving us strictly limited room for disbelief. It is difficult to see how this story could have been developed more effectively.

The care Wells took over his writing may be seen at a more local level in the final paragraph of 'The Lord of the Dynamos'. In manuscript this reads, 'So ended prematurely the worship of the Dynamo Deity, probably the most short lived of all religions, after the sacrifice of two burnt offerings and a poor half dozen of prayers. Let us hope it may never be revived.' This is a merely adequate conclusion. The version Wells finally published replaces 'probably' with the more judicious-sounding 'perhaps', then scraps everything after 'religions'. Wells may on second thoughts have judged the phrase 'burnt offerings' offensively callous as a description of the two dead men, 'poor half dozen of prayers' rather more sympathetic in tone than he had intended, the use of 'us' too obvious a device for imposing the author's point of view on the reader, and the concluding fear of dynamo revivalism a forced attempt at humour.

The simple thirteen-word sentence which replaces all this makes its point with a droll finality which brings the story to a much more satisfactory close: 'Yet withal it could at least boast a Martyrdom and a Human Sacrifice.' The capitals which highlight 'Martyrdom' and 'Human Sacrifice' invite us to wonder how often in the past these grand abstractions have been used by the authorities to dignify meaningless violence; the archaic 'withal' parodies the loftiness of sacred texts; 'at least' implies a distinctly negative evaluation of the impact of religion; the almost subliminal personification of the dynamo cult as a boastful person clinches our reaction. In one short sentence Wells insinuates that traditional forms of religion may be irrational, dangerous, and out of place in the modern world, and does so not in a strident, confrontational manner, but with wry humour. The ending in manuscript and the published ending hardly differ at all in their paraphrasable content, and each passes through our minds in a matter of seconds, yet the rewriting makes all the difference to the final impact of the story.

For further examples of Wells's craftsmanship, consider the attention-grabbing opening of 'Jimmy Goggles the God'; the brilliant comic stroke in 'Miss Winchelsea's Heart' by which Snooks's name-change occurs *gradually*; the use in 'The Star' of many different points of view to build up a global perspective adequate to the scale of the action; how the calculated absence of conventional plot in tales like 'The Remarkable Case of Davidson's Eyes' and 'The Crystal Egg' allows the strangeness of the events to stand in their own right; the rapid but seemingly inevitable escalation from slapstick comedy to apocalypse in 'The Man who could Work Miracles'; the shift from scientific discourse to the rhythms and imagery of the King James Bible in 'Under the Knife'; even the concise description of an observatory's structure in the fourth paragraph of 'In the Avu Observatory'. Such sureness of touch can be found throughout this volume.

It is necessary to emphasize Wells's craftsmanship because there are still critics and teachers inclined to dismiss any writer who is popular, accessible, and fun to read. As Wells implies in his original introduction, he does not aspire to what we might call the 'highbrow' tradition of short-story writing, typified by such authors as Maupassant, Chekhov, and Joyce. A Wells story is not a highly polished and subtle object, difficult to grasp at first reading, requiring to be contemplated over a period of time. Instead, it recalls a spoken anecdote or a news item: improvised, colourful, doubtful in veracity, but also memorable, thought-provoking, and above all entertaining. Among Wells's literary ancestors are Poe, Hoffmann, the Arabian Nights, Gothic fiction, Nathaniel Hawthorne, and Robert Louis Stevenson; among his descendants, not only Zamyatin, Orwell, and Borges, but any number of popular writers marketed under the label 'science fiction'. Such widely different short stories as Frederik Pohl's satirical fable of mass society 'The Tunnel under the World' and J. G. Ballard's poetic vision 'The Illuminated Man' might equally be classified as Wellsian in approach.

As Wells himself notes, the 1890s was a decade remarkable for the quality of its short-story writers. Kipling, Hardy, Crane, Conan Doyle, Conrad, Stevenson, Bierce, and James are among the names from this period still familiar after a century. Wells belongs in their front rank and is especially notable for combining his mastery of fantasy with a fondness for the comic heritage of nineteenth-century British fiction, recalling Charles Dickens as well as his own contemporaries like W. W. Jacobs and Jerome K. Jerome.

Probably the writer closest to Wells in the world of short fiction, however, is Rudyard Kipling. Kipling, too, mixes racy comedy and disturbing fantasy, uses rather stereotypical lower-class characters, and mimics the delivery of the spoken anecdote. Again like Wells, he makes frequent use of framing narratives, where stories are related at second or third hand, apparently artlessly but often to complex effect, creating a kind of twilight region where events with different or even conflicting claims to credibility can freely mingle. Unlike Wells, Kipling believes that there are traditions, rules, and lore which are too important to be questioned because they provide a crucial stability in a world which is in danger of disintegration. Associated with that belief we often find a knowing, manipulative tone and sometimes the withholding of key information as if to enforce the writer's authority over the reader. For Wells, in contrast, fiction is half-playroom, half-laboratory, a public space where ideas and intuitions can be tried out, permutated, even tested to destruction, then the results made public for the reader to make of them whatever he or she pleases.

While Kipling wrote short stories throughout his career, Wells had virtually ceased by 1909, with thirty-five years of fiction still ahead of him. He did so because by the time the last of the stories in this volume was published, he had moved away from the role of entertainer and (in the 'Miss Winchelsea' sense, at least) literary artist. In 1912 he rejected a nomination for the prestigious Academic Committee of the Royal Society of Literature, mistrustful, as he informed Henry James, of 'controls or fixed standards' in the arts.[5] Literature, in Wells's view, was valuable because of its freedom to challenge and stimulate. Once authors were assimilated to the establishment and their work became subject to the standards of academic connoisseurs, much of their value was lost. At the same time, Wells was also becoming what we would now call a 'media celebrity', one whose views were as often expressed in articles and speeches as in story form. While it is a mistake to dismiss the fiction of the later Wells (*Mr Blettsworthy on Rampole Island*, from as late as 1928, for example, is an outstanding piece of work), it is true to say that the general reader will find his most essential works to be those written before the end of the Great War. Wells knew that what he had to say thereafter would normally require explicit argument and lengthy development. 'A short story should go to its point as a man flees from a

[5] Quoted in Norman and Jeanne MacKenzie, *The Time Traveller: The Life of H. G. Wells* (London: Weidenfeld & Nicolson, and New York: Simon & Schuster, 1973), 278.

pursuing tiger', he observed. But he was now a discursive writer whose mission was to make the novel 'the social mediator, the vehicle of understanding, the instrument of self-examination, the parade of morals and the exchange of manners, the factory of customs, the criticism of laws and institutions and of social dogmas and ideas'.[6] This is the Wells of *Tono-Bungay*, the Wells who influenced, among others, Upton Sinclair and Saul Bellow. Undoubtedly, this Wells is a great writer, and one deserving of much more attention than he has received, but he is not great in quite the same magical way as the author of 'The Crystal Egg' or 'The Truth about Pyecraft'.

With five uncollected short stories on his hands, Wells decided to round off this phase of his writing by compiling a selection of his best pieces. His choice of what to include in *The Country of the Blind, and Other Stories* leaves little room for complaint. All the major stories are here, together with the majority of his really good ones, and a sprinkling of lesser ones for variety. Since the volume opens with some of these lesser items, newcomers may wish to turn straight to one of the most outstanding, 'Under the Knife', 'The Star', 'The Man who could Work Miracles', 'The Door in the Wall', or even 'The Country of the Blind' itself.

That Wells chose to name the whole collection after this piece suggests he rated it very highly, and justifiably so, for here he achieves what may well be his most perfect balance of the realistic and the fantastic. The fantasy derives from the 'parable of the cave' which opens book 7 of Plato's *Republic*, a work which Wells first read in his teens and from which he drew lifelong inspiration. Plato represents ordinary people as

---

[6] H. G. Wells, 'The Contemporary Novel', originally pub. in *An Englishman Looks at the World* (London: Cassell, 1914), pub. in the USA as *Social Forces in England and America* (New York: Harper, 1914); repr., abr., in Patrick Parrinder and Robert M. Philmus (eds.), *H. G. Wells's Literary Criticism* (Brighton: Harvester, and Totowa, NJ: Barnes & Noble, 1980), 192–215.

prisoners bound in a cave, able to see nothing but shadows cast on a wall whenever objects are passed in front of a fire behind them. The philosopher, seeking after truth, frees himself from his bonds, turns away from the blank wall, and goes in search of a greater reality. Unfortunately, when he returns with news of what he has found, he stumbles in the darkness and is mocked as a fool by those who remain trapped in their limited perceptions.

In Wells's story Nunez, a mountain guide, falls into a South American valley inhabited by blind people. At first he assumes that the possession of eyesight will enable him to rule over them, but in the outcome he is cruelly disappointed. The blind people take him to be subhuman and eventually decide that, for his own good, they must surgically remove those 'irritant bodies', his eyes. Nunez finally escapes to the freedom of the mountains, where he apparently meets a welcome death.

Summarized, the two stories have a strong resemblance: a lone visionary is rejected by a society which fails to appreciate his perception. To read the two stories, however, is to experience a profound contrast. Plato deals in simple images of light and darkness, and accordingly produces crude generalizations about truth and falsehood. Wells's more realistic treatment fruitfully complicates the issue by making us see people, objects, and events in their own right, as well as in their symbolic aspect: 'the little details of the rocks', the tender pressure of Medina-saroté's hand, the 'palaces and fountains and statues and white houses', remembrance of which lures Nunez back towards the world outside the valley. While we have an overriding sympathy for Nunez in his struggle for understanding and respect, it is none the less evident to us that the blind people live in a stable, contented society. The reign of King Nunez would bring considerably more benefit to him than to them, and might actually do them harm. 'The Country of the Blind' powerfully dramatizes the tyranny of the majority over the individual, but equally it shows the gifted individual tempted by conceit and by fantasies of power. Plato's parable is an idea with an illustration; 'The Country of the Blind' is a rich literary experience, in which each reader will find a slightly different significance, and which will mean something slightly different to us each time we return to it. T. S. Eliot described it as 'quite unforgettable'.[7]

It would have been interesting to have heard Eliot's view of the revised version which Wells produced thirty-five years later. In the revision, Nunez succeeds in escaping from the valley with his blind sweetheart, while behind them the remainder of her people perish in a huge landslide. Nunez had tried to warn them of the danger, only to be scorned. Bearing in mind the publication date of 1939, one needs little prompting to realize that the landslide parallels the coming of the Second World War. Nunez himself has become a surrogate for Wells, bitter that his two decades of propaganda against reactionary thinking and in favour of supranational organization had been answered by the rise of totalitarianism and the failure of the League of Nations to end nationalist warfare. While we may sympathize with Wells's frustration, there can be little doubt that artistically the revision is a step backwards toward the self-serving allegory of Plato. Since the revised 'Country of the Blind' has so rarely been reprinted, and affords a fascinating opportunity to compare the attitudes of Wells at 38 and 73 years of age, it is included here as Appendix 2.

Wells tells us, in his introduction, that *The Country of the Blind, and Other Stories* should be 'dipped in and dipped in again', rather than 'read severely through'. This is sound advice. It is also the case, however, that like 'The Door in the Wall', once this book has been opened and entered, it will not easily be closed, and these short stories may lead you to Wells's science fiction, which in turn may lead you to the comic novels, to the social novels, the autobiography, the

[7] 'Wells as Journalist', in Parrinder (ed.), *The Critical Heritage*, 320.

world histories, the essays . . . It would be gratifying to think that, for some readers at least, this 'miscellany of inventions' will offer not only first-rate entertainment, but also an introduction to one of the most thought-provoking and inspiring figures in modern literature.

NOTE ON THE TEXT

The majority of Wells's short stories first appeared in journals. For convenience, the details of their original publication have been incorporated in the Explanatory Notes at the end of this volume.

Wells collected most of his short stories in the following four books, sometimes revising the texts as he did so:

The Stolen Bacillus, and Other Incidents (London: Methuen, 1895)
The Plattner Story, and Others (London: Methuen, 1897)
Tales of Space and Time (London: Harper, 1900)
Twelve Stories and a Dream (London: Macmillan, 1903).

The first two collections did not appear in the USA. Instead, some of the stories from those volumes, plus three other tales otherwise uncollected, were issued under the title *Thirty Strange Stories* (New York: Arnold, 1897). This book has inferior texts and a higher incidence of typographical errors than its British counterparts.

Wells wrote few stories after *Twelve Stories and a Dream*. Eventually five were combined with twenty-eight from the previous four volumes to make up *The Country of the Blind, and Other Stories* (London: Nelson, 1911). Wells again revised the texts, making no drastic alterations, but consistently improving small details: for example, correcting misprints, removing awkward verbal repetitions, and clarifying ambiguities.

In the same year as *The Country of the Blind, and Other Stories*, Wells compiled a much briefer selection of his short stories, which was published in a limited edition, with photographic illustrations by Alvin Langdon Coburn: *The Door in the Wall, and Other Stories* (New York: Mitchell Kennerley, 1911). Of 600 copies, sixty were still available four years later to be imported and reissued as a British edition by the publisher Grant Richards. *The Door in the Wall, and Other Stories* shares seven of its eight tales with *The Country of the Blind, and Other Stories*, but does not incorporate the improvements made in the latter edition.

Thirteen years passed before Wells again turned his attention to the short stories. Then between 1924 and 1927 there appeared, in a limited edition of 1,670 sets, each signed by the author, an Atlantic Edition entitled *The Works of H. G. Wells* (London: T. Fisher Unwin; New York: Charles Scribner's Sons). Five of the twenty-eight volumes contain short stories. In all thirty-one stories are included, twenty-eight of them from *The Country of the Blind, and Other Stories*. These are based on the latter's texts, but contain a number of minor revisions and corrections, together with some new misprints.

In Wells's lifetime the short stories were reprinted in cheaper editions of his works (notably the Essex edition of 1926–7, published in London by Ernest Benn) and in *The Short Stories of H. G. Wells* (London: Ernest Benn, 1927), as well as in numerous magazines. These reprints invariably follow an earlier text. Their extremely rare deviations from those texts do not seem to have any authority from Wells.

The present edition of *The Country of the Blind and Other Stories* follows the Nelson edition of 1911, but accepts twenty corrections which are listed below, followed in each case by the original wording. With one exception, these corrections are taken from other texts authorized by Wells himself. The exception is 'euphemism', a word which is confused with 'euphuism' elsewhere in his work.

p. 17 rhythmic]   rhymthic
p. 19 then,']   then,
p. 65 Bellows']   Bellow's
p. 108 leading questions]   leading question
p. 111 Kümmel]   Kummel

p. 126 a butcher-boy's]   the butcher-boy's

p. 152 G.R.S., G.B.S., G.A.S.]   G.A.S., G.B.S., G.R.S.

p. 178 strange-lit]   strange lit

pp. 207–8 Wedderburn the eye specialist]   Wedderburn, the
eye specialist

p. 208 hunch back]   hunchback

p. 220 shifted the slip]   shifted the slips

p. 290 bit.]   bit."

p. 292 I tell you!]   I tell you?
Niggers!]   Niggers?

p. 298 missionaries close to]   missionary close to

p. 310 intellectual]   intellecual

p. 340 so be it!]   so be it?

p. 387 euphemism]   euphuism

p. 405 mission.]   mission,

p. 439 an even climate]   and even climate

SELECT BIBLIOGRAPHY

The most engaging and informative account of H. G. Wells's life and work is still his own *Experiment in Autobiography* (2 vols., London and New York, 1934). This may be supplemented by two excellent modern scholarly biographies, *The Time Traveller: The Life of H. G. Wells* by Norman and Jeanne MacKenzie (London and New York, 1973; revised edn., London, 1987) and *H. G. Wells: Desperately Mortal* by David C. Smith (New Haven and London, 1986). For a general guide to Wells's fiction see *An H. G. Wells Companion* by J. R. Hammond (London and New York, 1979). *H. G. Wells* by Michael Draper (Basingstoke and New York, 1987) is a general critical study.

For a collection of critical responses to Wells's writings during his lifetime see *H. G. Wells: The Critical Heritage*, ed. Patrick Parrinder (London and Boston, 1972). There are selections of more recent criticism in *H. G. Wells: A Collection of Critical Essays*, ed. Bernard Bergonzi (Englewood Cliffs, NJ, 1976), and *Critical Essays on H. G. Wells*, ed. John Huntington (Boston, 1991). The H. G. Wells Society publishes an annual journal, *The Wellsian*, as well as a *Comprehensive Bibliography* of Wells's writings (4th edn., London, 1986).

Bernard Bergonzi's study *The Early H. G. Wells* (Manchester and Toronto, 1961) contains some highly influential critical analysis of the short stories. For a more comprehensive account, see J. R. Hammond, *H. G. Wells and the Short Story* (Basingstoke and New York, 1992). J. R. Hammond has also edited H. G. Wells's *The Man with a Nose, and Other Uncollected Short Stories* (London, 1984). Wells's place in the tradition of the short story is discussed by H. E. Bates, *The Modern Short Story: A Critical Survey* (London, 1941) and Valerie Shaw, *The Short Story: A Critical Introduction* (London and New York, 1983).

A CHRONOLOGY OF H. G. WELLS

1866   21 Sept.: Herbert George Wells born at Bromley, Kent, England, the third son of a small shopkeeper.

1874–80 Attends Morley's Commercial Academy, Bromley.

1880   Wells's mother becomes housekeeper at Uppark. He works as a draper at Messrs Rodgers and Denyer, Windsor, but is dismissed after two months.

1880–1 Temporary posts in a school at Wookey, Somerset, and in a chemist's shop at Midhurst, Sussex.

1881   Feb.–Mar.: pupil at Midhurst Grammar School. May: starts work at Hyde's Drapery Emporium, Southsea, where he signs articles of apprenticeship in June.

1883   July: leaves his post in the drapery. Sept.: becomes student assistant at Midhurst Grammar School.

1884   Sept.: enters the Normal School of Science, South Kensington, to study biology under T. H. Huxley on a government scholarship.

1885   Success in first-year exams leads to renewal of scholarship. Sept.: studies physics under Professor Guthrie. Active in Debating Society.

1886   Studies geology under Professor Judd. Dec.: becomes founding editor of *Science Schools Journal*.

1887   June: leaves South Kensington without a degree. July: assistant at Holt Academy, Wrexham, North Wales. 30 Aug.: footballing accident leads to a crushed kidney and a lung haemorrhage. Nov.: returns to Uppark.

1888   Apr.–June: 'The Chronic Argonauts' serialized in *Science Schools Journal*.

1889   Jan.: assistant at Henley House School, Kilburn.

1890   B.Sc., University of London. Tutor at University Correspondence College, London.

1891   31 Oct.: marries his cousin, Isabel Mary Wells.

1893   17 May: recurrence of illness forces him to give up teaching. *Text-Book of Biology* published. Dec.: leaves Isabel to live with his student Amy Catherine Robbins.

1895   Publishes *Select Conversations with an Uncle, The Time Machine, The Wonderful Visit,* and *The Stolen Bacillus* (short stories). Jan.–May: drama critic for *Pall Mall Gazette.* May: moves to Woking, Surrey. 27 Oct.: marries Amy Catherine ('Jane').

1895–7 Chief fiction reviewer for *Saturday Review.*

1896   *The Island of Doctor Moreau* and *The Wheels of Chance* published. Moves to Worcester Park, Surrey.

1897   *The Invisible Man* published.

1898   Jan.: *The War of the Worlds* published. Mar.–Apr.: visits Rome in the company of George Gissing. Aug.: taken ill on holiday at Seaford. Advised not to return to Worcester Park. Sept.: moves to Sandgate, Kent.

1899   *When the Sleeper Wakes* published.

1900   *Love and Mr Lewisham* published. Dec.: moves into Spade House, Sandgate, designed by C. F. A. Voysey.

1901   Son, George Philip ('Gip'), born. Publishes *The First Men in the Moon* and *Anticipations.*

1902   Jan.: lectures on *The Discovery of the Future* at the Royal Institution.

1903   *Mankind in the Making* published. Son, Frank Richard, born. Joins Fabian Society.

1904   *The Food of the Gods* published.

1905   *A Modern Utopia* and *Kipps* published.

1906   Jan.: launches campaign to change Fabian Society constitution. Mar.–May: first visit to United States. *In the Days of the Comet* and *The Future in America* published.

1908   *New Worlds for Old, The War in the Air,* and *First and Last Things* published. Sept.: resigns from Fabian Society.

1909   *Tono-Bungay* and *Ann Veronica* published. Moves to Church Row, Hampstead. Dec.: daughter, Anna Jane, born to Amber Reeves after her marriage to G. R. Blanco-White.

1910   *The History of Mr Polly* published.

1911   *The New Machiavelli* and *The Country of the Blind, and Other Stories* published. Moves to Easton Glebe, Dunmow, Essex.

1912   *Marriage* published.

1913   *The Passionate Friends* published.

1914   Aug.: son, Anthony, born to Rebecca West. *The World Set Free, The Wife of Sir Isaac Harman*, and *The War That Will End War* published.

1915   *Boon, Bealby*, and *The Research Magnificent* published.

1916   *Mr Britling Sees It Through* published.

1917   *God the Invisible King* and *The Soul of a Bishop* published.

1918   *Joan and Peter* published.

1919   *The Undying Fire* published.

1920   Oct.: visits Russia and meets Lenin. *The Outline of History* and *Russia in the Shadows* published.

1922   *The Secret Places of the Heart* and *A Short History of the World* published.

1923   *Men Like Gods* published. Sept.: sets up house at Grasse, Alpes-Maritimes, with Odette Keun. Ends relationship with Rebecca West.

1924   *The Dream* published.

1924–7 *The Atlantic Edition of the Works of H. G. Wells* (28 volumes with prefaces by Wells) published.

1925   *Christina Alberta's Father* published.

1926   *The World of William Clissold* published.

1927   *Complete Short Stories* published. 6 Oct.: death of 'Jane' Wells.

1928   *The Open Conspiracy* and *Mr Blettsworthy on Rampole Island* published.

1930   *The Autocracy of Mr Parham* and *The Science of Life* published. Moves to London from Easton Glebe.

1931   *The Work, Wealth and Happiness of Mankind* published.

1932   *After Democracy* and *The Bulpington of Blup* published.

1933   Ends relationship with Odette Keun and abandons house at Grasse. *The Shape of Things to Come* published.

1934   Interviews Stalin and Roosevelt. *Experiment in Autobiography* published.

1935   Moves to his last home at Hanover Terrace, London.

1936   Feb.: film, *Things to Come*, premiered in London. *The Croquet Player* published.

1937   *Star Begotten* and *Brynhild* published.

1938   *World Brain* and *Apropos of Dolores* published. Dec.: visits Australia.

1939   *The Holy Terror* and *The New World Order* published.

1940   *The Rights of Man* and *Babes in the Darkling Wood* published.

1941   *You Can't Be Too Careful* published.

1942   *Phoenix* and *The Conquest of Time* published. D.Sc., University of London.

1943   *Crux Ansata* published.

1945   *The Happy Turning* and *Mind at the End of Its Tether* published.

1946   13 Aug.: dies in his house at Hanover Terrace.

THE COUNTRY
OF THE BLIND
and Other Stories

CONTENTS

Contents

I

THE JILTING OF JANE

As I sit writing in my study, I can hear our Jane bumping her way downstairs with a brush and dust-pan. She used in the old days to sing hymn tunes, or the British national song for the time being, to these instruments, but latterly she has been silent and even careful over her work. Time was when I prayed with fervour for such silence, and my wife with sighs for such care, but now they have come we are not so glad as we might have anticipated we should be. Indeed, I would rejoice secretly, though it may be unmanly weakness to admit it, even to hear Jane sing 'Daisy,'* or, by the fracture of any plate but one of Euphemia's best green ones, to learn that the period of brooding has come to an end.

Yet how we longed to hear the last of Jane's young man before we heard the last of him! Jane was always very free with her conversation to my wife, and discoursed admirably in the kitchen on a variety of topics—so well, indeed, that I sometimes left my study door open—our house is a small one—to partake of it. But after William came, it was always William, nothing but William; William this and William that; and when we thought William was worked out and exhausted altogether, then William all over again. The engagement lasted altogether three years; yet how she got introduced to William, and so became thus saturated with him, was always a secret. For my part, I believe it was at the street corner where the Rev. Barnabas Baux used to hold an open-air service after evensong on Sundays. Young Cupids were wont to flit like moths round the paraffin flare of that centre of High Church hymn-singing. I fancy she stood singing hymns there, out of memory and her imagination, instead of coming home to get supper, and William came up beside her and said, 'Hello!'

5

'Hello yourself!' she said; and etiquette being satisfied, they proceeded to talk together.

As Euphemia has a reprehensible way of letting her servants talk to her, she soon heard of him. 'He is *such* a respectable young man, ma'am,' said Jane, 'you don't know.' Ignoring the slur cast on her acquaintance, my wife inquired further about this William.

'He is second porter at Maynard's, the draper's,' said Jane, 'and gets eighteen shillings—nearly a pound—a week, m'm; and when the head porter leaves he will be head porter. His relatives are quite superior people, m'm. Not labouring people at all. His father was a greengrosher, m'm, and had a chumor, and he was bankrup' twice. And one of his sisters is in a Home for the Dying. It will be a very good match for me, m'm,' said Jane, 'me being an orphan girl.'

'Then you are engaged to him?' asked my wife.

'Not engaged, ma'am; but he is saving money to buy a ring—hammyfist.'

'Well, Jane, when you are properly engaged to him you may ask him round here on Sunday afternoons, and have tea with him in the kitchen;' for my Euphemia has a motherly conception of her duty towards her maid-servants. And presently the amethystine ring was being worn about the house, even with ostentation, and Jane developed a new way of bringing in the joint so that this gage* was evident. The elder Miss Maitland was aggrieved by it, and told my wife that servants ought not to wear rings. But my wife looked it up in *Enquire Within* and *Mrs Motherly's Book of Household Management*,* and found no prohibition. So Jane remained with this happiness added to her love.

The treasure of Jane's heart appeared to me to be what respectable people call a very deserving young man. 'William, ma'am,' said Jane one day suddenly, with ill-concealed complacency, as she counted out the beer bottles, 'William, ma'am, is a teetotaller. Yes, m'm; and he don't smoke. Smoking, ma'am,' said Jane, as one who reads the heart, '*do* make such a dust about. Beside the waste of money. *And* the smell. However, I suppose they got to do it—some of them . . .'

William was at first a rather shabby young man of the ready-made black coat school of costume. He had watery gray eyes, and a complexion appropriate to the brother of one in a Home for the Dying. Euphemia did not fancy him very much, even at the beginning. His eminent respectability was vouched for by an alpaca umbrella, from which he never allowed himself to be parted.

'He goes to chapel,' said Jane. 'His papa, ma'am——'

'His *what*, Jane?'

'His papa, ma'am, was Church; but Mr Maynard is a Plymouth Brother,* and William thinks it Policy, ma'am, to go there too. Mr Maynard comes and talks to him quite friendly when they ain't busy, about using up all the ends of string, and about his soul. He takes a lot of notice, do Mr Maynard, of William, and the way he saves his soul, ma'am.'

Presently we heard that the head porter at Maynard's had left, and that William was head porter at twenty-three shillings a week. 'He is really kind of over the man who drives the van,' said Jane, 'and him married, with three children.' And she promised in the pride of her heart to make interest for us with William to favour us so that we might get our parcels of drapery from Maynard's with exceptional promptitude.

After this promotion a rapidly-increasing prosperity came upon Jane's young man. One day we learned that Mr Maynard had given William a book. ' "Smiles' 'Elp Yourself," * it's called,' said Jane; 'but it ain't comic. It tells you how to get on in the world, and some what William read to me was *lovely*, ma'am.'

Euphemia told me of this, laughing, and then she became suddenly grave. 'Do you know, dear,' she said, 'Jane said one thing I did not like. She had been quiet for a minute, and then she suddenly remarked, "William is a lot above me, ma'am, ain't he?"'

7

'I don't see anything in that,' I said, though later my eyes were to be opened.

One Sunday afternoon about that time I was sitting at my writing-desk—possibly I was reading a good book—when a something went by the window. I heard a startled exclamation behind me, and saw Euphemia with her hands clasped together and her eyes dilated. 'George,' she said in an awe-stricken whisper, 'did you see?'

Then we both spoke to one another at the same moment, slowly and solemnly: '*A silk hat! Yellow gloves! A new umbrella!*'

'It may be my fancy, dear,' said Euphemia; 'but his tie was very like yours. I believe Jane keeps him in ties. She told me a little while ago, in a way that implied volumes about the rest of your costume, "The master *do* wear pretty ties, ma'am." And he echoes all your novelties.'

The young couple passed our window again on their way to their customary walk. They were arm in arm. Jane looked exquisitely proud, happy, and uncomfortable, with new white cotton gloves, and William, in the silk hat, singularly genteel!

That was the culmination of Jane's happiness. When she returned, 'Mr Maynard has been talking to William, ma'am,' she said, 'and he is to serve customers, just like the young shop gentlemen, during the next sale. And if he gets on, he is to be made an assistant, ma'am, at the first opportunity. He has got to be as gentlemanly as he can, ma'am; and if he ain't, ma'am, he says it won't be for want of trying. Mr Maynard has took a great fancy to him.'

'He *is* getting on, Jane,' said my wife.

'Yes, ma'am,' said Jane thoughtfully; 'he *is* getting on.'

And she sighed.

That next Sunday as I drank my tea I interrogated my wife. 'How is this Sunday different from all other Sundays, little woman? What has happened? Have you altered the curtains, or re-arranged the furniture, or where is the indefinable difference of it? Are you wearing your hair in a new way without warning me? I perceive a change clearly, and I cannot for the life of me say what it is.'

Then my wife answered in her most tragic voice, 'George,' she said, 'that William has not come near the place to-day! And Jane is crying her heart out upstairs.'

There followed a period of silence. Jane, as I have said, stopped singing about the house, and began to care for our brittle possessions, which struck my wife as being a very sad sign indeed. The next Sunday, and the next, Jane asked to go out, 'to walk with William,' and my wife, who never attempts to extort confidences, gave her permission, and asked no questions. On each occasion Jane came back looking flushed and very determined. At last one day she became communicative.

'William is being led away,' she remarked abruptly, with a catching of the breath, apropos of tablecloths. 'Yes, m'm. She is a milliner, and she can play on the piano.'

'I thought,' said my wife, 'that you went out with him on Sunday.'

'Not out with him, m'm—after him. I walked along by the side of them, and told her he was engaged to me.'

'Dear me, Jane, did you? What did they do?'

'Took no more notice of me than if I was dirt. So I told her she should suffer for it.'

'It could not have been a very agreeable walk, Jane.'

'Not for no parties, ma'am.'

'I wish,' said Jane, 'I could play the piano, ma'am. But anyhow, I don't mean to let *her* get him away from me. She's older than him, and her hair ain't gold to the roots, ma'am.'

It was on the August Bank Holiday that the crisis came. We do not clearly know the details of the fray, but only such fragments as poor Jane let fall. She came home dusty, excited, and with her heart hot within her.

The milliner's mother, the milliner, and William had made a party to the Art Museum at South Kensington, I think. Anyhow, Jane had calmly but firmly accosted them somewhere in the streets, and asserted her right to what, in spite of the consensus of literature, she held to be her inalienable property. She did, I think, go so far as to lay hands on him. They dealt with her in a crushingly superior way. They 'called a cab.' There was a 'scene,' William being pulled away into the four-wheeler by his future wife and mother-in-law from the reluctant hands of our discarded Jane. There were threats of giving her 'in charge.'

'My poor Jane!' said my wife, mincing veal as though she was mincing William. 'It's a shame of them. I would think no more of him. He is not worthy of you.'

'No, m'm,' said Jane. 'He *is* weak.'

'But it's that woman has done it,' said Jane. She was never known to bring herself to pronounce 'that woman's' name or to admit her girlishness. 'I can't think what minds some women must have—to try and get a girl's young man away from her. But there, it only hurts to talk about it,' said Jane.

Thereafter our house rested from William. But there was something in the manner of Jane's scrubbing the front door-step or sweeping out the rooms, a certain viciousness, that persuaded me that the story had not yet ended.

'Please, m'm, may I go and see a wedding to-morrow?' said Jane one day.

My wife knew by instinct whose wedding. 'Do you think it is wise, Jane?' she said.

'I would like to see the last of him,' said Jane.

'My dear,' said my wife, fluttering into my room about twenty minutes after Jane had started, 'Jane has been to the boot-hole and taken all the left-off boots and shoes, and gone off to the wedding with them in a bag. Surely she cannot mean——'

'Jane,' I said, 'is developing character. Let us hope for the best.'

Jane came back with a pale, hard face. All the boots seemed to be still in her bag, at which my wife heaved a premature sigh of relief. We heard her go upstairs and replace the boots with considerable emphasis.

'Quite a crowd at the wedding, ma'am,' she said presently, in a purely conversational style, sitting in our little kitchen, and scrubbing the potatoes; 'and such a lovely day for them.' She proceeded to numerous other details, clearly avoiding some cardinal incident.

'It was all extremely respectable and nice, ma'am; but *her* father didn't wear a black coat, and looked quite out of place, ma'am. Mr Piddingquirk——'

'*Who?*'

'Mr Piddingquirk—William that was, ma'am—had white gloves, and a coat like a clergyman, and a lovely chrysanthemum. He looked so nice, ma'am. And there was red carpet down, just like for gentlefolks. And they say he gave the clerk four shillings, ma'am. It was a real kerridge they had—not a fly.* When they came out of church there was rice-throwing, and her two little sisters dropping dead flowers. And someone threw a slipper, and then I threw a boot——'

'Threw a *boot*, Jane!'

'Yes, ma'am. Aimed at her. But it hit *him*. Yes, ma'am, hard. Gev him a black eye, I should think. I only threw that one. I hadn't the heart to try again. All the little boys cheered when it hit him.'

After an interval—'I am sorry the boot hit *him*.'

Another pause. The potatoes were being scrubbed violently. 'He always *was* a bit above me, you know, ma'am. And he was led away.'

The potatoes were more than finished. Jane rose sharply with a sigh, and rapped the basin down on the table.

'I don't care,' she said. 'I don't care a rap. He will find out his mistake yet. It serves me right. I was stuck up about him. I ought not to have looked so high. And I am glad things are as things are.'

My wife was in the kitchen, seeing to the higher cookery. After the confession of the boot-throwing, she must have watched poor Jane fuming with a certain dismay in those brown eyes of hers. But I imagine they softened again very quickly, and then Jane's must have met them.

'Oh, ma'am,' said Jane, with an astonishing change of note, 'think of all that *might* have been! Oh, ma'am, I *could* have been so happy! I ought to have known, but I didn't know. . . . You're very kind to let me talk to you, ma'am . . . for it's hard on me, ma'am . . . it's har-r-r-d——'

And I gather that Euphemia so far forgot herself as to let Jane sob out some of the fullness of her heart on a sympathetic shoulder. My Euphemia, thank Heaven, has never properly grasped the importance of 'keeping up her position.' And since that fit of weeping, much of the accent of bitterness has gone out of Jane's scrubbing and brush work.

Indeed, something passed the other day with the butcher-boy—but that scarcely belongs to this story. However, Jane is young still, and time and change are at work with her. We all have our sorrows, but I do not believe very much in the existence of sorrows that never heal.

II

THE CONE

THE night was hot and overcast, the sky red-rimmed with the lingering sunset of midsummer. They sat at the open window, trying to fancy the air was fresher there. The trees and shrubs of the garden stood stiff and dark; beyond in the roadway a gas-lamp burnt, bright orange against the hazy blue of the evening. Farther were the three lights of the railway signal against the lowering sky. The man and woman spoke to one another in low tones.

'He does not suspect?' said the man, a little nervously.

'Not he,' she said peevishly, as though that too irritated her. 'He thinks of nothing but the works and the prices of fuel. He has no imagination, no poetry.'

'None of these men of iron have,' he said sententiously. 'They have no hearts.'

'*He* has not,' she said. She turned her discontented face towards the window. The distant sound of a roaring and rushing drew nearer and grew in volume; the house quivered; one heard the metallic rattle of the tender. As the train passed, there was a glare of light above the cutting and a driving tumult of smoke; one, two, three, four, five, six, seven, eight black oblongs—eight trucks—passed across the dim grey of the embankment, and were suddenly extinguished one by one in the throat of the tunnel, which, with the last, seemed to swallow down train, smoke, and sound in one abrupt gulp.

'This country was all fresh and beautiful once,' he said; 'and now—it is Gehenna.* Down that way—nothing but pot-banks* and chimneys belching fire and dust into the face of heaven. . . . But what does it matter? An end comes, an end to all this cruelty. . . . *To-morrow.*' He spoke the last word in a whisper.

13

'*To-morrow*,' she said, speaking in a whisper too, and still staring out of the window.

'Dear!' he said, putting his hand on hers.

She turned with a start, and their eyes searched one another's. Hers softened to his gaze. 'My dear one!' she said, and then: 'It seems so strange—that you should have come into my life like this—to open——' She paused.

'To open?' he said.

'All this wonderful world'—she hesitated, and spoke still more softly—'this world of *love* to me.'

Then suddenly the door clicked and closed. They turned their heads, and he started violently back. In the shadow of the room stood a great shadowy figure—silent. They saw the face dimly in the half-light, with unexpressive dark patches under the pent-house brows. Every muscle in Raut's body suddenly became tense. When could the door have opened? What had he heard? Had he heard all? What had he seen? A tumult of questions.

The new-comer's voice came at last, after a pause that seemed interminable. 'Well?' he said.

'I was afraid I had missed you, Horrocks,' said the man at the window, gripping the window-ledge with his hand. His voice was unsteady.

The clumsy figure of Horrocks came forward out of the shadow. He made no answer to Raut's remark. For a moment he stood above them.

The woman's heart was cold within her. 'I told Mr Raut it was just possible you might come back,' she said in a voice that never quivered.

Horrocks, still silent, sat down abruptly in the chair by her little work-table. His big hands were clenched; one saw now the fire of his eyes under the shadow of his brows. He was trying to get his breath. His eyes went from the woman he had trusted to the friend he had trusted, and then back to the woman.

By this time and for the moment all three half understood

14

one another. Yet none dared say a word to ease the pent-up
things that choked them.

It was the husband's voice that broke the silence at last.

'You wanted to see me?' he said to Raut.

Raut started as he spoke. 'I came to see you,' he said,
resolved to lie to the last.

'Yes,' said Horrocks.

'You promised,' said Raut, 'to show me some fine effects
of moonlight and smoke.'

'I promised to show you some fine effects of moonlight
and smoke,' repeated Horrocks in a colourless voice.

'And I thought I might catch you to-night before you went
down to the works,' proceeded Raut, 'and come with you.'

There was another pause. Did the man mean to take the
thing coolly? Did he, after all, know? How long had he been
in the room? Yet even at the moment when they heard the
door, their attitudes . . . Horrocks glanced at the profile of
the woman, shadowy pallid in the half-light. Then he glanced
at Raut, and seemed to recover himself suddenly. 'Of course,'
he said, 'I promised to show you the works under their proper
dramatic conditions. It's odd how I could have forgotten.'

'If I am troubling you——' began Raut.

Horrocks started again. A new light had suddenly come
into the sultry gloom of his eyes. 'Not in the least,' he said.

'Have you been telling Mr Raut of all these contrasts of
flame and shadow you think so splendid?' said the woman,
turning now to her husband for the first time, her confidence
creeping back again, her voice just one half-note too high—
'that dreadful theory of yours that machinery is beautiful,
and everything else in the world ugly. I thought he would not
spare you, Mr Raut. It's his great theory, his one discovery in
art.'

'I am slow to make discoveries,' said Horrocks grimly,
damping her suddenly. 'But what I discover . . .' He stopped.

'Well?' she said.

'Nothing;' and suddenly he rose to his feet.

'I promised to show you the works,' he said to Raut, and put his big, clumsy hand on his friend's shoulder. 'And you are ready to go?'

'Quite,' said Raut, and stood up also.

There was another pause. Each of them peered through the indistinctness of the dusk at the other two. Horrocks' hand still rested on Raut's shoulder. Raut half fancied still that the incident was trivial after all. But Mrs Horrocks knew her husband better, knew that grim quiet in his voice, and the confusion in her mind took a vague shape of physical evil. 'Very well,' said Horrocks, and, dropping his hand, turned towards the door.

'My hat?' Raut looked round in the half-light.

'That's my work-basket,' said Mrs Horrocks with a gust of hysterical laughter. Their hands came together on the back of the chair. 'Here it is!' he said. She had an impulse to warn him in an undertone, but she could not frame a word. 'Don't go!' and 'Beware of him!' struggled in her mind, and the swift moment passed.

'Got it?' said Horrocks, standing with the door half open.

Raut stepped towards him. 'Better say good-bye to Mrs Horrocks,' said the ironmaster, even more grimly quiet in his tone than before.

Raut started and turned. 'Good-evening, Mrs Horrocks,' he said, and their hands touched.

Horrocks held the door open with a ceremonial politeness unusual in him towards men. Raut went out, and then, after a wordless look at her, her husband followed. She stood motionless while Raut's light footfall and her husband's heavy tread, like bass and treble, passed down the passage together. The front door slammed heavily. She went to the window, moving slowly, and stood watching, leaning forward. The two men appeared for a moment at the gateway in the road, passed under the street lamp, and were hidden by the black masses of the shrubbery. The lamplight fell for a moment on their faces, showing only unmeaning pale patches, telling nothing of what she still feared, and doubted, and craved vainly to know. Then she sank down into a crouching attitude in the big arm-chair, her eyes wide open and staring out at the red lights from the furnaces that flickered in the sky. An hour after she was still there, her attitude scarcely changed.

The oppressive stillness of the evening weighed heavily upon Raut. They went side by side down the road in silence, and in silence turned into the cinder-made by-way that presently opened out the prospect of the valley.

A blue haze, half dust, half mist, touched the long valley with mystery. Beyond were Hanley and Etruria,* grey and dark masses, outlined thinly by the rare golden dots of the street lamps, and here and there a gas-lit window, or the yellow glare of some late-working factory or crowded public-house. Out of the masses, clear and slender against the evening sky, rose a multitude of tall chimneys, many of them reeking, a few smokeless during a season of 'play.' Here and there a pallid patch and ghostly stunted beehive shapes showed the position of a pot-bank* or a wheel, black and sharp against the hot lower sky, marked some colliery where they raise the iridescent coal of the place. Nearer at hand was the broad stretch of railway, and half-invisible trains shunted—a steady puffing and rumbling, with every run a ringing concussion and a rhythmic series of impacts, and a passage of intermittent puffs of white steam across the further view. And to the left, between the railway and the dark mass of the low hill beyond, dominating the whole view, colossal, inky-black, and crowned with smoke and fitful flames, stood the great cylinders of the Jeddah Company Blast Furnaces, the central edifices of the big ironworks* of which Horrocks was the manager. They stood heavy and threatening, full of an incessant turmoil of flames and seething molten iron, and about the feet of them rattled the rolling-mills, and the steam-hammer beat heavily and splashed the white iron sparks hither and thither. Even as they looked, a truckful of fuel was shot into one of the giants, and the red flames gleamed out, and a confusion of smoke and black dust came boiling upwards towards the sky.

'Certainly you get some colour with your furnaces,' said Raut, breaking a silence that had become apprehensive.

Horrocks grunted. He stood with his hands in his pockets, frowning down at the dim steaming railway and the busy ironworks beyond, frowning as if he were thinking out some knotty problem.

Raut glanced at him and away again. 'At present your moonlight effect is hardly ripe,' he continued, looking upward; 'the moon is still smothered by the vestiges of daylight.'

Horrocks stared at him with the expression of a man who has suddenly awakened. 'Vestiges of daylight? . . . Of course, of course.' He too looked up at the moon, pale still in the midsummer sky. 'Come along,' he said suddenly, and gripping Raut's arm in his hand, made a move towards the path that dropped from them to the railway.

Raut hung back. Their eyes met and saw a thousand things in a moment that their lips came near to say. Horrocks's hand tightened and then relaxed. He let go, and before Raut was aware of it, they were arm in arm, and walking, one unwillingly enough, down the path.

'You see the fine effect of the railway signals towards Burslem,'* said Horrocks, suddenly breaking into loquacity, striding fast and tightening the grip of his elbow the while— 'little green lights and red and white lights, all against the haze. You have an eye for effect, Raut. It's fine. And look at those furnaces of mine, how they rise upon us as we come down the hill. That to the right is my pet—seventy feet of him. I packed him myself, and he's boiled away cheerfully with iron in his guts for five long years. I've a particular fancy for *him*. That line of red there—a lovely bit of warm orange you'd call it, Raut—that's the puddlers' furnaces,* and there, in the hot light, three black figures—did you see the white splash of the steam-hammer then?—that's the rolling mills.

Come along! Clang, clatter, how it goes rattling across the floor! Sheet tin, Raut,—amazing stuff. Glass mirrors are not in it when that stuff comes from the mill. And, squelch! there goes the hammer again. Come along!'

He had to stop talking to catch at his breath. His arm twisted into Raut's with benumbing tightness. He had come striding down the black path towards the railway as though he was possessed. Raut had not spoken a word, had simply hung back against Horrocks's pull with all his strength.

'I say,' he said now, laughing nervously, but with an undertone of snarl in his voice, 'why on earth are you nipping my arm off, Horrocks, and dragging me along like this?'

At length Horrocks released him. His manner changed again. 'Nipping your arm off?' he said. 'Sorry. But it's you taught me the trick of walking in that friendly way.'

'You haven't learnt the refinements of it yet then,' said Raut, laughing artificially again. 'By Jove! I'm black and blue.' Horrocks offered no apology. They stood now near the bottom of the hill, close to the fence that bordered the railway. The ironworks had grown larger and spread out with their approach. They looked up to the blast furnaces now instead of down; the further view of Etruria and Hanley had dropped out of sight with their descent. Before them, by the stile, rose a notice-board, bearing, still dimly visible, the words, 'BEWARE OF THE TRAINS,' half hidden by splashes of coaly mud.

'Fine effects,' said Horrocks, waving his arm. 'Here comes a train. The puffs of smoke, the orange glare, the round eye of light in front of it, the melodious rattle. Fine effects! But these furnaces of mine used to be finer, before we shoved cones in their throats, and saved the gas.'

'How?' said Raut. 'Cones?'

'Cones, my man, cones. I'll show you one nearer. The flames used to flare out of the open throats, great—what is it?—pillars of cloud by day, red and black smoke, and pillars of fire by night.* Now we run it off in pipes, and burn it to heat the blast, and the top is shut by a cone. You'll be interested in that cone.'

'But every now and then,' said Raut, 'you get a burst of fire and smoke up there.'

'The cone's not fixed, it's hung by a chain from a lever, and balanced by an equipoise. You shall see it nearer. Else, of course, there'd be no way of getting fuel into the thing. Every now and then the cone dips, and out comes the flare.'

'I see,' said Raut. He looked over his shoulder. 'The moon gets brighter,' he said.

'Come along,' said Horrocks abruptly, gripping his shoulder again, and moving him suddenly towards the railway crossing. And then came one of those swift incidents, vivid, but so rapid that they leave one doubtful and reeling. Half-way across, Horrocks's hand suddenly clenched upon him like a vice, and swung him backward and through a half-turn, so that he looked up the line. And there a chain of lamp-lit carriage windows telescoped swiftly as it came towards them, and the red and yellow lights of an engine grew larger and larger, rushing down upon them. As he grasped what this meant, he turned his face to Horrocks, and pushed with all his strength against the arm that held him back between the rails. The struggle did not last a moment. Just as certain as it was that Horrocks held him there, so certain was it that he had been violently lugged out of danger.

'Out of the way,' said Horrocks with a gasp, as the train came rattling by, and they stood panting by the gate into the ironworks.

'I did not see it coming,' said Raut, still, even in spite of his own apprehensions, trying to keep up an appearance of ordinary intercourse.

Horrocks answered with a grunt. 'The cone,' he said, and then, as one who recovers himself, 'I thought you did not hear.'

'I didn't,' said Raut.

'I wouldn't have had you run over then for the world,' said Horrocks.

'For a moment I lost my nerve,' said Raut.

Horrocks stood for half a minute, then turned abruptly towards the ironworks again. 'See how fine these great mounds of mine, these clinker-heaps,* look in the night! That truck yonder, up above there! Up it goes, and out-tilts the slag. See the palpitating red stuff go sliding down the slope. As we get nearer, the heap rises up and cuts the blast furnaces. See the quiver up above the big one. Not that way! This way, between the heaps. That goes to the puddling furnaces, but I want to show you the canal first.' He came and took Raut by the elbow, and so they went along side by side. Raut answered Horrocks vaguely. What, he asked himself, had really happened on the line? Was he deluding himself with his own fancies, or had Horrocks actually held him back in the way of the train? Had he just been within an ace of being murdered?

Suppose this slouching, scowling monster *did* know anything? For a minute or two then Raut was really afraid for his life, but the mood passed as he reasoned with himself. After all, Horrocks might have heard nothing. At any rate, he had pulled him out of the way in time. His odd manner might be due to the mere vague jealousy he had shown once before. He was talking now of the ash-heaps and the canal. 'Eigh?' said Horrocks.

'What?' said Raut. 'Rather! The haze in the moonlight. Fine!'

'Our canal,' said Horrocks, stopping suddenly. 'Our canal by moonlight and firelight is immense. You've never seen it? Fancy that! You've spent too many of your evenings philandering up in Newcastle* there. I tell you, for real florid quality—— But you shall see. Boiling water . . .'

As they came out of the labyrinth of clinker-heaps and mounds of coal and ore, the noises of the rolling-mill sprang upon them suddenly, loud, near, and distinct. Three shadowy workmen went by and touched their caps to Horrocks. Their faces were vague in the darkness. Raut felt a futile impulse to address them, and before he could frame his words they passed into the shadows. Horrocks pointed to the canal close before them now: a weird-looking place it seemed, in the blood-red reflections of the furnaces. The hot water that cooled the tuyères* came into it, some fifty yards up—a tumultuous, almost boiling affluent,* and the steam rose up from the water in silent white wisps and streaks, wrapping damply about them, an incessant succession of ghosts coming up from the black and red eddies, a white uprising that made the head swim. The shining black tower of the larger blast-furnace rose overhead out of the mist, and its tumultuous riot filled their ears. Raut kept away from the edge of the water, and watched Horrocks.

'Here it is red,' said Horrocks, 'blood-red vapour as red and hot as sin; but yonder there, where the moonlight falls on it, and it drives across the clinker-heaps, it is as white as death.'

Raut turned his head for a moment, and then came back hastily to his watch on Horrocks. 'Come along to the rolling-mills,' said Horrocks. The threatening hold was not so evident that time, and Raut felt a little reassured. But all the same, what on earth did Horrocks mean about 'white as death' and 'red as sin'? Coincidence, perhaps?

They went and stood behind the puddlers for a little while, and then through the rolling-mills, where amidst an incessant din the deliberate steam-hammer beat the juice out of the succulent iron, and black, half-naked Titans* rushed the plastic bars, like hot sealing-wax, between the wheels. 'Come on,' said Horrocks in Raut's ear; and they went and peeped through the little glass hole behind the tuyères, and saw the tumbled fire writhing in the pit of the blast-furnace. It left one eye blinded for a while. Then, with green and blue patches dancing across the dark, they went to the lift by which the trucks of ore and fuel and lime were raised to the top of the big cylinder.

And out upon the narrow rail that overhung the furnace Raut's doubts came upon him again. Was it wise to be here? If Horrocks did know—everything! Do what he would, he could not resist a violent trembling. Right under foot was a sheer depth of seventy feet. It was a dangerous place. They pushed by a truck of fuel to get to the railing that crowned the thing. The reek of the furnace, a sulphurous vapour streaked with pungent bitterness, seemed to make the distant hillside of Hanley quiver. The moon was riding out now from among a drift of clouds, half-way up the sky above the undulating wooded outlines of Newcastle. The steaming canal ran away from below them under an indistinct bridge, and vanished into the dim haze of the flat fields towards Burslem.

'That's the cone I've been telling you of,' shouted Horrocks; 'and, below that, sixty feet of fire and molten metal, with the air of the blast frothing through it like gas in soda-water.'

Raut gripped the hand-rail tightly, and stared down at the cone. The heat was intense. The boiling of the iron and the tumult of the blast made a thunderous accompaniment to Horrocks's voice. But the thing had to be gone through now. Perhaps, after all . . .

'In the middle,' bawled Horrocks, 'temperature near a thousand degrees. If *you* were dropped into it . . . flash into flame like a pinch of gunpowder in a candle. Put your hand out and feel the heat of his breath. Why, even up here I've seen the rain-water boiling off the trucks. And that cone there. It's a damned sight too hot for roasting cakes. The top side of it's three hundred degrees.'

'Three hundred degrees!' said Raut.

'Three hundred centigrade, mind!' said Horrocks. 'It will boil the blood out of you in no time.'

'Eigh?' said Raut, and turned.

'Boil the blood out of you in . . . No, you don't!'

'Let me go!' screamed Raut. 'Let go my arm!'

With one hand he clutched at the hand-rail, then with both. For a moment the two men stood swaying. Then suddenly, with a violent jerk, Horrocks had twisted him from his hold. He clutched at Horrocks and missed, his foot went back into empty air; in mid-air he twisted himself, and then cheek and shoulder and knee struck the hot cone together.

He clutched the chain by which the cone hung, and the thing sank an infinitesimal amount as he struck it. A circle of glowing red appeared about him, and a tongue of flame, released from the chaos within, flickered up towards him. An intense pain assailed him at the knees, and he could smell the singeing of his hands. He raised himself to his feet, and tried to climb up the chain, and then something struck his head. Black and shining with the moonlight, the throat of the furnace rose about him.

Horrocks, he saw, stood above him by one of the trucks of fuel on the rail. The gesticulating figure was bright and white in the moonlight, and shouting, 'Fizzle, you fool! Fizzle, you hunter of women! You hot-blooded hound! Boil! boil! boil!'

Suddenly he caught up a handful of coal out of the truck, and flung it deliberately, lump after lump, at Raut.

'Horrocks!' cried Raut. 'Horrocks!'

He clung, crying, to the chain, pulling himself up from the burning of the cone. Each missile Horrocks flung hit him. His clothes charred and glowed, and as he struggled the cone dropped, and a rush of hot, suffocating gas whooped out and burned round him in a swift breath of flame.

His human likeness departed from him. When the momentary red had passed, Horrocks saw a charred, blackened figure, its head streaked with blood, still clutching and fumbling with the chain, and writhing in agony—a cindery animal, an inhuman, monstrous creature that began a sobbing, intermittent shriek.

Abruptly at the sight the ironmaster's anger passed. A deadly sickness came upon him. The heavy odour of burning flesh came drifting up to his nostrils. His sanity returned to him.

'God have mercy upon me!' he cried. 'O God! what have I done?'

He knew the thing below him, save that it still moved and felt, was already a dead man—that the blood of the poor wretch must be boiling in his veins. An intense realisation of that agony came to his mind, and overcame every other feeling. For a moment he stood irresolute, and then, turning to the truck, he hastily tilted its contents upon the struggling thing that had once been a man. The mass fell with a thud, and went radiating over the cone. With the thud the shriek ended, and a boiling confusion of smoke, dust, and flame came rushing up towards him. As it passed, he saw the cone clear again.

Then he staggered back, and stood trembling, clinging to the rail with both hands. His lips moved, but no words came to them.

Down below was the sound of voices and running steps. The clangour of rolling in the shed ceased abruptly.

III

THE STOLEN BACILLUS

'THIS again,' said the Bacteriologist, slipping a glass slide under the microscope, 'is well,—a preparation of the Bacillus of cholera—the cholera germ.'

The pale-faced man peered down the microscope. He was evidently not accustomed to that kind of thing, and held a limp white hand over his disengaged eye. 'I see very little,' he said.

'Touch this screw,' said the Bacteriologist; 'perhaps the microscope is out of focus for you. Eyes vary so much. Just the fraction of a turn this way or that.'

'Ah! now I see,' said the visitor. 'Not so very much to see after all. Little streaks and shreds of pink. And yet those little particles, those mere atomies, might multiply and devastate a city! Wonderful!'

He stood up, and releasing the glass slip from the microscope, held it in his hand towards the window. 'Scarcely visible,' he said, scrutinising the preparation. He hesitated. 'Are these—alive? Are they dangerous now?'

'Those have been stained and killed,' said the Bacteriologist. 'I wish, for my own part, we could kill and stain every one of them in the universe.'

'I suppose,' the pale man said, with a slight smile, 'that you scarcely care to have such things about you in the living—in the active state?'

'On the contrary, we are obliged to,' said the Bacteriologist. 'Here, for instance——' He walked across the room and took up one of several sealed tubes. 'Here is the living thing. This is a cultivation of the actual living disease bacteria.' He hesitated. 'Bottled cholera, so to speak.'

A slight gleam of satisfaction appeared momentarily in the

face of the pale man. 'It's a deadly thing to have in your possession,' he said, devouring the little tube with his eyes. The Bacteriologist watched the morbid pleasure in his visitor's expression. This man, who had visited him that afternoon with a note of introduction from an old friend, interested him from the very contrast of their dispositions. The lank black hair and deep grey eyes, the haggard expression and nervous manner, the fitful yet keen interest of his visitor were a novel change from the phlegmatic deliberations of the ordinary scientific worker with whom the Bacteriologist chiefly associated. It was perhaps natural, with a hearer evidently so impressionable to the lethal nature of his topic, to take the most effective aspect of the matter.

He held the tube in his hand thoughtfully. 'Yes, here is the pestilence imprisoned. Only break such a little tube as this into a supply of drinking-water, say to these minute particles of life that one must needs stain and examine with the highest powers of the microscope even to see, and that one can neither smell nor taste—say to them, "Go forth, increase and multiply,* and replenish the cisterns," and death—mysterious, untraceable death, death swift and terrible, death full of pain and indignity—would be released upon this city, and go hither and thither seeking his victims. Here he would take the husband from the wife, here the child from its mother, here the statesman from his duty, and here the toiler from his trouble. He would follow the water-mains, creeping along streets, picking out and punishing a house here and a house there where they did not boil their drinking-water, creeping into the wells of the mineral water makers, getting washed into salad, and lying dormant in ices. He would wait ready to be drunk in the horse-troughs, and by unwary children in the public fountains. He would soak into the soil, to reappear in springs and wells at a thousand unexpected places. Once start him at the water supply, and before we could ring him in, and catch him again, he would have decimated the metropolis.'

He stopped abruptly. He had been told rhetoric was his weakness.

'But he is quite safe here, you know—quite safe.'

The pale-faced man nodded. His eyes shone. He cleared his throat. 'These Anarchist—rascals,' said he, 'are fools, blind fools—to use bombs when this kind of thing is attainable. I think——'

A gentle rap, a mere light touch of the finger-nails, was heard at the door. The Bacteriologist opened it. 'Just a minute, dear,' whispered his wife.

When he re-entered the laboratory his visitor was looking at his watch. 'I had no idea I had wasted an hour of your time,' he said. 'Twelve minutes to four. I ought to have left here by half-past three. But your things were really too interesting. No, positively I cannot stop a moment longer. I have an engagement at four.'

He passed out of the room reiterating his thanks, and the Bacteriologist accompanied him to the door, and then returned thoughtfully along the passage to his laboratory. He was musing on the ethnology of his visitor. Certainly the man was not a Teutonic type nor a common Latin one. 'A morbid product, anyhow, I am afraid,' said the Bacteriologist to himself. 'How he gloated over those cultivations of disease germs!' A disturbing thought struck him. He turned to the bench by the vapour bath, and then very quickly to his writing-table. Then he felt hastily in his pockets and then rushed to the door. 'I may have put it down on the hall table,' he said.

'Minnie!' he shouted hoarsely in the hall.

'Yes, dear,' came a remote voice.

'Had I anything in my hand when I spoke to you, dear, just now?'

Pause.

'Nothing, dear, because I remember——'

'Blue ruin!' cried the Bacteriologist, and incontinently ran to the front door and down the steps of his house to the street.

28

Minnie, hearing the door slam violently, ran in alarm to the window. Down the street a slender man was getting into a cab. The Bacteriologist, hatless, and in his carpet slippers, was running and gesticulating wildly towards this group. One slipper came off, but he did not wait for it. 'He has gone *mad*!' said Minnie; 'it's that horrid science of his'; and, opening the window, would have called after him. The slender man, suddenly glancing round, seemed struck with the same idea of mental disorder. He pointed hastily to the Bacteriologist, said something to the cabman, the apron of the cab slammed, the whip swished, the horse's feet clattered, and in a moment cab and Bacteriologist hotly in pursuit, had receded up the vista of the roadway and disappeared round the corner.

Minnie remained straining out of the window for a minute. Then she drew her head back into the room again. She was dumbfounded. 'Of course he is eccentric,' she meditated. 'But running about London—in the height of the season,* too—in his socks!' A happy thought struck her. She hastily put her bonnet on, seized his shoes, went into the hall, took down his hat and light overcoat from the pegs, emerged upon the doorstep, and hailed a cab that opportunely crawled by. 'Drive me up the road and round Havelock Crescent, and see if we can find a gentleman running about in a velveteen coat and no hat.'

'Velveteen coat, ma'am, and no 'at. Very good, ma'am.' And the cabman whipped up at once in the most matter-of-fact way, as if he drove to this address every day in his life.

Some few minutes later the little group of cabmen and loafers that collects round the cabman's shelter at Haverstock Hill were startled by the passing of a cab with a ginger-coloured screw* of a horse, driven furiously.

They were silent as it went by, and then as it receded— 'That's 'Arry 'Icks. Wot's *he* got?' said the stout gentleman known as Old Tootles.

'He's a-using his whip, he is, *to* rights,' said the ostler boy.

'Hullo!' said poor old Tommy Byles; 'here's another bloomin' loonatic. Blowed if there ain't.'

'It's old George,' said Old Tootles, 'and he's driving a loonatic, *as* you say. Ain't he a-clawin' out of the keb? Wonder if he's after 'Arry 'Icks?'

The group round the cabman's shelter became animated. Chorus: 'Go it, George!' 'It's a race.' 'You'll ketch 'em!' 'Whip up!'

'She's a goer, she is!' said the ostler boy.

'Strike me giddy!' cried Old Tootles. 'Here! *I'm* a-goin' to begin in a minute. Here's another comin'. If all the cabs in Hampstead ain't gone mad this morning!'

'It's a fieldmale this time,' said the ostler boy.

'She's a-followin' *him*,' said Old Tootles. 'Usually the other way about.'

'What's she got in her 'and?'

'Looks like a 'igh 'at.'

'What a bloomin' lark it is! Three to one on old George,' said the ostler boy. 'Nexst!'

Minnie went by in a perfect roar of applause. She did not like it, but she felt that she was doing her duty, and whirled on down Haverstock Hill and Camden Town High Street with her eyes ever intent on the animated back view of old George, who was driving her vagrant husband so incomprehensibly away from her.

The man in the foremost cab sat crouched in the corner, his arms tightly folded, and the little tube that contained such vast possibilities of destruction gripped in his hand. His mood was a singular mixture of fear and exultation. Chiefly he was afraid of being caught before he could accomplish his purpose, but behind this was a vaguer but larger fear of the awfulness of his crime. But his exultation far exceeded his fear. No Anarchist before him had ever approached this conception of his. Ravachol, Vaillant,* all those distinguished persons whose fame he had envied dwindled into insignificance beside him. He had only to make sure of the water supply, and break the little tube into a reservoir. How brilliantly he had planned it, forged the letter of introduction and got into the laboratory, and how brilliantly he had seized his opportunity! The world should hear of him at last. All those people who had sneered at him, neglected him, preferred other people to him, found his company undesirable, should consider him at last. Death, death, death! They had always treated him as a man of no importance. All the world had been in a conspiracy to keep him under. He would teach them yet what it is to isolate a man. What was this familiar street? Great Saint Andrew's Street, of course! How fared the chase? He craned out of the cab. The Bacteriologist was scarcely fifty yards behind. That was bad. He would be caught and stopped yet. He felt in his pocket for money, and found half a sovereign. This he thrust up through the trap in the top of the cab into the man's face. 'More,' he shouted, 'if only we get away.'

The money was snatched out of his hand. 'Right you are,' said the cabman, and the trap slammed, and the lash lay along the glistening side of the horse. The cab swayed, and the Anarchist, half-standing under the trap, put the hand containing the little glass tube upon the apron to preserve his balance. He felt the brittle thing crack, and the broken half of it rang upon the floor of the cab. He fell back into the seat with a curse, and stared dismally at the two or three drops of moisture on the apron.

He shuddered.

'Well, I suppose I shall be the first. *Phew!* Anyhow, I shall be a Martyr. That's something. But it is a filthy death, nevertheless. I wonder if it hurts us much as they say.'

Presently a thought occurred to him—he groped between his feet. A little drop was still in the broken end of the tube, and he drank that to make sure. It was better to make sure. At any rate, he would not fail.

Then it dawned upon him that there was no further need to escape the Bacteriologist. In Wellington Street he told the cabman to stop, and got out. He slipped on the step, and his head felt queer. It was rapid stuff, this cholera poison. He waved his cabman out of existence, so to speak, and stood on the pavement with his arms folded upon his breast awaiting the arrival of the Bacteriologist. There was something tragic in his pose. The sense of imminent death gave him a certain dignity. He greeted his pursuer with a defiant laugh.

'Vive l'Anarchie!* You are too late, my friend. I have drunk it. The cholera is abroad!'

The Bacteriologist from his cab beamed curiously at him through his spectacles. 'You have drunk it! An Anarchist! I see now.' He was about to say something more, and then checked himself. A smile hung in the corner of his mouth. He opened the apron of his cab as if to descend, at which the Anarchist waved him a dramatic farewell and strode off towards Waterloo Bridge, carefully jostling his infected body against as many people as possible. The Bacteriologist was so preoccupied with the vision of him that he scarcely manifested the slightest surprise at the appearance of Minnie upon the pavement with his hat and shoes and overcoat. 'Very good of you to bring my things,' he said, and remained lost in contemplation of the receding figure of the Anarchist.

'You had better get in,' he said, still staring. Minnie felt absolutely convinced now that he was mad, and directed the cabman home on her own responsibility. 'Put on my shoes? Certainly, dear,' said he, as the cab began to turn, and hid the strutting black figure, now small in the distance, from his eyes. Then suddenly something grotesque struck him, and he laughed. Then he remarked, 'It is really very serious, though.

'You see, that man came to my house to see me, and he is an Anarchist. No—don't faint, or I cannot possibly tell you the rest. And I wanted to astonish him, not knowing he was an Anarchist, and took up a cultivation of that new species of Bacterium I was telling you of that infest, and I think cause, the blue patches upon various monkeys; and, like a fool, I said it was Asiatic cholera. And he ran away with it to poison the water of London, and he certainly might have made things look blue for this civilised city. And now he has swallowed it. Of course, I cannot say what will happen, but you know it turned that kitten blue, and the three puppies—in patches, and the sparrow—bright blue. But the bother is, I shall have all the trouble and expense of preparing some more.

'Put on my coat on this hot day! Why? Because we might meet Mrs Jabber. My dear, Mrs Jabber is not a draught. But why should I wear a coat on a hot day because of Mrs ——. Oh! *very* well.'

IV

THE FLOWERING OF THE
STRANGE ORCHID

THE buying of orchids always has in it a certain speculative flavour. You have before you the brown shrivelled lump of tissue, and for the rest you must trust your judgment, or the auctioneer, or your good luck, 'as your taste may incline. The plant may be moribund or dead, or it may be just a respectable purchase, fair value for your money, or perhaps—for the thing has happened again and again—there slowly unfolds before the delighted eyes of the happy purchaser, day after day, some new variety, some novel richness, a strange twist of the labellum,* or some subtler colouration or unexpected mimicry. Pride, beauty, and profit blossom together on one delicate green spike, and, it may be, even immortality. For the new miracle of nature may stand in need of a new specific name, and what so convenient as that of its discoverer? 'John-smithia'! There have been worse names.

It was perhaps the hope of some such happy discovery that made Winter-Wedderburn such a frequent attendant at these sales—that hope, and also, maybe, the fact that he had nothing else of the slightest interest to do in the world. He was a shy, lonely, rather ineffectual man, provided with just enough income to keep off the spur of necessity, and not enough nervous energy to make him seek any exacting employments. He might have collected stamps or coins, or translated Horace,* or bound books, or invented new species of diatoms.* But, as it happened, he grew orchids, and had one ambitious little hothouse.

'I have a fancy,' he said over his coffee, 'that something is going to happen to me to-day.' He spoke—as he moved and thought—slowly.

'Oh, don't say *that*!' said his housekeeper—who was also his remote cousin. For 'something happening' was a euphemism that meant only one thing to her.

'You misunderstand me. I mean nothing unpleasant . . . though what I do mean I scarcely know.

'To-day,' he continued, after a pause, 'Peters' are going to sell a batch of plants from the Andamans and the Indies. I shall go up and see what they have. It may be I shall buy something good unawares. That may be it.'

He passed his cup for his second cupful of coffee.

'Are these the things collected by that poor young fellow you told me of the other day?' asked his cousin, as she filled his cup.

'Yes,' he said, and became meditative over a piece of toast.

'Nothing ever does happen to me,' he remarked presently, beginning to think aloud. 'I wonder why? Things enough happen to other people. There is Harvey. Only the other week; on Monday he picked up sixpence, on Wednesday his chicks all had the staggers,* on Friday his cousin came home from Australia, and on Saturday he broke his ankle. What a whirl of excitement!—compared to me.'

'I think I would rather be without so much excitement,' said his housekeeper. 'It can't be good for you.'

'I suppose it's troublesome. Still . . . you see, nothing ever happens to me. When I was a little boy I never had accidents. I never fell in love as I grew up. Never married. . . . I wonder how it feels to have something happen to you, something really remarkable.

'That orchid-collector was only thirty-six—twenty years younger than myself—when he died. And he had been married twice and divorced once; he had had malarial fever four times, and once he broke his thigh. He killed a Malay once, and once he was wounded by a poisoned dart. And in the end he was killed by jungle-leeches. It must have all been very troublesome, but then it must have been very interesting, you know—except, perhaps, the leeches.'

'I am sure it was not good for him,' said the lady with conviction.

'Perhaps not.' And then Wedderburn looked at his watch. 'Twenty-three minutes past eight. I am going up by the quarter to twelve train, so that there is plenty of time. I think I shall wear my alpaca jacket—it is quite warm enough—and my grey felt hat and brown shoes. I suppose——'

He glanced out of the window at the serene sky and sunlit garden, and then nervously at his cousin's face.

'I think you had better take an umbrella if you are going to London,' she said in a voice that admitted of no denial. 'There's all between here and the station coming back.'

When he returned he was in a state of mild excitement. He had made a purchase. It was rare that he could make up his mind quickly enough to buy, but this time he had done so.

'There are Vandas,' he said, 'and a Dendrobe and some Palæonophis.'* He surveyed his purchases lovingly as he consumed his soup. They were laid out on the spotless tablecloth before him, and he was telling his cousin all about them as he slowly meandered through his dinner. It was his custom to live all his visits to London over again in the evening for her and his own entertainment.

'I knew something would happen to-day. And I have bought all these. Some of them—some of them—I feel sure, do you know, that some of them will be remarkable. I don't know how it is, but I feel just as sure as if some one had told me that some of these will turn out remarkable.

'That one'—he pointed to a shrivelled rhizome*—'was not identified. It may be a Palæonophis—or it may not. It may be a new species, or even a new genus. And it was the last that poor Batten ever collected.'

'I don't like the look of it,' said his housekeeper. 'It's such an ugly shape.'

'To me it scarcely seems to have a shape.'

'I don't like those things that stick out,' said his housekeeper.

'It shall be put away in a pot to-morrow.'

'It looks,' said the housekeeper, 'like a spider shamming dead.'

Wedderburn smiled and surveyed the root with his head on one side. 'It is certainly not a pretty lump of stuff. But you can never judge of these things from their dry appearance. It may turn out to be a very beautiful orchid indeed. How busy I shall be to-morrow! I must see to-night just exactly what to do with these things, and to-morrow I shall set to work.'

'They found poor Batten lying dead, or dying, in a man-grove swamp—I forget which,' he began again presently, 'with one of these very orchids crushed up under his body. He had been unwell for some days with some kind of native fever, and I suppose he fainted. These mangrove swamps are very unwholesome. Every drop of blood, they say, was taken out of him by the jungle-leeches. It may be that very plant that cost him his life to obtain.'

'I think none the better of it for that.'

'Men must work though women may weep,'* said Wedder-burn with profound gravity.

'Fancy dying away from every comfort in a nasty swamp! Fancy being ill of fever with nothing to take but chlorodyne and quinine—if men were left to themselves they would live on chlorodyne and quinine*—and no one round you but horrible natives! They say the Andaman islanders are most disgusting wretches—and, anyhow, they can scarcely make good nurses, not having the necessary training. And just for people in England to have orchids!'

'I don't suppose it was comfortable, but some men seem to enjoy that kind of thing,' said Wedderburn. 'Anyhow, the natives of his party were sufficiently civilised to take care of all his collection until his colleague, who was an ornitholo-gist, came back again from the interior; though they could not tell the species of the orchid, and had let it wither. And it makes these things more interesting.'

'It makes them disgusting. I should be afraid of some of

the malaria clinging to them. And just think, there has been a dead body lying across that ugly thing! I never thought of that before. There! I declare I cannot eat another mouthful of dinner.'

'I will take them off the table if you like, and put them in the window-seat. I can see them just as well there.'

The next few days he was indeed singularly busy in his steamy little hothouse, fussing about with charcoal, lumps of teak, moss, and all the other mysteries of the orchid cultivator. He considered he was having a wonderfully eventful time. In the evening he would talk about these new orchids to his friends, and over and over again he reverted to his expectation of something strange.

Several of the Vandas and the Dendrobium died under his care, but presently the strange orchid began to show signs of life. He was delighted, and took his housekeeper right away from jam-making to see it at once, directly he made the discovery.

'That is a bud,' he said, 'and presently there will be a lot of leaves there, and those little things coming out here are aërial rootlets.'

'They look to me like little white fingers poking out of the brown,' said his housekeeper. 'I don't like them.'

'Why not?'

'I don't know. They look like fingers trying to get at you. I can't help my likes and dislikes.'

'I don't know for certain, but I don't *think* there are any orchids I know that have aërial rootlets quite like that. It may be my fancy, of course. You see they are a little flattened at the ends.'

'I don't like 'em,' said his housekeeper, suddenly shivering and turning away. 'I know it's very silly of me—and I'm very sorry, particularly as you like the thing so much. But I can't help thinking of that corpse.'

'But it may not be that particular plant. That was merely a guess of mine.'

His housekeeper shrugged her shoulders. 'Anyhow I don't like it,' she said.

Wedderburn felt a little hurt at her dislike to the plant. But that did not prevent his talking to her about orchids generally, and this orchid in particular, whenever he felt inclined.

'There are such queer things about orchids,' he said one day; 'such possibilities of surprises. You know, Darwin studied their fertilisation,* and showed that the whole structure of an ordinary orchid flower was contrived in order that moths might carry the pollen from plant to plant. Well, it seems that there are lots of orchids known the flower of which cannot possibly be used for fertilisation in that way. Some of the Cypripediums,* for instance; there are no insects known that can possibly fertilise them, and some of them have never been found with seed.'

'But how do they form new plants?'

'By runners and tubers, and that kind of outgrowth. That is easily explained. The puzzle is, what are the flowers for?'

'Very likely,' he added, '*my* orchid may be something extraordinary in that way. If so I shall study it. I have often thought of making researches as Darwin did. But hitherto I have not found the time, or something else has happened to prevent it. The leaves are beginning to unfold now. I do wish you would come and see them!'

But she said that the orchid-house was so hot it gave her the headache. She had seen the plant once again, and the aërial rootlets, which were now some of them more than a foot long, had unfortunately reminded her of tentacles reaching out after something; and they got into her dreams, growing after her with incredible rapidity. So that she had settled to her entire satisfaction that she would not see that plant again, and Wedderburn had to admire its leaves alone. They were of the ordinary broad form, and a deep glossy green, with splashes and dots of deep red towards the base. He knew of no other leaves quite like them. The plant was placed on a low bench near the thermometer, and close by was a simple arrangement by which a tap dripped on the hot-water pipes and kept the air steamy. And he spent his afternoons now with some regularity meditating on the approaching flowering of this strange plant.

And at last the great thing happened. Directly he entered the little glass house he knew that the spike had burst out, although his great *Palæonophis Lowii* hid the corner where his new darling stood. There was a new odour in the air, a rich, intensely sweet scent, that overpowered every other in that crowded, steaming little greenhouse.

Directly he noticed this he hurried down to the strange orchid. And, behold! the trailing green spikes bore now three great splashes of blossom, from which this overpowering sweetness proceeded. He stopped before them in an ecstasy of admiration.

The flowers were white, with streaks of golden orange upon the petals; the heavy labellum was coiled into an intricate projection, and a wonderful bluish purple mingled there with the gold. He could see at once that the genus was altogether a new one. And the insufferable scent! How hot the place was! The blossoms swam before his eyes.

He would see if the temperature was right. He made a step towards the thermometer. Suddenly everything appeared unsteady. The bricks on the floor were dancing up and down. Then the white blossoms, the green leaves behind them, the whole greenhouse, seemed to sweep sideways, and then in a curve upward.

*

At half-past four his cousin made the tea, according to their invariable custom. But Wedderburn did not come in for his tea.

'He is worshipping that horrid orchid,' she told herself, and waited ten minutes. 'His watch must have stopped. I will go and call him.'

She went straight to the hothouse, and, opening the door,

called his name. There was no reply. She noticed that the air was very close, and loaded with an intense perfume. Then she saw something lying on the bricks between the hot-water pipes.

For a minute, perhaps, she stood motionless.

He was lying, face upward, at the foot of the strange orchid. The tentacle-like aërial rootlets no longer swayed freely in the air, but were crowded together, a tangle of grey ropes, and stretched tight, with their ends closely applied to his chin and neck and hands.

She did not understand. Then she saw from under one of the exultant tentacles upon his cheek there trickled a little thread of blood.

With an inarticulate cry she ran towards him, and tried to pull him away from the leech-like suckers. She snapped two of these tentacles, and their sap dripped red.

Then the overpowering scent of the blossom began to make her head reel. How they clung to him! She tore at the tough ropes, and he and the white inflorescence* swam about her. She felt she was fainting, knew she must not. She left him and hastily opened the nearest door, and, after she had panted for a moment in the fresh air, she had a brilliant inspiration. She caught up a flower-pot and smashed in the windows at the end of the greenhouse. Then she re-entered. She tugged now with renewed strength at Wedderburn's motionless body, and brought the strange orchid crashing to the floor. It still clung with the grimmest tenacity to its victim. In a frenzy, she lugged it and him into the open air.

Then she thought of tearing through the sucker rootlets one by one, and in another minute she had released him and was dragging him away from the horror.

He was white and bleeding from a dozen circular patches.

The odd-job man was coming up the garden, amazed at the smashing of glass, and saw her emerge, hauling the inanimate body with red-stained hands. For a moment he thought impossible things.

'Bring some water!' she cried, and her voice dispelled his fancies. When, with unnatural alacrity, he returned with the water, he found her weeping with excitement, and with Wedderburn's head upon her knee, wiping the blood from his face.

'What's the matter?' said Wedderburn, opening his eyes feebly, and closing them again at once.

'Go and tell Annie to come out here to me, and then go for Dr Haddon at once,' she said to the odd-job man so soon as he brought the water; and added, seeing he hesitated, 'I will tell you all about it when you come back.'

Presently Wedderburn opened his eyes again, and, seeing that he was troubled by the puzzle of his position, she explained to him, 'You fainted in the hothouse.'

'And the orchid?'

'I will see to that,' she said.

Wedderburn had lost a good deal of blood, but beyond that he had suffered no very great injury. They gave him brandy mixed with some pink extract of meat, and carried him upstairs to bed. His housekeeper told her incredible story in fragments to Dr Haddon. 'Come to the orchid-house and see,' she said.

The cold outer air was blowing in through the open door, and the sickly perfume was almost dispelled. Most of the torn aërial rootlets lay already withered amidst a number of dark stains upon the bricks. The stem of the inflorescence was broken by the fall of the plant, and the flowers were growing limp and brown at the edges of the petals. The doctor stooped towards it, then saw that one of the aërial rootlets still stirred feebly, and hesitated.

The next morning the strange orchid still lay there, black now and putrescent. The door banged intermittently in the morning breeze, and all the array of Wedderburn's orchids was shrivelled and prostrate. But Wedderburn himself was bright and garrulous upstairs in the glory of his strange adventure.

V

IN THE AVU OBSERVATORY

THE observatory at Avu, in Borneo, stands on the spur of the mountain. To the north rises the old crater, black at night against the unfathomable blue of the sky. From the little circular building, with its mushroom dome, the slopes plunge steeply downward into the black mysteries of the tropical forest beneath. The little house in which the observer and his assistant live is about fifty yards from the observatory, and beyond this are the huts of their native attendants.

Thaddy, the chief observer, was down with a slight fever. His assistant, Woodhouse, paused for a moment in silent contemplation of the tropical night before commencing his solitary vigil. The night was very still. Now and then voices and laughter came from the native huts, or the cry of some strange animal was heard from the midst of the mystery of the forest. Nocturnal insects appeared in ghostly fashion out of the darkness, and fluttered round his light. He thought, perhaps, of all the possibilities of discovery that still lay in the black tangle beneath him; for to the naturalist the virgin forests of Borneo are still a wonderland full of strange questions and half-suspected discoveries. Woodhouse carried a small lantern in his hand, and its yellow glow contrasted vividly with the infinite series of tints between lavender-blue and black in which the landscape was painted. His hands and face were smeared with ointment against the attacks of the mosquitoes.

Even in these days of celestial photography, work done in a purely temporary erection, and with only the most primitive appliances in addition to the telescope, still involves a very large amount of cramped and motionless watching. He sighed as he thought of the physical fatigues before him, stretched himself, and entered the observatory.

The reader is probably familiar with the structure of an ordinary astronomical observatory. The building is usually cylindrical in shape, with a very light hemispherical roof capable of being turned round from the interior. The telescope is supported upon a stone pillar in the centre, and a clockwork arrangement compensates for the earth's rotation, and allows a star once found to be continuously observed. Besides this, there is a compact tracery of wheels and screws about its point of support, by which the astronomer adjusts it. There is, of course, a slit in the movable roof which follows the eye of the telescope in its survey of the heavens. The observer sits or lies on a sloping wooden arrangement, which he can wheel to any part of the observatory as the position of the telescope may require. Within it is advisable to have things as dark as possible, in order to enhance the brilliance of the stars observed.

The lantern flared as Woodhouse entered his circular den, and the general darkness fled into black shadows behind the big machine, from which it presently seemed to creep back over the whole place again as the light waned. The slit was a profound transparent blue, in which six stars shone with tropical brilliance, and their light lay, a pallid gleam, along the black tube of the instrument. Woodhouse shifted the roof, and then proceeding to the telescope, turned first one wheel and then another, the great cylinder slowly swinging into a new position. Then he glanced through the finder, the little companion telescope, moved the roof a little more, made some further adjustments, and set the clockwork in motion. He took off his jacket, for the night was very hot, and pushed into position the uncomfortable seat to which he was condemned for the next four hours. Then with a sigh he resigned himself to his watch upon the mysteries of space.

There was no sound now in the observatory, and the lantern waned steadily. Outside there was the occasional cry of some animal in alarm or pain, or calling to its mate, and the intermittent sounds of the Malay and Dyak servants. Presently one of the men began a queer chanting song, in which the others joined at intervals. After this it would seem that they turned in for the night, for no further sound came from their direction, and the whispering stillness became more and more profound.

The clockwork ticked steadily. The shrill hum of a mosquito explored the place and grew shriller in indignation at Woodhouse's ointment. Then the lantern went out and all the observatory was black.

Woodhouse shifted his position presently, when the slow movement of the telescope had carried it beyond the limits of his comfort.

He was watching a little group of stars in the Milky Way, in one of which his chief had seen or fancied a remarkable colour variability. It was not a part of the regular work for which the establishment existed, and for that reason perhaps Woodhouse was deeply interested. He must have forgotten things terrestrial. All his attention was concentrated upon the great blue circle of the telescope field—a circle powdered, so it seemed, with an innumerable multitude of stars, and all luminous against the blackness of its setting. As he watched he seemed to himself to become incorporeal, as if he too were floating in the ether* of space. Infinitely remote was the faint red spot he was observing.

Suddenly the stars were blotted out. A flash of blackness passed, and they were visible again.

'Queer,' said Woodhouse. 'Must have been a bird.'

The thing happened again, and immediately after the great tube shivered as though it had been struck. Then the dome of the observatory resounded with a series of thundering blows. The stars seemed to sweep aside as the telescope—which had been unclamped—swung round and away from the slit in the roof.

'Great Scott!' cried Woodhouse. 'What's this?'

45

Some huge vague black shape, with a flapping something like a wing, seemed to be struggling in the aperture of the roof. In another moment the slit was clear again, and the luminous haze of the Milky Way shone warm and bright.

The interior of the roof was perfectly black, and only a scraping sound marked the whereabouts of the unknown creature.

Woodhouse had scrambled from the seat to his feet. He was trembling violently and in a perspiration with the suddenness of the occurrence. Was the thing, whatever it was, inside or out? It was big, whatever else it might be. Something shot across the skylight, and the telescope swayed. He started violently and put his arm up. It was in the observatory, then, with him. It was clinging to the roof apparently. What the devil was it? Could it see him?

He stood for perhaps a minute in a state of stupefaction. The beast, whatever it was, clawed at the interior of the dome, and then something flapped almost into his face, and he saw the momentary gleam of starlight on a skin like oiled leather. His water-bottle was knocked off his little table with a smash.

The sense of some strange bird-creature hovering a few yards from his face in the darkness was indescribably unpleasant to Woodhouse. As his thought returned he concluded that it must be some night-bird or large bat. At any risk he would see what it was, and pulling a match from his pocket, he tried to strike it on the telescope seat. There was a smoking streak of phosphorescent light, the match flared for a moment, and he saw a vast wing sweeping towards him, a gleam of grey-brown fur, and then he was struck in the face and the match knocked out of his hand. The blow was aimed at his temple, and a claw tore sideways down to his cheek. He reeled and fell, and he heard the extinguished lantern smash. Another blow followed as he fell. He was partly stunned, he felt his own warm blood stream out upon his face. Instinctively he felt his eyes had been struck at, and,

turning over on his face to save them, tried to crawl under the protection of the telescope.

He was struck again upon the back, and he heard his jacket rip, and then the thing hit the roof of the observatory. He edged as far as he could between the wooden seat and the eyepiece of the instrument, and turned his body round so that it was chiefly his feet that were exposed. With these he could at least kick. He was still in a mystified state. The strange beast banged about in the darkness, and presently clung to the telescope, making it sway and the gear rattle. Once it flapped near him, and he kicked out madly and felt a soft body with his feet. He was horribly scared now. It must be a big thing to swing the telescope like that. He saw for a moment the outline of a head black against the starlight, with sharply-pointed upstanding ears and a crest between them. It seemed to him to be as big as a mastiff's. Then he began to bawl out as loudly as he could for help.

At that the thing came down upon him again. As it did so his hand touched something beside him on the floor. He kicked out, and the next moment his ankle was gripped and held by a row of keen teeth. He yelled again, and tried to free his leg by kicking with the other. Then he realised he had the broken water-bottle at his hand, and, snatching it, he struggled into a sitting posture, and feeling in the darkness towards his foot, gripped a velvety ear, like the ear of a big cat. He had seized the water-bottle by its neck and brought it down with a shivering crash upon the head of the strange beast. He repeated the blow, and then stabbed and jabbed with the jagged end of it, in the darkness, where he judged the face might be.

The small teeth relaxed their hold, and at once Woodhouse pulled his leg free and kicked hard. He felt the sickening feel of fur and bone giving under his boot. There was a tearing bite at his arm, and he struck over it at the face, as he judged, and hit damp fur.

There was a pause; then he heard the sound of claws

and the dragging of a heavy body away from him over the observatory floor. Then there was silence, broken only by his own sobbing breathing, and a sound like licking. Everything was black except the parallelogram of the blue skylight with the luminous dust of stars, against which the end of the telescope now appeared in silhouette. He waited, as it seemed, an interminable time.

Was the thing coming on again? He felt in his trouser-pocket for some matches, and found one remaining. He tried to strike this, but the floor was wet, and it spat and went out. He cursed. He could not see where the door was situated. In his struggle he had quite lost his bearings. The strange beast, disturbed by the splutter of the match, began to move again. 'Time!' called Woodhouse, with a sudden gleam of mirth, but the thing was not coming at him again. He must have hurt it, he thought, with the broken bottle. He felt a dull pain in his ankle. Probably he was bleeding there. He wondered if it would support him if he tried to stand up. The night outside was very still. There was no sound of any one moving. The sleepy fools had not heard those wings battering upon the dome, nor his shouts. It was no good wasting strength in shouting. The monster flapped its wings and startled him into a defensive attitude. He hit his elbow against the seat, and it fell over with a crash. He cursed this, and then he cursed the darkness.

Suddenly the oblong patch of starlight seemed to sway to and fro. Was he going to faint? It would never do to faint. He clenched his fists and set his teeth to hold himself together. Where had the door got to? It occurred to him he could get his bearings by the stars visible through the skylight. The patch of stars he saw was in Sagittarius and south-eastward; the door was north—or was it north by west? He tried to think. If he could get the door open he might retreat. It might be the thing was wounded. The suspense was beastly. 'Look here!' he said, 'if you don't come on, I shall come at you.'

Then the thing began clambering up the side of the observatory, and he saw its black outline gradually blot out the skylight. Was it in retreat? He forgot about the door, and watched as the dome shifted and creaked. Somehow he did not feel very frightened or excited now. He felt a curious sinking sensation inside him. The sharply-defined patch of light, with the black form moving across it, seemed to be growing smaller and smaller. That was curious. He began to feel very thirsty, and yet he did not feel inclined to get anything to drink. He seemed to be sliding down a long funnel.

He felt a burning sensation in his throat, and then he perceived it was broad daylight, and that one of the Dyak servants was looking at him with a curious expression. Then there was the top of Thaddy's face upside down. Funny fellow, Thaddy, to go about like that! Then he grasped the situation better, and perceived that his head was on Thaddy's knee, and Thaddy was giving him brandy. And then he saw the eyepiece of the telescope with a lot of red smears on it. He began to remember.

'You've made this observatory in a pretty mess,' said Thaddy.

The Dyak boy was beating up an egg in brandy. Woodhouse took this and sat up. He felt a sharp twinge of pain. His ankle was tied up, so were his arm and the side of his face. The smashed glass, red-stained, lay about the floor, the telescope seat was overturned, and by the opposite wall was a dark pool. The door was open, and he saw the grey summit of the mountain against a brilliant background of blue sky.

'Pah!' said Woodhouse. 'Who's been killing calves here? Take me out of it.'

Then he remembered the Thing, and the fight he had had with it.

'What *was* it?' he said to Thaddy—'the Thing I fought with?'

'*You* know that best,' said Thaddy. 'But, anyhow, don't worry yourself now about it. Have some more to drink.'

Thaddy, however, was curious enough, and it was a hard struggle between duty and inclination to keep Woodhouse quiet until he was decently put away in bed, and had slept upon the copious dose of meat extract Thaddy considered advisable. They then talked it over together.

'It was,' said Woodhouse, 'more like a big bat than anything else in the world. It had sharp, short ears, and soft fur, and its wings were leathery. Its teeth were little but devilish sharp, and its jaw could not have been very strong or else it would have bitten through my ankle.'

'It has pretty nearly,' said Thaddy.

'It seemed to me to hit out with its claws pretty freely. That is about as much as I know about the beast. Our conversation was intimate, so to speak, and yet not confidential.'

'The Dyak chaps talk about a Big Colugo, a Klang-utang—whatever that may be. It does not often attack man, but I suppose you made it nervous. They say there is a Big Colugo and a Little Colugo, and a something else that sounds like gobble. They all fly about at night. For my own part, I know there are flying foxes and flying lemurs about here, but they are none of them very big beasts.'

'There are more things in heaven and earth,' said Woodhouse—and Thaddy groaned at the quotation—'and more particularly in the forests of Borneo, than are dreamt of in our philosophies.* On the whole, if the Borneo fauna is going to disgorge any more of its novelties upon me, I should prefer that it did so when I was not occupied in the observatory at night and alone.'

50

VI

ÆPYORNIS ISLAND

THE man with the scarred face leant over the table and looked at my bundle.

'Orchids?' he asked.

'A few,' I said.

'Cypripediums,'* he said.

'Chiefly,' said I.

'Anything new? I thought not. I did these islands twenty-five—twenty-seven years ago. If you find anything new here—well, it's brand new. I didn't leave much.'

'I'm not a collector,' said I.

'I was young then,' he went on. 'Lord! how I used to fly round.' He seemed to take my measure. 'I was in the East Indies two years, and in Brazil seven. Then I went to Madagascar.'

'I know a few explorers by name,' I said, anticipating a yarn. 'Whom did you collect for?'

'Dawson's. I wonder if you've heard the name of Butcher ever?'

'Butcher—Butcher?' The name seemed vaguely present in my memory; then I recalled *Butcher* v. *Dawson.* 'Why!' said I, 'you are the man who sued them for four years' salary—got cast away on a desert island . . .'

'Your servant,' said the man with the scar, bowing. 'Funny case, wasn't it? Here was me, making a little fortune on that island, doing nothing for it neither, and them quite unable to give me notice. It often used to amuse me thinking over it while I was there. I did calculations of it—big—all over the blessed atoll in ornamental figuring.'

51

'How did it happen?' said I. 'I don't rightly remember the case.'

'Well. . . . You've heard of the Æpyornis?'*

'Rather. Andrews was telling me of a new species he was working on only a month or so ago. Just before I sailed. They've got a thigh bone, it seems, nearly a yard long. Monster the thing must have been!'

'I believe you,' said the man with the scar. 'It *was* a monster. Sindbad's roc* was just a legend of 'em. But when did they find these bones?'

'Three or four years ago—'91, I fancy. Why?'

'Why? Because *I* found them—Lord!—it's nearly twenty years ago. If Dawson's hadn't been silly about that salary they might have made a perfect ring* in 'em. . . . *I* couldn't help the infernal boat going adrift.'

He paused. 'I suppose it's the same place. A kind of swamp about ninety miles north of Antananarivo.* Do you happen to know? You have to go to it along the coast by boats. You don't happen to remember, perhaps?'

'I don't. I fancy Andrews said something about a swamp.'

'It must be the same. It's on the east coast. And somehow there's something in the water that keeps things from decaying. Like creosote it smells. It reminded me of Trinidad. Did they get any more eggs? Some of the eggs I found were a foot-and-a-half long. The swamp goes circling round, you know, and cuts off this bit. It's mostly salt, too. Well. . . . What a time I had of it! I found the things quite by accident. We went for eggs, me and two native chaps, in one of those rum* canoes all tied together, and found the bones at the same time. We had a tent and provisions for four days, and we pitched on one of the firmer places. To think of it brings that odd tarry smell back even now. It's funny work. You go probing into the mud with iron rods, you know. Usually the egg gets smashed. I wonder how long it is since these Æpyornises really lived. The missionaries say the natives have legends about when they were alive, but I never heard any such stories myself.[1] But certainly those eggs we got were as fresh as if they had been new laid. Fresh! Carrying them down to the boat one of my nigger chaps dropped one on a rock and it smashed. How I lammed into the beggar! But sweet it was, as if it was new laid, not even smelly, and its mother dead these four hundred years, perhaps. Said a centipede had bit him. However, I'm getting off the straight with the story. It had taken us all day to dig into the slush and get these eggs out unbroken, and we were all covered with beastly black mud, and naturally I was cross. So far as I knew they were the only eggs that have ever been got out not even cracked. I went afterwards to see the ones they have at the Natural History Museum in London; all of them were cracked and just stuck together like a mosaic, and bits missing. Mine were perfect, and I meant to blow them when I got back. Naturally I was annoyed at the silly duffer dropping three hours' work just on account of a centipede. I hit him about rather.'

The man with the scar took out a clay pipe. I placed my pouch before him. He filled up absent-mindedly.

'How about the others? Did you get those home? I don't remember——'

'That's the queer part of the story. I had three others. Perfectly fresh eggs. Well, we put 'em in the boat, and then I went up to the tent to make some coffee, leaving my two heathens down by the beach—the one fooling about with his sting and the other helping him. It never occurred to me that the beggars would take advantage of the peculiar position I was in to pick a quarrel. But I suppose the centipede poison and the kicking I had given him had upset the one—he was always a cantankerous sort—and he persuaded the other.

'I remember I was sitting and smoking and boiling up the water over a spirit-lamp business I used to take on these

---

[1] No European is known to have seen a live Æpyornis, with the doubtful exception of MacAndrew, who visited Madagascar in 1745.—H.G.W.

expeditions. Incidentally I was admiring the swamp under the sunset. All black and blood-red it was, in streaks—a beautiful sight. And up beyond the land rose grey and hazy to the hills, and the sky behind them red, like a furnace mouth. And fifty yards behind the back of me was these blessed heathens—quite regardless of the tranquil air of things—plotting to cut off with the boat and leave me all alone with three days' provisions and a canvas tent, and nothing to drink whatsoever beyond a little keg of water. I heard a kind of yelp behind me, and there they were in this canoe affair—it wasn't properly a boat—and, perhaps, twenty yards from land. I realised what was up in a moment. My gun was in the tent, and, besides, I had no bullets—only duck shot. They knew that. But I had a little revolver in my pocket, and I pulled that out as I ran down to the beach.

'"Come back!" says I, flourishing it.

'They jabbered something at me, and the man that broke the egg jeered. I aimed at the other—because he was un-wounded and had the paddle, and I missed. They laughed. However, I wasn't beat. I knew I had to keep cool, and I tried him again and made him jump with the whang of it. He didn't laugh that time. The third time I got his head, and over he went, and the paddle with him. It was a precious lucky shot for a revolver. I reckon it was fifty yards. He went right under. I don't know if he was shot, or simply stunned and drowned. Then I began to shout to the other chap to come back, but he huddled up in the canoe and refused to answer. So I fired out my revolver at him and never got near him.

'I felt a precious fool, I can tell you. There I was on this rotten, black beach, flat swamp all behind me, and the flat sea, cold after the sun set, and just this black canoe drifting steadily out to sea. I tell you I damned Dawson's and Jamrach's* and Museums and all the rest of it just to rights. I bawled to this nigger to come back, until my voice went up into a scream.

'There was nothing for it but to swim after him and take my luck with the sharks. So I opened my clasp-knife and put it in my mouth, and took off my clothes and waded in. As soon as I was in the water I lost sight of the canoe, but I aimed, as I judged, to head it off. I hoped the man in it was too bad to navigate it, and that it would keep on drifting in the same direction. Presently it came up over the horizon again to the south-westward about. The afterglow of sunset was well over now and the dim of night creeping up. The stars were coming through the blue. I swum like a champion, though my legs and arms were soon aching.

'However, I came up to him by the time the stars were fairly out. As it got darker I began to see all manner of glowing things in the water—phosphorescence, you know. At times it made me giddy. I hardly knew which was stars and which was phosphorescence, and whether I was swimming on my head or my heels. The canoe was as black as sin, and the ripple under the bows like liquid fire. I was naturally chary of clambering up into it. I was anxious to see what he was up to first. He seemed to be lying cuddled up in a lump in the bows, and the stern was all out of water. The thing kept turning round slowly as it drifted—kind of waltzing, don't you know. I went to the stern and pulled it down, expecting him to wake up. Then I began to clamber in with my knife in my hand, and ready for a rush. But he never stirred. So there I sat in the stern of the little canoe, drifting away over the calm phosphorescent sea, and with all the host of the stars above me, waiting for something to happen.

'After a long time I called him by name, but he never answered. I was too tired to take any risks by going along to him. So we sat there. I fancy I dozed once or twice. When the dawn came I saw he was as dead as a doornail and all puffed up and purple. My three eggs and the bones were lying in the middle of the canoe, and the keg of water and some coffee and biscuits wrapped in a Cape *Argus* by his feet, and a tin of methylated spirit underneath him. There was no paddle, nor, in fact, anything except the spirit-tin that I could use as one, so I settled to drift until I was picked up. I held an inquest on him, brought in a verdict against some snake, scorpion, or centipede unknown, and sent him overboard.

'After that I had a drink of water and a few biscuits, and took a look round. I suppose a man low down as I was don't see very far; leastways, Madagascar was clean out of sight, and any trace of land at all. I saw a sail going south-westward—looked like a schooner but her hull never came up. Presently the sun got high in the sky and began to beat down upon me. Lord! it pretty near made my brains boil. I tried dipping my head in the sea, but after a while my eye fell on the Cape *Argus*, and I lay down flat in the canoe and spread this over me. Wonderful things these newspapers! I never read one through thoroughly before, but it's odd what you get up to when you're alone, as I was. I suppose I read that blessed old Cape *Argus* twenty times. The pitch in the canoe simply reeked with the heat and rose up into big blisters.

'I drifted ten days,' said the man with the scar. 'It's a little thing in the telling, isn't it? Every day was like the last. Except in the morning and the evening I never kept a look-out even— the blaze was so infernal. I didn't see a sail after the first three days, and those I saw took no notice of me. About the sixth night a ship went by scarcely half a mile away from me, with all its lights ablaze and its ports open, looking like a big firefly. There was music aboard. I stood up and shouted and screamed at it. The second day I broached one of the Æpyornis eggs, scraped the shell away at the end bit by bit, and tried it, and I was glad to find it was good enough to eat. A bit flavoury—not bad, I mean—but with something of the taste of a duck's egg. There was a kind of circular patch, about six inches across, on one side of the yoke, and with streaks of blood and a white mark like a ladder in it that I thought queer, but I did not understand what this meant at the time, and I wasn't inclined to be particular. The egg lasted me three days, with biscuits and a drink of water. I chewed coffee berries too—invigorating stuff. The second egg I opened about the eighth day, and it scared me.'

The man with the scar paused. 'Yes,' he said, 'developing.'

'I daresay you find it hard to believe. *I* did, with the thing before me. There the egg had been, sunk in that cold black mud, perhaps three hundred years. But there was no mistaking it. There was the—what is it?—embryo, with its big head and curved back, and its heart beating under its throat, and the yolk shrivelled up and great membranes spreading inside of the shell and all over the yolk. Here was I hatching out the eggs of the biggest of all extinct birds, in a little canoe in the midst of the Indian Ocean. If old Dawson had known that! It was worth four years' salary. What do *you* think?

'However, I had to eat that precious thing up, every bit of it, before I sighted the reef, and some of the mouthfuls were beastly unpleasant. I left the third one alone. I held it up to the light, but the shell was too thick for me to get any notion of what might be happening inside; and though I fancied I heard blood pulsing, it might have been the rustle in my own ears, like what you listen to in a seashell.

'Then came the atoll. Came out of the sunrise, as it were, suddenly, close up to me. I drifted straight towards it until I was about half a mile from shore, not more, and then the current took a turn, and I had to paddle as hard as I could with my hands and bits of the Æpyornis shell to make the place. However, I got there. It was just a common atoll about four miles round, with a few trees growing and a spring in one place, and the lagoon full of parrot-fish. I took the egg ashore and put it in a good place, well above the tide lines and in the sun, to give it all the chance I could, and pulled the canoe up safe, and loafed about prospecting. It's rum how dull an atoll is. As soon as I had found a spring all the interest seemed to vanish. When I was a kid I thought nothing could be finer or more adventurous than the Robinson Crusoe business, but that place was as monotonous as a book of sermons. I went round finding eatable things and generally thinking; but I tell you I was bored to death before the first day was out. It shows my luck—the very day I landed the weather changed. A thunderstorm went by to the north and flicked its wing over the island, and in the night there came a drencher and a howling wind slap over us. It wouldn't have taken much, you know, to upset that canoe.

'I was sleeping under the canoe, and the egg was luckily among the sand higher up the beach, and the first thing I remember was a sound like a hundred pebbles hitting the boat at once, and a rush of water over my body. I'd been dreaming of Antananarivo, and I sat up and holloaed to Intoshi to ask her what the devil was up, and clawed out at the chair where the matches used to be. Then I remembered where I was. There were phosphorescent waves rolling up as if they meant to eat me, and all the rest of the night as black as pitch. The air was simply yelling. The clouds seemed down on your head almost, and the rain fell as if heaven was sinking and they were baling out the waters above the firmament.* One great roller came writhing at me, like a fiery serpent, and I bolted. Then I thought of the canoe, and ran down to it as the water went hissing back again; but the thing had gone. I wondered about the egg then, and felt my way to it. It was all right and well out of reach of the maddest waves, so I sat down beside it and cuddled it for company. Lord! what a night that was!

'The storm was over before the morning. There wasn't a rag of cloud left in the sky when the dawn came, and all along the beach there were bits of plank scattered—which was the disarticulated skeleton, so to speak, of my canoe. However, that gave me something to do, for, taking advantage of two of the trees being together, I rigged up a kind of storm-shelter with these vestiges. And that day the egg hatched.

'Hatched, sir, when my head was pillowed on it and I was

asleep. I heard a whack and felt a jar and sat up, and there was the end of the egg pecked out and a rum little brown head looking out at me. "Lord!" I said, "you're welcome"; and with a little difficulty he came out.

'He was a nice friendly little chap at first, about the size of a small hen—very much like most other young birds, only bigger. His plumage was a dirty brown to begin with, with a sort of grey scab that fell off it very soon, and scarcely feathers—a kind of downy hair. I can hardly express how pleased I was to see him. I tell you, Robinson Crusoe don't make near enough of his loneliness. But here was interesting company. He looked at me and winked his eye from the front backwards, like a hen, and gave a chirp and began to peck about at once, as though being hatched three hundred years too late was just nothing. "Glad to see you, Man Friday!" says I, for I had naturally settled he was to be called Man Friday if ever he was hatched, as soon as ever I found the egg in the canoe had developed. I was a bit anxious about his feed, so I gave him a lump of raw parrot-fish at once. He took it, and opened his beak for more. I was glad of that for, under the circumstances, if he'd been at all fanciful, I should have had to eat him after all.

'You'd be surprised what an interesting bird that Æpyornis chick was. He followed me about from the very beginning. He used to stand by me and watch while I fished in the lagoon, and go shares in anything I caught. And he was sensible, too. There were nasty green warty things, like pickled gherkins, used to lie about on the beach, and he tried one of these and it upset him. He never even looked at any of them again.

'And he grew. You could almost see him grow. And as I was never much of a society man, his quiet, friendly ways suited me to a T. For nearly two years we were as happy as we could be on that island. I had no business worries, for I knew my salary was mounting up at Dawsons'. We would see a sail now and then, but nothing ever came near us. I amused myself, too, by decorating the island with designs worked in sea-urchins and fancy shells of various kinds. I put ÆPYORNIS ISLAND all round the place very nearly, in big letters, like what you see done with coloured stones at railway stations in the old country, and mathematical calculations and drawings of various sorts. And I used to lie watching the blessed bird stalking round and growing, growing; and think how I could make a living out of him by showing him about if I ever got taken off. After his first moult he began to get handsome, with a crest and a blue wattle,* and a lot of green feathers at the behind of him. And then I used to puzzle whether Dawsons' had any right to claim him or not. Stormy weather and in the rainy season we lay snug under the shelter I had made out of the old canoe, and I used to tell him lies about my friends at home. And after a storm we would go round the island together to see if there was any drift. It was a kind of idyll, you might say. If only I had had some tobacco it would have been simply just like heaven.

'It was about the end of the second year our little paradise went wrong. Friday was then about fourteen feet high to the bill of him, with a big, broad head like the end of a pickaxe, and two huge brown eyes with yellow rims, set together like a man's—not out of sight of each other like a hen's. His plumage was fine—none of the half-mourning style of your ostrich—more like a cassowary* as far as colour and texture go. And then it was he began to cock his comb at me and give himself airs, and show signs of a nasty temper. . . .

'At last came a time when my fishing had been rather unlucky, and he began to hang about me in a queer, meditative way. I thought he might have been eating sea-cucumbers or something, but it was really just discontent on his part. I was hungry too, and when at last I landed a fish I wanted it for myself. Tempers were short that morning on both sides. He pecked at it and grabbed it, and I gave him a whack on the head to make him leave go. And at that he went for me. Lord! . . .

'He gave me this in the face.' The man indicated his scar. 'Then he kicked me. It was like a cart-horse. I got up, and seeing he hadn't finished, I started off full tilt with my arms doubled up over my face. But he ran on those gawky legs of his faster than a racehorse, and kept landing out at me with sledgehammer kicks, and bringing his pickaxe down on the back of my head. I made for the lagoon, and went in up to my neck. He stopped at the water, for he hated getting his feet wet, and began to make a shindy, something like a peacock's, only hoarser. He started strutting up and down the beach. I'll admit I felt small to see this blessed fossil lording it there. And my head and face were all bleeding, and—well, my body just one jelly of bruises.

'I decided to swim across the lagoon and leave him alone for a bit, until the affair blew over. I shinned up the tallest palm-tree, and sat there thinking of it all. I don't suppose I ever felt so hurt by anything before or since. It was the brutal ingratitude of the creature. I'd been more than a brother to him. I'd hatched him, educated him. A great gawky, out-of-date bird! And me a human being—heir of the ages and all that.*

'I thought after a time he'd begin to see things in that light himself, and feel a little sorry for his behaviour. I thought if I was to catch some nice little bits of fish, perhaps, and go to him presently in a casual kind of way, and offer them to him, he might do the sensible thing. It took me some time to learn how unforgiving and cantankerous an extinct bird can be. Malice!

'I won't tell you all the little devices I tried to get that bird round again. I simply can't. It makes my cheek burn with shame even now to think of the snubs and buffets I had from this infernal curiosity. I tried violence. I chucked lumps of coral at him from a safe distance, but he only swallowed them. I shied my open knife at him and almost lost it, though it was too big for him to swallow. I tried starving him out and struck fishing, but he took to picking along the beach at low water after worms, and rubbed along on that. Half my time I spent up to my neck in the lagoon, and the rest up the palm-trees. One of them was scarcely high enough, and when he caught me up it he had a regular Bank Holiday with the calves of my legs. It got unbearable. I don't know if you have ever tried sleeping up a palm-tree. It gave me the most horrible nightmares. Think of the shame of it, too! Here was this extinct animal mooning about my island like a sulky duke, and me not allowed to rest the sole of my foot on the place. I used to cry with weariness and vexation. I told him straight that I didn't mean to be chased about a desert island by any damned anachronisms. I told him to go and peck a navigator of his own age. But he only snapped his beak at me. Great ugly bird, all legs and neck!

'I shouldn't like to say how long that went on altogether. I'd have killed him sooner if I'd known how. However, I hit on a way of settling him at last. It is a South American dodge. I joined all my fishing-lines together with stems of seaweed and things, and made a stoutish string, perhaps twelve yards in length or more, and I fastened two lumps of coral rock to the ends of this. It took me some time to do, because every now and then I had to go into the lagoon or up a tree as the fancy took me. This I whirled rapidly round my head, and then let it go at him. The first time I missed, but the next time the string caught his legs beautifully, and wrapped round them again and again. Over he went. I threw it standing waist-deep in the lagoon, and as soon as he went down I was out of the water and sawing at his neck with my knife . . .

'I don't like to think of that even now. I felt like a murderer while I did it, though my anger was hot against him. When I stood over him and saw him bleeding on the white sand, and his beautiful great legs and neck writhing in his last agony . . . Pah!

'With that tragedy loneliness came upon me like a curse. Good Lord! you can't imagine how I missed that bird. I sat by his corpse and sorrowed over him, and shivered as I looked round the desolate, silent reef. I thought of what a jolly little bird he had been when he was hatched, and of a thousand pleasant tricks he had played before he went wrong. I thought if I'd only wounded him I might have nursed him round into a better understanding. If I'd had any means of digging into the coral rock I'd have buried him. I felt exactly as if he was human. As it was, I couldn't think of eating him, so I put him in the lagoon, and the little fishes picked him clean. I didn't even save the feathers. Then one day a chap cruising about in a yacht had a fancy to see if my atoll still existed.

'He didn't come a moment too soon, for I was about sick enough of the desolation of it, and only hesitating whether I should walk out into the sea and finish up the business that way, or fall back on the green things. . . .

'I sold the bones to a man named Winslow—a dealer near the British Museum, and he says he sold them to old Havers. It seems Havers didn't understand they were extra large, and it was only after his death they attracted attention. They called 'em Æpyornis—what was it?'

'*Æpyornis vastus*,' said I. 'It's funny, the very thing was mentioned to me by a friend of mine. When they found an Æpyornis, with a thigh a yard long, they thought they had reached the top of the scale, and called him *Æpyornis maximus*. Then some one turned up another thigh-bone four feet six or more, and that they called *Æpyornis Titan*. Then your *vastus* was found after old Havers died, in his collection, and then a *vastissimus* turned up.'

'Winslow was telling me as much,' said the man with the scar. 'If they get any more Æpyornises, he reckons some scientific swell will go and burst a blood-vessel. But it was a queer thing to happen to a man; wasn't it—altogether?'

VII

THE REMARKABLE CASE OF
DAVIDSON'S EYES

I

THE transitory mental aberration of Sidney Davidson, remarkable enough in itself, is still more remarkable if Wade's explanation is to be credited. It sets one dreaming of the oddest possibilities of intercommunication in the future, of spending an intercalary* five minutes on the other side of the world, or being watched in our most secret operations by unsuspected eyes. It happened that I was the immediate witness of Davidson's seizure, and so it falls naturally to me to put the story upon paper.

When I say that I was the immediate witness of his seizure, I mean that I was the first on the scene. The thing happened at the Harlow Technical College, just beyond the Highgate Archway. He was alone in the larger laboratory when the thing happened. I was in a smaller room, where the balances are, writing up some notes. The thunderstorm had completely upset my work, of course. It was just after one of the louder peals that I thought I heard some glass smash in the other room. I stopped writing, and turned round to listen. For a moment I heard nothing; the hail was playing the devil's tattoo on the corrugated zinc of the roof. Then came another sound, a smash—no doubt of it this time. Something heavy had been knocked off the bench. I jumped up at once and went and opened the door leading into the big laboratory.

I was surprised to hear a queer sort of laugh, and saw Davidson standing unsteadily in the middle of the room, with a dazzled look on his face. My first impression was that he was drunk. He did not notice me. He was clawing out at something invisible a yard in front of his face. He put out his hand, slowly, rather hesitatingly, and then clutched nothing. 'What's come to it?' he said. He held up his hands to his face, fingers spread out. 'Great Scott!' he said. The thing happened three or four years ago, when every one swore by that personage. Then he began raising his feet clumsily, as though he had expected to find them glued to the floor.

'Davidson!' cried I. 'What's the matter with you?' He turned round in my direction and looked about for me. He looked over me and at me and on either side of me, without the slightest sign of seeing me. 'Waves,' he said; 'and a remarkably neat schooner. I'd swear that was Bellows'* voice. *Hullo!*' He shouted suddenly at the top of his voice.

I thought he was up to some foolery. Then I saw littered about his feet the shattered remains of the best of our electrometers. 'What's up, man?' said I. 'You've smashed the electrometer!'

'Bellows again!' said he. 'Friends left, if my hands are gone. Something about electrometers. Which way *are* you, Bellows?' He suddenly came staggering towards me. 'The damned stuff cuts like butter,' he said. He walked straight into the bench and recoiled. 'None so buttery that!' he said, and stood swaying.

I felt scared. 'Davidson,' said I, 'what on earth's come over you?'

He looked round him in every direction. 'I could swear that was Bellows. Why don't you show yourself like a man, Bellows?'

It occurred to me that he must be suddenly struck blind. I walked round the table and laid my hand upon his arm. I never saw a man more startled in my life. He jumped away from me, and came round into an attitude of self-defence, his face fairly distorted with terror. 'Good God!' he cried. 'What was that?'

'It's I—Bellows. Confound it, Davidson!'

He jumped when I answered him and stared—how can I

express it?—right through me. He began talking, not to me, but to himself. 'Here in broad daylight on a clear beach. Not a place to hide in.' He looked about him wildly. 'Here! I'm *off.*' He suddenly turned and ran headlong into the big electromagnet—so violently that, as we found afterwards, he bruised his shoulder and jawbone cruelly. At that he stepped back a pace, and cried out with almost a whimper, 'What, in Heaven's name, has come over me?' He stood, blanched with terror and trembling violently, with his right arm clutching his left, where that had collided with the magnet.

By that time I was excited and fairly scared. 'Davidson,' said I, 'don't be afraid.'

He was startled at my voice, but not so excessively as before. I repeated my words in as clear and as firm a tone as I could assume. 'Bellows,' he said, 'is that you?'

'Can't you see it's me?'

He laughed. 'I can't even see it's myself. Where the devil are we?'

'Here,' said I, 'in the laboratory.'

'The laboratory!' he answered in a puzzled tone, and put his hand to his forehead. 'I *was* in the laboratory—till that flash came, but I'm hanged if I'm there now. What ship is that?'

'There's no ship,' said I. 'Do be sensible, old chap.'

'No ship!' he repeated, and seemed to forget my denial forthwith. 'I suppose,' said he slowly, 'we're both dead. But the rummy part is I feel just as though I still had a body. Don't get used to it all at once, I suppose. The old shop was struck by lightning, I suppose. Jolly quick thing, Bellows—eigh?'

'Don't talk nonsense. You're very much alive. You are in the laboratory, blundering about. You've just smashed a new electrometer. I don't envy you when Boyce arrives.'

He stared away from me towards the diagrams of cryo-hydrates.* 'I must be deaf,' said he. 'They've fired a gun, for there goes the puff of smoke, and I never heard a sound.'

I put my hand on his arm again, and this time he was less alarmed. 'We seem to have a sort of invisible bodies,' said he.

'By Jove! there's a boat coming round the headland. It's very much like the old life after all—in a different climate.'

I shook his arm. 'Davidson,' I cried, 'wake up!'

II

IT was just then that Boyce came in. So soon as he spoke Davidson exclaimed: 'Old Boyce! Dead too! What a lark!' I hastened to explain that Davidson was in a kind of somnambulistic trance. Boyce was interested at once. We both did all we could to rouse the fellow out of his extraordinary state. He answered our questions, and asked us some of his own, but his attention seemed distracted by his hallucination about a beach and a ship. He kept interpolating observations concerning some boat and the davits, and sails filling with the wind. It made one feel queer, in the dusky laboratory, to hear him saying such things.

He was blind and helpless. We had to walk him down the passage, one at each elbow, to Boyce's private room, and while Boyce talked to him there, and humoured him about this ship idea, I went along the corridor and asked old Wade to come and look at him. The voice of our Dean sobered him a little, but not very much. He asked where his hands were, and why he had to walk about up to his waist in the ground. Wade thought over him a long time—you know how he knits his brows—and then made him feel the couch, guiding his hands to it. 'That's a couch,' said Wade. 'The couch in the private room of Professor Boyce. Horse-hair stuffing.'

Davidson felt about, and puzzled over it, and answered presently that he could feel it all right, but he couldn't see it.

'What *do* you see?' asked Wade. Davidson said he could see nothing but a lot of sand and broken-up shells. Wade gave him some other things to feel, telling him what they were, and watching him keenly.

'The ship is almost hull down,' said Davidson presently, *apropos* of nothing.

'Never mind the ship,' said Wade. 'Listen to me, Davidson. Do you know what hallucination means?'

'Rather,' said Davidson.

'Well, everything you see is hallucinatory.'

'Bishop Berkeley,'* said Davidson.

'Don't mistake me,' said Wade. 'You are alive and in this room of Boyce's. But something has happened to your eyes. You cannot see; you can feel and hear, but not see. Do you follow me?'

'It seems to me that I see too much.' Davidson rubbed his knuckles into his eyes. 'Well?' he said.

'That's all. Don't let it perplex you. Bellows here and I will take you home in a cab.'

'Wait a bit.' Davidson thought. 'Help me to sit down,' said he presently; 'and now—I'm sorry to trouble you—but will you tell me all that over again?'

Wade repeated it very patiently. Davidson shut his eyes, and pressed his hands upon his forehead. 'Yes,' said he. 'It's quite right. Now my eyes are shut I know you're right. That's you, Bellows, sitting by me on the couch. I'm in England again. And we're in the dark.'

Then he opened his eyes. 'And there,' said he, 'is the sun just rising, and the yards of the ship, and a tumbled sea, and a couple of birds flying. I never saw anything so real. And I'm sitting up to my neck in a bank of sand.'

He bent forward and covered his face with his hands. Then he opened his eyes again. 'Dark sea and sunrise! And yet I'm sitting on a sofa in old Boyce's room! . . . God help me!'

III

THAT was the beginning. For three weeks this strange affection of Davidson's eyes continued unabated. It was far worse than being blind. He was absolutely helpless, and had to be fed like a newly-hatched bird, and led about and undressed. If he attempted to move, he fell over things or struck

68

himself against walls or doors. After a day or so he got used to hearing our voices without seeing us, and willingly admitted he was at home, and that Wade was right in what he told him. My sister, to whom he was engaged, insisted on coming to see him, and would sit for hours every day while he talked about this beach of his. Holding her hand seemed to comfort him immensely. He explained that when we left the College and drove home—he lived in Hampstead village—it appeared to him as if we drove right through a sandhill—it was perfectly black until he emerged again—and through rocks and trees and solid obstacles, and when he was taken to his own room it made him giddy and almost frantic with the fear of falling, because going upstairs seemed to lift him thirty or forty feet above the rocks of his imaginary island. He kept saying he should smash all the eggs. The end was that he had to be taken down into his father's consulting room and laid upon a couch that stood there.

He described the island as being a bleak kind of place on the whole, with very little vegetation, except some peaty stuff, and a lot of bare rock. There were multitudes of penguins, and they made the rocks white and disagreeable to see. The sea was often rough, and once there was a thunderstorm, and he lay and shouted at the silent flashes. Once or twice seals pulled up on the beach, but only on the first two or three days. He said it was very funny the way in which the penguins used to waddle right through him, and how he seemed to lie among them without disturbing them.

I remember one odd thing, and that was when he wanted very badly to smoke. We put a pipe in his hands—he almost poked his eye out with it—and lit it. But he couldn't taste anything. I've since found it's the same with me—I don't know if it's the usual case—that I cannot enjoy tobacco at all unless I can see the smoke.

But the queerest part of his vision came when Wade sent him out in a Bath-chair to get fresh air. The Davidsons hired a chair, and got that deaf and obstinate dependant of theirs,

Widgery, to attend to it. Widgery's ideas of healthy expeditions were peculiar. My sister, who had been to the Dogs' Home, met them in Camden Town, towards King's Cross, Widgery trotting along complacently, and Davidson, evidently most distressed, trying in his feeble, blind way to attract Widgery's attention.

He positively wept when my sister spoke to him. 'Oh, get me out of this horrible darkness!' he said, feeling for her hand. 'I must get out of it, or I shall die.' He was quite incapable of explaining what was the matter, but my sister decided he must go home, and presently, as they went uphill towards Hampstead, the horror seemed to drop from him. He said it was good to see the stars again, though it was then about noon and a blazing day.

'It seemed,' he told me afterwards, 'as if I was being carried irresistibly towards the water. I was not very much alarmed at first. Of course it was night there—a lovely night.'

'Of course?' I asked, for that struck me as odd.

'Of course,' said he. 'It's always night there when it is day here. . . . Well, we went right into the water, which was calm and shining under the moonlight—just a broad swell that seemed to grow broader and flatter as I came down into it. The surface glistened just like a skin—it might have been empty space underneath for all I could tell to the contrary. Very slowly, for I rode slanting into it, the water crept up to my eyes. Then I went under and the skin seemed to break and heal again about my eyes. The moon gave a jump up in the sky and grew green and dim, and fish, faintly glowing, came darting round me—and things that seemed made of luminous glass; and I passed through a tangle of seaweeds that shone with an oily lustre. And so I drove down into the sea, and the stars went out one by one, and the moon grew greener and darker, and the seaweed became a luminous purple-red. It was all very faint and mysterious, and everything seemed to quiver. And all the while I could hear the wheels of the Bath-chair creaking, and the footsteps of people going by, and a man in the distance selling the special *Pall Mall.**

'I kept sinking down deeper and deeper into the water. It became inky black about me, not a ray from above came down into that darkness, and the phosphorescent things grew brighter and brighter. The snaky branches of the deeper weeds flickered like the flames of spirit-lamps; but, after a time, there were no more weeds. The fishes came staring and gaping towards me, and into me and through me. I never imagined such fishes before. They had lines of fire along the sides of them as though they had been outlined with a luminous pencil. And there was a ghastly thing swimming backwards with a lot of twining arms. And then I saw, coming very slowly towards me through the gloom, a hazy mass of light that resolved itself as it drew nearer into multitudes of fishes, struggling and darting round something that drifted. I drove on straight towards it, and presently I saw in the midst of the tumult, and by the light of the fish, a bit of splintered spar looming over me, and a dark hull tilting over, and some glowing phosphorescent forms that were shaken and writhed as the fish bit at them. Then it was I began to try to attract Widgery's attention. A horror came upon me. Ugh! I should have driven right into those half-eaten —— things. If your sister had not come! They had great holes in them, Bellows, and . . . Never mind. But it was ghastly!'

IV

FOR three weeks Davidson remained in this singular state, seeing what at the time we imagined was an altogether phantasmal world, and stone blind to the world around him. Then, one Tuesday, when I called I met old Davidson in the passage. 'He can see his thumb!' the old gentleman said, in a perfect transport. He was struggling into his overcoat. 'He can see his thumb, Bellows!' he said, with the tears in his eyes. 'The lad will be all right yet.'

I rushed in to Davidson. He was holding up a little book before his face, and looking at it and laughing in a weak kind of way.

'It's amazing,' said he. 'There's a kind of patch come there.' He pointed with his finger. 'I'm on the rocks as usual, and the penguins are staggering and flapping about as usual, and there's been a whale showing every now and then, but it's got too dark now to make him out. But put something *there*, and I see it—I do see it. It's very dim and broken in places, but I see it all the same, like a faint spectre of itself. I found it out this morning while they were dressing me. It's like a hole in this infernal phantom world. Just put your hand by mine. No—not there. Ah! Yes! I see it. The base of your thumb and a bit of cuff! It looks like the ghost of a bit of your hand sticking out of the darkling sky. Just by it there's a group of stars like a cross coming out.'

From that time Davidson began to mend. His account of the change, like his account of the vision, was oddly convincing. Over patches of his field of vision, the phantom world grew fainter, grew transparent, as it were, and through these translucent gaps he began to see dimly the real world about him. The patches grew in size and number, ran together and spread until only here and there were blind spots left upon his eyes. He was able to get up and steer himself about, feed himself once more, read, smoke, and behave like an ordinary citizen again. At first it was very confusing to him to have these two pictures overlapping each other like the changing views of a lantern,* but in a little while he began to distinguish the real from the illusory.

At first he was unfeignedly glad, and seemed only too anxious to complete his cure by taking exercise and tonics. But as that odd island of his began to fade away from him, he became queerly interested in it. He wanted particularly to go down into the deep sea again, and would spend half his time wandering about the low-lying parts of London, trying to find the water-logged wreck he had seen drifting. The glare of real daylight very soon impressed him so vividly as to blot out everything of his shadowy world, but of a night-time, in a darkened room, he could still see the white-splashed rocks of the island, and the clumsy penguins staggering to and fro. But even these grew fainter and fainter, and, at last, soon after he married my sister, he saw them for the last time.

V

AND now to tell of the queerest thing of all. About two years after his cure I dined with the Davidsons, and after dinner a man named Atkins called in. He is a lieutenant in the Royal Navy, and a pleasant, talkative man. He was on friendly terms with my brother-in-law, and was soon on friendly terms with me. It came out that he was engaged to Davidson's cousin, and incidentally he took out a kind of pocket photograph case to show us a new rendering of his *fiancée*. 'And, by-the-by,' said he, 'here's the old *Fulmar*.'

Davidson looked at it casually. Then suddenly his face lit up. 'Good heavens!' said he. 'I could almost swear——'

'What?' said Atkins.

'That I had seen that ship before.'

'Don't see how you can have. She hasn't been out of the South Seas for six years, and before then——'

'But,' began Davidson, and then, 'Yes—that's the ship I dreamt of; I'm sure that's the ship I dreamt of. She was standing off an island that swarmed with penguins, and she fired a gun.'

'Good Lord!' said Atkins, who had now heard the particulars of the seizure. 'How the deuce could you dream that?'

And then, bit by bit, it came out that on the very day Davidson was seized, H.M.S. *Fulmar* had actually been off a little rock to the south of Antipodes Island.* A boat had landed overnight to get penguins' eggs, had been delayed, and a thunderstorm drifting up, the boat's crew had waited until the morning before rejoining the ship. Atkins had been one of them, and he corroborated, word for word, the descriptions Davidson had given of the island and the boat. There is not the slightest doubt in any of our minds that Davidson has really seen the place. In some unaccountable way, while he moved hither and thither in London, his sight moved hither and thither in a manner that corresponded, about this distant island. *How* is absolutely a mystery.

That completes the remarkable story of Davidson's eyes. It's perhaps the best authenticated case in existence of real vision at a distance. Explanation there is none forthcoming, except what Professor Wade has thrown out. But his explanation invokes the Fourth Dimension, and a dissertation on theoretical kinds of space. To talk of there being 'a kink in space' seems mere nonsense to me; it may be because I am no mathematician. When I said that nothing would alter the fact that the place is eight thousand miles away, he answered that two points might be a yard away on a sheet of paper, and yet be brought together by bending the paper round. The reader may grasp his argument, but I certainly do not. His idea seems to be that Davidson, stooping between the poles of the big electro-magnet, had some extraordinary twist given to his retinal elements* through the sudden change in the field of force due to the lightning.

He thinks, as a consequence of this, that it may be possible to live visually in one part of the world, while one lives bodily in another. He has even made some experiments in support of his views; but, so far, he has simply succeeded in blinding a few dogs. I believe that is the net result of his work, though I have not seen him for some weeks. Latterly I have been so busy with my work in connection with the Saint Pancras installation that I have had little opportunity of calling to see him. But the whole of his theory seems fantastic to me. The facts concerning Davidson stand on an altogether different footing, and I can testify personally to the accuracy of every detail I have given.

VIII

THE LORD OF THE DYNAMOS

THE chief attendant of the three dynamos that buzzed and rattled at Camberwell,* and kept the electric railway going, came out of Yorkshire, and his name was James Holroyd. He was a practical electrician, but fond of whisky, a heavy, red-haired brute with irregular teeth. He doubted the existence of the Deity, but accepted Carnot's cycle,* and he had read Shakespeare and found him weak in chemistry. His helper came out of the mysterious East, and his name was Azuma-zi. But Holroyd called him Pooh-bah.* Holroyd liked a nigger help because he would stand kicking—a habit with Holroyd—and did not pry into the machinery and try to learn the ways of it. Certain odd possibilities of the negro mind brought into abrupt contact with the crown of our civilisation Holroyd never fully realised, though just at the end he got some inkling of them.

To define Azuma-zi was beyond ethnology. He was, per-haps, more negroid than anything else, though his hair was curly rather than frizzy, and his nose had a bridge. Moreover, his skin was brown rather than black, and the whites of his eyes were yellow. His broad cheek-bones and narrow chin gave his face something of the viperine V. His head, too, was broad behind, and low and narrow at the forehead, as if his brain had been twisted round in the reverse way to a Euro-pean's. He was short of stature and still shorter of English. In conversation he made numerous odd noises of no known marketable value, and his infrequent words were carved and wrought into heraldic grotesqueness.* Holroyd tried to elucidate his religious beliefs, and—especially after whisky—lectured to him against superstition and missionaries.

75

Azuma-zi, however, shirked the discussion of his gods, even though he was kicked for it.

Azuma-zi had come, clad in white but insufficient raiment, out of the stoke-hole of the *Lord Clive*,* from the Straits Settlements* and beyond, into London. He had heard even is his youth of the greatness and riches of London, where all the women are white and fair, and even the beggars in the streets are white, and he had arrived, with newly-earned gold coins in his pocket, to worship at the shrine of civilisation. The day of his landing was a dismal one; the sky was dun, and a wind-worried drizzle filtered down to the greasy streets, but he plunged boldly into the delights of Shadwell,* and was presently cast up, shattered in health, civilised in costume, penniless, and, except in matters of the direst necessity, practically a dumb animal, to toil for James Holroyd, and to be bullied by him in the dynamo shed at Camberwell. And to James Holroyd bullying was a labour of love.

There were three dynamos with their engines at Camberwell. The two that have been there since the beginning are small machines; the larger one was new. The smaller machines made a reasonable noise; their straps hummed over the drums, every now and then the brushes buzzed and fizzled, and the air churned steadily, whoo! whoo! whoo! between their poles. One was loose in its foundations and kept the shed vibrating. But the big dynamo drowned these little noises altogether with the sustained drone of its iron core, which somehow set part of the ironwork humming. The place made the visitor's head reel with the throb, throb, throb of the engines, the rotation of the big wheels, the spinning ball-valves, the occasional spittings of the steam, and over all the deep, unceasing, surging note of the big dynamo. This last noise was from an engineering point of view a defect, but Azuma-zi accounted it unto the monster for mightiness and pride.

If it were possible we would have the noises of that shed always about the reader as he reads, we would tell all our story to such an accompaniment. It was a steady stream of din, from which the ear picked out first one thread and then another; there was the intermittent snorting, panting, and seething of the steam engines, the suck and thud of their pistons, the dull beat on the air as the spokes of the great driving wheels came round, a note the leather straps made as they ran tighter and looser, and a fretful tumult from the dynamos; and, over all, sometimes inaudible, as the ear tired of it, and then creeping back upon the senses again, was this trombone note of the big machine. The floor never felt steady and quiet beneath one's feet, but quivered and jarred. It was a confusing, unsteady place, and enough to send anyone's thoughts jerking into odd zigzags. And for three months, while the big strike of the engineers was in progress, Holroyd, who was a blackleg,* and Azuma-zi, who was a mere black, were never out of the stir and eddy of it, but slept and fed in the little wooden shanty between the shed and the gates.

Holroyd delivered a theological lecture on the text of his big machine soon after Azuma-zi came. He had to shout to be heard in the din. 'Look at that,' said Holroyd; 'where's your 'eathen idol to match 'im?' And Azuma-zi looked. For a moment Holroyd was inaudible, and then Azuma-zi heard: 'Kill a hundred men. Twelve per cent. on the ordinary shares,'* said Holroyd, 'and that's something like a Gord.'

Holroyd was proud of his big dynamo, and expatiated upon its size and power to Azuma-zi until heaven knows what odd currents of thought that and the incessant whirling and shindy set up within the curly black cranium. He would explain in the most graphic manner the dozen or so ways in which a man might be killed by it, and once he gave Azuma-zi a shock as a sample of its quality. After that, in the breathing-times of his labour—it was heavy labour, being not only his own, but most of Holroyd's—Azuma-zi would sit and watch the big machine. Now and then the brushes would sparkle and spit blue flashes, at which Holroyd would swear, but all the rest was as smooth and rhythmic as breathing. The band ran shouting over the shaft, and ever behind one as one watched was the complacent thud of the piston. So it lived all day in this big airy shed, with him and Holroyd to wait upon it; not prisoned up and slaving to drive a ship as the other engines he knew—mere captive devils of the British Solomon*—had been, but a machine enthroned. Those two smaller dynamos Azuma-zi by force of contrast despised; the large one he privately christened the Lord of the Dynamos. They were fretful and irregular, but the big dynamo was steady. How great it was! How serene and easy in its working! Greater and calmer even than the Buddhas he had seen at Rangoon, and yet not motionless, but living! The great black coils spun, spun, spun, the rings ran round under the brushes, and the deep note of its coil steadied the whole. It affected Azuma-zi queerly.

Azuma-zi was not fond of labour. He would sit about and watch the Lord of the Dynamos while Holroyd went away to persuade the yard porter to get whisky, although his proper place was not in the dynamo shed but behind the engines, and, moreover, if Holroyd caught him skulking he got hit for it with a rod of stout copper wire. He would go and stand close to the colossus, and look up at the great leather band running overhead. There was a black patch on the band that came round, and it pleased him somehow among all the clatter to watch this return again and again. Odd thoughts spun with the whirl of it. Scientific people tell us that savages give souls to rocks and trees,—and a machine is a thousand times more alive than a rock or a tree. And Azuma-zi was practically a savage still; the veneer of civilisation lay no deeper than his slop suit,* his bruises, and the coal grime on his face and hands. His father before him had worshipped a meteoric stone, kindred blood, it may be, had splashed the broad wheels of Juggernaut.*

He took every opportunity Holroyd gave him of touching and handling the great dynamo that was fascinating him. He polished and cleaned it until the metal parts were blinding in the sun. He felt a mysterious sense of service in doing this. He would go up to it and touch its spinning coils gently. The gods he had worshipped were all far away. The people in London hid their gods.

At last his dim feelings grew more distinct, and took shape in thoughts, and at last in acts. When he came into the roaring shed one morning he salaamed to the Lord of the Dynamos, and then, when Holroyd was away, he went and whispered to the thundering machine that he was its servant, and prayed it to have pity on him and save him from Holroyd. As he did so a rare gleam of light came in through the open archway of the throbbing machine-shed, and the Lord of the Dynamos, as he whirled and roared, was radiant with pale gold. Then Azuma-zi knew that his service was acceptable to his Lord. After that he did not feel so lonely as he had done, and he had indeed been very much alone in London. And even when his work-time was over, which was rare, he loitered about the shed.

Then, the next time Holroyd maltreated him, Azuma-zi went presently to the Lord of the Dynamos and whispered, 'Thou seest, O my Lord!' and the angry whirr of the machinery seemed to answer him. Thereafter it appeared to him that whenever Holroyd came into the shed a different note came into the sounds of the dynamo. 'My Lord bides his time,' said Azuma-zi to himself. 'The iniquity of the fool is not yet ripe.' And he waited and watched for the day of reckoning. One day there was evidence of short circuiting, and Holroyd, making an unwary examination—it was in the afternoon— got a rather severe shock. Azuma-zi from behind the engine saw him jump off and curse at the peccant* coil.

'He is warned,' said Azuma-zi to himself. 'Surely my Lord is very patient.'

Holroyd had at first initiated his 'nigger' into such elementary conceptions of the dynamo's working as would enable him to take temporary charge of the shed in his absence. But when he noticed the manner in which Azuma-zi hung about the monster he became suspicious. He dimly perceived his assistant was 'up to something,' and connecting him with the anointing of the coils with oil that had rotted the varnish in one place, he issued an edict, shouted above the confusion of the machinery, 'Don't 'ee go nigh that big dynamo any more, Pooh-bah, or a'll take thy skin off!' Besides, if it pleased Azuma-zi to be near the big machine, it was plain sense and decency to keep him away from it.

Azuma-zi obeyed at the time, but later he was caught bowing before the Lord of the Dynamos. At which Holroyd twisted his arm and kicked him as he turned to go away. As Azuma-zi presently stood behind the engine and glared at the back of the hated Holroyd, the noises of the machinery took a new rhythm, and sounded like four words in his native tongue.

It is hard to say exactly what madness is. I fancy Azuma-zi was mad. The incessant din and whirl of the dynamo shed may have churned up his little store of knowledge and big store of superstitious fancy, at last, into something akin to frenzy. At any rate, when the idea of making Holroyd a sacrifice to the Dynamo Fetich* was thus suggested to him, it filled him with a strange tumult of exultant emotion.

That night the two men and their black shadows were alone in the shed together. The shed was lit with one big arc light that winked and flickered purple. The shadows lay black behind the dynamos, the ball governors of the engines whirled from light to darkness, and their pistons beat loud and steady. The world outside seen through the open end of the shed seemed incredibly dim and remote. It seemed absolutely silent, too, since the riot of the machinery drowned every external sound. Far away was the black fence of the yard with grey shadowy houses behind, and above was the deep blue sky and the pale little stars. Azuma-zi suddenly walked across the centre of the shed above which the leather bands were running, and went into the shadow by the big dynamo. Holroyd heard a click, and the spin of the armature* changed.

'What are you dewin' with that switch?' he bawled in surprise. 'Han't I told you——'

Then he saw the set expression of Azuma-zi's eyes as the Asiatic came out of the shadow towards him.

In another moment the two men were grappling fiercely in front of the great dynamo.

'You coffee-headed fool!' gasped Holroyd, with a brown hand at his throat. 'Keep off those contact rings.' In another moment he was tripped and reeling back upon the Lord of the Dynamos. He instinctively loosened his grip upon his antagonist to save himself from the machine.

The messenger, sent in furious haste from the station to find out what had happened in the dynamo shed, met Azuma-zi at the porter's lodge by the gate. Azuma-zi tried to explain something, but the messenger could make nothing of the black's incoherent English, and hurried on to the shed. The machines were all noisily at work, and nothing seemed to be disarranged. There was, however, a queer smell of singed hair. Then he saw an odd-looking crumpled mass clinging to the front of the big dynamo, and, approaching, recognised the distorted remains of Holroyd.

The man stared and hesitated a moment. Then he saw the face, and shut his eyes convulsively. He turned on his heel before he opened them, so that he should not see Holroyd again, and went out of the shed to get advice and help.

When Azuma-zi saw Holroyd die in the grip of the Great Dynamo he had been a little scared about the consequences of his act. Yet he felt strangely elated, and knew that the favour of the Lord Dynamo was upon him. His plan was already settled when he met the man coming from the station, and the scientific manager who speedily arrived on the scene jumped at the obvious conclusion of suicide. This expert scarcely noticed Azuma-zi, except to ask a few questions. Did he see Holroyd kill himself? Azuma-zi explained he had been out of sight at the engine furnace until he heard a difference in the noise from the dynamo. It was not a difficult examination, being untinctured by suspicion.

The distorted remains of Holroyd, which the electrician removed from the machine, were hastily covered by the porter with a coffee-stained table-cloth. Somebody, by a happy inspiration, fetched a medical man. The expert was chiefly anxious to get the machine at work again, for seven or eight trains had stopped midway in the stuffy tunnels of the electric railway. Azuma-zi, answering or misunderstanding the questions of the people who had by authority or impudence come into the shed, was presently sent back to the stoke-hole by the scientific manager. Of course a crowd collected outside the gates of the yard—a crowd, for no known reason, always hovers for a day or two near the scene of a sudden death in London—two or three reporters percolated somehow into the engine-shed, and one even got to Azuma-zi; but the scientific expert cleared them out again, being himself an amateur journalist.

Presently the body was carried away, and public interest departed with it. Azuma-zi remained very quietly at his furnace, seeing over and over again in the coals a figure that wriggled violently and became still. An hour after the murder, to any one coming into the shed it would have looked exactly as if nothing remarkable had ever happened there. Peeping presently from his engine-room the black saw the Lord Dynamo spin and whirl beside his little brothers, and the driving wheels were beating round, and the steam in the pistons went thud, thud, exactly as it had been earlier in the evening. After all, from the mechanical point of view, it had been a most insignificant incident—the mere temporary deflection of a current. But now the slender form and slender shadow of the scientific manager replaced the sturdy outline of Holroyd travelling up and down the lane of light upon the vibrating floor under the straps between the engines and the dynamos.

'Have I not served my Lord?' said Azuma-zi inaudibly,

from his shadow, and the note of the great dynamo rang out full and clear. As he looked at the big whirling mechanism the strange fascination of it that had been a little in abeyance since Holroyd's death resumed its sway.

Never had Azuma-zi seen a man killed so swiftly and pitilessly. The big humming machine had slain its victim without wavering for a second from its steady beating. It was indeed a mighty god.

The unconscious scientific manager stood with his back to him, scribbling on a piece of paper. His shadow lay at the foot of the monster.

Was the Lord Dynamo still hungry? His servant was ready.

Azuma-zi made a stealthy step forward; then stopped. The scientific manager suddenly ceased his writing, walked down the shed to the endmost of the dynamos, and began to examine the brushes.

Azuma-zi hesitated, and then slipped across noiselessly into the shadow by the switch. There he waited. Presently the manager's footsteps could be heard returning. He stopped in his old position, unconscious of the stoker crouching ten feet away from him. Then the big dynamo suddenly fizzled, and in another moment Azuma-zi had sprung out of the darkness upon him.

First, the scientific manager was gripped round the body and swung towards the big dynamo, then, kicking with his knee and forcing his antagonist's head down with his hands, he loosened the grip on his waist and swung round away from the machine. Then the black grasped him again, putting a curly head against his chest, and they swayed and panted as it seemed for an age or so. Then the scientific manager was impelled to catch a black ear in his teeth and bite furiously. The black yelled hideously.

They rolled over on the floor, and the black, who had apparently slipped from the vice of the teeth or parted with some ear—the scientific manager wondered which at the time—tried to throttle him. The scientific manager was making some ineffectual efforts to claw something with his hands and to kick, when the welcome sound of quick footsteps sounded on the floor. The next moment Azuma-zi had left him and darted towards the big dynamo. There was a splutter amid the roar.

The officer of the company who had entered stood staring as Azuma-zi caught the naked terminals in his hands, gave one horrible convulsion, and then hung motionless from the machine, his face violently distorted.

'I'm jolly glad you came in when you did,' said the scientific manager, still sitting on the floor.

He looked at the still quivering figure. 'It is not a nice death to die, apparently—but it is quick.'

The official was still staring at the body. He was a man of slow apprehension.

There was a pause.

The scientific manager got up on his feet rather awkwardly. He ran his fingers along his collar thoughtfully, and moved his head to and fro several times.

'Poor Holroyd! I see now.' Then almost mechanically he went towards the switch in the shadow and turned the current into the railway circuit again. As he did so the singed body loosened its grip upon the machine and fell forward on its face. The core of the dynamo roared out loud and clear, and the armature beat the air.

So ended prematurely the worship of the Dynamo Deity, perhaps the most short-lived of all religions. Yet withal it could at least boast a Martyrdom and a Human Sacrifice.

IX

THE MOTH

PROBABLY you have heard of Hapley—not W. T. Hapley, the son, but the celebrated Hapley, the Hapley of *Periplaneta Hapliia*, Hapley the entomologist.

If so you know at least of the great feud between Hapley and Professor Pawkins, though certain of its consequences may be new to you. For those who have not, a word or two of explanation is necessary, which the idle reader may go over with a glancing eye, if his indolence so incline him.

It is amazing how very widely diffused is the ignorance of such really important matters as this Hapley-Pawkins feud. Those epoch-making controversies, again, that have convulsed the Geological Society are, I verily believe, almost entirely unknown outside the fellowship of that body. I have heard men of fair general education even refer to the great scenes at these meetings as vestry-meeting squabbles. Yet the great hate of the English and Scotch geologists* has lasted now half a century, and has 'left deep and abundant marks upon the body of the science.' And this Hapley-Pawkins business, though perhaps a more personal affair, stirred passions as profound, if not profounder. Your common man has no conception of the zeal that animates a scientific investigator, the fury of contradiction you can arouse in him. It is the *odium theologicum** in a new form. There are men, for instance, who would gladly burn Professor Ray Lankester* at Smithfield* for his treatment of the Mollusca in the Encyclopædia. That fantastic extension of the Cephalopods to cover the Pteropods* ... But I wander from Hapley and Pawkins.

It began years and years ago, with a revision of the Microlepidoptera* (whatever these may be) by Pawkins, in which he extinguished a new species created by Hapley.

Hapley, who was always quarrelsome, replied by a stinging impeachment of the entire classification of Pawkins.[1] Pawkins in his 'Rejoinder'[2] suggested that Hapley's microscope was as defective as his power of observation, and called him an 'irresponsible meddler'—Hapley was not a professor at that time. Hapley in his retort,[3] spoke of 'blundering collectors,' and described, as if inadvertently, Pawkins' revision as a 'miracle of ineptitude.' It was war to the knife. However, it would scarcely interest the reader to detail how these two great men quarrelled, and how the split between them widened until from the Microlepidoptera they were at war upon every open question in entomology. There were memorable occasions. At times the Royal Entomological Society meetings resembled nothing so much as the Chamber of Deputies.* On the whole, I fancy Pawkins was nearer the truth than Hapley. But Hapley was skilful with his rhetoric, had a turn for ridicule rare in a scientific man, was endowed with vast energy, and had a fine sense of injury in the matter of the extinguished species; while Pawkins was a man of dull presence, prosy of speech, in shape not unlike a water-barrel, over conscientious with testimonials, and suspected of jobbing museum appointments.* So the young men gathered round Hapley and applauded him. It was a long struggle, vicious from the beginning and growing at last to pitiless antagonism. The successive turns of fortune, now an advantage to one side and now to another—now Hapley tormented by some success of Pawkins, and now Pawkins outshone by Hapley, belong rather to the history of entomology than to this story.

But in 1891 Pawkins, whose health had been bad for some time, published some work upon the 'mesoblast'* of the Death's Head Moth. What the mesoblast of the Death's Head Moth may be does not matter a rap in this story. But

[1] 'Remarks on a Recent Revision of Microlepidoptera.' *Quart. Journ. Entomological Soc.*, 1863.

[2] 'Rejoinder to certain Remarks,' etc. *Ibid.* 1864.

[3] 'Further Remarks,' etc. *Ibid.*

the work was far below his usual standard, and gave Hapley an opening he had coveted for years. He must have worked night and day to make the most of his advantage.

In an elaborate critique he rent Pawkins to tatters—one can fancy the man's disordered black hair, and his queer dark eyes flashing as he went for his antagonist—and Pawkins made a reply, halting, ineffectual, with painful gaps of silence, and yet malignant. There was no mistaking his will to wound Hapley, nor his incapacity to do it. But few of those who heard him—I was absent from that meeting—realised how ill the man was.

Hapley got his opponent down, and meant to finish him. He followed with a simply brutal attack upon Pawkins, in the form of a paper upon the development of moths in general, a paper showing evidence of a most extraordinary amount of mental labour, and yet couched in a violently controversial tone. Violent as it was, an editorial note witnesses that it was modified. It must have covered Pawkins with shame and confusion of face. It left no loophole; it was murderous in argument, and utterly contemptuous in tone; an awful thing for the declining years of a man's career.

The world of entomologists waited breathlessly for the rejoinder from Pawkins. He would try one, for Pawkins had always been game. But when it came it surprised them. For the rejoinder of Pawkins was to catch influenza, proceed to pneumonia, and die.

It was perhaps as effectual a reply as he could make under the circumstances, and largely turned the current of feeling against Hapley. The very people who had most gleefully cheered on those gladiators became serious at the consequence. There could be no reasonable doubt the fret of the defeat had contributed to the death of Pawkins. There was a limit even to scientific controversy, said serious people. Another crushing attack was already in the press and appeared on the day before the funeral. I don't think Hapley exerted himself to stop it. People remembered how Hapley had hounded down his rival, and forgot that rival's defects. Scathing satire reads ill over fresh mould. The thing provoked comment in the daily papers. This it was that made me think that you had probably heard of Hapley and this controversy. But, as I have already remarked, scientific workers live very much in a world of their own; half the people, I dare say, who go along Piccadilly to the Academy* every year, could not tell you where the learned societies abide. Many even think that research is a kind of happy-family cage in which all kinds of men lie down together in peace.

In his private thoughts Hapley could not forgive Pawkins for dying. In the first place, it was a mean dodge to escape the absolute pulverisation Hapley had in hand for him, and in the second, it left Hapley's mind with a queer gap in it. For twenty years he had worked hard, sometimes far into the night, and seven days a week, with microscope, scalpel, collecting-net, and pen, and almost entirely with reference to Pawkins. The European reputation he had won had come as an incident in that great antipathy. He had gradually worked up to a climax in this last controversy. It had killed Pawkins, but it had also thrown Hapley out of gear, so to speak, and his doctor advised him to give up work for a time, and rest. So Hapley went down into a quiet village in Kent, and thought day and night of Pawkins, and good things it was now impossible to say about him.

At last Hapley began to realise in what direction the preoccupation tended. He determined to make a fight for it, and started by trying to read novels. But he could not get his mind off Pawkins, white in the face and making his last speech—every sentence a beautiful opening for Hapley. He turned to fiction—and found it had no grip on him. He read the 'Island Nights' Entertainments'* until his 'sense of causation' was shocked beyond endurance by the Bottle Imp. Then he went to Kipling, and found he 'proved nothing,' besides being irreverent and vulgar. These scientific people have their limitations. Then unhappily, he tried Besant's

'Inner House,'* and the opening chapter set his mind upon learned societies and Pawkins at once.

So Hapley turned to chess, and found it a little more soothing. He soon mastered the moves and the chief gambits and commoner closing positions, and began to beat the Vicar. But then the cylindrical contours of the opposite king began to resemble Pawkins standing up and gasping ineffectually against check-mate, and Hapley decided to give up chess.

Perhaps the study of some new branch of science would after all be better diversion. The best rest is change of occupation. Hapley determined to plunge at diatoms,* and had one of his smaller microscopes and Halibut's monograph sent down from London. He thought that perhaps if he could get up a vigorous quarrel with Halibut, he might be able to begin life afresh and forget Pawkins. And very soon he was hard at work in his habitual strenuous fashion, at these microscopic denizens of the way-side pool.

It was on the third day of the diatoms that Hapley became aware of a novel addition to the local fauna. He was working late at the microscope, and the only light in the room was the brilliant little lamp with the special form of green shade. Like all experienced microscopists, he kept both eyes open. It is the only way to avoid excessive fatigue. One eye was over the instrument, and bright and distinct before that was the circular field of the microscope, across which a brown diatom was slowly moving. With the other eye Hapley saw, as it were, without seeing. He was only dimly conscious of the brass side of the instrument, the illuminated part of the table-cloth, a sheet of note-paper, the foot of the lamp, and the darkened room beyond.

Suddenly his attention drifted from one eye to the other. The table-cloth was of the material called tapestry by shopmen, and rather brightly coloured. The pattern was in gold, with a small amount of crimson and pale blue upon a greyish ground. At one point the pattern seemed displaced, and there was a vibrating movement of the colours at this point.

Hapley suddenly moved his head back and looked with both eyes. His mouth fell open with astonishment.

It was a large moth or butterfly; its wings spread in butterfly fashion!

It was strange it should be in the room at all, for the windows were closed. Strange that it should not have attracted his attention when fluttering to its present position. Strange that it should match the table-cloth. Stranger far that to him, Hapley, the great entomologist, it was altogether unknown. There was no delusion. It was crawling slowly towards the foot of the lamp.

'New Genus, by heavens! And in England!' said Hapley, staring.

Then he suddenly thought of Pawkins. Nothing would have maddened Pawkins more. . . . And Pawkins was dead!

Something about the head and body of the insect became singularly suggestive of Pawkins, just as the chess king had been.

'Confound Pawkins!' said Hapley. 'But I must catch this.' And looking round him for some means of capturing the moth, he rose slowly out of his chair. Suddenly the insect rose, struck the edge of the lampshade—Hapley heard the 'ping'—and vanished into the shadow.

In a moment Hapley had whipped off the shade, so that the whole room was illuminated. The thing had disappeared, but soon his practised eye detected it upon the wall-paper near the door. He went towards it poising the lamp-shade for capture. Before he was within striking distance, however, it had risen and was fluttering round the room. After the fashion of its kind, it flew with sudden starts and turns, seeming to vanish here and reappear there. Once Hapley struck, and missed; then again.

The third time he hit his microscope. The instrument swayed, struck and overturned the lamp, and fell noisily upon the floor. The lamp turned over on the table and, very luckily, went out. Hapley was left in the dark. With a start he felt the strange moth blunder into his face.

It was maddening. He had no lights. If he opened the door of the room the thing would get away. In the darkness he saw Pawkins quite distinctly laughing at him. Pawkins had ever an oily laugh. He swore furiously and stamped his foot on the floor.

There was a timid rapping at the door.

Then it opened, perhaps a foot, and very slowly. The alarmed face of the landlady appeared behind a pink candle flame; she wore a night-cap over her grey hair and had some purple garment over her shoulders. 'What *was* that fearful smash?' she said. 'Has anything——' The strange moth appeared fluttering about the chink of the door. 'Shut that door!' said Hapley, and suddenly rushed at her.

The door slammed hastily. Hapley was left alone in the dark. Then in the pause he heard his landlady scuttle upstairs, lock her door, and drag something heavy across the room and put against it.

It became evident to Hapley that his conduct and appearance had been strange and alarming. Confound the moth! and Pawkins! However, it was a pity to lose the moth now. He felt his way into the hall and found the matches, after sending his hat down upon the floor with a noise like a drum. With the lighted candle he returned to the sitting-room. No moth was to be seen. Yet once for a moment it seemed that the thing was fluttering round his head. Hapley very suddenly decided to give up the moth and go to bed. But he was excited. All night long his sleep was broken by dreams of the moth, Pawkins, and his landlady. Twice in the night he turned out and soused his head in cold water.

One thing was very clear to him. His landlady could not possibly understand about the strange moth, especially as he had failed to catch it. No one but an entomologist would understand quite how he felt. She was probably frightened at his behaviour, and yet he failed to see how he could explain it. He decided to say nothing further about the events of last night. After breakfast he saw her in her garden, and decided to go out and talk to reassure her. He talked to her about beans and potatoes, bees, caterpillars, and the price of fruit. She replied in her usual manner, but she looked at him a little suspiciously, and kept walking as he walked, so that there was always a bed of flowers, or a row of beans, or something of the sort, between them. After a while he began to feel singularly irritated at this, and to conceal his vexation went indoors and presently went out for a walk.

The moth, or butterfly, trailing an odd flavour of Pawkins with it, kept coming into that walk, though he did his best to keep his mind off it. Once he saw it quite distinctly, with its wings flattened out, upon the old stone wall that runs along the west edge of the park, but going up to it he found it was only two lumps of grey and yellow lichen. 'This,' said Hapley, 'is the reverse of mimicry. Instead of a butterfly looking like a stone, here is a stone looking like a butterfly!' Once something hovered and fluttered round his head, but by an effort of will he drove that impression out of his mind again.

In the afternoon Hapley called upon the Vicar, and argued with him upon theological questions. They sat in the little arbour covered with briar, and smoked as they wrangled. 'Look at that moth!' said Hapley, suddenly, pointing to the edge of the wooden table.

'Where?' said the Vicar.

'You don't see a moth on the edge of the table there?' said Hapley.

'Certainly not,' said the Vicar.

Hapley was thunderstruck. He gasped. The Vicar was staring at him. Clearly the man saw nothing. 'The eye of faith is no better than the eye of science,' said Hapley awkwardly.

'I don't see your point,' said the Vicar, thinking it was part of the argument.

That night Hapley found the moth crawling over his

counterpane. He sat on the edge of the bed in his shirt sleeves and reasoned with himself. Was it pure hallucination? He knew he was slipping, and he battled for his sanity with the same silent energy he had formerly displayed against Pawkins. So persistent is mental habit, that he felt as if it were still a struggle with Pawkins. He was well versed in psychology. He knew that such visual illusions do come as a result of mental strain. But the point was, he did not only *see* the moth, he had heard it when it touched the edge of the lampshade, and afterwards when it hit against the wall, and he had felt it strike his face in the dark.

He looked at it. It was not at all dreamlike, but perfectly clear and solid-looking in the candle-light. He saw the hairy body, and the short feathery antennæ, the jointed legs, even a place where the down was rubbed from the wing. He suddenly felt angry with himself for being afraid of a little insect.

His landlady had got the servant to sleep with her that night, because she was afraid to be alone. In addition she had locked the door, and put the chest of drawers against it. They listened and talked in whispers after they had gone to bed, but nothing occurred to alarm them. About eleven they had ventured to put the candle out, and had both dozed off to sleep. They woke up with a start, and sat up in bed, listening in the darkness.

Then they heard slippered feet going to and fro in Hapley's room. A chair was overturned, and there was a violent dab at the wall. Then a china mantel ornament smashed upon the fender. Suddenly the door of the room opened, and they heard him upon the landing. They clung to one another, listening. He seemed to be dancing upon the staircase. Now he would go down three or four steps quickly, then up again, then hurry down into the hall. They heard the umbrella stand go over, and the fanlight break. Then the bolt shot and the chain rattled. He was opening the door.

They hurried to the window. It was a dim grey night; an almost unbroken sheet of watery cloud was sweeping across the moon, and the hedge and trees in front of the house were black against the pale roadway. They saw Hapley, looking like a ghost in his shirt and white trousers, running to and fro in the road, and beating the air. Now he would stop, now he would dart very rapidly at something invisible, now he would move upon it with stealthy strides. At last he went out of sight up the road towards the down. Then, while they argued who should go down and lock the door, he returned. He was walking very fast, and he came straight into the house, closed the door carefully, and went quietly up to his bedroom. Then everything was silent.

'Mrs Colville,' said Hapley, calling down the staircase next morning, 'I hope I did not alarm you last night.'

'You may well ask that!' said Mrs Colville.

'The fact is, I am a sleep-walker, and the last two nights I have been without my sleeping mixture. There is nothing to be alarmed about, really. I am sorry I made such an ass of myself. I will go over the down to Shoreham, and get some stuff to make me sleep soundly. I ought to have done that yesterday.'

But half-way over the down, by the chalk pits, the moth came upon Hapley again. He went on, trying to keep his mind upon chess problems, but it was no good. The thing fluttered into his face, and he struck at it with his hat in self-defence. Then rage, the old rage—the rage he had so often felt against Pawkins—came upon him again. He went on, leaping and striking at the eddying insect. Suddenly he trod on nothing, and fell headlong.

There was a gap in his sensations, and Hapley found himself sitting on the heap of flints in front of the opening of the chalk-pits, with a leg twisted back under him. The strange moth was still fluttering round his head. He struck at it with his hand, and turning his head saw two men approaching him. One was the village doctor. It occurred to Hapley that this was lucky. Then it came into his mind with extraordinary vividness, that no one would ever be able to see the strange moth except himself, and that it behoved him to keep silent about it.

Late that night, however, after his broken leg was set, he was feverish and forgot his self-restraint. He was lying flat on his bed, and he began to run his eyes round the room to see if the moth was still about. He tried not to do this, but it was no good. He soon caught sight of the thing resting close to his hand, by the night-light, on the green table-cloth. The wings quivered. With a sudden wave of anger he smote at it with his fist, and the nurse woke up with a shriek. He had missed it.

'That moth!' he said; and then, 'It was fancy. Nothing!'

All the time he could see quite clearly the insect going round the cornice and darting across the room, and he could also see that the nurse saw nothing of it and looked at him strangely. He must keep himself in hand. He knew he was a lost man if he did not keep himself in hand. But as the night waned the fever grew upon him, and the very dread he had of seeing the moth made him see it. About five, just as the dawn was grey, he tried to get out of bed and catch it, though his leg was afire with pain. The nurse had to struggle with him.

On account of this, they tied him down to the bed. At this the moth grew bolder, and once he felt it settle in his hair. Then, because he struck out violently with his arms, they tied these also. At this the moth came and crawled over his face, and Hapley wept, swore, screamed, prayed for them to take it off him, unavailingly.

The doctor was a blockhead, a just-qualified general practitioner, and quite ignorant of mental science. He simply said there was no moth. Had he possessed the wit, he might still, perhaps, have saved Hapley from his fate by entering into his delusion, and covering his face with gauze, as he prayed might be done. But, as I say, the doctor was a blockhead, and until the leg was healed Hapley was kept tied to his bed, and with the imaginary moth crawling over him. It never left him while he was awake and it grew to a monster in his dreams. While he was awake he longed for sleep, and from sleep he awoke screaming.

So now Hapley is spending the remainder of his days in a padded room, worried by a moth that no one else can see. The asylum doctor calls it hallucination; but Hapley, when he is in his easier mood, and can talk, says it is the ghost of Pawkins, and consequently a unique specimen and well worth the trouble of catching.

X

THE TREASURE IN THE FOREST

THE canoe was now approaching the land. The bay opened out, and a gap in the white surf of the reef marked where the little river ran out to the sea; the thicker and deeper green of the virgin forest showed its course down the distant hill slope. The forest here came close to the beach. Far beyond, dim and almost cloudlike in texture, rose the mountains, like suddenly frozen waves. The sea was still save for an almost imperceptible swell. The sky blazed.

The man with the carved paddle stopped. 'It should be somewhere here,' he said. He shipped the paddle and held his arms out straight before him.

The other man had been in the fore part of the canoe, closely scrutinising the land. He had a sheet of yellow paper on his knee.

'Come and look at this, Evans,' he said.

Both men spoke in low tones, and their lips were hard and dry.

The man called Evans came swaying along the canoe until he could look over his companion's shoulder.

The paper had the appearance of a rough map. By much folding it was creased and worn to the pitch of separation, and the second man held the discoloured fragments together where they had parted. On it one could dimly make out, in almost obliterated pencil, the outline of the bay.

'Here,' said Evans, 'is the reef, and here is the gap.' He ran his thumb-nail over the chart.

'This curved and twisting line is the river—I could do with a drink now!—and this star is the place.'

'You see this dotted line,' said the man with the map; 'it is a straight line, and runs from the opening of the reef to a clump of palm-trees. The star comes just where it cuts the river. We must mark the place as we go into the lagoon.'

'It's queer,' said Evans, after a pause, 'what these little marks down here are for. It looks like the plan of a house or something; but what all these little dashes, pointing this way and that, may mean I can't get a notion. And what's the writing?'

'Chinese,' said the man with the map.

'Of course! *He* was a Chinee,' said Evans.

'They all were,' said the man with the map.

They both sat for some minutes staring at the land, while the canoe drifted slowly. Then Evans looked towards the paddle.

'Your turn with the paddle now, Hooker,' said he.

And his companion quietly folded up his map, put it in his pocket, passed Evans carefully, and began to paddle. His movements were languid, like those of a man whose strength was nearly exhausted.

Evans sat with his eyes half closed, watching the frothy breakwater of the coral creep nearer and nearer. The sky was like a furnace, for the sun was near the zenith. Though they were so near the Treasure he did not feel the exaltation he had anticipated. The intense excitement of the struggle for the plan, and the long night voyage from the mainland in the unprovisioned canoe had, to use his own expression, 'taken it out of him.' He tried to arouse himself by directing his mind to the ingots the Chinamen had spoken of, but it would not rest there; it came back headlong to the thought of sweet water rippling in the river, and to the almost unendurable dryness of his lips and throat. The rhythmic wash of the sea upon the reef was becoming audible now, and it had a pleasant sound in his ears; the water washed along the side of the canoe, and the paddle dripped between each stroke. Presently he began to doze.

He was still dimly conscious of the island, but a queer dream texture interwove with his sensations. Once again it

was the night when he and Hooker had hit upon the Chinamen's secret; he saw the moonlit trees, the little fire burning, and the black figures of the three Chinamen—silvered
on one side by moonlight, and on the other glowing from
the firelight—and heard them talking together in pigeon-
English*—for they came from different provinces. Hooker
had caught the drift of their talk first, and had motioned to
him to listen. Fragments of the conversation were inaudible,
and fragments incomprehensible. A Spanish galleon from the
Philippines hopelessly aground, and its treasure buried against
the day of return, lay in the background of the story; a ship-
wrecked crew thinned by disease, a quarrel or so, and the
needs of discipline, and at last taking to their boats never to
be heard of again. Then Chang-hi, only a year since, wandering ashore, had happened upon the ingots hidden for two
hundred years, had deserted his junk,* and reburied them
with infinite toil, single-handed but very safe. He laid great
stress on the safety—it was a secret of his. Now he wanted
help to return and exhume them. Presently the little map
fluttered and the voices sank. A fine story for two stranded
British wastrels to hear! Evans' dream shifted to the moment
when he had Chang-hi's pigtail in his hand. The life of a
Chinaman is scarcely sacred like a European's. The cunning
little face of Chang-hi, first keen and furious like a startled
snake, and then fearful, treacherous, and pitiful, became over-
whelmingly prominent in the dream. At the end Chang-hi
had grinned, a most incomprehensible and startling grin.
Abruptly things became very unpleasant, as they will do at
times in dreams. Chang-hi gibbered and threatened him. He
saw in his dream heaps and heaps of gold, and Chang-hi
intervening and struggling to hold him back from it. He took
Chang-hi by the pig-tail—how big the yellow brute was, and
how he struggled and grinned! He kept growing bigger, too.
Then the bright heaps of gold turned to a roaring furnace,
and a vast devil, surprisingly like Chang-hi, but with a huge
black tail, began to feed him with coals. They burnt his mouth

horribly. Another devil was shouting his name: 'Evans, Evans, you sleepy fool!'—or was it Hooker?

He woke up. They were in the mouth of the lagoon.

'There are the three palm-trees. It must be in a line with that clump of bushes,' said his companion. 'Mark that. If we go to those bushes and then strike into the bush in a straight line from here, we shall come to it when we come to the stream.'

They could see now where the mouth of the stream opened out. At the sight of it Evans revived. 'Hurry up, man,' he said, 'or by heaven I shall have to drink sea water!' He gnawed his hand and stared at the gleam of silver among the rocks and green tangle.

Presently he turned almost fiercely upon Hooker. 'Give *me* the paddle,' he said.

So they reached the river mouth. A little way up Hooker took some water in the hollow of his hand, tasted it, and spat it out. A little further he tried again. 'This will do,' he said, and they began drinking eagerly.

'Curse this!' said Evans suddenly. 'It's too slow.' And, leaning dangerously over the fore part of the canoe, he began to suck up the water with his lips.

Presently they made an end of drinking, and, running the canoe into a little creek, were about to land among the thick growth that overhung the water.

'We shall have to scramble through this to the beach to find our bushes and get the line to the place,' said Evans.

'We had better paddle round,' said Hooker.

So they pushed out again into the river and paddled back down it to the sea, and along the shore to the place where the clump of bushes grew. Here they landed, pulled the light canoe far up the beach, and then went up towards the edge of the jungle until they could see the opening of the reef and the bushes in a straight line. Evans had taken a native implement out of the canoe. It was L-shaped, and the transverse piece was armed with polished stone. Hooker carried the paddle. 'It is straight now in this direction,' said he; 'we must push through this till we strike the stream. Then we must prospect.'

They pushed through a close tangle of reeds, broad fronds, and young trees, and at first it was toilsome going, but very speedily the trees became larger and the ground beneath them opened out. The blaze of the sunlight was replaced by insensible degrees by cool shadow. The trees became at last vast pillars that rose up to a canopy of greenery far overhead. Dim white flowers hung from their stems, and ropy creepers swung from tree to tree. The shadow deepened. On the ground, blotched fungi and a red-brown incrustation became frequent.

Evans shivered. 'It seems almost cold here after the blaze outside.'

'I hope we are keeping to the straight,' said Hooker.

Presently they saw, far ahead, a gap in the sombre darkness where white shafts of hot sunlight smote into the forest. There also was brilliant green undergrowth and coloured flowers. Then they heard the rush of water.

'Here is the river. We should be close to it now,' said Hooker.

The vegetation was thick by the river bank. Great plants, as yet unnamed, grew among the roots of the big trees, and spread rosettes of huge green fans towards the strip of sky. Many flowers and a creeper with shiny foliage clung to the exposed stems. On the water of the broad, quiet pool which the treasure-seekers now overlooked there floated big oval leaves and a waxen, pinkish-white flower not unlike a water-lily. Further, as the river bent away from them, the water suddenly frothed and became noisy in a rapid.

'Well?' said Evans.

'We have swerved a little from the straight,' said Hooker. 'That was to be expected.'

He turned and looked into the dim cool shadows of the

silent forest behind them. 'If we beat a little way up and down the stream we should come to something.'

'You said——' began Evans.

'*He* said there was a heap of stones,' said Hooker.

The two men looked at each other for a moment.

'Let us try a little down-stream first,' said Evans.

They advanced slowly, looking curiously about them. Suddenly Evans stopped. 'What the devil's that?' he said.

Hooker followed his finger. 'Something blue,' he said. It had come into view as they topped a gentle swell of the ground. Then he began to distinguish what it was.

He advanced suddenly with hasty steps, until the body that belonged to the limp hand and arm had become visible. His grip tightened on the implement he carried. The thing was the figure of a Chinaman lying on his face. The *abandon* of the pose was unmistakable.

The two men drew closer together, and stood staring silently at this ominous dead body. It lay in a clear space among the trees. Near by was a spade after the Chinese pattern, and further off lay a scattered heap of stones, close to a freshly dug hole.

'Somebody has been here before,' said Hooker, clearing his throat.

Then suddenly Evans began to swear and rave, and stamp upon the ground.

Hooker turned white but said nothing. He advanced towards the prostrate body. He saw the neck was puffed and purple, and the hands and ankles swollen. 'Pah!' he said, and suddenly turned away and went towards the excavation. He gave a cry of surprise. He shouted to Evans, who was following him slowly.

'You fool! It's all right. It's here still.' Then he turned again and looked at the dead Chinaman, and then again at the hole.

Evans hurried to the hole. Already half exposed by the ill-fated wretch beside them lay a number of dull yellow bars.

He bent down in the hole, and, clearing off the soil with his bare hands, hastily pulled one of the heavy masses out. As he did so a little thorn pricked his hand. He pulled the delicate spike out with his fingers and lifted the ingot.

'Only gold or lead could weigh like this,' he said exultantly.

Hooker was still looking at the dead Chinaman. He was puzzled.

'He stole a march on his friends,' he said at last. 'He came here alone, and some poisonous snake has killed him. . . . I wonder how he found the place.'

Evans stood with the ingot in his hands. What did a dead Chinaman signify? 'We shall have to take this stuff to the mainland piecemeal, and bury it there for a while. How shall we get it to the canoe?'

He took his jacket off and spread it on the ground, and flung two or three ingots into it. Presently he found that another little thorn had punctured his skin.

'This is as much as we can carry,' said he. Then suddenly, with a queer rush of irritation, 'What are you staring at?'

Hooker turned to him. 'I can't stand him . . .' He nodded towards the corpse. 'It's so like——'

'Rubbish!' said Evans. 'All Chinamen are alike.'

Hooker looked into his face. 'I'm going to bury *that*, anyhow, before I lend a hand with this stuff.'

'Don't be a fool, Hooker,' said Evans. 'Let that mass of corruption bide.'

Hooker hesitated, and then his eye went carefully over the brown soil about them. 'It scares me somehow,' he said.

'The thing is,' said Evans, 'what to do with these ingots. Shall we re-bury them over here, or take them across the strait in the canoe?'

Hooker thought. His puzzled gaze wandered among the tall tree-trunks, and up into the remote sunlit greenery overhead. He shivered again as his eye rested upon the blue figure of the Chinaman. He stared searchingly among the grey depths between the trees.

'What's come to you, Hooker?' said Evans. 'Have you lost your wits?'

'Let's get the gold out of this place, anyhow,' said Hooker.

He took the ends of the collar of the coat in his hands, and Evans took the opposite corners, and they lifted the mass. 'Which way?' said Evans. 'To the canoe?'

'It's queer,' said Evans, when they had advanced only a few steps, 'but my arms ache still with that paddling.'

'Curse it!' he said. 'But they ache! I must rest.'

They let the coat down. Evans' face was white, and little drops of sweat stood out upon his forehead. 'It's stuffy, somehow, in this forest.'

Then with an abrupt transition to unreasonable anger: 'What is the good of waiting here all the day? Lend a hand, I say! You have done nothing but moon since we saw the dead Chinaman.'

Hooker was looking steadfastly at his companion's face. He helped raise the coat bearing the ingots, and they went forward perhaps a hundred yards in silence. Evans began to breathe heavily. 'Can't you speak?' he said.

'What's the matter with you?' said Hooker.

Evans stumbled, and then with a sudden curse flung the coat from him. He stood for a moment staring at Hooker, and then with a groan clutched at his own throat.

'Don't come near me,' he said, and went and leant against a tree. Then in a steadier voice, 'I'll be better in a minute.'

Presently his grip upon the trunk loosened, and he slipped slowly down the stem of the tree until he was a crumpled heap at its foot. His hands were clenched convulsively. His face became distorted with pain. Hooker approached him.

'Don't touch me! Don't touch me!' said Evans in a stifled voice. 'Put the gold back on the coat.'

'Can't I do anything for you?' said Hooker.

'Put the gold back on the coat.'

As Hooker handled the ingots he felt a little prick on the

ball of his thumb. He looked at his hand and saw a slender thorn, perhaps two inches in length.

Evans gave an inarticulate cry and rolled over.

Hooker's jaw dropped. He stared at the thorn for a moment with dilated eyes. Then he looked at Evans, who was now crumpled together on the ground, his back bending and straightening spasmodically. Then he looked through the pillars of the trees and net-work of creeper stems, to where in the dim grey shadow the blue-clad body of the Chinaman was still indistinctly visible. He thought of the little dashes in the corner of the plan, and in a moment he understood.

'God help me!' he said. For the thorns were similar to those the Dyaks poison and use in their blowing-tubes. He understood now what Chang-hi's assurance of the safety of his treasure meant. He understood that grin now.

'Evans!' he cried.

But Evans was silent and motionless, save for a horrible spasmodic twitching of his limbs. A profound silence brooded over the forest.

Then Hooker began to suck furiously at the little pink spot on the ball of his thumb—sucking for dear life. Presently he felt a strange aching pain in his arms and shoulders, and his fingers seemed difficult to bend. Then he knew that sucking was no good.

Abruptly he stopped, and sitting down by the pile of ingots, and resting his chin upon his hands and his elbows upon his knees, stared at the distorted but still quivering body of his companion. Chang-hi's grin came into his mind again. The dull pain spread towards his throat and grew slowly in intensity. Far above him a faint breeze stirred the greenery, and the white petals of some unknown flower came floating down through the gloom.

XI

THE STORY OF THE LATE
MR ELVESHAM

I SET this story down, not expecting it will be believed, but, if possible, to prepare a way of escape for the next victim. He, perhaps, may profit by my misfortune. My own case, I know, is hopeless, and I am now in some measure prepared to meet my fate.

My name is Edward George Eden. I was born at Trentham,* in Staffordshire, my father being employed in the gardens there. I lost my mother when I was three years old, and my father when I was five, my uncle, George Eden, then adopting me as his own son. He was a single man, self-educated, and well-known in Birmingham as an enterprising journalist; he educated me generously, fired my ambition to succeed in the world, and at his death, which happened four years ago, left me his entire fortune, a matter of about five hundred pounds after all outgoing charges were paid. I was then eighteen. He advised me in his will to expend the money in completing my education. I had already chosen the profession of medicine, and through his posthumous generosity and my good fortune in a scholarship competition, I became a medical student at University College, London. At the time of the beginning of my story I lodged at 11A University Street in a little upper room, very shabbily furnished and draughty, overlooking the back of Shoolbred's premises.* I used this little room both to live in and sleep in, because I was anxious to eke out my means to the very last shillings-worth.

I was taking a pair of shoes to be mended at a shop in the Tottenham Court Road when I first encountered the little old man with the yellow face, with whom my life has now become so inextricably entangled. He was standing on the kerb, and staring at the number on the door in a doubtful way, as I opened it. His eyes—they were dull grey eyes, and reddish under the rims—fell to my face, and his countenance immediately assumed an expression of corrugated amiability.

'You come,' he said, 'apt to the moment. I had forgotten the number of your house. How do you do, Mr Eden?'

I was a little astonished at his familiar address, for I had never set eyes on the man before. I was a little annoyed, too, at his catching me with my boots under my arm. He noticed my lack of cordiality.

'Wonder who the deuce I am, eh? A friend, let me assure you. I have seen you before, though you haven't seen me. Is there anywhere where I can talk to you?'

I hesitated. The shabbiness of my room upstairs was not a matter for every stranger. 'Perhaps,' said I, 'we might walk down the street. I'm unfortunately prevented——' My gesture explained the sentence before I had spoken it.

'The very thing,' he said, and faced this way, and then that. 'The street? Which way shall we go?' I slipped my boots down in the passage. 'Look here!' he said abruptly; 'this business of mine is a rigmarole. Come and lunch with me, Mr Eden. I'm an old man, a very old man, and not good at explanations, and what with my piping voice and the clatter of the traffic——'

He laid a persuasive skinny hand that trembled a little upon my arm.

I was not so old that an old man might not treat me to a lunch. Yet at the same time I was not altogether pleased by this abrupt invitation. 'I had rather——' I began. 'But I had rather,' he said, catching me up, 'and a certain civility is surely due to my grey hairs.'

And so I consented, and went with him.

He took me to Blavitiski's; I had to walk slowly to accommodate myself to his paces; and over such a lunch as I had never tasted before, he fended off my leading questions, and I took a better note of his appearance. His clean-shaven face was lean and wrinkled, his shrivelled lips fell over a set of false teeth, and his white hair was thin and rather long; he seemed small to me,—though indeed, most people seemed small to me,—and his shoulders were rounded and bent. And watching him, I could not help but observe that he too was taking note of me, running his eyes, with a curious touch of greed in them, over me, from my broad shoulders to my sun-tanned hands, and up to my freckled face again. 'And now,' said he, as we lit our cigarettes, 'I must tell you of the business in hand.

'I must tell you, then, that I am an old man, a very old man.' He paused momentarily. 'And it happens that I have money that I must presently be leaving, and never a child have I to leave it to.' I thought of the confidence trick, and resolved I would be on the alert for the vestiges of my five hundred pounds. He proceeded to enlarge on his loneliness, and the trouble he had to find a proper disposition of his money. 'I have weighed this plan and that plan, charities, institutions, and scholarships, and libraries, and I have come to this conclusion at last,'—he fixed his eyes on my face, —'that I will find some young fellow, ambitious, pure-minded, and poor, healthy in body and healthy in mind, and, in short, make him my heir, give him all that I have.' He repeated, 'Give him all that I have. So that he will suddenly be lifted out of all the trouble and struggle in which his sympathies have been educated, to freedom and influence.'

I tried to seem disinterested. With a transparent hypocrisy I said, 'And you want my help, my professional services maybe, to find that person.'

He smiled, and looked at me over his cigarette, and I laughed at his quiet exposure of my modest pretence.

'What a career such a man might have!' he said. 'It fills me with envy to think how I have accumulated that another man may spend——

'But there are conditions, of course, burdens to be imposed. He must, for instance, take my name. You cannot expect everything without some return. And I must go into all the circumstances of his life before I can accept him. He *must* be sound. I must know his heredity, how his parents and grandparents died, have the strictest inquiries made into his private morals.'

This modified my secret congratulations a little.

'And do I understand,' said I, 'that I——'

'Yes,' he said, almost fiercely. 'You. *You*.'

I answered never a word. My imagination was dancing wildly, my innate scepticism was useless to modify its transports. There was not a particle of gratitude in my mind—I did not know what to say nor how to say it. 'But why me in particular?' I said at last.

He had chanced to hear of me from Professor Haslar, he said, as a typically sound and sane young man, and he wished, as far as possible, to leave his money where health and integrity were assured.

That was my first meeting with the little old man. He was mysterious about himself; he would not give his name yet, he said, and after I had answered some questions of his, he left me at the Blavitiski portal. I noticed that he drew a handful of gold coins from his pocket when it came to paying for the lunch. His insistence upon bodily health was curious. In accordance with an arrangement we had made I applied that day for a life policy in the Loyal Insurance Company for a large sum, and I was exhaustively overhauled by the medical advisers of that company in the subsequent week. Even that did not satisfy him, and he insisted I must be re-examined by the great Doctor Henderson.

It was Friday in Whitsun week before he came to a decision. He called me down, quite late in the evening,—nearly nine it was,—from cramming chemical equations for my Preliminary Scientific examination. He was standing in the passage under the feeble gas-lamp, and his face was a grotesque interplay of shadows. He seemed more bowed than when I had first seen him, and his cheeks had sunk in a little.

His voice shook with emotion. 'Everything is satisfactory, Mr Eden,' he said. 'Everything is quite, quite satisfactory. And this night of all nights, you must dine with me and celebrate your—accession.' He was interrupted by a cough. 'You won't have long to wait, either,' he said, wiping his handkerchief across his lips, and gripping my hand with his long bony claw that was disengaged. 'Certainly not very long to wait.'

We went into the street and called a cab. I remember every incident of that drive vividly, the swift, easy motion, the vivid contrast of gas and oil and electric light, the crowds of people in the streets, the place in Regent Street to which we went, and the sumptuous dinner we were served with there. I was disconcerted at first by the well-dressed waiter's glances at my rough clothes, bothered by the stones of the olives, but as the champagne warmed my blood, my confidence revived. At first the old man talked of himself. He had already told me his name in the cab; he was Egbert Elvesham, the great philosopher, whose name I had known since I was a lad at school. It seemed incredible to me that this man, whose intelligence had so early dominated mine, this great abstraction, should suddenly realise itself as this decrepit, familiar figure. I daresay every young fellow who has suddenly fallen among celebrities has felt something of my disappointment. He told me now of the future that the feeble streams of his life would presently leave dry for me, houses, copyrights, investments; I had never suspected that philosophers were so rich. He watched me drink and eat with a touch of envy. 'What a capacity for living you have!' he said; and then with a sigh, a sigh of relief I could have thought it, 'it will not be long.'

'Ay,' said I, my head swimming now with champagne; 'I have a future perhaps—of a passing agreeable sort, thanks to you. I shall now have the honour of your name. But you have a past. Such a past as is worth all my future.'

He shook his head and smiled, as I thought, with half sad appreciation of my flattering admiration. 'That future,' he said, 'would you in truth change it?' The waiter came with liqueurs. 'You will not perhaps mind taking my name, taking my position, but would you indeed—willingly—take my years?'

'With your achievements,' said I gallantly.

He smiled again. 'Kümmel—both,' he said to the waiter, and turned his attention to a little paper packet he had taken from his pocket. 'This hour,' said he, 'this after-dinner hour is the hour of small things. Here is a scrap of my unpublished wisdom.' He opened the packet with his shaking yellow fingers, and showed a little pinkish powder on the paper. 'This,' said he—'well, you must guess what it is. But Kümmel—put but a dash of this powder in it—is Himmel.'*

His large greyish eyes watched mine with an inscrutable expression.

It was a bit of a shock to me to find this great teacher gave his mind to the flavour of liqueurs. However, I feigned an interest in his weakness, for I was drunk enough for such small sycophancy.

He parted the powder between the little glasses, and, rising suddenly, with a strange unexpected dignity, held out his hand towards me. I imitated his action, and the glasses rang. 'To a quick succession,' said he, and raised his glass towards his lips.

'Not that,' I said hastily. 'Not that.'

He paused with the liqueur at the level of his chin, and his eyes blazing into mine.

'To a long life,' said I.

He hesitated. 'To a long life,' said he, with a sudden bark of laughter, and with eyes fixed on one another we tilted the little glasses. His eyes looked straight into mine, and as I drained the stuff off, I felt a curiously intense sensation. The first touch of it set my brain in a furious tumult; I seemed to feel an actual physical stirring in my skull, and a seething humming filled my ears. I did not notice the flavour in my mouth, the aroma that filled my throat; I saw only the grey intensity of his gaze that burnt into mine. The draught, the mental confusion, the noise and stirring in my head, seemed to last an interminable time. Curious vague impressions of half-forgotten things danced and vanished on the edge of my consciousness. At last he broke the spell. With a sudden explosive sigh he put down his glass.

'Well?' he said.

'It's glorious,' said I, though I had not tasted the stuff.

My head was spinning. I sat down. My brain was chaos. Then my perception grew clear and minute as though I saw things in a concave mirror. His manner seemed to have changed into something nervous and hasty. He pulled out his watch and grimaced at it. 'Eleven-seven! And to-night I must—Seven-twenty-five. Waterloo! I must go at once.' He called for the bill, and struggled with his coat. Officious waiters came to our assistance. In another moment I was wishing him good-bye, over the apron of a cab, and still with an absurd feeling of minute distinctness, as though—how can I express it?—I not only saw but *felt* through an inverted opera-glass.

'That stuff,' he said. He put his hand to his forehead. 'I ought not to have given it to you. It will make your head split to-morrow. Wait a minute. Here.' He handed me out a little flat thing like a seidlitz-powder.* 'Take that in water as you are going to bed. The other thing was a drug. Not till you're ready to go to bed, mind. It will clear your head. That's all. One more shake—Futurus!'*

I gripped his shrivelled claw. 'Good-bye,' he said, and by the droop of his eyelids I judged he too was a little under the influence of that brain-twisting cordial.

He recollected something else with a start, felt in his breast-pocket, and produced another packet, this time a cylinder the size and shape of a shaving-stick. 'Here,' said he. 'I'd almost forgotten. Don't open this until I come to-morrow—but take it now.'

It was so heavy that I wellnigh dropped it. 'All ri'!' said I, and he grinned at me through the cab window as the cabman flicked his horse into wakefulness. It was a white packet he had given me, with red seals at either end and along its edge. 'If this isn't money,' said I, 'it's platinum or lead.'

I stuck it with elaborate care into my pocket, and with a whirling brain walked home through the Regent Street loiterers and the dark back streets beyond Portland Road. I remember the sensations of that walk very vividly, strange as they were. I was still so far myself that I could notice my strange mental state, and wonder whether this stuff I had had was opium—a drug beyond my experience. It is hard now to describe the peculiarity of my mental strangeness—mental doubling vaguely expresses it. As I was walking up Regent Street I found in my mind a queer persuasion that it was Waterloo Station, and had an odd impulse to get into the Polytechnic as a man might get into a train. I put a knuckle in my eye, and it was Regent Street. How can I express it? You see a skilful actor looking quietly at you, he pulls a grimace, and lo!—another person. Is it too extravagant if I tell you that it seemed to me as if Regent Street had, for the moment, done that? Then, being persuaded it was Regent Street again, I was oddly muddled about some fantastic reminiscences that cropped up. 'Thirty years ago,' thought I, 'it was here that I quarrelled with my brother.' Then I burst out laughing, to the astonishment and encouragement of a group of night prowlers. Thirty years ago I did not exist, and never in my life had I boasted a brother. The stuff was surely liquid folly, for the poignant regret for that lost brother still clung to me. Along Portland Road the madness took another turn. I began to recall vanished shops, and to compare the street with what it used to be. Confused, troubled thinking is comprehensible enough after the drink I had taken, but what puzzled me were these curiously vivid phantasm memories that had crept into my mind, and not only the memories that had crept in, but also the memories that had slipped out. I stopped opposite Stevens', the natural history dealer's, and cudgelled my brains to think what he had to do with me. A 'bus went by, and sounded exactly like the rumbling of a train. I seemed to be dipping into some dark, remote pit for the recollection. 'Of course,' said I, at last, 'he has promised me three frogs to-morrow. Odd I should have forgotten.'

Do they still show children dissolving views?* In those I remember one view would begin like a faint ghost, and grow and oust another. In just that way it seemed to me that a ghostly set of new sensations was struggling with those of my ordinary self.

I went on through Euston Road to Tottenham Court Road, puzzled, and a little frightened, and scarcely noticed the unusual way I was taking, for commonly I used to cut through the intervening network of back streets. I turned into University Street, to discover that I had forgotten my number. Only by a strong effort did I recall 11A, and even then it seemed to me that it was a thing some forgotten person had told me. I tried to steady my mind by recalling the incidents of the dinner, and for the life of me I could conjure up no picture of my host's face; I saw him only as a shadowy outline, as one might see oneself reflected in a window through which one was looking. In his place, however, I had a curious exterior vision of myself, sitting at a table, flushed, bright-eyed, and talkative.

'I must take this other powder,' said I. 'This is getting impossible.'

I tried the wrong side of the hall for my candle and the matches, and had a doubt of which landing my room might be on. 'I'm drunk,' I said, 'that's certain,' and blundered needlessly on the staircase to sustain the proposition.

At the first glance my room seemed unfamiliar. 'What rot!' I said, and stared about me. I seemed to bring myself back by the effort, and the odd phantasmal quality passed into the concrete familiar. There was the old glass still, with my notes on the albumens* stuck in the corner of the frame, my old everyday suit of clothes pitched about the floor. And yet it was not so real after all. I felt an idiotic persuasion trying to creep into my mind, as it were, that I was in a railway carriage in a train just stopping, that I was peering out of the window at some unknown station. I gripped the bed-rail firmly to reassure myself. 'It's clairvoyance, perhaps,' I said. 'I must write to the Psychical Research Society.'

I put the rouleau* on my dressing-table, sat on my bed, and began to take off my boots. It was as if the picture of my present sensations was painted over some other picture that was trying to show through. 'Curse it!' said I; 'my wits are going, or am I in two places at once?' Half-undressed, I tossed the powder into a glass and drank it off. It effervesced, and became a fluorescent amber colour. Before I was in bed my mind was already tranquillised. I felt the pillow at my cheek, and thereupon I must have fallen asleep.

I awoke abruptly out of a dream of strange beasts, and found myself lying on my back. Probably every one knows that dismal, emotional dream from which one escapes, awake indeed, but strangely cowed. There was a curious taste in my mouth, a tired feeling in my limbs, a sense of cutaneous discomfort. I lay with my head motionless on my pillow, expecting that my feeling of strangeness and terror would pass away, and that I should then doze off again to sleep. But instead of that, my uncanny sensations increased. At first I could perceive nothing wrong about me. There was a faint light in the room, so faint that it was the very next thing to darkness, and the furniture stood out in it as vague blots of absolute darkness. I stared with my eyes just over the bedclothes.

It came into my mind that some one had entered the room to rob me of my rouleau of money, but after lying for some moments, breathing regularly to simulate sleep, I realised this was mere fancy. Nevertheless, the uneasy assurance of something wrong kept fast hold of me. With an effort I raised my head from the pillow, and peered about me at the dark. What it was I could not conceive. I looked at the dim shapes around me, the greater and lesser darknesses that indicated curtains, table, fireplace, bookshelves, and so forth. Then I began to perceive something unfamiliar in the forms of the darkness. Had the bed turned round? Yonder should be the bookshelves, and something shrouded and pallid rose there, something that would not answer to the bookshelves, however I looked at it. It was far too big to be my shirt thrown on a chair.

Overcoming a childish terror, I threw back the bedclothes and thrust my leg out of bed. Instead of coming out of my truckle-bed* upon the floor, I found my foot scarcely reached the edge of the mattress. I made another step, as it were, and sat up on the edge of the bed. By the side of my bed should be the candle, and the matches upon the broken chair. I put out my hand and touched—nothing. I waved my hand in the darkness, and it came against some heavy hanging, soft and thick in texture, which gave a rustling noise at my touch. I grasped this and pulled it; it appeared to be a curtain suspended over the head of my bed.

I was now thoroughly awake, and beginning to realise that I was in a strange room. I was puzzled. I tried to recall the overnight circumstances, and I found them now, curiously enough, vivid in my memory: the supper, my reception of the little packages, my wonder whether I was intoxicated, my slow undressing, the coolness to my flushed face of my pillow. I felt a sudden distrust. Was that last night, or the night before? At any rate, this room was strange to me, and I could not imagine how I had got into it. The dim, pallid outline was growing paler, and I perceived it was a window, with the dark shape of an oval toilet-glass against the weak intimation of the dawn that filtered through the blind. I stood up, and was surprised by a curious feeling of weakness and unsteadiness. With trembling hands outstretched, I walked slowly towards the window, getting, nevertheless, a bruise on the knee from a chair by the way. I fumbled round the glass, which was large, with handsome brass sconces, to find the blind-cord. I could not find any. By chance I took hold of the tassel, and with the click of a spring the blind ran up.

I found myself looking out upon a scene that was altogether strange to me. The night was overcast, and through the flocculent grey of the heaped clouds there filtered a faint half-light of dawn. Just at the edge of the sky the cloud-canopy had a blood-red rim. Below, everything was dark and indistinct, dim hills in the distance, a vague mass of buildings running up into pinnacles, trees like spilt ink, and below the window a tracery of black bushes and pale grey paths. It was so unfamiliar that for the moment I thought myself still dreaming. I felt the toilet-table; it appeared to be made of some polished wood, and was rather elaborately furnished—there were little cut-glass bottles and a brush upon it. There was also a queer little object, horse-shoe shape it felt, with smooth, hard projections, lying in a saucer. I could find no matches nor candlestick.

I turned my eyes to the room again. Now the blind was up, faint spectres of its furnishing came out of the darkness. There was a huge curtained bed, and the fireplace at its foot had a large white mantel with something of the shimmer of marble.

I leant against the toilet-table, shut my eyes and opened them again, and tried to think. The whole thing was far too real for dreaming. I was inclined to imagine there was still some hiatus in my memory, as a consequence of my draught of that strange liqueur; that I had come into my inheritance perhaps, and suddenly lost my recollection of everything since my good fortune had been announced. Perhaps if I waited a little, things would be clearer to me again. Yet my dinner with old Elvesham was now singularly vivid and recent. The champagne, the observant waiters, the powder, and the liqueurs—I could have staked my soul it all happened a few hours ago.

And then occurred a thing so trivial and yet so terrible to me that I shiver now to think of that moment. I spoke aloud. I said, 'How the devil did I get here?' . . . *And the voice was not my own.*

It was not my own, it was thin, the articulation was slurred, the resonance of my facial bones was different. Then, to reassure myself I ran one hand over the other, and felt loose folds of skin, the bony laxity of age. 'Surely,' I said, in that horrible voice that had somehow established itself in my throat, 'surely this thing is a dream!' Almost as quickly as if I did it involuntarily, I thrust my fingers into my mouth. My teeth had gone. My finger-tips ran on the flaccid surface of an even row of shrivelled gums. I was sick with dismay and disgust.

I felt then a passionate desire to see myself, to realise at once in its full horror the ghastly change that had come upon me. I tottered to the mantel, and felt along it for matches. As I did so, a barking cough sprang up in my throat, and I clutched the thick flannel nightdress I found about me. There were no matches there, and I suddenly realised that my extremities were cold. Sniffing and coughing, whimpering a little, perhaps, I fumbled back to bed. 'It is surely a dream,' I whispered to myself as I clambered back, 'surely a dream.' It was a senile repetition. I pulled the bedclothes over my shoulders, over my ears, I thrust my withered hand under the pillow, and determined to compose myself to sleep. Of course it was a dream. In the morning the dream would be over, and I should wake up strong and vigorous again to my youth and studies. I shut my eyes, breathed regularly, and, finding myself wakeful, began to count slowly through the powers of three.*

But the thing I desired would not come. I could not get to sleep. And the persuasion of the inexorable reality of the change that had happened to me grew steadily. Presently I found myself with my eyes wide open, the powers of three forgotten, and my skinny fingers upon my shrivelled gums. I was, indeed, suddenly and abruptly, an old man. I had in some unaccountable manner fallen through my life and come to old age, in some way I had been cheated of all the best of my life, of love, of struggle, of strength, and hope. I grovelled into the pillow and tried to persuade myself that such hallucination was possible. Imperceptibly, steadily, the dawn grew clearer.

At last, despairing of further sleep, I sat up in bed and looked about me. A chill twilight rendered the whole chamber visible. It was spacious and well-furnished, better furnished than any room I had ever slept in before. A candle and matches became dimly visible upon a little pedestal in a recess. I threw back the bedclothes, and, shivering with the rawness of the early morning, albeit it was summer-time, I got out and lit the candle. Then, trembling horribly, so that the extinguisher rattled on its spike, I tottered to the glass and saw—*Elvesham's face!* It was none the less horrible because I had already dimly feared as much. He had already seemed physically weak and pitiful to me, but seen now, dressed only in a coarse flannel nightdress, that fell apart and showed the stringy neck, seen now as my own body, I cannot describe its desolate decrepitude. The hollow cheeks, the straggling tail of dirty grey hair, the rheumy bleared eyes, the quivering, shrivelled lips, the lower displaying a gleam of the pink interior lining, and those horrible dark gums showing. You who are mind and body together, at your natural years, cannot imagine what this fiendish imprisonment meant to me. To be young and full of the desire and energy of youth, and to be caught, and presently to be crushed in this tottering ruin of a body. . . .

But I wander from the course of my story. For some time I must have been stunned at this change that had come upon me. It was daylight when I did so far gather myself together as to think. In some inexplicable way I had been changed, though how, short of magic, the thing had been done, I could not say. And as I thought, the diabolical ingenuity of Elvesham came home to me. It seemed plain to me that as I found myself in his, so he must be in possession of *my* body, of my strength, that is, and my future. But how to prove it? Then, as I thought, the thing became so incredible, even to me, that my mind reeled, and I had to pinch myself, to feel my toothless gums, to see myself in the glass, and touch the things about me, before I could steady myself to face the facts again. Was all life hallucination? Was I indeed Elvesham, and he me? Had I been dreaming of Eden overnight? Was there any Eden? But if I was Elvesham, I should remember where I was on the previous morning, the name of the town in which I lived, what happened before the dream began. I struggled with my thoughts. I recalled the queer doubleness of my memories overnight. But now my mind was clear. Not the ghost of any memories but those proper to Eden could I raise.

'This way lies insanity!' I cried in my piping voice. I staggered to my feet, dragged my feeble, heavy limbs to the washhand-stand, and plunged my grey head into a basin of cold water. Then, towelling myself, I tried again. It was no good. I felt beyond all question that I was indeed Eden, not Elvesham. But Eden in Elvesham's body!

Had I been a man of any other age, I might have given myself up to my fate as one enchanted. But in these sceptical days miracles do not pass current. Here was some trick of psychology. What a drug and a steady stare could do, a drug and a steady stare, or some similar treatment, could surely undo. Men have lost their memories before. But to exchange memories as one does umbrellas! I laughed. Alas! not a healthy laugh, but a wheezing, senile titter. I could have fancied old Elvesham laughing at my plight, and a gust of petulant anger, unusual to me, swept across my feelings. I began dressing eagerly in the clothes I found lying about on the floor, and only realised when I was dressed that it was an evening suit I had assumed. I opened the wardrobe and found some more ordinary clothes, a pair of plaid trousers, and an old-fashioned dressing-gown. I put a venerable smoking-cap on my venerable head, and, coughing a little from my exertions, tottered out upon the landing.

It was then, perhaps, a quarter to six, and the blinds were closely drawn and the house quite silent. The landing was a spacious one, a broad, richly-carpeted staircase went down into the darkness of the hall below, and before me a door ajar showed me a writing-desk, a revolving bookcase, the back of a study chair, and a fine array of bound books, shelf upon shelf.

'My study,' I mumbled, and walked across the landing. Then at the sound of my voice a thought struck me, and I went back to the bedroom and put in the set of false teeth. They slipped in with the ease of old habit. 'That's better,' said I, gnashing them, and so returned to the study.

The drawers of the writing-desk were locked. Its revolving top was also locked. I could see no indications of the keys, and there were none in the pockets of my trousers. I shuffled back at once to the bedroom, and went through the dress suit, and afterwards the pockets of all the garments I could find. I was very eager, and one might have imagined that burglars had been at work, to see my room when I had done. Not only were there no keys to be found, but not a coin, nor a scrap of paper—save only the receipted bill of the overnight dinner.

A curious weariness asserted itself. I sat down and stared at the garments flung here and there, their pockets turned inside out. My first frenzy had already flickered out. Every moment I was beginning to realise the immense intelligence of the plans of my enemy, to see more and more clearly the hopelessness of my position. With an effort I rose and hurried hobbling into the study again. On the staircase was a housemaid pulling up the blinds. She stared, I think, at the expression of my face. I shut the door of the study behind me, and, seizing a poker, began an attack upon the desk. That is how they found me. The cover of the desk was split, the lock smashed, the letters torn out of the pigeon-holes, and tossed about the room. In my senile rage I had flung about the pens and other such light stationery, and overturned the ink. Moreover, a large vase upon the mantel had got broken—I do not know how. I could find no cheque-book, no money, no indications of the slightest use for the recovery of my body. I was battering madly at the drawers, when the butler, backed by two women-servants, intruded upon me.

That simply is the story of my change. No one will believe my frantic assertions. I am treated as one demented, and even at this moment I am under restraint. But I am sane, absolutely sane, and to prove it I have sat down to write this story minutely as the things happened to me. I appeal to the reader, whether there is any trace of insanity in the style or method of the story he has been reading. I am a young man locked away in an old man's body. But the clear fact is incredible to everyone. Naturally I appear demented to those who will not believe this, naturally I do not know the names of my secretaries, of the doctors who come to see me, of my servants and neighbours, of this town (wherever it is) where I find myself. Naturally I lose myself in my own house, and suffer inconveniences of every sort. Naturally I ask the oddest questions. Naturally I weep and cry out, and have paroxysms of despair. I have no money and no cheque-book. The bank will not recognise my signature, for I suppose that, allowing for the feeble muscles I now have, my handwriting is still Eden's. These people about me will not let me go to the bank personally. It seems, indeed, that there is no bank in this town, and that I have an account in some part of London. It seems that Elvesham kept the name of his solicitor secret from all his household. I can ascertain nothing. Elvesham was, of course, a profound student of mental science, and all my declarations of the facts of the case merely confirm the theory that my insanity is the outcome of overmuch brooding upon psychology. Dreams of the personal identity indeed!

Two days ago I was a healthy youngster, with all life before me; now I am a furious old man, unkempt, and desperate, and miserable, prowling about a great, luxurious, strange house, watched, feared, and avoided as a lunatic by everyone about me. And in London is Elvesham beginning life again in a vigorous body, and with all the accumulated knowledge and wisdom of threescore and ten. He has stolen my life.

What has happened I do not clearly know. In the study are volumes of manuscript notes referring chiefly to the psychology of memory, and parts of what may be either calculations or ciphers in symbols absolutely strange to me. In some passages there are indications that he was also occupied with the philosophy of mathematics. I take it he has transferred the whole of his memories, the accumulation that makes up his personality, from this old withered brain of his to mine, and, similarly, that he has transferred mine to his discarded tenement. Practically, that is, he has changed bodies. But how such a change may be possible is without the range of my philosophy. I have been a materialist for all my thinking life, but here, suddenly, is a clear case of man's detachability from matter.

One desperate experiment I am about to try. I sit writing here before putting the matter to issue. This morning, with the help of a table-knife that I had secreted at breakfast, I succeeded in breaking open a fairly obvious secret drawer in this wrecked writing-desk. I discovered nothing save a little green glass phial containing a white powder. Round the neck of the phial was a label, and thereon was written this one word, '*Release*.' This may be—is most probably—poison. I can understand Elvesham placing poison in my way, and I should be sure that it was his intention so to get rid of the only living witness against him, were it not for this careful concealment. The man has practically solved the problem of immortality. Save for the spite of chance, he will live in my body until it has aged, and then, again, throwing that aside, he will assume some other victim's youth and strength. When one remembers his heartlessness, it is terrible to think of the ever-growing experience that . . . How long has he been leaping from body to body? . . . But I tire of writing. The powder appears to be soluble in water. The taste is not unpleasant.

There the narrative found upon Mr Elvesham's desk ends. His dead body lay between the desk and the chair. The latter had been pushed back, probably by his last convulsions. The story was written in pencil, and in a crazy hand, quite unlike his usual minute characters. There remain only two curious facts to record. Indisputably there was some connection between Eden and Elvesham, since the whole of Elvesham's property was bequeathed to the young man. But he never inherited. When Elvesham committed suicide, Eden was, strangely enough, already dead. Twenty-four hours before, he had been knocked down by a cab and killed instantly, at the crowded crossing at the intersection of Gower Street and Euston Road. So that the only human being who could have thrown light upon this fantastic narrative is beyond the reach of questions. Without further comment I leave this extraordinary matter to the reader's individual judgment.

XII

UNDER THE KNIFE

'WHAT if I die under it?' The thought recurred again and again, as I walked home from Haddon's. It was a purely personal question. I was spared the deep anxieties of a married man, and I knew there were few of my intimate friends but would find my death troublesome chiefly on account of their duty of regret. I was surprised indeed, and perhaps a little humiliated, as I turned the matter over, to think how few could possibly exceed the conventional requirement. Things came before me stripped of glamour, in a clear dry light, during that walk from Haddon's house over Primrose Hill. There were the friends of my youth: I perceived now that our affection was a tradition, which we foregathered rather laboriously to maintain. There were the rivals and helpers of my later career: I suppose I had been cold-blooded or undemonstrative—one perhaps implies the other. It may be that even the capacity for friendship is a question of physique. There had been a time in my own life when I had grieved bitterly enough at the loss of a friend; but as I walked home that afternoon the emotional side of my imagination was dormant. I could not pity myself, nor feel sorry for my friends, nor conceive of them as grieving for me.

I was interested in this deadness of my emotional nature—no doubt a concomitant of my stagnating physiology; and my thoughts wandered off along the line it suggested. Once before, in my hot youth, I had suffered a sudden loss of blood, and had been within an ace of death. I remembered now that my affections as well as my passions had drained out of me, leaving scarce anything but a tranquil resignation, a dreg of self-pity. It had been weeks before the old ambitions and tendernesses and all the complex moral interplay of a man had reasserted themselves. It occurred to me that the real meaning of this numbness might be a gradual slipping away from the pleasure-pain guidance of the animal man. It has been proven, I take it, as thoroughly as anything can be proven in this world, that the higher emotions, the moral feelings, even the subtle unselfishness of love, are evolved from the elemental desires and fears of the simple animal: they are the harness in which man's mental freedom goes. And it may be that as death overshadows us, as our possibility of acting diminishes, this complex growth of balanced impulse, propensity and aversion, whose interplay inspires our acts, goes with it. Leaving what?

I was suddenly brought back to reality by an imminent collision with a butcher-boy's tray. I found that I was crossing the bridge over the Regent's Park Canal, which runs parallel with that in the Zoological Gardens. The boy in blue had been looking over his shoulder at a black barge advancing slowly, towed by a gaunt white horse.* In the Gardens a nurse was leading three happy little children over the bridge. The trees were bright green; the spring hopefulness was still unstained by the dusts of summer; the sky in the water was bright and clear, but broken by long waves, by quivering bands of black, as the barge drove through. The breeze was stirring; but it did not stir me as the spring breeze used to do.

Was this dulness of feeling in itself an anticipation? It was curious that I could reason and follow out a network of suggestion as clearly as ever: so, at least, it seemed to me. It was calmness rather than dulness that was coming upon me. Was there any ground for the belief in the presentiment of death? Did a man near to death begin instinctively to withdraw himself from the meshes of matter and sense, even before the cold hand was laid upon his? I felt strangely isolated—isolated without regret—from the life and existence about me. The children playing in the sun and gathering strength and experience for the business of life, the park-keeper gossiping with a nursemaid, the nursing mother, the young couple intent upon each other as they passed me, the trees by the wayside spreading new pleading leaves to the sunlight, the stir in their branches—I had been part of it all, but I had nearly done with it now.

Some way down the Broad Walk I perceived that I was tired, and that my feet were heavy. It was hot that afternoon, and I turned aside and sat down on one of the green chairs that line the way. In a minute I had dozed into a dream, and the tide of my thoughts washed up a vision of the resurrection. I was still sitting in the chair, but I thought myself actually dead, withered, tattered, dried, one eye (I saw) pecked out by birds. 'Awake!' cried a voice; and incontinently the dust of the path and the mould under the grass became insurgent. I had never before thought of Regent's Park as a cemetery, but now, through the trees, stretching as far as eye could see, I beheld a flat plain of writhing graves and heeling tombstones. There seemed to be some trouble: the rising dead appeared to stifle as they struggled upward, they bled in their struggles, the red flesh was torn away from the white bones. 'Awake!' cried a voice; but I determined I would not rise to such horrors. 'Awake!' They would not let me alone. 'Wike up!' said an angry voice. A cockney angel! The man who sells the tickets was shaking me, demanding my penny.

I paid my penny, pocketed my ticket, yawned, stretched my legs, and, feeling now rather less torpid, got up and walked on towards Langham Place. I speedily lost myself again in a shifting maze of thoughts about death. Going across Marylebone Road into that crescent at the end of Langham Place, I had the narrowest escape from the shaft of a cab, and went on my way with a palpitating heart and a bruised shoulder. It struck me that it would have been curious if my meditations on my death on the morrow had led to my death that day.

But I will not weary you with more of my experiences that day and the next. I knew more and more certainly that I should die under the operation; at times I think I was inclined to pose to myself. The doctors were coming at eleven, and I did not get up. It seemed scarce worth while to trouble about washing and dressing, and though I read my newspapers and the letters that came by the first post, I did not find them very interesting. There was a friendly note from Addison, my old schoolfriend, calling my attention to two discrepancies and a printer's error in my new book, with one from Langridge venting some vexation over Minton. The rest were business communications. I breakfasted in bed. The glow of pain at my side seemed more massive. I knew it was pain, and yet, if you can understand, I did not find it very painful. I had been awake and hot and thirsty in the night, but in the morning bed felt comfortable. In the night-time I had lain thinking of things that were past; in the morning I dozed over the question of immortality. Haddon came, punctual to the minute, with a neat black bag; and Mowbray soon followed. Their arrival stirred me up a little. I began to take a more personal interest in the proceedings. Haddon moved the little octagonal table close to the bedside, and, with his broad back to me, began taking things out of his bag. I heard the light click of steel upon steel. My imagination, I found, was not altogether stagnant. 'Will you hurt me much?' I said in an off-hand tone.

'Not a bit,' Haddon answered over his shoulder. 'We shall chloroform you. Your heart's as sound as a bell.' And as he spoke, I had a whiff of the pungent sweetness of the anæsthetic.

They stretched me out, with a convenient exposure of my side, and, almost before I realised what was happening, the chloroform was being administered. It stings the nostrils, and there is a suffocating sensation at first. I knew I should die—that this was the end of consciousness for me. And suddenly I felt that I was not prepared for death: I had a vague sense of a duty overlooked—I knew not what. What was it I had not done? I could think of nothing more to do, nothing desirable left in life; and yet I had the strangest disinclination to death. And the physical sensation was painfully oppressive. Of course the doctors did not know they were going to kill me. Possibly I struggled. Then I fell motionless, and a great silence, a monstrous silence, and an impenetrable blackness came upon me.

There must have been an interval of absolute unconsciousness, seconds or minutes. Then with a chilly, unemotional clearness, I perceived that I was not yet dead. I was still in my body; but all the multitudinous sensations that come sweeping from it to make up the background of consciousness had gone, leaving me free of it all. No, not free of it all; for as yet something still held me to the poor stark flesh upon the bed—held me, yet not so closely that I did not feel myself external to it, independent of it, straining away from it. I do not think I saw, I do not think I heard; but I perceived all that was going on, and it was as if I both heard and saw. Haddon was bending over me, Mowbray behind me; the scalpel—it was a large scalpel—was cutting my flesh at the side under the flying ribs. It was interesting to see myself cut like cheese, without a pang, without even a qualm. The interest was much of a quality with that one might feel in a game of chess between strangers. Haddon's face was firm and his hand steady; but I was surprised to perceive (*how* I know not) that he was feeling the gravest doubt as to his own wisdom in the conduct of the operation.

Mowbray's thoughts, too, I could see. He was thinking that Haddon's manner showed too much of the specialist. New suggestions came up like bubbles through a stream of frothing meditation, and burst one after another in the little bright spot of his consciousness. He could not help noticing and admiring Haddon's swift dexterity, in spite of his envious quality and his disposition to detract. I saw my liver exposed. I was puzzled at my own condition. I did not feel that I was dead, but I was different in some way from my living self. The grey depression, that had weighed on me for a year or more and coloured all my thoughts, was gone. I perceived and thought without any emotional tint at all. I wondered if everyone perceived things in this way under chloroform, and forgot it again when he came out of it. It would be inconvenient to look into some heads, and not forget.

Although I did not think that I was dead, I still perceived quite clearly that I was soon to die. This brought me back to the consideration of Haddon's proceedings. I looked into his mind, and saw that he was afraid of cutting a branch of the portal vein.* My attention was distracted from details by the curious changes going on in his mind. His consciousness was like the quivering little spot of light which is thrown by the mirror of a galvanometer. His thoughts ran under it like a stream, some through the focus bright and distinct, some shadowy in the half-light of the edge. Just now the little glow was steady; but the least movement on Mowbray's part, the slightest sound from outside, even a faint difference in the slow movement of the living flesh he was cutting, set the light-spot shivering and spinning. A new sense-impression came rushing up through the flow of thoughts; and lo! the light-spot jerked away towards it, swifter than a frightened fish. It was wonderful to think that upon that unstable, fitful thing depended all the complex motions of the man; that for the next five minutes, therefore, my life hung upon its movements. And he was growing more and more nervous in his work. It was as if a little picture of a cut vein grew brighter, and struggled to oust from his brain another picture of a cut falling short of the mark. He was afraid: his dread of cutting too little was battling with his dread of cutting too far.

Then, suddenly, like an escape of water from under a lock-gate, a great uprush of horrible realisation set all his thoughts swirling, and simultaneously I perceived that the vein was cut. He started back with a hoarse exclamation, and I saw the brown-purple blood gather in a swift bead, and run trickling. He was horrified. He pitched the red-stained scalpel on to the octagonal table; and instantly both doctors flung themselves upon me, making hasty and ill-conceived efforts to remedy the disaster. 'Ice!' said Mowbray, gasping. But I knew that I was killed, though my body still clung to me.

I will not describe their belated endeavours to save me, though I perceived every detail. My perceptions were sharper and swifter than they had ever been in life; my thoughts rushed through my mind with incredible swiftness, but with perfect definition. I can only compare their crowded clarity to the effects of a reasonable dose of opium. In a moment it would all be over, and I should be free. I knew I was immortal, but what would happen I did not know. Should I drift off presently, like a puff of smoke from a gun, in some kind of half-material body, an attenuated version of my material self? Should I find myself suddenly among the innumerable hosts of the dead, and know the world about me for the phantasmagoria it had always seemed? Should I drift to some spiritualistic *séance*, and there make foolish, incomprehensible attempts to affect a purblind medium? It was a state of unemotional curiosity, of colourless expectation. And then I realised a growing stress upon me, a feeling as though some huge human magnet was drawing me upward out of my body. The stress grew and grew. I seemed an atom for which monstrous forces were fighting. For one brief, terrible moment sensation came back to me. That feeling of falling headlong which comes in nightmares, that feeling a thousand times intensified, that and a black horror swept across my thoughts in a torrent. Then the two doctors, the naked body with its cut side, the little room, swept away from under me and vanished, as a speck of foam vanishes down an eddy.

I was in mid-air. Far below was the West End of London, receding rapidly,—for I seemed to be flying swiftly upward,—and as it receded, passing westward like a panorama. I could see, through the faint haze of smoke, the innumerable roofs chimney-set, the narrow roadways, stippled with people and conveyances, the little specks of squares, and the church steeples like thorns sticking out of the fabric. But it spun away as the earth rotated on its axis, and in a few seconds (as it seemed) I was over the scattered clumps of town about Ealing, the little Thames a thread of blue to the south, and the Chiltern Hills and the North Downs coming up like the rim of a basin, far away and faint with haze. Up I rushed. And at first I had not the faintest conception what this headlong rush upward could mean.

Every moment the circle of scenery beneath me grew wider and wider, and the details of town and field, of hill and valley, got more and more hazy and pale and indistinct, a luminous grey was mingled more and more with the blue of the hills and the green of the open meadows; and a little patch of cloud, low and far to the west, shone ever more dazzlingly white. Above, as the veil of atmosphere between myself and outer space grew thinner, the sky, which had been a fair springtime blue at first, grew deeper and richer in colour, passing steadily through the intervening shades, until presently it was as dark as the blue sky of midnight, and presently as black as the blackness of a frosty starlight, and at last as black as no blackness I had ever beheld. And first one star, and then many, and at last an innumerable host broke out upon the sky: more stars than anyone has ever seen from the face of the earth. For the blueness of the sky is the light of the sun and stars sifted and spread abroad blindingly: there is diffused light even in the darkest skies of winter, and we do not see the stars by day only because of the dazzling irradiation of the sun. But now I saw things—I know not how; assuredly with no mortal eyes—and that defect of bedazzlement blinded me no longer. The sun was incredibly strange and wonderful. The body of it was a disc of blinding white light: not yellowish, as it seems to those who live upon the earth, but livid white, all streaked with scarlet streaks and rimmed about with a fringe of writhing tongues of red fire. And shooting half-way across the heavens from either side of it and brighter than the Milky Way, were two pinions of silver white, making it look more like those winged globes I have seen in Egyptian sculpture than anything else I can remember upon earth. These I knew for the solar corona, though I had never seen anything of it but a picture during the days of my earthly life.

When my attention came back to the earth again, I saw that it had fallen very far away from me. Field and town were long since indistinguishable, and all the varied hues of the country were merging into a uniform bright grey, broken only by the brilliant white of the clouds that lay scattered in flocculent masses over Ireland and the west of England. For now I could see the outlines of the north of France and Ireland, and all this Island of Britain, save where Scotland passed over the horizon to the north, or where the coast was blurred or obliterated by cloud. The sea was a dull grey, and darker than the land; and the whole panorama was rotating slowly towards the east.

All this had happened so swiftly that until I was some thousand miles or so from the earth I had no thought for myself. But now I perceived I had neither hands nor feet, neither parts nor organs, and that I felt neither alarm nor pain. All about me I perceived that the vacancy (for I had already left the air behind) was cold beyond the imagination of man; but it troubled me not. The sun's rays shot through the void, powerless to light or heat until they should strike on matter in their course. I saw things with a serene self-forgetfulness, even as if I were God. And down below there, rushing away from me,—countless miles in a second,—where a little dark spot on the grey marked the position of London, two doctors were struggling to restore life to the poor hacked and outworn shell I had abandoned. I felt then such release, such serenity as I can compare to no mortal delight I have ever known.

It was only after I had perceived all these things that the meaning of that headlong rush of the earth grew into comprehension. Yet it was so simple, so obvious, that I was amazed at my never anticipating the thing that was happening to me.

I had suddenly been cut adrift from matter: all that was
material of me was there upon earth, whirling away through
space, held to the earth by gravitation, partaking of the
earth-inertia, moving in its wreath of epicycles round the
sun, and with the sun and the planets on their vast march
through space. But the immaterial has no inertia, feels nothing of the pull of matter for matter: where it parts from its
garment of flesh, there it remains (so far as space concerns
it any longer) immovable in space. *I* was not leaving the
earth: the earth was leaving *me*, and not only the earth but
the whole solar system was streaming past. And about me in
space, invisible to me, scattered in the wake of the earth
upon its journey, there must be an innumerable multitude
of souls, stripped like myself of the material, stripped like
myself of the passions of the individual and the generous
emotions of the gregarious brute, naked intelligences, things
of new-born wonder and thought, marvelling at the strange
release that had suddenly come on them!

As I receded faster and faster from the strange white sun
in the black heavens, and from the broad and shining earth
upon which my being had begun, I seemed to grow in some
incredible manner vast: vast as regards this world I had left,
vast as regards the moments and periods of a human life.
Very soon I saw the full circle of the earth, slightly gibbous,*
like the moon when she nears her full, but very large; and
the silvery shape of America was now in the noonday blaze
wherein (as it seemed) little England had been basking but
a few minutes ago. At first the earth was large, and shone in
the heavens, filling a great part of them; but every moment
she grew smaller and more distant. As she shrank, the broad
moon in its third quarter crept into view over the rim of her
disc. I looked for the constellations. Only that part of Aries
directly behind the sun and the Lion, which the earth covered,
were hidden. I recognised the tortuous, tattered band of the
Milky Way with Vega very bright between sun and earth; and
Sirius and Orion shone splendid against the unfathomable

blackness in the opposite quarter of the heavens. The Pole Star was overhead, and the Great Bear hung over the circle of the earth. And away beneath and beyond the shining corona of the sun were strange groupings of stars I had never seen in my life—notably a dagger-shaped group that I knew for the Southern Cross. All these were no larger than when they had shone on earth, but the little stars that one scarce sees shone now against the setting of black vacancy as brightly as the first-magnitudes had done, while the larger worlds were points of indescribable glory and colour. Aldebaran was a spot of blood-red fire, and Sirius condensed to one point the light of innumerable sapphires. And they shone steadily: they did not scintillate, they were calmly glorious. My impressions had an adamantine hardness and brightness: there was no blurring softness, no atmosphere, nothing but infinite darkness set with the myriads of these acute and brilliant points and specks of light. Presently, when I looked again, the little earth seemed no bigger than the sun, and it dwindled and turned as I looked, until in a second's space (as it seemed to me), it was halved; and so it went on swiftly dwindling. Far away in the opposite direction, a little pinkish pin's head of light, shining steadily, was the planet Mars. I swam motionless in vacancy, and, without a trace of terror or astonishment, watched the speck of cosmic dust we call the world fall away from me.

Presently it dawned upon me that my sense of duration had changed; that my mind was moving not faster but infinitely slower, that between each separate impression there was a period of many days. The moon spun once round the earth as I noted this; and I perceived clearly the motion of Mars in his orbit. Moreover, it appeared as if the time between thought and thought grew steadily greater, until at last a thousand years was but a moment in my perception.

At first the constellations had shone motionless against the black background of infinite space; but presently it seemed as though the group of stars about Hercules and the

Scorpion was contracting, while Orion and Aldebaran and their neighbours were scattering apart. Flashing suddenly out of the darkness there came a flying multitude of particles of rock, glittering like dust-specks in a sunbeam, and encompassed in a faintly luminous cloud. They swirled all about me, and vanished again in a twinkling far behind. And then I saw that a bright spot of light, that shone a little to one side of my path, was growing very rapidly larger, and perceived that it was the planet Saturn rushing towards me. Larger and larger it grew, swallowing up the heavens behind it, and hiding every moment a fresh multitude of stars. I perceived its flattened, whirling body, its disc-like belt, and seven of its little satellites. It grew and grew, till it towered enormous; and then I plunged amid a streaming multitude of clashing stones and dancing dust-particles and gas-eddies, and saw for a moment the mighty triple belt like three concentric arches of moonlight above me, its shadow black on the boiling tumult below. These things happened in one-tenth of the time it takes to tell them. The planet went by like a flash of lightning; for a few seconds it blotted out the sun, and there and then became a mere black, dwindling, winged patch against the light. The earth, the mother mote of my being, I could no longer see.

So with a stately swiftness, in the profoundest silence, the solar system fell from me as it had been a garment, until the sun was a mere star amid the multitude of stars, with its eddy of planet-specks lost in the confused glittering of the remoter light. I was no longer a denizen of the solar system: I had come to the outer Universe, I seemed to grasp and comprehend the whole world of matter. Ever more swiftly the stars closed in about the spot where Antares and Vega had vanished in a phosphorescent haze, until that part of the sky had the semblance of a whirling mass of nebulæ, and ever before me yawned vaster gaps of vacant blackness, and the stars shone fewer and fewer. It seemed as if I moved towards a point between Orion's belt and sword; and the void about that region opened vaster and vaster every second, an incredible gulf of nothingness into which I was falling. Faster and ever faster the universe rushed by, a hurry of whirling motes at last, speeding silently into the void. Stars glowing brighter and brighter, with their circling planets catching the light in a ghostly fashion as I neared them, shone out and vanished again into inexistence; faint comets, clusters of meteorites, winking specks of matter, eddying light-points, whizzed past, some perhaps a hundred millions of miles or so from me at most, few nearer, travelling with unimaginable rapidity, shooting constellations, momentary darts of fire, through that black, enormous night. More than anything else it was like a dusty draught, sunbeam-lit. Broader and wider and deeper grew the starless space, the vacant Beyond, into which I was being drawn. At last a quarter of the heavens was black and blank, and the whole headlong rush of stellar universe closed in behind me like a veil of light that is gathered together. It drove away from me like a monstrous jack-o'-lantern* driven by the wind. I had come out into the wilderness of space. Ever the vacant blackness grew broader, until the hosts of the stars seemed only like a swarm of fiery specks hurrying away from me, inconceivably remote, and the darkness, the nothingness and emptiness, was about me on every side. Soon the little universe of matter, the cage of points in which I had begun to be, was dwindling, now to a whirling disc of luminous glittering, and now to one minute disc of hazy light. In a little while it would shrink to a point, and at last would vanish altogether.

Suddenly feeling came back to me—feeling in the shape of overwhelming terror; such a dread of those dark vastitudes as no words can describe, a passionate resurgence of sympathy and social desire. Were there other souls, invisible to me as I to them, about me in the blackness? or was I indeed, even as I felt, alone? Had I passed out of being into something that was neither being nor not-being? The covering of the body, the covering of matter, had been torn from me, and the hallucinations of companionship and security. Everything was black and silent. I had ceased to be. I was nothing. There was nothing, save only that infinitesimal dot of light that dwindled in the gulf. I strained myself to hear and see, and for a while there was naught but infinite silence, intolerable darkness, horror, and despair.

Then I saw that about the spot of light into which the whole world of matter had shrunk there was a faint glow. And in a band on either side of that the darkness was not absolute. I watched it for ages, as it seemed to me, and through the long waiting the haze grew imperceptibly more distinct. And then about the band appeared an irregular cloud of the faintest, palest brown. I felt a passionate impatience; but the things grew brighter so slowly that they scarce seemed to change. What was unfolding itself? What was this strange reddish dawn in the interminable night of space?

The cloud's shape was grotesque. It seemed to be looped along its lower side into four projecting masses, and, above, it ended in a straight line. What phantom was it? I felt assured I had seen that figure before; but I could not think what, nor where, nor when it was. Then the realisation rushed upon me. *It was a clenched Hand.* I was alone in space, alone with this huge, shadowy Hand, upon which the whole Universe of Matter lay like an unconsidered speck of dust. It seemed as though I watched it through vast periods of time. On the forefinger glittered a ring; and the universe from which I had come was but a spot of light upon the ring's curvature. And the thing that the hand gripped had the likeness of a black rod.* Through a long eternity I watched this Hand, with the ring and the rod, marvelling and fearing and waiting helplessly on what might follow. It seemed as though nothing could follow: that I should watch for ever, seeing only the Hand and the thing it held, and understanding nothing of its import. Was the whole universe but a refracting speck upon some greater Being? Were our worlds but the atoms of another universe, and those again of another, and so on through an

endless progression? And what was I? Was I indeed immaterial? A vague persuasion of a body gathering about me
came into my suspense. The abysmal darkness about the
Hand filled with impalpable suggestions, with uncertain,
fluctuating shapes.

Then, suddenly, came a sound, like the sound of a tolling
bell: faint, as if infinitely far; muffled, as though heard through
thick swathings of darkness: a deep, vibrating resonance,
with vast gulfs of silence between each stroke. And the
Hand appeared to tighten on the rod. And I saw far above
the Hand, towards the apex of the darkness, a circle of dim
phosphorescence, a ghostly sphere whence these sounds came
throbbing; and at the last stroke the Hand vanished, for the
hour had come, and I heard a noise of many waters.* But the
black rod remained as a great band across the sky. And then
a voice, which seemed to run to the uttermost parts of space,
spoke, saying, 'There will be no more pain.'*

At that an almost intolerable gladness and radiance rushed
in upon me, and I saw the circle shining white and bright,
and the rod black and shining, and many things else distinct
and clear. And the circle was the face of the clock, and the
rod the rail of my bed. Haddon was standing at the foot,
against the rail, with a small pair of scissors on his fingers;
and the hands of my clock on the mantel over his shoulder
were clasped together over the hour of twelve. Mowbray was
washing something in a basin at the octagonal table, and at
my side I felt a subdued feeling that could scarce be spoken
of as pain.

The operation had not killed me. And I perceived, suddenly,
that the dull melancholy of half a year was lifted from my
mind.

XIII

THE SEA RAIDERS

I

Until the extraordinary affair at Sidmouth, the peculiar species *Haploteuthis ferox* was known to science only generically, on the strength of a half-digested tentacle obtained near the Azores, and a decaying body pecked by birds and nibbled by fish, found early in 1896 by Mr Jennings, near Land's End.

In no department of zoological science, indeed, are we quite so much in the dark as with regard to the deep-sea cephalopods.* A mere accident, for instance, it was that led to the Prince of Monaco's discovery of nearly a dozen new forms in the summer of 1895, a discovery in which the before-mentioned tentacle was included. It chanced that a cachalot* was killed off Terceira by some sperm whalers, and in its last struggles charged almost to the Prince's yacht, missed it, rolled under, and died within twenty yards of his rudder. And in its agony it threw up a number of large objects, which the Prince, dimly perceiving they were strange and important, was, by a happy expedient, able to secure before they sank. He set his screws in motion, and kept them circling in the vortices thus created until a boat could be lowered. And these specimens were whole cephalopods and fragments of cephalopods, some of gigantic proportions, and almost all of them unknown to science!

It would seem, indeed, that these large and agile creatures, living in the middle depths of the sea, must, to a large extent, for ever remain unknown to us, since under water they are too nimble for nets, and it is only by such rare, unlooked-for accidents that specimens can be obtained. In the case of *Haploteuthis ferox*, for instance, we are still altogether ignorant of its habitat, as ignorant as we are of the breeding-ground of the herring or the sea-ways of the salmon. And zoologists are altogether at a loss to account for its sudden appearance on our coast. Possibly it was the stress of a hunger migration that drove it hither out of the deep. But it will be, perhaps, better to avoid necessarily inconclusive discussion, and to proceed at once with our narrative.

The first human being to set eyes upon a living *Haploteuthis*—the first human being to survive, that is, for there can be little doubt now that the wave of bathing fatalities and boating accidents that travelled along the coast of Cornwall and Devon in early May was due to this cause—was a retired tea-dealer of the name of Fison, who was stopping at a Sidmouth boarding-house. It was in the afternoon, and he was walking along the cliff path between Sidmouth and Ladram Bay. The cliffs in this direction are very high, but down the rod face of them in one place a kind of ladder staircase has been made. He was near this when his attention was attracted by what at first he thought to be a cluster of birds struggling over a fragment of food that caught the sunlight, and glistened pinkish-white. The tide was right out, and this object was not only far below him, but remote across a broad waste of rock reefs covered with dark seaweed and interspersed with silvery shining tidal pools. And he was, moreover, dazzled by the brightness of the further water.

In a minute, regarding this again, he perceived that his judgment was in fault, for over this struggle circled a number of birds, jackdaws and gulls for the most part, the latter gleaming blindingly when the sunlight smote their wings, and they seemed minute in comparison with it. And his curiosity was, perhaps, aroused all the more strongly because of his first insufficient explanations.

As he had nothing better to do than amuse himself, he decided to make this object, whatever it was, the goal of his afternoon walk, instead of Ladram Bay, conceiving it might perhaps be a great fish of some sort, stranded by some chance, and flapping about in its distress. And so he hurried down the long steep ladder, stopping at intervals of thirty feet or so to take breath and scan the mysterious movement.

At the foot of the cliff he was, of course, nearer his object than he had been; but, on the other hand, it now came up against the incandescent sky, beneath the sun, so as to seem dark and indistinct. Whatever was pinkish of it was now hidden by a skerry* of weedy boulders. But he perceived that it was made up of seven rounded bodies distinct or connected, and that the birds kept up a constant croaking and screaming, but seemed afraid to approach it too closely.

Mr Fison, torn by curiosity, began picking his way across the wave-worn rocks, and finding the wet seaweed that covered them thickly rendered them extremely slippery, he stopped, removed his shoes and socks, and rolled his trousers above his knees. His object was, of course, merely to avoid stumbling into the rocky pools about him, and perhaps he was rather glad, as all men are, of an excuse to resume, even for a moment, the sensations of his boyhood. At any rate, it is to this, no doubt, that he owes his life.

He approached his mark with all the assurance which the absolute security of this country against all forms of animal life gives its inhabitants. The round bodies moved to and fro, but it was only when he surmounted the skerry of boulders I have mentioned that he realised the horrible nature of the discovery. It came upon him with some suddenness.

The rounded bodies fell apart as he came into sight over the ridge, and displayed the pinkish object to be the partially devoured body of a human being, but whether of a man or woman he was unable to say. And the rounded bodies were new and ghastly-looking creatures, in shape somewhat resembling an octopus, with huge and very long and flexible tentacles, coiled copiously on the ground. The skin had a glistening texture, unpleasant to see, like shiny leather. The downward bend of the tentacle-surrounded mouth, the curious excrescence at the bend, the tentacles, and the large intelligent eyes, gave the creatures a grotesque suggestion of a face. They were the size of a fair-sized swine about the body, and the tentacles seemed to him to be many feet in length. There were, he thinks, seven or eight at least of the creatures. Twenty yards beyond them, amid the surf of the now returning tide, two others were emerging from the sea.

Their bodies lay flatly on the rocks, and their eyes regarded him with evil interest; but it does not appear that Mr Fison was afraid, or that he realised that he was in any danger. Possibly his confidence is to be ascribed to the limpness of their attitudes. But he was horrified, of course, and intensely excited and indignant, at such revolting creatures preying upon human flesh. He thought they had chanced upon a drowned body. He shouted to them, with the idea of driving them off, and finding they did not budge, cast about him, picked up a big rounded lump of rock, and flung it at one.

And then, slowly uncoiling their tentacles, they all began moving towards him—creeping at first deliberately, and making a soft purring sound to each other.

In a moment Mr Fison realised that he was in danger. He shouted again, threw both his boots, and started off, with a leap, forthwith. Twenty yards off he stopped and faced about, judging them slow, and behold! the tentacles of their leader were already pouring over the rocky ridge on which he had just been standing!

At that he shouted again, but this time not threatening, but a cry of dismay, and began jumping, striding, slipping, wading across the uneven expanse between him and the beach. The tall red cliffs seemed suddenly at a vast distance, and he saw, as though they were creatures in another world, two minute workmen engaged in the repair of the ladder-way, and little suspecting the race for life that was beginning below them. At one time he could hear the creatures splashing in the pools not a dozen feet behind him, and once he slipped and almost fell.

They chased him to the very foot of the cliffs, and desisted only when he had been joined by the workmen at the foot of the ladder-way up the cliff. All three of the men pelted them with stones for a time, and then hurried to the cliff top and along the path towards Sidmouth, to secure assistance and a boat, and to rescue the desecrated body from the clutches of these abominable creatures.

II

AND, as if he had not already been in sufficient peril that day, Mr Fison went with the boat to point out the exact spot of his adventure.

As the tide was down, it required a considerable detour to reach the spot, and when at last they came off the ladder-way, the mangled body had disappeared. The water was now running in, submerging first one slab of slimy rock and then another, and the four men in the boat—the workmen, that is, the boatman, and Mr Fison—now turned their attention from the bearings off shore to the water beneath the keel.

At first they could see little below them, save a dark jungle of laminaria,* with an occasional darting fish. Their minds were set on adventure, and they expressed their disappointment freely. But presently they saw one of the monsters swimming through the water seaward, with a curious rolling motion that suggested to Mr Fison the spinning roll of a captive balloon. Almost immediately after, the waving streamers of laminaria were extraordinarily perturbed, parted for a moment, and three of these beasts became darkly visible, struggling for what was probably some fragment of the drowned man. In a moment the copious olive-green ribbons had poured again over this writhing group.

At that all four men, greatly excited, began beating the water with oars and shouting, and immediately they saw a tumultuous movement among the weeds. They desisted to see more clearly, and as soon as the water was smooth, they saw, as it seemed to them, the whole sea bottom among the weeds set with eyes.

'Ugly swine!' cried one of the men. 'Why, there's dozens!'

And forthwith the things began to rise through the water about them. Mr Fison has since described to the writer this startling eruption out of the waving laminaria meadows. To him it seemed to occupy a considerable time, but it is probable that really it was an affair of a few seconds only. For a time nothing but eyes, and then he speaks of tentacles streaming out and parting the weed fronds this way and that. Then these things, growing larger, until at last the bottom was hidden by their intercoiling forms, and the tips of tentacles rose darkly here and there into the air above the swell of the waters.

One came up boldly to the side of the boat, and clinging to this with three of its sucker-set tentacles, threw four others over the gunwale, as if with an intention either of oversetting the boat or of clambering into it. Mr Fison at once caught up the boat-hook, and, jabbing furiously at the soft tentacles, forced it to desist. He was struck in the back and almost pitched overboard by the boatman, who was using his oar to resist a similar attack on the other side of the boat. But the tentacles on either side at once relaxed their hold, slid out of sight, and splashed into the water.

'We'd better get out of this,' said Mr Fison, who was trembling violently. He went to the tiller, while the boatman and one of the workmen seated themselves and began rowing. The other workman stood up in the fore part of the boat, with the boat-hook, ready to strike any more tentacles that might appear. Nothing else seems to have been said. Mr Fison had expressed the common feeling beyond amendment. In a hushed, scared mood, with faces white and drawn, they set about escaping from the position into which they had so recklessly blundered.

But the oars had scarcely dropped into the water before dark, tapering, serpentine ropes had bound them, and were about the rudder; and creeping up the sides of the boat with a looping motion came the suckers again. The men gripped their oars and pulled, but it was like trying to move a boat in a floating raft of weeds. 'Help here!' cried the boatman, and Mr Fison and the second workman rushed to help lug at the oar.

Then the man with the boat-hook—his name was Ewan, or Ewen—sprang up with a curse and began striking downward over the side, as far as he could reach, at the bank of tentacles that now clustered along the boat's bottom. And, at the same time, the two rowers stood up to get a better purchase for the recovery of their oars. The boatman handed his to Mr Fison, who lugged desperately, and, meanwhile, the boatman opened a big clasp-knife, and leaning over the side of the boat, began hacking at the spiring arms upon the oar shaft.

Mr Fison, staggering with the quivering rocking of the boat, his teeth set, his breath coming short, and the veins starting on his hands as he pulled at his oar, suddenly cast his eyes seaward. And there, not fifty yards off, across the long rollers of the incoming tide, was a large boat standing in* towards them, with three women and a little child in it. A boatman was rowing, and a little man in a pink-ribboned straw hat and whites stood in the stern hailing them. For a moment, of course, Mr Fison thought of help, and then he thought of the child. He abandoned his oar forthwith, threw up his arms in a frantic gesture, and screamed to the party in the boat to keep away 'for God's sake!' It says much for the modesty and courage of Mr Fison that he does not seem to be aware that there was any quality of heroism in his action at this juncture. The oar he had abandoned was at once drawn under, and presently reappeared floating about twenty yards away.

At the same moment Mr Fison felt the boat under him lurch violently, and a hoarse scream, a prolonged cry of terror from Hill, the boatman, caused him to forget the party of excursionists altogether. He turned, and saw Hill crouching by the forward row-lock, his face convulsed with terror, and his right arm over the side and drawn tightly down. He gave now a succession of short, sharp cries, 'Oh! oh! oh!—oh!' Mr Fison believes that he must have been hacking at the tentacles below the water-line, and have been grasped by them, but, of course, it is quite impossible to say now certainly what had happened. The boat was heeling over, so that the gunwale was within ten inches of the water, and both Ewan and the other labourer were striking down into the water, with oar and boat-hook, on either side of Hill's arm. Mr Fison instinctively placed himself to counterpoise them.

Then Hill, who was a burly, powerful man, made a strenuous effort, and rose almost to a standing position. He lifted his arm, indeed, clean out of the water. Hanging to it was a complicated tangle of brown ropes, and the eyes of one of the brutes that had hold of him, glaring straight and resolute, showed momentarily above the surface. The boat heeled more and more, and the green-brown water came pouring in a cascade over the side. Then Hill slipped and fell with his ribs across the side, and his arm and the mass of tentacles about it splashed back into the water. He rolled over; his boot kicked Mr Fison's knee as that gentleman rushed forward to seize him, and in another moment fresh tentacles had whipped about his waist and neck, and after a brief, convulsive struggle, in which the boat was nearly capsized, Hill was lugged overboard. The boat righted with a violent jerk that all but sent Mr Fison over the other side, and hid the struggle in the water from his eyes.

He stood staggering to recover his balance for a moment, and as he did so he became aware that the struggle and the inflowing tide had carried them close upon the weedy rocks again. Not four yards off a table of rock still rose in rhythmic movements above the inwash of the tide. In a moment Mr Fison seized the oar from Ewan, gave one vigorous stroke, then dropping it, ran to the bows and leapt. He felt his feet slide over the rock, and, by a frantic effort, leapt again towards a further mass. He stumbled over this, came to his knees, and rose again.

'Look out!' cried someone, and a large drab* body struck him. He was knocked flat into a tidal pool by one of the workmen, and as he went down he heard smothered, choking cries, that he believed at the time came from Hill. Then he found himself marvelling at the shrillness and variety of Hill's voice. Someone jumped over him, and a curving rush of foamy water poured over him, and passed. He scrambled to his feet dripping, and without looking seaward, ran as fast as his terror would let him shoreward. Before him, over the flat space of scattered rocks, stumbled the two workmen— one a dozen yards in front of the other.

He looked over his shoulder at last, and seeing that he was not pursued, faced about. He was astonished. From the moment of the rising of the cephalopods out of the water he had been acting too swiftly to fully comprehend his actions. Now it seemed to him as if he had suddenly jumped out of an evil dream.

For there were the sky, cloudless and blazing with the afternoon sun, the sea weltering under its pitiless brightness, the soft creamy foam of the breaking water, and the low, long, dark ridges of rock. The righted boat floated, rising and falling gently on the swell about a dozen yards from shore. Hill and the monsters, all the stress and tumult of that fierce fight for life, had vanished as though they had never been.

Mr Fison's heart was beating violently; he was throbbing to the finger-tips, and his breath came deep.

There was something missing. For some seconds he could not think clearly enough what this might be. Sun, sky, sea, rocks—what was it? Then he remembered the boat-load of excursionists. It had vanished. He wondered whether he had imagined it. He turned, and saw the two workmen standing side by side under the projecting masses of the tall pink cliffs. He hesitated whether he should make one last attempt to save the man Hill. His physical excitement seemed to desert him suddenly, and leave him aimless and helpless. He turned shoreward, stumbling and wading towards his two companions.

He looked back again, and there were now two boats floating, and the one farthest out at sea pitched clumsily, bottom upward.

III

So it was *Haploteuthis ferox* made its appearance upon the Devonshire coast. So far, this has been its most serious aggression. Mr Fison's account, taken together with the wave of boating and bathing casualties to which I have already alluded, and the absence of fish from the Cornish coasts that year, points clearly to a shoal of these voracious deep-sea monsters prowling slowly along the sub-tidal coast-line. Hunger migration has, I know, been suggested as the force that drove them hither; but, for my own part, I prefer to believe the alternative theory of Hemsley. Hemsley holds that a pack or shoal of these creatures may have become enamoured of human flesh by the accident of a foundered ship sinking among them, and have wandered in search of it out of their accustomed zone; first waylaying and following ships, and so coming to our shores in the wake of the Atlantic traffic. But to discuss Hemsley's cogent and admirably-stated arguments would be out of place here.

It would seem that the appetites of the shoal were satisfied by the catch of eleven people—for, so far as can be ascertained, there were ten people in the second boat, and certainly these creatures gave no further signs of their presence off Sidmouth that day. The coast between Seaton and Budleigh Salterton was patrolled all that evening and night by four Preventive Service boats, the men in which were armed with harpoons and cutlasses, and as the evening advanced, a number of more or less similarly equipped expeditions, organised by private individuals, joined them. Mr Fison took no part in any of these expeditions.

About midnight excited hails were heard from a boat about a couple of miles out at sea to the south-east of Sidmouth, and a lantern was seen waving in a strange manner to and fro and up and down. The nearer boats at once hurried towards the alarm. The venturesome occupants of the boat—a seaman, a curate, and two schoolboys—had actually seen the monsters passing under their boat. The creatures, it seems, like most deep-sea organisms, were phosphorescent, and they had been floating, five fathoms deep or so, like creatures of moonshine through the blackness of the water, their tentacles retracted and as if asleep, rolling over and over, and moving slowly in a wedge-like formation towards the south-east.

These people told their story in gesticulated fragments, as first one boat drew alongside and then another. At last there was a little fleet of eight or nine boats collected together, and from them a tumult, like the chatter of a market-place, rose into the stillness of the night. There was little or no disposition to pursue the shoal, the people had neither weapons nor experience for such a dubious chase, and presently—even with a certain relief, it may be—the boats turned shoreward.

And now to tell what is perhaps the most astonishing fact in this whole astonishing raid. We have not the slightest knowledge of the subsequent movements of the shoal, although the whole south-west coast was now alert for it. But it may, perhaps, be significant that a cachalot was stranded off Sark on June 3. Two weeks and three days after this Sidmouth affair, a living *Haploteuthis* came ashore on Calais sands. It was alive, because several witnesses saw its tentacles moving in a convulsive way. But it is probable that it was dying. A gentleman named Pouchet obtained a rifle and shot it.

That was the last appearance of a living *Haploteuthis*. No others were seen on the French coast. On the 15th of June a dead carcass, almost complete, was washed ashore near Torquay, and a few days later a boat from the Marine Biological station, engaged in dredging off Plymouth, picked up a rotting specimen, slashed deeply with a cutlass wound. How the former had come by its death it is impossible to say. And on the last day of June, Mr Egbert Caine, an artist, bathing near Newlyn,* threw up his arms, shrieked, and was drawn under. A friend bathing with him made no attempt to save him, but swam at once for the shore. This is the last fact to tell of this extraordinary raid from the deeper sea. Whether it is really the last of these horrible creatures it is, as yet, premature to say. But it is believed, and certainly it is to be hoped, that they have returned now, and returned for good, to the sunless depths of the middle seas, out of which they have so strangely and so mysteriously arisen.

XIV

THE OBLITERATED MAN

I WAS—you shall hear immediately why I am not now—
Egbert Craddock Cummins. The name remains. I am still
(Heaven help me!) Dramatic Critic to the *Fiery Cross*.* What
I shall be in a little while I do not know. I write in great
trouble and confusion of mind. I will do what I can to make
myself clear in the face of terrible difficulties. You must bear
with me a little. When a man is rapidly losing his own identity, he naturally finds a difficulty in expressing himself. I will
make it perfectly plain in a minute, when once I get my grip
upon the story. Let me see—where *am* I? I wish I knew. Ah,
I have it! Dead self! Egbert Craddock Cummins!

In the past I should have disliked writing anything quite so
full of 'I' as this story must be. It is full of 'I's' before and
behind, like the beast in Revelation*—the one with a head
like a calf, I am afraid. But my tastes have changed since I
became a Dramatic Critic and studied the masters—G.R.S.,
G.B.S., G.A.S.,* and the others. Everything has changed since
then. At least the story is about myself—so that there is
some excuse for me. And it is really not egotism, because, as
I say, since those days my identity has undergone an entire
alteration.

That past! . . . I was—in those days—rather a nice fellow,
rather shy—taste for grey in my clothes, weedy little moustache, face 'interesting,' slight stutter which I had caught in
my early life from a schoolfellow. Engaged to a very nice girl,
named Delia. Fairly new, she was*—cigarettes—liked me
because I was human and original. Considered I was like
Lamb*—on the strength of the stutter, I believe. Father, an
eminent authority on postage stamps. She read a great deal
in the British Museum. (A perfect pairing ground for literary

people, that British Museum—you should read George
Egerton and Justin Huntly M'Carthy and Gissing* and the
rest of them.) We loved in our intellectual way, and shared
the brightest hopes. (All gone now.) And her father liked me
because I seemed honestly eager to hear about stamps. She
had no mother. Indeed, I had the happiest prospects a young
man could have. I never went to theatres in those days. My
Aunt Charlotte before she died had told me not to.

Then Barnaby, the editor of the *Fiery Cross*, made me—
in spite of my spasmodic efforts to escape—Dramatic Critic.*
He is a fine, healthy man, Barnaby, with an enormous head
of frizzy black hair and a convincing manner, and he caught
me on the staircase going to see Wembly. He had been dining,
and was more than usually buoyant. 'Hullo, Cummins!' he
said. 'The very man I want!' He caught me by the shoulder
or the collar or something, ran me up the little passage, and
flung me over the waste-paper basket into the arm-chair in
his office. 'Pray be seated,' he said, as he did so. Then he ran
across the room and came back with some pink and yellow
tickets and pushed them into my hand. 'Opera Comique,' he
said, 'Thursday; Friday, the Surrey; Saturday, the Frivolity.*
That's all, I think.'

'But——' I began.

'Glad you're free,' he said, snatching some proofs off the
desk and beginning to read.

'I don't quite understand,' I said.

'*Eigh?*' he said, at the top of his voice, as though he thought
I had gone and was startled at my remark.

'Do you want me to criticise these plays?'

'Do something with 'em. . . . Did you think it was a treat?'

'But I can't.'

'Did you call me a fool?'

'Well, I've never been to a theatre in my life.'

'Virgin soil.'

'But I don't know anything about it, you know.'

'That's just it. New view. No habits. No *clichés* in stock.

153

Ours is a live paper, not a bag of tricks. None of your clock-work professional journalism in this office. And I can rely on your integrity——'

'But I've conscientious scruples——'

He caught me up suddenly and put me outside his door. 'Go and talk to Wembly about that,' he said. 'He'll explain.'

As I stood perplexed, he opened the door again, said, 'I forgot this,' thrust a fourth ticket into my hand (it was for that night—in twenty minutes' time) and slammed the door upon me. His expression was quite calm, but I caught his eye.

I hate arguments. I decided that I would take his hint and become (to my own destruction) a Dramatic Critic. I walked slowly down the passage to Wembly. That Barnaby has a remarkable persuasive way. He has made few suggestions during our very pleasant intercourse of four years that he has not ultimately won me round to adopting. It may be, of course, that I am of a yielding disposition; certainly I am too apt to take my colour from my circumstances. It is, indeed, to my unfortunate susceptibility to vivid impressions that all my misfortunes are due. I have already alluded to the slight stammer I had acquired from a schoolfellow in my youth. However, this is a digression. . . . I went home in a cab to dress.

I will not trouble the reader with my thoughts about the first-night audience, strange assembly as it is,—those I reserve for my Memoirs,—nor the humiliating story of how I got lost during the *entr'acte* in a lot of red plush passages, and saw the third act from the gallery. The only point upon which I wish to lay stress was the remarkable effect of the acting upon me. You must remember I had lived a quiet and retired life, and had never been to the theatre before, and that I am extremely sensitive to vivid impressions. At the risk of repetition I must insist upon these points.

The first effect was a profound amazement, not untinctured by alarm. The phenomenal unnaturalness of acting is a thing

discounted in the minds of most people by early visits to the
theatre. They get used to the fantastic gestures, the flamboyant
emotions, the weird mouthings, melodious snortings, agonis-
ing yelps, lip-gnawings, glaring horrors, and other emotional
symbolism of the stage. It becomes at last a mere deaf-and-
dumb language to them, which they read intelligently *pari
passu** with the hearing of the dialogue. But all this was new
to me. The thing was called a modern comedy, the people
were supposed to be English and were dressed like fashionable Americans of the current epoch, and I fell into the
natural error of supposing that the actors were trying to
represent human beings. I looked round on my first-night
audience with a kind of wonder, discovered—as all new Dramatic Critics do—that it rested with me to reform the Drama,
and, after a supper choked with emotion, went off to the
office to write a column, piebald with 'new paragraphs' (as
all my stuff is—it fills out so) and purple with indignation.
Barnaby was delighted.

But I could not sleep that night. I dreamt of actors—actors
glaring, actors smiting their chests, actors flinging out a
handful of extended fingers, actors smiling bitterly, laughing
despairingly, falling hopelessly, dying idiotically. I got up at
eleven with a slight headache, read my notice in the *Fiery
Cross*, breakfasted, and went back to my room to shave. (It's
my habit to do so.) Then an odd thing happened. I could
not find my razor. Suddenly it occurred to me that I had
not unpacked it the day before.

'Ah!' said I, in front of the looking-glass. Then 'Hullo!'

Quite involuntarily, when I had thought of my portmanteau, I had flung up the left arm (fingers fully extended)
and clutched at my diaphragm with my right hand. I am
an acutely self-conscious man at all times. The gesture
struck me as absolutely novel for me. I repeated it, for my
own satisfaction. 'Odd!' Then (rather puzzled) I turned to
my portmanteau.

After shaving, my mind reverted to the acting I had

seen, and I entertained myself before the cheval glass* with some imitations of Jafferay's more exaggerated gestures. 'Really, one might think it a disease,' I said—'Stage-Walkitis!' (There's many a truth spoken in jest.) Then, if I remember rightly, I went off to see Wembly, and afterwards lunched at the British Museum with Delia. We actually spoke about our prospects, in the light of my new appointment.

But that appointment was the beginning of my downfall. From that day I necessarily became a persistent theatre-goer, and almost insensibly I began to change. The next thing I noticed after the gesture about the razor was to catch myself bowing ineffably when I met Delia, and stooping in an old-fashioned, courtly way over her hand. Directly I caught myself, I straightened myself up and became very uncomfortable. I remember she looked at me curiously. Then, in the office, I found myself doing 'nervous business,' fingers on teeth, when Barnaby asked me a question I could not very well answer. Then, in some trifling difference with Delia, I clasped my hand to my brow. And I pranced through my social trans-actions at times singularly like an actor! I tried not to—no one could be more keenly alive to the arrant absurdity of the histrionic bearing. And I did!

It began to dawn on me what it all meant. The acting, I saw, was too much for my delicately-strung nervous system. I have always, I know, been too amenable to the sugges-tions of my circumstances. Night after night of concen-trated attention to the conventional attitudes and intonation of the English stage was gradually affecting my speech and carriage. I was giving way to the infection of sympathetic imitation. Night after night my plastic nervous system took the print of some new amazing gesture, some new emotional exaggeration—and retained it. A kind of theatrical veneer threatened to plate over and obliterate my private individu-ality altogether. I saw myself in a kind of vision. Sitting by myself one night, my new self seemed to me to glide, posing and gesticulating, across the room. He clutched his throat, he opened his fingers, he opened his legs in walking like a high-class marionette. He went from attitude to attitude. He might have been clockwork. Directly after this I made an ineffectual attempt to resign my theatrical work. But Barnaby persisted in talking about the Polywhiddle Divorce all the time I was with him, and I could get no opportunity of saying what I wished.

And then Delia's manner began to change towards me. The ease of our intercourse vanished. I felt she was learning to dislike me. I grinned, and capered, and scowled, and posed at her in a thousand ways, and knew—with what a voiceless agony!—that I did it all the time. I tried to resign again, and Barnaby talked about 'X' and 'Z' and 'Y' in the *New Review*, and gave me a strong cigar to smoke, and so routed me. And then I walked up the Assyrian Gallery in the manner of Irving* to meet Delia, and so precipitated the crisis.

'Ah!—*Dear!*' I said, with more sprightliness and emotion in my voice than had ever been in all my life before I became (to my own undoing) a Dramatic Critic.

She held out her hand rather coldly, scrutinising my face as she did so. I prepared, with a new-won grace, to walk by her side.

'Egbert,' she said, standing still, and thought. Then she looked at me.

I said nothing. I felt what was coming. I tried to be the old Egbert Craddock Cummins of shambling gait and stammering sincerity, whom she loved, but I felt even as I did so that I was a new thing, a thing of surging emotions and mysterious fixity—like no human being that ever lived, except upon the stage. 'Egbert,' she said, 'you are not yourself.'

'Ah!' Involuntarily I clutched my diaphragm and averted my head (as is the way with them).

'There!' she said.

'*What do you mean?*' I said, whispering in vocal italics— you know how they do it—turning on her, perplexity on face, right hand down, left on brow. I knew quite well what she meant. I knew quite well the dramatic unreality of my behaviour. But I struggled against it in vain. 'What do you mean?' I said, and, in a kind of hoarse whisper, 'I don't understand!'

She really looked as though she disliked me. 'What do you keep on posing for?' she said. 'I don't like it. You didn't use to.'

'Didn't use to!' I said slowly, repeating this twice. I glared up and down the gallery with short, sharp glances. 'We are alone,' I said swiftly. *'Listen!'* I poked my forefinger towards her, and glared at her. 'I am under a curse.'

I saw her hand tighten upon her sunshade. 'You are under some bad influence or other,' said Delia. 'You should give it up. I never knew anyone change as you have done.'

'Delia!' I said, lapsing into the pathetic. 'Pity me. Augh! Delia! *Pit*—y me!'

She eyed me critically. *'Why* you keep playing the fool like this I don't know,' she said. 'Anyhow, I really cannot go about with a man who behaves as you do. You made us both ridiculous on Wednesday. Frankly, I dislike you, as you are now. I met you here to tell you so—as it's about the only place where we can be sure of being alone together——'

'Delia!' said I, with intensity, knuckles of clenched hands white. 'You don't mean——'

'I do,' said Delia. 'A woman's lot is sad enough at the best of times. But with you——'

I clapped my hand on my brow.

'So, good-bye,' said Delia, without emotion.

'Oh, Delia!' I said. 'Not *this*?'

'Good-bye, Mr Cummins,' she said.

By a violent effort I controlled myself and touched her hand. I tried to say some word of explanation to her. She looked into my working face and winced. 'I *must* do it,' she said hopelessly. Then she turned from me and began walking rapidly down the gallery.

Heavens! How the human agony cried within me! I loved

Delia. But nothing found expression—I was already too deeply crusted with my acquired self.

'Good-baye!'* I said at last, watching her retreating figure. How I hated myself for doing it! After she had vanished, I repeated in a dreamy way, 'Good-baye!' looking hopelessly round me. Then, with a kind of heart-broken cry, I shook my clenched fists in the air, staggered to the pedestal of a winged figure, buried my face in my arms, and made my shoulders heave. Something within me said 'Ass!' as I did so. (I had the greatest difficulty in persuading the Museum policeman, who was attracted by my cry of agony, that I was not intoxicated, but merely suffering from a transient indisposition.)

But even this great sorrow has not availed to save me from my fate. I see it; everyone sees it: I grow more 'theatrical' every day. And no one could be more painfully aware of the pungent silliness of theatrical ways. The quiet, nervous, but pleasing E. C. Cummins vanishes. I cannot save him. I am driven like a dead leaf before the winds of March. My tailor even enters into the spirit of my disorder. He has a peculiar sense of what is fitting. I tried to get a dull grey suit from him this spring, and he foisted a brilliant blue upon me, and I see he has put braid down the sides of my new dress trousers. My hairdresser insists upon giving me a 'wave.'

I am beginning to associate with actors. I detest them, but it is only in their company that I can feel I am not glaringly conspicuous. Their talk infects me. I notice a growing tendency to dramatic brevity, to dashes and pauses in my style, to a punctuation of bows and attitudes. Barnaby has remarked it too. I offended Wembly by calling him 'Dear Boy' yesterday. I dread the end, but I cannot escape from it.

The fact is, I am being obliterated. Living a grey, retired life all my youth, I came to the theatre a delicate sketch of a man, a thing of tints and faint lines. Their gorgeous colouring has effaced me altogether. People forget how much mode of expression, method of movement, are a matter of contagion. I have heard of stage-struck people before, and thought it a figure of speech. I spoke of it jestingly, as a disease. It is no jest. It is a disease. And I have got it badly! Deep down within me I protest against the wrong done to my personality—unavailingly. For three hours or more a week I have to go and concentrate my attention on some fresh play, and the suggestions of the drama strengthen their awful hold upon me. My manners grow so flamboyant, my passions so professional, that I doubt, as I said at the outset, whether it is really myself that behaves in such a manner. I feel merely the core to this dramatic casing, that grows thicker and presses upon me—me and mine. I feel like King John's abbot in his cope of lead.*

I doubt, indeed, whether I should not abandon the struggle altogether—leave this sad world of ordinary life for which I am so ill fitted, abandon the name of Cummins for some professional pseudonym, complete my self-effacement, and— a thing of tricks and tatters, of posing and pretence—go upon the stage. It seems my only resort—'to hold the mirror up to Nature.'* For in the ordinary life, I will confess, no one now seems to regard me as both sane and sober. Only upon the stage, I feel convinced, will people take me seriously. That will be the end of it. I *know* that will be the end of it. And yet . . . I will frankly confess . . . all that marks off your actor from your common man . . . I *detest*. I am still largely of my Aunt Charlotte's opinion, that play-acting is unworthy of a pure-minded man's attention, much more participation. Even now I would resign my dramatic criticism and try a rest. Only I can't get hold of Barnaby. Letters of resignation he never notices. He says it is against the etiquette of journalism to write to your Editor. And when I go to see him, he gives me another big cigar and some strong whisky and soda, and then something always turns up to prevent my explanation.

XV

THE PLATTNER STORY

WHETHER the story of Gottfried Plattner is to be credited or not is a pretty question in the value of evidence. On the one hand, we have seven witnesses—to be perfectly exact, we have six and a half pairs of eyes, and one undeniable fact; and on the other we have—what is it?—prejudice, common-sense, the inertia of opinion. Never were there seven more honest-seeming witnesses; never was there a more undeniable fact than the inversion of Gottfried Plattner's anatomical structure, and—never was there a more preposterous story than the one they have to tell! The most preposterous part of the story is the worthy Gottfried's contribution (for I count him as one of the seven). Heaven forbid that I should be led into giving countenance to superstition by a passion for impartiality, and so come to share the fate of Eusapia's patrons!* Frankly, I believe there is something crooked about this business of Gottfried Plattner; but what that crooked factor is, I will admit as frankly, I do not know. I have been surprised at the credit accorded to the story in the most unexpected and authoritative quarters. The fairest way to the reader, however, will be for me to tell it without further comment.

Gottfried Plattner is, in spite of his name, a freeborn Englishman. His father was an Alsatian who came to England in the 'sixties, married a respectable English girl of unexceptionable antecedents, and died, after a wholesome and uneventful life (devoted, I understand, chiefly to the laying of parquet flooring), in 1887. Gottfried's age is seven-and-twenty. He is, by virtue of his heritage of three languages, Modern Languages Master in a small private school in the south of England. To the casual observer he is singularly like any other Modern Languages Master in any other small private school. His costume is neither very costly nor very fashionable, but, on the other hand, it is not markedly cheap or shabby; his complexion, like his height and his bearing, is inconspicuous. You would notice, perhaps, that, like the majority of people, his face was not absolutely symmetrical, his right eye a little larger than the left, and his jaw a trifle heavier on the right side. If you, as an ordinary careless person, were to bare his chest and feel his heart beating, you would probably find it quite like the heart of anyone else. But here you and the trained observer would part company. If you found his heart quite ordinary, the trained observer would find it quite otherwise. And once the thing was pointed out to you, you too would perceive the peculiarity easily enough. It is that Gottfried's heart beats on the right side of his body.

Now, that is not the only singularity of Gottfried's structure, although it is the only one that would appeal to the untrained mind. Careful sounding of Gottfried's internal arrangements by a well-known surgeon seems to point to the fact that all the other unsymmetrical parts of his body are similarly misplaced. The right lobe of his liver is on the left side, the left on his right; while his lungs, too, are similarly contraposed. What is still more singular, unless Gottfried is a consummate actor, we must believe that his right hand has recently become his left. Since the occurrences we are about to consider (as impartially as possible), he has found the utmost difficulty in writing, except from right to left across the paper with his left hand. He cannot throw with his right hand, he is perplexed at meal-times between knife and fork, and his ideas of the rule of the road—he is a cyclist—are still a dangerous confusion. And there is not a scrap of evidence to show that before these occurrences Gottfried was at all left-handed.

There is yet another wonderful fact in this preposterous business. Gottfried produces three photographs of himself. You have him at the age of five or six, thrusting fat legs at you from under a plaid frock, and scowling. In that photograph his left eye is a little larger than his right, and his jaw is a trifle heavier on the left side. This is the reverse of his present living condition. The photograph of Gottfried at fourteen seems to contradict these facts, but that is because it is one of those cheap 'Gem' photographs that were then in vogue, taken direct upon metal, and therefore reversing things just as a looking-glass would. The third photograph represents him at one-and-twenty, and confirms the record of the others. There seems here evidence of the strongest confirmatory character that Gottfried has exchanged his left side for his right. Yet how a human being can be so changed, short of a fantastic and pointless miracle, it is exceedingly hard to suggest.

In one way, of course, these facts might be explicable on the supposition that Plattner has undertaken an elaborate mystification, on the strength of his heart's displacement. Photographs may be faked, and left-handedness imitated. But the character of the man does not lend itself to any such theory. He is quiet, practical, unobtrusive, and thoroughly sane, from the Nordau standpoint.* He likes beer, and smokes moderately, takes walking exercise daily, and has a healthily high estimate of the value of his teaching. He has a good but untrained tenor voice, and takes a pleasure in singing airs of a popular and cheerful character. He is fond, but not morbidly fond, of reading,—chiefly fiction pervaded with a vaguely pious optimism,—sleeps well, and rarely dreams. He is, in fact, the very last person to evolve a fantastic fable. Indeed, so far from forcing this story upon the world, he has been singularly reticent on the matter. He meets enquirers with a certain engaging—bashfulness is almost the word, that disarms the most suspicious. He seems genuinely ashamed that anything so unusual has occurred to him.

It is to be regretted that Plattner's aversion to the idea of post-mortem dissection may postpone, perhaps for ever, the positive proof that his entire body has had its left and right sides transposed. Upon that fact mainly the credibility of his story hangs. There is no way of taking a man and moving him about in space as ordinary people understand space, that will result in our changing his sides. Whatever you do, his right is still his right, his left his left. You can do that with a perfectly thin and flat thing, of course. If you were to cut a figure out of paper, any figure with a right and left side, you could change its sides simply by lifting it up and turning it over. But with a solid it is different. Mathematical theorists tell us that the only way in which the right and left sides of a solid body can be changed is by taking that body clean out of space as we know it,—taking it out of ordinary existence, that is, and turning it somewhere outside space. This is a little abstruse, no doubt, but anyone with any knowledge of mathematical theory will assure the reader of its truth. To put the thing in technical language, the curious inversion of Plattner's right and left sides is proof that he has moved out of our space into what is called the Fourth Dimension, and that he has returned again to our world. Unless we choose to consider ourselves the victims of an elaborate and motiveless fabrication, we are almost bound to believe that this has occurred.

So much for the tangible facts. We come now to the account of the phenomena that attended his temporary disappearance from the world. It appears that in the Sussexville Proprietary School, Plattner not only discharged the duties of Modern Languages Master, but also taught chemistry, commercial geography, book-keeping, shorthand, drawing, and any other additional subject to which the changing fancies of the boys' parents might direct attention. He knew little or nothing of these various subjects, but in secondary as distinguished from Board or elementary schools, knowledge in the teacher is, very properly, by no means so necessary as high moral character and gentlemanly tone. In chemistry he was particularly deficient, knowing, he says, nothing beyond the Three Gases* (whatever the three gases may be). As, however, his pupils began by knowing nothing, and derived all their information from him, this caused him (or anyone) but little inconvenience for several terms. Then a little boy named Whibble joined the school, who had been educated (it seems) by some mischievous relative into an inquiring habit of mind. This little boy followed Plattner's lessons with marked and sustained interest, and in order to exhibit his zeal on the subject, brought, at various times, substances for Plattner to analyse. Plattner, flattered by this evidence of his power of awakening interest, and trusting to the boy's ignorance, analysed these, and even made general statements as to their composition. Indeed, he was so far stimulated by his pupil as to obtain a work upon analytical chemistry, and study it during his supervision of the evening's preparation. He was surprised to find chemistry quite an interesting subject.

So far the story is absolutely commonplace. But now the greenish powder comes upon the scene. The source of that greenish powder seems, unfortunately, lost. Master Whibble tells a tortuous story of finding it done up in a packet in a disused limekiln near the Downs. It would have been an excellent thing for Plattner, and possibly for Master Whibble's family, if a match could have been applied to that powder there and then. The young gentleman certainly did not bring it to school in a packet, but in a common eight-ounce graduated medicine bottle, plugged with masticated newspaper. He gave it to Plattner at the end of the afternoon school. Four boys had been detained after school prayers in order to complete some neglected tasks, and Plattner was supervising these in the small class-room in which the chemical teaching was conducted. The appliances for the practical teaching of chemistry in the Sussexville Proprietary School, as in most small schools in this country, are characterised by a severe simplicity. They are kept in a small cupboard standing in a recess, and having about the same capacity as a common travelling trunk. Plattner, being bored with his passive superintendence, seems to have welcomed the intervention of Whibble with his green powder as an agreeable diversion, and, unlocking this cupboard, proceeded at once with his analytical experiments. Whibble sat, luckily for himself, at a safe distance, regarding him. The four malefactors, feigning a profound absorption in their work, watched him furtively with the keenest interest. For even within the limits of the Three Gases, Plattner's practical chemistry was, I understand, temerarious.*

They are practically unanimous in their account of Plattner's proceedings. He poured a little of the green powder into a test-tube, and tried the substance with water, hydrochloric acid, nitric acid, and sulphuric acid in succession. Getting no result, he emptied out a little heap—nearly half the bottleful, in fact—upon a slate and tried a match. He held the medicine bottle in his left hand. The stuff began to smoke and melt, and then exploded with deafening violence and a blinding flash.

The five boys, seeing the flash and being prepared for catastrophes, ducked below their desks, and were none of them seriously hurt. The window was blown out into the playground, and the blackboard on its easel was upset. The slate was smashed to atoms. Some plaster fell from the ceiling. No other damage was done to the school edifice or appliances, and the boys at first, seeing nothing of Plattner, fancied he was knocked down and lying out of their sight below the desks. They jumped out of their places to go to his assistance, and were amazed to find the space empty. Being still confused by the sudden violence of the report, they hurried to the open door, under the impression that he must have been hurt, and have rushed out of the room. But Carson, the foremost, nearly collided in the doorway with the principal, Mr Lidgett.

Mr Lidgett is a corpulent, excitable man with one eye. The boys describe him as stumbling into the room mouthing some of those tempered expletives irritable schoolmasters accustom themselves to use—lest worse befall. 'Wretched mumchancer!'* he said. 'Where's Mr Plattner?' The boys are agreed on the very words. ('Wobbler,' 'snivelling puppy,' and 'mumchancer' are, it seems, among the ordinary small change of Mr Lidgett's scholastic commerce.)

Where's Mr Plattner? That was a question that was to be repeated many times in the next few days. It really seemed as though that frantic hyperbole, 'blown to atoms,' had for once realised itself. There was not a visible particle of Plattner to be seen; not a drop of blood nor a stitch of clothing to be found. Apparently he had been blown clean out of existence and left not a wrack behind.* Not so much as would cover a sixpenny piece, to quote a proverbial expression! The evidence of his absolute disappearance as a consequence of that explosion is indubitable.

It is not necessary to enlarge here upon the commotion excited in the Sussexville Proprietary School, and in Sussexville and elsewhere, by this event. It is quite possible, indeed, that some of the readers of these pages may recall the hearing of some remote and dying version of that excitement during the last summer holidays. Lidgett, it would seem, did everything in his power to suppress and minimise the story. He instituted a penalty of twenty-five lines for any mention of Plattner's name among the boys, and stated in the schoolroom that he was clearly aware of his assistant's whereabouts. He was afraid, he explains, that the possibility of an explosion happening, in spite of the elaborate precautions taken to minimise the practical teaching of chemistry, might injure the reputation of the school; and so might any mysterious quality in Plattner's departure. Indeed, he did everything in his power to make the occurrence seem as ordinary as possible. In particular, he cross-examined the five eye-witnesses of the occurrence so searchingly that they began to doubt the plain evidence of their senses. But, in spite of these efforts, the tale, in a magnified and distorted state, made a nine days' wonder in the district, and several parents withdrew their sons on colourable pretexts. Not the least remarkable point in the matter is the fact that a large number of people in the neighbourhood dreamed singularly vivid dreams of Plattner during the period of excitement before his return, and that these dreams had a curious uniformity. In almost all of them Plattner was seen, sometimes singly, sometimes in company, wandering about through a coruscating iridescence. In all cases his face was pale and distressed, and in some he gesticulated towards the dreamer. One or two of the boys, evidently under the influence of nightmare, fancied that Plattner approached them with remarkable swiftness, and seemed to look closely into their very eyes. Others fled with Plattner from the pursuit of vague and extraordinary creatures of a globular shape. But all these fancies were forgotten in inquiries and speculations when on the Wednesday next but one after the Monday of the explosion, Plattner returned.

The circumstances of his return were as singular as those of his departure. So far as Mr Lidgett's somewhat choleric outline can be filled in from Plattner's hesitating statements, it would appear that on Wednesday evening, towards the hour of sunset, the former gentleman, having dismissed evening preparation, was engaged in his garden, picking and eating strawberries, a fruit of which he is inordinately fond. It is a large old-fashioned garden, secured from observation, fortunately, by a high and ivy-covered red-brick wall. Just as he was stooping over a particularly prolific plant, there was a flash in the air and a heavy thud, and before he could look round, some heavy body struck him violently from behind. He was pitched forward, crushing the strawberries he held in his hand, and that so roughly, that his silk hat—Mr Lidgett adheres to the older ideas of scholastic costume—was driven violently down upon his forehead, and almost over one eye. This heavy missile, which slid over him sideways and collapsed into a sitting posture among the strawberry plants, proved to be our long-lost Mr Gottfried Plattner, in an extremely dishevelled condition. He was collarless and hatless, his linen was dirty, and there was blood upon his hands. Mr Lidgett was so indignant and surprised that he remained on all-fours, and with his hat jammed down on his eye, while he expostulated vehemently with Plattner for his disrespectful and unaccountable conduct.

This scarcely idyllic scene completes what I may call the exterior version of the Plattner story—its exoteric aspect. It is quite unnecessary to enter here into all the details of his dismissal by Mr Lidgett. Such details, with the full names and dates and references, will be found in the larger report of these occurrences that was laid before the Society for the Investigation of Abnormal Phenomena. The singular transposition of Plattner's right and left sides was scarcely observed for the first day or so, and then first in connection with his disposition to write from right to left across the blackboard. He concealed rather than ostended this curious confirmatory circumstance, as he considered it would unfavourably affect his prospects in a new situation. The displacement of his heart was discovered some months after, when he was having a tooth extracted under anæsthetics. He then, very unwillingly, allowed a cursory surgical examination to be made of himself, with a view to a brief account in the *Journal of Anatomy*. That exhausts the statement of the material facts; and we may now go on to consider Plattner's account of the matter.

But first let us clearly differentiate between the preceding portion of this story and what is to follow. All I have told thus far is established by such evidence as even a criminal lawyer would approve. Every one of the witnesses is still alive; the reader, if he have the leisure, may hunt the lads out to-morrow, or even brave the terrors of the redoubtable Lidgett, and cross-examine and trap and test to his heart's content; Gottfried Plattner himself, and his twisted heart and his three photographs, are producible. It may be taken as proved that he did disappear for nine days as the consequence of an explosion; that he returned almost as violently, under circumstances in their nature annoying to Mr

Lidgett, whatever the details of those circumstances may be; and that he returned inverted, just as a reflection returns from a mirror. From the last fact, as I have already stated, it follows almost inevitably that Plattner, during those nine days, must have been in some state of existence altogether out of space. The evidence to these statements is, indeed, far stronger than that upon which most murderers are hanged. But for his own particular account of where he had been, with its confused explanations and wellnigh self-contradictory details, we have only Mr Gottfried Plattner's word. I do not wish to discredit that, but I must point out—what so many writers upon obscure psychic phenomena fail to do—that we are passing here from the practically undeniable to that kind of matter which any reasonable man is entitled to believe or reject as he thinks proper. The previous statements render it plausible; its discordance with common experience tilts it towards the incredible. I would prefer not to sway the beam of the reader's judgment either way, but simply to tell the story as Plattner told it me.

He gave me his narrative, I may state, at my house at Chislehurst, and so soon as he had left me that evening, I went into my study and wrote down everything as I remembered it. Subsequently he was good enough to read over a type-written copy, so that its substantial correctness is undeniable.

He states that at the moment of the explosion he distinctly thought he was killed. He felt lifted off his feet and driven forcibly backward. It is a curious fact for psychologists that he thought clearly during his backward flight, and wondered whether he should hit the chemistry cupboard or the blackboard easel. His heels struck ground, and he staggered and fell heavily into a sitting position on something soft and firm. For a moment the concussion stunned him. He became aware at once of a vivid scent of singed hair, and he seemed to hear the voice of Lidgett asking for him. You will understand that for a time his mind was greatly confused.

At first he was under the impression that he was still standing in the class-room. He perceived quite distinctly the surprise of the boys and the entry of Mr Lidgett. He is quite positive upon that score. He did not hear their remarks; but that he ascribed to the deafening effect of the experiment. Things about him seemed curiously dark and faint, but his mind explained that on the obvious but mistaken idea that the explosion had engendered a huge volume of dark smoke. Through the dimness the figures of Lidgett and the boys moved, as faint and silent as ghosts. Plattner's face still tingled with the stinging heat of the flash. He was, he says, 'all muddled.' His first definite thoughts seem to have been of his personal safety. He thought he was perhaps blinded and deafened. He felt his limbs and face in a gingerly manner. Then his perceptions grew clearer, and he was astonished to miss the old familiar desks and other schoolroom furniture about him. Only dim, uncertain, grey shapes stood in the place of these. Then came a thing that made him shout aloud, and awoke his stunned faculties to instant activity. *Two of the boys, gesticulating, walked one after the other clean through him!* Neither manifested the slightest consciousness of his presence. It is difficult to imagine the sensation he felt. They came against him, he says, with no more force than a wisp of mist.

Plattner's first thought after that was that he was dead. Having been brought up with thoroughly sound views in these matters, however, he was a little surprised to find his body still about him. His second conclusion was that he was not dead, but that the others were: that the explosion had destroyed the Sussexville Proprietary School and every soul in it except himself. But that, too, was scarcely satisfactory. He was thrown back upon astonished observation.

Everything about him was profoundly dark: at first it seemed to have an altogether ebony blackness. Overhead was a black firmament. The only touch of light in the scene was a faint greenish glow at the edge of the sky in one direction, which threw into prominence a horizon of un-dulating black hills. This, I say, was his impression at first. As his eye grew accustomed to the darkness, he began to distinguish a faint quality of differentiating greenish colour in the circumambient night. Against this background the furniture and occupants of the class-room, it seems, stood out like phosphorescent spectres, faint and impalpable. He extended his hand, and thrust it without an effort through the wall of the room by the fireplace.

He describes himself as making a strenuous effort to at-tract attention. He shouted to Lidgett, and tried to seize the boys as they went to and fro. He only desisted from these attempts when Mrs Lidgett, whom he (as an Assistant Mas-ter) naturally disliked, entered the room. He says the sensa-tion of being in the world, and yet not a part of it, was an extraordinarily disagreeable one. He compared his feelings, not inaptly, to those of a cat watching a mouse through a window. Whenever he made a motion to communicate with the dim, familiar world about him, he found an invisible, incomprehensible barrier preventing intercourse.

He then turned his attention to his solid environment. He found the medicine bottle still unbroken in his hand, with the remainder of the green powder therein. He put this in his pocket, and began to feel about him. Apparently he was sitting on a boulder of rock covered with a velvety moss. The dark country about him he was unable to see, the faint, misty picture of the schoolroom blotting it out, but he had a feeling (due perhaps to a cold wind) that he was near the crest of a hill, and that a steep valley fell away beneath his feet. The green glow along the edge of the sky seemed to be growing in extent and intensity. He stood up, rubbing his eyes.

It would seem that he made a few steps, going steeply downhill, and then stumbled, nearly fell, and sat down again upon a jagged mass of rock to watch the dawn. He became aware that the world about him was absolutely silent. It was as still as it was dark, and though there was a cold wind blowing up the hill-face, the rustle of grass, the soughing of the boughs that should have accompanied it, were absent. He could hear, therefore, if he could not see, that the hillside upon which he stood was rocky and desolate. The green grew brighter every moment, and as it did so a faint, transparent blood-red mingled with, but did not mitigate, the blackness of the sky overhead and the rocky desolations about him. Having regard to what follows, I am inclined to think that that redness may have been an optical effect due to contrast. Something black fluttered momentarily against the livid yellow-green of the lower sky, and then the thin and penetrating voice of a bell rose out of the black gulf below him. An oppressive expectation grew with the growing light.

It is probable that an hour or more elapsed while he sat there, the strange green light growing brighter every moment, and spreading slowly, in flamboyant fingers, upward towards the zenith. As it grew, the spectral vision of *our* world became relatively or absolutely fainter. Probably both, for the time must have been about that of our earthly sunset. So far as his vision of our world went, Plattner, by his few steps downhill, had passed through the floor of the class-room, and was now, it seemed, sitting in mid-air in the larger schoolroom downstairs. He saw the boarders distinctly, but much more faintly than he had seen Lidgett. They were preparing their evening tasks, and he noticed with interest that several were cheating with their Euclid riders* by means of a crib,* a compilation whose existence he had hitherto never suspected. As the time passed, they faded steadily, as steadily as the light of the green dawn increased.

Looking down into the valley, he saw that the light had crept far down its rocky sides, and that the profound blackness of the abyss was now broken by a minute green glow, like the light of a glow-worm. And almost immediately the limb of a huge heavenly body of blazing green rose over the basaltic undulations of the distant hills, and the monstrous hill-masses about him came out gaunt and desolate, in green light and deep, ruddy black shadows. He became aware of a vast number of ball-shaped objects drifting as thistledown drifts over the high ground. There were none of these nearer to him than the opposite side of the gorge. The bell below twanged quicker and quicker with something like impatient insistence, and several lights moved hither and thither. The boys at work at their desks were now almost imperceptibly faint.

This extinction of our world, when the green sun of this other universe rose, is a curious point upon which Plattner insists. During the Other-World night it is difficult to move about, on account of the vividness with which the things of this world are visible. It becomes a riddle to explain why, if this is the case, we in this world catch no glimpse of the Other-World. It is due, perhaps, to the comparatively vivid illumination of this world of ours. Plattner describes the mid-day of the Other-World, at its brightest, as not being nearly so bright as this world at full moon, while its night is profoundly black. Consequently, the amount of light, even in an ordinary dark room, is sufficient to render the things of the Other-World invisible, on the same principle that faint phosphorescence is only visible in the profoundest darkness. I have tried, since he told me his story, to see something of the Other-World by sitting for a long space in a photographer's dark room at night. I have certainly seen indistinctly the form of greenish slopes and rocks, but only, I must admit, very indistinctly indeed. The reader may possibly be more successful. Plattner tells me that since his return he has dreamt and seen and recognised places in the Other-World, but this is probably due to his memory of these scenes. It seems quite possible that people with unusually keen eyesight may occasionally catch a glimpse of this strange Other-World about us.

However, this is a digression. As the green sun rose, a long street of black buildings became perceptible, though only darkly and indistinctly, in the gorge, and after some hesitation, Plattner began to clamber down the precipitous descent towards them. The descent was long and exceedingly tedious, being so not only by the extraordinary steepness, but also by reason of the looseness of the boulders with which the whole face of the hill was strewn. The noise of his descent—now and then his heels struck fire from the rocks—seemed now the only sound in the universe, for the beating of the bell had ceased. As he drew nearer, he perceived that the various edifices had a singular resemblance to tombs and mausoleums and monuments, saving only that they were all uniformly black instead of being white, as most sepulchres are. And then he saw, crowding out of the largest building, very much as people disperse from church, a number of pallid, rounded, pale-green figures. These dispersed in several directions about the broad street of the place, some going through side alleys and reappearing upon the steepness of the hill, others entering some of the small black buildings which lined the way.

At the sight of these things drifting up towards him, Plattner stopped, staring. They were not walking, they were indeed limbless, and they had the appearance of human heads, beneath which a tadpole-like body swung. He was too astonished at their strangeness, too full, indeed, of strangeness, to be seriously alarmed by them. They drove towards him, in front of the chill wind that was blowing uphill, much as soap-bubbles drive before a draught. And as he looked at the nearest of those approaching, he saw it was indeed a human head, albeit with singularly large eyes, and wearing such an expression of distress and anguish as he had never seen before upon mortal countenance. He was surprised to find that it did not turn to regard him, but seemed to be watching and following some unseen moving thing. For a moment he was puzzled, and then it occurred to him that this creature was watching with its enormous eyes something that was happening in the world he had just left. Nearer it came, and nearer, and he was too astonished to cry out. It made a very faint fretting sound as it came close to him. Then it struck his face with a gentle pat—its touch was very cold—and drove past him, and upward towards the crest of the hill.

An extraordinary conviction flashed across Plattner's mind that this head had a strong likeness to Lidgett. Then he turned his attention to the other heads that were now swarming thickly up the hill-side. None made the slightest sign of recognition. One or two, indeed, came close to his head and almost followed the example of the first, but he dodged convulsively out of the way. Upon most of them he saw the same expression of unavailing regret he had seen upon the first, and heard the same faint sounds of wretchedness from them. One or two wept, and one rolling swiftly uphill wore an expression of diabolical rage. But others were cold, and several had a look of gratified interest in their eyes. One, at least, was almost in an ecstasy of happiness. Plattner does not remember that he recognised any more likenesses in those he saw at this time.

For several hours, perhaps, Plattner watched these strange things dispersing themselves over the hills, and not till long after they had ceased to issue from the clustering black buildings in the gorge, did he resume his downward climb. The darkness about him increased so much that he had a difficulty in stepping true. Overhead the sky was now a bright, pale green. He felt neither hunger nor thirst. Later, when he did, he found a chilly stream running down the centre of the gorge, and the rare moss upon the boulders, when he tried it at last in desperation, was good to eat.

He groped about among the tombs that ran down the gorge, seeking vaguely for some clue to these inexplicable things. After a long time he came to the entrance of the big mausoleum-like building from which the heads had issued. In this he found a group of green lights burning upon a kind of basaltic altar, and a bell-rope from a belfry overhead hanging down into the centre of the place. Round the wall ran a lettering of fire in a character unknown to him. While he was still wondering at the purport of these things, he heard the receding tramp of heavy feet echoing far down the street. He ran out into the darkness again, but he could see nothing. He had a mind to pull the bell-rope, and finally decided to follow the footsteps. But, although he ran far, he never overtook them; and his shouting was of no avail. The gorge seemed to extend an interminable distance. It was as dark as earthly starlight throughout its length, while the ghastly green day lay along the upper edge of its precipices. There were none of the heads, now, below. They were all, it seemed, busily occupied along the upper slopes. Looking up, he saw them drifting hither and thither, some hovering stationary, some flying swiftly through the air. It reminded him, he said, of 'big snowflakes'; only these were black and pale green.

In pursuing the firm, undeviating footsteps that he never overtook, in groping into new regions of this endless devil's dyke,* in clambering up and down the pitiless heights, in wandering about the summits, and in watching the drifting faces, Plattner states that he spent the better part of seven or eight days. He did not keep count, he says. Though once or twice he found eyes watching him, he had word with no living soul. He slept among the rocks on the hillside. In the gorge things earthly were invisible, because, from the earthly standpoint, it was far underground. On the altitudes, so soon as the earthly day began, the world became visible to him. He found himself sometimes stumbling over the dark green rocks, or arresting himself on a precipitous brink, while all about him the green branches of the Sussexville lanes were swaying; or, again, he seemed to be walking through the Sussexville streets, or watching unseen the private business of some household. And then it was he discovered, that to almost every human being in our world there pertained some of these drifting heads; that everyone in the world is watched intermittently by these helpless disembodiments.

What are they—these Watchers of the Living? Plattner never learned. But two, that presently found and followed him, were like his childhood's memory of his father and mother. Now and then other faces turned their eyes upon him: eyes like those of dead people who had swayed him, or injured him, or helped him in his youth and manhood. Whenever they looked at him, Plattner was overcome with a strange sense of responsibility. To his mother he ventured to speak; but she made no answer. She looked sadly, steadfastly, and tenderly—a little reproachfully, too, it seemed—into his eyes.

He simply tells this story: he does not endeavour to explain. We are left to surmise who these Watchers of the Living may be, or, if they are indeed the Dead, why they should so closely and passionately watch a world they have left for ever. It may be—indeed to my mind it seems just—that, when our life has closed, when evil or good is no longer a choice for us, we may still have to witness the working out of the train of consequences we have laid. If human souls continue after death, then surely human interests continue after death. But that is merely my own guess at the meaning of the things seen. Plattner offers no interpretation, for none was given him. It is well the reader should understand this clearly. Day after day, with his head reeling, he wandered about this strange-lit world outside the world, weary and, towards the end, weak and hungry. By day—by our earthly day, that is—the ghostly vision of the old familiar scenery of Sussexville, all about him, irked and worried him. He could not see where to put his feet, and ever and again with a chilly touch one of these Watching Souls would come against his face. And after dark the multitude of these Watchers about him, and their intent distress, confused his mind beyond describing. A great longing to return to the earthly life that was so near and yet so remote consumed him. The unearthliness of things about him produced a positively painful mental distress. He was worried beyond describing by his own particular followers. He would shout at them to desist from staring at him, scold at them, hurry away from them. They were always mute and intent. Run as he might over the uneven ground, they followed his destinies.

On the ninth day, towards evening, Plattner heard the invisible footsteps approaching, far away down the gorge. He was then wandering over the broad crest of the same hill upon which he had fallen in his entry into this strange Other-World of his. He turned to hurry down into the gorge, feeling his way hastily, and was arrested by the sight of the thing that was happening in a room in a back street near the school. Both of the people in the room he knew by sight. The windows were open, the blinds up, and the setting sun shone clearly into it, so that it came out quite brightly at first, a vivid oblong of room, lying like a magic-lantern picture upon the black landscape and the livid green dawn. In addition to the sunlight, a candle had just been lit in the room.

On the bed lay a lank man, his ghastly white face terrible upon the tumbled pillow. His clenched hands were raised above his head. A little table beside the bed carried a few medicine bottles, some toast and water, and an empty glass. Every now and then the lank man's lips fell apart, to indicate a word he could not articulate. But the woman did not notice that he wanted anything, because she was busy turning out papers from an old-fashioned bureau in the opposite corner of the room. At first the picture was very vivid indeed, but as the green dawn behind it grew brighter and brighter, so it became fainter and more and more transparent.

As the echoing footsteps paced nearer and nearer, those footsteps that sound so loud in that Other-World and come so silently in this, Plattner perceived about him a great multitude of dim faces gathering together out of the darkness and watching the two people in the room. Never before had he seen so many of the Watchers of the Living. A multitude had eyes only for the sufferer in the room, another multitude, in infinite anguish, watched the woman as she hunted with greedy eyes for something she could not find. They crowded about Plattner, they came across his sight and buffeted his face, the noise of their unavailing regrets was all about him. He saw clearly only now and then. At other times the picture quivered dimly, through the veil of green reflections upon their movements. In the room it must have been very still, and Plattner says the candle flame streamed up into a perfectly vertical line of smoke, but in his ears each footfall and its echoes beat like a clap of thunder. And the faces! Two, more particularly near the woman's: one a woman's also, white and clear-featured, a face which might have once been cold and hard, but which was now softened by the touch of a wisdom strange to earth. The other might have been the woman's father. Both were evidently absorbed in the contemplation of some act of hateful meanness, so it seemed, which they could no longer guard against and prevent. Behind were others, teachers, it may be, who had taught ill, friends whose influence had failed. And over the man, too—a multitude, but none that seemed to be parents or teachers! Faces that might once have been coarse, now purged to strength by sorrow! And in the forefront one face, a girlish one, neither angry nor remorseful, but merely patient and weary, and, as it seemed to Plattner, waiting for relief. His powers of description fail him at the memory of this multitude of ghastly countenances. They gathered on the stroke of the bell. He saw them all in the space of a second. It would seem that he was so worked on by his excitement that, quite involuntarily, his restless fingers took the bottle of green powder out of his pocket and held it before him. But he does not remember that.

Abruptly the footsteps ceased. He waited for the next, and there was silence, and then suddenly, cutting through the unexpected stillness like a keen, thin blade, came the first stroke of the bell. At that the multitudinous faces swayed to and fro, and a louder crying began all about him. The woman did not hear; she was burning something now in the candle flame. At the second stroke everything grew dim, and a breath of wind, icy cold, blew through the host of watchers. They swirled about him like an eddy of dead leaves in the spring, and at the third stroke something was extended through them to the bed. You have heard of a beam of light. This was like a beam of darkness, and looking again at it, Plattner saw that it was a shadowy arm and hand.

The green sun was now topping the black desolations of the horizon, and the vision of the room was very faint. Plattner could see that the white of the bed struggled, and was convulsed; and that the woman looked round over her shoulder at it, startled.

The cloud of watchers lifted high like a puff of green dust before the wind, and swept swiftly downward towards the temple in the gorge. Then suddenly Plattner understood the meaning of the shadowy black arm that stretched across his shoulder and clutched its prey. He did not dare turn his head to see the Shadow behind the arm. With a violent effort, and covering his eyes, he set himself to run, made, perhaps, twenty strides, then slipped on a boulder, and fell. He fell forward on his hands; and the bottle smashed and exploded as he touched the ground.

In another moment he found himself, stunned and bleeding, sitting face to face with Lidgett in the old walled garden behind the school.

There the story of Plattner's experiences ends. I have resisted, I believe successfully, the natural disposition of a writer of fiction to dress up incidents of this sort. I have told the thing as far as possible in the order in which Plattner told it to me. I have carefully avoided any attempt at style, effect, or construction. It would have been easy, for instance, to have worked the scene of the death-bed into a kind of plot in which Plattner might have been involved. But, quite apart from the objectionableness of falsifying a most extraordinary true story, any such trite devices would spoil, to my mind, the peculiar effect of this dark world, with its livid green illumination and its drifting Watchers of the Living, which, unseen and unapproachable to us, is yet lying all about us.

It remains to add that a death did actually occur in Vincent Terrace, just beyond the school garden, and, so far as can be proved, at the moment of Plattner's return. Deceased was a rate-collector and insurance agent. His widow, who was much younger than himself, married last month a Mr Whymper, a veterinary surgeon of Allbeeding. As the portion of this story given here has in various forms circulated orally in Sussexville, she has consented to my use of her name, on condition that I make it distinctly known that she emphatically contradicts every detail of Plattner's account of her husband's last moments. She burnt no will, she says, although Plattner never accused her of doing so; her husband made but one will, and that just after their marriage. Certainly, from a man who had never seen it, Plattner's account of the furniture of the room was curiously accurate.

One other thing, even at the risk of an irksome repetition, I must insist upon, lest I seem to favour the credulous, superstitious view. Plattner's absence from the world for nine days is, I think, proved. But that does not prove his story. It is quite conceivable that even outside space hallucinations may be possible. That, at least, the reader must bear distinctly in mind.

XVI

THE RED ROOM

'I CAN assure you,' said I, 'that it will take a very tangible ghost to frighten me.' And I stood up before the fire with my glass in my hand.

'It is your own choosing,' said the man with the withered arm, and glanced at me askance.

'Eight-and-twenty years,' said I, 'I have lived, and never a ghost have I seen as yet.'

The old woman sat staring hard into the fire, her pale eyes wide open. 'Ay,' she broke in; 'and eight-and-twenty years you have lived and never seen the likes of this house, I reckon. There's a many things to see, when one's still but eight-and-twenty.' She swayed her head slowly from side to side. 'A many things to see and sorrow for.'

I half suspected the old people were trying to enhance the spiritual terrors of their house by their droning insistence. I put down my empty glass on the table and looked about the room, and caught a glimpse of myself, abbreviated and broadened to an impossible sturdiness, in the queer old mirror at the end of the room. 'Well,' I said, 'if I see anything to-night, I shall be so much the wiser. For I come to the business with an open mind.'

'It's your own choosing,' said the man with the withered arm once more.

I heard the sound of a stick and a shambling step on the flags in the passage outside, and the door creaked on its hinges as a second old man entered, more bent, more wrinkled, more aged even than the first. He supported himself by a single crutch, his eyes were covered by a shade, and his lower lip, half averted, hung pale and pink from his decaying yellow teeth. He made straight for an arm-chair on the opposite side of the table, sat down clumsily, and began to cough. The man with the withered arm gave this new-comer a short glance of positive dislike; the old woman took no notice of his arrival, but remained with her eyes fixed steadily on the fire.

'I said—it's your own choosing,' said the man with the withered arm, when the coughing had ceased for a while.

'It's my own choosing,' I answered.

The man with the shade became aware of my presence for the first time, and threw his head back for a moment and sideways, to see me. I caught a momentary glimpse of his eyes, small and bright and inflamed. Then he began to cough and splutter again.

'Why don't you drink?' said the man with the withered arm, pushing the beer towards him. The man with the shade poured out a glassful with a shaky hand that splashed half as much again on the deal table. A monstrous shadow of him crouched upon the wall and mocked his action as he poured and drank. I must confess I had scarce expected these grotesque custodians. There is to my mind something inhuman in senility, something crouching and atavistic; the human qualities seem to drop from old people insensibly day by day. The three of them made me feel uncomfortable, with their gaunt silences, their bent carriage, their evident unfriendliness to me and to one another.

'If,' said I, 'you will show me to this haunted room of yours, I will make myself comfortable there.'

The old man with the cough jerked his head back so suddenly that it startled me, and shot another glance of his red eyes at me from under the shade; but no one answered me. I waited a minute, glancing from one to the other.

'If,' I said a little louder, 'if you will show me to this haunted room of yours, I will relieve you from the task of entertaining me.'

'There's a candle on the slab outside the door,' said the man with the withered arm, looking at my feet as he addressed me. 'But if you go to the red room to-night——'

('This night of all nights!' said the old woman.)

'You go alone.'

'Very well,' I answered. 'And which way do I go?'

'You go along the passage for a bit,' said he, 'until you come to a door, and through that is a spiral staircase, and half-way up that is a landing and another door covered with baize. Go through that and down the long corridor to the end, and the red room is on your left up the steps.'

'Have I got that right?' I said, and repeated his directions. He corrected me in one particular.

'And are you really going?' said the man with the shade, looking at me again for the third time, with that queer, unnatural tilting of the face.

('This night of all nights!' said the old woman.)

'It is what I came for,' I said, and moved towards the door. As I did so, the old man with the shade rose and staggered round the table, so as to be closer to the others and to the fire. At the door I turned and looked at them, and saw they were all close together, dark against the firelight, staring at me over their shoulders, with an intent expression on their ancient faces.

'Good-night,' I said, setting the door open.

'It's your own choosing,' said the man with the withered arm.

I left the door wide open until the candle was well alight, and then I shut them in and walked down the chilly, echoing passage.

I must confess that the oddness of these three old pensioners in whose charge her ladyship had left the castle, and the deep-toned, old-fashioned furniture of the house-keeper's room in which they foregathered, affected me in spite of my efforts to keep myself at a matter-of-fact phase. They seemed to belong to another age, an older age, an age when things spiritual were different from this of ours, less certain; an age when omens and witches were credible, and ghosts beyond denying. Their very existence was spectral;

the cut of their clothing, fashions born in dead brains. The ornaments and conveniences of the room about them were ghostly—the thoughts of vanished men, which still haunted rather than participated in the world of to-day. But with an effort I sent such thoughts to the right-about. The long, draughty subterranean passage was chilly and dusty, and my candle flared and made the shadows cower and quiver. The echoes rang up and down the spiral staircase, and a shadow came sweeping up after me, and one fled before me into the darkness overhead. I came to the landing and stopped there for a moment, listening to a rustling that I fancied I heard; then, satisfied of the absolute silence, I pushed open the baize-covered door and stood in the corridor.

The effect was scarcely what I expected, for the moonlight, coming in by the great window on the grand staircase, picked out everything in vivid black shadow or silvery illumination. Everything was in its place: the house might have been deserted on the yesterday instead of eighteen months ago. There were candles in the sockets of the sconces, and whatever dust had gathered on the carpets or upon the polished flooring was distributed so evenly as to be invisible in the moonlight. I was about to advance, and stopped abruptly. A bronze group stood upon the landing, hidden from me by the corner of the wall, but its shadow fell with marvellous distinctness upon the white panelling, and gave me the impression of someone crouching to waylay me. I stood rigid for half a minute perhaps. Then, with my hand in the pocket that held my revolver, I advanced, only to discover a Ganymede and Eagle* glistening in the moonlight. That incident for a time restored my nerve, and a porcelain Chinaman on a buhl table,* whose head rocked silently as I passed him, scarcely startled me.

The door to the red room and the steps up to it were in a shadowy corner. I moved my candle from side to side, in order to see clearly the nature of the recess in which I stood before opening the door. Here it was, thought I, that my predecessor was found, and the memory of that story gave me a sudden twinge of apprehension. I glanced over my shoulder at the Ganymede in the moonlight, and opened the door of the red room rather hastily, with my face half turned to the pallid silence of the landing.

I entered, closed the door behind me at once, turned the key I found in the lock within, and stood with the candle held aloft, surveying the scene of my vigil, the great red room of Lorraine Castle, in which the young duke had died. Or, rather, in which he had begun his dying, for he had opened the door and fallen headlong down the steps I had just ascended. That had been the end of his vigil, of his gallant attempt to conquer the ghostly tradition of the place, and never, I thought, had apoplexy* better served the ends of superstition. And there were other and older stories that clung to the room, back to the half-credible beginning of it all, the tale of a timid wife and the tragic end that came to her husband's jest of frightening her. And looking around that large sombre room, with its shadowy window bays, its recesses and alcoves, one could well understand the legends that had sprouted in its black corners, its germinating darkness. My candle was a little tongue of light in its vastness, that failed to pierce the opposite end of the room, and left an ocean of mystery and suggestion beyond its island of light.

I resolved to make a systematic examination of the place at once, and dispel the fanciful suggestions of its obscurity before they obtained a hold upon me. After satisfying myself of the fastening of the door, I began to walk about the room, peering round each article of furniture, tucking up the valances of the bed, and opening its curtains wide. I pulled up the blinds and examined the fastenings of the several windows before closing the shutters, leant forward and looked up the blackness of the wide chimney, and tapped the dark oak panelling for any secret opening. There were two big mirrors in the room, each with a pair of sconces bearing candles, and on the mantelshelf, too, were more candles in china candlesticks. All these I lit one after the other. The fire was laid, an unexpected consideration from the old housekeeper,—and I lit it, to keep down any disposition to shiver, and when it was burning well, I stood round with my back to it and regarded the room again. I had pulled up a chintz-covered arm-chair and a table, to form a kind of barricade before me, and on this lay my revolver ready to hand. My precise examination had done me good, but I still found the remoter darkness of the place, and its perfect stillness, too stimulating for the imagination. The echoing of the stir and crackling of the fire was no sort of comfort to me. The shadow in the alcove at the end in particular, had that undefinable quality of a presence, that odd suggestion of a lurking, living thing, that comes so easily in silence and solitude. At last, to reassure myself, I walked with a candle into it, and satisfied myself that there was nothing tangible there. I stood that candle upon the floor of the alcove, and left it in that position.

By this time I was in a state of considerable nervous tension, although to my reason there was no adequate cause for the condition. My mind, however, was perfectly clear. I postulated quite unreservedly that nothing supernatural could happen, and to pass the time I began to string some rhymes together, Ingoldsby* fashion, of the original legend of the place. A few I spoke aloud, but the echoes were not pleasant. For the same reason I also abandoned, after a time, a conversation with myself upon the impossibility of ghosts and haunting. My mind reverted to the three old and distorted people downstairs, and I tried to keep it upon that topic. The sombre reds and blacks of the room troubled me; even with seven candles the place was merely dim. The one in the alcove flared in a draught, and the fire-flickering kept the shadows and penumbra perpetually shifting and stirring. Casting about for a remedy, I recalled the candles I had seen in the passage, and, with a slight effort, walked out into the moonlight, carrying a candle and leaving the door open, and presently returned with as many as ten. These I put in various knick-knacks of china with which the room was sparsely adorned, lit and placed where the shadows had lain deepest, some on the floor, some in the window recesses, until at last my seventeen candles were so arranged that not an inch of the room but had the direct light of at least one of them. It occurred to me that when the ghost came, I could warn him not to trip over them. The room was now quite brightly illuminated. There was something very cheery and reassuring in these little streaming flames, and snuffing them gave me an occupation, and afforded a helpful sense of the passage of time.

Even with that, however, the brooding expectation of the vigil weighed heavily upon me. It was after midnight that the candle in the alcove suddenly went out, and the black shadow sprang back to its place there. I did not see the candle go out; I simply turned and saw that the darkness was there, as one might start and see the unexpected presence of a stranger. 'By Jove!' said I aloud; 'that draught's a strong one!' and, taking the matches from the table, I walked across the room in a leisurely manner, to relight the corner again. My first match would not strike, and as I succeeded with the second, something seemed to blink on the wall before me. I turned my head involuntarily, and saw that the two candles on the little table by the fireplace were extinguished. I rose at once to my feet.

'Odd!' I said. 'Did I do that myself in a flash of absent-mindedness?'

I walked back, relit one, and as I did so, I saw the candle in the right sconce of one of the mirrors wink and go right out, and almost immediately its companion followed it. There was no mistake about it. The flame vanished, as if the wicks had been suddenly nipped between a finger and a thumb, leaving the wick neither glowing nor smoking, but black. While I stood gaping, the candle at the foot of the bed went out, and the shadows seemed to take another step towards me.

'This won't do!' said I, and first one and then another candle on the mantelshelf followed.

'What's up?' I cried, with a queer high note getting into my voice somehow. At that the candle on the wardrobe went out, and the one I had relit in the alcove followed.

'Steady on!' I said. 'These candles are wanted,' speaking with a half-hysterical facetiousness, and scratching away at a match the while for the mantel candlesticks. My hands trembled so much that twice I missed the rough paper of the matchbox. As the mantel emerged from darkness again, two candles in the remoter end of the window were eclipsed. But with the same match I also relit the larger mirror candles, and those on the floor near the doorway, so that for the moment I seemed to gain on the extinctions. But then in a volley there vanished four lights at once in different corners of the room, and I struck another match in quivering haste, and stood hesitating whither to take it.

As I stood undecided, an invisible hand seemed to sweep out the two candles on the table. With a cry of terror, I dashed at the alcove, then into the corner, and then into the window, relighting three, as two more vanished by the fire-place; then, perceiving a better way, I dropped the matches on the iron-bound deed-box in the corner, and caught up the bedroom candlestick. With this I avoided the delay of striking matches; but for all that the steady process of extinction went on, and the shadows I feared and fought against returned, and crept in upon me, first a step gained on this side of me and then on that. It was like a ragged storm-cloud sweeping out the stars. Now and then one returned for a minute, and was lost again. I was now almost frantic with the horror of the coming darkness, and my self-possession deserted me. I leaped panting and dishevelled from candle to candle, in a vain struggle against that remorseless advance.

I bruised myself on the thigh against the table, I sent a chair headlong, I stumbled and fell and whisked the cloth from the table in my fall. My candle rolled away from me, and I snatched another as I rose. Abruptly this was blown out, as I swung it off the table by the wind of my sudden movement, and immediately the two remaining candles followed. But there was light still in the room, a red light that staved off the shadows from me. The fire! Of course I could still thrust my candle between the bars and relight it!

I turned to where the flames were still dancing between the glowing coals, and splashing red reflections upon the furniture, made two steps towards the grate, and incontinently the flames dwindled and vanished, the glow vanished, the reflections rushed together and vanished, and as I thrust the candle between the bars darkness closed upon me like the shutting of an eye, wrapped about me in a stifling embrace, sealed my vision, and crushed the last vestiges of reason from my brain. The candle fell from my hand. I flung out my arms in a vain effort to thrust that ponderous blackness away from me, and, lifting up my voice, screamed with all my might—once, twice, thrice. Then I think I must have staggered to my feet. I know I thought suddenly of the moonlit corridor, and, with my head bowed and my arms over my face, made a run for the door.

But I had forgotten the exact position of the door, and struck myself heavily against the corner of the bed. I staggered back, turned, and was either struck or struck myself against some other bulky furniture. I have a vague memory of battering myself thus, to and fro in the darkness, of a cramped struggle, and of my own wild crying as I darted to and fro, of a heavy blow at last upon my forehead, a horrible sensation of falling that lasted an age, of my last frantic effort to keep my footing, and then I remember no more.

I opened my eyes in daylight. My head was roughly bandaged, and the man with the withered arm was watching my face. I looked about me, trying to remember what had happened, and for a space I could not recollect. I rolled my eyes into the corner, and saw the old woman, no longer abstracted, pouring out some drops of medicine from a little blue phial into a glass. 'Where am I?' I asked; 'I seem to remember you, and yet I cannot remember who you are.'

They told me then, and I heard of the haunted Red Room as one who hears a tale. 'We found you at dawn,' said he, 'and there was blood on your forehead and lips.'

It was very slowly I recovered my memory of my experience. 'You believe now,' said the old man, 'that the room is haunted?' He spoke no longer as one who greets an intruder, but as one who grieves for a broken friend.

'Yes,' said I; 'the room is haunted.'

'And you have seen it. And we, who have lived here all our lives, have never set eyes upon it. Because we have never dared. . . . Tell us, is it truly the old earl who——'

'No,' said I; 'it is not.'

'I told you so,' said the old lady, with the glass in her hand. 'It is his poor young countess who was frightened——'

'It is not,' I said. 'There is neither ghost of earl nor ghost of countess in that room, there is no ghost there at all; but worse, far worse——'

'Well?' they said.

'The worst of all the things that haunt poor mortal man,' said I; 'and that is, in all its nakedness—*Fear!* Fear that will not have light nor sound, that will not bear with reason, that deafens and darkens and overwhelms. It followed me through the corridor, it fought against me in the room——'

I stopped abruptly. There was an interval of silence. My hand went up to my bandages.

Then the man with the shade sighed and spoke. 'That is it,' said he. 'I knew that was it. A power of darkness. To put such a curse upon a woman! It lurks there always. You can feel it even in the daytime, even of a bright summer's day, in the hangings, in the curtains keeping behind you however you face about. In the dusk it creeps along the corridor and follows you, so that you dare not turn. There is Fear in that room of hers—black Fear, and there will be—so long as this house of sin endures.'

XVII

THE PURPLE PILEUS

MR COOMBES was sick of life. He walked away from his unhappy home, and, sick not only of his own existence but of everybody else's, turned aside down Gaswork Lane to avoid the town, and, crossing the wooden bridge that goes over the canal to Starling's Cottages, was presently alone in the damp pine woods and out of sight and sound of human habitation. He would stand it no longer. He repeated aloud with blasphemies unusual to him that he would stand it no longer.

He was a pale-faced little man, with dark eyes and a fine and very black moustache. He had a very stiff, upright collar slightly frayed, that gave him an illusory double chin, and his overcoat (albeit shabby) was trimmed with astrachan. His gloves were a bright brown with black stripes over the knuckles, and split at the finger ends. His appearance, his wife had said once in the dear, dead days beyond recall*— before he married her, that is—was military. But now she called him—it seems a dreadful thing to tell of between husband and wife, but she called him 'a little grub.' It wasn't the only thing she had called him, either.

The row had arisen about that beastly Jennie again. Jennie was his wife's friend, and, by no invitation of Mr Coombes, she came in every blessed Sunday to dinner, and made a shindy all the afternoon. She was a big, noisy girl, with a taste for loud colours and a strident laugh; and this Sunday she had outdone all her previous intrusions by bringing in a fellow with her, a chap as showy as herself. And Mr Coombes, in a starchy, clean collar and his Sunday frock-coat, had sat dumb and wrathful at his own table, while his wife and her guests talked foolishly and undesirably, and laughed aloud. Well, he stood that, and after dinner (which, 'as usual,' was late), what must Miss Jennie do but go to the piano and play banjo tunes, for all the world as if it were a week-day! Flesh and blood could not endure such goings on. They would hear next door, they would hear in the road, it was a public announcement of their disrepute. He had to speak.

He had felt himself go pale, and a kind of rigour had affected his respiration as he delivered himself. He had been sitting on one of the chairs by the window—the new guest had taken possession of the arm-chair. He turned his head. 'Sun Day!' he said over the collar, in the voice of one who warns. 'Sun Day!' What people call a 'nasty' tone, it was.

Jennie had kept on playing, but his wife, who was looking through some music that was piled on the top of the piano, had stared at him. 'What's wrong now?' she said; 'can't people enjoy themselves?'

'I don't mind rational 'njoyment, at all,' said little Coombes, 'but I ain't a-going to have week-day tunes playing on a Sunday in this house.'

'What's wrong with my playing now?' said Jennie, stopping and twirling round on the music-stool with a monstrous rustle of flounces.*

Coombes saw it was going to be a row, and opened too vigorously, as is common with your timid, nervous men all the world over. 'Steady on with that music-stool!' said he; 'it ain't made for 'eavy-weights.'

'Never you mind about weights,' said Jennie, incensed. 'What was you saying behind my back about my playing?'

'Surely you don't 'old with not having a bit of music on a Sunday, Mr Coombes?' said the new guest, leaning back in the arm-chair, blowing a cloud of cigarette smoke and smiling in a kind of pitying way. And simultaneously his wife said something to Jennie about 'Never mind 'im. You go on, Jinny.'

'I do,' said Mr Coombes, addressing the new guest.

'May I arst why?' said the new guest, evidently enjoying both his cigarette and the prospect of an argument. He was, by-the-by, a lank young man, very stylishly dressed in bright drab,* with a white cravat and a pearl and silver pin. It had been better taste to come in a black coat, Mr Coombes thought.

'Because,' began Mr Coombes, 'it don't suit me. I'm a business man. I 'ave to study my connection.* Rational 'njoyment——'

'His connection!' said Mrs Coombes scornfully. 'That's what he's always a-saying. We got to do this, and we got to do that——'

'If you don't mean to study my connection,' said Mr Coombes, 'what did you marry me for?'

'I wonder,' said Jennie, and turned back to the piano.

'I never saw such a man as you,' said Mrs Coombes. 'You've altered all round since we were married. Before——'

Then Jennie began at the tum, tum, tum again.

'Look here!' said Mr Coombes, driven at last to revolt, standing up and raising his voice. 'I tell you I won't have that.' The frock-coat heaved with his indignation.

'No vi'lence, now,' said the long young man in drab, sitting up.

'Who the juice are you?' said Mr Coombes fiercely.

Whereupon they all began talking at once. The new guest said he was Jennie's 'intended,' and meant to protect her, and Mr Coombes said he was welcome to do so anywhere but in his (Mr Coombes') house; and Mrs Coombes said he ought to be ashamed of insulting his guests, and (as I have already mentioned) that he was getting a regular little grub; and the end was, that Mr Coombes ordered his visitors out of the house, and they wouldn't go, and so he said he would go himself. With his face burning and tears of excitement in his eyes, he went into the passage, and as he struggled with his overcoat—his frock-coat sleeves got concertinaed up his arm—and gave a brush at his silk hat, Jennie began again at the piano, and strummed him insultingly out of the house. Tum, tum, tum. He slammed the shop door so that the house quivered. That, briefly, was the immediate making of his mood. You will perhaps begin to understand his disgust with existence.

As he walked along the muddy path under the firs,—it was late October, and the ditches and heaps of fir needles were gorgeous with clumps of fungi,—he recapitulated the melancholy history of his marriage. It was brief and commonplace enough. He now perceived with sufficient clearness that his wife had married him out of a natural curiosity and in order to escape from her worrying, laborious, and uncertain life in the workroom; and, like the majority of her class, she was far too stupid to realise that it was her duty to co-operate with him in his business. She was greedy of enjoyment, loquacious, and socially-minded, and evidently disappointed to find the restraints of poverty still hanging about her. His worries exasperated her, and the slightest attempt to control her proceedings resulted in a charge of 'grumbling.' Why couldn't he be nice—as he used to be? And Coombes was such a harmless little man, too, nourished mentally on *Self-Help*,* and with a meagre ambition of self-denial and competition, that was to end in a 'sufficiency.' Then Jennie came in as a female Mephistopheles,* a gabbling chronicle of 'fellers,' and was always wanting his wife to go to theatres, and 'all that.' And in addition were aunts of his wife, and cousins (male and female) to eat up capital, insult him personally, upset business arrangements, annoy good customers, and generally blight his life. It was not the first occasion by many that Mr Coombes had fled his home in wrath and indignation, and something like fear, vowing furiously and even aloud that he wouldn't stand it, and so frothing away his energy along the line of least resistance. But never before had he been quite so sick of life as on this particular Sunday afternoon. The Sunday dinner may have had its share in his despair—and the greyness of the sky. Perhaps, too, he was beginning to realise his unendurable frustration as a business man as the consequence of his marriage. Presently bankruptcy, and after that—— Perhaps she might have reason to repent when it was too late. And destiny, as I have already intimated, had planted the path through the wood with evil-smelling fungi, thickly and variously planted it, not only on the right side, but on the left.

A small shopman is in such a melancholy position, if his wife turns out a disloyal partner. His capital is all tied up in his business, and to leave her means to join the unemployed in some strange part of the earth. The luxuries of divorce are beyond him altogether. So that the good old tradition of marriage for better or worse holds inexorably for him, and things work up to tragic culminations. Bricklayers kick their wives to death, and dukes betray theirs; but it is among the small clerks and shopkeepers nowadays that it comes most often to a cutting of throats. Under the circumstances it is not so very remarkable—and you must take it as charitably as you can—that the mind of Mr Coombes ran for a while on some such glorious close to his disappointed hopes, and that he thought of razors, pistols, bread-knives, and touching letters to the coroner denouncing his enemies by name, and praying piously for forgiveness. After a time his fierceness gave way to melancholia. He had been married in this very overcoat, in his first and only frock-coat that was buttoned up beneath it. He began to recall their courting along this very walk, his years of penurious saving to get capital, and the bright hopefulness of his marrying days. For it all to work out like this! Was there no sympathetic ruler anywhere in the world? He reverted to death as a topic.

He thought of the canal he had just crossed, and doubted whether he shouldn't stand with his head out, even in the middle, and it was while drowning was in his mind that the purple pileus* caught his eye. He looked at it mechanically for a moment, and stopped and stooped towards it to pick it up, under the impression that it was some such small leather object as a purse. Then he saw that it was the purple top of a fungus, a peculiarly poisonous-looking purple: slimy, shiny, and emitting a sour odour. He hesitated with his hand an inch or so from it, and the thought of poison crossed his mind. With that he picked the thing, and stood up again with it in his hand.

The odour was certainly strong—acrid, but by no means disgusting. He broke off a piece, and the fresh surface was a creamy white, that changed like magic in the space of ten seconds to a yellowish-green colour. It was even an inviting-looking change. He broke off two other pieces to see it repeated. They were wonderful things these fungi, thought Mr Coombes, and all of them the deadliest poisons, as his father had often told him. Deadly poisons!

There is no time like the present for a rash resolve. Why not here and now? thought Mr Coombes. He tasted a little piece, a very little piece indeed—a mere crumb. It was so pungent that he almost spat it out again, then merely hot and full-flavoured: a kind of German mustard with a touch of horse-radish and—well, mushroom. He swallowed it in the excitement of the moment. Did he like it or did he not? His mind was curiously careless. He would try another bit. It really wasn't bad—it was good. He forgot his troubles in the interest of the immediate moment. Playing with death it was. He took another bite, and then deliberately finished a mouthful. A curious, tingling sensation began in his finger-tips and toes. His pulse began to move faster. The blood in his ears sounded like a mill-race. 'Try bi' more,' said Mr Coombes. He turned and looked about him, and found his feet unsteady. He saw, and struggled towards, a little patch of purple a dozen yards away. 'Jol' goo' stuff,' said Mr Coombes. 'E—lomore ye'.' He pitched forward and fell on his face, his hands outstretched towards the cluster of pilei. But he did not eat any more of them. He forgot forthwith.

He rolled over and sat up with a look of astonishment on his face. His carefully brushed silk hat had rolled away towards the ditch. He pressed his hand to his brow. Something had happened, but he could not rightly determine what it was. Anyhow, he was no longer dull—he felt bright, cheerful. And his throat was afire. He laughed in the sudden gaiety of his heart. Had he been dull? He did not know; but at anyrate he would be dull no longer. He got up and stood unsteadily, regarding the universe with an agreeable smile. He began to remember. He could not remember very well, because of a steam roundabout that was beginning in his head. And he knew he had been disagreeable at home, just because they wanted to be happy. They were quite right; life should be as gay as possible. He would go home and make it up, and reassure them. And why not take some of this delightful toadstool with him, for them to eat? A hatful, no less. Some of those red ones with white spots as well, and a few yellow. He had been a dull dog, an enemy to merriment; he would make up for it. It would be gay to turn his coat-sleeves inside out, and stick some yellow gorse into his waistcoat pockets. Then home—singing—for a jolly evening.

After the departure of Mr Coombes, Jennie discontinued playing, and turned round on the music-stool again. 'What a fuss about nothing!' said Jennie.

'You see, Mr Clarence, what I've got to put up with,' said Mrs Coombes.

'He is a bit hasty,' said Mr Clarence judicially.

'He ain't got the slightest sense of our position,' said Mrs Coombes; 'that's what I complain of. He cares for nothing but his old shop, and if I have a bit of company, or buy anything to keep myself decent, or get any little thing I want out of the housekeeping money, there's disagreeables. "Economy," he says; "struggle for life," and all that. He lies awake of nights about it, worrying how he can screw me out of a shilling. He wanted us to eat Dorset butter once. If once I was to give in to him—there!'

'Of course,' said Jennie.

'If a man values a woman,' said Mr Clarence, lounging back in the arm-chair, 'he must be prepared to make sacrifices for her. For my own part,' said Mr Clarence, with his eye on Jennie, 'I shouldn't think of marrying till I was in a position to do the thing in style. It's downright selfishness. A man ought to go through the rough-and-tumble by himself, and not drag her——'

'I don't agree altogether with that,' said Jennie. 'I don't see why a man shouldn't have a woman's help, provided he doesn't treat her meanly, you know. It's meanness——'

'You wouldn't believe,' said Mrs Coombes. 'But I was a fool to 'ave 'im. I might 'ave known. If it 'adn't been for my father, we shouldn't 'ave 'ad not a carriage to our wedding.'

'Lord! he didn't stick out at that?' said Mr Clarence, quite shocked.

'Said he wanted the money for his stock, or some such rubbish. Why, he wouldn't have a woman in to help me once a week if it wasn't for my standing out plucky. And the fusses he makes about money—comes to me, well, pretty near crying, with sheets of paper and figgers. "If only we can tide over this year," he says, "the business is bound to go." "If only we can tide over this year," I says; "then it'll be, if only we can tide over next year. I know you," I says. "And you don't catch me screwing myself lean and ugly. Why didn't you marry a slavey?"* I says, "if you wanted one—instead of a respectable girl," I says.'

So Mrs Coombes. But we will not follow this unedifying conversation further. Suffice it that Mr Coombes was very satisfactorily disposed of, and they had a snug little time round the fire. Then Mrs Coombes went to get the tea, and Jennie sat coquettishly on the arm of Mr Clarence's chair until the tea-things clattered outside. 'What was that I heard?' asked Mrs Coombes playfully, as she entered, and there was badinage about kissing. They were just sitting down to the little circular table when the first intimation of Mr Coombes' return was heard.

This was a fumbling at the latch of the front door.

''Ere's my lord,' said Mrs Coombes. 'Went out like a lion and comes back like a lamb, I'll lay.'

Something fell over in the shop: a chair, it sounded like. Then there was a sound as of some complicated step exercise in the passage. Then the door opened and Coombes appeared. But it was Coombes transfigured. The immaculate collar had been torn carelessly from his throat. His carefully-brushed silk hat, half-full of a crush of fungi, was under one arm; his coat was inside out, and his waistcoat adorned with bunches of yellow-blossomed furze. These little eccentricities of Sunday costume, however, were quite overshadowed by the change in his face; it was livid white, his eyes were unnaturally large and bright, and his pale blue lips were drawn back in a cheerless grin. 'Merry!' he said. He had stopped dancing to open the door. 'Rational 'njoyment. Dance.' He made three fantastic steps into the room, and stood bowing.

'Jim!' shrieked Mrs Coombes, and Mr Clarence sat petrified, with a dropping lower jaw.

'Tea,' said Mr Coombes. 'Jol' thing, tea. Tose-stools, too. Brosher.'

'He's drunk,' said Jennie in a weak voice. Never before had she seen this intense pallor in a drunken man, or such shining, dilated eyes.

Mr Coombes held out a handful of scarlet agaric* to Mr Clarence. 'Jo' stuff,' said he; 'ta' some.'

At that moment he was genial. Then at the sight of their startled faces he changed, with the swift transition of insanity, into overbearing fury. And it seemed as if he had suddenly recalled the quarrel of his departure. In such a huge voice as Mrs Coombes had never heard before, he shouted, 'My house. I'm master 'ere. Eat what I give yer!' He bawled this, as it seemed, without an effort, without a violent gesture, standing there as motionless as one who whispers, holding out a handful of fungus.

Clarence approved himself a coward. He could not meet the mad fury in Coombes' eyes; he rose to his feet, pushing back his chair, and turned, stooping. At that Coombes rushed at him. Jennie saw her opportunity, and, with the ghost of a shriek, made for the door. Mrs Coombes followed her. Clarence tried to dodge. Over went the tea-table with a smash as Coombes clutched him by the collar and tried to thrust the fungus into his mouth. Clarence was content to leave his collar behind him, and shot out into the passage with red patches of fly agaric still adherent to his face. 'Shut 'im in!' cried Mrs Coombes, and would have closed the door, but her supports deserted her; Jennie saw the shop door open, and vanished thereby, locking it behind her, while Clarence went on hastily into the kitchen. Mr Coombes came heavily against the door, and Mrs Coombes, finding the key was inside, fled upstairs and locked herself in the spare bedroom.

So the new convert to *joie de vivre* emerged upon the passage, his decorations a little scattered, but that respectable hatful of fungi still under his arm. He hesitated at the three ways, and decided on the kitchen. Whereupon Clarence, who was fumbling with the key, gave up the attempt to imprison his host, and fled into the scullery, only to be captured before he could open the door into the yard. Mr Clarence is singularly reticent of the details of what occurred. It seems that Mr Coombes' transitory irritation had vanished again, and he was once more a genial playfellow. And as there were knives and meat choppers about, Clarence very generously resolved to humour him and so avoid anything tragic. It is beyond dispute that Mr Coombes played with Mr Clarence to his heart's content; they could not have been more playful and familiar if they had known each other for years. He insisted gaily on Clarence trying the fungi, and, after a friendly tussle, was smitten with remorse at the mess he was making of his guest's face. It also appears that Clarence was dragged under the sink and his face scrubbed with the blacking brush—he being still resolved to humour the lunatic at any cost—and that finally, in a somewhat dishevelled, chipped, and discoloured condition, he was assisted to his coat and shown out by the back door, the shopway being barred by Jennie. Mr Coombes' wandering thoughts then turned to Jennie. Jennie had been unable to unfasten the shop door, but she shot the bolts against Mr Coombes' latch-key, and remained in possession of the shop for the rest of the evening.

It would appear that Mr Coombes then returned to the kitchen, still in pursuit of gaiety, and, albeit a strict Good Templar,* drank (or spilt down the front of the first and only frock-coat) no less than five bottles of the stout Mrs Coombes insisted upon having for her health's sake. He made cheerful noises by breaking off the necks of the bottles with several of his wife's wedding-present dinner-plates, and during the earlier part of this great drunk he sang divers* merry ballads. He cut his finger rather badly with one of the bottles—the only bloodshed in this story—and what with that, and the systematic convulsion of his inexperienced physiology by the liquorish brand of Mrs Coombes' stout, it may be the evil of the fungus poison was somehow allayed. But we prefer to draw a veil over the concluding incidents of this Sunday afternoon. They ended in the coal cellar, in a deep and healing sleep.

An interval of five years elapsed. Again it was a Sunday afternoon in October, and again Mr Coombes walked through the pine wood beyond the canal. He was still the same dark-eyed, black-moustached little man that he was at the outset of the story, but his double chin was now scarcely so illusory as it had been. His overcoat was new, with a velvet lapel, and a stylish collar with turn-down corners, free of any coarse starchiness, had replaced the original all-round article. His hat was glossy, his gloves newish—though one finger had split and been carefully mended. And a casual observer would have noticed about him a certain rectitude of bearing, a certain erectness of head that marks the man who thinks well of himself. He was a master now, with three assistants. Beside him walked a larger sunburnt parody of himself, his brother Tom, just back from Australia. They were recapitulating their early struggles, and Mr Coombes had just been making a financial statement.

'It's a very nice little business, Jim,' said brother Tom. 'In these days of competition you're jolly lucky to have worked it up so. And you're jolly lucky, too, to have a wife who's willing to help like yours does.'

'Between ourselves,' said Mr Coombes, 'it wasn't always so. It wasn't always like this. To begin with, the missus was a bit giddy. Girls are funny creatures.'

'Dear me!'

'Yes. You'd hardly think it, but she was downright extravagant, and always having slaps at me. I was a bit too easy and loving, and all that, and she thought the whole blessed show was run for her. Turned the 'ouse into a regular caravansery,* always having her relations and girls from business in, and their chaps. Comic songs a' Sunday, it was getting to, and driving trade away. And she was making eyes at the chaps, too! I tell you, Tom, the place wasn't my own.'

'Shouldn't 'a' thought it.'

'It was so. Well—I reasoned with her. I said, "I ain't a duke, to keep a wife like a pet animal. I married you for 'elp and company," I said, "You got to 'elp and pull the business through." She wouldn't 'ear of it. "Very well," I says; "I'm a mild man till I'm roused," I says, "and it's getting to that." But she wouldn't 'ear of no warnings.'

'Well?'

'It's the way with women. She didn't think I 'ad it in me to be roused. Women of her sort (between ourselves, Tom) don't respect a man until they're a bit afraid of him. So I just broke out to show her. In comes a girl named Jennie, that used to work with her, and her chap. We 'ad a bit of a row, and I came out 'ere—it was just such another day as this— and I thought it all out. Then I went back and pitched into them.'

'You did?'

'I did. I was mad, I can tell you. I wasn't going to 'it 'er, if I could 'elp it, so I went back and licked into this chap, just to show 'er what I could do. 'E was a big chap, too. Well, I chucked him, and smashed things about, and gave 'er a scaring, and she ran up and locked 'erself into the spare room.'

'Well?'

'That's all. I says to 'er the next morning, "Now you know," I says, "what I'm like when I'm roused." And I didn't have to say anything more.'

'And you've been happy ever after, eh?'

'So to speak. There's nothing like putting your foot down with them. If it 'adn't been for that afternoon I should 'a' been tramping the roads now, and she'd 'a' been grumbling at me, and all her family grumbling for bringing her to poverty—I know their little ways. But we're all right now. And it's a very decent little business, as you say.'

They proceeded on their way meditatively. 'Women are funny creatures,' said Brother Tom.

'They want a firm hand,' says Coombes.

'What a lot of these funguses there are about here!' remarked Brother Tom presently. 'I can't see what use they are in the world.'

Mr Coombes looked. 'I dessay they're sent for some wise purpose,' said Mr Coombes.

And that was as much thanks as the purple pileus ever got for maddening this absurd little man to the pitch of decisive action, and so altering the whole course of his life.

XVIII

A SLIP UNDER THE MICROSCOPE

OUTSIDE the laboratory windows was a watery-grey fog, and within a close warmth and the yellow light of the green-shaded gas lamps that stood two to each table down its narrow length. On each table stood a couple of glass jars containing the mangled vestiges of the crayfish, mussels, frogs, and guinea-pigs upon which the students had been working, and down the side of the room, facing the windows, were shelves bearing bleached dissections in spirits, surmounted by a row of beautifully executed anatomical drawings in white-wood frames and overhanging a row of cubical lockers. All the doors of the laboratory were panelled with blackboard, and on these were the half-erased diagrams of the previous day's work. The laboratory was empty, save for the demonstrator, who sat near the preparation-room door, and silent, save for a low, continuous murmur and the clicking of the rocker microtome* at which he was working. But scattered about the room were traces of numerous students: hand-bags, polished boxes of instruments, in one place a large drawing covered by newspaper, and in another a prettily bound copy of *News from Nowhere*,* a book oddly at variance with its surroundings. These things had been put down hastily as the students had arrived and hurried at once to secure their seats in the adjacent lecture theatre. Deadened by the closed door, the measured accents of the professor sounded as a featureless muttering.

Presently, faint through the closed windows came the sound of the Oratory clock* striking the hour of eleven. The clicking of the microtome ceased, and the demonstrator looked at his watch, rose, thrust his hands into his pockets, and walked slowly down the laboratory towards the lecture theatre door.

He stood listening for a moment, and then his eye fell on the little volume by William Morris. He picked it up, glanced at the title, smiled, opened it, looked at the name on the fly-leaf, ran the leaves through with his hand, and put it down. Almost immediately the even murmur of the lecturer ceased, there was a sudden burst of pencils rattling on the desks in the lecture theatre, a stirring, a scraping of feet, and a number of voices speaking together. Then a firm footfall approached the door, which began to open, and stood ajar, as some indistinctly heard question arrested the new-comer.

The demonstrator turned, walked slowly back past the microtome, and left the laboratory by the preparation-room door. As he did so, first one, and then several students carrying notebooks entered the laboratory from the lecture theatre, and distributed themselves among the little tables, or stood in a group about the doorway. They were an exceptionally heterogeneous assembly, for while Oxford and Cambridge still recoil from the blushing prospect of mixed classes, the College of Science anticipated America in the matter years ago—mixed socially, too, for the prestige of the College is high, and its scholarships, free of any age limit, dredge deeper even than do those of the Scotch universities.* The class numbered one-and-twenty, but some remained in the theatre questioning the professor, copying the black-board diagrams before they were washed off, or examining the special specimens he had produced to illustrate the day's teaching. Of the nine who had come into the laboratory three were girls, one of whom, a little fair woman, wearing spectacles and dressed in greyish-green, was peering out of the window at the fog, while the other two, both wholesome-looking, plain-faced schoolgirls, unrolled and put on the brown holland* aprons they wore while dissecting. Of the men, two went down the laboratory to their places, one a pallid, dark-bearded man, who had once been a tailor; the other a pleasant-featured, ruddy young man of twenty, dressed in a well-fitting brown suit; young Wedderburn, the son of Wedderburn

the eye specialist. The others formed a little knot near the
theatre door. One of these, a dwarfed, spectacled figure, with
a hunch back, sat on a bent wood stool; two others, one a
short, dark youngster, and the other a flaxen-haired, reddish-
complexioned young man, stood leaning side by side against
the slate sink, while the fourth stood facing them, and maintained the larger share of the conversation.

This last person was named Hill. He was a sturdily built
young fellow, of the same age as Wedderburn; he had a
white face, dark grey eyes, hair of an indeterminate colour,
and prominent, irregular features. He talked rather louder
than was needful, and thrust his hands deeply into his pockets.
His collar was frayed and blue with the starch of a careless
laundress, his clothes were evidently ready-made, and there
was a patch on the side of his boot near the toe. And as he
talked or listened to the others, he glanced now and again
towards the lecture theatre door. They were discussing the
depressing peroration of the lecture they had just heard, the
last lecture it was in the introductory course in zoology. 'From
ovum to ovum is the goal of the higher vertebrata,'* the
lecturer had said in his melancholy tones, and so had neatly
rounded off the sketch of comparative anatomy he had been
developing. The spectacled hunchback had repeated it, with
noisy appreciation, had tossed it towards the fair-haired
student with an evident provocation, and had started one
of these vague, rambling discussions on generalities, so un-
accountably dear to the student mind all the world over.

'That is our goal, perhaps—I admit it, as far as science
goes,' said the fair-haired student, rising to the challenge.
'But there are things above science.'

'Science,' said Hill confidently, 'is systematic knowledge.
Ideas that don't come into the system—must anyhow—be
loose ideas.' He was not quite sure whether that was a clever
saying or a fatuity until his hearers took it seriously.

'The thing I cannot understand,' said the hunchback, at
large, 'is whether Hill is a materialist or not.'

'There is one thing above matter,' said Hill promptly, feeling he had a better thing this time; aware, too, of someone in the doorway behind him, and raising his voice a trifle for her benefit, 'and that is, the delusion that there is something above matter.'

'So we have your gospel at last,' said the fair student. 'It's all a delusion, is it? All our aspirations to lead something more than dogs' lives, all our work for anything beyond ourselves. But see how inconsistent you are. Your socialism, for instance. Why do you trouble about the interests of the race? Why do you concern yourself about the beggar in the gutter? Why are you bothering yourself to lend that book'— he indicated William Morris by a movement of the head—'to everyone in the lab.?'

'Girl,' said the hunchback indistinctly, and glanced guiltily over his shoulder.

The girl in brown, with the brown eyes, had come into the laboratory, and stood on the other side of the table behind him, with her rolled-up apron in one hand, looking over her shoulder, listening to the discussion. She did not notice the hunchback, because she was glancing from Hill to his interlocutor. Hill's consciousness of her presence betrayed itself to her only in his studious ignorance of the fact; but she understood that, and it pleased her. 'I see no reason,' said he, 'why a man should live like a brute because he knows of nothing beyond matter, and does not expect to exist a hundred years hence.'

'Why shouldn't he?' said the fair-haired student.

'Why *should* he?' said Hill.

'What inducement has he?'

'That's the way with all you religious people. It's all a business of inducements. Cannot a man seek after righteousness for righteousness' sake?'

There was a pause. The fair man answered, with a kind of vocal padding, 'But—you see—inducement—when I said inducement,' to gain time. And then the hunchback came to his rescue and inserted a question. He was a terrible person in the debating society with his questions, and they invariably took one form—a demand for a definition. 'What's your definition of righteousness?' said the hunchback at this stage.

Hill experienced a sudden loss of complacency at this question, but even as it was asked, relief came in the person of Brooks, the laboratory attendant, who entered by the preparation-room door, carrying a number of freshly killed guinea-pigs by their hind legs. 'This is the last batch of material this session,' said the youngster who had not previously spoken. Brooks advanced up the laboratory, smacking down a couple of guinea-pigs at each table. The rest of the class, scenting the prey from afar, came crowding in by the lecture theatre door, and the discussion perished abruptly as the students who were not already in their places hurried to them to secure the choice of a specimen. There was a noise of keys rattling on split rings as lockers were opened and dissecting instruments taken out. Hill was already standing by his table, and his box of scalpels was sticking out of his pocket. The girl in brown came a step towards him, and, leaning over his table, said softly, 'Did you see that I returned your book, Mr Hill?'

During the whole scene she and the book had been vividly present in his consciousness; but he made a clumsy pretence of looking at the book and seeing it for the first time. 'Oh, yes,' he said, taking it up. 'I see. Did you like it?'

'I want to ask you some questions about it—some time.'

'Certainly,' said Hill. 'I shall be glad.' He stopped awkwardly. 'You liked it?' he said.

'It's a wonderful book. Only some things I don't understand.'

Then suddenly the laboratory was hushed by a curious, braying noise. It was the demonstrator. He was at the blackboard ready to begin the day's instruction, and it was his custom to demand silence by a sound midway between the 'Er' of common intercourse and the blast of a trumpet. The girl in brown slipped back to her place: it was immediately in front of Hill's, and Hill, forgetting her forthwith, took a notebook out of the drawer of his table, turned over its leaves hastily, drew a stumpy pencil from his pocket, and prepared to make a copious note of the coming demonstration. For demonstrations and lectures are the sacred text of the College students. Books, saving only the Professor's own, you may—it is even expedient to—ignore.

Hill was the son of a Landport* cobbler, and had been hooked by a chance blue paper* the authorities had thrown out to the Landport Technical College. He kept himself in London on his allowance of a guinea a week, and found that, with proper care, this also covered his clothing allowance, an occasional waterproof collar, that is; and ink and needles and cotton, and such-like necessaries for a man about town. This was his first year and his first session, but the brown old man in Landport had already got himself detested in many public-houses by boasting of his son, 'the Professor.' Hill was a vigorous youngster, with a serene contempt for the clergy of all denominations, and a fine ambition to reconstruct the world. He regarded his scholarship as a brilliant opportunity. He had begun to read at seven, and had read steadily whatever came in his way, good or bad, since then. His worldly experience had been limited to the island of Portsea,* and acquired chiefly in the wholesale boot factory in which he had worked by day, after passing the seventh standard of the Board school.* He had a considerable gift of speech, as the College Debating Society, which met amidst the crushing machines and mine models in the metallurgical theatre downstairs, already recognised—recognised by a violent battering of desks whenever he rose. And he was just at that fine emotional age when life opens at the end of a narrow pass like a broad valley at one's feet, full of the promise of wonderful discoveries and tremendous achievements. And his own limitations, save that he knew that he knew neither Latin nor French, were all unknown to him.

At first his interest had been divided pretty equally between his biological work at the College and social and theological theorising, an employment which he took in deadly earnest. Of a night, when the big museum library was not open, he would sit on the bed of his room in Chelsea with his coat and a muffler on, and write out the lecture notes and revise his dissection memoranda, until Thorpe called him out by a whistle—the landlady objected to open the door to attic visitors*—and then the two would go prowling about the shadowy, shiny, gas-lit streets, talking, very much in the fashion of the sample just given, of the God idea, and Righteousness, and Carlyle,* and the Reorganisation of Society. And in the midst of it all, Hill, arguing not only for Thorpe, but for the casual passer-by, would lose the thread of his argument glancing at some pretty painted face that looked meaningly at him as he passed. Science and Righteousness! But once or twice lately there had been signs that a third interest was creeping into his life, and he had found his attention wandering from the fate of the mesoblastic somites* or the probable meaning of the blastopore,* to the thought of the girl with the brown eyes who sat at the table before him.

She was a paying student;* she descended inconceivable social altitudes to speak to him. At the thought of the education she must have had, and the accomplishments she must possess, the soul of Hill became abject within him. She had spoken to him first over a difficulty about the alisphenoid* of a rabbit's skull, and he had found that, in biology at least, he had no reason for self-abasement. And from that, after the manner of young people starting from any starting-point, they got to generalities, and while Hill attacked her upon the question of socialism—some instinct told him to spare her a direct assault upon her religion—she was gathering resolution to undertake what she told herself was his æsthetic education. She was a year or two older than he, though the thought never occurred to him. The loan of *News from Nowhere* was the beginning of a series of cross loans. Upon some absurd first principle of his, Hill had never 'wasted time' upon poetry, and it seemed an appalling deficiency to her. One day in the lunch hour, when she chanced upon him alone in the little museum where the skeletons were arranged, shamefully eating the bun that constituted his midday meal, she retreated, and returned to lend him, with a slightly furtive air, a volume of Browning.* He stood sideways towards her and took the book rather clumsily, because he was holding the bun in the other hand. And in the retrospect his voice lacked the cheerful clearness he could have wished.

That occurred after the examination in comparative anatomy, on the day before the College turned out its students, and was carefully locked up by the officials, for the Christmas holidays. The excitement of cramming for the first trial of strength had for a little while dominated Hill, to the exclusion of his other interests. In the forecasts of the result in which everyone indulged he was surprised to find that no one regarded him as a possible competitor for the Harvey Commemoration Medal, of which this and the two subsequent examinations disposed. It was about this time that Wedderburn, who so far had lived inconspicuously on the uttermost margin of Hill's perceptions, began to take on the appearance of an obstacle. By a mutual agreement, the nocturnal prowlings with Thorpe ceased for the three weeks before the examination, and his landlady pointed out that she really could not supply so much lamp oil at the price. He walked to and fro from the College with little slips of mnemonics in his hand, lists of crayfish appendages, rabbits' skull-bones, and vertebrate nerves, for example, and became a positive nuisance to foot passengers in the opposite direction.

But, by a natural reaction, Poetry and the girl with the brown eyes ruled the Christmas holiday. The pending results of the examination became such a secondary consideration that Hill marvelled at his father's excitement. Even had he wished it, there was no comparative anatomy to read in Landport, and he was too poor to buy books, but the stock of poets in the library was extensive, and Hill's attack was magnificently sustained. He saturated himself with the fluent numbers of Longfellow and Tennyson, and fortified himself with Shakespeare; found a kindred soul in Pope, and a master in Shelley, and heard and fled the siren voices of Eliza Cook and Mrs Hemans.* But he read no more Browning, because he hoped for the loan of other volumes from Miss Haysman when he returned to London.

He walked from his lodgings to the College with that volume of Browning in his shiny black bag, and his mind teeming with the finest general propositions about poetry. Indeed, he framed first this little speech and then that with which to grace the return. The morning was an exceptionally pleasant one for London; there was a clear, hard frost and undeniable blue in the sky, a thin haze softened every outline, and warm shafts of sunlight struck between the house blocks and turned the sunny side of the street to amber and gold. In the hall of the College he pulled off his glove and signed his name with fingers so stiff with cold that the characteristic dash under the signature he cultivated became a quivering line. He imagined Miss Haysman about him everywhere. He turned at the staircase, and there, below, he saw a crowd struggling at the foot of the notice-board. This, possibly, was the biology list. He forgot Browning and Miss Haysman for the moment, and joined the scrimmage. And at last, with his cheek flattened against the sleeve of the man on the step above him, he read the list—

CLASS I

H. J. Somers Wedderburn
William Hill

and thereafter followed a second class that is outside our present sympathies. It was characteristic that he did not trouble to look for Thorpe on the physics list, but backed out of the struggle at once, and in a curious, emotional state between pride over common second-class humanity and acute disappointment at Wedderburn's success, went on his way upstairs. At the top, as he was hanging up his coat in the passage, the zoological demonstrator, a young man from Oxford, who secretly regarded him as a blatant 'mugger'* of the very worst type, offered his heartiest congratulations.

At the laboratory door Hill stopped for a second to get his breath, and then entered. He looked straight up the laboratory and saw all five girl students grouped in their places, and Wedderburn, the once retiring Wedderburn, leaning rather gracefully against the window, playing with the blind tassel and talking, apparently, to the five of them. Now, Hill could talk bravely enough and even overbearingly to one girl, and he could have made a speech to a roomful of girls, but this business of standing at ease and appreciating, fencing, and returning quick remarks round a group was, he knew, altogether beyond him. Coming up the staircase his feelings for Wedderburn had been generous, a certain admiration perhaps, a willingness to shake his hand conspicuously and heartily as one who had fought but the first round. But before Christmas Wedderburn had never gone up to that end of the room to talk. In a flash Hill's mist of vague excitement condensed abruptly to a vivid dislike of Wedderburn. Possibly his expression changed. As he came up to his place, Wedderburn nodded carelessly to him, and the others glanced round. Miss Haysman looked at him and away again, the faintest touch of her eyes. 'I can't agree with you, Mr Wedderburn,' she said.

'I must congratulate you on your first-class, Mr Hill,' said the spectacled girl in green, turning round and beaming at him.

'It's nothing,' said Hill, staring at Wedderburn and Miss Haysman talking together, and eager to hear what they talked about.

'We poor folks in the second class don't think so,' said the girl in spectacles.

What was it Wedderburn was saying? Something about William Morris! Hill did not answer the girl in spectacles, and the smile died out of his face. He could not hear, and failed to see how he could 'cut in.' Confound Wedderburn! He sat down, opened his bag, hesitated whether to return the volume of Browning forthwith, in the sight of all, and instead drew out his new notebooks for the short course in elementary botany that was now beginning, and which would terminate in February. As he did so, a fat, heavy man, with a white face and pale grey eyes—Bindon, the professor of botany, who came up from Kew* for January and February— came in by the lecture theatre door, and passed, rubbing his hands together and smiling, in silent affability down the laboratory.

In the subsequent six weeks Hill experienced some very rapid and curiously complex emotional developments. For the most part he had Wedderburn in focus—a fact that Miss Haysman never suspected. She told Hill (for in the comparative privacy of the museum she talked a good deal to him of socialism and Browning and general propositions) that she had met Wedderburn at the house of some people she knew, and 'he's inherited his cleverness; for his father, you know, is the great eye-specialist.'

'*My* father is a cobbler,' said Hill, quite irrelevantly, and perceived the want of dignity even as he said it. But the gleam of jealousy did not offend her. She conceived herself the fundamental source of it. He suffered bitterly from a sense of Wedderburn's unfairness, and a realisation of his own handicap. Here was this Wedderburn had picked up a prominent man for a father, and instead of his losing so many marks on the score of that advantage, it was counted to him for righteousness! And while Hill had to introduce himself and talk to Miss Haysman clumsily over mangled guinea-pigs in the laboratory, this Wedderburn, in some backstairs way, had access to her social altitudes, and could converse in a polished argot that Hill understood perhaps, but felt incapable of speaking. Not, of course, that he wanted to. Then it seemed to Hill that for Wedderburn to come there day after day with cuffs unfrayed, neatly tailored, precisely barbered, quietly perfect, was in itself an ill-bred, sneering sort of proceeding. Moreover, it was a stealthy thing for Wedderburn to behave insignificantly for a space, to mock modesty, to lead Hill to fancy that he himself was beyond dispute the man of the year, and then suddenly to dart in front of him, and incontinently to swell up in this fashion. In addition to these things, Wedderburn displayed an increasing disposition to join in any conversational grouping that included Miss Haysman, and would venture, and indeed seek occasion, to pass opinions derogatory to socialism and atheism. He goaded Hill to incivilities by neat, shallow, and exceedingly effective personalities* about the socialist leaders, until Hill hated Bernard Shaw's graceful egotisms, William Morris's limited editions and luxurious wall-papers, and Walter Crane's* charmingly absurd ideal working men, about as much as he hated Wedderburn. The dissertations in the laboratory, that had been his glory in the previous term, became a danger, degenerated into inglorious tussels with Wedderburn, and Hill kept to them only out of an obscure perception that his honour was involved. In the debating society Hill knew quite clearly that, to a thunderous accompaniment of banged desks, he could have pulverised Wedderburn. Only Wedderburn never attended the debating society to be pulverised, because—nauseous affectation!—he 'dined late.'

You must not imagine that these things presented themselves in quite such a crude form to Hill's perception. Hill was a born generaliser. Wedderburn to him was not so much an individual obstacle as a type, the salient angle of a class. The economic theories that, after infinite ferment, had shaped themselves in Hill's mind, became abruptly concrete at the contact. The world became full of easy-mannered, graceful, gracefully-dressed, conversationally dexterous, finally shallow Wedderburns, Bishops Wedderburn, Wedderburn M.P.s, Professors Wedderburn, Wedderburn landlords, all with finger-bowl shibboleths* and epigrammatic cities of refuge* from a sturdy debater. And everyone ill-clothed or ill-dressed, from the cobbler to the cab-runner,* was a man and a brother, a fellow-sufferer, to Hill's imagination. So that he became, as it were, a champion of the fallen and oppressed, albeit to outward seeming only a self-assertive, ill-mannered young man, and an unsuccessful champion at that. Again and again a skirmish over the afternoon tea that the girl students had inaugurated left Hill with flushed cheeks and a tattered temper, and the debating society noticed a new quality of sarcastic bitterness in his speeches.

You will understand now how it was necessary, if only in the interests of humanity, that Hill should demolish Wedderburn in the forthcoming examination and outshine him in the eyes of Miss Haysman; and you will perceive, too, how Miss Haysman fell into some common feminine misconceptions. The Hill-Wedderburn quarrel, for in his unostentatious way Wedderburn reciprocated Hill's ill-veiled rivalry, became a tribute to her indefinable charm; she was the Queen of Beauty in a tournament of scalpels and stumpy pencils. To her confidential friend's secret annoyance, it even troubled her conscience, for she was a good girl, and painfully aware, from Ruskin and contemporary fiction,* how entirely men's activities are determined by women's attitudes. And if Hill never by any chance mentioned the topic of love to her, she only credited him with the finer modesty for that omission.

So the time came on for the second examination, and Hill's increasing pallor confirmed the general rumour that he was working hard. In the aërated bread shop* near South Kensington Station you would see him, breaking his bun and sipping his milk, with his eyes intent upon a paper of closely written notes. In his bedroom there were propositions about buds and stems round his looking-glass, a diagram to catch his eye, if soap should chance to spare it, above his washing basin. He missed several meetings of the debating society, but he found the chance encounters with Miss Haysman in the spacious ways of the adjacent art museum, or in the little museum at the top of the College, or in the College corridors, more frequent and very restful. In particular, they used to meet in a little gallery full of wrought-iron chests and gates, near the art library, and there Hill used to talk, under the gentle stimulus of her flattering attention, of Browning and his personal ambitions. A characteristic she found remarkable in him was his freedom from avarice. He contemplated quite calmly the prospect of living all his life on an income below a hundred pounds a year. But he was determined to be famous, to make, recognisably in his own proper person, the world a better place to live in. He took Bradlaugh and John Burns* for his leaders and models, poor, even impecunious, great men. But Miss Haysman thought that such lives were deficient on the æsthetic side, by which, though she did not know it, she meant good wall-paper and upholstery, pretty books, tasteful clothes, concerts, and meals nicely cooked and respectfully served.

At last came the day of the second examination, and the professor of botany, a fussy, conscientious man, rearranged all the tables in a long narrow laboratory to prevent copying, and put his demonstrator on a chair on a table (where he felt, he said, like a Hindoo god*), to see all the cheating, and stuck a notice outside the door, 'Door closed,' for no earthly reason that any human being could discover. And all the morning from ten till one the quill of Wedderburn shrieked defiance at Hill's, and the quills of the others chased their leaders in a tireless pack, and so also it was in the afternoon. Wedderburn was a little quieter than usual, and Hill's face was hot all day, and his overcoat bulged with textbooks and notebooks against the last moment's revision. And the next day, in the morning and in the afternoon, was the practical examination, when sections had to be cut and slides identified. In the morning Hill was depressed because he knew he had cut a thick section, and in the afternoon came the mysterious slip.

It was just the kind of thing that the botanical professor was always doing. Like the income tax, it offered a premium to the cheat. It was a preparation under the microscope, a little glass slip, held in its place on the stage of the instrument by light steel clips, and the inscription set forth that the slip was not to be moved. Each student was to go in turn to it, sketch it, write in his book of answers what he considered it to be, and return to his place. Now, to move such a slip is a thing one can do by a chance movement of the finger, and in a fraction of a second. The professor's reason for decreeing that the slip should not be moved depended on the fact that the object he wanted identified was characteristic of a certain tree stem. In the position in which it was placed it was a difficult thing to recognise, but once the slip was moved so as to bring other parts of the preparation into view, its nature was obvious enough.

Hill came to this, flushed from a contest with staining reagents,* sat down on the little stool before the microscope, turned the mirror to get the best light, and then, out of sheer habit, shifted the slip. At once he remembered the prohibition, and, with an almost continuous motion of his hands, moved it back, and sat paralysed with astonishment at his action.

Then, slowly, he turned his head. The professor was out of the room; the demonstrator sat aloft on his impromptu rostrum, reading the *Q. Jour. Mi. Sci.*;* the rest of the examinees were busy, and with their backs to him. Should he own up to the accident now? He knew quite clearly what the thing was. It was a lenticel,* a characteristic preparation from the elder-tree. His eyes roved over his intent fellow-students, and Wedderburn suddenly glanced over his shoulder at him with a queer expression in his eyes. The mental excitement that had kept Hill at an abnormal pitch of vigour these two days gave way to a curious nervous tension. His book of answers was beside him. He did not write down what the thing was, but with one eye at the microscope he began making a hasty sketch of it. His mind was full of this grotesque puzzle in ethics that had suddenly been sprung upon him. Should he identify it? or should he leave this question unanswered? In that case Wedderburn would probably come out first in the second result. How could he tell now whether he might not have identified the thing without shifting it? It was possible that Wedderburn had failed to recognise it, of course. Suppose Wedderburn too had shifted the slide? He looked up at the clock. There were fifteen minutes in which to make up his mind. He gathered up his book of answers and the coloured pencils he used in illustrating his replies and walked back to his seat.

He read through his manuscript, and then sat thinking and gnawing his knuckle. It would look queer now if he owned up. He *must* beat Wedderburn. He forgot the examples of those starry gentlemen, John Burns and Bradlaugh. Besides, he reflected, the glimpse of the rest of the slip he had had was, after all, quite accidental, forced upon him by chance, a kind of providential revelation rather than an unfair advantage. It was not nearly so dishonest to avail himself of that as it was of Broome, who believed in the efficacy of prayer, to pray daily for a first-class. 'Five minutes more,' said the demonstrator, folding up his paper and becoming observant. Hill watched the clock hands until two minutes remained; then he opened the book of answers, and, with hot ears and an affectation of ease, gave his drawing of the lenticel its name.

When the second pass list appeared, the previous positions of Wedderburn and Hill were reversed, and the spectacled girl in green, who knew the demonstrator in private life (where he was practically human), said that in the result of the two examinations taken together Hill had the advantage of a mark—167 to 166 out of a possible 200. Everyone admired Hill in a way, though the suspicion of 'mugging' clung to him. But Hill was to find congratulations and Miss Haysman's enhanced opinion of him, and even the decided decline in the crest of Wedderburn, tainted by an unhappy memory. He felt a remarkable access of energy at first, and the note of a democracy marching to triumph returned to his debating-society speeches; he worked at his comparative anatomy with tremendous zeal and effect, and he went on with his æsthetic education. But through it all, a vivid little picture was continually coming before his mind's eye—of a sneakish person manipulating a slide.

No human being had witnessed the act, and he was cocksure that no higher power existed to see it; but for all that it worried him. Memories are not dead things but alive; they dwindle in disuse, but they harden and develop in all sorts of queer ways if they are being continually fretted. Curiously enough, though at the time he perceived clearly that the shifting was accidental, as the days wore on, his memory became confused about it, until at last he was not sure—although he assured himself that he *was* sure—whether the movement had been absolutely involuntary. Then it is possible that Hill's dietary was conducive to morbid conscientiousness; a breakfast frequently eaten in a hurry, a midday bun, and, at such hours after five as chanced to be convenient, such meat as his means determined, usually in a chop-house* in a back street off the Brompton Road. Occasionally he treated himself to threepenny or ninepenny classics,* and they usually represented a suppression of potatoes or chops. It is indisputable that outbreaks of self-abasement and emotional revival have a distinct relation to periods of scarcity. But apart from this influence on the feelings, there was in Hill a distinct aversion to falsity that the blasphemous Landport cobbler had inculcated by strap and tongue* from his earliest years. Of one fact about professed atheists I am convinced; they may be—they usually are—fools, void of subtlety, revilers of holy institutions, brutal speakers, and mischievous knaves, but they lie with difficulty. If it were not so, if they had the faintest grasp of the idea of compromise, they would simply be liberal churchmen.* And, moreover, this memory poisoned his regard for Miss Haysman. For she now so evidently preferred him to Wedderburn that he felt sure he cared for her, and began reciprocating her attentions by timid marks of personal regard; at one time he even bought a bunch of violets, carried it about in his pocket, and produced it, with a stumbling explanation, withered and dead, in the gallery of old iron. It poisoned, too, the denunciation of capitalist dishonesty that had been one of his life's pleasures. And, lastly, it poisoned his triumph in Wedderburn. Previously he had been Wedderburn's superior in his own eyes, and had raged simply at a want of recognition. Now he began to fret at the darker suspicion of positive inferiority. He fancied he found justifications for his position in Browning, but they vanished on analysis. At last—moved, curiously enough, by exactly the same motive forces that had resulted in his dishonesty—he went to Professor Bindon, and made a clean breast of the whole affair. As Hill was a paid student, Professor Bindon did not ask him to sit down, and he stood before the professor's desk as he made his confession.

'It's a curious story,' said Professor Bindon, slowly realising how the thing reflected on himself, and then letting his anger rise,—'a most remarkable story. I can't understand your doing it, and I can't understand this avowal. You're a type of student—Cambridge men would never dream—I suppose I ought to have thought—why *did* you cheat?'

'I didn't cheat,' said Hill.

'But you have just been telling me you did.'

'I thought I explained——'

'Either you cheated or you did not cheat.'

'I said my motion was involuntary.'

'I am not a metaphysician, I am a servant of science—of

223

fact. You were told not to move the slip. You did move the slip. If that is not cheating——'

'If I was a cheat,' said Hill, with the note of hysterics in his voice, 'should I come here and tell you?'

'Your repentance, of course, does you credit,' said Professor Bindon, 'but it does not alter the original facts.'

'No, sir,' said Hill, giving in in utter self-abasement.

'Even now you cause an enormous amount of trouble. The examination list will have to be revised.'

'I suppose so, sir.'

'Suppose so? Of course it must be revised. And I don't see how I can conscientiously pass you.'

'Not pass me?' said Hill. 'Fail me?'

'It's the rule in all examinations. Or where should we be? What else did you expect? You don't want to shirk the consequences of your own acts?'

'I thought, perhaps——' said Hill. And then, 'Fail me? I thought, as I told you, you would simply deduct the marks given for that slip.'

'Impossible!' said Bindon. 'Besides, it would still leave you above Wedderburn. Deduct only the marks! Preposterous! The Departmental Regulations distinctly say——'

'But it's my own admission, sir.'

'The Regulations say nothing whatever of the manner in which the matter comes to light. They simply provide——'

'It will ruin me. If I fail this examination, they won't renew my scholarship.'

'You should have thought of that before.'

'But, sir, consider all my circumstances——'

'I cannot consider anything. Professors in this College are machines. The Regulations will not even let us recommend our students for appointments. I am a machine, and you have worked me. I have to do——'

'It's very hard, sir.'

'Possibly it is.'

'If I am to be failed this examination, I might as well go home at once.'

'That is as you think proper.' Bindon's voice softened a little; he perceived he had been unjust, and, provided he did not contradict himself, he was disposed to amelioration. 'As a private person,' he said, 'I think this confession of yours goes far to mitigate your offence. But you have set the machinery in motion, and now it must take its course. I—I am really sorry you gave way.'

A wave of emotion prevented Hill from answering. Suddenly, very vividly, he saw the heavily-lined face of the old Landport cobbler, his father. 'Good God! What a fool I have been!' he said hotly and abruptly.

'I hope,' said Bindon, 'that it will be a lesson to you.'

But, curiously enough, they were not thinking of quite the same indiscretion.

There was a pause.

'I would like a day to think, sir, and then I will let you know—about going home, I mean,' said Hill, moving towards the door.

The next day Hill's place was vacant. The spectacled girl in green was, as usual, first with the news. Wedderburn and Miss Haysman were talking of a performance of *The Meistersingers** when she came up to them.

'Have you heard?' she said.

'Heard what?'

'There was cheating in the examination.'

'Cheating!' said Wedderburn, with his face suddenly hot. 'How?'

'That slide——'

'Moved? Never!'

'It was. That slide that we weren't to move——'.

'Nonsense!' said Wedderburn. 'Why! How could they find out? Who do they say——?'

225

'It was Mr Hill.'

'*Hill!*'

'Mr Hill!'

'Not—surely not the immaculate Hill?' said Wedderburn, recovering.

'I don't believe it,' said Miss Haysman. 'How do you know?'

'I *didn't*,' said the girl in spectacles. 'But I know it now for a fact. Mr Hill went and confessed to Professor Bindon himself.'

'By Jove!' said Wedderburn. 'Hill of all people. But I am always inclined to distrust these philanthropists-on-principle——'

'Are you quite sure?' said Miss Haysman, with a catch in her breath.

'Quite. It's dreadful, isn't it? But, you know, what can you expect? His father is a cobbler.'

Then Miss Haysman astonished the girl in spectacles.

'I don't care. I will not believe it,' she said, flushing darkly under her warm-tinted skin. 'I will not believe it until he has told me so himself—face to face. I would scarcely believe it then,' and abruptly she turned her back on the girl in spectacles, and walked to her own place.

'It's true, all the same,' said the girl in spectacles, peering and smiling at Wedderburn.

But Wedderburn did not answer her. She was indeed one of those people who seemed destined to make unanswered remarks.

The Country of the Blind and Other Stories

XIX

THE CRYSTAL EGG

THERE was, until a year ago, a little and very grimy-looking shop near Seven Dials,* over which, in weather-worn yellow lettering, the name of 'C. Cave, Naturalist and Dealer in Antiquities,' was inscribed. The contents of its window were curiously variegated. They comprised some elephant tusks and an imperfect set of chessmen, beads and weapons, a box of eyes, two skulls of tigers and one human, several moth-eaten stuffed monkeys (one holding a lamp), an old-fashioned cabinet, a fly-blown ostrich egg or so, some fishing-tackle, and an extraordinarily dirty, empty glass fish-tank. There was also, at the moment the story begins, a mass of crystal, worked into the shape of an egg and brilliantly polished. And at that two people who stood outside the window were looking, one of them a tall, thin clergyman, the other a black-bearded young man of dusky complexion and unobtrusive costume. The dusky young man spoke with eager gesticulation, and seemed anxious for his companion to purchase the article.

While they were there, Mr Cave came into his shop, his beard still wagging with the bread and butter of his tea. When he saw these men and the object of their regard, his countenance fell. He glanced guiltily over his shoulder, and softly shut the door. He was a little old man, with pale face and peculiar watery blue eyes; his hair was a dirty grey, and he wore a shabby blue frock-coat, an ancient silk hat, and carpet slippers very much down at heel. He remained watching the two men as they talked. The clergyman went deep into his trouser pocket, examined a handful of money, and showed his teeth in an agreeable smile. Mr Cave seemed still more depressed when they came into the shop.

The clergyman, without any ceremony, asked the price of

the crystal egg. Mr Cave glanced nervously towards the door leading into the parlour, and said five pounds. The clergyman protested that the price was high, to his companion as well as to Mr Cave—it was, indeed, very much more than Mr Cave had intended to ask when he had stocked the article—and an attempt at bargaining ensued. Mr Cave stepped to the shop door, and held it open. 'Five pounds is my price,' he said, as though he wished to save himself the trouble of unprofitable discussion. As he did so, the upper portion of a woman's face appeared above the blind in the glass upper panel of the door leading into the parlour, and stared curiously at the two customers. 'Five pounds is my price,' said Mr Cave, with a quiver in his voice.

The swarthy young man had so far remained a spectator, watching Cave keenly. Now he spoke. 'Give him five pounds,' he said. The clergyman glanced at him to see if he were in earnest, and when he looked at Mr Cave again, he saw that the latter's face was white. 'It's a lot of money,' said the clergyman, and, diving into his pocket, began counting his resources. He had little more than thirty shillings, and he appealed to his companion, with whom he seemed to be on terms of considerable intimacy. This gave Mr Cave an opportunity of collecting his thoughts, and he began to explain in an agitated manner that the crystal was not, as a matter of fact, entirely free for sale. His two customers were naturally surprised at this, and inquired why he had not thought of that before he began to bargain. Mr Cave became confused, but he stuck to his story, that the crystal was not in the market that afternoon, that a probable purchaser of it had already appeared. The two, treating this as an attempt to raise the price still further, made as if they would leave the shop. But at this point the parlour door opened, and the owner of the dark fringe and the little eyes appeared.

She was a coarse-featured, corpulent woman, younger and very much larger than Mr Cave; she walked heavily, and her face was flushed. 'That crystal *is* for sale,' she said. 'And five pounds is a good enough price for it. I can't think what you're about, Cave, not to take the gentleman's offer!'

Mr Cave, greatly perturbed by the irruption, looked angrily at her over the rims of his spectacles, and, without excessive assurance, asserted his right to manage his business in his own way. An altercation began. The two customers watched the scene with interest and some amusement, occasionally assisting Mrs Cave with suggestions. Mr Cave, hard driven, persisted in a confused and impossible story of an inquiry for the crystal that morning, and his agitation became painful. But he stuck to his point with extraordinary persistence. It was the young Oriental who ended this curious controversy. He proposed that they should call again in the course of two days—so as to give the alleged inquirer a fair chance. 'And then we must insist,' said the clergyman. 'Five pounds.' Mrs Cave took it on herself to apologise for her husband, explaining that he was sometimes 'a little odd,' and as the two customers left, the couple prepared for a free discussion of the incident in all its bearings.

Mrs Cave talked to her husband with singular directness. The poor little man, quivering with emotion, muddled himself between his stories, maintaining on the one hand that he had another customer in view, and on the other asserting that the crystal was honestly worth ten guineas. 'Why did you ask five pounds?' said his wife. '*Do* let me manage my business my own way!' said Mr Cave.

Mr Cave had living with him a step-daughter and a step-son, and at supper that night the transaction was re-discussed. None of them had a high opinion of Mr Cave's business methods, and this action seemed a culminating folly.

'It's my opinion he's refused that crystal before,' said the step-son, a loose-limbed lout of eighteen.

'But *Five Pounds*!' said the step-daughter, an argumentative young woman of six-and-twenty.

Mr Cave's answers were wretched; he could only mumble weak assertions that he knew his own business best. They drove him from his half-eaten supper into the shop, to close it for the night, his ears aflame and tears of vexation behind his spectacles. Why had he left the crystal in the window so long? The folly of it! That was the trouble closest in his mind. For a time he could see no way of evading sale.

After supper his step-daughter and step-son smartened themselves up and went out and his wife retired upstairs to reflect upon the business aspects of the crystal, over a little sugar and lemon and so forth* in hot water. Mr Cave went into the shop, and stayed there until late, ostensibly to make ornamental rockeries for gold-fish cases, but really for a private purpose that will be better explained later. The next day Mrs Cave found that the crystal had been removed from the window, and was lying behind some second-hand books on angling. She replaced it in a conspicuous position. But she did not argue further about it, as a nervous headache disinclined her from debate. Mr Cave was always disinclined. The day passed disagreeably. Mr Cave was, if anything, more absent-minded than usual, and uncommonly irritable withal. In the afternoon, when his wife was taking her customary sleep, he removed the crystal from the window again.

The next day Mr Cave had to deliver a consignment of dog-fish at one of the hospital schools, where they were needed for dissection. In his absence Mrs Cave's mind reverted to the topic of the crystal, and the methods of expenditure suitable to a windfall of five pounds. She had already devised some very agreeable expedients, among others a dress of green silk for herself and a trip to Richmond, when a jangling of the front door bell summoned her into the shop. The customer was an examination coach who came to complain of the non-delivery of certain frogs asked for the previous day. Mrs Cave did not approve of this particular branch of Mr Cave's business, and the gentleman, who had called in a somewhat aggressive mood, retired after a brief exchange of words—entirely civil, so far as he was concerned. Mrs Cave's eye then naturally turned to the window; for the sight of the crystal was an assurance of the five pounds and of her dreams. What was her surprise to find it gone!

She went to the place behind the locker on the counter, where she had discovered it the day before. It was not there; and she immediately began an eager search about the shop.

When Mr Cave returned from his business with the dog-fish, about a quarter to two in the afternoon, he found the shop in some confusion, and his wife, extremely exasperated and on her knees behind the counter, routing among his taxidermic material. Her face came up hot and angry over the counter, as the jangling bell announced his return, and she forthwith accused him of 'hiding it.'

'Hid *what*?' asked Mr Cave.

'The crystal!'

At that Mr Cave, apparently much surprised, rushed to the window. 'Isn't it here?' he said. 'Great Heavens! what has become of it?'

Just then Mr Cave's step-son re-entered the shop from the inner room—he had come home a minute or so before Mr Cave—and he was blaspheming freely. He was apprenticed to a second-hand furniture dealer down the road, but he had his meals at home, and he was naturally annoyed to find no dinner ready.

But when he heard of the loss of the crystal, he forgot his meal, and his anger was diverted from his mother to his step-father. Their first idea, of course, was that he had hidden it. But Mr Cave stoutly denied all knowledge of its fate, freely offering his bedabbled affidavit* in the matter—and at last was worked up to the point of accusing, first, his wife and then his step-son of having taken it with a view to a private sale. So began an exceedingly acrimonious and emotional discussion, which ended for Mrs Cave in a peculiar nervous condition midway between hysterics and amuck, and caused the step-son to be half-an-hour late at the furniture establishment in the afternoon. Mr Cave took refuge from his wife's emotions in the shop.

In the evening the matter was resumed, with less passion and in a judicial spirit, under the presidency of the step-daughter. The supper passed unhappily and culminated in a painful scene. Mr Cave gave way at last to extreme exasperation, and went out banging the front door violently. The rest of the family, having discussed him with the freedom his absence warranted, hunted the house from garret to cellar, hoping to light upon the crystal.

The next day the two customers called again. They were received by Mrs Cave almost in tears. It transpired that no one *could* imagine all that she had stood from Cave at various times in her married pilgrimage. . . . She also gave a garbled account of the disappearance. The clergyman and the Oriental laughed silently at one another, and said it was very extraordinary. As Mrs Cave seemed disposed to give them the complete history of her life they made to leave the shop. Thereupon Mrs Cave, still clinging to hope, asked for the clergyman's address, so that, if she could get anything out of Cave, she might communicate it. The address was duly given, but apparently was afterwards mislaid. Mrs Cave can remember nothing about it.

In the evening of that day the Caves seem to have exhausted their emotions, and Mr Cave, who had been out in the afternoon, supped in a gloomy isolation that contrasted pleasantly with the impassioned controversy of the previous days. For some time matters were very badly strained in the Cave household, but neither crystal nor customer reappeared.

Now, without mincing the matter, we must admit that Mr Cave was a liar. He knew perfectly well where the crystal was. It was in the rooms of Mr Jacoby Wace, Assistant Demonstrator at St Catherine's Hospital, Westbourne Street. It stood on the sideboard partially covered by a black velvet cloth, and beside a decanter of American whisky. It is from Mr Wace, indeed, that the particulars upon which this narrative is based were derived. Cave had taken off the thing to the hospital hidden in the dog-fish sack, and there had pressed the young investigator to keep it for him. Mr Wace was a little dubious at first. His relationship to Cave was peculiar. He had a taste for singular characters, and he had more than once invited the old man to smoke and drink in his rooms, and to unfold his rather amusing views of life in general and of his wife in particular. Mr Wace had encountered Mrs Cave, too, on occasions when Mr Cave was not at home to attend to him. He knew the constant interference to which Cave was subjected, and having weighed the story judicially, he decided to give the crystal a refuge. Mr Cave promised to explain the reasons for his remarkable affection for the crystal more fully on a later occasion, but he spoke distinctly of seeing visions therein. He called on Mr Wace the same evening.

He told a complicated story. The crystal he said had come into his possession with other oddments at the forced sale of another curiosity dealer's effects, and not knowing what its value might be, he had ticketed it at ten shillings. It had hung upon his hands at that price for some months, and he was thinking of 'reducing the figure,' when he made a singular discovery.

At that time his health was very bad—and it must be borne in mind that, throughout all this experience, his physical condition was one of ebb—and he was in considerable distress by reason of the negligence, the positive ill-treatment even, he received from his wife and step-children. His wife was vain, extravagant, unfeeling, and had a growing taste for private drinking; his step-daughter was mean and over-reaching; and his step-son had conceived a violent dislike for him, and lost no chance of showing it. The requirements of his business pressed heavily upon him, and Mr Wace does not think that he was altogether free from occasional intemperance. He had begun life in a comfortable position, he was a man of fair education, and he suffered, for weeks at a stretch, from melancholia and insomnia. Afraid to disturb his family, he would slip quietly from his wife's side, when his thoughts became intolerable, and wander about the house. And about three o'clock one morning, late in August, chance directed him into the shop.

The dirty little place was impenetrably black except in one spot, where he perceived an unusual glow of light. Approaching this, he discovered it to be the crystal egg, which was standing on the corner of the counter towards the window. A thin ray smote through a crack in the shutters, impinged upon the object, and seemed as it were to fill its entire interior.

It occurred to Mr Cave that this was not in accordance with the laws of optics as he had known them in his younger days. He could understand the rays being refracted by the crystal and coming to a focus in its interior, but this diffusion jarred with his physical conceptions. He approached the crystal nearly, peering into it and round it, with a transient revival of the scientific curiosity that in his youth had determined his choice of a calling. He was surprised to find the light not steady, but writhing within the substance of the egg, as though that object was a hollow sphere of some luminous vapour. In moving about to get different points of view, he suddenly found that he had come between it and the ray, and that the crystal none the less remained luminous. Greatly astonished, he lifted it out of the light ray and carried it to the darkest part of the shop. It remained bright for some four or five minutes, when it slowly faded and went out. He placed it in the thin streak of daylight, and its luminousness was almost immediately restored.

So far, at least, Mr Wace was able to verify the remarkable story of Mr Cave. He has himself repeatedly held this crystal in a ray of light (which had to be of a less diameter than one millimetre). And in a perfect darkness, such as could be produced by velvet wrapping, the crystal did undoubtedly appear very faintly phosphorescent. It would seem, however, that the luminousness was of some exceptional sort, and not equally visible to all eyes; for Mr Harbinger—whose name will be familiar to the scientific reader in connection with the

Pasteur Institute—was quite unable to see any light whatever. And Mr Wace's own capacity for its appreciation was out of comparison inferior to that of Mr Cave's. Even with Mr Cave the power varied very considerably: his vision was most vivid during states of extreme weakness and fatigue.

Now, from the outset, this light in the crystal exercised a curious fascination upon Mr Cave. And it says more for his loneliness of soul than a volume of pathetic* writing could do, that he told no human being of his curious observations. He seems to have been living in such an atmosphere of petty spite that to admit the existence of a pleasure would have been to risk the loss of it. He found that as the dawn advanced, and the amount of diffused light increased, the crystal became to all appearance non-luminous. And for some time he was unable to see anything in it, except at night-time, in dark corners of the shop.

But the use of an old velvet cloth, which he used as a background for a collection of minerals, occurred to him, and by doubling this, and putting it over his head and hands, he was able to get a sight of the luminous movement within the crystal even in the day-time. He was very cautious lest he should be thus discovered by his wife, and he practised this occupation only in the afternoons, while she was asleep upstairs, and then circumspectly in a hollow under the counter. And one day, turning the crystal about in his hands, he saw something. It came and went like a flash, but it gave him the impression that the object had for a moment opened to him the view of a wide and spacious and strange country; and turning it about, he did, just as the light faded, see the same vision again.

Now it would be tedious and unnecessary to state all the phases of Mr Cave's discovery from this point. Suffice that the effect was this: the crystal, being peered into at an angle of about 137 degrees from the direction of the illuminating ray, gave a clear and consistent picture of a wide and peculiar country-side. It was not dream-like at all: it produced a definite impression of reality, and the better the light the more real and solid it seemed. It was a moving picture: that is to say, certain objects moved in it, but slowly in an orderly manner like real things, and, according as the direction of the lighting and vision changed, the picture changed also. It must, indeed, have been like looking through an oval glass at a view, and turning the glass about to get at different aspects.

Mr Cave's statements, Mr Wace assures me, were extremely circumstantial, and entirely free from any of that emotional quality that taints hallucinatory impressions. But it must be remembered that all the efforts of Mr Wace to see any similar clarity in the faint opalescence of the crystal were wholly unsuccessful, try as he would. The difference in intensity of the impressions received by the two men was very great, and it is quite conceivable that what was a view to Mr Cave was a mere blurred nebulosity to Mr Wace.

The view, as Mr Cave described it, was invariably of an extensive plain, and he seemed always to be looking at it from a considerable height, as if from a tower or a mast. To the east and to the west the plain was bounded at a remote distance by vast reddish cliffs, which reminded him of those he had seen in some picture; but what the picture was Mr Wace was unable to ascertain. These cliffs passed north and south—he could tell the points of the compass by the stars that were visible of a night—receding in an almost illimitable perspective and fading into the mists of the distance before they met. He was nearer the eastern set of cliffs; on the occasion of his first vision the sun was rising over them, and black against the sunlight and pale against their shadow appeared a multitude of soaring forms that Mr Cave regarded as birds. A vast range of buildings spread below him; he seemed to be looking down upon them; and as they approached the blurred and refracted edge of the picture they became indistinct. There were also trees curious in shape, and in colouring a deep mossy green and an exquisite grey, beside a wide and shining canal. And something great and brilliantly coloured flew across the picture. But the first time Mr Cave saw these pictures he saw only in flashes, his hands shook, his head moved, the vision came and went, and grew foggy and indistinct. And at first he had the greatest difficulty in finding the picture again once the direction of it was lost.

His next clear vision, which came about a week after the first, the interval having yielded nothing but tantalising glimpses and some useful experience, showed him the view down the length of the valley. The view was different, but he had a curious persuasion, which his subsequent observations abundantly confirmed, that he was regarding the strange world from exactly the same spot, although he was looking in a different direction. The long façade of the great building, whose roof he had looked down upon before, was now receding in perspective. He recognised the roof. In the front of the façade was a terrace of massive proportions and extraordinary length, and down the middle of the terrace, at certain intervals, stood huge but very graceful masts, bearing small shiny objects which reflected the setting sun. The import of these small objects did not occur to Mr Cave until some time after, as he was describing the scene to Mr Wace. The terrace overhung a thicket of the most luxuriant and graceful vegetation, and beyond this was a wide grassy lawn on which certain broad creatures, in form like beetles but enormously larger, reposed. Beyond this again was a richly decorated causeway of pinkish stone; and beyond that, and lined with dense red weeds, and passing up the valley exactly parallel with the distant cliffs, was a broad and mirror-like expanse of water. The air seemed full of squadrons of great birds, manœuvring in stately curves; and across the river was a multitude of splendid buildings, richly coloured and glittering with metallic tracery and facets, among a forest of moss-like and lichenous trees. And suddenly something flapped repeatedly across the vision, like the fluttering of a jewelled fan or the beating of a wing, and a face, or rather the upper part of a face with very large eyes, came as it were close to his own and as if on the other side of the crystal. Mr Cave was so startled and so impressed by the absolute reality of these eyes that he drew his head back from the crystal to look behind it. He had become so absorbed in watching that he was quite surprised to find himself in the cool darkness of his little shop, with its familiar odour of methyl, mustiness, and decay. And as he blinked about him, the glowing crystal faded and went out.

Such were the first general impressions of Mr Cave. The story is curiously direct and circumstantial. From the outset, when the valley first flashed momentarily on his senses, his imagination was strangely affected, and as he began to appreciate the details of the scene he saw, his wonder rose to the point of a passion. He went about his business listless and distraught, thinking only of the time when he should be able to return to his watching. And then a few weeks after his first sight of the valley came the two customers, the stress and excitement of their offer, and the narrow escape of the crystal from sale, as I have already told.

Now, while the thing was Mr Cave's secret, it remained a mere wonder, a thing to creep to covertly and peep at, as a child might peep upon a forbidden garden. But Mr Wace has, for a young scientific investigator, a particularly lucid and consecutive habit of mind. Directly the crystal and its story came to him, and he had satisfied himself, by seeing the phosphorescence with his own eyes, that there really was a certain evidence for Mr Cave's statements, he proceeded to develop the matter systematically. Mr Cave was only too eager to come and feast his eyes on this wonderland he saw, and he came every night from half-past eight until half-past ten, and sometimes, in Mr Wace's absence, during the day. On Sunday afternoons, also, he came. From the outset Mr Wace made copious notes, and it was due to his scientific method that the relation between the direction from which the initiating ray entered the crystal and the orientation of the picture were proved. And, by covering the crystal in a box perforated only with a small aperture to admit the exciting ray, and by substituting black holland* for his buff* blinds, he greatly improved the conditions of the observations; so that in a little while they were able to survey the valley in any direction they desired.

So having cleared the way, we may give a brief account of this visionary world within the crystal. The things were in all cases seen by Mr Cave, and the method of working was invariably for him to watch the crystal and report what he saw, while Mr Wace (who as a science student had learnt the trick of writing in the dark) wrote a brief note of his report. When the crystal faded, it was put into its box in the proper position and the electric light turned on. Mr Wace asked questions, and suggested observations to clear up difficult points. Nothing, indeed, could have been less visionary and more matter-of-fact.

The attention of Mr Cave had been speedily directed to the bird-like creatures he had seen so abundantly present in each of his earlier visions. His first impression was soon corrected, and he considered for a time that they might represent a diurnal* species of bat. Then he thought, grotesquely enough, that they might be cherubs. Their heads were round and curiously human, and it was the eyes of one of them that had so startled him on his second observation. They had broad, silvery wings, not feathered, but glistening almost as brilliantly as new-killed fish and with the same subtle play of colour, and these wings were not built on the plan of bird-wing or bat, Mr Wace learned, but supported by curved ribs radiating from the body. (A sort of butterfly wing with curved ribs seems best to express their appearance.) The body was small, but fitted with two bunches of prehensile* organs, like long tentacles, immediately under the mouth. Incredible as it appeared to Mr Wace, the persuasion at last became irresistible that it was these creatures which owned the great quasi-human buildings and the magnificent garden that made the broad valley so splendid. And Mr Cave perceived that the buildings, with other peculiarities, had no doors, but that the great circular windows, which opened freely, gave the creatures egress and entrance. They would alight upon their tentacles, fold their wings to a smallness almost rod-like, and hop into the interior. But among them was a multitude of smaller-winged creatures, like great dragon-flies and moths and flying beetles, and across the greensward* brilliantly-coloured gigantic ground-beetles crawled lazily to and fro. Moreover, on the causeways and terraces, large-headed creatures similar to the greater winged flies, but wingless, were visible, hopping busily upon their hand-like tangle of tentacles.

Allusion has already been made to the glittering objects upon masts that stood upon the terrace of the nearer building. It dawned upon Mr Cave, after regarding one of these masts very fixedly on one particularly vivid day that the glittering object there was a crystal exactly like that into which he peered. And a still more careful scrutiny convinced him that each one in a vista of nearly twenty carried a similar object.

Occasionally one of the large flying creatures would flutter up to one, and folding its wings and coiling a number of its tentacles about the mast, would regard the crystal fixedly for a space,—sometimes for as long as fifteen minutes. And a series of observations, made at the suggestion of Mr Wace, convinced both watchers that, so far as this visionary world was concerned, the crystal into which they peered actually stood at the summit of the end-most mast on the terrace, and that on one occasion at least one of these inhabitants of this other world had looked into Mr Cave's face while he was making these observations.

So much for the essential facts of this very singular story. Unless we dismiss it all as the ingenious fabrication of Mr Wace, we have to believe one of two things: either that Mr Cave's crystal was in two worlds at once, and that while it was carried about in one, it remained stationary in the other, which seems altogether absurd; or else that it had some peculiar relation of sympathy with another and exactly similar crystal in this other world, so that what was seen in the interior of the one in this world was, under suitable conditions, visible to an observer in the corresponding crystal in the other world; and *vice versa*. At present, indeed, we do not know of any way in which two crystals could so come *en rapport*, but nowadays we know enough to understand that the thing is not altogether impossible. This view of the crystals as *en rapport* was the supposition that occurred to Mr Wace, and to me at least it seems extremely plausible. . . .

And where was this other world? On this, also, the alert intelligence of Mr Wace speedily threw light. After sunset, the sky darkened rapidly—there was a very brief twilight interval indeed—and the stars shone out. They were recognisably the same as those we see, arranged in the same constellations. Mr Cave recognised the Bear, the Pleiades, Aldebaran, and Sirius; so that the other world must be somewhere in the solar system, and, at the utmost, only a few hundreds of millions of miles from our own. Following up this clue, Mr Wace learned that the midnight sky was a darker blue even than our midwinter sky, and that the sun seemed a little smaller. *And there were two small moons!* 'like our moon but smaller, and quite differently marked,' one of which moved so rapidly that its motion was clearly visible as one regarded it. These moons were never high in the sky, but vanished as they rose: that is, every time they revolved they were eclipsed because they were so near their primary planet. And all this answers quite completely, although Mr Cave did not know it, to what must be the condition of things on Mars.

Indeed, it seems an exceedingly plausible conclusion that peering into this crystal Mr Cave did actually see the planet Mars and its inhabitants. And if that be the case, then the evening star that shone so brilliantly in the sky of that distant vision was neither more nor less than our own familiar earth.

For a time the Martians—if they were Martians—do not seem to have known of Mr Cave's inspection. Once or twice one would come to peer, and go away very shortly to some other mast, as though the vision was unsatisfactory. During this time Mr Cave was able to watch the proceedings of these winged people without being disturbed by their attentions, and although his report is necessarily vague and fragmentary, it is nevertheless very suggestive. Imagine the impression of humanity a Martian observer would get who, after a difficult process of preparation and with considerable fatigue to the eyes, was able to peer at London from the steeple of St Martin's Church* for stretches, at longest, of four minutes at a time. Mr Cave was unable to ascertain if the winged Martians were the same as the Martians who hopped about the causeways and terraces, and if the latter could put on wings at will. He several times saw certain clumsy bipeds, dimly suggestive of apes, white and partially translucent, feeding among certain of the lichenous trees, and once some of these fled before one of the hopping, round-headed Martians. The latter caught one in its tentacles, and then the picture faded suddenly and left Mr Cave most tantalisingly in the dark. On another occasion a vast thing, that Mr Cave thought at first was some gigantic insect, appeared advancing along the causeway beside the canal with extraordinary rapidity. As this drew nearer Mr Cave perceived that it was a mechanism of shining metals and of extraordinary complexity. And then, when he looked again, it had passed out of sight.

After a time Mr Wace aspired to attract the attention of the Martians, and the next time that the strange eyes of one of them appeared close to the crystal Mr Cave cried out and sprang away, and they immediately turned on the light and began to gesticulate in a manner suggestive of signalling. But when at last Mr Cave examined the crystal again the Martian had departed.

Thus far these observations had progressed in early November, and then Mr Cave, feeling that the suspicions of his family about the crystal were allayed, began to take it to and fro with him in order that, as occasion arose in the daytime or night, he might comfort himself with what was fast becoming the most real thing in his existence.

In December Mr Wace's work in connection with a forthcoming examination became heavy, the sittings were reluctantly suspended for a week, and for ten or eleven days—he is not quite sure which—he saw nothing of Cave. He then grew anxious to resume these investigations, and, the stress of his seasonal labours being abated, he went down to Seven Dials. At the corner he noticed a shutter before a bird fancier's window, and then another at a cobbler's. Mr Cave's shop was closed.

He rapped and the door was opened by the step-son in black. He at once called Mrs Cave, who was, Mr Wace could not but observe, in cheap but ample widow's weeds of the most imposing pattern. Without any very great surprise Mr Wace learnt that Cave was dead and already buried. She was in tears, and her voice was a little thick. She had just returned from Highgate.* Her mind seemed occupied with her own prospects and the honourable details of the obsequies,* but Mr Wace was at last able to learn the particulars of Cave's death. He had been found dead in his shop in the early morning, the day after his last visit to Mr Wace, and the crystal had been clasped in his stone cold hands. His face was smiling, said Mrs Cave, and the velvet cloth from the minerals lay on the floor at his feet. He must have been dead five or six hours when he was found.

This came as a great shock to Wace, and he began to reproach himself bitterly for having neglected the plain symptoms of the old man's ill-health. But his chief thought was of the crystal. He approached that topic in a gingerly manner, because he knew Mrs Cave's peculiarities. He was dumbfounded to learn that it was sold.

Mrs Cave's first impulse, directly Cave's body had been

taken upstairs, had been to write to the mad clergyman who had offered five pounds for the crystal, informing him of its recovery; but after a violent hunt, in which her daughter joined her, they were convinced of the loss of his address. As they were without the means required to mourn and bury Cave in the elaborate style the dignity of an old Seven Dials inhabitant demands, they had appealed to a friendly fellow-tradesman in Great Portland Street. He had very kindly taken over a portion of the stock at a valuation. The valuation was his own, and the crystal egg was included in one of the lots. Mr Wace, after a few suitable condolences, a little off-handedly proffered perhaps, hurried at once to Great Portland Street. But there he learned that the crystal egg had already been sold to a tall, dark man in grey. And there the material facts in this curious, and to me at least very suggestive, story come abruptly to an end. The Great Portland Street dealer did not know who the tall dark man in grey was, nor had he observed him with sufficient attention to describe him minutely. He did not even know which way this person had gone after leaving the shop. For a time Mr Wace remained in the shop, trying the dealer's patience with hopeless questions, venting his own exasperation. And at last, realising abruptly that the whole thing had passed out of his hands, had vanished like a vision of the night, he returned to his own rooms, a little astonished to find the notes he had made still tangible and visible upon his untidy table.

His annoyance and disappointment were naturally very great. He made a second call (equally ineffectual) upon the Great Portland Street dealer, and he resorted to advertisements in such periodicals as were likely to come into the hands of a *bric-a-brac* collector. He also wrote letters to *The Daily Chronicle* and *Nature*,* but both those periodicals, suspecting a hoax, asked him to reconsider his action before they printed, and he was advised that such a strange story, unfortunately so bare of supporting evidence, might imperil his reputation as an investigator. Moreover, the calls of his proper work were urgent. So that after a month or so, save for an occasional reminder to certain dealers, he had reluctantly to abandon the quest for the crystal egg, and from that day to this it remains undiscovered. Occasionally, however, he tells me, and I can quite believe him, he has bursts of zeal, in which he abandons his more urgent occupation and resumes the search.

Whether or not it will remain lost for ever, with the material and origin of it, are things equally speculative at the present time. If the present purchaser is a collector, one would have expected the enquiries of Mr Wace to have reached him through the dealers. He has been able to discover Mr Cave's clergyman and 'Oriental'—no other than the Rev. James Parker and the young Prince of Bosso-Kuni in Java. I am obliged to them for certain particulars. The object of the Prince was simply curiosity—and extravagance. He was so eager to buy because Cave was so oddly reluctant to sell. It is just as possible that the buyer in the second instance was simply a casual purchaser and not a collector at all, and the crystal egg, for all I know, may at the present moment be within a mile of me, decorating a drawing-room or serving as a paper-weight—its remarkable functions all unknown. Indeed, it is partly with the idea of such a possibility that I have thrown this narrative into a form that will give it a chance of being read by the ordinary consumer of fiction.

My own ideas in the matter are practically identical with those of Mr Wace. I believe the crystal on the mast in Mars and the crystal egg of Mr Cave's to be in some physical, but at present quite inexplicable, way *en rapport*, and we both believe further that the terrestrial crystal must have been—possibly at some remote date—sent hither from that planet, in order to give the Martians a near view of our affairs. Possibly the fellows to the crystals on the other masts are also on our globe. No theory of hallucination suffices for the facts.

XX

THE STAR

IT was on the first day of the new year that the announcement was made, almost simultaneously from three observatories, that the motion of the planet Neptune, the outermost of all the planets* that wheel about the sun, had become very erratic. Ogilvy* had already called attention to a suspected retardation in its velocity in December. Such a piece of news was scarcely calculated to interest a world the greater portion of whose inhabitants were unaware of the existence of the planet Neptune, nor outside the astronomical profession did the subsequent discovery of a faint remote speck of light in the region of the perturbed planet cause any very great excitement. Scientific people, however, found the intelligence remarkable enough, even before it became known that the new body was rapidly growing larger and brighter, that its motion was quite different from the orderly progress of the planets, and that the deflection of Neptune and its satellite was becoming now of an unprecedented kind.

Few people without a training in science can realise the huge isolation of the solar system. The sun with its specks of planets, its dust of planetoids,* and its impalpable comets, swims in a vacant immensity that almost defeats the imagination. Beyond the orbit of Neptune there is space, vacant so far as human observation has penetrated, without warmth or light or sound, blank emptiness, for twenty million times a million miles. That is the smallest estimate of the distance to be traversed before the very nearest of the stars is attained. And, saving a few comets more unsubstantial than the thinnest flame, no matter had ever to human knowledge crossed this gulf of space until early in the twentieth century this strange wanderer appeared. A vast mass of matter it was, bulky, heavy, rushing without warning out of the black mystery of the sky into the radiance of the sun. By the second day it was clearly visible to any decent instrument, as a speck with a barely sensible diameter, in the constellation Leo near Regulus. In a little while an opera glass could attain it.

On the third day of the new year the newspaper readers of two hemispheres were made aware for the first time of the real importance of this unusual apparition in the heavens. 'A Planetary Collision,' one London paper headed the news, and proclaimed Duchaine's opinion that this strange new planet would probably collide with Neptune. The leader-writers enlarged upon the topic. So that in most of the capitals of the world, on January 3rd, there was an expectation, however vague, of some imminent phenomenon in the sky; and as the night followed the sunset round the globe, thousands of men turned their eyes skyward to see—the old familiar stars just as they had always been.

Until it was dawn in London and Pollux setting and the stars overhead grown pale. The Winter's dawn it was, a sickly filtering accumulation of daylight, and the light of gas and candles shone yellow in the windows to show where people were astir. But the yawning policeman saw the thing, the busy crowds in the markets stopped agape, workmen going to their work betimes, milkmen, the drivers of news-carts, dissipation going home jaded and pale, homeless wanderers, sentinels on their beats, and, in the country, labourers trudging afield, poachers slinking home, all over the dusky quickening* country it could be seen—and out at sea by seamen watching for the day—a great white star, come suddenly into the westward sky!

Brighter it was than any star in our skies; brighter than the evening star at its brightest. It still glowed out white and large, no mere twinkling spot of light, but a small, round, clear shining disc, an hour after the day had come. And where science has not reached, men stared and feared, telling one another of the wars and pestilences that are foreshadowed by these fiery signs in the Heavens. Sturdy Boers, dusky Hottentots,* Gold Coast* negroes, Frenchmen, Spaniards, Portuguese, stood in the warmth of the sunrise watching the setting of this strange new star.

And in a hundred observatories there had been suppressed excitement, rising almost to shouting pitch, as the two remote bodies had rushed together, and a hurrying to and fro, to gather photographic apparatus and spectroscope,* and this appliance and that, to record this novel, astonishing sight, the destruction of a world. For it was a world, a sister planet of our earth, far greater than our earth* indeed, that had so suddenly flashed into flaming death. Neptune it was had been struck, fairly and squarely, by the strange planet from outer space, and the heat of the concussion had incontinently turned two solid globes into one vast mass of incandescence. Round the world that day, two hours before the dawn, went the pallid great white star, fading only as it sank westward and the sun mounted above it. Everywhere men marvelled at it, but of all those who saw it none could have marvelled more than those sailors, habitual watchers of the stars, who far away at sea had heard nothing of its advent and saw it now rise like a pigmy moon and climb zenithward and hang overhead and sink westward with the passing of the night.

And when next it rose over Europe everywhere were crowds of watchers on hilly slopes, on house-roofs, in open spaces, staring eastward for the rising of the great new star. It rose with a white glow in front of it, like the glare of a white fire, and those who had seen it come into existence the night before cried out at the sight of it. 'It is larger,' they cried. 'It is brighter!' And indeed the moon, a quarter full and sinking in the west, was in its apparent size beyond comparison, but scarcely in all its breadth had it as much brightness now as the little circle of the strange new star.

'It is brighter!' cried the people clustering in the streets. But in the dim observatories the watchers held their breath and peered at one another. '*It is nearer!*' they said. '*Nearer!*'

And voice after voice repeated, 'It is nearer,' and the clicking telegraph took that up, and it trembled along telephone wires, and in a thousand cities grimy compositors* fingered the type. 'It is nearer.' Men writing in offices, struck with a strange realisation, flung down their pens, men talking in a thousand places suddenly came upon a grotesque possibility in those words, 'It is nearer.' It hurried along awakening streets, it was shouted down the frost-stilled ways of quiet villages, men who had read these things from the throbbing tape stood in yellow-lit doorways shouting the news to the passers-by. 'It is nearer.' Pretty women, flushed and glittering, heard the news told jestingly between the dances, and feigned an intelligent interest they did not feel. 'Nearer! Indeed. How curious! How very, very clever people must be to find out things like that!'

Lonely tramps faring through the wintry night murmured those words to comfort themselves—looking skyward. 'It has need to be nearer, for the night's as cold as charity. Don't seem much warmth from it if it *is* nearer, all the same.'

'What is a new star to me?' cried the weeping woman, kneeling beside her dead.

The schoolboy, rising early for his examination work, puzzled it out for himself—with the great white star shining broad and bright through the frost-flowers of his window. 'Centrifugal, centripetal,'* he said, with his chin on his fist. 'Stop a planet in its flight, rob it of its centrifugal force, what then? Centripetal has it, and down it falls into the sun! And this——!

'Do *we* come in the way? I wonder——'

The light of that day went the way of its brethren, and with the later watches of the frosty darkness rose the strange star again. And it was now so bright that the waxing moon seemed but a pale yellow ghost of itself, hanging huge in the sunset. In a South African city a great man had married, and the streets were alight to welcome his return with his bride. 'Even the skies have illuminated,' said the flatterer. Under

Capricorn, two negro lovers, daring the wild beasts and evil spirits for love of one another, crouched together in a cane brake where the fire-flies hovered. 'That is our star,' they whispered, and felt strangely comforted by the sweet brilliance of its light.

The master mathematican sat in his private room and pushed the papers from him. His calculations were already finished. In a small white phial there still remained a little of the drug that had kept him awake and active for four long nights. Each day, serene, explicit, patient as ever, he had given his lecture to his students, and then had come back at once to this momentous calculation. His face was grave, a little drawn and hectic* from his drugged activity. For some time he seemed lost in thought. Then he went to the window, and the blind went up with a click. Half-way up the sky, over the clustering roofs, chimneys, and steeples of the city, hung the star.

He looked at it as one might look into the eyes of a brave enemy. 'You may kill me,' he said after a silence. 'But I can hold you—and all the universe for that matter—in the grip of this small brain. I would not change. Even now.'

He looked at the little phial. 'There will be no need of sleep again,' he said. The next day at noon, punctual to the minute, he entered his lecture theatre, put his hat on the end of the table as his habit was, and carefully selected a large piece of chalk. It was a joke among his students that he could not lecture without that piece of chalk to fumble in his fingers, and once he had been stricken to impotence by their hiding his supply. He came and looked under his grey eyebrows at the rising tiers of young fresh faces, and spoke with his accustomed studied commonness of phrasing. 'Circumstances have arisen—circumstances beyond my control,' he said, and paused, 'which will debar me from completing the course I had designed. It would seem, gentlemen, if I may put the thing clearly and briefly, that—Man has lived in vain.'

The students glanced at one another. Had they heard

aright? Mad? Raised eyebrows and grinning lips there were, but one or two faces remained intent upon his calm grey-fringed face. 'It will be interesting,' he was saying, 'to devote this morning to an exposition, so far as I can make it clear to you, of the calculations that have led me to this conclusion. Let us assume——'

He turned towards the blackboard, meditating a diagram in the way that was usual to him. 'What was that about "lived in vain"?' whispered one student to another. 'Listen,' said the other, nodding towards the lecturer.

And presently they began to understand.

That night the star rose later, for its proper eastward motion had carried it some way across Leo towards Virgo, and its brightness was so great that the sky became a luminous blue as it rose, and every star was hidden in its turn, save only Jupiter near the zenith, Capella, Aldebaran, Sirius, and the pointers of the Bear. It was very white and beautiful. In many parts of the world that night a pallid halo encircled it about. It was perceptibly larger; in the clear refractive* sky of the tropics it seemed as if it were nearly a quarter the size of the moon. The frost was still on the ground in England, but the world was as brightly lit as if it were midsummer moonlight. One could see to read quite ordinary print by that cold, clear light, and in the cities the lamps burnt yellow and wan.

And everywhere the world was awake that night, and throughout Christendom a sombre murmur hung in the keen air over the country-side like the belling of bees in the heather, and this murmurous tumult grew to a clangour in the cities. It was the tolling of the bells in a million belfry towers and steeples, summoning the people to sleep no more, to sin no more, but to gather in their churches and pray. And overhead, growing larger and brighter, as the earth rolled on its way and the night passed, rose the dazzling star.

And the streets and houses were alight in all the cities, the shipyards glared, and whatever roads led to high country were lit and crowded all night long. And in all the seas about the civilized lands, ships with throbbing engines, and ships with bellying sails, crowded with men and living creatures, were standing out to ocean and the north. For already the warning of the master mathematician had been telegraphed all over the world and translated into a hundred tongues. The new planet and Neptune, locked in a fiery embrace, were whirling headlong, ever faster and faster towards the sun. Already every second this blazing mass flew a hundred miles, and every second its terrific velocity increased. As it flew now, indeed, it must pass a hundred million of miles wide of the earth and scarcely affect it. But near its destined path, as yet only slightly perturbed, spun the mighty planet Jupiter and his moons sweeping splendid round the sun. Every moment now the attraction between the fiery star and the greatest of the planets grew stronger. And the result of that attraction? Inevitably Jupiter would be deflected from its orbit into an elliptical path, and the burning star, swung by his attraction wide of its sunward rush, would 'describe a curved path,' and perhaps collide with, and certainly pass very close to, our earth. 'Earthquakes, volcanic outbreaks, cyclones, sea waves, floods, and a steady rise in temperature to I know not what limit'—so prophesied the master mathematician.

And overhead, to carry out his words, lonely and cold and livid blazed the star of the coming doom.

To many who stared at it that night until their eyes ached it seemed that it was visibly approaching. And that night, too, the weather changed, and the frost that had gripped all Central Europe and France and England softened towards a thaw.

But you must not imagine, because I have spoken of people praying through the night and people going aboard ships and people fleeing towards mountainous country, that the whole world was already in a terror because of the star. As a matter of fact, use and wont still ruled the world, and save

for the talk of idle moments and the splendour of the night,
nine human beings out of ten were still busy at their common occupations. In all the cities the shops, save one here
and there, opened and closed at their proper hours, the doctor
and the undertaker plied their trades, the workers gathered
in the factories, soldiers drilled, scholars studied, lovers sought
one another, thieves lurked and fled, politicians planned their
schemes. The presses of the newspapers roared through the
nights, and many a priest of this church and that would not
open his holy building to further what he considered a foolish panic. The newspapers insisted on the lesson of the year
1000*—for then, too, people had anticipated the end. The
star was no star—mere gas—a comet; and were it a star it
could not possibly strike the earth. There was no preced-
ent for such a thing. Common-sense was sturdy everywhere,
scornful, jesting, a little inclined to persecute the obdurate
fearful. That night, at seven-fifteen by Greenwich time, the
star would be at its nearest to Jupiter. Then the world would
see the turn things would take. The master mathematician's
grim warnings were treated by many as so much mere elaborate self-advertisement. Common-sense at last, a little heated
by argument, signified its unalterable convictions by going
to bed. So, too, barbarism and savagery, already tired of
the novelty, went about their nightly business, and, save for
a howling dog here and there, the beast world left the star
unheeded.

And yet, when at last the watchers in the European States
saw the star rise, an hour later, it is true, but no larger than
it had been the night before, there were still plenty awake to
laugh at the master mathematician—to take the danger as if
it had passed.

But hereafter the laughter ceased. The star grew—it grew
with a terrible steadiness hour after hour, a little larger each
hour, a little nearer the midnight zenith,* and brighter and
brighter, until it had turned night into a second day. Had it
come straight to the earth instead of in a curved path, had it

lost no velocity to Jupiter, it must have leapt the intervening gulf in a day; but as it was, it took five days altogether to come by our planet. The next night it had become a third the size of the moon before it set to English eyes, and the thaw was assured. It rose over America near the size of the moon, but blinding white to look at, and *hot*; and a breath of hot wind blew now with its rising and gathering strength, and in Virginia, and Brazil, and down the St Lawrence valley, it shone intermittently through a driving reek of thunder-clouds, flickering violet lightning, and hail unprecedented. In Manitoba was a thaw and devastating floods. And upon all the mountains of the earth the snow and ice began to melt that night, and all the rivers coming out of high country flowed thick and turbid, and soon—in their upper reaches—with swirling trees and the bodies of beasts and men. They rose steadily, steadily in the ghostly brilliance, and came trickling over their banks at last, behind the flying population of their valleys.

And along the coast of Argentina and up the South Atlantic the tides were higher than had ever been in the memory of man, and the storms drove the waters in many cases scores of miles inland, drowning whole cities. And so great grew the heat during the night that the rising of the sun was like the coming of a shadow. The earthquakes began and grew until all down America from the Arctic Circle to Cape Horn, hillsides were sliding, fissures were opening, and houses and walls crumbling to destruction. The whole side of Cotopaxi* slipped out in one vast convulsion, and a tumult of lava poured out so high and broad and swift and liquid that in one day it reached the sea.

So the star, with the wan moon in its wake, marched across the Pacific, trailed the thunder-storms like the hem of a robe, and the growing tidal wave that toiled behind it, frothing and eager, poured over island and island and swept them clear of men: until that wave came at last—in a blinding light and with the breath of a furnace, swift and terrible it came—a wall of water, fifty feet high, roaring hungrily, upon the long coasts of Asia, and swept inland across the plains of China. For a space the star, hotter now and larger and brighter than the sun in its strength, showed with pitiless brilliance the wide and populous country; towns and villages with their pagodas and trees, roads, wide cultivated fields, millions of sleepless people staring in helpless terror at the incandescent sky; and then, low and growing, came the murmur of the flood. And thus it was with millions of men that night—a flight nowhither, with limbs heavy with heat and breath fierce and scant, and the flood like a wall swift and white behind. And then death.

China was lit glowing white, but over Japan and Java and all the islands of Eastern Asia the great star was a ball of dull red fire because of the steam and smoke and ashes the volcanoes were spouting forth to salute its coming. Above was the lava, hot gases and ash, and below the seething floods, and the whole earth swayed and rumbled with the earthquake shocks. Soon the immemorial snows of Thibet and the Himalaya were melting and pouring down by ten million deepening converging channels upon the plains of Burmah and Hindostan. The tangled summits of the Indian jungles were aflame in a thousand places, and below the hurrying waters around the stems were dark objects that still struggled feebly and reflected the blood-red tongues of fire. And in a rudderless confusion a multitude of men and women fled down the broad river-ways to that one last hope of men—the open sea.

Larger grew the star, and larger, hotter, and brighter with a terrible swiftness now. The tropical ocean had lost its phosphorescence, and the whirling steam rose in ghostly wreaths from the black waves that plunged incessantly, speckled with storm-tossed ships.

And then came a wonder. It seemed to those who in Europe watched for the rising of the star that the world must have ceased its rotation. In a thousand open spaces of down and upland the people who had fled thither from the floods and the falling houses and sliding slopes of hill watched for that rising in vain. Hour followed hour through a terrible suspense, and the star rose not. Once again men set their eyes upon the old constellations they had counted lost to them for ever. In England it was hot and clear overhead, though the ground quivered perpetually, but in the tropics, Sirius and Capella and Aldebaran showed through a veil of steam. And when at last the great star rose near ten hours late, the sun rose close upon it, and in the centre of its white heart was a disc of black.

Over Asia it was the star had begun to fall behind the movement of the sky, and then suddenly, as it hung over India, its light had been veiled. All the plain of India from the mouth of the Indus to the mouths of the Ganges was a shallow waste of shining water that night, out of which rose temples and palaces, mounds and hills, black with people. Every minaret was a clustering mass of people, who fell one by one into the turbid waters, as heat and terror overcame them. The whole land seemed a-wailing, and suddenly there swept a shadow across that furnace of despair, and a breath of cold wind, and a gathering of clouds, out of the cooling air. Men looking up, near blinded, at the star, saw that a black disc was creeping across the light. It was the moon, coming between the star and the earth. And even as men cried to God at this respite, out of the East with a strange inexplicable swiftness sprang the sun. And then star, sun, and moon rushed together across the heavens.

So it was that presently to the European watchers star and sun rose close upon each other, drove headlong for a space and then slower, and at last came to rest, star and sun merged into one glare of flame at the zenith of the sky. The moon no longer eclipsed the star but was lost to sight in the brilliance of the sky. And though those who were still alive regarded it for the most part with that dull stupidity that hunger, fatigue, heat and despair engender, there were still men who could perceive the meaning of these signs. Star and earth had been at their nearest, had swung about one another, and the star had passed. Already it was receding, swifter and swifter, in the last stage of its headlong journey downward into the sun.

And then the clouds gathered, blotting out the vision of the sky, the thunder and lightning wove a garment round the world; all over the earth was such a downpour of rain as men had never before seen, and where the volcanoes flared red against the cloud canopy there descended torrents of mud. Everywhere the waters were pouring off the land, leaving mud-silted ruins, and the earth littered like a storm-worn beach with all that had floated, and the dead bodies of the men and brutes, its children. For days the water streamed off the land, sweeping away soil and trees and houses in the way, and piling huge dykes and scooping out Titanic gullies over the country-side. Those were the days of darkness that followed the star and the heat. All through them, and for many weeks and months, the earthquakes continued.

But the star had passed, and men, hunger-driven and gathering courage only slowly, might creep back to their ruined cities, buried granaries, and sodden fields. Such few ships as had escaped the storms of that time came stunned and shattered and sounding their way cautiously through the new marks and shoals of once familiar ports. And as the storms subsided men perceived that everywhere the days were hotter than of yore, and the sun larger, and the moon, shrunk to a third of its former size, took now fourscore days between its new and new.

But of the new brotherhood that grew presently among men, of the saving of laws and books and machines, of the strange change that had come over Iceland and Greenland and the shores of Baffin's Bay, so that the sailors coming there presently found them green and gracious, and could scarce believe their eyes, this story does not tell. Nor of the movement of mankind, now that the earth was hotter, northward and southward towards the poles of the earth. It concerns itself only with the coming and the passing of the star.

The Martian astronomers—for there are astronomers on Mars, although they are very different beings from men—were naturally profoundly interested by these things. They saw them from their own standpoint of course. 'Considering the mass and temperature of the missile that was flung through our solar system into the sun,' one wrote, 'it is astonishing what a little damage the earth, which it missed so narrowly, has sustained. All the familiar continental markings and the masses of the seas remain intact, and indeed the only difference seems to be a shrinkage of the white discolouration (supposed to be frozen water) round either pole.' Which only shows how small the vastest of human catastrophes may seem at a distance of a few million miles.

XXI

THE MAN WHO COULD WORK MIRACLES

A Pantoum in Prose*

IT is doubtful whether the gift was innate. For my own part, I think it came to him suddenly. Indeed, until he was thirty he was a sceptic, and did not believe in miraculous powers. And here, since it is the most convenient place, I must mention that he was a little man, and had eyes of a hot brown, very erect red hair, a moustache with ends that he twisted up, and freckles. His name was George McWhirter Fotheringay—not the sort of name by any means to lead to any expectation of miracles—and he was clerk at Gomshott's. He was greatly addicted to assertive argument. It was while he was asserting the impossibility of miracles that he had his first intimation of his extraordinary powers. This particular argument was being held in the bar of the Long Dragon, and Toddy Beamish was conducting the opposition by a monotonous but effective 'So *you* say,' that drove Mr Fotheringay to the very limit of his patience.

There were present, besides these two, a very dusty cyclist, landlord Cox, and Miss Maybridge, the perfectly respectable and rather portly barmaid of the Dragon. Miss Maybridge was standing with her back to Mr Fotheringay, washing glasses; the others were watching him, more or less amused by the present ineffectiveness of the assertive method. Goaded by the Torres Vedras tactics* of Mr Beamish, Mr Fotheringay determined to make an unusual rhetorical effort. 'Looky here, Mr Beamish,' said Mr Fotheringay. 'Let us clearly understand what a miracle is. It's something contrariwise to the course of nature, done by power of will, something what couldn't happen without being specially willed.'

'So *you* say,' said Mr Beamish, repulsing him.

Mr Fotheringay appealed to the cyclist, who had hitherto been a silent auditor, and received his assent—given with a hesitating cough and a glance at Mr Beamish. The landlord would express no opinion, and Mr Fotheringay, returning to Mr Beamish, received the unexpected concession of a qualified assent to his definition of a miracle.

'For instance,' said Mr Fotheringay, greatly encouraged. 'Here would be a miracle. That lamp, in the natural course of nature, couldn't burn like that upsy-down, could it, Beamish?'

'*You* say it couldn't,' said Beamish.

'And you?' said Fotheringay. 'You don't mean to say—eh?'

'No,' said Beamish reluctantly. 'No, it couldn't.'

'Very well,' said Mr Fotheringay. 'Then here comes someone, as it might be me, along here, and stands as it might be here, and says to that lamp, as I might do, collecting all my will—Turn upsy-down without breaking, and go on burning steady, and—Hullo!'

It was enough to make anyone say 'Hullo!' The impossible, the incredible, was visible to them all. The lamp hung inverted in the air, burning quietly with its flame pointing down. It was as solid, as indisputable as ever a lamp was, the prosaic common lamp of the Long Dragon bar.

Mr Fotheringay stood with an extended forefinger and the knitted brows of one anticipating a catastrophic smash. The cyclist, who was sitting next the lamp, ducked and jumped across the bar. Everybody jumped, more or less. Miss Maybridge turned and screamed. For nearly three seconds the lamp remained still. A faint cry of mental distress came from Mr Fotheringay. 'I can't keep it up,' he said, 'any longer.' He staggered back, and the inverted lamp suddenly flared, fell against the corner of the bar, bounced aside, smashed upon the floor, and went out.

It was lucky it had a metal receiver, or the whole place would have been in a blaze. Mr Cox was the first to speak, and his remark, shorn of needless excrescences, was to the effect that Fotheringay was a fool. Fotheringay was beyond disputing even so fundamental a proposition as that! He was astonished beyond measure at the thing that had occurred. The subsequent conversation threw absolutely no light on the matter so far as Fotheringay was concerned; the general opinion not only followed Mr Cox very closely but very vehemently. Everyone accused Fotheringay of a silly trick, and presented him to himself as a foolish destroyer of comfort and security. His mind was in a tornado of perplexity, he was himself inclined to agree with them, and he made a remarkably ineffectual opposition to the proposal of his departure.

He went home flushed and heated, coat-collar crumpled, eyes smarting, and ears red. He watched each of the ten street lamps nervously as he passed it. It was only when he found himself alone in his little bedroom in Church Row that he was able to grapple seriously with his memories of the occurrence, and ask, 'What on earth happened?'

He had removed his coat and boots, and was sitting on the bed with his hands in his pockets repeating the text of his defence for the seventeenth time, '*I* didn't want the confounded thing to upset,' when it occurred to him that at the precise moment he had said the commanding words he had inadvertently willed the thing he said, and that when he had seen the lamp in the air he had felt that it depended on him to maintain it there without being clear how this was to be done. He had not a particularly complex mind, or he might have stuck for a time at that 'inadvertently willed,' embracing, as it does, the abstrusest problems of voluntary action; but as it was, the idea came to him with a quite acceptable haziness. And from that, following, as I must admit, no clear logical path, he came to the test of experiment.

He pointed resolutely to his candle and collected his mind,

though he felt he did a foolish thing. 'Be raised up,' he said. But in a second that feeling vanished. The candle was raised, hung in the air one giddy moment, and as Mr Fotheringay gasped, fell with a smash on his toilet-table, leaving him in darkness save for the expiring glow of its wick.

For a time Mr Fotheringay sat in the darkness, perfectly still. 'It did happen, after all,' he said. 'And 'ow *I'm* to explain it I *don't* know.' He sighed heavily, and began feeling in his pockets for a match. He could find none, and he rose and groped about the toilet-table. 'I wish I had a match,' he said. He resorted to his coat, and there was none there, and then it dawned upon him that miracles were possible even with matches. He extended a hand and scowled at it in the dark. 'Let there be a match in that hand,' he said. He felt some light object fall across his palm and his fingers closed upon a match.

After several ineffectual attempts to light this, he discovered it was a safety match. He threw it down, and then it occurred to him that he might have willed it lit. He did, and perceived it burning in the midst of his toilet-table mat. He caught it up hastily, and it went out. His perception of possibilities enlarged, and he felt for and replaced the candle in its candlestick. 'Here! *you* be lit,' said Mr Fotheringay, and forthwith the candle was flaring, and he saw a little black hole in the toilet-cover, with a wisp of smoke rising from it. For a time he stared from this to the little flame and back, and then looked up and met his own gaze in the looking-glass. By this help he communed with himself in silence for a time.

'How about miracles now?' said Mr Fotheringay at last, addressing his reflection.

The subsequent meditations of Mr Fotheringay were of a severe but confused description. So far, he could see it was a case of pure willing with him. The nature of his experiences so far disinclined him for any further experiments, at least until he had reconsidered them. But he lifted a sheet of paper, and turned a glass of water pink and then green, and he created a snail, which he miraculously annihilated, and got himself a miraculous new tooth-brush. Somewhere in the small hours he had reached the fact that his will-power must be of a particularly rare and pungent quality, a fact of which he had indeed had inklings before, but no certain assurance. The scare and perplexity of his first discovery was now qualified by pride in this evidence of singularity and by vague intimations of advantage. He became aware that the church clock was striking one, and as it did not occur to him that his daily duties at Gomshott's might be miraculously dispensed with, he resumed undressing, in order to get to bed without further delay. As he struggled to get his shirt over his head, he was struck with a brilliant idea. 'Let me be in bed,' he said, and found himself so. 'Undressed,' he stipulated; and, finding the sheets cold, added hastily, 'and in my nightshirt— no, in a nice soft woollen nightshirt. Ah!' he said with immense enjoyment. 'And now let me be comfortably asleep. . . .'

He awoke at his usual hour and was pensive all through breakfast-time, wondering whether his over-night experience might not be a particularly vivid dream. At length his mind turned again to cautious experiments. For instance, he had three eggs for breakfast; two his landlady had supplied, good, but shoppy,* and one was a delicious fresh goose-egg, laid, cooked, and served by his extraordinary will. He hurried off to Gomshott's in a state of profound but carefully concealed excitement, and only remembered the shell of the third egg when his landlady spoke of it that night. All day he could do no work because of this astonishing new self-knowledge, but this caused him no inconvenience, because he made up for it miraculously in his last ten minutes.

As the day wore on his state of mind passed from wonder to elation, albeit the circumstances of his dismissal from the Long Dragon were still disagreeable to recall, and a garbled account of the matter that had reached his colleagues led to some badinage. It was evident he must be careful how he lifted frangible articles, but in other ways his gift promised more and more as he turned it over in his mind. He intended among other things to increase his personal property by unostentatious acts of creation. He called into existence a pair of very splendid diamond studs,* and hastily annihilated them again as young Gomshott came across the counting-house to his desk. He was afraid young Gomshott might wonder how he had come by them. He saw quite clearly the gift required caution and watchfulness in its exercise, but so far as he could judge the difficulties attending its mastery would be no greater than those he had already faced in the study of cycling. It was that analogy, perhaps, quite as much as the feeling that he would be unwelcome in the Long Dragon, that drove him out after supper into the lane beyond the gasworks, to rehearse a few miracles in private.

There was possibly a certain want of originality in his attempts, for, apart from his will-power, Mr Fotheringay was not a very exceptional man. The miracle of Moses' rod* came to his mind, but the night was dark and unfavourable to the proper control of large miraculous snakes. Then he recollected the story of 'Tannhäuser'* that he had read on the back of the Philharmonic* programme. That seemed to him singularly attractive and harmless. He stuck his walking-stick—a very nice Poona-Penang lawyer*—into the turf that edged the footpath, and commanded the dry wood to blossom. The air was immediately full of the scent of roses, and by means of a match he saw for himself that this beautiful miracle was indeed accomplished. His satisfaction was ended by advancing footsteps. Afraid of a premature discovery of his powers, he addressed the blossoming stick hastily: 'Go back.' What he meant was 'Change back;' but of course he was confused. The stick receded at a considerable velocity, and incontinently came a cry of anger and a bad word from the approaching person. 'Who are you throwing brambles at, you fool?' cried a voice. 'That got me on the shin.'

'I'm sorry, old chap,' said Mr Fotheringay, and then, realising the awkward nature of the explanation, caught nervously at his moustache. He saw Winch, one of the three Immering constables, advancing.

'What d'yer mean by it?' asked the constable. 'Hullo! it's you, is it? The gent that broke the lamp at the Long Dragon!'

'I don't mean anything by it,' said Mr Fotheringay. 'Nothing at all.'

'What d'yer do it for then?'

'Oh, bother!' said Mr Fotheringay.

'Bother indeed! D'yer know that stick hurt? What d'yer do it for, eh?'

For the moment Mr Fotheringay could not think what he had done it for. His silence seemed to irritate Mr Winch. 'You've been assaulting the police, young man, this time. That's what *you* done.'

'Look here, Mr Winch,' said Mr Fotheringay, annoyed and confused, 'I'm sorry, very. The fact is——'

'Well?'

He could think of no way but the truth. 'I was working a miracle.' He tried to speak in an off-hand way, but try as he would he couldn't.

'Working a ——! 'Ere, don't you talk rot. Working a miracle, indeed! Miracle! Well, that's downright funny! Why, you's the chap that don't believe in miracles. . . . Fact is, this is another of your silly conjuring tricks—that's what this is. Now, I tell you——'

But Mr Fotheringay never heard what Mr Winch was going to tell him. He realised he had given himself away, flung his valuable secret to all the winds of heaven. A violent gust of irritation swept him to action. He turned on the constable swiftly and fiercely. 'Here,' he said, 'I've had enough of this, I have! I'll show you a silly conjuring trick, I will! Go to Hades! Go, now!'

He was alone!

Mr Fotheringay performed no more miracles that night, nor did he trouble to see what had become of his flowering stick. He returned to the town, scared and very quiet, and went to his bedroom. 'Lord!' he said, 'it's a powerful gift—an extremely powerful gift. I didn't hardly mean as much as that. Not really. . . . I wonder what Hades is like!'

He sat on the bed taking off his boots. Struck by a happy thought he transferred the constable to San Francisco, and without any more interference with normal causation went soberly to bed. In the night he dreamt of the anger of Winch.

The next day Mr Fotheringay heard two interesting items of news. Someone had planted a most beautiful climbing rose against the elder Mr Gomshott's private house in the Lullaborough Road, and the river as far as Rawling's Mill was to be dragged for Constable Winch.

Mr Fotheringay was abstracted and thoughtful all that day, and performed no miracles except certain provisions for Winch, and the miracle of completing his day's work with punctual perfection in spite of all the bee-swarm of thoughts that hummed through his mind. And the extraordinary abstraction and meekness of his manner was remarked by several people, and made a matter for jesting. For the most part he was thinking of Winch.

On Sunday evening he went to chapel, and oddly enough, Mr Maydig, who took a certain interest in occult matters, preached about 'things that are not lawful.' Mr Fotheringay was not a regular chapel-goer, but the system of assertive scepticism, to which I have already alluded, was now very much shaken. The tenor of the sermon threw an entirely new light on these novel gifts, and he suddenly decided to consult Mr Maydig immediately after the service. So soon as that was determined, he found himself wondering why he had not done so before.

Mr Maydig, a lean, excitable man with quite remarkably long wrists and neck, was gratified at a request for a private conversation from a young man whose carelessness in religious matters was a subject for general remark in the town. After a few necessary delays, he conducted him to the study of the manse,* which was contiguous to the chapel, seated him comfortably, and, standing in front of a cheerful fire—his legs threw a Rhodian arch* of shadow on the opposite wall—requested Mr Fotheringay to state his business.

At first Mr Fotheringay was a little abashed, and found some difficulty in opening the matter. 'You will scarcely believe me, Mr Maydig, I am afraid'—and so forth for some time. He tried a question at last, and asked Mr Maydig his opinion of miracles.

Mr Maydig was still saying 'Well' in an extremely judicial tone, when Mr Fotheringay interrupted again: 'You don't believe, I suppose, that some common sort of person—like myself, for instance—as it might be sitting here now, might have some sort of twist inside him that made him able to do things by his will.'

'It's possible,' said Mr Maydig. 'Something of the sort, perhaps, is possible.'

'If I might make free with something here, I think I might show you by a sort of experiment,' said Mr Fotheringay. 'Now, take that tobacco-jar on the table, for instance. What I want to know is whether what I am going to do with it is a miracle or not. Just half a minute, Mr Maydig, please.'

He knitted his brows, pointed to the tobacco-jar and said: 'Be a bowl of vi'lets.'

The tobacco-jar did as it was ordered.

Mr Maydig started violently at the change, and stood looking from the thaumaturgist* to the bowl of flowers. He said nothing. Presently he ventured to lean over the table and smell the violets; they were fresh-picked and very fine ones. Then he stared at Mr Fotheringay again.

'How did you do that?' he asked.

Mr Fotheringay pulled his moustache. 'Just told it—and there you are. Is that a miracle, or is it black art, or what is it? And what do you think's the matter with me? That's what I want to ask.'

'It's a most extraordinary occurrence.'

'And this day last week I knew no more that I could do

267

things like that than you did. It came quite sudden. It's something odd about my will, I suppose, and that's as far as I can see.'

'Is that—the only thing. Could you do other things besides that?'

'Lord, yes!' said Mr Fotheringay. 'Just anything.' He thought, and suddenly recalled a conjuring entertainment he had seen. 'Here!' he pointed, 'change into a bowl of fish—no, not that—change into a glass bowl full of water with goldfish swimming in it. That's better! You see that, Mr Maydig?'

'It's astonishing. It's incredible. You are either a most extraordinary . . . But no——'

'I could change it into anything,' said Mr Fotheringay. 'Just anything. Here! be a pigeon, will you?'

In another moment a blue pigeon was fluttering round the room and making Mr Maydig duck every time it came near him. 'Stop there, will you?' said Mr Fotheringay; and the pigeon hung motionless in the air. 'I could change it back to a bowl of flowers,' he said, and after replacing the pigeon on the table worked that miracle. 'I expect you will want your pipe in a bit,' he said, and restored the tobacco-jar.

Mr Maydig had followed all these later changes in a sort of ejaculatory silence. He stared at Mr Fotheringay and in a very gingerly manner picked up the tobacco-jar, examined it, replaced it on the table. '*Well!*' was the only expression of his feelings.

'Now, after that it's easier to explain what I came about,' said Mr Fotheringay; and proceeded to a lengthy and involved narrative of his strange experiences, beginning with the affair of the lamp in the Long Dragon and complicated by persistent allusions to Winch. As he went on, the transient pride Mr Maydig's consternation had caused passed away; he became the very ordinary Mr Fotheringay of everyday intercourse again. Mr Maydig listened intently, the tobacco-jar in his hand, and his bearing changed also with the course of the narrative. Presently, while Mr Fotheringay was dealing with the miracle of the third egg, the minister interrupted with a fluttering, extended hand.

'It is possible,' he said. 'It is credible. It is amazing, of course, but it reconciles a number of amazing difficulties. The power to work miracles is a gift—a peculiar quality like genius or second sight; hitherto it has come very rarely and to exceptional people. But in this case . . . I have always wondered at the miracles of Mahomet, and at Yogi's miracles, and the miracles of Madame Blavatsky.* But, of course—— Yes, it is simply a gift! It carries out so beautifully the arguments of that great thinker'—Mr Maydig's voice sank—'his Grace the Duke of Argyll.* Here we plumb some profounder law—deeper than the ordinary laws of nature. Yes—yes. Go on. Go on!'

Mr Fotheringay proceeded to tell of his misadventure with Winch, and Mr Maydig, no longer overawed or scared, began to jerk his limbs about and interject astonishment. 'It's this what troubled me most,' proceeded Mr Fotheringay; 'it's this I'm most mijitly in want of advice for; of course he's at San Francisco—wherever San Francisco may be—but of course it's awkward for both of us, as you'll see, Mr Maydig. I don't see how he can understand what has happened, and I daresay he's scared and exasperated something tremendous, and trying to get at me. I daresay he keeps on starting off to come here. I send him back, by a miracle, every few hours, when I think of it. And, of course, that's a thing he won't be able to understand, and it's bound to annoy him; and, of course, if he takes a ticket every time it will cost him a lot of money. I done the best I could for him, but, of course, it's difficult for him to put himself in my place. I thought afterwards that his clothes might have got scorched, you know—if Hades is all it's supposed to be—before I shifted him. In that case I suppose they'd have locked him up in San Francisco. Of course I willed him a new suit of clothes on him directly I thought of it. But, you see, I'm already in a deuce of a tangle——'

Mr Maydig looked serious. 'I see you are in a tangle. Yes, it's a difficult position. How you are to end it . . .' He became diffuse and inconclusive.

'However, we'll leave Winch for a little and discuss the larger question. I don't think this is a case of the black art* or anything of the sort. I don't think there is any taint of criminality about it at all, Mr Fotheringay—none whatever, unless you are suppressing material facts. No, it's miracles— pure miracles—miracles, if I may say so, of the very highest class.'

He began to pace the hearthrug and gesticulate, while Mr Fotheringay sat with his arm on the table and his head on his arm, looking worried. 'I don't see how I'm to manage about Winch,' he said.

'A gift of working miracles—apparently a very powerful gift,' said Mr Maydig, 'will find a way about Winch—never fear. My dear sir, you are a most important man—a man of the most astonishing possibilities. As evidence, for example! And in other ways, the things you may do. . . .'

'Yes, *I've* thought of a thing or two,' said Mr Fotheringay. 'But—some of the things came a bit twisty. You saw that fish at first? Wrong sort of bowl and wrong sort of fish. And I thought I'd ask someone.'

'A proper course,' said Mr Maydig, 'a very proper course— altogether the proper course.' He stopped and looked at Mr Fotheringay. 'It's practically an unlimited gift. Let us test your powers, for instance. If they really *are* . . . If they really are all they seem to be.'

And so, incredible as it may seem, in the study of the little house behind the Congregational* Chapel, on the evening of Sunday, Nov. 10, 1896,* Mr Fotheringay, egged on and inspired by Mr Maydig, began to work miracles. The reader's attention is specially and definitely called to the date. He will object, probably has already objected, that certain points in this story are improbable, that if any things of the sort already described had indeed occurred, they would have been in all the papers at that time. The details immediately following he will find particularly hard to accept, because among other things they involve the conclusion that he or she, the reader in question, must have been killed in a violent and unprecedented manner more than a year ago. Now a miracle is nothing if not improbable, and as a matter of fact the reader *was* killed in a violent and unprecedented manner in 1896. In the subsequent course of this story that will become perfectly clear and credible, as every right-minded and reasonable reader will admit. But this is not the place for the end of the story, being but little beyond the hither side of the middle. And at first the miracles worked by Mr Fotheringay were timid little miracles—little things with the cups and parlour fitments, as feeble as the miracles of Theosophists,* and, feeble as they were, they were received with awe by his collaborator. He would have preferred to settle the Winch business out of hand, but Mr Maydig would not let him. But after they had worked a dozen of these domestic trivialities, their sense of power grew, their imagination began to show signs of stimulation, and their ambition enlarged. Their first larger enterprise was due to hunger and the negligence of Mrs Minchin, Mr Maydig's housekeeper. The meal to which the minister conducted Mr Fotheringay was certainly ill-laid and uninviting as refreshment for two industrious miracle-workers; but they were seated, and Mr Maydig was descanting in sorrow rather than in anger upon his housekeeper's shortcomings, before it occurred to Mr Fotheringay that an opportunity lay before him. 'Don't you think, Mr Maydig,' he said, 'if it isn't a liberty, I——'

'My dear Mr Fotheringay! Of course! No—I didn't think.'

Mr Fotheringay waved his hand. 'What shall we have?' he said, in a large, inclusive spirit, and, at Mr Maydig's order, revised the supper very thoroughly. 'As for me,' he said, eyeing Mr Maydig's selection, 'I am always particularly fond of a tankard of stout and a nice Welsh rarebit,* and I'll order that. I ain't much given to Burgundy,' and forthwith stout and Welsh rarebit promptly appeared at his command. They sat long at their supper, talking like equals, as Mr Fotheringay presently perceived, with a glow of surprise and gratification, of all the miracles they would presently do. 'And, by-the-by, Mr Maydig,' said Mr Fotheringay, 'I might perhaps be able to help you—in a domestic way.'

'Don't quite follow,' said Mr Maydig, pouring out a glass of miraculous old Burgundy.

Mr Fotheringay helped himself to a second Welsh rarebit out of vacancy, and took a mouthful. 'I was thinking,' he said, 'I might be able (*chum, chum*) to work (*chum, chum*) a miracle with Mrs Minchin (*chum, chum*)—make her a better woman.'

Mr Maydig put down the glass and looked doubtful. 'She's—— She strongly objects to interference, you know, Mr Fotheringay. And—as a matter of fact—it's well past eleven and she's probably in bed and asleep. Do you think, on the whole——'

Mr Fotheringay considered these objections. 'I don't see that it shouldn't be done in her sleep.'

For a time Mr Maydig opposed the idea, and then he yielded. Mr Fotheringay issued his orders, and a little less at their ease, perhaps, the two gentlemen proceeded with their repast. Mr Maydig was enlarging on the changes he might expect in his housekeeper next day, with an optimism that seemed even to Mr Fotheringay's supper senses a little forced and hectic, when a series of confused noises from upstairs began. Their eyes exchanged interrogations, and Mr Maydig left the room hastily. Mr Fotheringay heard him calling up to his housekeeper and then his footsteps going softly up to her.

In a minute or so the minister returned, his step light, his face radiant. 'Wonderful!' he said, 'and touching! Most touching!'

He began pacing the hearthrug. 'A repentance—a most touching repentance—through the crack of the door. Poor woman! A most wonderful change! She had got up. She must have got up at once. She had got up out of her sleep to smash a private bottle of brandy in her box. And to confess it too! ... But this gives us—it opens—a most amazing vista of possibilities. If we can work this miraculous change in *her* ...'

'The thing's unlimited seemingly,' said Mr Fotheringay. 'And about Mr Winch——'

'Altogether unlimited.' And from the hearthrug Mr Maydig, waving the Winch difficulty aside, unfolded a series of wonderful proposals—proposals he invented as he went along.

Now what those proposals were does not concern the essentials of this story. Suffice it that they were designed in a spirit of infinite benevolence, the sort of benevolence that used to be called post-prandial.* Suffice it, too, that the problem of Winch remained unsolved. Nor is it necessary to describe how far that series got to its fulfilment. There were astonishing changes. The small hours found Mr Maydig and Mr Fotheringay careering across the chilly market square under the still moon, in a sort of ecstasy of thaumaturgy, Mr Maydig all flap and gesture, Mr Fotheringay short and bristling, and no longer abashed at his greatness. They had reformed every drunkard in the Parliamentary division, changed all the beer and alcohol to water (Mr Maydig had overruled Mr Fotheringay on this point); they had, further, greatly improved the railway communication of the place, drained Flinder's swamp, improved the soil of One Tree Hill, and cured the vicar's wart. And they were going to see what could be done with the injured pier at South Bridge. 'The place,' gasped Mr Maydig, 'won't be the same place to-morrow. How surprised and thankful everyone will be!' And just at that moment the church clock struck three.

'I say,' said Mr Fotheringay, 'that's three o'clock! I must be getting back. I've got to be at business by eight. And besides, Mrs Wimms——'

'We're only beginning,' said Mr Maydig, full of the

sweetness of unlimited power. 'We're only beginning. Think of all the good we're doing. When people wake——'

"But——,' said Mr Fotheringay.

Mr Maydig gripped his arm suddenly. His eyes were bright and wild. 'My dear chap,' he said, 'there's no hurry. Look'— he pointed to the moon at the zenith—'Joshua!'*

'Joshua?' said Mr Fotheringay.

'Joshua,' said Mr Maydig. 'Why not? Stop it.'

Mr Fotheringay looked at the moon.

'That's a bit tall,' he said, after a pause.

'Why not?' said Mr Maydig. 'Of course it doesn't stop. You stop the rotation of the earth, you know. Time stops. It isn't as if we were doing harm.'

'H'm!' said Mr Fotheringay. 'Well,' he sighed, 'I'll try. Here!'

He buttoned up his jacket and addressed himself to the habitable globe, with as good an assumption of confidence as lay in his power. 'Jest stop rotating, will you?' said Mr Fotheringay.

Incontinently he was flying head over heels through the air at the rate of dozens of miles a minute. In spite of the innumerable circles he was describing per second, he thought; for thought is wonderful—sometimes as sluggish as flowing pitch, sometimes as instantaneous as light. He thought in a second, and willed. 'Let me come down safe and sound. Whatever else happens, let me down safe and sound.'

He willed it only just in time, for his clothes, heated by his rapid flight through the air, were already beginning to singe. He came down with a forcible, but by no means injurious, bump in what appeared to be a mound of fresh-turned earth. A large mass of metal and masonry, extraordinarily like the clock-tower in the middle of the market square, hit the earth near him, ricochetted over him, and flew into stonework, bricks, and cement, like a bursting bomb. A hurtling cow hit one of the larger blocks and smashed like an egg. There was a crash that made all the most violent crashes of his past life

seem like the sound of falling dust, and this was followed
by a descending series of lesser crashes. A vast wind roared
throughout earth and heaven, so that he could scarcely lift
his head to look. For a while he was too breathless and astonished even to see where he was or what had happened.
And his first movement was to feel his head and reassure
himself that his streaming hair was still his own.

'Lord!' gasped Mr Fotheringay, scarce able to speak for
the gale, 'I've had a squeak! What's gone wrong? Storms and
thunder. And only a minute ago a fine night. It's Maydig set
me on to this sort of thing. *What* a wind! If I go on fooling
in this way I'm bound to have a thundering accident! . . .
'Where's Maydig?

'What a confounded mess everything's in!'

He looked about him so far as his flapping jacket would
permit. The appearance of things was really extremely strange.
'The sky's all right anyhow,' said Mr Fotheringay. 'And that's
about all that is all right. And even there it looks like a terrific gale coming up. But there's the moon overhead. Just as
it was just now. Bright as midday. But as for the rest——
Where's the village? Where's—where's anything? And what
on earth set this wind a-blowing? *I* didn't order no wind.'

Mr Fotheringay struggled to get to his feet in vain, and
after one failure, remained on all fours, holding on. He
surveyed the moonlit world to leeward,* with the tails of his
jacket streaming over his head. 'There's something seriously
wrong,' said Mr Fotheringay. 'And what it is—goodness
knows.'

Far and wide nothing was visible in the white glare through
the haze of dust that drove before a screaming gale but
tumbled masses of earth and heaps of inchoate ruins, no
trees, no houses, no familiar shapes, only a wilderness of
disorder, vanishing at last into the darkness beneath the whirling columns and streamers, the lightnings and thunderings
of a swiftly rising storm. Near him in the livid glare was

something that might once have been an elm-tree, a smashed mass of splinters, shivered from boughs to base, and further a twisted mass of iron girders—only too evidently the via-duct—rose out of the piled confusion.

You see, when Mr Fotheringay had arrested the rotation of the solid globe, he had made no stipulation concerning the trifling movables upon its surface. And the earth spins so fast that the surface at its equator is travelling at rather more than a thousand miles an hour, and in these latitudes at more than half that pace. So that the village, and Mr Maydig, and Mr Fotheringay, and everybody and everything had been jerked violently forward at about nine miles per second*—that is to say, much more violently than if they had been fired out of a cannon. And every human being, every living creature, every house, and every tree—all the world as we know it—had been so jerked and smashed and utterly des-troyed. That was all.

These things Mr Fotheringay did not, of course, fully appreciate. But he perceived that his miracle had miscarried, and with that a great disgust of miracles came upon him. He was in darkness now, for the clouds had swept together and blotted out his momentary glimpse of the moon, and the air was full of fitful struggling tortured wraiths of hail. A great roaring of wind and waters filled earth and sky, and peering under his hand through the dust and sleet to windward,* he saw by the play of the lightnings a vast wall of water pouring towards him.

'Maydig!' screamed Mr Fotheringay's feeble voice amid the elemental uproar. 'Here!—Maydig!'

'Stop!' cried Mr Fotheringay to the advancing water. 'Oh, for goodness' sake, stop!

'Just a moment,' said Mr Fotheringay to the lightnings and thunder. 'Stop jest a moment while I collect my thoughts. . . . And now what shall I do?' he said. 'What *shall* I do? Lord! I wish Maydig was about.'

'I know,' said Mr Fotheringay. 'And for goodness' sake let's have it right *this* time.'

He remained on all fours, leaning against the wind, very intent to have everything right.

'Ah!' he said. 'Let nothing what I'm going to order happen until I say "Off!" . . . Lord! I wish I'd thought of that before!'

He lifted his little voice against the whirlwind, shouting louder and louder in the vain desire to hear himself speak. 'Now then!—here goes! Mind about that what I said just now. In the first place, when all I've got to say is done, let me lose my miraculous power, let my will become just like anybody else's will, and all these dangerous miracles be stopped. I don't like them. I'd rather I didn't work 'em. Ever so much. That's the first thing. And the second is—let me be back just before the miracles begin; let everything be just as it was before that blessed lamp turned up. It's a big job, but it's the last. Have you got it? No more miracles, everything as it was—me back in the Long Dragon just before I drank my half-pint. That's it! Yes.'

He dug his fingers into the mould, closed his eyes, and said 'Off!'

Everything became perfectly still. He perceived that he was standing erect.

'So *you* say,' said a voice.

He opened his eyes. He was in the bar of the Long Dragon, arguing about miracles with Toddy Beamish. He had a vague sense of some great thing forgotten that instantaneously passed. You see that, except for the loss of his miraculous powers, everything was back as it had been, his mind and memory therefore were now just as they had been at the time when this story began. So that he knew absolutely nothing of all that is told here—knows nothing of all that is told here to this day. And among other things, of course, he still did not believe in miracles.

'I tell you that miracles, properly speaking, can't possibly happen,' he said, 'whatever you like to hold. And I'm prepared to prove it up to the hilt.'

'That's what *you* think,' said Toddy Beamish, and 'Prove it if you can.'

'Looky here, Mr Beamish,' said Mr Fotheringay. 'Let us clearly understand what a miracle is. It's something contrariwise to the course of nature done by power of Will . . .'

XXII

A VISION OF JUDGMENT

I

Bru-a-a-a.

I listened, not understanding.

Wa-ra-ra-ra.

'Good Lord!' said I, still only half awake. 'What an infernal shindy!'

Ra-ra-ra-ra-ra-ra-ra-ra-ra Ta-ra-rra-ra.

'It's enough,' said I, 'to wake——' and stopped short. Where was I?

Ta-rra-rara—louder and louder.

'It's either some new invention——'

Toora-toora-toora! Deafening!

'No,' said I, speaking loud in order to hear myself. 'That's the Last Trump.'*

Tooo-rraa!

II

THE last note jerked me out of my grave like a hooked minnow.

I saw my monument (rather a mean little affair, and I wished I knew who'd done it), and the old elm tree and the sea view vanished like a puff of steam, and then all about me—a multitude no man could number, nations, tongues, kingdoms, peoples—children of all the ages, in an amphitheatral space as vast as the sky. And over against us, seated on a throne of dazzling white cloud, the Lord God and all the host of his angels. I recognised Azrael by his darkness and Michael* by his sword, and the great angel

279

who had blown the trumpet stood with the trumpet still half raised.

III

'Prompt,' said the little man beside me. 'Very prompt. Do you see the angel with the book?'

He was ducking and craning his head about to see over and under and between the souls that crowded round us. 'Everybody's here,' he said. 'Everybody. And now we shall know——

'There's Darwin,'* he said, going off at a tangent. '*He'll* catch it! And there—you see?—that tall, important-looking man trying to catch the eye of the Lord God, that's the Duke. But there's a lot of people one doesn't know.

'Oh! there's Priggles, the publisher. I have always wondered about printers' overs.* Priggles was a clever man . . . But we shall know now—even about him.

'I shall hear all that. I shall get most of the fun before . . . *My* letter's S.'

He drew the air in between his teeth.

'Historical characters, too. See? That's Henry the Eighth.* There'll be a good bit of evidence. Oh, damn! He's Tudor.'

He lowered his voice. 'Notice this chap, just in front of us, all covered with hair. Paleolithic,* you know. And there again——'

But I did not heed him, because I was looking at the Lord God.

IV

'Is this *all*?' asked the Lord God.

The angel at the book—it was one of countless volumes, like the British Museum Reading-room Catalogue, glanced at us and seemed to count us in the instant.

'That's all,' he said, and added: 'It was, O God, a very little planet.'

The eyes of God surveyed us.

'Let us begin,' said the Lord God.

V

THE angel opened the book and read a name. It was a name full of As, and the echoes of it came back out of the uttermost parts of space. I did not catch it clearly, because the little man beside me said, in a sharp jerk, *'What's* that?' It sounded like 'Ahab' to me; but it could not have been the Ahab of Scripture.

Instantly a small black figure was lifted up to a puffy cloud at the very feet of God. It was a stiff little figure, dressed in rich outlandish robes and crowned, and it folded its arms and scowled.

'Well?' said God, looking down at him.

We were privileged to hear the reply, and indeed the acoustic properties of the place were marvellous.

'I plead guilty,' said the little figure.

'Tell them what you have done,' said the Lord God.

'I was a king,' said the little figure, 'a great king, and I was lustful and proud and cruel. I made wars, I devastated countries, I built palaces, and the mortar was the blood of men. Hear, O God, the witnesses against me, calling to you for vengeance. Hundreds and thousands of witnesses.' He waved his hands towards us. 'And worse! I took a prophet— one of your prophets——'

'One of my prophets,' said the Lord God.

'And because he would not bow to me, I tortured him for four days and nights, and in the end he died. I did more, O God, I blasphemed. I robbed you of your honours——'

'Robbed me of my honours,' said the Lord God.

'I caused myself to be worshipped in your stead. No evil

was there but I practised it; no cruelty wherewith I did not stain my soul. And at last you smote me, O God!'

God raised his eyebrows slightly.

'And I was slain in battle. And so I stand before you, meet for your nethermost Hell! Out of your greatness daring no lies, daring no pleas, but telling the truth of my iniquities before all mankind.'

He ceased. His face I saw distinctly, and it seemed to me white and terrible and proud and strangely noble. I thought of Milton's Satan.*

'Most of that is from the Obelisk,'* said the Recording Angel, finger on page.

'It is,' said the Tyrannous Man, with a faint touch of surprise.

Then suddenly God bent forward and took this man in his hand, and held him up on his palm as if to see him better. He was just a little dark stroke in the middle of God's palm.

'*Did* he do all this?' said the Lord God.

The Recording Angel flattened his book with his hand.

'In a way,' said the Recording Angel, carelessly.

Now when I looked again at the little man his face had changed in a very curious manner. He was looking at the Recording Angel with a strange apprehension in his eyes, and one hand fluttered to his mouth. Just the movement of a muscle or so, and all that dignity of defiance was gone.

'Read,' said the Lord God.

And the angel read, explaining very carefully and fully all the wickedness of the Wicked Man. It was quite an intellectual treat.—A little 'daring' in places, I thought, but of course Heaven has its privileges. . . .

VI

EVERYBODY was laughing. Even the prophet of the Lord whom the Wicked Man had tortured had a smile on his face. The Wicked Man was really such a preposterous little fellow.

'And then,' read the Recording Angel, with a smile that set us all agog, 'one day, when he was a little irascible from over-eating, he——'

'Oh, not *that*,' cried the Wicked Man, 'nobody knew of *that*.

'It didn't happen,' screamed the Wicked Man. 'I was bad—I was really bad. Frequently bad, but there was nothing so silly—so absolutely silly——'

The angel went on reading.

'O God!' cried the Wicked Man. 'Don't let them know that! I'll repent! I'll apologise. . . .'

The Wicked Man on God's hand began to dance and weep. Suddenly shame overcame him. He made a wild rush to jump off the ball of God's little finger, but God stopped him by a dexterous turn of the wrist. Then he made a rush for the gap between hand and thumb, but the thumb closed. And all the while the angel went on reading—reading. The Wicked Man rushed to and fro across God's palm, and then suddenly turned about and fled up the sleeve of God.

I expected God would turn him out, but the mercy of God is infinite.

The Recording Angel paused.

'Eh?' said the Recording Angel.

'Next,' said God, and before the Recording Angel could call the name a hairy creature in filthy rags stood upon God's palm.

VII

'HAS God got Hell up his sleeve then?' said the little man beside me.

'*Is* there a Hell?' I asked.

'If you notice,' he said—he peered between the feet of the great angels—'there's no particular indication of a Celestial City.'

"Ssh!' said a little woman near us, scowling. 'Hear this blessed Saint!'

VIII

'HE was Lord of the Earth, but I was the prophet of the God of Heaven,' cried the Saint, 'and all the people marvelled at the sign. For I, O God, knew of the glories of thy Paradise. No pain, no hardship, gashing with knives, splinters thrust under my nails, strips of flesh flayed off, all for the glory and honour of God.'

God smiled.

'And at last I went, I in my rags and sores, smelling of my holy discomforts——'

Gabriel laughed abruptly.

'And lay outside his gates, as a sign, as a wonder——'

'As a perfect nuisance,' said the Recording Angel, and began to read, heedless of the fact that the saint was still speaking of the gloriously unpleasant things he had done that Paradise might be his.

And behold, in that book the record of the Saint also was a revelation, a marvel.

It seemed not ten seconds before the Saint also was rushing to and fro over the great palm of God. Not ten seconds! And at last he also shrieked beneath that pitiless and cynical exposition, and fled also, even as the Wicked Man had fled, into the shadow of the sleeve. And it was permitted us to see into the shadow of the sleeve. And the two sat side by side, stark of all delusions, in the shadow of the robe of God's charity, like brothers.

And thither also I fled in my turn.

IX

'AND now,' said God, as he shook us out of his sleeve upon the planet he had given us to live upon, the planet that whirled about green Sirius* for a sun, 'now that you understand me and each other a little better, . . . try again.'

Then he and his great angels turned themselves about and suddenly had vanished. . . .

The Throne had vanished.

All about me was a beautiful land, more beautiful than any I had ever seen before—waste, austere, and wonderful; and all about me were the enlightened souls of men in new clean bodies. . . .

XXIII

JIMMY GOGGLES THE GOD

'IT isn't every one who's been a god,' said the sunburnt man. 'But it's happened to me—among other things.'

I intimated my sense of his condescension.

'It don't leave much for ambition, does it?' said the sunburnt man.

'I was one of those men who were saved from the *Ocean Pioneer*. Gummy! how time flies! It's twenty years ago. I doubt if you'll remember anything of the *Ocean Pioneer*?'

The name was familiar, and I tried to recall when and where I had read it. The *Ocean Pioneer*? 'Something about gold dust,' I said vaguely, 'but the precise——'

'That's it,' he said. 'In a beastly little channel she hadn't no business in—dodging pirates. It was before they'd put the kybosh on* that business. And there'd been volcanoes or something and all the rocks was wrong. There's places about by Soona where you fair have to follow the rocks about to see where they're going next. Down she went in twenty fathoms before you could have dealt for whist,* with fifty thousand pounds worth of gold aboard, it was said, in one form or another.'

'Survivors?'

'Three.'

'I remember the case now,' I said. 'There was something about salvage——'

But at the word salvage the sunburnt man exploded into language so extraordinarily horrible that I stopped aghast. He came down to more ordinary swearing, and pulled himself up abruptly. 'Excuse me,' he said, 'but—salvage!'

He leant over towards me. 'I was in that job,' he said.

'Tried to make myself a rich man, and got made a god instead. I've got my feelings——

'It ain't all jam being a god,' said the sunburnt man, and for some time conversed by means of such pithy but unprogressive axioms. At last he took up his tale again.

'There was me,' said the sunburnt man, 'and a seaman named Jacobs, and Always, the mate of the *Ocean Pioneer*. And him it was that set the whole thing going. I remember him now, when we was in the jolly-boat,* suggesting it all to our minds just by one sentence. He was a wonderful hand at suggesting things. "There was forty thousand pounds," he said, "on that ship, and it's for me to say just where she went down." It didn't need much brains to tumble to that. And he was the leader from the first to the last. He got hold of the Sanderses and their brig;* they were brothers, and the brig was the *Pride of Banya*, and he it was bought the diving dress—a second-hand one with a compressed air apparatus instead of pumping. He'd have done the diving too, if it hadn't made him sick going down. And the salvage people were mucking about with a chart he'd cooked up, as solemn as could be, at Starr Race, a hundred and twenty miles away.

'I can tell you we was a happy lot aboard that brig, jokes and drink and bright hopes all the time. It all seemed so neat and clean and straightforward, and what rough chaps call a "cert." And we used to speculate how the other blessed lot, the proper salvagers, who'd started two days before us, were getting on, until our sides fairly ached. We all messed together in the Sanderses' cabin—it was a curious crew, all officers and no men—and there stood the diving-dress waiting its turn. Young Sanders was a humorous sort of chap, and there certainly was something funny in the confounded thing's great fat head and its stare, and he made us see it too. "Jimmy Goggles," he used to call it, and talk to it like a Christian. Asked if he was married, and how Mrs Goggles was, and all the little Goggleses. Fit to make you split. And every blessed day all of us used to drink the health of Jimmy Goggles in rum, and unscrew his eye and pour a glass of rum in him, until, instead of that nasty mackintosheriness,* he smelt as nice in his inside as a cask of rum. It was jolly times we had in those days, I can tell you—little suspecting, poor chaps! what was a-coming.

'We weren't going to throw away our chances by any blessed hurry, you know, and we spent a whole day sounding* our way towards where the *Ocean Pioneer* had gone down, right between two chunks of ropy grey rock—lava rocks that rose nearly out of the water. We had to lay off about half a mile to get a safe anchorage, and there was a thundering row who should stop on board. And there she lay just as she had gone down, so that you could see the top of the masts that was still standing perfectly distinctly. The row ended in all coming in the boat. I went down in the diving-dress on Friday morning directly it was light.

'What a surprise it was! I can see it all now quite distinctly. It was a queer-looking place, and the light was just coming. People over here think every blessed place in the tropics is a flat shore and palm-trees and surf, bless 'em! This place, for instance, wasn't a bit that way. Not common rocks they were, undermined by waves; but great curved banks like iron-work cinder heaps, with green slime below, and thorny shrubs and things just waving upon them here and there, and the water glassy calm and clear, and showing you a kind of dirty gray-black shine, with huge flaring red-brown weeds spreading motionless, and crawling and darting things going through it. And far away beyond the ditches and pools and the heaps was a forest on the mountain flank, growing again after the fires and cinder showers of the last eruption. And the other way forest, too, and a kind of broken—what is it?—amby-theatre* of black and rusty cinders rising out of it all, and the sea in a kind of bay in the middle.

'The dawn, I say, was just coming, and there wasn't much colour about things, and not a human being but ourselves anywhere in sight up or down the channel. Except the *Pride of Banya*, lying out beyond a lump of rocks towards the line of the sea.

'Not a human being in sight,' he repeated, and paused.

'*I* don't know where they came from, not a bit. And we were feeling so safe that we were all alone that poor young Sanders was a-singing. I was in Jimmy Goggles, all except the helmet. "Easy," says Always, "there's her mast." And after I'd had just one squint over the gunwale,* I caught up the bogey, and almost tipped out as old Sanders brought the boat round. When the windows were screwed and everything was all right, I shut the valve from the air-belt in order to help my sinking, and jumped overboard, feet foremost— for we hadn't a ladder. I left the boat pitching, and all of them staring down into water after me, as my head sank down into the weeds and blackness that lay about the mast. I suppose nobody, not the most cautious chap in the world, would have bothered about a look-out at such a desolate place. It stunk of solitude.

'Of course you must understand that I was a greenhorn* at diving. None of us were divers. We'd had to muck about with the thing to get the way of it, and this was the first time I'd been deep. It feels damnable. Your ears hurt beastly. I don't know if you've ever hurt yourself yawning or sneezing, but it takes you like that, only ten times worse. And a pain over the eyebrows here—splitting—and a feeling like influenza in the head. And it isn't all heaven in your lungs and things. And going down feels like the beginning of a lift, only it keeps on. And you can't turn your head to see what's above you, and you can't get a fair squint at what's happening to your feet without bending down something painful. And being deep it was dark, let alone the blackness of the ashes and mud that formed the bottom. It was like going down out of the dawn back into the night, so to speak.

'The mast came up like a ghost out of the black, and then a lot of fishes, and then a lot of flapping red seaweed, and then whack I came with a kind of dull bang on the deck of the *Ocean Pioneer*, and the fishes that had been feeding on the dead rose about me like a swarm of flies from road stuff in summer-time. I turned on the compressed air again— for the suit was a bit thick and mackintoshery after all, in spite of the rum—and stood recovering myself. It struck coolish down there, and that helped take off the stuffiness a bit.

'When I began to feel easier, I started looking about me. It was an extraordinary sight. Even the light was extraordinary, a kind of reddy-coloured twilight, on account of the streamers of seaweed that floated up on either side of the ship. And far overhead just a moony, deep green blue. The deck of the ship, except for a slight list to starboard, was level, and lay all dark and long between the weeds, clear except where the masts had snapped when she rolled, and vanishing into black night towards the forecastle.* There wasn't any dead on the decks, most were in the weeds alongside, I suppose; but afterwards I found two skeletons lying in the passengers' cabins, where death had come to them. It was curious to stand on that deck and recognise it all, bit by bit; a place against the rail where I'd been fond of smoking by starlight, and the corner where an old chap from Sydney used to flirt with a widow we had aboard. A comfortable couple they'd been, only a month ago, and now you couldn't have got a meal for a baby crab off either of them.

'I've always had a bit of a philosophical turn, and I daresay I spent the best part of five minutes in such thoughts before I went below to find where the blessed dust was stored. It was slow work hunting, feeling it was for the most part, pitchy dark, with confusing blue gleams down the companion.* And there were things moving about, a dab at my glass once, and once a pinch at my leg. Crabs, I expect. I kicked a lot of loose stuff that puzzled me, and stooped and picked up something all knobs and spikes. What do you think? Backbone! But I never had any particular feeling for bones. We had talked the affair over pretty thoroughly, and Always knew just where the stuff was stowed. I found it that trip. I lifted a box one end an inch or more.'

He broke off in his story. 'I've lifted it,' he said, 'as near as that! Forty thousand pounds' worth of pure gold! Gold! I shouted inside my helmet as a kind of cheer, and hurt my ears. I was getting confounded stuffy and tired by this time—I must have been down twenty-five minutes or more—and I thought this was good enough. I went up the companion again, and as my eyes came up flush with the deck, a thundering great crab gave a kind of hysterical jump and went scuttling off sideways. Quite a start it gave me. I stood up clear on deck and shut the valve behind the helmet to let the air accumulate to carry me up again—I noticed a kind of whacking from above, as though they were hitting the water with an oar, but I didn't look up. I fancied they were signalling me to come up.

'And then something shot down by me—something heavy, and stood a-quiver in the planks. I looked, and there was a long knife I'd seen young Sanders handling. Thinks I, he's dropped it, and I was still calling him this kind of fool and that—for it might have hurt me serious—when I began to lift and drive up towards the daylight. Just about the level of the top spars of the *Ocean Pioneer*, whack! I came against something sinking down, and a boot knocked in front of my helmet. Then something else, struggling frightful. It was a big weight atop of me, whatever it was, and moving and twisting about. I'd have thought it a big octopus, or some such thing, if it hadn't been for the boot. But octopuses don't wear boots. It was all in a moment, of course. I felt myself sinking down again, and I threw my arms about to keep steady, and the whole lot rolled free of me and shot down as I went up——'

He paused.

'I saw young Sanders's face, over a naked black shoulder, and a spear driven clean through his neck, and out of his mouth and neck what looked like spirts of pink smoke in the water. And down they went clutching one another, and turning over, and both too far gone to leave go. And in another second my helmet came a whack, fit to split, against the niggers' canoe. It was niggers! Two canoes full.

'It was lively times I tell you! Overboard came Always with three spears in him. There was the legs of three or four black chaps kicking about me in the water. I couldn't see much, but I saw the game was up at a glance, gave my valve a tremendous twist, and went bubbling down again after poor Always, in as awful a state of scare and astonishment as you can well imagine. I passed young Sanders and the nigger going up again and struggling still a bit, and in another moment I was standing in the dim again on the deck of the *Ocean Pioneer*.

'Gummy, thinks I, here's a fix! Niggers! At first I couldn't see anything for it but Stifle below or Stabs above. I didn't properly understand how much air there was to last me out, but I didn't feel like standing very much more of it down below. I was hot and frightfully heady, quite apart from the blue funk* I was in. We'd never reckoned with these beastly natives, filthy Papuan beasts. It wasn't any good coming up where I was, but I had to do something. On the spur of the moment, I clambered over the side of the brig and landed among the weeds, and set off through the darkness as fast as I could. I just stopped once and knelt, and twisted back my head in the helmet and had a look up. It was a most extraordinary bright green-blue above, and the two canoes and the boat floating there very small and distant like a kind of twisted H. And it made me feel sick to squint up at it, and think what the pitching and swaying of the three meant.

'It was just about the most horrible ten minutes I ever had, blundering about in that darkness—pressure something awful, like being buried in sand, pain across the chest, sick with funk, and breathing nothing as it seemed but the smell of rum and mackintosh. Gummy! After a bit, I found myself going up a steepish sort of slope. I had another squint to see if anything was visible of the canoes and boats, and then kept on. I stopped with my head a foot from the surface, and tried to see where I was going, but, of course, nothing was to be seen but the reflection of the bottom. Then out I dashed, like knocking my head through a mirror. Directly I got my eyes out of the water, I saw I'd come up a kind of beach near the forest. I had a look round, but the natives and the brig were both hidden by a big hummucky heap of twisted lava. The born fool in me suggested a run for the woods. I didn't take the helmet off, but I eased open one of the windows, and, after a bit of a pant, went on out of the water. You'd hardly imagine how clean and light the air tasted.

'Of course, with four inches of lead in your boot soles, and your head in a copper knob the size of a football, and been thirty-five minutes under water, you don't break any records running. I ran like a ploughboy going to work. And half-way to the trees I saw a dozen niggers or more, coming out in a gaping, astonished sort of way to meet me.

'I just stopped dead, and cursed myself for all the fools out of London. I had about as much chance of cutting back to the water as a turned turtle.* I just screwed up my window again to leave my hands free, and waited for them. There wasn't anything else for me to do.

'But they didn't come on very much. I began to suspect why. "Jimmy Goggles," I says, "it's your beauty does it." I was inclined to be a little light-headed, I think, with all these dangers about and the change in the pressure of the blessed air. "Who're ye staring at?" I said, as if the savages could hear me. "What d'ye take me for? I'm hanged if I don't give you something to stare at," I said, and with that I screwed up the escape valve and turned on the compressed air from the belt, until I was swelled out like a blown frog. Regular imposing it must have been. I'm blessed if they'd come on a step; and presently one and then another went down on their hands and knees. They didn't know what to make of me, and they was doing the extra polite, which was very wise and reasonable of them. I had half a mind to edge back seaward and cut and run, but it seemed too hopeless. A step back and they'd have been after me. And out of sheer desperation I began to march towards them up the beach, with slow, heavy steps, and waving my blown-out arms about, in a dignified manner. And inside of me I was singing as small as a tomtit.*

'But there's nothing like a striking appearance to help a man over a difficulty,—I've found that before and since. People like ourselves, who're up to diving dresses by the time we're seven, can scarcely imagine the effect of one on a simple-minded savage. One or two of these niggers cut and run, the others started in a great hurry trying to knock their brains out on the ground. And on I went as slow and solemn and silly-looking and artful as a jobbing plumber.* It was evident they took me for something immense.

'Then up jumped one and began pointing, making extraordinary gestures to me as he did so, and all the others began sharing their attention between me and something out at sea. "What's the matter now?" I said. I turned slowly on account of my dignity, and there I saw, coming round a point, the poor old *Pride of Banya* towed by a couple of canoes. The sight fairly made me sick. But they evidently expected some recognition, so I waved my arms in a striking sort of non-committal manner. And then I turned and stalked on towards the trees again. At that time I was praying like mad, I remember, over and over again; "Lord help me through with it! Lord help me through with it!" It's only fools who know nothing of danger can afford to laugh at praying.

'But these niggers weren't going to let me walk through and away like that. They started a kind of bowing dance about me, and sort of pressed me to take a pathway that lay through the trees. It was clear to me they didn't take me for a British citizen, whatever else they thought of me, and for my own part I was never less anxious to own up to the old country.

'You'd hardly believe it, perhaps, unless you're familiar with savages, but these poor, misguided, ignorant creatures took me straight to their kind of joss* place to present me to the blessed old black stone there. By this time I was beginning to sort of realise the depth of their ignorance, and directly I set eyes on this deity I took my cue. I started a baritone howl, "wow-wow," very long on one note, and began waving my arms about a lot, and then very slowly and ceremoniously turned their image over on its side and sat down on it. I wanted to sit down badly, for diving dresses ain't much wear in the tropics. Or, to put it different like, they're a sight too much. It took away their breath, I could see, my sitting on their joss, but in less time than a minute they made up their minds and were hard at work worshipping me. And I can tell you I felt a bit relieved to see things turning out so well, in spite of the weight on my shoulders and feet.

'But what made me anxious was what the chaps in the canoes might think when they came back. If they'd seen me in the boat before I went down, and without the helmet on—for they might have been spying and hiding since over night—they would very likely take a different view from the others. I was in a deuce of a stew about that for hours, as it seemed, until the shindy of the arrival began.

'But they took it down—the whole blessed village took it down. At the cost of sitting up stiff and stern, as much like those sitting Egyptian images one sees as I could manage, for pretty nearly twelve hours, I should guess at least, on end, I got over it. You'd hardly think what it meant in that heat and stink. I don't think any of them dreamt of the man inside. I was just a wonderful leathery great joss that had come up with luck out of the water. But the fatigue! the heat! the beastly closeness! the mackintosheriness and the rum! and the fuss! They lit a stinking fire on a kind of lava slab there was before me, and brought in a lot of gory muck—the worst parts of what they were feasting on outside, the Beasts—and burnt it all in my honour. I was getting a bit hungry, but I understand now how gods manage to do without eating, what with the smell of burnt-offerings about them. And they brought in a lot of the stuff they'd got off the brig and, among other stuff, what I was a bit relieved to see, the kind of pneumatic pump that was used for the compressed air affair, and then a lot of chaps and girls came in and danced about me something disgraceful. It's extraordinary the different ways different people have of showing respect. If I'd had a hatchet handy I'd have gone for the lot of them—they made me feel that wild. All this time I sat as stiff as company, not knowing anything better to do. And at last, when nightfall came, and the wattle* joss-house place got a bit too shadowy for their taste—all these here savages are afraid of the dark, you know—and I started a sort of "Moo" noise, they built big bonfires outside and left me alone in peace in the darkness of my hut, free to unscrew my windows a bit and think things over, and feel just as bad as I liked. And Lord! I was sick.

'I was weak and hungry, and my mind kept on behaving like a beetle on a pin, tremendous activity and nothing done at the end of it. Come round just where it was before. There was sorrowing for the other chaps, beastly drunkards certainly, but not deserving such a fate, and young Sanders with the spear through his neck wouldn't go out of my mind. There was the treasure down there in the *Ocean Pioneer*, and how one might get it and hide it somewhere safer, and get away and come back for it. And there was the puzzle where to get anything to eat. I tell you I was fair rambling. I was afraid to ask by signs for food, for fear of behaving too human, and so there I sat and hungered until very near the dawn. Then the village got a bit quiet, and I couldn't stand it any longer, and I went out and got some stuff like artichokes in a bowl and some sour milk. What was left of these I put away among the other offerings, just to give them a hint of my tastes. And in the morning they came to worship, and found me sitting up stiff and respectable on their previous god, just as they'd left me overnight. I'd got my back against the central pillar of the hut, and, practically, I was asleep. And that's how I became a god among the heathen—a false god, no doubt, and blasphemous, but one can't always pick and choose.

'Now, I don't want to crack myself up as a god beyond my merits, but I must confess that while I was god to these people they was extraordinary successful. I don't say there's anything in it, mind you. They won a battle with another tribe—I got a lot of offerings I didn't want through it—they had wonderful fishing, and their crop of pourra* was exceptional fine. And they counted the capture of the brig among the benefits I brought 'em. I must say I don't think that was a poor record for a perfectly new hand. And, though perhaps you'd scarcely credit it, I was the tribal god of those beastly savages for pretty nearly four months. . . .

'What else could I do, man? But I didn't wear that diving-dress all the time. I made 'em rig me up a sort of holy of holies, and a deuce of a time I had too, making them understand what it was I wanted them to do. That indeed was the great difficulty—making them understand my wishes. I couldn't let myself down by talking their lingo* badly, even if I'd been able to speak at all, and I couldn't go flapping a lot of gestures at them. So I drew pictures in sand and sat down beside them and hooted like one o'clock.* Sometimes they did the things I wanted all right, and sometimes they did them all wrong. They was always very willing, certainly. All the while I was puzzling how I was to get the confounded business settled. Every night before the dawn I used to march out in full rig and go off to a place where I could see the channel in which the *Ocean Pioneer* lay sunk, and once even, one moonlight night, I tried to walk out to her, but the weeds and rocks and dark clean beat me. I didn't get back till full day, and then I found all those silly niggers out on the beach praying their sea-god to return to them. I was that vexed and tired, messing and tumbling about, and coming up and going down again, I could have punched their silly heads all round when they started rejoicing. Hanged if I like so much ceremony.

'And then came the missionary. That missionary! *What* a Guy!* Gummy! It was in the afternoon, and I was sitting in state in my outer temple place, sitting on that old black stone of theirs, when he came. I heard a row outside and jabbering, and then his voice speaking to an interpreter. "They worship stocks and stones,"* he said, and I knew what was up, in a flash. I had one of my windows out for comfort, and I sang out straight away on the spur of the moment. "Stocks and stones!" I says. "You come inside," I says, "and I'll punch your blooming Exeter Hall* of a head."

'There was a kind of silence and more jabbering, and in he came, Bible in hand, after the manner of them—a little sandy* chap in specks and a pith helmet.* I flatter myself that me sitting there in the shadows, with my copper head and my big goggles, struck him a bit of a heap at first. "Well," I says, "how's the trade in scissors?"* for I don't hold with missionaries.

'I had a lark with that missionary. He was a raw hand, and quite outclassed by a man like me. He gasped out who was I, and I told him to read the inscription at my feet if he wanted to know. There wasn't no inscription; why should there be? but down he goes to read, and his interpreter, being of course as superstitious as any of them, more so by reason of his seeing missionaries close to, took it for an act of worship and plumped down like a shot. All my people gave a howl of triumph, and there wasn't any more business to be done in my village after that journey, not by the likes of him.

'But, of course, I was a fool to choke him off like that. If I'd had any sense I should have told him straight away of the treasure and taken him into Co. I've no doubt he'd have come into Co. A child, with a few hours to think it over, could have seen the connection between my diving dress and the loss of the *Ocean Pioneer*. A week after he left I went out one morning and saw the *Motherhood*, the salver's ship from Starr Race, towing up the channel and sounding. The whole blessed game was up, and all my trouble thrown away. Gummy! How wild I felt! And guying it in that stinking silly dress! Four months!'

The sunburnt man's story degenerated again. 'Think of it,' he said, when he emerged to linguistic purity once more. 'Forty thousand pounds' worth of gold.'

'Did the little missionary come back?' I asked.

'Oh yes! bless him! And he pledged his reputation there was a man inside the god, and started out to see as much with tremendous ceremony. But there wasn't—he got sold again. I always did hate scenes and explanations, and long before he came I was out of it all—going home to Banya* along the coast, hiding in bushes by day, and thieving food from the villages by night. Only weapon, a spear. No clothes, no money. Nothing. My face, my fortune, as the saying is. And just a squeak of eight thousand pounds of gold—fifth share. But the natives cut up rusty,* thank goodness, because they thought it was him had driven their luck away.'

XXIV

MISS WINCHELSEA'S HEART

MISS WINCHELSEA was going to Rome. The matter had filled her mind for a month or more, and had overflowed so abundantly into her conversation that quite a number of people who were not going to Rome, and who were not likely to go to Rome, had made it a personal grievance against her. Some indeed had attempted quite unavailingly to convince her that Rome was not nearly such a desirable place as it was reported to be, and others had gone so far as to suggest behind her back that she was dreadfully 'stuck up' about 'that Rome of hers.' And little Lily Hardhurst had told her friend Mr Binns that so far as she was concerned Miss Winchelsea might 'go to her old Rome and stop there; *she* (Miss Lily Hardhurst) wouldn't grieve.' And the way in which Miss Winchelsea put herself upon terms of personal tenderness with Horace and Benvenuto Cellini and Raphael and Shelley and Keats*—if she had been Shelley's widow* she could not have professed a keener interest in his grave— was a matter of universal astonishment. Her dress was a triumph of tactful discretion, sensible, but not too 'touristy'— Miss Winchelsea had a great dread of being 'touristy'—and her Baedeker* was carried in a cover of grey to hide its glaring red. She made a prim and pleasant little figure on the Charing Cross platform, in spite of her swelling pride, when at last the great day dawned, and she could start for Rome. The day was bright, the Channel passage would be pleasant, and all the omens promised well. There was the gayest sense of adventure in this unprecedented departure.

She was going with two friends who had been fellow-students with her at the training college, nice honest girls both, though not so good at history and literature as Miss

Winchelsea. They both looked up to her immensely, though physically they had to look down, and she anticipated some pleasant times to be spent in 'stirring them up' to her own pitch of æsthetic and historical enthusiasm. They had secured seats already, and welcomed her effusively at the carriage door. In the instant criticism of the encounter she noted that Fanny had a slightly 'touristy' leather strap, and that Helen had succumbed to a serge jacket with side pockets, into which her hands were thrust. But they were much too happy with themselves and the expedition for their friend to attempt any hint at the moment about these things. As soon as the first ecstasies were over—Fanny's enthusiasm was a little noisy and crude, and consisted mainly in emphatic repetitions of 'Just *fancy*! we're going to Rome, my dear!—Rome!'—they gave their attention to their fellow-travellers. Helen was anxious to secure a compartment to themselves, and, in order to discourage intruders, got out and planted herself firmly on the step. Miss Winchelsea peeped out over her shoulder, and made sly little remarks about the accumulating people on the platform, at which Fanny laughed gleefully.

They were travelling with one of Mr Thomas Gunn's parties*—fourteen days in Rome for fourteen pounds. They did not belong to the personally-conducted party, of course—Miss Winchelsea had seen to that—but they travelled with it because of the convenience of that arrangement. The people were the oddest mixture, and wonderfully amusing. There was a vociferous red-faced polyglot personal conductor in a pepper-and-salt* suit, very long in the arms and legs and very active. He shouted proclamations. When he wanted to speak to people he stretched out an arm and held them until his purpose was accomplished. One hand was full of papers, tickets, counterfoils of tourists. The people of the personally-conducted party were, it seemed, of two sorts; people the conductor wanted and could not find, and people he did not want and who followed him in a steadily growing tail up and down the platform. These people seemed, indeed, to think that their one chance of reaching Rome lay in keeping close to him. Three little old ladies were particularly energetic in his pursuit, and at last maddened him to the pitch of clapping them into a carriage and daring them to emerge again. For the rest of the time, one, two, or three of their heads protruded from the window wailing inquiries about 'a little wicker-work box' whenever he drew near. There was a very stout man with a very stout wife in shiny black; there was a little old man like an aged hostler.*

'What *can* such people want in Rome?' asked Miss Winchelsea. 'What can it mean to them?' There was a very tall curate in a very small straw hat, and a very short curate encumbered by a long camera stand. The contrast amused Fanny very much. Once they heard some one calling for 'Snooks.' 'I always thought that name was invented by novelists,' said Miss Winchelsea. 'Fancy! Snooks. I wonder which *is* Mr Snooks.' Finally they picked out a very stout and resolute little man in a large check suit. 'If he isn't Snooks, he ought to be,' said Miss Winchelsea.

Presently the conductor discovered Helen's attempt at a corner in carriages. 'Room for five,' he bawled with a parallel translation on his fingers. A party of four together—mother, father, and two daughters—blundered in, all greatly excited. 'It's all right, Ma—you let me,' said one of the daughters, hitting her mother's bonnet with a handbag she struggled to put in the rack. Miss Winchelsea detested people who banged about and called their mother 'Ma.' A young man travelling alone followed. He was not at all 'touristy' in his costume, Miss Winchelsea observed; his Gladstone bag* was of good pleasant leather with labels reminiscent of Luxembourg and Ostend, and his boots, though brown, were not vulgar. He carried an overcoat on his arm. Before these people had properly settled in their places, came an inspection of tickets and a slamming of doors, and behold! they were gliding out of Charing Cross Station on their way to Rome.

'Fancy!' cried Fanny, 'we are going to Rome, my dear! Rome! I don't seem to believe it, even now.'

Miss Winchelsea suppressed Fanny's emotions with a little smile, and the lady who was called 'Ma' explained to people in general why they had 'cut it so close' at the station. The two daughters called her 'Ma' several times, toned her down in a tactless, effective way, and drove her at last to the muttered inventory of a basket of travelling requisites. Presently she looked up. 'Lor'!' she said, 'I didn't bring *them*!' Both the daughters said 'Oh, Ma!' But what 'them' was did not appear. Presently Fanny produced Hare's *Walks in Rome*,* a sort of mitigated guide-book very popular among Roman visitors; and the father of the two daughters began to examine his books of tickets minutely, apparently in a search after English words. When he had looked at the tickets for a long time right way up, he turned them upside down. Then he produced a fountain pen and dated them with considerable care. The young man having completed an unostentatious survey of his fellow-travellers produced a book and fell to reading. When Helen and Fanny were looking out of the window at Chislehurst*—the place interested Fanny because the poor dear Empress of the French used to live there— Miss Winchelsea took the opportunity to observe the book the young man held. It was not a guide-book but a little thin volume of poetry—*bound*. She glanced at his face—it seemed a refined, pleasant face to her hasty glance. He wore a little gilt *pince-nez*.* 'Do you think she lives there now?' said Fanny, and Miss Winchelsea's inspection came to an end.

For the rest of the journey Miss Winchelsea talked little, and what she said was as agreeable and as stamped with refinement as she could make it. Her voice was always low and clear and pleasant, and she took care that on this occasion it was particularly low and clear and pleasant. As they came under the white cliffs the young man put his book of poetry away, and when at last the train stopped beside the boat, he displayed a graceful alacrity with the impedimenta of Miss Winchelsea and her friends. Miss Winchelsea 'hated nonsense,' but she was pleased to see the young man perceived at once that they were ladies, and helped them without any violent geniality; and how nicely he showed that his civilities were to be no excuse for further intrusions. None of her little party had been out of England before, and they were all excited and a little nervous at the Channel passage. They stood in a little group in a good place near the middle of the boat—the young man had taken Miss Winchelsea's carry-all there and had told her it was a good place—and they watched the white shores of Albion* recede and quoted Shakespeare and made quiet fun of their fellow-travellers in the English way.

They were particularly amused at the precautions the bigger-sized people had taken against the little waves—cut lemons and flasks prevailed, one lady lay full length in a deck chair with a handkerchief over her face, and a very broad resolute man in a bright brown 'touristy' suit walked all the way from England to France along the deck, with his legs as widely apart as Providence permitted. These were all excellent precautions, and nobody was ill. The personally-conducted party pursued the conductor about the deck with inquiries, in a manner that suggested to Helen's mind the rather vulgar image of hens with a piece of bacon rind, until at last he went into hiding below. And the young man with the thin volume of poetry stood at the stern watching England receding, looking rather lonely and sad to Miss Winchelsea's eye.

And then came Calais and tumultuous novelties, and the young man had not forgotten Miss Winchelsea's hold-all and the other little things. All three girls, though they had passed Government examinations in French to any extent, were stricken with a dumb shame of their accents, and the young man was very useful. And he did not intrude. He put them in a comfortable carriage and raised his hat and went away.

Miss Winchelsea thanked him in her best manner—a pleasing, cultivated manner—and Fanny said he was 'nice' almost before he was out of earshot. 'I wonder what he can be,' said Helen. 'He's going to Italy, because I noticed green tickets in his book.' Miss Winchelsea almost told them of the poetry, and decided not to do so. And presently the carriage windows seized hold upon them and the young man was forgotten. It made them feel that they were doing an educated sort of thing to travel through a country whose commonest advertisements were in idiomatic French, and Miss Winchelsea made unpatriotic comparisons because there were weedy little sign-board advertisements by the rail side instead of the broad hoardings that deface the landscape in our land. But the north of France is really uninteresting country, and after a time Fanny reverted to Hare's *Walks*, and Helen initiated lunch. Miss Winchelsea awoke out of a happy reverie; she had been trying to realise, she said, that she was actually going to Rome, but she perceived at Helen's suggestion that she was hungry, and they lunched out of their baskets very cheerfully. In the afternoon they were tired and silent until Helen made tea. Miss Winchelsea might have dozed, only she knew Fanny slept with her mouth open; and as their fellow-passengers were two rather nice, critical-looking ladies of uncertain age—who knew French well enough to talk it—she employed herself in keeping Fanny awake. The rhythm of the train became insistent, and the streaming landscape outside became at last quite painful to the eye. They were already dreadfully tired of travelling before their night's stoppage came.

The stoppage for the night was brightened by the appearance of the young man, and his manners were all that could be desired and his French quite serviceable. His coupons availed for the same hotel as theirs, and by chance, as it seemed, he sat next Miss Winchelsea at the *table d'hôte*. In spite of her enthusiasm for Rome, she had thought out some such possibility very thoroughly, and when he ventured to make a remark upon the tediousness of travelling—he let the soup and fish go by before he did this—she did not simply assent to his proposition, but responded with another. They were soon comparing their journeys, and Helen and Fanny were cruelly overlooked in the conversation. It was to be the same journey, they found; one day for the galleries at Florence—'from what I hear,' said the young man, 'it is barely enough,'—and the rest at Rome. He talked of Rome very pleasantly; he was evidently quite well read, and he quoted Horace about Soracte.* Miss Winchelsea had 'done' that book of Horace for her matriculation,* and was delighted to cap his quotation. It gave a sort of tone to things, this incident— a touch of refinement to mere chatting. Fanny expressed a few emotions, and Helen interpolated a few sensible remarks, but the bulk of the talk on the girls' side naturally fell to Miss Winchelsea.

Before they reached Rome this young man was tacitly of their party. They did not know his name nor what he was, but it seemed he taught, and Miss Winchelsea had a shrewd idea he was an extension lecturer.* At any rate he was something of that sort, something gentlemanly and refined without being opulent and impossible. She tried once or twice to ascertain whether he came from Oxford or Cambridge, but he missed her timid opportunities. She tried to get him to make remarks about those places to see if he would say 'come up' to them instead of 'go down,'—she knew that was how you told a 'Varsity man. He used the word "Varsity'— not university—in quite the proper way.

They saw as much of Mr Ruskin's Florence* as the brief time permitted; he met them in the Pitti Gallery* and went round with them, chatting brightly, and evidently very grateful for their recognition. He knew a great deal about art, and all four enjoyed the morning immensely. It was fine to go round recognising old favourites and finding new beauties, especially while so many people fumbled helplessly with Baedeker. Nor was he a bit of a prig, Miss Winchelsea said, and indeed she detested prigs. He had a distinct undertone of humour, and was funny, for example, without being vulgar, at the expense of the quaint work of Beato Angelico. He had a grave seriousness beneath it all, and was quick to seize the moral lessons of the pictures. Fanny went softly among these masterpieces; she admitted 'she knew so little about them,' and she confessed that to her they were 'all beautiful.' Fanny's 'beautiful' inclined to be a little monotonous, Miss Winchelsea thought. She had been quite glad when the last sunny Alp had vanished, because of the staccato* of Fanny's admiration. Helen said little, but Miss Winchelsea had found her a trifle wanting on the æsthetic side in the old days and was not surprised; sometimes she laughed at the young man's hesitating, delicate jests and sometimes she didn't, and sometimes she seemed quite lost to the art about them in the contemplation of the dresses of the other visitors.

At Rome the young man was with them intermittently. A rather 'touristy' friend of his took him away at times. He complained comically to Miss Winchelsea. 'I have only two short weeks in Rome,' he said, 'and my friend Leonard wants to spend a whole day at Tivoli* looking at a waterfall.'

'What is your friend Leonard?' asked Miss Winchelsea abruptly.

'He's the most enthusiastic pedestrian I ever met,' the young man replied—amusingly, but a little unsatisfactorily, Miss Winchelsea thought.

They had some glorious times, and Fanny could not think what they would have done without him. Miss Winchelsea's interest and Fanny's enormous capacity for admiration were insatiable. They never flagged—through pictures and sculpture galleries, immense crowded churches, ruins and museums, Judas trees and prickly pears, wine carts and palaces, they admired their way unflinchingly. They never saw a stone pine or a eucalyptus but they named and admired it; they never glimpsed Soracte but they exclaimed. Their common ways were made wonderful by imaginative play. 'Here

Cæsar may have walked,' they would say. 'Raphael may have seen Soracte from this very point.' They happened on the tomb of Bibulus. 'Old Bibulus,' said the young man. 'The oldest monument of Republican Rome!' said Miss Winchelsea.

'I'm dreadfully stupid,' said Fanny, 'but who *was* Bibulus?'

There was a curious little pause.

'Wasn't he the person who built the wall?' said Helen.

The young man glanced quickly at her and laughed. 'That was Balbus,'* he said. Helen reddened, but neither he nor Miss Winchelsea threw any light upon Fanny's ignorance about Bibulus.

Helen was more taciturn than the other three, but then she was always taciturn, and usually she took care of the tram tickets and things like that, or kept her eye on them if the young man took them, and told him where they were when he wanted them. Glorious times they had, these young people, in that pale brown cleanly city of memories that was once the world. Their only sorrow was the shortness of the time. They said indeed that the electric trams and the '70 buildings,* and that criminal advertisement that glares upon the Forum, outraged their æsthetic feelings unspeakably; but that was only part of the fun. And indeed Rome is such a wonderful place that it made Miss Winchelsea forget some of her most carefully prepared enthusiasms at times, and Helen, taken unawares, would suddenly admit the beauty of unexpected things. Yet Fanny and Helen would have liked a shop window or so in the English quarter if Miss Winchelsea's uncompromising hostility to all other English visitors had not rendered that district impossible.

The intellectual and æsthetic fellowship of Miss Winchelsea and the scholarly young man passed insensibly towards a deeper feeling. The exuberant Fanny did her best to keep pace with their recondite admiration by playing her 'beautiful' with vigour, and saying 'Oh! *let's* go,' with enormous appetite whenever a new place of interest was mentioned. But Helen developed a certain want of sympathy towards the end that disappointed Miss Winchelsea a little. She refused to see 'anything' in the face of Beatrice Cenci—Shelley's Beatrice Cenci!—in the Barberini Gallery;* and one day, when they were deploring the electric trams, she said rather snappishly that 'people must get about somehow, and it's better than torturing horses up these horrid little hills.' She spoke of the Seven Hills of Rome as 'horrid little hills'!

And the day they went on the Palatine*—though Miss Winchelsea did not know of this—she remarked suddenly to Fanny, 'Don't hurry like that, my dear; *they* don't want us to overtake them. And we don't say the right things for them when we *do* get near.'

'I wasn't trying to overtake them,' said Fanny, slackening her excessive pace; 'I wasn't indeed.' And for a minute she was short of breath.

But Miss Winchelsea had come upon happiness. It was only when she came to look back across an intervening tragedy that she quite realised how happy she had been pacing among the cypress-shadowed ruins, and exchanging the very highest class of information the human mind can possess, the most refined impressions it is possible to convey. Insensibly emotion crept into their intercourse, sunning itself openly and pleasantly at last when Helen's modernity was not too near. Insensibly their interest drifted from the wonderful associations about them to their more intimate and personal feelings. In a tentative way information was supplied; she spoke allusively of her school, of her examination successes, of her gladness that the days of 'Cram' were over. He made it quite clear that he also was a teacher. They spoke of the greatness of their calling, of the necessity of sympathy to face its irksome details, of a certain loneliness they sometimes felt.

That was in the Colosseum, and it was as far as they got that day, because Helen returned with Fanny—she had taken her into the upper galleries. Yet the private dreams of Miss Winchelsea, already vivid and concrete enough, became now realistic in the highest degree. She figured that pleasant young man lecturing in the most edifying way to his students, herself modestly prominent as his intellectual mate and helper; she figured a refined little home, with two bureaus, with white shelves of high-class books, and autotypes* of the pictures of Rossetti and Burne Jones,* with Morris's wall-papers and flowers in pots of beaten copper. Indeed she figured many things. On the Pincio* the two had a few precious moments together, while Helen marched Fanny off to see the *muro Torto*,* and he spoke at once plainly. He said he hoped their friendship was only beginning, that he already found her company very precious to him, that indeed it was more than that.

He became nervous, thrusting at his glasses with trembling fingers as though he fancied his emotions made them unstable. 'I should of course,' he said, 'tell you things about myself. I know it is rather unusual my speaking to you like this. Only our meeting has been so accidental—or providential—and I am snatching at things. I came to Rome expecting a lonely tour . . . and I have been so very happy, so very happy. Quite recently I have found myself in a position—I have dared to think——. And——'

He glanced over his shoulder and stopped. He said 'Demn!' quite distinctly—and she did not condemn him for that manly lapse into profanity. She looked and saw his friend Leonard advancing. He drew nearer; he raised his hat to Miss Winchelsea, and his smile was almost a grin. 'I've been looking for you everywhere, Snooks,' he said. 'You promised to be on the Piazza steps half-an-hour ago.'

Snooks! The name struck Miss Winchelsea like a blow in the face. She did not hear his reply. She thought afterwards that Leonard must have considered her the vaguest-minded person. To this day she is not sure whether she was introduced to Leonard or not, nor what she said to him. A sort of mental paralysis was upon her. Of all offensive surnames—Snooks!

Helen and Fanny were returning, there were civilities, and the young men were receding. By a great effort she controlled herself to face the inquiring eyes of her friends. All that afternoon she lived the life of a heroine under the indescribable outrage of that name, chatting, observing, with 'Snooks' gnawing at her heart. From the moment that it first rang upon her ears, the dream of her happiness was prostrate in the dust. All the refinement she had figured was ruined and defaced by that cognomen's unavoidable vulgarity.

What was that refined little home to her now, spite of autotypes, Morris papers, and bureaus? Athwart it in letters of fire ran an incredible inscription: 'Mrs Snooks.' That may seem a little thing to the reader, but consider the delicate refinement of Miss Winchelsea's mind. Be as refined as you can and then think of writing yourself down:—'Snooks.' She conceived herself being addressed as Mrs Snooks by all the people she liked least, conceived the patronymic touched with a vague quality of insult. She figured a card of grey and silver bearing 'Winchelsea' triumphantly effaced by an arrow, Cupid's arrow, in favour of 'Snooks.' Degrading confession of feminine weakness! She imagined the terrible rejoicings of certain girl friends, of certain grocer cousins from whom her growing refinement had long since estranged her. How they would make it sprawl across the envelope that would bring their sarcastic congratulations. Would even his pleasant company compensate her for that? 'It is impossible,' she muttered; 'impossible! *Snooks!*'

She was sorry for him, but not so sorry as she was for herself. For him she had a touch of indignation. To be so nice, so refined, while all the time he was 'Snooks,' to hide under a pretentious gentility of demeanour the badge sinister* of his surname seemed a sort of treachery. To put it in the language of sentimental science she felt he had 'led her on.'

There were, of course, moments of terrible vacillation, a period even when something almost like passion bid her throw refinement to the winds. And there was something in her, an unexpurgated vestige of vulgarity that made a strenuous attempt at proving that Snooks was not so very bad a name after all. Any hovering hesitation flew before Fanny's manner, when Fanny came with an air of catastrophe to tell that she also knew the horror. Fanny's voice fell to a whisper when she said *Snooks*. Miss Winchelsea would not give him any answer when at last, in the Borghese,* she could have a minute with him; but she promised him a note.

She handed him that note in the little book of poetry he had lent her; the little book that had first drawn them together. Her refusal was ambiguous, allusive. She could no more tell him why she rejected him than she could have told a cripple of his hump. He too must feel something of the unspeakable quality of his name. Indeed he had avoided a dozen chances of telling it, she now perceived. So she spoke of 'obstacles she could not reveal'—'reasons why the thing he spoke of was impossible.' She addressed the note with a shiver, 'E. K. Snooks.'

Things were worse than she had dreaded; he asked her to explain. How *could* she explain? Those last two days in Rome were dreadful. She was haunted by his air of astonished perplexity. She knew she had given him intimate hopes, she had not the courage to examine her mind thoroughly for the extent of her encouragement. She knew he must think her the most changeable of beings. Now that she was in full retreat, she would not even perceive his hints of a possible correspondence. But in that matter he did a thing that seemed to her at once delicate and romantic. He made a go-between of Fanny. Fanny could not keep the secret, and came and told her that night under a transparent pretext of needed advice. 'Mr Snooks,' said Fanny, 'wants to write to me. Fancy! I had no idea. But should I let him?' They talked it over long and earnestly, and Miss Winchelsea was careful to keep the veil over her heart. She was already repenting his disregarded hints. Why should she not hear of him sometimes—painful though his name must be to her? Miss Winchelsea decided it might be permitted, and Fanny kissed her good-night with unusual emotion. After she had gone Miss Winchelsea sat for

a long time at the window of her little room. It was moonlight, and down the street a man sang 'Santa Lucia' with
almost heart-dissolving tenderness. . . . She sat very still.

She breathed a word very softly to herself. The word was
'*Snooks*.' Then she got up with a profound sigh, and went to
bed. The next morning he said to her meaningly, 'I shall hear
of you through your friend.'

Mr Snooks saw them off from Rome with that pathetic
interrogative perplexity still on his face, and if it had not
been for Helen he would have retained Miss Winchelsea's
hold-all in his hand as a sort of encyclopædic keepsake. On
their way back to England Miss Winchelsea on six separate
occasions made Fanny promise to write to her the longest of
long letters. Fanny, it seemed, would be quite near Mr Snooks.
Her new school—she was always going to new schools—
would be only five miles from Steely Bank, and it was in the
Steely Bank Polytechnic, and one or two first-class schools,
that Mr Snooks did his teaching. He might even see her at
times. They could not talk much of him—she and Fanny
always spoke of 'him,' never of Mr Snooks—because Helen
was apt to say unsympathetic things about him. Her nature
had coarsened very much, Miss Winchelsea perceived, since
the old Training College days; she had become hard and
cynical. She thought he had a weak face, mistaking refinement
for weakness as people of her stamp are apt to do, and when
she heard his name was Snooks, she said she had expected
something of the sort. Miss Winchelsea was careful to spare
her own feelings after that, but Fanny was less circumspect.

The girls parted in London, and Miss Winchelsea returned,
with a new interest in life, to the Girls' High School in which
she had been an increasingly valuable assistant for the last
three years. Her new interest in life was Fanny as a correspondent, and to give her a lead she wrote her a lengthy
descriptive letter within a fortnight of her return. Fanny
answered, very disappointingly. Fanny indeed had no literary gift, but it was new to Miss Winchelsea to find herself

deploring the want of gifts in a friend. That letter was even criticised aloud in the safe solitude of Miss Winchelsea's study, and her criticism, spoken with great bitterness, was 'Twaddle!' It was full of just the things Miss Winchelsea's letter had been full of, particulars of the school. And of Mr Snooks, only this much: 'I have had a letter from Mr Snooks, and he has been over to see me on two Saturday afternoons running. He talked about Rome and you; we both talked about you. Your ears must have burnt, my dear. . . .'

Miss Winchelsea repressed a desire to demand more explicit information, and wrote the sweetest, long letter again. 'Tell me all about yourself, dear. That journey has quite refreshed our ancient friendship, and I do so want to keep in touch with you.' About Mr Snooks she simply wrote on the fifth page that she was glad Fanny had seen him, and that if he *should* ask after her, she was to be remembered to him *very kindly* (underlined). And Fanny replied most obtusely in the key of that 'ancient friendship,' reminding Miss Winchelsea of a dozen foolish things of those old schoolgirl days at the Training College, and saying not a word about Mr Snooks!

For nearly a week Miss Winchelsea was so angry at the failure of Fanny as a go-between that she could not write to her. And then she wrote less effusively, and in her letter she asked point-blank, 'Have you seen Mr Snooks?' Fanny's letter was unexpectedly satisfactory. 'I *have* seen Mr Snooks,' she wrote, and having once named him she kept on about him; it was all Snooks—Snooks this and Snooks that. He was to give a public lecture, said Fanny, among other things. Yet Miss Winchelsea, after the first glow of gratification, still found this letter a little unsatisfactory. Fanny did not report Mr Snooks as saying anything about Miss Winchelsea, nor as looking a little white and worn, as he ought to have been dong. And behold! before she had replied, came a second letter from Fanny on the same theme, quite a gushing letter, and covering six sheets with her loose feminine hand.

And about this second letter was a rather odd little thing that Miss Winchelsea only noticed as she re-read it the third time. Fanny's natural femininity had prevailed even against the round and clear traditions of the Training College; she was one of those she-creatures born to make all her *m*s and *n*s and *u*s and *r*s and *e*s alike, and to leave her *o*s and *a*s open and her *i*s undotted. So that it was only after an elaborate comparison of word with word that Miss Winchelsea felt assured Mr Snooks was not really 'Mr Snooks' at all! In Fanny's first letter of gush he was Mr 'Snooks,' in her second the spelling was changed to Mr 'Senoks.' Miss Winchelsea's hand positively trembled as she turned the sheet over—it meant so much to her. For it had already begun to seem to her that even the name of Mrs Snooks might be avoided at too great a price, and suddenly—this possibility! She turned over the six sheets, all dappled with that critical name, and everywhere the first letter had the form of an *e*! For a time she walked the room with a hand pressed upon her heart.

She spent a whole day pondering this change, weighing a letter of inquiry that should be at once discreet and effectual; weighing, too, what action she should take after the answer came. She was resolved that if this altered spelling was anything more than a quaint fancy of Fanny's, she would write forthwith to Mr Snooks. She had now reached a stage when the minor refinements of behaviour disappear. Her excuse remained uninvented, but she had the subject of her letter clear in her mind, even to the hint that 'circumstances in my life have changed very greatly since we talked together.' But she never gave that hint. There came a third letter from that fitful correspondent Fanny. The first line proclaimed her 'the happiest girl alive.'

Miss Winchelsea crushed the letter in her hand—the rest unread—and sat with her face suddenly very still. She had received it just before morning school, and had opened it when the junior mathematicians were well under way.

Presently she resumed reading with an appearance of great calm. But after the first sheet she went on reading the third without discovering the error:—'told him frankly I did not like his name,' the third sheet began. 'He told me he did not like it himself—you know that sort of sudden, frank way he has'—Miss Winchelsea did know. 'So I said, "couldn't you change it?" He didn't see it at first. Well, you know, dear, he had told me what it really meant; it means Sevenoaks, only it has got down to Snooks—both Snooks and Noaks, dreadfully vulgar surnames though they be, are really worn forms of Sevenoaks. So I said—even I have my bright ideas at times— "If it got down from Sevenoaks to Snooks, why not get it back from Snooks to Sevenoaks?" And the long and the short of it is, dear, he couldn't refuse me, and he changed his spelling there and then to Senoks for the bills of the new lecture. And afterwards, when we are married, we shall put in the apostrophe and make it Se'noks. Wasn't it kind of him to mind that fancy of mine, when many men would have taken offence? But it is just like him all over; he is as kind as he is clever. Because he knew as well as I did that I would have had him in spite of it, had he been ten times Snooks. But he did it all the same.'

The class was startled by the sound of paper being viciously torn, and looked up to see Miss Winchelsea white in the face and with some very small pieces of paper clenched in one hand. For a few seconds they stared at her stare, and then her expression changed back to a more familiar one. 'Has any one finished number three?' she asked in an even tone. She remained calm after that. But impositions ruled high* that day. And she spent two laborious evenings writing letters of various sorts to Fanny, before she found a decent congratulatory vein. Her reason struggled hopelessly against the persuasion that Fanny had behaved in an exceedingly treacherous manner.

One may be extremely refined and still capable of a very

sore heart. Certainly Miss Winchelsea's heart was very sore. She had moods of sexual hostility, in which she generalised uncharitably about mankind. 'He forgot himself with me,' she said. 'But Fanny is pink and pretty and soft and a fool—a very excellent match for a Man.' And by way of a wedding present she sent Fanny a gracefully bound volume of poetry by George Meredith,* and Fanny wrote back a grossly happy letter to say that it was '*all* beautiful.' Miss Winchelsea hoped that some day Mr Senoks might take up that slim book and think for a moment of the donor. Fanny wrote several times before and about her marriage, pursuing that fond legend of their 'ancient friendship,' and giving her happiness in the fullest detail. And Miss Winchelsea wrote to Helen for the first time after the Roman journey, saying nothing about the marriage, but expressing very cordial feelings.

They had been in Rome at Easter, and Fanny was married in the August vacation. She wrote a garrulous letter to Miss Winchelsea, describing her home-coming and the astonishing arrangements of their 'teeny, weeny' little house. Mr Se'noks was now beginning to assume a refinement in Miss Winchelsea's memory out of all proportion to the facts of the case, and she tried in vain to imagine his cultured greatness in a 'teeny weeny' little house. 'Am busy enamelling* a cosy corner,' said Fanny, sprawling to the end of her third sheet, 'so excuse more.' Miss Winchelsea answered in her best style, gently poking fun at Fanny's arrangements, and hoping intensely that Mr Se'noks might see the letter. Only this hope enabled her to write at all, answering not only that letter but one in November and one at Christmas.

The two latter communications contained urgent invitations for her to come to Steely Bank on a visit during the Christmas holidays. She tried to think that *he* had told her to ask that, but it was too much like Fanny's opulent good-nature. She could not but believe that he must be sick of his blunder by this time; and she had more than a hope that he would presently write her a letter beginning 'Dear Friend.' Something subtly tragic in the separation was a great support to her, a sad misunderstanding. To have been jilted would have been intolerable. But he never wrote that letter beginning 'Dear Friend.'

For two years Miss Winchelsea could not go to see her friends, in spite of the reiterated invitations of Mrs Sevenoaks —it became full Sevenoaks in the second year. Then one day near the Easter rest she felt lonely and without a soul to understand her in the world, and her mind ran once more on what is called Platonic friendship. Fanny was clearly happy and busy in her new sphere of domesticity, but no doubt *he* had his lonely hours. Did he ever think of those days in Rome, gone now beyond recalling? No one had understood her as he had done; no one in all the world. It would be a sort of melancholy pleasure to talk to him again, and what harm could it do? Why should she deny herself? That night she wrote a sonnet, all but the last two lines of the octave*— which would not come; and the next day she composed a graceful little note to tell Fanny she was coming down.

And so she saw him again.

Even at the first encounter it was evident he had changed; he seemed stouter and less nervous, and it speedily appeared that his conversation had already lost much of its old delicacy. There even seemed a justification for Helen's description of weakness in his face—in certain lights it *was* weak. He seemed busy and preoccupied about his affairs, and almost under the impression that Miss Winchelsea had come for the sake of Fanny. He discussed his dinner with Fanny in an intelligent way. They only had one good long talk together, and that came to nothing. He did not refer to Rome, and spent some time abusing a man who had stolen an idea he had had for a text-book. It did not seem a very wonderful idea to Miss Winchelsea. She discovered he had forgotten the names of more than half the painters whose work they had rejoiced over in Florence.

It was a sadly disappointing week, and Miss Winchelsea was glad when it came to an end. Under various excuses she avoided visiting them again. After a time the visitor's room was occupied by their two little boys, and Fanny's invitations ceased. The intimacy of her letters had long since faded away.

XXV

A DREAM OF ARMAGEDDON*

THE man with the white face entered the carriage at Rugby. He moved slowly in spite of the urgency of his porter, and even while he was still on the platform I noted how ill he seemed. He dropped into the corner over against me with a sigh, made an incomplete attempt to arrange his travelling shawl, and became motionless, with his eyes staring vacantly. Presently he was moved by a sense of my observation, looked up at me, and put out a spiritless hand for his newspaper. Then he glanced again in my direction.

I feigned to read. I feared I had unwittingly embarrassed him, and in a moment I was surprised to find him speaking.

'I beg your pardon?' said I.

'That book,' he repeated, pointing a lean finger, 'is about dreams.'

'Obviously,' I answered, for it was Fortnum-Roscoe's *Dream States*, and the title was on the cover.

He hung silent for a space as if he sought words. 'Yes,' he said, at last, 'but they tell you nothing.'

I did not catch his meaning for a second.

'They don't know,' he added.

I looked a little more attentively at his face.

'There are dreams,' he said, 'and dreams.'

That sort of proposition I never dispute.

'I suppose——' he hesitated. 'Do you ever dream? I mean vividly.'

'I dream very little,' I answered. 'I doubt if I have three vivid dreams in a year.'

'Ah!' he said, and seemed for a moment to collect his thoughts.

'Your dreams don't mix with your memories?' he asked

320

abruptly. 'You don't find yourself in doubt: did this happen or did it not?'

'Hardly ever. Except just for a momentary hesitation now and then. I suppose few people do.'

'Does *he* say——' he indicated the book.

'Says it happens at times and gives the usual explanation about intensity of impression and the like to account for its not happening as a rule. I suppose you know something of these theories——'

'Very little—except that they are wrong.'

His emaciated hand played with the strap of the window for a time. I prepared to resume reading, and that seemed to precipitate his next remark. He leant forward almost as though he would touch me.

'Isn't there something called consecutive dreaming—that goes on night after night?'

'I believe there is. There are cases given in most books on mental trouble.'

'Mental trouble! Yes. I daresay there are. It's the right place for them. But what I mean——' He looked at his bony knuckles. 'Is that sort of thing always dreaming? *Is* it dreaming? Or is it something else? Mightn't it be something else?'

I should have snubbed his persistent conversation but for the drawn anxiety of his face. I remember now the look of his faded eyes and the lids red stained—perhaps you know that look.

'I'm not just arguing about a matter of opinion,' he said. 'The thing's killing me.'

'Dreams?'

'If you call them dreams. Night after night. Vivid!—so vivid . . . this——' (he indicated the landscape that went streaming by the window) 'seems unreal in comparison! I can scarcely remember who I am, what business I am on . . .'

He paused. 'Even now——'

'The dream is always the same—do you mean?' I asked.

'It's over.'

'You mean?'

'I died.'

'Died?'

'Smashed and killed, and now so much of me as that dream was is dead. Dead for ever. I dreamt I was another man, you know, living in a different part of the world and in a different time. I dreamt that night after night. Night after night I woke into that other life. Fresh scenes and fresh happenings—until I came upon the last——'

'When you died?'

'When I died.'

'And since then——'

'No,' he said. 'Thank God! that was the end of the dream. . . .'

It was clear I was in for this dream. And, after all, I had an hour before me, the light was fading fast, and Fortnum-Roscoe has a dreary way with him. 'Living in a different time,' I said: 'do you mean in some different age?'

'Yes.'

'Past?'

'No, to come—to come.'

'The year three thousand, for example?'

'I don't know what year it was. I did when I was asleep, when I was dreaming, that is, but not now—not now that I am awake. There's a lot of things I have forgotten since I woke out of these dreams, though I knew them at the time when I was—I suppose it was dreaming. They called the year differently from our way of calling the year. . . . What *did* they call it?' He put his hand to his forehead. 'No,' said he, 'I forget.'

He sat smiling weakly. For a moment I feared he did not mean to tell me his dream. As a rule, I hate people who tell their dreams, but this struck me differently. I proffered assistance even. 'It began——' I suggested.

'It was vivid from the first. I seemed to wake up in it

suddenly. And it's curious that in these dreams I am speaking of I never remembered this life I am living now. It seemed as if the dream life was enough while it lasted. Perhaps—— But I will tell you how I find myself when I do my best to recall it all. I don't remember anything clearly until I found myself sitting in a sort of loggia looking out over the sea. I had been dozing, and suddenly I woke up—fresh and vivid—not a bit dreamlike—because the girl had stopped fanning me.'

'The girl?'

'Yes, the girl. You must not interrupt or you will put me out.'

He stopped abruptly. 'You won't think I'm mad?' he said.

'No,' I answered; 'you've been dreaming. Tell me your dream.'

'I woke up, I say, because the girl had stopped fanning me. I was not surprised to find myself there or anything of that sort, you understand. I did not feel I had fallen into it suddenly. I simply took it up at that point. Whatever memory I had of *this* life, this nineteenth-century life, faded as I woke, vanished like a dream. I knew all about myself, knew that my name was no longer Cooper but Hedon, and all about my position in the world. I've forgotten a lot since I woke—there's a want of connection—but it was all quite clear and matter-of-fact then.'

He hesitated again, gripping the window strap, putting his face forward, and looking up to me appealingly.

'This seems bosh to you?'

'No, no!' I cried. 'Go on. Tell me what this loggia was like.'

'It was not really a loggia—I don't know what to call it. It faced south. It was small. It was all in shadow except the semicircle above the balcony that showed the sky and sea and the corner where the girl stood. I was on a couch—it was a metal couch with light striped cushions—and the girl was leaning over the balcony with her back to me. The light of the sunrise fell on her ear and cheek. Her pretty white neck and the little curls that nestled there, and her white shoulder were in the sun, and all the grace of her body was in the cool blue shadow. She was dressed—how can I describe it? It was easy and flowing. And altogether there she stood, so that it came to me how beautiful and desirable she was, as though I had never seen her before. And when at last I sighed and raised myself upon my arm she turned her face to me——'

He stopped.

'I have lived three-and-fifty years in this world. I have had mother, sisters, friends, wife and daughters—all their faces, the play of their faces, I know. But the face of this girl—it is much more real to me. I can bring it back into memory so that I see it again—I could draw it or paint it. And after all——'

He stopped—but I said nothing.

'The face of a dream—the face of a dream. She was beautiful. Not that beauty which is terrible, cold, and worshipful, like the beauty of a saint; nor that beauty that stirs fierce passions; but a sort of radiation, sweet lips that softened into smiles, and grave gray eyes. And she moved gracefully, she seemed to have part with all pleasant and gracious things——'

He stopped, and his face was downcast and hidden. Then he looked up at me and went on, making no further attempt to disguise his absolute belief in the reality of his story.

'You see, I had thrown up my plans and ambitions, thrown up all I had ever worked for or desired, for her sake. I had been a master man away there in the north, with influence and property and a great reputation, but none of it had seemed worth having beside her. I had come to the place, this city of sunny pleasures, with her, and left all those things to wreck and ruin just to save a remnant at least of my life. While I had been in love with her before I knew that she had any care for me, before I had imagined that she would dare—that we should dare—all my life had seemed vain and hollow, dust and ashes. It *was* dust and ashes. Night after night, and through the long days I had longed and desired—my soul had beaten against the thing forbidden!

'But it is impossible for one man to tell another just these things. It's emotion, it's a tint, a light that comes and goes. Only while it's there, everything changes, everything. The thing is I came away and left them in their crisis to do what they could.'

'Left whom?' I asked, puzzled.

'The people up in the north there. You see—in this dream, anyhow—I had been a big man, the sort of man men come to trust in, to group themselves about. Millions of men who had never seen me were ready to do things and risk things because of their confidence in me. I had been playing that game for years, that big laborious game, that vague, monstrous political game amidst intrigues and betrayals, speech and agitation. It was a vast weltering world, and at last I had a sort of leadership against the Gang—you know it was called the Gang—a sort of compromise of scoundrelly projects and base ambitions and vast public emotional stupidities and catchwords—the Gang that kept the world noisy and blind year by year, and all the while that it was drifting, drifting towards infinite disaster. But I can't expect you to understand the shades and complications of the year—the year something or other ahead. I had it all—down to the smallest details—in my dream. I suppose I had been dreaming of it before I awoke, and the fading outline of some queer new development I had imagined still hung about me as I rubbed my eyes. It was some grubby affair that made me thank God for the sunlight. I sat up on the couch and remained looking at the woman, and rejoicing—rejoicing that I had come away out of all that tumult and folly and violence before it was too late. After all, I thought, this is life—love and beauty, desire and delight, are they not worth all those dismal struggles for vague, gigantic ends? And I blamed myself for having ever sought to be a leader when I might have given my days to love. But then, thought I, if I had not spent my early days sternly and austerely, I might have wasted myself upon vain and worthless women, and at the thought all my being went out in love and tenderness to my dear mistress, my dear lady, who had come at last and compelled me—compelled me by her invincible charm for me—to lay that life aside.

'"You are worth it," I said, speaking without intending her to hear; "you are worth it, my dearest one; worth pride and praise and all things. Love! to have *you* is worth them all together." And at the murmur of my voice she turned about.

'"Come and see," she cried—I can hear her now—"come and see the sunrise upon Monte Solaro."

'I remember how I sprang to my feet and joined her at the balcony. She put a white hand upon my shoulder and pointed towards great masses of limestone flushing, as it were, into life. I looked. But first I noted the sunlight on her face caressing the lines of her cheeks and neck. How can I describe to you the scene we had before us? We were at Capri——'

'I have been there,' I said. 'I have clambered up Monte Solaro and drunk *vero Capri*—muddy stuff like cider—at the summit.'

'Ah!' said the man with the white face; 'then perhaps you can tell me—you will know if this was indeed Capri. For in this life I have never been there. Let me describe it. We were in a little room, one of a vast multitude of little rooms, very cool and sunny, hollowed out of the limestone of a sort of cape, very high above the sea. The whole island, you know, was one enormous hotel, complex beyond explaining, and on the other side there were miles of floating hotels, and huge floating stages to which the flying machines came. They called it a Pleasure City. Of course, there was none of that in your time—rather, I should say, *is* none of that *now*. Of course. Now!—yes.

'Well, this room of ours was at the extremity of the cape, so that one could see east and west. Eastward was a great cliff—a thousand feet high perhaps, coldly grey except for one bright edge of gold, and beyond it the Isle of the Sirens, and a falling coast that faded and passed into the hot sunrise. And when one turned to the west, distinct and near was a little bay, a little beach still in shadow. And out of that shadow rose Solaro, straight and tall, flushed and golden-crested, like a beauty throned, and the white moon was floating behind her in the sky. And before us from east to west stretched the many-tinted sea all dotted with little sailing-boats.

'To the eastward, of course, these little boats were gray and very minute and clear, but to the westward they were little boats of gold—shining gold—almost like little flames. And just below us was a rock with an arch worn through it. The blue sea-water broke to green and foam all round the rock, and a galley came gliding out of the arch.'

'I know that rock,' I said. 'I was nearly drowned there. It is called the Faraglioni.'

'*Faraglioni?* Yes, *she* called it that,' answered the man with the white face. 'There was some story—but that——'

He put his hand to his forehead again. 'No,' he said, 'I forget that story.'

'Well, that is the first thing I remember, the first dream I had, that little shaded room and the beautiful air and sky and that dear lady of mine, with her shining arms and her graceful robe, and how we sat and talked in half whispers to one another. We talked in whispers, not because there was any one to hear, but because there was still such a freshness of mind between us that our thoughts were a little frightened, I think, to find themselves at last in words. And so they went softly.

'Presently we were hungry, and we went from our apartment, going by a strange passage with a moving floor, until we came to the great breakfast-room—there was a fountain and music. A pleasant and joyful place it was, with its sunlight and splashing, and the murmur of plucked strings. And we sat and ate and smiled at one another, and I would not heed a man who was watching me from a table near by.

'And afterwards we went on to the dancing-hall. But I

cannot describe that hall. The place was enormous, larger than any building you have ever seen—and in one place there was the old gate of Capri, caught into the wall of a gallery high overhead. Light girders, stems and threads of gold, burst from the pillars like fountains, streamed like an Aurora* across the roof and interlaced, like—like conjuring tricks. All about the great circle for the dancers there were beautiful figures, strange dragons, and intricate and wonderful grotesques bearing lights. The place was inundated with artificial light that shamed the newborn day. And as we went through the throng the people turned about and looked at us, for all through the world my name and face were known, and how I had suddenly thrown up pride and struggle to come to this place. And they looked also at the lady beside me, though half the story of how at last she had come to me was unknown or mistold. And few of the men who were there, I know, but judged me a happy man, in spite of all the shame and dishonour that had come upon my name.

'The air was full of music, full of harmonious scents, full of the rhythm of beautiful motions. Thousands of beautiful people swarmed about the hall, crowded the galleries, sat in a myriad recesses; they were dressed in splendid colours and crowned with flowers; thousands danced about the great circle beneath the white images of the ancient gods, and glorious processions of youths and maidens came and went. We two danced, not the dreary monotonies of your days—of this time, I mean—but dances that were beautiful, intoxicating. And even now I can see my lady dancing—dancing joyously. She danced, you know, with a serious face; she danced with a serious dignity, and yet she was smiling at me and caressing me—smiling and caressing with her eyes.

'The music was different,' he murmured. 'It went—I cannot describe it; but it was infinitely richer and more varied than any music that has ever come to me awake.

'And then—it was when we had done dancing—a man came to speak to me. He was a lean, resolute man, very soberly clad for that place, and already I had marked his face watching me in the breakfasting hall, and afterwards as we went along the passage I had avoided his eye. But now, as we sat in a little alcove smiling at the pleasure of all the people who went to and fro across the shining floor, he came and touched me, and spoke to me so that I was forced to listen. And he asked that he might speak to me for a little time apart.

'"No," I said. "I have no secrets from this lady. What do you want to tell me?"

'He said it was a trivial matter, or at least a dry matter, for a lady to hear.

'"Perhaps for me to hear," said I.

'He glanced at her, as though almost he would appeal to her. Then he asked me suddenly if I had heard of a great and avenging declaration that Gresham* had made. Now, Gresham had always before been the man next to myself in the leadership of that great party in the north. He was a forcible, hard, and tactless man, and only I had been able to control and soften him. It was on his account even more than my own, I think, that the others had been so dismayed at my retreat. So this question about what he had done re-awakened my old interest in the life I had put aside just for a moment.

'"I have taken no heed of any news for many days," I said. "What has Gresham been saying?"

'And with that the man began, nothing loth, and I must confess even I was struck by Gresham's reckless folly in the wild and threatening words he had used. And this messenger they had sent to me not only told me of Gresham's speech, but went on to ask counsel and to point out what need they had of me. While he talked, my lady sat a little forward and watched his face and mine.

'My old habits of scheming and organising reasserted themselves. I could even see myself suddenly returning to the north, and all the dramatic effect of it. All that this man said witnessed to the disorder of the party indeed, but not to its damage. I should go back stronger than I had come. And then I thought of my lady. You see—how can I tell you? There were certain peculiarities of our relationship—as things are I need not tell about that—which would render her presence with me impossible. I should have had to leave her; indeed, I should have had to renounce her clearly and openly, if I was to do all that I could do in the north. And the man knew *that*, even as he talked to her and me, knew it as well as she did, that my steps to duty were—first, separation, then abandonment. At the touch of that thought my dream of a return was shattered. I turned on the man suddenly, as he was imagining his eloquence was gaining ground with me.

' "What have I to do with these things now?" I said. "I have done with them. Do you think I am coquetting with your people in coming here?"

' "No," he said; "but——"

' "Why cannot you leave me alone? I have done with these things. I have ceased to be anything but a private man."

' "Yes," he answered. "But have you thought?—this talk of war, these reckless challenges, these wild aggressions——"

'I stood up.

' "No," I cried. "I won't hear you. I took count of all those things, I weighed them—and I have come away."

'He seemed to consider the possibility of persistence. He looked from me to where the lady sat regarding us.

' "War," he said, as if he were speaking to himself, and then turned slowly from me and walked away.

'I stood, caught in the whirl of thoughts his appeal had set going.

'I heard my lady's voice.

' "Dear," she said; "but if they have need of you——"

'She did not finish her sentence, she let it rest there. I turned to her sweet face, and the balance of my mood swayed and reeled.

' "They want me only to do the thing they dare not do

themselves," I said. "If they distrust Gresham they must settle with him themselves."

'She looked at me doubtfully.

'"But war——" she said.

'I saw a doubt on her face that I had seen before, a doubt of herself and me, the first shadow of the discovery that, seen strongly and completely, must drive us apart for ever.

'Now, I was an older mind than hers, and I could sway her to this belief or that.

'"My dear one," I said, "you must not trouble over these things. There will be no war. Certainly there will be no war. The age of wars is past. Trust me to know the justice of this case. They have no right upon me, dearest, and no one has a right upon me. I have been free to choose my life, and I have chosen this."

'"But *war*——" she said.

'I sat down beside her. I put an arm behind her and took her hand in mine. I set myself to drive that doubt away—I set myself to fill her mind with pleasant things again. I lied to her, and in lying to her I lied also to myself. And she was only too ready to believe me, only too ready to forget.

'Very soon the shadow had gone again, and we were hastening to our bathing-place in the Grotta del Bovo Marino, where it was our custom to bathe every day. We swam and splashed one another, and in that buoyant water I seemed to become something lighter and stronger than a man. And at last we came out dripping and rejoicing and raced among the rocks. And then I put on a dry bathing-dress, and we sat to bask in the sun, and presently I nodded, resting my head against her knee, and she put her hand upon my hair and stroked it softly and I dozed. And behold! as it were with the snapping of the string of a violin, I was awakening, and I was in my own bed in Liverpool, in the life of to-day.

'Only for a time I could not believe that all these vivid moments had been no more than the substance of a dream.

'In truth, I could not believe it a dream, for all the sobering reality of things about me. I bathed and dressed as it were by habit, and as I shaved I argued why I of all men should leave the woman I loved to go back to fantastic politics in the hard and strenuous north. Even if Gresham did force the world back to war, what was that to me? I was a man, with the heart of a man, and why should I feel the responsibility of a deity for the way the world might go?

'You know that is not quite the way I think about affairs, about my real affairs. I am a solicitor, you know, with a point of view.

'The vision was so real, you must understand, so utterly unlike a dream, that I kept perpetually recalling little irrelevant details; even the ornament of a book-cover that lay on my wife's sewing-machine in the breakfast-room recalled with the utmost vividness the gilt line that ran about the seat in the alcove where I had talked with the messenger from my deserted party. Have you ever heard of a dream that had a quality like that?'

'Like——?'

'So that afterwards you remembered little details you had forgotten.'

I thought. I had never noticed the point before, but he was right.

'Never,' I said. 'That is what you never seem to do with dreams.'

'No,' he answered. 'But that is just what I did. I am a solicitor, you must understand, in Liverpool, and I could not help wondering what the clients and business people I found myself talking to in my office would think if I told them suddenly I was in love with a girl who would be born a couple of hundred years or so hence, and worried about the politics of my great-great-great-grandchildren. I was chiefly busy that day negotiating a ninety-nine-year building lease. It was a private builder in a hurry, and we wanted to tie him in every possible way. I had an interview with him, and he showed a certain want of temper that sent me to bed still irritated. That night I had no dream. Nor did I dream the next night, at least, to remember.

'Something of that intense reality of conviction vanished. I began to feel sure it *was* a dream. And then it came again.

'When the dream came again, nearly four days later, it was very different. I think it certain that four days had also elapsed in the dream. Many things had happened in the north, and the shadow of them was back again between us, and this time it was not so easily dispelled. I began, I know, with moody musings. Why, in spite of all, should I go back, go back for all the rest of my days, to toil and stress, insults, and perpetual dissatisfaction, simply to save hundreds of millions of common people, whom I did not love, whom too often I could not do other than despise, from the stress and anguish of war and infinite misrule? And, after all, I might fail. *They* all sought their own narrow ends, and why should not I— why should not I also live as a man? And out of such thoughts her voice summoned me, and I lifted my eyes.

'I found myself awake and walking. We had come out above the Pleasure City, we were near the summit of Monte Solaro and looking towards the bay. It was the late afternoon and very clear. Far away to the left Ischia hung in a golden haze between sea and sky, and Naples was coldly white against the hills, and before us was Vesuvius with a tall and slender streamer feathering at last towards the south, and the ruins of Torre dell' Annunziata and Castellammare glittering and near.'

I interrupted suddenly: 'You have been to Capri, of course?'

'Only in this dream,' he said, 'only in this dream. All across the bay beyond Sorrento were the floating palaces of the Pleasure City moored and chained. And northward were the broad floating stages that received the aeroplanes. Aeroplanes fell out of the sky every afternoon, each bringing its thousands of pleasure-seekers from the uttermost parts of the earth to Capri and its delights. All these things, I say, stretched below.

'But we noticed them only incidentally because of an un-usual sight that evening had to show. Five war aeroplanes that had long slumbered useless in the distant arsenals of the Rhine-mouth were manœuvring now in the eastward sky. Gresham had astonished the world by producing them and others, and sending them to circle here and there. It was the threat material in the great game of bluff he was playing, and it had taken even me by surprise. He was one of those incredibly stupid energetic people who seem sent by heaven to create disasters. His energy to the first glance seemed so wonderfully like capacity! But he had no imagination, no invention, only a stupid, vast, driving force of will, and a mad faith in his stupid idiot "luck" to pull him through. I remember how we stood out upon the headland watching the squadron circling far away, and how I weighed the full meaning of the sight, seeing clearly the way things must go. And then even it was not too late. I might have gone back, I think, and saved the world. The people of the north would follow me, I knew, granted only that in one thing I respected their moral standards. The east and south would trust me as they would trust no other northern man. And I knew I had only to put it to her and she would have let me go. . . . Not because she did not love me!

'Only I did not want to go; my will was all the other way about. I had so newly thrown off the incubus of responsibility: I was still so fresh a renegade from duty that the daylight clearness of what I *ought* to do had no power at all to touch my will. My will was to live, to gather pleasures, and make my dear lady happy. But though this sense of vast neglected duties had no power to draw me, it could make me silent and preoccupied, it robbed the days I had spent of half their brightness and roused me into dark meditations in the silence of the night. And as I stood and watched Gresham's aeroplanes sweep to and fro—those birds of infinite ill omen—she stood beside me, watching me, perceiving the trouble indeed, but not perceiving it clearly—her eyes questioning my face, her

334

expression shaded with perplexity. Her face was grey because the sunset was fading out of the sky. It was no fault of hers that she held me. She had asked me to go from her, and again in the night-time and with tears she had asked me to go.

'At last it was the sense of her that roused me from my mood. I turned upon her suddenly and challenged her to race down the mountain slopes. "No," she said, as if I jarred with her gravity, but I was resolved to end that gravity and made her run—no one can be very grey and sad who is out of breath—and when she stumbled I ran with my hand beneath her arm. We ran down past a couple of men, who turned back staring in astonishment at my behaviour—they must have recognised my face. And half-way down the slope came a tumult in the air—clang-clank, clang-clank—and we stopped, and presently over the hill-crest those war things came flying one behind the other.'

The man seemed hesitating on the verge of a description.

'What were they like?' I asked.

'They had never fought,' he said. 'They were just like our ironclads* are nowadays; they had never fought. No one knew what they might do, with excited men inside them; few even cared to speculate. They were great driving things shaped like spear-heads without a shaft, with a propeller in the place of the shaft.'

'Steel?'

'Not steel.'

'Aluminium?'

'No, no, nothing of that sort. An alloy that was very common—as common as brass, for example. It was called— let me see——' He squeezed his forehead with the fingers of one hand. 'I am forgetting everything,' he said.

'And they carried guns?'

'Little guns, firing high explosive shells. They fired the guns backwards, out of the base of the leaf, so to speak, and rammed with the beak. That was the theory, you know, but they had never been fought. No one could tell exactly what was going to happen. And meanwhile I suppose it was very fine to go whirling through the air like a flight of young swallows, swift and easy. I guess the captains tried not to think too clearly what the real thing would be like. And these flying war machines, you know, were only one sort of the endless war contrivances that had been invented and had fallen into abeyance during the long peace. There were all sorts of these things that people were routing out and furbishing up; infernal things, silly things; things that had never been tried; big engines, terrible explosives, great guns. You know the silly way of these ingenious sort of men who make these things; they turn 'em out as beavers build dams, and with no more sense of the rivers they're going to divert and the lands they're going to flood!

'As we went down the winding stepway to our hotel again in the twilight I foresaw it all: I saw how clearly and inevitably things were driving for war in Gresham's silly, violent hands, and I had some inkling of what war was bound to be under these new conditions. And even then, though I knew it was drawing near the limit of my opportunity, I could find no will to go back.'

He sighed.

'That was my last chance.

'We did not go into the city until the sky was full of stars, so we walked out upon the high terrace, to and fro, and—she counselled me to go back.

'"My dearest," she said, and her sweet face looked up to me, "this is Death. This life you lead is Death. Go back to them, go back to your duty——"

'She began to weep, saying between her sobs, and clinging to my arm as she said it, "Go back—go back."

'Then suddenly she fell mute, and glancing down at her face, I read in an instant the thing she had thought to do. It was one of those moments when one *sees*.

'"No!" I said.

336

'"No?" she asked, in surprise, and I think a little fearful at the answer to her thought.

'"Nothing," I said, "shall send me back. Nothing! I have chosen. Love, I have chosen, and the world must go. Whatever happens, I will live this life—I will live for *you*! It—nothing shall turn me aside; nothing, my dear one. Even if you died—even if you died——"

'"Yes?" she murmured, softly.

'"Then—I also would die."

'And before she could speak again I began to talk, talking eloquently—as I *could* do in that life—talking to exalt love, to make the life we were living seem heroic and glorious; and the thing I was deserting something hard and enormously ignoble that it was a fine thing to set aside. I bent all my mind to throw that glamour upon it, seeking not only to convert her but myself to that. We talked, and she clung to me, torn too between all that she deemed noble and all that she knew was sweet. And at last I did make it heroic, made all the thickening disaster of the world only a sort of glorious setting to our unparalleled love, and we two poor foolish souls strutted there at last, clad in that splendid delusion, drunken rather with that glorious delusion, under the still stars.

'And so my moment passed.

'It was my last chance. Even as we went to and fro there, the leaders of the south and east were gathering their resolve, and the hot answer that shattered Gresham's bluffing for ever took shape and waited. And all over Asia, and the ocean, and the south, the air and the wires were throbbing with their warnings to prepare—prepare.

'No one living, you know, knew what war was; no one could imagine, with all these new inventions, what horror war might bring. I believe most people still believed it would be a matter of bright uniforms and shouting charges and triumphs and flags and bands—in a time when half the world drew its food-supply from regions ten thousand miles away——'

The man with the white face paused. I glanced at him, and his face was intent on the floor of the carriage. A little railway station, a string of loaded trucks, a signal-box, and the back of a cottage shot by the carriage window, and a bridge passed with a clap of noise, echoing the tumult of the train.

'After that,' he said, 'I dreamt often. For three weeks of nights that dream was my life. And the worst of it was there were nights when I could not dream, when I lay tossing on a bed in *this* accursed life; and *there*—somewhere lost to me—things were happening—momentous, terrible things. . . . I lived at nights—my days, my waking days, this life I am living now, became a faded, far-away dream, a drab setting, the cover of the book.'

He thought.

'I could tell you all, tell you every little thing in the dream, but as to what I did in the daytime—no. I could not tell—I do not remember. My memory—my memory has gone. The business of life slips from me——'

He leant forward, and pressed his hands upon his eyes. For a long time he said nothing.

'And then?' said I.

'The war burst like a hurricane.'

He stared before him at unspeakable things.

'And then?' I urged again.

'One touch of unreality,' he said, in the low tone of a man who speaks to himself, 'and they would have been nightmares. But they were not nightmares—they were not nightmares. *No!*'

He was silent for so long that it dawned upon me that there was a danger of losing the rest of the story. But he went on talking again in the same tone of questioning self-communion.

'What was there to do but flight? I had not thought the war would touch Capri—I had seemed to see Capri as being out of it all, as the contrast to it all; but two nights after the whole place was shouting and bawling, every woman almost and every other man wore a badge—Gresham's badge—and there was no music but a jangling war-song over and over again, and everywhere men enlisting, and in the dancing halls they were drilling. The whole island was a-whirl with rumours; it was said, again and again, that fighting had begun. I had not expected this. I had seen so little of the life of pleasure that I had failed to reckon with this violence of the amateurs. And as for me, I was out of it. I was like a man who might have prevented the firing of a magazine.* The time had gone. I was no one; the vainest stripling with a badge counted for more than I. The crowd jostled us and bawled in our ears; that accursed song deafened us; a woman shrieked at my lady because no badge was on her, and we two went back to our own place again, ruffled and insulted— my lady white and silent, and I a-quiver with rage. So furious was I, I could have quarrelled with her if I could have found one shade of accusation in her eyes.

'All my magnificence had gone from me. I walked up and down our rock cell, and outside was the darkling sea and a light to the southward that flared and passed and came again.

'"We must get out of this place," I said over and over. "I have made my choice, and I will have no hand in these troubles. I will have nothing of this war. We have taken our lives out of all these things. This is no refuge for us. Let us go."

'And the next day we were already in flight from the war that covered the world.

'And all the rest was Flight—all the rest was Flight.'

He mused darkly.

'How much was there of it?'

He made no answer.

'How many days?'

His face was white and drawn and his hands were clenched. He took no heed of my curiosity.

I tried to draw him back to his story with questions.

'Where did you go?' I said.

'When?'

'When you left Capri.'

'South-west,' he said, and glanced at me for a second. 'We went in a boat.'

'But I should have thought an aeroplane?'

'They had been seized.'

I questioned him no more. Presently I thought he was beginning again. He broke out in an argumentative monotone:

'But why should it be? If, indeed, this battle, this slaughter and stress, *is* life, why have we this craving for pleasure and beauty? If there *is* no refuge, if there is no place of peace, and if all our dreams of quiet places are a folly and a snare, why have we such dreams? Surely it was no ignoble cravings, no base intentions, had brought us to this; it was love had isolated us. Love had come to me with her eyes and robed in her beauty, more glorious than all else in life, in the very shape and colour of life, and summoned me away. I had silenced all the voices, I had answered all the questions—I had come to her. And suddenly there was nothing but War and Death!'

I had an inspiration. 'After all,' I said, 'it could have been only a dream.'

'A dream!' he cried, flaming upon me, 'a dream—when, even now——'

For the first time he became animated. A faint flush crept into his cheek. He raised his open hand and clenched it, and dropped it to his knee. He spoke, looking away from me, and for all the rest of the time he looked away. 'We are but phantoms,' he said, 'and the phantoms of phantoms, desires like cloud shadows and wills of straw that eddy in the wind; the days pass, use and wont carry us through as a train carries the shadow of its lights—so be it! But one thing is real and certain, one thing is no dream stuff, but eternal and enduring. It is the centre of my life, and all other things about it are subordinate or altogether vain. I loved her, that woman of a dream. And she and I are dead together!'

'A dream! How can it be a dream, when it drenched a living life with unappeasable sorrow, when it makes all that I have lived for and cared for worthless and unmeaning?

'Until that very moment when she was killed I believed we had still a chance of getting away,' he said. 'All through the night and morning that we sailed across the sea from Capri to Salerno we talked of escape. We were full of hope, and it clung about us to the end, hope for the life together we should lead, out of it all, out of the battle and struggle, the wild and empty passions, the empty, arbitrary "thou shalt" and "thou shalt not" of the world. We were uplifted, as though our quest was a holy thing, as though love for one another was a mission. . . .

'Even when from our boat we saw the fair face of that great rock Capri—already scarred and gashed by the gun emplacements and hiding-places that were to make it a fastness—we reckoned nothing of the imminent slaughter, though the fury of preparation hung about in puffs and clouds of dust at a hundred points amidst the grey; but, indeed, I made a text of that and talked. There, you know, was the rock, still beautiful for all its scars, with its countless windows and arches and ways, tier upon tier, for a thousand feet, a vast carving of grey, broken by vine-clad terraces, and lemon and orange groves, and masses of agave and prickly pear, and puffs of almond blossom. And out under the archway that is built over the Piccola Marina other boats were coming; and as we came round the cape and within sight of the mainland, another little string of boats came into view, driving before the wind towards the south-west. In a little while a multitude had come out, the remoter just little specks of ultramarine in the shadow of the eastward cliff.

'"It is love and reason," I said, "fleeing from all this madness of war."

'And though we presently saw a squadron of aeroplanes flying across the southern sky we did not heed it. There it was—a line of little dots in the sky—and then more, dotting the south-eastern horizon, and then still more, until all that quarter of the sky was stippled with blue specks. Now they were all thin little strokes of blue, and now one and now a multitude would heel and catch the sun and become short flashes of light. They came, rising and falling and growing larger, like some huge flight of gulls or rooks or such-like birds, moving with a marvellous uniformity, and ever as they drew nearer they spread over a greater width of sky. The southward wing flung itself in an arrow-headed cloud athwart the sun. And then suddenly they swept round to the eastward and streamed eastward, growing smaller and smaller and clearer and clearer again until they vanished from the sky. And after that we noted to the northward, and very high, Gresham's fighting machines hanging high over Naples like an evening swarm of gnats.

'It seemed to have no more to do with us than a flight of birds.

'Even the mutter of guns far away in the south-east seemed to us to signify nothing. . . .

'Each day, each dream after that, we were still exalted, still seeking that refuge where we might live and love. Fatigue had come upon us, pain and many distresses. For though we were dusty and stained by our toilsome tramping, and half starved, and with the horror of the dead men we had seen and the flight of the peasants—for very soon a gust of fighting swept up the peninsula*—with these things haunting our minds it still resulted only in a deepening resolution to escape. Oh, but she was brave and patient! She who had never faced hardship and exposure had courage for herself—and me. We went to and fro seeking an outlet, over a country all commandeered and ransacked by the gathering hosts of war. Always we went on foot. At first there were other fugitives, but we did not mingle with them. Some escaped northward, some were caught in the torrent of peasantry that swept along the main roads; many gave themselves into the hands of the soldiery and were sent northward. Many of the men were impressed.* But we kept away from these things; we had brought no money to bribe a passage north, and I feared for my lady at the hands of these conscript crowds. We had landed at Salerno, and we had been turned back from Cava, and we had tried to cross towards Taranto by a pass over Mount Alburno, but we had been driven back for want of food, and so we had come down among the marshes by Pæstum, where those great temples stand alone. I had some vague idea that by Pæstum it might be possible to find a boat or something, and take once more to sea. And there it was the battle overtook us.

'A sort of soul-blindness had me. Plainly I could see that we were being hemmed in; that the great net of that giant Warfare had us in its toils. Many times we had seen the levies that had come down from the north going to and fro, and had come upon them in the distance amidst the mountains making ways for the ammunition and preparing the mounting of the guns. Once we fancied they had fired at us, taking us for spies—at any rate a shot had gone shuddering over us. Several times we had hidden in woods from hovering aeroplanes.

'But all these things do not matter now, these nights of flight and pain. . . . We were in an open place near those great temples at Pæstum, at last, on a blank stony place dotted with spiky bushes, empty and desolate and so flat that a grove of eucalyptus far away showed to the feet of its stems. How I can see it! My lady was sitting down under a bush resting a little, for she was very weak and weary, and I was standing up watching to see if I could tell the distance of the firing that came and went. They were still, you know, fighting far from each other, with these terrible new weapons that had never before been used: guns that would carry beyond sight, and aeroplanes that would do—— What *they* would do no man could foretell.

343

'I knew that we were between the two armies, and that they drew together. I knew we were in danger, and that we could not stop there and rest!

'Though all those things were in my mind, they were in the background. They seemed to be affairs beyond our concern. Chiefly, I was thinking of my lady. An aching distress filled me. For the first time she had owned herself beaten and had fallen a-weeping. Behind me I could hear her sobbing, but I would not turn round to her because I knew she had need of weeping, and had held herself so far and so long for me. It was well, I thought, that she would weep and rest, and then we would toil on again, for I had no inkling of the thing that hung so near. Even now I can see her as she sat there, her lovely hair upon her shoulder, can mark again the deepening hollow of her cheek.

'"If we had parted," she said, "if I had let you go——"

'"No," said I. "Even now I do not repent. I will not repent; I made my choice, and I will hold on to the end."

'And then——

'Overhead in the sky flashed something and burst, and all about us I heard the bullets making a noise like a handful of peas suddenly thrown. They chipped the stones about us, and whirled fragments from the bricks and passed. . . .'

He put his hand to his mouth, and then moistened his lips.

'At the flash I had turned about. . . .

'You know—she stood up——

'She stood up, you know, and moved a step towards me——

'As though she wanted to reach me——

'And she had been shot through the heart.'

He stopped and stared at me. I felt all that foolish incapacity an Englishman feels on such occasions. I met his eyes for a moment, and then stared out of the window. For a long space we kept silence. When at last I looked at him he was sitting back in his corner, his arms folded and his teeth gnawing at his knuckles.

He bit his nail suddenly, and stared at it.

'I carried her,' he said, 'towards the temples, in my arms—as though it mattered. I don't know why. They seemed a sort of sanctuary, you know, they had lasted so long, I suppose.

'She must have died almost instantly. Only—I talked to her—all the way.'

Silence again.

'I have seen those temples,' I said abruptly, and indeed he had brought those still, sunlit arcades of worn sandstone very vividly before me.

'It was the brown one, the big brown one. I sat down on a fallen pillar and held her in my arms. . . . Silent after the first babble was over. And after a little while the lizards came out and ran about again, as though nothing unusual was going on, as though nothing had changed. . . . It was tremendously still there, the sun high and the shadows still; even the shadows of the weeds upon the entablature were still—in spite of the thudding and banging that went all about the sky.

'I seem to remember that the aeroplanes came up out of the south, and that the battle went away to the west. One aeroplane was struck, and overset and fell. I remember that—though it didn't interest me in the least. It didn't seem to signify. It was like a wounded gull, you know—flapping for a time in the water. I could see it down the aisle of the temple—a black thing in the bright blue water.

'Three or four times shells burst about the beach, and then that ceased. Each time that happened all the lizards scuttled in and hid for a space. That was all the mischief done, except that once a stray bullet gashed the stone hard by—made just a fresh bright surface.

'As the shadows grew longer, the stillness seemed greater.

'The curious thing,' he remarked, with the manner of a man who makes a trivial conversation, 'is that I didn't *think*—I didn't think at all. I sat with her in my arms amidst the stones—in a sort of lethargy—stagnant.

'And I don't remember waking up. I don't remember

dressing that day. I know I found myself in my office, with my letters all slit open in front of me, and how I was struck by the absurdity of being there, seeing that in reality I was sitting, stunned, in that Pæstum Temple with a dead woman in my arms. I read my letters like a machine. I have forgotten what they were about.'

He stopped, and there was a long silence.

Suddenly I perceived that we were running down the incline from Chalk Farm to Euston. I started at this passing of time. I turned on him with a brutal question with the tone of 'Now or never.'

'And did you dream again?'

'Yes.'

He seemed to force himself to finish. His voice was very low.

'Once more, and as it were only for a few instants. I seemed to have suddenly awakened out of a great apathy, to have risen into a sitting position, and the body lay there on the stones beside me. A gaunt body. Not her, you know. So soon—it was not her. . . .

'I may have heard voices. I do not know. Only I knew clearly that men were coming into the solitude and that that was a last outrage.

'I stood up and walked through the temple, and then there came into sight—first one man with a yellow face, dressed in a uniform of dirty white, trimmed with blue, and then several, climbing to the crest of the old wall of the vanished city, and crouching there. They were little bright figures in the sunlight, and there they hung, weapon in hand, peering cautiously before them.

'And further away I saw others, and then more at another point in the wall. It was a long lax line of men in open order.

'Presently the man I had first seen stood up and shouted a command, and his men came tumbling down the wall and into the high weeds towards the temple. He scrambled down

346

with them and led them. He came facing towards me, and when he saw me he stopped.

'At first I had watched these men with a mere curiosity, but when I had seen they meant to come to the temple I was moved to forbid them. I shouted to the officer.

'"You must not come here," I cried, "*I* am here. I am here with my dead."

'He stared, and then shouted a question back to me in some unknown tongue.

'I repeated what I had said.

'He shouted again, and I folded my arms and stood still. Presently he spoke to his men and came forward. He carried a drawn sword.

'I signed to him to keep away, but he continued to advance. I told him again very patiently and clearly: "You must not come here. These are old temples, and I am here with my dead."

'Presently he was so close I could see his face clearly. It was a narrow face, with dull grey eyes, and a black moustache. He had a scar on his upper lip, and he was dirty and unshaven. He kept shouting unintelligible things, questions perhaps, at me.

'I know now that he was afraid of me, but at the time that did not occur to me. As I tried to explain to him he interrupted me in imperious tones, bidding me, I suppose, stand aside.

'He made to go past me, and I caught hold of him.

'I saw his face change at my grip.

'"You fool," I cried. "Don't you know? She is dead!"

'He started back. He looked at me with cruel eyes. I saw a sort of exultant resolve leap into them—delight. Then suddenly, with a scowl, he swept his sword back—*so*—and thrust.'

He stopped abruptly.

I became aware of a change in the rhythm of the train. The brakes lifted their voices and the carriage jarred and jerked. This present world insisted upon itself, became clamorous. I saw through the steamy window huge electric lights glaring down from tall masts upon a fog, saw rows of

347

stationary empty carriages passing by, and then a signal-box, hoisting its constellation of green and red into the murky London twilight, marched after them. I looked again at his drawn features.

'He ran me through the heart. It was with a sort of astonishment—no fear, no pain—but just amazement, that I felt it pierce me, felt the sword drive home into my body. It didn't hurt, you know. It didn't hurt at all.'

The yellow platform lights came into the field of view, passing first rapidly, then slowly, and at last stopping with a jerk. Dim shapes of men passed to and fro without.

'Euston!' cried a voice.

'Do you mean——?'

'There was no pain, no sting or smart. Amazement and then darkness sweeping over everything. The hot, brutal face before me, the face of the man who had killed me, seemed to recede. It swept out of existence——'

'Euston!' clamoured the voices outside; 'Euston!'

The carriage door opened, admitting a flood of sound, and a porter stood regarding us. The sounds of doors slamming, and the hoof-clatter of cab-horses, and behind these things the featureless remote roar of the London cobble-stones, came to my ears. A truck-load of lighted lamps blazed along the platform.

'A darkness, a flood of darkness that opened and spread and blotted out all things.'

'Any luggage, sir?' said the porter.

'And that was the end?' I asked.

He seemed to hesitate. Then, almost inaudibly, he answered, '*No.*'

'You mean?'

'I couldn't get to her. She was there on the other side of the temple—— And then——'

'Yes,' I insisted. 'Yes?'

'Nightmares,' he cried; 'nightmares indeed! My God! Great birds that fought and tore.'

XXVI

THE VALLEY OF SPIDERS

TOWARDS mid-day the three pursuers came abruptly round a bend in the torrent bed upon the sight of a very broad and spacious valley. The difficult and winding trench of pebbles along which they had tracked the fugitives for so long expanded to a broad slope, and with a common impulse the three men left the trail, and rode to a little eminence set with olive-dun trees, and there halted, the two others, as became them, a little behind the man with the silver-studded bridle.

For a space they scanned the great expanse below them with eager eyes. It spread remoter and remoter, with only a few clusters of sere thorn bushes here and there, and the dim suggestions of some now waterless ravine to break its desolation of yellow grass. Its purple distances melted at last into the bluish slopes of the further hills—hills it might be of a greener kind—and above them, invisibly supported, and seeming indeed to hang in the blue, were the snow-clad summits of mountains—that grew larger and bolder to the north-westward as the sides of the valley drew together. And westward the valley opened until a distant darkness under the sky told where the forests began. But the three men looked neither east nor west, but only steadfastly across the valley.

The gaunt man with the scarred lip was the first to speak. 'Nowhere,' he said, with a sigh of disappointment in his voice. 'But, after all, they had a full day's start.'

'They don't know we are after them,' said the little man on the white horse.

'*She* would know,' said the leader bitterly, as if speaking to himself.

'Even then they can't go fast. They've got no beast but the mule, and all to-day the girl's foot has been bleeding——'

The man with the silver bridle flashed a quick intensity of rage on him. 'Do you think I haven't seen that?' he snarled.

'It helps, anyhow,' whispered the little man to himself.

The gaunt man with the scarred lip stared impassively. 'They can't be over the valley,' he said. 'If we ride hard——'

He glanced at the white horse and paused.

'Curse all white horses!' said the man with the silver bridle, and turned to scan the beast his curse included.

The little man looked down between the melancholy ears of his steed.

'I did my best,' he said.

The two others stared again across the valley for a space. The gaunt man passed the back of his hand across the scarred lip.

'Come up!'* said the man who owned the silver bridle, suddenly. The little man started and jerked his rein, and the horse hoofs of the three made a multitudinous faint pattering upon the withered grass as they turned back towards the trail. . . .

They rode cautiously down the long slope before them, and so came through a waste of prickly twisted bushes and strange dry shapes of thorny branches that grew amongst the rocks, into the levels below. And there the trail grew faint, for the soil was scanty, and the only herbage was this scorched dead straw that lay upon the ground. Still, by hard scanning, by leaning beside the horses' necks and pausing ever and again, even these white men could contrive to follow after their prey.

There were trodden places, bent and broken blades of the coarse grass, and ever and again the sufficient intimation of a footmark. And once the leader saw a brown smear of blood where the half-caste girl may have trod. And at that under his breath he cursed her for a fool.

The gaunt man checked his leader's tracking, and the little

man on the white horse rode behind, a man lost in a dream. They rode one after another, the man with the silver bridle led the way, and they spoke never a word. After a time it came to the little man on the white horse that the world was very still. He started out of his dream. Besides the little noises of their horses and equipment, the whole great valley kept the brooding quiet of a painted scene.

Before him went his master and his fellow, each intently leaning forward to the left, each impassively moving with the paces of his horse; their shadows went before them—still, noiseless, tapering attendants; and nearer a crouched cool shape was his own. He looked about him. What was it had gone? Then he remembered the reverberation from the banks of the gorge and the perpetual accompaniment of shifting, jostling pebbles. And, moreover——? There was no breeze. That was it! What a vast, still place it was, a monotonous afternoon slumber! And the sky open and blank except for a sombre veil of haze that had gathered in the upper valley.

He straightened his back, fretted with his bridle, puckered his lips to whistle, and simply sighed. He turned in his saddle for a time, and stared at the throat of the mountain gorge out of which they had come. Blank! Blank slopes on either side, with never a sign of a decent beast or tree—much less a man. What a land it was! What a wilderness! He dropped again into his former pose.

It filled him with a momentary pleasure to see a wry stick of purple black flash out into the form of a snake, and vanish amidst the brown. After all, the infernal valley *was* alive. And then, to rejoice him still more, came a little breath across his face, a whisper that came and went, the faintest inclination of a stiff black-antlered bush upon a little crest, the first intimations of a possible breeze. Idly he wetted his finger, and held it up.

He pulled up sharply to avoid a collision with the gaunt man, who had stopped at fault upon the trail. Just at that guilty moment he caught his master's eye looking towards him.

For a time he forced an interest in the tracking. Then, as they rode on again, he studied his master's shadow and hat and shoulder, appearing and disappearing behind the gaunt man's nearer contours. They had ridden four days out of the very limits of the world into this desolate place, short of water, with nothing but a strip of dried meat under their saddles, over rocks and mountains, where surely none but these fugitives had ever been before—for *that*!

And all this was for a girl, a mere wilful child! And the man had whole cityfuls of people to do his basest bidding— girls, women! Why in the name of passionate folly *this* one in particular? asked the little man, and scowled at the world, and licked his parched lips with a blackened tongue. It was the way of the master, and that was all he knew. Just because she sought to evade him . . .

His eye caught a whole row of high-plumed canes bending in unison, and then the tails of silk that hung before his neck flapped and fell. The breeze was growing stronger. Somehow it took the stiff stillness out of things—and that was well.

'Hullo!' said the gaunt man.

All three stopped abruptly.

'What?' asked the master. 'What?'

'Over there,' said the gaunt man, pointing up the valley. 'What?'

'Something coming towards us.'

And as he spoke a yellow animal crested a rise and came bearing down upon them. It was a big wild dog, coming before the wind, tongue out, at a steady pace, and running with such an intensity of purpose that he did not seem to see the horsemen he approached. He ran with his nose up, following, it was plain, neither scent nor quarry. As he drew nearer the little man felt for his sword. 'He's mad,' said the gaunt rider.

'Shout!' said the little man, and shouted.

The dog came on. Then when the little man's blade was already out, it swerved aside and went panting by them and passed. The eyes of the little man followed its flight. 'There was no foam,'* he said. For a space the man with the silver-studded bridle stared up the valley. 'Oh, come on!' he cried at last. 'What does it matter?' and jerked his horse into movement again.

The little man left the insoluble mystery of a dog that fled from nothing but the wind, and lapsed into profound musings on human character. 'Come on!' he whispered to himself. 'Why should it be given to one man to say "Come on!" with that stupendous violence of effect? Always, all his life, the man with the silver bridle has been saying that. If *I* said it——!' thought the little man. But people marvelled when the master was disobeyed even in the wildest things. This half-caste girl seemed to him, seemed to every one, mad—blasphemous almost. The little man, by way of comparison, reflected on the gaunt rider with the scarred lip, as stalwart as his master, as brave and, indeed, perhaps braver, and yet for him there was obedience, nothing but to give obedience duly and stoutly. . . .

Certain sensations of the hands and knees called the little man back to more immediate things. He became aware of something. He rode up beside his gaunt fellow. 'Do you notice the horses?' he said in an undertone.

The gaunt face looked interrogation.

'They don't like this wind,' said the little man, and dropped behind as the man with the silver bridle turned upon him.

'It's all right,' said the gaunt-faced man.

They rode on again for a space in silence. The foremost two rode downcast upon the trail, the hindmost man watched the haze that crept down the vastness of the valley, nearer and nearer, and noted how the wind grew in strength moment by moment. Far away on the left he saw a line of dark bulks—wild hog, perhaps, galloping down the valley, but of that he said nothing, nor did he remark again upon the uneasiness of the horses

And then he saw first one and then a second great white

ball, a great shining white ball like a gigantic head of thistle-down, that drove before the wind athwart the path. These balls soared high in the air, and dropped and rose again and caught for a moment, and hurried on and passed, but at the sight of them the restlessness of the horses increased.

Then presently he saw that more of these drifting globes—and then soon very many more—were hurrying towards him down the valley.

They became aware of a squealing. Athwart the path a huge boar rushed, turning his head but for one instant to glance at them, and then hurling on down the valley again. And at that all three stopped and sat in their saddles, staring into the thickening haze that was coming upon them.

'If it were not for this thistle-down——' began the leader.

But now a big globe came drifting past within a score of yards of them. It was really not an even sphere at all, but a vast, soft, ragged, filmy thing, a sheet gathered by the corners, an aerial jelly-fish, as it were, but rolling over and over as it advanced, and trailing long cobwebby threads and streamers that floated in its wake.

'It isn't thistle-down,' said the little man.

'I don't like the stuff,' said the gaunt man.

And they looked at one another.

'Curse it!' cried the leader. 'The air's full of it up there. If it keeps on at this pace long, it will stop us altogether.'

An instinctive feeling, such as lines out a herd of deer at the approach of some ambiguous thing, prompted them to turn their horses to the wind, ride forward for a few paces, and stare at that advancing multitude of floating masses. They came on before the wind with a sort of smooth swift-ness, rising and falling noiselessly, sinking to earth, rebound-ing high, soaring—all with a perfect unanimity, with a still, deliberate assurance.

Right and left of the horsemen the pioneers of this strange army passed. At one that rolled along the ground, breaking shapelessly and trailing out reluctantly into long grappling ribbons and bands, all three horses began to shy and dance. The master was seized with a sudden, unreasonable impatience. He cursed the drifting globes roundly. 'Get on!' he cried; 'get on! What do these things matter? How *can* they matter? Back to the trail!' He fell swearing at his horse and sawed the bit across its mouth.

He shouted aloud with rage. 'I will follow that trail, I tell you,' he cried. 'Where is the trail?'

He gripped the bridle of his prancing horse and searched amidst the grass. A long and clinging thread fell across his face, a grey streamer dropped about his bridle arm, some big, active thing with many legs ran down the back of his head. He looked up to discover one of those grey masses anchored as it were above him by these things and flapping out ends as a sail flaps when a boat comes about*—but noiselessly.

He had an impression of many eyes, of a dense crew of squat bodies, of long, many-jointed limbs hauling at their mooring ropes to bring the thing down upon him. For a space he stared up, reining in his prancing horse with the instinct born of years of horsemanship. Then the flat of a sword smote his back, and a blade flashed overhead and cut the drifting balloon of spider-web free, and the whole mass lifted softly and drove clear and away.

'Spiders!' cried the voice of the gaunt man. 'The things are full of big spiders! Look, my lord!'

The man with the silver bridle still followed the mass that drove away.

'Look, my lord!'

The master found himself staring down at a red smashed thing on the ground that, in spite of partial obliteration, could still wriggle unavailing legs. Then, when the gaunt man pointed to another mass that bore down upon them, he drew his sword hastily. Up the valley now it was like a fog bank torn to rags. He tried to grasp the situation.

'Ride for it!' the little man was shouting. 'Ride for it down the valley.'

What happened then was like the confusion of a battle. The man with the silver bridle saw the little man go past him, slashing furiously at imaginary cobwebs, saw him cannon into the horse of the gaunt man and hurl it and its rider to earth. His own horse went a dozen paces before he could rein it in. Then he looked up to avoid imaginary dangers, and then back again to see a horse rolling on the ground, the gaunt man standing and slashing over it at a rent and fluttering mass of grey that streamed and wrapped about them both. And thick and fast as thistle-down on waste land on a windy day in July the cobweb masses were coming on.

The little man had dismounted, but he dared not release his horse. He was endeavouring to lug the struggling brute back with the strength of one arm, while with the other he slashed aimlessly. The tentacles of a second grey mass had entangled themselves with the struggle, and this second grey mass came to its moorings, and slowly sank.

The master set his teeth, gripped his bridle, lowered his head, and spurred his horse forward. The horse on the ground rolled over, there was blood and moving shapes upon the flanks, and the gaunt man suddenly leaving it, ran forward towards his master, perhaps ten paces. His legs were swathed and encumbered with grey; he made ineffectual movements with his sword. Grey streamers waved from him; there was a thin veil of grey across his face. With his left hand he beat at something on his body, and suddenly he stumbled and fell. He struggled to rise, and fell again, and suddenly, horribly, began to howl, 'Oh—ohoo, ohooh!'

The master could see the great spiders upon him, and others upon the ground.

As he strove to force his horse nearer to this gesticulating, screaming grey object that struggled up and down, there came a clatter of hoofs, and the little man, in act of mounting, swordless, balanced on his belly athwart the white horse, and clutching its mane, whirled past. And again a clinging thread of grey gossamer swept across the master's face. All about him, and over him, it seemed this drifting, noiseless cobweb circled and drew nearer him. . . .

To the day of his death he never knew just how the event of that moment happened. Did he, indeed, turn his horse, or did it really of its own accord stampede after its fellow? Suffice it that in another second he was galloping full tilt down the valley with his sword whirling furiously overhead. And all about him on the quickening breeze, the spiders' air-ships, their air bundles and air sheets, seemed to him to hurry in a conscious pursuit.

Clatter, clatter, thud, thud,—the man with the silver bridle rode, heedless of his direction, with his fearful face looking up now right, now left, and his sword arm ready to slash. And a few hundred yards ahead of him, with a tail of torn cobweb trailing behind him, rode the little man on the white horse, still but imperfectly in the saddle. The reeds bent before them, the wind blew fresh and strong, over his shoulder the master could see the webs hurrying to overtake. . . .

He was so intent to escape the spiders' webs that only as his horse gathered together for a leap did he realise the ravine ahead. And then he realised it only to misunderstand and interfere. He was leaning forward on his horse's neck and sat up and back all too late.

But if in his excitement he had failed to leap, at any rate he had not forgotten how to fall. He was horseman again in mid-air. He came off clear with a mere bruise upon his shoulder, and his horse rolled, kicking spasmodic legs, and lay still. But the master's sword drove its point into the hard soil, and snapped clean across, as though Chance refused him any longer as her Knight, and the splintered end missed his face by an inch or so.

He was on his feet in a moment, breathlessly scanning the

on-rushing spider-webs. For a moment he was minded to run, and then thought of the ravine, and turned back. He ran aside once to dodge one drifting terror, and then he was swiftly clambering down the precipitous sides, and out of the touch of the gale.

There, under the lee* of the dry torrent's steeper banks, he might crouch and watch these strange, grey masses pass and pass in safety till the wind fell, and it became possible to escape. And there for a long time he crouched, watching the strange, grey ragged masses trail their streamers across his narrowed sky.

Once a stray spider fell into the ravine close beside him— a full foot it measured from leg to leg and its body was half a man's hand—and after he had watched its monstrous alacrity of search and escape for a little while and tempted it to bite his broken sword, he lifted up his iron-heeled boot and smashed it into a pulp. He swore as he did so, and for a time sought up and down for another.

Then presently, when he was surer these spider swarms could not drop into the ravine, he found a place where he could sit down, and sat and fell into deep thought and began, after his manner, to gnaw his knuckles and bite his nails. And from this he was moved by the coming of the man with the white horse.

He heard him long before he saw him, as a clattering of hoofs, stumbling footsteps, and a reassuring voice. Then the little man appeared, a rueful figure, still with a tail of white cobweb trailing behind him. They approached each other without speaking, without a salutation. The little man was fatigued and shamed to the pitch of hopeless bitterness, and came to a stop at last, face to face with his seated master. The latter winced a little under his dependent's eye. 'Well?' he said at last, with no pretence of authority.

'You left him?'

'My horse bolted.'

'I know. So did mine.'

He laughed at his master mirthlessly.

'I say my horse bolted,' said the man who once had a silver-studded bridle.

'Cowards both,' said the little man.

The other gnawed his knuckle through some meditative moments, with his eye on his inferior.

'Don't call me a coward,' he said at length.

'You are a coward, like myself.'

'A coward possibly. There is a limit beyond which every man must fear. That I have learnt at last. But not like yourself. That is where the difference comes in.'

'I never could have dreamt you would have left him. He saved your life two minutes before. . . . Why are you our lord?'

The master gnawed his knuckles again, and his countenance was dark.

'No man calls me a coward,' he said. 'No. . . . A broken sword is better than none. . . . One spavined* white horse cannot be expected to carry two men a four days' journey. I hate white horses, but this time it cannot be helped. You begin to understand me? I perceive that you are minded, on the strength of what you have seen and fancy, to taint my reputation. It is men of your sort who unmake kings. Besides which—I never liked you.'

'My lord!' said the little man.

'No,' said the master. '*No!*'

He stood up sharply as the little man moved. For a minute perhaps they faced one another. Overhead the spiders' balls went driving. There was a quick movement among the pebbles; a running of feet, a cry of despair, a gasp and a blow. . . .

Towards nightfall the wind fell. The sun set in a calm serenity, and the man who had once possessed the silver bridle came at last very cautiously and by an easy slope out of the ravine again; but now he led the white horse that once belonged to the little man. He would have gone back to his horse to get his silver-mounted bridle again, but he feared night and a quickening breeze might still find him in the valley, and besides, he disliked greatly to think he might discover his horse all swathed in cobwebs and perhaps unpleasantly eaten.

And as he thought of those cobwebs, and of all the dangers he had been through, and the manner in which he had been preserved that day, his hand sought a little reliquary* that hung about his neck, and he clasped it for a moment with heartfelt gratitude. As he did so his eyes went across the valley.

'I was hot with passion,' he said, 'and now she has met her reward. They also, no doubt——'

And behold! far away out of the wooded slopes across the valley, but in the clearness of the sunset, distinct and unmistakable, he saw a little spire of smoke.

At that his expression of serene resignation changed to an amazed anger. Smoke? He turned the head of the white horse about, and hesitated. And as he did so a little rustle of air went through the grass about him. Far away upon some reeds swayed a tattered sheet of grey. He looked at the cobwebs; he looked at the smoke.

'Perhaps, after all, it is not them,' he said at last.

But he knew better.

After he had stared at the smoke for some time, he mounted the white horse.

As he rode, he picked his way amidst stranded masses of web. For some reason there were many dead spiders on the ground, and those that lived feasted guiltily on their fellows. At the sound of his horse's hoofs they fled.

Their time had passed. From the ground, without either a wind to carry them or a winding-sheet ready, these things, for all their poison, could do him little evil.

He flicked with his belt at those he fancied came too near. Once, where a number ran together over a bare place, he was minded to dismount and trample them with his boots, but this impulse he overcame. Ever and again he turned in his saddle, and looked back at the smoke.

'Spiders,' he muttered over and over again. 'Spiders. Well, well . . . The next time I must spin a web.'

XXVII

THE NEW ACCELERATOR

CERTAINLY, if ever a man found a guinea when he was looking for a pin, it is my good friend Professor Gibberne. I have heard before of investigators overshooting the mark, but never quite to the extent that he has done. He has really, this time at anyrate, without any touch of exaggeration in the phrase, found something to revolutionise human life. And that when he was simply seeking an all-round nervous stimulant to bring languid people up to the stresses of these pushful days. I have tasted the stuff now several times, and I cannot do better than describe the effect the thing had on me. That there are astonishing experiences in store for all in search of new sensations will become apparent enough.

Professor Gibberne, as many people know, is my neighbour in Folkestone.* Unless my memory plays me a trick, his portrait at various ages has already appeared in *The Strand Magazine*—I think late in 1899; but I am unable to look it up because I have lent that volume to someone who has never sent it back. The reader may, perhaps, recall the high forehead and the singularly long black eyebrows that give such a Mephistophelian* touch to his face. He occupies one of those pleasant little detached houses in the mixed style that make the western end of the Upper Sandgate Road so interesting. His is the one with the Flemish gables and the Moorish portico, and it is in the little room with the mullioned bay window that he works when he is down here, and in which of an evening we have so often smoked and talked together. He is a mighty jester, but, besides, he likes to talk to me about his work; he is one of those men who find a help and stimulus in talking, and so I have been able to follow the conception of the New Accelerator right up from a very early stage. Of course, the greater portion of his experimental work is not done in Folkestone, but in Gower Street, in the fine new laboratory next to the hospital that he has been the first to use.

As every one knows, or at least as all intelligent people know, the special department in which Gibberne has gained so great and deserved a reputation among physiologists is the action of drugs upon the nervous system. Upon soporifics, sedatives, and anæsthetics he is, I am told, unequalled. He is also a chemist of considerable eminence, and I suppose in the subtle and complex jungle of riddles that centres about the ganglion cell and the axis fibre* there are little cleared places of his making, little glades of illumination, that, until he sees fit to publish his results, are still inaccessible to every other living man. And in the last few years he has been particularly assiduous upon this question of nervous stimulants, and already, before the discovery of the New Accelerator, very successful with them. Medical science has to thank him for at least three distinct and absolutely safe invigorators of unrivalled value to practising men. In cases of exhaustion the preparation known as Gibberne's B Syrup has, I suppose, saved more lives already than any lifeboat round the coast.

'But none of these little things begin to satisfy me yet,' he told me nearly a year ago. 'Either they increase the central energy without affecting the nerves, or they simply increase the available energy by lowering the nervous conductivity; and all of them are unequal and local in their operation. One wakes up the heart and viscera and leaves the brain stupefied, one gets at the brain champagne fashion, and does nothing good for the solar plexus,* and what I want—and what, if it's an earthly possibility, I mean to have—is a stimulant that stimulates all round, that wakes you up for a time from the crown of your head to the tip of your great toe, and makes you go two—or even three—to everybody else's one. Eh? That's the thing I'm after.'

'It would tire a man,' I said.

'Not a doubt of it. And you'd eat double or treble—and all that. But just think what the thing would mean. Imagine yourself with a little phial like this'—he held up a little bottle of green glass and marked his points with it—'and in this precious phial is the power to think twice as fast, move twice as quickly, do twice as much work in a given time as you could otherwise do.'

'But is such a thing possible?'

'I believe so. If it isn't, I've wasted my time for a year. These various preparations of the hypophosphites, for example, seem to show that something of the sort . . . Even if it was only one and a half times as fast it would do.'

'It *would* do,' I said.

'If you were a statesman in a corner, for example, time rushing up against you, something urgent to be done, eh?'

'He could dose his private secretary,' I said.

'And gain—double time. And think if *you*, for example, wanted to finish a book.'

'Usually,' I said, 'I wish I'd never begun 'em.'

'Or a doctor, driven to death, wants to sit down and think out a case. Or a barrister—or a man cramming for an examination.'

'Worth a guinea a drop,' said I, 'and more—to men like that.'

'And in a duel, again,' said Gibberne, 'where it all depends on your quickness in pulling the trigger.'

'Or in fencing,' I echoed.

'You see,' said Gibberne, 'if I get it as an all-round thing, it will really do you no harm at all—except perhaps to an infinitesimal degree it brings you nearer old age. You will just have lived twice to other people's once——'

'I suppose,' I meditated, 'in a duel—it would be fair?'

'That's a question for the seconds,' said Gibberne.

I harked back further. 'And you really think such a thing *is* possible?' I said.

'As possible,' said Gibberne, and glanced at something

that went throbbing by the window, 'as a motor-bus. As a matter of fact——'

He paused and smiled at me deeply, and tapped slowly on the edge of his desk with the green phial. 'I think I know the stuff. . . . Already I've got something coming.' The nervous smile upon his face betrayed the gravity of his revelation. He rarely talked of his actual experimental work unless things were very near the end. 'And it may be, it may be— I shouldn't be surprised—it may even do the thing at a greater rate than twice.'

'It will be rather a big thing,' I hazarded.

'It will be, I think, rather a big thing.'

But I don't think he quite knew what a big thing it was to be, for all that.

I remember we had several talks about the stuff after that. 'The New Accelerator' he called it, and his tone about it grew more confident on each occasion. Sometimes he talked nervously of unexpected physiological results its use might have, and then he would get a little unhappy; at others he was frankly mercenary, and we debated long and anxiously how the preparation might be turned to commercial account. 'It's a good thing,' said Gibberne, 'a tremendous thing. I know I'm giving the world something, and I think it only reasonable we should expect the world to pay. The dignity of science is all very well, but I think somehow I must have the monopoly of the stuff for, say, ten years. I don't see why *all* the fun in life should go to the dealers in ham.'

My own interest in the coming drug certainly did not wane in the time. I have always had a queer little twist towards metaphysics in my mind. I have always been given to paradoxes about space and time, and it seemed to me that Gibberne was really preparing no less than the absolute acceleration of life. Suppose a man repeatedly dosed with such a preparation: he would live an active and record life indeed, but he would be an adult at eleven, middle-aged at twenty-five, and by thirty well on the road to senile decay. It seemed to me that so far Gibberne was only going to do for any one who took his drug exactly what Nature has done for the Jews and Orientals, who are men in their teens and aged by fifty, and quicker in thought and act than we are all the time. The marvel of drugs has always been great to my mind; you can madden a man, calm a man, make him incredibly strong and alert or a helpless log, quicken this passion and allay that, all by means of drugs, and here was a new miracle to be added to this strange armoury of phials the doctors use! But Gibberne was far too eager upon his technical points to enter very keenly into my aspect of the question.

It was the 7th or 8th of August when he told me the distillation that would decide his failure or success for a time was going forward as we talked, and it was on the 10th that he told me the thing was done and the New Accelerator a tangible reality in the world. I met him as I was going up the Sandgate Hill towards Folkestone—I think I was going to get my hair cut, and he came hurrying down to meet me—I suppose he was coming to my house to tell me at once of his success. I remember that his eyes were unusually bright and his face flushed, and I noted even then the swift alacrity of his step.

'It's done,' he cried, and gripped my hand, speaking very fast; 'it's more than done. Come up to my house and see.'

'Really?'

'Really!' he shouted. 'Incredibly! Come up and see.'

'And it does—twice?'

'It does more, much more. It scares me. Come up and see the stuff. Taste it! Try it! It's the most amazing stuff on earth.' He gripped my arm and, walking at such a pace that he forced me into a trot, went shouting with me up the hill. A whole *char-à-banc*-ful* of people turned and stared at us in unison after the manner of people in *chars-à-banc*. It was one of those hot, clear days that Folkestone sees so much of, every colour incredibly bright and every outline hard. There was a breeze, of course, but not so much breeze as sufficed under these conditions to keep me cool and dry. I panted for mercy.

'I'm not walking fast, am I?' cried Gibberne, and slackened his pace to a quick march.

'You've been taking some of this stuff,' I puffed.

'No,' he said. 'At the utmost a drop of water that stood in a beaker from which I had washed out the last traces of the stuff. I took some last night, you know. But that is ancient history now.'

'And it goes twice?' I said, nearing his doorway in a grateful perspiration.

'It goes a thousand times, many thousand times!' cried Gibberne, with a dramatic gesture, flinging open his Early English carved oak gate.

'Phew!' said I, and followed him to the door.

'I don't know how many times it goes,' he said, with his latch-key in his hand.

'And you——'

'It throws all sorts of light on nervous physiology, it kicks the theory of vision into a perfectly new shape! . . . Heaven knows how many thousand times. We'll try all that after—— The thing is to try the stuff now.'

'Try the stuff?' I said, as we went along the passage.

'Rather,' said Gibberne, turning on me in his study. 'There it is in that little green phial there! Unless you happen to be afraid?'

I am a careful man by nature, and only theoretically adventurous. I *was* afraid. But on the other hand, there is pride.

'Well,' I haggled. 'You say you've tried it?'

'I've tried it,' he said, 'and I don't look hurt by it, do I? I don't even look livery, and I *feel*——'

I sat down. 'Give me the potion,' I said. 'If the worst comes to the worst it will save having my hair cut, and that, I think, is one of the most hateful duties of a civilised man. How do you take the mixture?'

'With water,' said Gibberne, whacking down a carafe.

He stood up in front of his desk and regarded me in his easy-chair; his manner was suddenly affected by a touch of the Harley Street* specialist. 'It's rum* stuff, you know,' he said.

I made a gesture with my hand.

'I must warn you, in the first place, as soon as you've got it down to shut your eyes, and open them very cautiously in a minute or so's time. One still sees. The sense of vision is a question of length of vibration, and not of multitude of impacts; but there's a kind of shock to the retina,* a nasty giddy confusion just at the time if the eyes are open. Keep 'em shut.'

'Shut,' I said. 'Good!'

'And the next thing is, keep still. Don't begin to whack about. You may fetch something a nasty rap if you do. Remember you will be going several thousand times faster than you ever did before, heart, lungs, muscles, brain— everything—and you will hit hard without knowing it. You won't know it, you know. You'll feel just as you do now. Only everything in the world will seem to be going ever so many thousand times slower than it ever went before. That's what makes it so deuced queer.'

'Lor,' I said. 'And you mean——'

'You'll see,' said he, and took up a little measure. He glanced at the material on his desk. 'Glasses,' he said, 'water. All here. Mustn't take too much for the first attempt.'

The little phial glucked out its precious contents. 'Don't forget what I told you,' he said, turning the contents of the measure into a glass in the manner of an Italian waiter measuring whisky. 'Sit with the eyes tightly shut and in absolute stillness for two minutes,' he said. 'Then you will hear me speak.'

He added an inch or so of water to the little dose in each glass.

'By-the-by,' he said, 'don't put your glass down. Keep it in your hand and rest your hand on your knee. Yes—so. And now——'

He raised his glass.

'The New Accelerator,' I said.

'The New Accelerator,' he answered, and we touched glasses and drank, and instantly I closed my eyes.

You know that blank non-existence into which one drops when one has taken 'gas.'* For an indefinite interval it was like that. Then I heard Gibberne telling me to wake up, and I stirred and opened my eyes. There he stood as he had been standing, glass still in hand. It was empty, that was all the difference.

'Well?' said I.

'Nothing out of the way?'

'Nothing. A slight feeling of exhilaration, perhaps. Nothing more.'

'Sounds?'

'Things are still,' I said. 'By Jove! yes! They *are* still. Except the sort of faint pat, patter, like rain falling on different things. What is it?'

'Analysed sounds,' I think he said, but I am not sure. He glanced at the window. 'Have you ever seen a curtain before a window fixed in that way before?'

I followed his eyes, and there was the end of the curtain, frozen, as it were, corner high, in the act of flapping briskly in the breeze.

'No,' said I; 'that's odd.'

'And here,' he said, and opened the hand that held the glass. Naturally I winced, expecting the glass to smash. But so far from smashing, it did not even seem to stir; it hung in mid-air—motionless. 'Roughly speaking,' said Gibberne, 'an object in these latitudes falls 16 feet in the first second. This glass is falling 16 feet in a second now. Only, you see, it hasn't been falling yet for the hundredth part of a second. That gives you some idea of the pace of my Accelerator.'

And he waved his hand round and round, over and under

the slowly sinking glass. Finally he took it by the bottom, pulled it down and placed it very carefully on the table. 'Eh?' he said to me, and laughed.

'That seems all right,' I said, and began very gingerly to raise myself from my chair. I felt perfectly well, very light and comfortable, and quite confident in my mind. I was going fast all over. My heart, for example, was beating a thousand times a second, but that caused me no discomfort at all. I looked out of the window. An immovable cyclist, head down and with a frozen puff of dust behind his driving-wheel, scorched to overtake a galloping *char-à-banc* that did not stir. I gaped in amazement at this incredible spectacle. 'Gibberne,' I cried, 'how long will this confounded stuff last?'

'Heaven knows!' he answered. 'Last time I took it I went to bed and slept it off. I tell you, I was frightened. It must have lasted some minutes, I think—it seemed like hours. But after a bit it slows down rather suddenly, I believe.'

I was proud to observe that I did not feel frightened— I suppose because there were two of us. 'Why shouldn't we go out?' I asked.

'Why not?'

'They'll see us.'

'Not they. Goodness, no! Why, we shall be going a thousand times faster than the quickest conjuring trick that was ever done. Come along! Which way shall we go? Window, or door?'

And out by the window we went.

Assuredly of all the strange experiences that I have ever had, or imagined, or read of other people having or imagining, that little raid I made with Gibberne on the Folkestone Leas, under the influence of the New Accelerator, was the strangest and maddest of all. We went out by his gate into the road, and there we made a minute examination of the statuesque passing traffic. The tops of the wheels and some of the legs of the horses of this *char-à-banc*, the end of the whip-lash and the lower jaw of the conductor—who was just beginning to yawn—were perceptibly in motion, but all the rest of the lumbering conveyance seemed still. And quite noiseless except for a faint rattling that came from one man's throat. And as parts of this frozen edifice there were a driver, you know, and a conductor, and eleven people! The effect as we walked about the thing began by being madly queer and ended by being—disagreeable. There they were, people like ourselves and yet not like ourselves, frozen in careless attitudes, caught in mid-gesture. A girl and a man smiled at one another, a leering smile that threatened to last for evermore; a woman in a floppy capelline* rested her arm on the rail and stared at Gibberne's house with the unwinking stare of eternity; a man stroked his moustache like a figure of wax, and another stretched a tiresome stiff hand with extended fingers towards his loosened hat. We stared at them, we laughed at them, we made faces at them, and then a sort of disgust of them came upon us, and we turned away and walked round in front of the cyclist towards the Leas.

'Goodness!' cried Gibberne, suddenly; 'look there!'

He pointed, and there at the tip of his finger and sliding down the air with wings flapping slowly and at the speed of an exceptionally languid snail—was a bee.

And so we came out upon the Leas. There the thing seemed madder than ever. The band was playing in the upper stand, though all the sound it made for us was a low-pitched, wheezy rattle, a sort of prolonged last sigh that passed at times into a sound like the slow, muffled ticking of some monstrous clock. Frozen people stood erect, strange, silent, self-conscious-looking dummies hung unstably in mid-stride, promenading upon the grass. I passed close to a little poodle dog suspended in the act of leaping, and watched the slow movement of his legs as he sank to earth. 'Lord, look *here*!' cried Gibberne, and we halted for a moment before a magnificent person in white faint-striped flannels, white shoes, and a Panama hat, who turned back to wink at two gaily dressed ladies he had passed. A wink, studied with such leisurely deliberation as we could afford, is an unattractive thing. It loses any quality of alert gaiety, and one remarks that the winking eye does not completely close, that under its drooping lid appears the lower edge of an eyeball and a little line of white. 'Heaven give me memory,' said I, 'and I will never wink again.'

'Or smile,' said Gibberne, with his eye on the lady's answering teeth.

'It's infernally hot, somehow,' said I, 'Let's go slower.'

'Oh, come along!' said Gibberne.

We picked our way among the bath-chairs* in the path. Many of the people sitting in the chairs seemed almost natural in their passive poses, but the contorted scarlet of the bandsmen was not a restful thing to see. A purple-faced little gentleman was frozen in the midst of a violent struggle to refold his newspaper against the wind; there were many evidences that all these people in their sluggish way were exposed to a considerable breeze, a breeze that had no existence so far as our sensations went. We came out and walked a little way from the crowd, and turned and regarded it. To see all that multitude changed to a picture, smitten rigid, as it were, into the semblance of realistic wax, was impossibly wonderful. It was absurd, of course; but it filled me with an irrational, an exultant sense of superior advantage. Consider the wonder of it! All that I had said, and thought, and done since the stuff had begun to work in my veins had happened, so far as those people, so far as the world in general went, in the twinkling of an eye. 'The New Accelerator——' I began, but Gibberne interrupted me.

'There's that infernal old woman!' he said.

'What old woman?'

'Lives next door to me,' said Gibberne. 'Has a lapdog that yaps. Gods! The temptation is strong!'

There is something very boyish and impulsive about Gibberne at times. Before I could expostulate with him he had dashed forward, snatched the unfortunate animal out of visible existence, and was running violently with it towards the cliff of the Leas. It was most extraordinary. The little brute, you know, didn't bark or wriggle or make the slightest sign of vitality. It kept quite stiffly in an attitude of somnolent repose, and Gibberne held it by the neck. It was like running about with a dog of wood. 'Gibberne,' I cried, 'put it down!' Then I said something else. 'If you run like that, Gibberne,' I cried, 'you'll set your clothes on fire. Your linen trousers are going brown as it is!'

He clapped his hand on his thigh and stood hesitating on the verge. 'Gibberne,' I cried, coming up, 'put it down. This heat is too much! It's our running so! Two or three miles a second! Friction of the air!'

'What?' he said, glancing at the dog.

'Friction of the air,' I shouted. 'Friction of the air. Going too fast. Like meteorites and things. Too hot. And, Gibberne! Gibberne! I'm all over pricking and a sort of perspiration. You can see people stirring slightly. I believe the stuff's working off! Put that dog down.'

'Eh?' he said.

'It's working off,' I repeated. 'We're too hot and the stuff's working off! I'm wet through.'

He stared at me, then at the band, the wheezy rattle of whose performance was certainly going faster. Then with a tremendous sweep of the arm he hurled the dog away from him and it went spinning upward, still inanimate, and hung at last over the grouped parasols of a knot of chattering people. Gibberne was gripping my elbow. 'By Jove!' he cried, 'I believe it is! A sort of hot pricking and—yes. That man's moving his pocket-handkerchief! Perceptibly. We must get out of this sharp.'

But we could not get out of it sharply enough. Luckily, perhaps! For we might have run, and if we had run we should, I believe, have burst into flames.* Almost certainly we should have burst into flames! You know we had neither of us thought of that. . . . But before we could even begin to run the action of the drug had ceased. It was the business of a minute fraction of a second. The effect of the New Accelerator passed like the drawing of a curtain, vanished in the movement of a hand. I heard Gibberne's voice in infinite alarm. 'Sit down,' he said, and flop, down upon the turf at the edge of the Leas I sat—scorching as I sat. There is a patch of burnt grass there still where I sat down. The whole stagnation seemed to wake up as I did so, the disarticulated vibration of the band rushed together into a blast of music, the promenaders put their feet down and walked their ways, the papers and flags began flapping, smiles passed into words, the winker finished his wink and went on his way complacently, and all the seated people moved and spoke.

The whole world had come alive again, was going as fast as we were, or rather we were going no faster than the rest of the world. It was like slowing down as one comes into a railway station. Everything seemed to spin round for a second or two, I had the most transient feeling of nausea, and that was all. And the little dog, which had seemed to hang for a moment when the force of Gibberne's arm was expended, fell with a swift acceleration clean through a lady's parasol!

That was the saving of us. Unless it was for one corpulent old gentleman in a bath-chair, who certainly did start at the sight of us, and afterwards regarded us at intervals with a darkly suspicious eye, and, finally, I believe, said something to his nurse about us, I doubt if a solitary person remarked our sudden appearance among them. Plop! We must have appeared abruptly. We ceased to smoulder almost at once, though the turf beneath me was uncomfortably hot. The attention of every one—including even the Amusements' Association band, which on this occasion, for the only time in its history, got out of tune—was arrested by the amazing fact, and the still more amazing yapping and uproar caused by the fact, that a respectable, over-fed lapdog sleeping quietly to the east of the bandstand should suddenly fall through

the parasol of a lady on the west—in a slightly singed condition due to the extreme velocity of its movements through
the air. In these absurd days, too, when we are all trying to
be as psychic, and silly, and superstitious as possible! People
got up and trod on other people, chairs were overturned, the
Leas policeman ran. How the matter settled itself I do not
know—we were much too anxious to disentangle ourselves
from the affair and get out of range of the eye of the old
gentleman in the bath-chair to make minute inquiries. As
soon as we were sufficiently cool and sufficiently recovered
from our giddiness and nausea and confusion of mind to
do so we stood up, and skirting the crowd, directed our
steps back along the road below the Metropole towards
Gibberne's house. But amidst the din I heard very distinctly
the gentleman who had been sitting beside the lady of the
ruptured sunshade using quite unjustifiable threats and language to one of those chair-attendants who have 'Inspector'
written on their caps: 'If you didn't throw the dog,' he said,
'who *did?*'

The sudden return of movement and familiar noises, and
our natural anxiety about ourselves (our clothes were still
dreadfully hot, and the fronts of the thighs of Gibberne's
white trousers were scorched a drabbish brown), prevented
the minute observations I should have liked to make on all
these things. Indeed, I really made no observations of any
scientific value on that return. The bee, of course, had gone.
I looked for that cyclist, but he was already out of sight as
we came into the Upper Sandgate Road or hidden from us
by traffic; the *char-à-banc*, however, with its people now all
alive and stirring, was clattering along at a spanking pace
almost abreast of the nearer church.

We noted, however, that the window-sill on which we had
stepped in getting out of the house was slightly singed, and
that the impressions of our feet on the gravel of the path
were unusually deep.

So it was I had my first experience of the New Accelerator.

Practically we had been running about and saying and doing all sorts of things in the space of a second or so of time. We had lived half an hour while the band had played, perhaps, two bars. But the effect it had upon us was that the whole world had stopped for our convenient inspection. Considering all things, and particularly considering our rashness in venturing out of the house, the experience might certainly have been much more disagreeable than it was. It showed, no doubt, that Gibberne has still much to learn before his preparation is a manageable convenience, but its practicability it certainly demonstrated beyond all cavil.

Since that adventure he has been steadily bringing its use under control, and I have several times, and without the slightest bad result, taken measured doses under his direction; though I must confess I have not yet ventured abroad again while under its influence. I may mention, for example, that this story has been written at one sitting and without interruption, except for the nibbling of some chocolate, by its means. I began at 6.25, and my watch is now very nearly at the minute past the half-hour. The convenience of securing a long, uninterrupted spell of work in the midst of a day full of engagements cannot be exaggerated. Gibberne is now working at the quantitative handling of his preparation, with especial reference to its distinctive effects upon different types of constitution. He then hopes to find a Retarder, with which to dilute its present rather excessive potency. The Retarder will, of course, have the reverse effect to the Accelerator; used alone it should enable the patient to spread a few seconds over many hours of ordinary time, and so to maintain an apathetic inaction, a glacier-like absence of alacrity, amidst the most animated or irritating surroundings. The two things together must necessarily work an entire revolution in civilised existence. It is the beginning of our escape from that Time Garment of which Carlyle speaks.* While this Accelerator will enable us to concentrate ourselves with tremendous impact upon any moment or occasion that demands our utmost sense and vigour, the Retarder will enable us to pass in passive tranquillity through infinite hardship and tedium. Perhaps I am a little optimistic about the Retarder, which has indeed still to be discovered, but about the Accelerator there is no possible sort of doubt whatever. Its appearance upon the market in a convenient, controllable, and assimilable form is a matter of the next few months. It will be obtainable of all chemists and druggists, in small green bottles, at a high but, considering its extraordinary qualities, by no means excessive price. Gibberne's Nervous Accelerator it will be called, and he hopes to be able to supply it in three strengths: one in 200, one in 900, and one in 2000, distinguished by yellow, pink, and white labels respectively.

No doubt its use renders a great number of very extraordinary things possible; for, of course, the most remarkable and, possibly, even criminal proceedings may be effected with impunity by thus dodging, as it were, into the interstices of time. Like all potent preparations, it will be liable to abuse. We have, however, discussed this aspect of the question very thoroughly, and we have decided that this is purely a matter of medical jurisprudence and altogether outside our province. We shall manufacture and sell the Accelerator, and as for the consequences—we shall see.

XXVIII

THE TRUTH ABOUT PYECRAFT

HE sits not a dozen yards away. If I glance over my shoulder I can see him. And if I catch his eye—and usually I catch his eye—it meets me with an expression——

It is mainly an imploring look—and yet with suspicion in it.

Confound his suspicion! If I wanted to tell on him I should have told long ago. I don't tell and I don't tell, and he ought to feel at his ease. As if anything so gross and fat as he could feel at ease! Who would believe me if I did tell?

Poor old Pyecraft! Great, uneasy jelly of substance! The fattest clubman in London.

He sits at one of the little club tables in the huge bay by the fire, stuffing. What is he stuffing? I glance judiciously, and catch him biting at a round of hot buttered teacake, with his eyes on me. Confound him!—with his eyes on me!

That settles it, Pyecraft! Since you *will* be abject, since you *will* behave as though I was not a man of honour, here, right under your embedded* eyes, I write the thing down—the plain truth about Pyecraft. The man I helped, the man I shielded, and who has requited me by making my club un-endurable, absolutely unendurable, with his liquid appeal, with the perpetual 'don't tell' of his looks.

And, besides, why does he keep on eternally eating?

Well, here goes for the truth, the whole truth, and nothing but the truth!*

Pyecraft——. I made the acquaintance of Pyecraft in this very smoking-room. I was a young, nervous new member, and he saw it. I was sitting all alone, wishing I knew more of the members, and suddenly he came, a great rolling front of chins and abdomina, towards me, and grunted and sat down in a chair close by me and wheezed for a space, and scraped for a space with a match and lit a cigar, and then addressed me. I forget what he said—something about the matches not lighting properly, and afterwards as he talked he kept stopping the waiters one by one as they went by, and telling them about the matches in that thin, fluty voice he has. But, anyhow, it was in some such way we began our talking.

He talked about various things and came round to games. And thence to my figure and complexion. '*You* ought to be a good cricketer,' he said. I suppose I am slender, slender to what some people would call lean, and I suppose I am rather dark, still—— I am not ashamed of having a Hindu great-grandmother, but, for all that, I don't want casual strangers to see through me at a glance to *her*. So that I was set against Pyecraft from the beginning.

But he only talked about me in order to get to himself.

'I expect,' he said, 'you take no more exercise than I do, and probably you eat no less.' (Like all excessively obese people he fancied he ate nothing.) 'Yet'—and he smiled an oblique smile—'we differ.'

And then he began to talk about his fatness and his fatness; all he did for his fatness and all he was going to do for his fatness: what people had advised him to do for his fatness and what he had heard of people doing for fatness similar to his. 'A *priori*,'* he said, 'one would think a question of nutrition could be answered by dietary and a question of assimilation by drugs.' It was stifling. It was dumpling talk. It made me feel swelled to hear him.

One stands that sort of thing once in a way at a club, but a time came when I fancied I was standing too much. He took to me altogether too conspicuously. I could never go into the smoking-room but he would come wallowing towards me, and sometimes he came and gormandised round and about me while I had my lunch. He seemed at times almost to be clinging to me. He was a bore, but not so fearful a bore as to be limited to me; and from the first there was something in his manner—almost as though he knew, almost as though he penetrated to the fact that I *might*—that there was a remote, exceptional chance in me that no one else presented.

'I'd give anything to get it down,' he would say—'anything,' and peer at me over his vast cheeks and pant. Poor old Pyecraft! He has just gonged; no doubt to order another buttered teacake!

He came to the actual thing one day. 'Our Pharmacopœia,' he said, 'our Western Pharmacopœia, is anything but the last word of medical science. In the East, I've been told——'

He stopped and stared at me. It was like being at an aquarium.

I was quite suddenly angry with him. 'Look here,' I said, 'who told you about my great-grandmother's recipes?'

'Well,' he fenced.

'Every time we've met for a week,' I said—'and we've met pretty often—you've given me a broad hint or so about that little secret of mine.'

'Well,' he said, 'now the cat's out of the bag, I'll admit, yes, it is so. I had it——'

'From Pattison?'

'Indirectly,' he said, which I believe was lying, 'yes.'

'Pattison,' I said, 'took that stuff at his own risk.'

He pursed his mouth and bowed.

'My great-grandmother's recipes,' I said, 'are queer things to handle. My father was near making me promise——'

'He didn't?'

'No. But he warned me. He himself used one—once.'

'Ah! . . . But do you think——? Suppose—suppose there did happen to be one——'

'The things are curious documents,' I said. 'Even the smell of 'em . . . No!'

But after going so far Pyecraft was resolved I should go farther. I was always a little afraid if I tried his patience too much he would fall on me suddenly and smother me. I own

I was weak. But I was also annoyed with Pyecraft. I had got to that state of feeling for him that disposed me to say, 'Well, *take* the risk!' The little affair of Pattison to which I have alluded was a different matter altogether. What it was doesn't concern us now, but I knew, anyhow, that the particular recipe I used then was safe. The rest I didn't know so much about, and, on the whole, I was inclined to doubt their safety pretty completely.

Yet even if Pyecraft got poisoned——

I must confess the poisoning of Pyecraft struck me as an immense undertaking.

That evening I took that queer, odd-scented sandalwood box out of my safe, and turned the rustling skins over. The gentleman who wrote the recipes for my great-grandmother evidently had a weakness for skins of a miscellaneous origin, and his handwriting was cramped to the last degree. Some of the things are quite unreadable to me—though my family, with its Indian Civil Service associations, has kept up a knowledge of Hindustani from generation to generation—and none are absolutely plain sailing. But I found the one that I knew was there soon enough, and sat on the floor by my safe for some time looking at it.

'Look here,' said I to Pyecraft next day, and snatched the slip away from his eager grasp.

'So far as I can make it out, this is a recipe for Loss of Weight. ('Ah!' said Pyecraft.) I'm not absolutely sure, but I think it's that. And if you take my advice you'll leave it alone. Because, you know—I blacken my blood in your interest, Pyecraft—my ancestors on that side were, so far as I can gather, a jolly queer lot. See?'

'Let me try it,' said Pyecraft.

I leant back in my chair. My imagination made one mighty effort and fell flat within me. 'What in Heaven's name, Pyecraft,' I asked, 'do you think you'll look like when you get thin?'

He was impervious to reason. I made him promise never

to say a word to me about his disgusting fatness again whatever happened—never, and then I handed him that little
piece of skin.

'It's nasty stuff,' I said.

'No matter,' he said, and took it.

He goggled at it. 'But—but——' he said.

He had just discovered that it wasn't English.

'To the best of my ability,' I said, 'I will do you a translation.'

I did my best. After that we didn't speak for a fortnight.
Whenever he approached me I frowned and motioned him
away, and he respected our compact, but at the end of the
fortnight he was as fat as ever. And then he got a word in.

'I must speak,' he said. 'It isn't fair. There's something
wrong. It's done me no good. You're not doing your great-
grandmother justice.'

'Where's the recipe?'

He produced it gingerly from his pocket-book.

I ran my eye over the items. 'Was the egg addled?' I
asked.

'No. Ought it to have been?'

'That,' I said, 'goes without saying in all my poor dear
great-grandmother's recipes. When condition or quality is
not specified you must get the worst. She was drastic or
nothing. . . . And there's one or two possible alternatives to
some of these other things. You got *fresh* rattlesnake venom?'

'I got a rattlesnake from Jamrach's.* It cost—it cost——'

'That's your affair anyhow. This last item——'

'I know a man who——'

'Yes. H'm. Well, I'll write the alternatives down. So far as
I know the language, the spelling of this recipe is particularly
atrocious. By-the-by, dog here probably means pariah dog.'*

For a month after that I saw Pyecraft constantly at the
club and as fat and anxious as ever. He kept our treaty, but
at times he broke the spirit of it by shaking his head
despondently. Then one day in the cloakroom he said, 'Your
great-grandmother——'

'Not a word against her,' I said; and he held his peace.

I could have fancied he had desisted, and I saw him one day talking to three new members about his fatness as though he was in search of other recipes. And then, quite unexpectedly, his telegram came.

'Mr Formalyn!' bawled a page-boy under my nose, and I took the telegram and opened it at once.

'For Heaven's sake come.—Pyecraft.'

'H'm,' said I, and to tell the truth I was so pleased at the rehabilitation of my great-grandmother's reputation this evidently promised that I made a most excellent lunch.

I got Pyecraft's address from the hall porter. Pyecraft inhabited the upper half of a house in Bloomsbury, and I went there so soon as I had done my coffee and Trappistine.* I did not wait to finish my cigar.

'Mr Pyecraft?' said I, at the front door.

They believed he was ill; he hadn't been out for two days.

'He expects me,' said I, and they sent me up.

I rang the bell at the lattice-door upon the landing.

'He shouldn't have tried it, anyhow,' I said to myself. 'A man who eats like a pig ought to look like a pig.'

An obviously worthy woman, with an anxious face and a carelessly placed cap, came and surveyed me through the lattice.

I gave my name and she let me in in a dubious fashion.

'Well?' said I, as we stood together inside Pyecraft's piece of the landing.

''E said you was to come in if you came,' she said, and regarded me, making no motion to show me anywhere. And then, confidentially, ''E's locked in, sir.'

'Locked in?'

'Locked 'imself in yesterday morning and 'asn't let any one in since, sir. And ever and again *swearing*. Oh, my!'

I stared at the door she indicated by her glances. 'In there?' I said.

'Yes, sir.'

'What's up?'

She shook her head sadly. ''E keeps on calling for vittles, sir. *'Eavy* vittles 'e wants. I get 'im what I can. Pork 'e's had, sooit puddin', sossiges, noo bread. Everythink like that. Left outside, if you please, and me go away. 'E's eatin', sir, something *awful.*'

There came a piping bawl from inside the door: 'That Formalyn?'

'That you, Pyecraft?' I shouted, and went and banged the door.

'Tell her to go away.'

I did.

Then I could hear a curious pattering upon the door, almost like some one feeling for the handle in the dark, and Pyecraft's familiar grunts.

'It's all right,' I said, 'she's gone.'

But for a long time the door didn't open.

I heard the key turn. Then Pyecraft's voice said, 'Come in.'

I turned the handle and opened the door. Naturally I expected to see Pyecraft.

Well, you know, he wasn't there!

I never had such a shock in my life. There was his sitting-room in a state of untidy disorder, plates and dishes among the books and writing things, and several chairs overturned, but Pyecraft——

'It's all right, old man; shut the door,' he said, and then I discovered him.

There he was, right up close to the cornice in the corner by the door, as though some one had glued him to the ceiling. His face was anxious and angry. He panted and gesticulated. 'Shut the door,' he said. 'If that woman gets hold of it——'

I shut the door, and went and stood away from him and stared.

'If anything gives way and you tumble down,' I said, 'you'll break your neck, Pyecraft.'

'I wish I could,' he wheezed.

'A man of your age and weight getting up to kiddish gymnastics——'

'Don't,' he said, and looked agonised.

'I'll tell you,' he said, and gesticulated.

'How the deuce,' said I, 'are you holding on up there?'

And then abruptly I realised that he was not holding on at all, that he was floating up there—just as a gas-filled bladder might have floated in the same position. He began a struggle to thrust himself away from the ceiling and to clamber down the wall to me. 'It's that prescription,' he panted, as he did so. 'Your great-gran——'

He took hold of a framed engraving rather carelessly as he spoke and it gave way, and he flew back to the ceiling again, while the picture smashed on to the sofa. Bump he went against the ceiling, and I knew then why he was all over white on the more salient curves and angles of his person. He tried again more carefully, coming down by way of the mantel.

It was really a most extraordinary spectacle, that great, fat, apoplectic-looking* man upside down and trying to get from the ceiling to the floor. 'That prescription,' he said. 'Too successful.'

'How?'

'Loss of weight—almost complete.'

And then, of course, I understood.

'By Jove, Pyecraft,' said I, 'what you wanted was a cure for fatness! But you always called it weight. You would call it weight.'

Somehow I was extremely delighted. I quite liked Pyecraft for the time. 'Let me help you!' I said, and took his hand and pulled him down. He kicked about, trying to get foothold somewhere. It was very like holding a flag on a windy day.

'That table,' he said, pointing, 'is solid mahogany and very heavy. If you can put me under that——'

I did, and there he wallowed about like a captive balloon, while I stood on his hearthrug and talked to him.

I lit a cigar. 'Tell me,' I said, 'what happened?'

'I took it,' he said.

'How did it taste?'

'Oh, *beastly*!'

I should fancy they all did. Whether one regards the ingredients or the probable compound or the possible results, almost all my great-grandmother's remedies appear to me at least to be extraordinarily uninviting. For my own part——

'I took a little sip first.'

'Yes?'

'And as I felt lighter and better after an hour, I decided to take the draught.'

'My dear Pyecraft!'

'I held my nose,' he explained. 'And then I kept on getting lighter and lighter—and helpless, you know.'

He gave way suddenly to a burst of passion. 'What the goodness am I to *do*?' he said.

'There's one thing pretty evident,' I said, 'that you mustn't do. If you go out of doors you'll go up and up.' I waved an arm upward. 'They'd have to send Santos-Dumont* after you to bring you down again.'

'I suppose it will wear off?'

I shook my head. 'I don't think you can count on that,' I said.

And then there was another burst of passion, and he kicked out at adjacent chairs and banged the floor. He behaved just as I should have expected a great, fat, self-indulgent man to behave under trying circumstances—that is to say, very badly. He spoke of me and of my great-grandmother with an utter want of discretion.

'I never asked you to take the stuff,' I said.

And generously disregarding the insults he was putting upon me, I sat down in his armchair and began to talk to him in a sober, friendly fashion.

I pointed out to him that this was a trouble he had brought upon himself, and that it had almost an air of poetical justice. He had eaten too much. This he disputed, and for a time we argued the point.

He became noisy and violent, so I desisted from this aspect of his lesson. 'And then,' said I, 'you committed the sin of euphemism. You called it, not Fat, which is just and inglorious, but Weight. You——'

He interrupted to say that he recognised all that. What was he to *do*?

I suggested he should adapt himself to his new conditions. So we came to the really sensible part of the business. I suggested that it would not be difficult for him to learn to walk about on the ceiling with his hands——

'I can't sleep,' he said.

But that was no great difficulty. It was quite possible, I pointed out, to make a shake-up under a wire mattress, fasten the under things on with tapes, and have a blanket, sheet, and coverlet to button at the side. He would have to confide in his housekeeper, I said; and after some squabbling he agreed to that. (Afterwards it was quite delightful to see the beautifully matter-of-fact way with which the good lady took all these amazing inversions.) He could have a library ladder in his room, and all his meals could be laid on the top of his bookcase. We also hit on an ingenious device by which he could get to the floor whenever he wanted, which was simply to put the *British Encylopædia* (tenth edition) on the top of his open shelves. He just pulled out a couple of volumes and held on, and down he came. And we agreed there must be iron staples along the skirting, so that he could cling to those whenever he wanted to get about the room on the lower level.

As we got on with the thing I found myself almost keenly interested. It was I who called in the housekeeper and broke matters to her, and it was I chiefly who fixed up the inverted bed. In fact, I spent two whole days at his flat. I am a handy, interfering sort of man with a screw-driver, and I made all sorts of ingenious adaptations for him—ran a wire to bring his bells within reach, turned all his electric lights up instead of down, and so on. The whole affair was extremely curious and interesting to me, and it was delightful to think of Pyecraft like some great, fat blow-fly, crawling about on his ceiling and clambering round the lintel of his doors from one room to another, and never, never, never coming to the club any more. . . .

Then, you know, my fatal ingenuity got the better of me. I was sitting by his fire drinking his whisky, and he was up in his favourite corner by the cornice, tacking a Turkey carpet to the ceiling, when the idea struck me. 'By Jove, Pyecraft!' I said, 'all this is totally unnecessary.'

And before I could calculate the complete consequences of my notion I blurted it out. 'Lead underclothing,' said I, and the mischief was done.

Pyecraft received the thing almost in tears. 'To be right ways up again——' he said.

I gave him the whole secret before I saw where it would take me. 'Buy sheet lead,' I said, 'stamp it into discs. Sew 'em all over your underclothes until you have enough. Have lead-soled boots, carry a bag of solid lead, and the thing is done! Instead of being a prisoner here you may go abroad again, Pyecraft; you may travel——'

A still happier idea came to me. 'You need never fear a shipwreck. All you need do is just slip off some or all of your clothes, take the necessary amount of luggage in your hand, and float up in the air——'

In his emotion he dropped the tack-hammer within an ace of my head. 'By Jove!' he said, 'I shall be able to come back to the club again.'

The thing pulled me up short. 'By Jove!' I said, faintly. 'Yes. Of course—you will.'

He did. He does. There he sits behind me now, stuffing—as I live!—a third go of buttered teacake. And no one in the whole world knows—except his housekeeper and me—that he weighs practically nothing; that he is a mere boring mass of assimilatory matter, mere clouds in clothing, *niente, nefas*,* the most inconsiderable of men. There he sits watching until I have done this writing. Then, if he can, he will waylay me. He will come billowing up to me. . . .

He will tell me over again all about it, how it feels, how it doesn't feel, how he sometimes hopes it is passing off a little. And always somewhere in that fat, abundant discourse he will say, 'The secret's keeping, eh? If any one knew of it—I should be so ashamed. . . . Makes a fellow look such a fool, you know. Crawling about on a ceiling and all that. . . .'

And now to elude Pyecraft, occupying, as he does, an admirable strategic position between me and the door.

XXIX

THE MAGIC SHOP

I HAD seen the Magic Shop from afar several times; I had passed it once or twice, a shop window of alluring little objects, magic balls, magic hens, wonderful cones, ventriloquist dolls, the material of the basket trick, packs of cards that *looked* all right, and all that sort of thing, but never had I thought of going in until one day, almost without warning, Gip* hauled me by my finger right up to the window, and so conducted himself that there was nothing for it but to take him in. I had not thought the place was there, to tell the truth—a modest-sized frontage in Regent Street, between the picture shop and the place where the chicks run about just out of patent incubators,—but there it was sure enough. I had fancied it was down nearer the Circus, or round the corner in Oxford Street, or even in Holborn;* always over the way and a little inaccessible it had been, with something of the mirage in its position; but here it was now quite indisputably, and the fat end of Gip's pointing finger made a noise upon the glass.

'If I was rich,' said Gip, dabbing a finger at the Disappearing Egg, 'I'd buy myself that. And that'—which was The Crying Baby, Very Human—'and that,' which was a mystery, and called, so a neat card asserted, 'Buy One and Astonish Your Friends.'

'Anything,' said Gip, 'will disappear under one of those cones. I have read about it in a book.

'And there, dadda, is the Vanishing Halfpenny—only they've put it this way up so's we can't see how it's done.'

Gip, dear boy, inherits his mother's breeding, and he did not propose to enter the shop or worry in any way; only, you know, quite unconsciously, he lugged my finger doorward, and he made his interest clear.

'That,' he said, and pointed to the Magic Bottle.

'If you had that?' I said; at which promising inquiry he looked up with a sudden radiance.

'I could show it to Jessie,'* he said, thoughtful as ever of others.

'It's less than a hundred days to your birthday, Gibbles,' I said, and laid my hand on the door-handle.

Gip made no answer, but his grip tightened on my finger, and so we came into the shop.

It was no common shop this; it was a magic shop, and all the prancing precedence Gip would have taken in the matter of mere toys was wanting. He left the burthen of the conversation to me.

It was a little, narrow shop, not very well lit, and the door-bell pinged again with a plaintive note as we closed it behind us. For a moment or so we were alone and could glance about us. There was a tiger in *papier-mâché* on the glass case that covered the low counter—a grave, kind-eyed tiger that waggled his head in a methodical manner; there were several crystal spheres, a china hand holding magic cards, a stock of magic fish-bowls in various sizes, and an immodest magic hat that shamelessly displayed its springs. On the floor were magic mirrors; one to draw you out long and thin, one to swell your head and vanish your legs, and one to make you short and fat like a draught; and while, we were laughing at these the shopman, as I suppose, came in.

At any rate, there he was behind the counter—a curious, sallow, dark man, with one ear larger than the other and a chin like the toe-cap of a boot.

'What can we have the pleasure?' he said, spreading his long magic fingers on the glass case; and so with a start we were aware of him.

'I want,' I said, 'to buy my little boy a few simple tricks.'

'Legerdemain?' he asked. 'Mechanical? Domestic?'

'Anything amusing?' said I.

'Um!' said the shopman, and scratched his head for a

moment as if thinking. Then, quite distinctly, he drew from his head a glass ball. 'Something in this way?' he said, and held it out.

The action was unexpected. I had seen the trick done at entertainments endless times before—it's part of the common stock of conjurers—but I had not expected it here. 'That's good,' I said, with a laugh.

'Isn't it?' said the shopman.

Gip stretched out his disengaged hand to take this object and found merely a blank palm.

'It's in your pocket,' said the shopman, and there it was!

'How much will that be?' I asked.

'We make no charge for glass balls,' said the shopman politely. 'We get them'—he picked one out of his elbow as he spoke—'free.' He produced another from the back of his neck, and laid it beside its predecessor on the counter. Gip regarded his glass ball sagely, then directed a look of inquiry at the two on the counter, and finally brought his round-eyed scrutiny to the shopman, who smiled. 'You may have those two,' said the shopman, 'and, if you *don't* mind one from my mouth. *So!*'

Gip counselled me mutely for a moment, and then in a profound silence put away the four balls, resumed my reassuring finger, and nerved himself for the next event.

'We get all our smaller tricks in that way,' the shopman remarked.

I laughed in the manner of one who subscribes to a jest. 'Instead of going to the wholesale shop,' I said. 'Of course, it's cheaper.'

'In a way,' the shopman said. 'Though we pay in the end. But not so heavily—as people suppose. . . . Our larger tricks, and our daily provisions and all the other things we want, we get out of that hat. . . . And you know, sir, if you'll excuse my saying it, there *isn't* a wholesale shop, not for Genuine Magic goods, sir. I don't know if you noticed our inscription—the Genuine Magic Shop.' He drew a business card from his

cheek and handed it to me. 'Genuine,' he said, with his finger
on the word, and added, 'There is absolutely no deception,
sir.'

He seemed to be carrying out the joke pretty thoroughly,
I thought.

He turned to Gip with a smile of remarkable affability.
'You, you know, are the Right Sort of Boy.'

I was surprised at his knowing that, because, in the interests
of discipline, we keep it rather a secret even at home; but
Gip received it in unflinching silence, keeping a steadfast
eye on him.

'It's only the Right Sort of Boy gets through that doorway.'

And, as if by way of illustration, there came a rattling at
the door, and a squeaking little voice could be faintly heard.
'Nyar! I *warn* 'a go in there, dadda, I WARN 'a go in there.
Ny-a-a-ah!' and then the accents of a downtrodden parent,
urging consolations and propitiations. 'It's locked, Edward,'
he said.

'But it isn't,' said I.

'It is, sir,' said the shopman, 'always—for that sort of child,'
and as he spoke we had a glimpse of the other youngster, a
little, white face, pallid from sweet-eating and over-sapid*
food, and distorted by evil passions, a ruthless little egotist,
pawing at the enchanted pane. 'It's no good, sir,' said the
shopman, as I moved, with my natural helpfulness, doorward,
and presently the spoilt child was carried off howling.

'How do you manage that?' I said, breathing a little more
freely.

'Magic!' said the shopman, with a careless wave of the
hand, and behold! sparks of coloured fire flew out of his
fingers and vanished into the shadows of the shop.

'You were saying,' he said, addressing himself to Gip, 'before you came in, that you would like one of our "Buy One
and Astonish your Friends" boxes?'

Gip, after a gallant effort, said 'Yes.'

'It's in your pocket.'

And leaning over the counter—he really had an extraordinary long body—this amazing person produced the article in the customary conjurer's manner. 'Paper,' he said, and took a sheet out of the empty hat with the springs; 'string,' and behold his mouth was a string box, from which he drew an unending thread, which when he had tied his parcel he bit off—and, it seemed to me, swallowed the ball of string. And then he lit a candle at the nose of one of the ventriloquist's dummies, stuck one of his fingers (which had become sealing-wax red) into the flame, and so sealed the parcel. 'Then there was the Disappearing Egg,' he remarked, and produced one from within my coat-breast and packed it, and also The Crying Baby, Very Human. I handed each parcel to Gip as it was ready, and he clasped them to his chest.

He said very little, but his eyes were eloquent; the clutch of his arms was eloquent. He was the playground of unspeakable emotions. These, you know, were *real* Magics.

Then, with a start, I discovered something moving about in my hat—something soft and jumpy. I whipped it off, and a ruffled pigeon—no doubt a confederate—dropped out and ran on the counter, and went, I fancy, into a cardboard box behind the *papier-mâché* tiger.

'Tut, tut!' said the shopman, dexterously relieving me of my headdress; 'careless bird, and—as I live—nesting!'

He shook my hat, and shook out into his extended hand, two or three eggs, a large marble, a watch, about half a dozen of the inevitable glass balls, and then crumpled, crinkled paper, more and more and more, talking all the time of the way in which people neglect to brush their hats *inside* as well as out—politely, of course, but with a certain personal application. 'All sorts of things accumulate, sir. . . . Not *you*, of course, in particular. . . . Nearly every customer. . . . Astonishing what they carry about with them. . . .' The crumpled paper rose and billowed on the counter more and more and more, until he was nearly hidden from us, until he was altogether hidden, and still his voice went on and on. 'We none of us know what the fair semblance of a human being may conceal, Sir. Are we all then no better than brushed exteriors, whited sepulchres——'*

His voice stopped—exactly like when you hit a neighbour's gramophone with a well-aimed brick, the same instant silence—and the rustle of the paper stopped, and everything was still. . . .

'Have you done with my hat?' I said, after an interval.

There was no answer.

I stared at Gip, and Gip stared at me, and there were our distortions in the magic mirrors, looking very rum,* and grave, and quiet. . . .

'I think we'll go now,' I said. 'Will you tell me how much all this comes to? . . .

'I say,' I said, on a rather louder note, 'I want the bill; and my hat, please.'

It might have been a sniff from behind the paper pile. . . .

'Let's look behind the counter, Gip,' I said. 'He's making fun of us.'

I led Gip round the head-wagging tiger, and what do you think there was behind the counter? No one at all! Only my hat on the floor, and a common conjurer's lop-eared white rabbit lost in meditation, and looking as stupid and crumpled as only a conjurer's rabbit can do. I resumed my hat, and the rabbit lolloped a lollop or so out of my way.

'Dadda!' said Gip, in a guilty whisper.

'What is it, Gip?' said I.

'I *do* like this shop, dadda.'

'So should I,' I said to myself, 'if the counter wouldn't suddenly extend itself to shut one off from the door.' But I didn't call Gip's attention to that. 'Pussy!' he said, with a hand out to the rabbit as it came lolloping past us; 'Pussy, do Gip a magic!' and his eyes followed it as it squeezed through a door I had certainly not remarked a moment before. Then this door opened wider, and the man with one ear larger than the other appeared again. He was smiling still, but his eye met mine with something between amusement and defiance. 'You'd like to see our showroom, sir,' he said, with an innocent suavity. Gip tugged my finger forward. I glanced at the counter and met the shopman's eye again. I was beginning to think the magic just a little too genuine. 'We haven't *very* much time,' I said. But somehow we were inside the showroom before I could finish that.

'All goods of the same quality,' said the shopman, rubbing his flexible hands together, 'and that is the Best. Nothing in the place that isn't genuine Magic, and warranted thoroughly rum. Excuse me, sir!'

I felt him pull at something that clung to my coat-sleeve, and then I saw he held a little, wriggling red demon by the tail—the little creature bit and fought and tried to get at his hand—and in a moment he tossed it carelessly behind a counter. No doubt the thing was only an image of twisted indiarubber, but for the moment——! And his gesture was exactly that of a man who handles some petty biting bit of vermin. I glanced at Gip, but Gip was looking at a magic rocking-horse. I was glad he hadn't seen the thing. 'I say,' I said, in an undertone, and indicating Gip and the red demon with my eyes, 'you haven't many things like *that* about, have you?'

'None of ours! Probably brought it with you,' said the shopman—also in an undertone, and with a more dazzling smile than ever. 'Astonishing what people *will* carry about with them unawares!' And then to Gip, 'Do you see anything you fancy here?'

There were many things that Gip fancied there.

He turned to this astonishing tradesman with mingled confidence and respect. 'Is that a Magic Sword?' he said.

'A Magic Toy Sword. It neither bends, breaks, nor cuts the fingers. It renders the bearer invincible in battle against any one under eighteen. Half a crown to seven and sixpence, according to size. These panoplies* on cards are for juvenile knights-errant and very useful—shield of safety, sandals of swiftness, helmet of invisibility.'

'Oh, dadda!' gasped Gip.

I tried to find out what they cost, but the shopman did not heed me. He had got Gip now; he had got him away from my finger; he had embarked upon the exposition of all his confounded stock, and nothing was going to stop him. Presently I saw with a qualm of distrust and something very like jealousy that Gip had hold of this person's finger as usually he has hold of mine. No doubt the fellow was interesting, I thought, and had an interestingly faked lot of stuff, really *good* faked stuff, still——

I wandered after them, saying very little, but keeping an eye on this prestidigital fellow. After all, Gip was enjoying it. And no doubt when the time came to go we should be able to go quite easily.

It was a long, rambling place, that showroom, a gallery broken up by stands and stalls and pillars, with archways leading off to other departments, in which the queerest-looking assistants loafed and stared at one, and with perplexing mirrors and curtains. So perplexing, indeed, were these that I was presently unable to make out the door by which we had come.

The shopman showed Gip magic trains that ran without steam or clockwork, just as you set the signals, and then some very, very valuable boxes of soldiers that all came alive directly you took off the lid and said—— I myself haven't a very quick ear, and it was a tongue-twisting sound, but Gip—he has his mother's ear—got it in no time. 'Bravo!' said the shopman, putting the men back into the box unceremoniously and handing it to Gip. 'Now,' said the shopman, and in a moment Gip had made them all alive again.

'You'll take that box?' asked the shopman.

'We'll take that box,' said I, 'unless you charge its full value. In which case it would need a Trust Magnate——'

'Dear heart! *No!*' and the shopman swept the little men back again, shut the lid, waved the box in the air, and there it was, in brown paper, tied up and—*with Gip's full name and address on the paper!*

The shopman laughed at my amazement.

'This is the genuine magic,' he said. 'The real thing.'

'It's a little too genuine for my taste,' I said again.

After that he fell to showing Gip tricks, odd tricks, and still odder the way they were done. He explained them, he turned them inside out, and there was the dear little chap nodding his busy bit of a head in the sagest manner.

I did not attend as well as I might. 'Hey, presto!' said the Magic Shopman, and then would come the clear, small 'Hey, presto!' of the boy. But I was distracted by other things. It was being borne in upon me just how tremendously rum this place was; it was, so to speak, inundated by a sense of rumness. There was something a little rum about the fixtures even, about the ceiling, about the floor, about the casually distributed chairs. I had a queer feeling that whenever I wasn't looking at them straight they went askew, and moved about, and played a noiseless puss-in-the-corner* behind my back. And the cornice had a serpentine design with masks—masks altogether too expressive for proper plaster.

Then abruptly my attention was caught by one of the odd-looking assistants. He was some way off and evidently unaware of my presence—I saw a sort of three-quarter length of him over a pile of toys and through an arch—and, you know, he was leaning against a pillar in an idle sort of way doing the most horrid things with his features! The particular horrid thing he did was with his nose. He did it just as though he was idle and wanted to amuse himself. First of all it was a short, blobby nose, and then suddenly he shot it out like a telescope, and then out it flew and became thinner and thinner until it was like a long, red flexible whip. Like a thing in a nightmare it was! He flourished it about and flung it forth as a fly-fisher flings his line.

My instant thought was that Gip mustn't see him. I turned about, and there was Gip quite preoccupied with the shop-man, and thinking no evil. They were whispering together and looking at me. Gip was standing on a little stool, and the shopman was holding a sort of big drum in his hand.

'Hide and seek, dadda!' cried Gip. 'You're He!'

And before I could do anything to prevent it, the shop-man had clapped the big drum over him.

I saw what was up directly. 'Take that off,' I cried, 'this instant! You'll frighten the boy. Take it off!'

The shopman with the unequal ears did so without a word, and held the big cylinder towards me to show its emptiness. And the little stool was vacant! In that instant my boy had utterly disappeared! . . .

You know, perhaps, that sinister something that comes like a hand out of the unseen and grips your heart about. You know it takes your common self away and leaves you tense and deliberate, neither slow nor hasty, neither angry nor afraid. So it was with me.

I came up to this grinning shopman and kicked his stool aside.

'Stop this folly!' I said. 'Where is my boy?'

'You see,' he said, still displaying the drum's interior, 'there is no deception——'

I put out my hand to grip him, and he eluded me by a dexterous movement. I snatched again, and he turned from me and pushed open a door to escape. 'Stop!' I said, and he laughed, receding. I leapt after him into utter darkness.

Thud!

'Lor' bless my 'eart! I didn't see you coming, sir!'

I was in Regent Street, and I had collided with a decent-looking working man; and a yard away, perhaps, and looking a little perplexed with himself, was Gip. There was some sort of apology, and then Gip had turned and come to me with a bright little smile, as though for a moment he had missed me.

And he was carrying four parcels in his arm!

He secured immediate possession of my finger.

For the second I was rather at a loss. I stared round to see the door of the Magic Shop, and, behold, it was not there! There was no door, no shop, nothing, only the common pilaster between the shop where they sell pictures and the window with the chicks! . . .

I did the only thing possible in that mental tumult; I walked straight to the kerbstone and held up my umbrella for a cab.

"Ansoms,'* said Gip, in a note of culminating exultation.

I helped him in, recalled my address with an effort, and got in also. Something unusual proclaimed itself in my tail-coat pocket, and I felt and discovered a glass ball. With a petulant expression I flung it into the street.

Gip said nothing.

For a space neither of us spoke.

'Dadda!' said Gip, at last, 'that *was* a proper shop!'

I came round with that to the problem of just how the whole thing had seemed to him. He looked completely undamaged—so far, good; he was neither scared nor un-hinged, he was simply tremendously satisfied with the afternoon's entertainment, and there in his arms were the four parcels.

Confound it! what could be in them?

'Um!' I said. 'Little boys can't go to shops like that every day.'

He received this with his usual stoicism, and for a moment I was sorry I was his father and not his mother, and so couldn't suddenly there, *coram publico*,* in our hansom, kiss him. After all, I thought, the thing wasn't so very bad.

But it was only when we opened the parcels that I really began to be reassured. Three of them contained boxes of soldiers, quite ordinary lead soldiers, but of so good a quality as to make Gip altogether forget that originally these parcels had been Magic Tricks of the only genuine sort, and the fourth contained a kitten, a little living white kitten, in excellent health and appetite and temper.

I saw this unpacking with a sort of provisional relief. I hung about in the nursery for quite an unconscionable time. . . .

That happened six months ago. And now I am beginning to believe it is all right. The kitten had only the magic natural to all kittens, and the soldiers seemed as steady a company as any colonel could desire. And Gip——?

The intelligent parent will understand that I have to go cautiously with Gip.

But I went so far as this one day. I said, 'How would you like your soldiers to come alive, Gip, and march about by themselves?'

'Mine do,' said Gip. 'I just have to say a word I know before I open the lid.'

'Then they march about alone?'

'Oh, *quite*, dadda. I shouldn't like them if they didn't do that.'

I displayed no unbecoming surprise, and since then I have taken occasion to drop in upon him once or twice, unannounced, when the soldiers were about, but so far I have never discovered them performing in anything like a magical manner. . . .

It's so difficult to tell.

There's also a question of finance. I have an incurable habit of paying bills. I have been up and down Regent Street several times looking for that shop. I am inclined to think, indeed, that in that matter honour is satisfied, and that, since Gip's name and address are known to them, I may very well leave it to these people, whoever they may be, to send in their bill in their own time.

THE EMPIRE OF THE ANTS

I

WHEN Captain Gerilleau received instructions to take his new gunboat, the *Benjamin Constant*,* to Badama on the Batemo arm of the Guaramadema and there assist the inhabitants against a plague of ants, he suspected the authorities of mockery. His promotion had been romantic and irregular, the affections of a prominent Brazilian lady and the captain's liquid eyes had played a part in the process, and the *Diario* and *O Futuro* had been lamentably disrespectful in their comments. He felt he was to give further occasion for disrespect.

He was a Creole,* his conceptions of etiquette and discipline were pure-blooded Portuguese, and it was only to Holroyd, the Lancashire engineer who had come over with the boat, and as an exercise in the use of English—his 'th' sounds were very uncertain—that he opened his heart.

'It is in effect,' he said, 'to make me absurd! What can a man do against ants? Dey come, dey go.'

'They say,' said Holroyd, 'that these don't go. That chap you said was a Sambo——'

'Zambo;*—it is a sort of mixture of blood.'

'Sambo. He said the people are going!'

The captain smoked fretfully for a time. 'Dese tings 'ave to happen,' he said at last. 'What is it? Plagues of ants and suchlike as God wills. Dere was a plague in Trinidad—the little ants that carry leaves. Orl der orange-trees, all der mangoes! What does it matter? Sometimes ant armies come into your houses—fighting ants; a different sort. You go and they clean the house. Then you come back again;—the house is clean, like new! No cockroaches, no fleas, no jiggers in the floor.'

'That Sambo chap,' said Holroyd, 'says these are a different sort of ant.'

The captain shrugged his shoulders, fumed, and gave his attention to a cigarette.

Afterwards he reopened the subject. 'My dear 'Olroyd, what am I to do about dese infernal ants?'

The captain reflected. 'It is ridiculous,' he said. But in the afternoon he put on his full uniform and went ashore, and jars and boxes came back to the ship and subsequently he did. And Holroyd sat on deck in the evening coolness and smoked profoundly and marvelled at Brazil. They were six days up the Amazon, some hundreds of miles from the ocean, and east and west of him there was a horizon like the sea, and to the south nothing but a sand-bank island with some tufts of scrub. The water was always running like a sluice, thick with dirt, animated with crocodiles and hovering birds, and fed by some inexhaustible source of tree trunks; and the waste of it, the headlong waste of it, filled his soul. The town of Alemquer, with its meagre church, its thatched sheds for houses, its discoloured ruins of ampler days, seemed a little thing lost in this wilderness of Nature, a sixpence dropped on Sahara. He was a young man, this was his first sight of the tropics, he came straight from England, where Nature is hedged, ditched, and drained into the perfection of submission, and he had suddenly discovered the insignificance of man. For six days they had been steaming up from the sea by unfrequented channels, and man had been as rare as a rare butterfly. One saw one day a canoe, another day a distant station, the next no men at all. He began to perceive that man is indeed a rare animal, having but a precarious hold upon this land.

He perceived it more clearly as the days passed, and he made his devious way to the Batemo, in the company of this remarkable commander, who ruled over one big gun, and was forbidden to waste his ammunition. Holroyd was learning Spanish industriously, but he was still in the present tense and substantive stage of speech, and the only other person who had any words of English was a negro stoker, who had them all wrong. The second in command was a Portuguese, da Cunha, who spoke French, but it was a different sort of French from the French Holroyd had learnt in Southport, and their intercourse was confined to politenesses and simple propositions about the weather. And the weather, like everything else in this amazing new world, the weather had no human aspect, and was hot by night and hot by day, and the air steam, even the wind was hot steam, smelling of vegetation in decay: and the alligators and the strange birds, the flies of many sorts and sizes, the beetles, the ants, the snakes and monkeys seemed to wonder what man was doing in an atmosphere that had no gladness in its sunshine and no coolness in its night. To wear clothing was intolerable, but to cast it aside was to scorch by day, and expose an ampler area to the mosquitoes by night; to go on deck by day was to be blinded by glare and to stay below was to suffocate. And in the daytime came certain flies, extremely clever and noxious about one's wrist and ankle. Captain Gerilleau, who was Holroyd's sole distraction from these physical distresses, developed into a formidable bore, telling the simple story of his heart's affections day by day, a string of anonymous women, as if he was telling beads. Sometimes he suggested sport, and they shot at alligators, and at rare intervals they came to human aggregations in the waste of trees, and stayed for a day or so, and drank and sat about, and, one night, danced with Creole girls, who found Holroyd's poor elements of Spanish, without either past tense or future, amply sufficient for their purposes. But these were mere luminous chinks in the long grey passage of the streaming river, up which the throbbing engines beat. A certain liberal heathen deity, in the shape of a demi-john,* held seductive court aft, and, it is probable, forward.

But Gerilleau learnt things about the ants, more things and more, at this stopping-place and that, and became interested in his mission.

'Dey are a new sort of ant,' he said. 'We have got to be—what do you call it?—entomologie? Big. Five centimetres! Some bigger! It is ridiculous. We are like the monkeys—sent to pick insects. . . . But dey are eating up the country.'

He burst out indignantly. 'Suppose—suddenly, there are complications with Europe. Here am I—soon we shall be above the Rio Negro—and my gun, useless!'

He nursed his knee and mused.

'Dose people who were dere at de dancing place, dey 'ave come down. Dey 'ave lost all they got. De ants come to deir house one afternoon. Everyone run out. You know when de ants come one must—everyone runs out and they go over the house. If you stayed they'd eat you. See? Well, presently dey go back; dey say, "The ants 'ave gone." . . . De ants *aven't* gone. Dey try to go in—de son, 'e goes in. De ants fight.'

'Swarm over him?'

'Bite 'im. Presently he comes out again—screaming and running. He runs past them to the river. See? He gets into de water and drowns de ants—yes.' Gerilleau paused, brought his liquid eyes close to Holroyd's face, tapped Holroyd's knee with his knuckle. 'That night he dies, just as if he was stung by a snake.'

'Poisoned—by the ants?'

'Who knows?' Gerilleau shrugged his shoulders. 'Perhaps they bit him badly. . . . When I joined dis service I joined to fight men. Dese things, dese ants, dey come and go. It is no business for men.'

After that he talked frequently of the ants to Holroyd, and whenever they chanced to drift against any speck of humanity in that waste of water and sunshine and distant trees, Holroyd's improving knowledge of the language enabled him to recognise the ascendant word *Saüba*, more and more completely dominating the whole.

He perceived the ants were becoming interesting, and the nearer he drew to them the more interesting they became. Gerilleau abandoned his old themes almost suddenly, and the Portuguese lieutenant became a conversational figure; he knew something about the leaf-cutting ant, and expanded his knowledge. Gerilleau sometimes rendered what he had to tell to Holroyd. He told of the little workers that swarm and fight, and the big workers that command and rule, and how these latter always crawled to the neck and how their bites drew blood. He told how they cut leaves and made fungus beds, and how their nests in Caracas are sometimes a hundred yards across. Two days the three men spent disputing whether ants have eyes. The discussion grew dangerously heated on the second afternoon, and Holroyd saved the situation by going ashore in a boat to catch ants and see. He captured various specimens and returned, and some had eyes and some hadn't. Also, they argued, do ants bite or sting?

'Dese ants,' said Gerilleau, after collecting information at a rancho, 'have big eyes. They don't run about blind—not as most ants do. No! Dey get in corners and watch what you do.'

'And they sting?' asked Holroyd.

'Yes. Dey sting. Dere is poison in the sting.' He meditated. 'I do not see what men can do against ants. Dey come and go.'

'But these don't go.'

'They will,' said Gerilleau.

Past Tamandu there is a long low coast of eighty miles without any population, and then one comes to the confluence of the main river and the Batemo arm like a great lake, and then the forest came nearer, came at last intimately near. The character of the channel changes, snags* abound, and the *Benjamin Constant* moored by a cable that night, under the very shadow of dark trees. For the first time for many days came a spell of coolness, and Holroyd and Gerilleau sat late, smoking cigars and enjoying this delicious sensation.

Gerilleau's mind was full of ants and what they could do. He decided to sleep at last, and lay down on a mattress on deck, a man hopelessly perplexed, his last words, when he already seemed asleep, were to ask, with a flourish of despair, 'What can one do with ants? . . . De whole thing is absurd.'

Holroyd was left to scratch his bitten wrists, and meditate alone.

He sat on the bulwark and listened to the little changes in Gerilleau's breathing until he was fast asleep, and then the ripple and lap of the stream took his mind, and brought back that sense of immensity that had been growing upon him since first he had left Para and come up the river. The monitor* showed but one small light, and there was first a little talking forward and then stillness. His eyes went from the dim black outlines of the middle works of the gunboat towards the bank, to the black overwhelming mysteries of forest, lit now and then by a fire-fly, and never still from the murmur of alien and mysterious activities. . . .

It was the inhuman immensity of this land that astonished and oppressed him. He knew the skies were empty of men, the stars were specks in an incredible vastness of space; he knew the ocean was enormous and untamable, but in England he had come to think of the land as man's. In England it is indeed man's, the wild things live by sufferance, grow on lease, everywhere the roads, the fences, and absolute security runs. In an atlas, too, the land is man's, and all coloured to show his claim to it—in vivid contrast to the universal independent blueness of the sea. He had taken it for granted that a day would come when everywhere about the earth, plough and culture, light tramways and good roads, an ordered security, would prevail. But now, he doubted.

This forest was interminable, it had an air of being invincible, and Man seemed at best an infrequent precarious intruder. One travelled for miles, amidst the still, silent struggle of giant trees, of strangulating creepers, of assertive flowers, everywhere the alligator, the turtle, and endless varieties of birds and insects seemed at home, dwelt irreplaceably—but man, man at most held a footing upon resentful clearings, fought weeds, fought beasts and insects for the barest foothold, fell a prey to snake and beast, insect and fever, and was presently carried away. In many places down the river he had been manifestly driven back, this deserted creek or that preserved the name of a *casa*,* and here and there ruinous white walls and a shattered tower enforced the lesson. The puma, the jaguar, were more the masters here. . . .

Who were the real masters?

In a few miles of this forest there must be more ants than there are men in the whole world! This seemed to Holroyd a perfectly new idea. In a few thousand years men had emerged from barbarism to a stage of civilisation that made them feel lords of the future and masters of the earth! But what was to prevent the ants evolving also? Such ants as one knew lived in little communities of a few thousand individuals, made no concerted efforts against the greater world. But they had a language, they had an intelligence! Why should things stop at that any more than men had stopped at the barbaric stage? Suppose presently the ants began to store knowledge, just as men had done by means of books and records, use weapons, form great empires, sustain a planned and organised war?

Things came back to him that Gerilleau had gathered about these ants they were approaching. They used a poison like the poison of snakes. They obeyed greater leaders even as the leaf-cutting ants do. They were carnivorous, and where they came they stayed. . . .

The forest was very still. The water lapped incessantly against the side. About the lantern overhead there eddied a noiseless whirl of phantom moths.

Gerilleau stirred in the darkness and sighed. 'What can one *do*?' he murmured, and turned over and was still again.

Holroyd was roused from meditations that were becoming sinister by the hum of a mosquito.

II

THE next morning Holroyd learnt they were within forty kilometres of Badama, and his interest in the banks intensified. He came up whenever an opportunity offered to examine his surroundings. He could see no signs of human occupation whatever, save for a weedy ruin of a house and the green-stained façade of the long-deserted monastery at Mojû, with a forest tree growing out of a vacant window space, and great creepers netted across its vacant portals. Several flights of strange yellow butterflies with semi-transparent wings crossed the river that morning, and many alighted on the monitor and were killed by the men. It was towards afternoon that they came upon the derelict *cuberta*.

She did not at first appear to be derelict; both her sails were set and hanging slack in the afternoon calm, and there was the figure of a man sitting on the fore planking beside the shipped sweeps.* Another man appeared to be sleeping face downwards on the sort of longitudinal bridge these big canoes have in the waist. But it was presently apparent, from the sway of her rudder and the way she drifted into the course of the gunboat, that something was out of order with her. Gerilleau surveyed her through a field-glass, and became interested in the queer darkness of the face of the sitting man, a red-faced man he seemed, without a nose—crouching he was rather than sitting, and the longer the captain looked the less he liked to look at him, and the less able he was to take his glasses away.

But he did so at last, and went a little way to call up Holroyd. Then he went back to hail the cuberta. He hailed her again, and so she drove past him. *Santa Rosa* stood out clearly as her name.

As she came by and into the wake of the monitor, she pitched a little, and suddenly the figure of the crouching man collapsed as though all its joints had given way. His hat

409

fell off, his head was not nice to look at, and his body flopped lax and rolled out of sight behind the bulwarks.

'Caramba!' cried Gerilleau, and resorted to Holroyd forthwith.

Holroyd was half-way up the companion. 'Did you see dat?' said the captain.

'Dead!' said Holroyd. 'Yes. You'd better send a boat aboard. There's something wrong.'

'Did you—by any chance—see his face?'

'What was it like?'

'It was—ugh!—I have no words.' And the captain suddenly turned his back on Holroyd and became an active and strident commander.

The gunboat came about, steamed parallel to the erratic course of the canoe, and dropped the boat with Lieutenant da Cunha and three sailors to board her. Then the curiosity of the captain made him draw up almost alongside as the lieutenant got aboard, so that the whole of the *Santa Rosa*, deck and hold, was visible to Holroyd.

He saw now clearly that the sole crew of the vessel was these two dead men, and though he could not see their faces, he saw by their outstretched hands, which were all of ragged flesh, that they had been subjected to some strange exceptional process of decay. For a moment his attention concentrated on those two enigmatical bundles of dirty clothes and laxly flung limbs, and then his eyes went forward to discover the open hold piled high with trunks and cases, and aft, to where the little cabin gaped inexplicably empty. Then he became aware that the planks of the middle decking were dotted with moving black specks.

His attention was riveted by these specks. They were all walking in directions radiating from the fallen man in a manner—the image came unsought to his mind—like the crowd dispersing from a bull-fight.

He became aware of Gerilleau beside him. 'Capo,' he said,

'have you your glasses? Can you focus as closely as those planks there?'

Gerilleau made an effort, grunted, and handed him the glasses.

There followed a moment of scrutiny. 'It's ants,' said the Englishman, and handed the focused field-glass back to Gerilleau.

His impression of them was of a crowd of large black ants, very like ordinary ants except for their size, and for the fact that some of the larger of them bore a sort of clothing of grey. But at the time his inspection was too brief for particulars. The head of Lieutenant da Cunha appeared over the side of the cuberta, and a brief colloquy ensued.

'You must go aboard,' said Gerilleau.

The lieutenant objected that the boat was full of ants.

'You have your boots,' said Gerilleau.

The lieutenant changed the subject. 'How did these men die?' he asked.

Captain Gerilleau embarked upon speculations that Holroyd could not follow, and the two men disputed with a certain increasing vehemence. Holroyd took up the field-glass and resumed his scrutiny, first of the ants and then of the dead man amidships.

He has described these ants to me very particularly.

He says they were as large as any ants he has ever seen, black and moving with a steady deliberation very different from the mechanical fussiness of the common ant. About one in twenty was much larger than its fellows, and with an exceptionally large head. These reminded him at once of the master workers who are said to rule over the leaf-cutter ants; like them they seemed to be directing and co-ordinating the general movements. They tilted their bodies back in a manner altogether singular as if they made some use of the fore feet. And he had a curious fancy that he was too far off to verify, that most of these ants of both kinds were wearing

411

accoutrements, had things strapped about their bodies by bright white bands like white metal threads. . . .

He put down the glasses abruptly, realising that the question of discipline between the captain and his subordinate had become acute.

'It is your duty,' said the captain, 'to go aboard. It is my instructions.'

The lieutenant seemed on the verge of refusing. The head of one of the mulatto* sailors appeared beside him.

'I believe these men were killed by the ants,' said Holroyd abruptly in English.

The captain burst into a rage. He made no answer to Holroyd. 'I have commanded you to go aboard,' he screamed to his subordinate in Portuguese. 'If you do not go aboard forthwith it is mutiny—rank mutiny. Mutiny and cowardice! Where is the courage that should animate us? I will have you in irons, I will have you shot like a dog.' He began a torrent of abuse and curses, he danced to and fro. He shook his fists, he behaved as if beside himself with rage, and the lieutenant, white and still, stood looking at him. The crew appeared forward, with amazed faces.

Suddenly, in a pause of this outbreak, the lieutenant came to some heroic decision, saluted, drew himself together and clambered upon the deck of the cuberta.

'Ah!' said Gerilleau, and his mouth shut like a trap. Holroyd saw the ants retreating before da Cunha's boots. The Portuguese walked slowly to the fallen man, stooped down, hesitated, clutched his coat and turned him over. A black swarm of ants rushed out of the clothes, and da Cunha stepped back very quickly and trod two or three times on the deck.

Holroyd put up the glasses. He saw the scattered ants about the invader's feet, and doing what he had never seen ants doing before. They had nothing of the blind movements of the common ant; they were looking at him—as a rallying crowd of men might look at some gigantic monster that had dispersed it.

'How did he die?' the captain shouted.

Holroyd understood the Portuguese to say the body was too much eaten to tell.

'What is there forward?' asked Gerilleau.

The lieutenant walked a few paces, and began his answer in Portuguese. He stopped abruptly and beat off something from his leg. He made some peculiar steps as if he was trying to stamp on something invisible, and went quickly towards the side. Then he controlled himself, turned about, walked deliberately forward to the hold, clambered up to the fore decking, from which the sweeps are worked, stooped for a time over the second man, groaned audibly, and made his way back and aft to the cabin, moving very rigidly. He turned and began a conversation with his captain, cold and respectful in tone on either side, contrasting vividly with the wrath and insult of a few moments before. Holroyd gathered only fragments of its purport.

He reverted to the field-glass, and was surprised to find the ants had vanished from all the exposed surfaces of the deck. He turned towards the shadows beneath the decking, and it seemed to him they were full of watching eyes.

The cuberta, it was agreed, was derelict, but too full of ants to put men aboard to sit and sleep: it must be towed. The lieutenant went forward to take in and adjust the cable, and the men in the boat stood up to be ready to help him. Holroyd's glasses searched the canoe.

He became more and more impressed by the fact that a great if minute and furtive activity was going on. He perceived that a number of gigantic ants—they seemed nearly a couple of inches in length—carrying oddly-shaped burthens for which he could imagine no use—were moving in rushes from one point of obscurity to another. They did not move in columns across the exposed places, but in open, spaced-out lines, oddly suggestive of the rushes of modern infantry advancing under fire. A number were taking cover under the dead man's clothes, and a perfect swarm was gathering along the side over which da Cunha must presently go.

He did not see them actually rush for the lieutenant as he returned, but he has no doubt they did make a concerted rush. Suddenly the lieutenant was shouting and cursing and beating at his legs. 'I'm stung!' he shouted, with a face of hate and accusation towards Gerilleau.

Then he vanished over the side, dropped into his boat, and plunged at once into the water. Holroyd heard the splash.

The three men in the boat pulled him out and brought him aboard, and that night he died.

III

HOLROYD and the captain came out of the cabin in which the swollen and contorted body of the lieutenant lay and stood together at the stern of the monitor, staring at the sinister vessel they trailed behind them. It was a close, dark night that had only phantom flickerings of sheet lightning to illuminate it. The cuberta, a vague black triangle, rocked about in the steamer's wake, her sails bobbing and flapping, and the black smoke from the funnels, spark-lit ever and again, streamed over her swaying masts.

Gerilleau's mind was inclined to run on the unkind things the lieutenant had said in the heat of his last fever.

'He says I murdered 'im,' he protested. 'It is simply absurd. Someone '*ad* to go aboard. Are we to run away from these confounded ants whenever they show up?'

Holroyd said nothing. He was thinking of a disciplined rush of little black shapes across bare sunlit planking.

'It was his place to go,' harped Gerilleau. 'He died in the execution of his duty. What has he to complain of? Murdered! . . . But the poor fellow was—what is it?—demented. He was not in his right mind. The poison swelled him. . . . U'm.'

They came to a long silence.

'We will sink that canoe—burn it.'

'And then?'

The inquiry irritated Gerilleau. His shoulders went up, his hands flew out at right angles from his body. 'What is one to *do*?' he said, his voice going up to an angry squeak.

'Anyhow,' he broke out vindictively, 'every ant in dat cuberta!—I will burn dem alive!'

Holroyd was not moved to conversation. A distant ululation of howling monkeys filled the sultry night with foreboding sounds, and as the gunboat drew near the black mysterious banks this was reinforced by a depressing clamour of frogs.

'What is one to *do*?' the captain repeated after a vast interval, and suddenly becoming active and savage and blasphemous, decided to burn the *Santa Rosa* without further delay. Everyone aboard was pleased by that idea, everyone helped with zest; they pulled in the cable, cut it, and dropped the boat and fired her with tow and kerosene, and soon the cuberta was crackling and flaring merrily amidst the immensities of the tropical night. Holroyd watched the mounting yellow flare against the blackness, and the livid flashes of sheet lightning that came and went above the forest summits, throwing them into momentary silhouette, and his stoker stood behind him watching also.

The stoker was stirred to the depths of his linguistics. '*Satlba* go pop, pop,' he said, 'Wahaw!' and laughed richly.

But Holroyd was thinking that these little creatures on the decked canoe had also eyes and brains.

The whole thing impressed him as incredibly foolish and wrong, but—what was one to *do*? This question came back enormously reinforced on the morrow, when at last the gunboat reached Badama.

This place, with its leaf-thatch-covered houses and sheds, its creeper-invaded sugar-mill, its little jetty of timber and canes, was very still in the morning heat, and showed never a sign of living men. Whatever ants there were at that distance were too small to see.

'All the people have gone,' said Gerilleau, 'but we will do one thing anyhow. We will 'oot and vissel.'

So Holroyd hooted and whistled.

Then the captain fell into a doubting fit of the worst kind. 'Dere is one thing we can do,' he said presently.

'What's that?' said Holroyd.

''Oot and vissel again.'

So they did.

The captain walked his deck and gesticulated to himself. He seemed to have many things on his mind. Fragments of speeches came from his lips. He appeared to be addressing some imaginary public tribunal either in Spanish or Portuguese. Holroyd's improving ear detected something about ammunition. He came out of these preoccupations suddenly into English. 'My dear 'Olroyd!' he cried, and broke off with 'But what *can* one do?'

They took the boat and the field-glasses, and went close in to examine the place. They made out a number of big ants, whose still postures had a certain effect of watching them, dotted about the edge of the rude embarkation jetty. Gerilleau tried ineffectual pistol shots at these. Holroyd thinks he distinguished curious earthworks running between the nearer houses, that may have been the work of the insect conquerors of those human habitations. The explorers pulled past the jetty, and became aware of a human skeleton wearing a loin cloth, and very bright and clean and shining, lying beyond. They came to a pause regarding this. . . .

'I 'ave all dose lives to consider,' said Gerilleau suddenly.

Holroyd turned and stared at the captain, realising slowly that he referred to the unappetising mixture of races that constituted his crew.

'To send a landing party—it is impossible—impossible. They will be poisoned, they will swell, they will swell up and abuse me and die. It is totally impossible. . . . If we land, I must land alone, alone, in thick boots and with my life in my hand. Perhaps I should live. Or again—I might not land. I do not know. I do not know.'

Holroyd thought he did, but he said nothing.

'De whole thing,' said Gerilleau suddenly, ''as been got up to make me ridiculous. De whole thing!'

They paddled about and regarded the clean white skeleton from various points of view, and then they returned to the gunboat. Then Gerilleau's indecisions became terrible. Steam was got up, and in the afternoon the monitor went on up the river with an air of going to ask somebody something, and by sunset came back again and anchored. A thunderstorm gathered and broke furiously, and then the night became beautifully cool and quiet and everyone slept on deck. Except Gerilleau, who tossed about and muttered. In the dawn he awakened Holroyd.

'Lord!' said Holroyd, 'what now?'

'I have decided,' said the captain.

'What—to land?' said Holroyd, sitting up brightly.

'No!' said the captain, and was for a time very reserved. 'I have decided,' he repeated, and Holroyd manifested symptoms of impatience.

'Well,—yes,' said the captain, '*I shall fire de big gun!*'

And he did! Heaven knows what the ants thought of it, but he did. He fired it twice with great sternness and ceremony. All the crew had wadding in their ears, and there was an effect of going into action about the whole affair, and first they hit and wrecked the old sugar-mill, and then they smashed the abandoned store behind the jetty. And the Gerilleau experienced the inevitable reaction.

'It is no good,' he said to Holroyd; 'no good at all. No sort of bally good. We must go back—for instructions. Dere will be de devil of a row about dis ammunition—oh! de *devil* of a row! You don't know, 'Olroyd. . . .'

He stood regarding the world in infinite perplexity for a space.

'But what else was there to *do*?' he cried.

In the afternoon the monitor started down stream again, and in the evening a landing party took the body of the lieutenant and buried it on the bank upon which the new ants have so far not appeared. . . .

IV

I HEARD this story in a fragmentary state from Holroyd not three weeks ago.

These new ants have got into his brain, and he has come back to England with the idea, as he says, of 'exciting people' about them 'before it is too late.' He says they threaten British Guiana,* which cannot be much over a trifle of a thousand miles from their present sphere of activity, and that the Colonial Office ought to get to work upon them at once. He declaims with great passion: 'These are intelligent ants. Just think what that means!'

There can be no doubt they are a serious pest, and that the Brazilian Government is well advised in offering a prize of five hundred pounds for some effectual method of extirpation. It is certain too that since they first appeared in the hills beyond Badama, about three years ago, they have achieved extraordinary conquests. The whole of the south bank of the Batemo River, for nearly sixty miles, they have in their effectual occupation; they have driven men out completely, occupied plantations and settlements, and boarded and captured at least one ship. It is even said they have in some inexplicable way bridged the very considerable Capuarana arm and pushed many miles towards the Amazon itself. There can be little doubt that they are far more reasonable and with a far better social organisation than any previously known ant species; instead of being in dispersed societies they are organised into what is in effect a single nation; but their peculiar and immediate formidableness lies not so much in this as in the intelligent use they make of poison against their larger enemies. It would seem this poison of theirs is closely akin to snake poison, and it is highly probable they actually manufacture it, and that the larger individuals among them carry the needle-like crystals of it in their attacks upon men.

Of course it is extremely difficult to get any detailed information about these new competitors for the sovereignty of the globe. No eye-witnesses of their activity, except for such glimpses as Holroyd's, have survived the encounter. The most extraordinary legends of their prowess and capacity are in circulation in the region of the Upper Amazon, and grow daily as the steady advance of the invader stimulates men's imaginations through their fears. These strange little creatures are credited not only with the use of implements and a knowledge of fire and metals and with organised feats of engineering that stagger our northern minds—unused as we are to such feats as that of the Saübas of Rio de Janeiro, who in 1841 drove a tunnel under the Parahyba where it is as wide as the Thames at London Bridge—but with an organised and detailed method of record and communication analogous to our books. So far their action has been a steady progressive settlement, involving the flight or slaughter of every human being in the new areas they invade. They are increasing rapidly in numbers, and Holroyd at least is firmly convinced that they will finally dispossess man over the whole of tropical South America.

And why should they stop at tropical South America?

Well, there they are, anyhow. By 1911 or thereabouts, if they go on as they are going, they ought to strike the Capuarana Extension Railway, and force themselves upon the attention of the European capitalist.

By 1920 they will be half-way down the Amazon. I fix 1950 or '60 at the latest for the discovery of Europe.

XXXI

THE DOOR IN THE WALL

I

ONE confidential evening, not three months ago, Lionel Wallace told me this story of the Door in the Wall. And at the time I thought that so far as he was concerned it was a true story.

He told it me with such a direct simplicity of conviction that I could not do otherwise than believe in him. But in the morning, in my own flat, I woke to a different atmosphere, and as I lay in bed and recalled the things he had told me, stripped of the glamour of his earnest slow voice, denuded of the focussed, shaded table light, the shadowy atmosphere that wrapped about him and me, and the pleasant bright things, the dessert and glasses and napery* of the dinner we had shared, making them for the time a bright little world quite cut off from everyday realities, I saw it all as frankly incredible. 'He was mystifying!' I said, and then: 'How well he did it! . . . It isn't quite the thing I should have expected him, of all people, to do well.'

Afterwards as I sat up in bed and sipped my morning tea, I found myself trying to account for the flavour of reality that perplexed me in his impossible reminiscences, by supposing they did in some way suggest, present, convey—I hardly know which word to use—experiences it was otherwise impossible to tell.

Well, I don't resort to that explanation now. I have got over my intervening doubts. I believe now, as I believed at the moment of telling, that Wallace did to the very best of his ability strip the truth of his secret for me. But whether he himself saw, or only thought he saw, whether he himself was the possessor of an inestimable privilege or the victim of a fantastic dream, I cannot pretend to guess. Even the facts of his death, which ended my doubts for ever, throw no light on that.

That much the reader must judge for himself.

I forget now what chance comment or criticism of mine moved so reticent a man to confide in me. He was, I think, defending himself against an imputation of slackness and unreliability I had made in relation to a great public movement, in which he had disappointed me. But he plunged suddenly. 'I have,' he said, 'a preoccupation——

'I know,' he went on, after a pause, 'I have been negligent. The fact is—it isn't a case of ghosts or apparitions—but—it's an odd thing to tell of, Redmond—I am haunted. I am haunted by something—that rather takes the light out of things, that fills me with longings . . .'

He paused, checked by that English shyness that so often overcomes us when we would speak of moving or grave or beautiful things. 'You were at Saint Æthelstan's all through,' he said, and for a moment that seemed to me quite irrelevant. 'Well'—and he paused. Then very haltingly at first, but afterwards more easily, he began to tell of the thing that was hidden in his life, the haunting memory of a beauty and a happiness that filled his heart with insatiable longings, that made all the interests and spectacle of worldly life seem dull and tedious and vain to him.

Now that I have the clue to it, the thing seems written visibly in his face. I have a photograph in which that look of detachment has been caught and intensified. It reminds me of what a woman once said of him—a woman who had loved him greatly. 'Suddenly,' she said, 'the interest goes out of him. He forgets you. He doesn't care a rap for you—under his very nose . . .'

Yet the interest was not always out of him, and when he was holding his attention to a thing Wallace could contrive to be an extremely successful man. His career, indeed, is set with successes. He left me behind him long ago: he soared up over my head, and cut a figure in the world that I couldn't cut—anyhow. He was still a year short of forty, and they say now that he would have been in office and very probably in the new Cabinet if he had lived. At school he always beat me without effort—as it were by nature. We were at school together at Saint Æthelstan's College in West Kensington for almost all our school-time. He came into the school as my co-equal, but he left far above me, in a blaze of scholarships and brilliant performance. Yet I think I made a fair average running. And it was at school I heard first of the 'Door in the Wall'—that I was to hear of a second time only a month before his death.

To him at least the Door in the Wall was a real door, leading through a real wall to immortal realities. Of that I am now quite assured.

And it came into his life quite early, when he was a little fellow between five and six. I remember how, as he sat making his confession to me with a slow gravity, he reasoned and reckoned the date of it. 'There was,' he said, 'a crimson Virginia creeper in it—all one bright uniform crimson, in a clear amber sunshine against a white wall. That came into the impression somehow, though I don't clearly remember how, and there were horse-chestnut leaves upon the clean pavement outside the green door. They were blotched yellow and green, you know, not brown nor dirty, so that they must have been new fallen. I take it that means October. I look out for horse-chestnut leaves every year and I ought to know.

'If I'm right in that, I was about five years and four months old.'

He was, he said, rather a precocious little boy—he learnt to talk at an abnormally early age, and he was so sane and 'old-fashioned,' as people say, that he was permitted an amount of initiative that most children scarcely attain by seven or eight. His mother died when he was two, and he was under the less vigilant and authoritative care of a nursery governess. His father was a stern, preoccupied lawyer, who gave him little attention, and expected great things of him. For all his brightness he found life a little grey and dull, I think. And one day he wandered.

He could not recall the particular neglect that enabled him to get away, nor the course he took among the West Kensington roads. All that had faded among the incurable blurs of memory. But the white wall and the green door stood out quite distinctly.

As his memory of that childish experience ran, he did at the very first sight of that door experience a peculiar emotion, an attraction, a desire to get to the door and open it and walk in. And at the same time he had the clearest conviction that either it was unwise or it was wrong of him—he could not tell which—to yield to this attraction. He insisted upon it as a curious thing that he knew from the very beginning—unless memory has played him the queerest trick—that the door was unfastened, and that he could go in as he chose.

I seem to see the figure of that little boy, drawn and repelled. And it was very clear in his mind, too, though why it should be so was never explained, that his father would be very angry if he went in through that door.

Wallace described all these moments of hesitation to me with the utmost particularity. He went right past the door, and then, with his hands in his pockets and making an infantile attempt to whistle, strolled right along beyond the end of the wall. There he recalls a number of mean dirty shops, and particularly that of a plumber and decorator with a dusty disorder of earthenware pipes, sheet lead, ball taps, pattern books of wall paper, and tins of enamel. He stood pretending to examine these things, and *coveting*, passionately desiring, the green door.

Then, he said, he had a gust of emotion. He made a run for it, lest hesitation should grip him again; he went plump with outstretched hand through the green door and let it

slam behind him. And so, in a trice, he came into the garden
that has haunted all his life.

It was very difficult for Wallace to give me his full sense
of that garden into which he came.

There was something in the very air of it that exhilarated,
that gave one a sense of lightness and good happening and
well-being; there was something in the sight of it that made
all its colour clean and perfect and subtly luminous. In the
instant of coming into it one was exquisitely glad—as only in
rare moments, and when one is young and joyful one can be
glad in this world. And everything was beautiful there. . . .

Wallace mused before he went on telling me. 'You see,' he
said, with the doubtful inflection of a man who pauses at
incredible things, 'there were two great panthers there. . . .
Yes, spotted panthers. And I was not afraid. There was a long
wide path with marble-edged flower borders on either side,
and these two huge velvety beasts were playing there with a
ball. One looked up and came towards me, a little curious as
it seemed. It came right up to me, rubbed its soft round ear
very gently against the small hand I held out, and purred. It
was, I tell you, an enchanted garden. I know. And the size?
Oh! it stretched far and wide, this way and that. I believe
there were hills far away. Heaven knows where West Kensington had suddenly got to. And somehow it was just like
coming home.

'You know, in the very moment the door swung to behind
me, I forgot the road with its fallen chestnut leaves, its cabs
and tradesmen's carts, I forgot the sort of gravitational pull
back to the discipline and obedience of home, I forgot all
hesitations and fear, forgot discretion, forgot all the intimate
realities of this life. I became in a moment a very glad and
wonder-happy little boy—in another world. It was a world
with a different quality, a warmer, more penetrating and
mellower light, with a faint clear gladness in its air, and wisps
of sun-touched cloud in the blueness of its sky. And before
me ran this long wide path, invitingly, with weedless beds

on either side, rich with untended flowers, and these two
great panthers. I put my little hands fearlessly on their soft
fur, and caressed their round ears and the sensitive corners
under their ears, and played with them, and it was as though
they welcomed me home. There was a keen sense of home-
coming in my mind, and when presently a tall, fair girl appeared in the pathway and came to meet me, smiling, and
said "Well?" to me, and lifted me, and kissed me, and put
me down, and led me by the hand, there was no amazement, but only an impression of delightful rightness, of being
reminded of happy things that had in some strange way been
overlooked. There were broad red steps, I remember, that
came into view between spikes of delphinium, and up these
we went to a great avenue between very old and shady dark
trees. All down this avenue, you know between the red
chapped stems, were marble seats of honour and statuary,
and very tame and friendly white doves . . .

'Along this cool avenue my girl-friend led me, looking
down—I recall the pleasant lines, the finely-modelled chin
of her sweet kind face—asking me questions in a soft, agreeable voice, and telling me things, pleasant things I know,
though what they were I was never able to recall. . . . Presently
a little Capuchin monkey, very clean, with a fur of ruddy
brown and kindly hazel eyes, came down a tree to us and
ran beside me, looking up at me and grinning, and presently
leapt to my shoulder. So we two went on our way in great
happiness.'

He paused.

'Go on,' I said.

'I remember little things. We passed an old man musing
among laurels, I remember, and a place gay with paroquets,*
and came through a broad shaded colonnade to a spacious
cool palace, full of pleasant fountains, full of beautiful things,
full of the quality and promise of heart's desire. And there
were many things and many people, some that still seem to
stand out clearly and some that are a little vague; but all

these people were beautiful and kind. In some way—I don't know how—it was conveyed to me that they all were kind to me, glad to have me there, and filling me with gladness by their gestures, by the touch of their hands, by the welcome and love in their eyes. Yes——'

He mused for a while. 'Playmates I found there. That was very much to me, because I was a lonely little boy. They played delightful games in a grass-covered court where there was a sun-dial set about with flowers. And as one played one loved. . . .

'But—it's odd—there's a gap in my memory. I don't remember the games we played. I never remembered. Afterwards, as a child, I spent long hours trying, even with tears, to recall the form of that happiness. I wanted to play it all over again—in my nursery—by myself. No! All I remember is the happiness and two dear playfellows who were most with me. . . . Then presently came a sombre dark woman, with a grave, pale face and dreamy eyes, a sombre woman, wearing a soft long robe of pale purple, who carried a book, and beckoned and took me aside with her into a gallery above a hall—though my playmates were loth to have me go, and ceased their game and stood watching as I was carried away. "Come back to us!" they cried. "Come back to us soon!" I looked up at her face, but she heeded them not at all. Her face was very gentle and grave. She took me to a seat in the gallery, and I stood beside her, ready to look at her book as she opened it upon her knee. The pages fell open. She pointed, and I looked, marvelling, for in the living pages of that book I saw myself; it was a story about myself, and in it were all the things that had happened to me since ever I was born. . . .

'It was wonderful to me, because the pages of that book were not pictures, you understand, but realities.'

Wallace paused gravely—looked at me doubtfully.

'Go on,' I said. 'I understand.'

'They were realities—yes, they must have been; people

moved and things came and went in them; my dear mother, whom I had near forgotten; then my father, stern and upright, the servants, the nursery, all the familiar things of home. Then the front door and the busy streets, with traffic to and fro. I looked and marvelled, and looked half doubtfully again into the woman's face and turned the pages over, skipping this and that, to see more of this book and more, and so at last I came to myself hovering and hesitating outside the green door in the long white wall, and felt again the conflict and the fear.

' "And next?" I cried; and would have turned on, but the cool hand of the grave woman delayed me.

' "Next?" I insisted, and struggled gently with her hand, pulling up her fingers with all my childish strength, and as she yielded and the page came over she bent down upon me like a shadow and kissed my brow.

'But the page did not show the enchanted garden, nor the panthers, nor the girl who had led me by the hand, nor the playfellows who had been so loth to let me go. It showed a long grey street in West Kensington, in that chill hour of afternoon before the lamps are lit, and I was there, a wretched little figure, weeping aloud, for all that I could do to restrain myself, and I was weeping because I could not return to my dear playfellows who had called after me, "Come back to us! Come back to us soon!" I was there. This was no page in a book, but harsh reality; that enchanted place and the restraining hand of the grave mother at whose knee I stood had gone—whither had they gone?'

He halted again, and remained for a time staring into the fire.

'Oh! the woefulness of that return!' he murmured.

'Well?' I said, after a minute or so.

'Poor little wretch I was!—brought back to this grey world again! As I realised the fulness of what had happened to me, I gave way to quite ungovernable grief. And the shame and humiliation of that public weeping and my disgraceful home-coming remain with me still. I see again the benevolent-looking old gentleman in gold spectacles who stopped and spoke to me—prodding me first with his umbrella. "Poor little chap," said he; "and are you lost then?"—and me a London boy of five and more! And he must needs bring in a kindly young policeman and make a crowd of me, and so march me home. Sobbing, conspicuous, and frightened, I came back from the enchanted garden to the steps of my father's house.

'That is as well as I can remember my vision of that garden—the garden that haunts me still. Of course, I can convey nothing of that indescribable quality of translucent unreality, that *difference* from the common things of experience that hung about it all; but that—that is what happened. If it was a dream, I am sure it was a day-time and altogether extraordinary dream. . . . H'm!—naturally there followed a terrible questioning, by my aunt, my father, the nurse, the governess—everyone. . . .

'I tried to tell them, and my father gave me my first thrashing for telling lies. When afterwards I tried to tell my aunt, she punished me again for my wicked persistence. Then, as I said, everyone was forbidden to listen to me, to hear a word about it. Even my fairy-tale books were taken away from me for a time—because I was too "imaginative." Eh? Yes, they did that! My father belonged to the old school. . . . And my story was driven back upon myself. I whispered it to my pillow—my pillow that was often damp and salt to my whispering lips with childish tears. And I added always to my official and less fervent prayers this one heartfelt request: "Please God I may dream of the garden. Oh! take me back to my garden!" Take me back to my garden! I dreamt often of the garden. I may have added to it, I may have changed it; I do not know. . . . All this, you understand, is an attempt to reconstruct from fragmentary memories a very early experience. Between that and the other consecutive memories of my boyhood there is a gulf. A time came when it seemed impossible I should ever speak of that wonder glimpse again.'

I asked an obvious question.

'No,' he said. 'I don't remember that I ever attempted to find my way back to the garden in those early years. This seems odd to me now, but I think that very probably a closer watch was kept on my movements after this misadventure to prevent my going astray. No, it wasn't till you knew me that I tried for the garden again. And I believe there was a period—incredible as it seems now—when I forgot the garden altogether—when I was about eight or nine it may have been. Do you remember me as a kid at Saint Æthelstan's?'

'Rather!'

'I didn't show any signs, did I, in those days of having a secret dream?'

II

HE looked up with a sudden smile.

'Did you ever play North-West Passage* with me? . . . No, of course you didn't come my way!'

'It was the sort of game,' he went on, 'that every imaginative child plays all day. The idea was the discovery of a North-West Passage to school. The way to school was plain enough; the game consisted in finding some way that wasn't plain, starting off ten minutes early in some almost hopeless direction, and working my way round through unaccustomed streets to my goal. And one day I got entangled among some rather low-class streets on the other side of Campden Hill, and I began to think that for once the game would be against me and that I should get to school late. I tried rather desperately a street that seemed a *cul-de-sac*, and found a passage at the end. I hurried through that with renewed hope. 'I shall do it yet,' I said, and passed a row of frowsy little shops that were inexplicably familiar to me, and behold!

there was my long white wall and the green door that led to the enchanted garden!

'The thing whacked upon me suddenly. Then, after all, that garden, that wonderful garden, wasn't a dream!'

He paused.

'I suppose my second experience with the green door marks the world of difference there is between the busy life of a schoolboy and the infinite leisure of a child. Anyhow, this second time I didn't for a moment think of going in straight away. You see——. For one thing, my mind was full of the idea of getting to school in time—set on not breaking my record for punctuality. I must surely have felt *some* little desire at least to try the door—yes. I must have felt that. . . . But I seem to remember the attraction of the door mainly as another obstacle to my overmastering determination to get to school. I was immensely interested by this discovery I had made, of course—I went on with my mind full of it— but I went on. It didn't check me. I ran past, tugging out my watch, found I had ten minutes still to spare, and then I was going downhill into familiar surroundings. I got to school, breathless, it is true, and wet with perspiration, but in time. I can remember hanging up my coat and hat. . . . Went right by it and left it behind me. Odd, eh?'

He looked at me thoughtfully. 'Of course I didn't know then that it wouldn't always be there. Schoolboys have limited imaginations. I suppose I thought it was an awfully jolly thing to have it there, to know my way back to it, but there was the school tugging at me. I expect I was a good deal distraught and inattentive that morning, recalling what I could of the beautiful strange people I should presently see again. Oddly enough I had no doubt in my mind that they would be glad to see me. . . . Yes, I must have thought of the garden that morning just as a jolly sort of place to which one might resort in the interludes of a strenuous scholastic career.

'I didn't go that day at all. The next day was a half holiday, and that may have weighed with me. Perhaps, too, my state of inattention brought down impositions* upon me, and docked the margin of time necessary for the *détour*. I don't know. What I do know is that in the meantime the enchanted garden was so much upon my mind that I could not keep it to myself.

'I told. What was his name?—a ferrety-looking youngster we used to call Squiff.'

'Young Hopkins,' said I.

'Hopkins it was. I did not like telling him. I had a feeling that in some way it was against the rules to tell him, but I did. He was walking part of the way home with me; he was talkative, and if we had not talked about the enchanted garden we should have talked of something else, and it was intolerable to me to think about any other subject. So I blabbed.

'Well, he told my secret. The next day in the play interval I found myself surrounded by half a dozen bigger boys, half teasing, and wholly curious to hear more of the enchanted garden. There was that big Fawcett—you remember him?—and Carnaby and Morley Reynolds. You weren't there by any chance? No, I think I should have remembered if you were. . . .

'A boy is a creature of odd feelings. I was, I really believe, in spite of my secret self-disgust, a little flattered to have the attention of these big fellows. I remember particularly a moment of pleasure caused by the praise of Crawshaw—you remember Crawshaw major, the son of Crawshaw the composer?—who said it was the best lie he had ever heard. But at the same time there was a really painful undertow of shame at telling what I felt was indeed a sacred secret. That beast Fawcett made a joke about the girl in green——'

Wallace's voice sank with the keen memory of that shame. 'I pretended not to hear,' he said. 'Well, then Carnaby suddenly called me a young liar, and disputed with me when I said the thing was true. I said I knew where to find the green door, could lead them all there in ten minutes. Carnaby became outrageously virtuous, and said I'd have to—and bear out my words or suffer. Did you ever have Carnaby twist your arm? Then perhaps you'll understand how it went with me. I swore my story was true. There was nobody in the school then to save a chap from Carnaby, though Crawshaw put in a word or so. Carnaby had got his game. I grew excited and red-eared, and a little frightened. I behaved altogether like a silly little chap, and the outcome of it all was that instead of starting alone for my enchanted garden, I led the way presently—cheeks flushed, ears hot, eyes smarting, and my soul one burning misery and shame—for a party of six mocking, curious, and threatening schoolfellows.

'We never found the white wall and the green door. . . .'

'You mean——?'

'I mean I couldn't find it. I would have found it if I could.

'And afterwards when I could go alone I couldn't find it. I never found it. I seem now to have been always looking for it through my school-boy days, but I never came upon it—never.'

'Did the fellows—make it disagreeable?'

'Beastly. . . . Carnaby held a council over me for wanton lying. I remember how I sneaked home and upstairs to hide the marks of my blubbering. But when I cried myself to sleep at last it wasn't for Carnaby, but for the garden, for the beautiful afternoon I had hoped for, for the sweet friendly women and the waiting playfellows, and the game I had hoped to learn again, that beautiful forgotten game. . . .

'I believed firmly that if I had not told—. . . . I had bad times after that—crying at night and wool-gathering* by day. For two terms I slackened and had bad reports. Do you remember? Of course you would! It was *you*—your beating me in mathematics that brought me back to the grind again.'

III

FOR a time my friend stared silently into the red heart of the fire. Then he said: 'I never saw it again until I was seventeen.

'It leapt upon me for the third time—as I was driving to Paddington on my way to Oxford and a scholarship. I had just one momentary glimpse. I was leaning over the apron of my hansom* smoking a cigarette, and no doubt thinking myself no end of a man of the world, and suddenly there was the door, the wall, the dear sense of unforgettable and still attainable things.

'We clattered by—I too taken by surprise to stop my cab until we were well past and round a corner. Then I had a queer moment, a double and divergent movement of my will: I tapped the little door in the roof of the cab, and brought my arm down to pull out my watch. "Yes, sir!" said the cabman, smartly. "Er—well—it's nothing," I cried. "*My* mistake! We haven't much time! Go on!" And he went on. . . .

'I got my scholarship. And the night after I was told of that I sat over my fire in my little upper room, my study, in my father's house, with his praise—his rare praise—and his sound counsels ringing in my ears, and I smoked my favourite pipe—the formidable bulldog* of adolescence—and thought of that door in the long white wall. "If I had stopped," I thought, "I should have missed my scholarship, I should have missed Oxford—muddled all the fine career before me! I begin to see things better!" I fell musing deeply, but I did not doubt then this career of mine was a thing that merited sacrifice.

'Those dear friends and that clear atmosphere seemed very sweet to me, very fine but remote. My grip was fixing now upon the world. I saw another door opening—the door of my career.'

He stared again into the fire. Its red light picked out a stubborn strength in his face for just one flickering moment, and then it vanished again.

'Well,' he said and sighed, 'I have served that career. I have done—much work, much hard work. But I have dreamt of the enchanted garden a thousand dreams, and seen its door, or at least glimpsed its door, four times since then. Yes—four times. For a while this world was so bright and

433

interesting, seemed so full of meaning and opportunity, that the half-effaced charm of the garden was by comparison gentle and remote. Who wants to pat panthers on the way to dinner with pretty women and distinguished men? I came down to London from Oxford, a man of bold promise that I have done something to redeem. Something—and yet there have been disappointments. . . .

'Twice I have been in love—I will not dwell on that—but once, as I went to someone who, I knew, doubted whether I dared to come, I took a short cut at a venture through an unfrequented road near Earl's Court, and so happened on a white wall and a familiar green door. "Odd!" said I to myself, "but I thought this place was on Campden Hill. It's the place I never could find somehow—like counting Stonehenge*— the place of that queer daydream of mine." And I went by it intent upon my purpose. It had no appeal to me that afternoon.

'I had just a moment's impulse to try the door, three steps aside were needed at the most—though I was sure enough in my heart that it would open to me—and then I thought that doing so might delay me on the way to that appointment in which I thought my honour was involved. Afterwards I was sorry for my punctuality—I might at least have peeped in, I thought, and waved a hand to those panthers, but I knew enough by this time not to seek again belatedly that which is not found by seeking. Yes, that time made me very sorry. . . .

'Years of hard work after that, and never a sight of the door. It's only recently it has come back to me. With it there has come a sense as though some thin tarnish had spread itself over my world. I began to think of it as a sorrowful and bitter thing that I should never see that door again. Perhaps I was suffering a little from overwork—perhaps it was what I've heard spoken of as the feeling of forty. I don't know. But certainly the keen brightness that makes effort easy has gone out of things recently, and that just at a time—with all these new political developments—when I ought to be working. Odd, isn't it? But I do begin to find life toilsome, its rewards, as I come near them, cheap. I began a little while ago to want the garden quite badly. Yes—and I've seen it three times.'

'The garden?'

'No—the door! And I haven't gone in!'

He leant over the table to me, with an enormous sorrow in his voice as he spoke. 'Thrice I have had my chance— *thrice!* If ever that door offers itself to me again, I swore, I will go in, out of this dust and heat, out of this dry glitter of vanity, out of these toilsome futilities. I will go and never return. This time I will stay.... I swore it, and when the time came—*I didn't go*.

'Three times in one year have I passed that door and failed to enter. Three times in the last year.

'The first time was on the night of the snatch division* on the Tenants' Redemption Bill, on which the Government was saved by a majority of three. You remember? No one on our side—perhaps very few on the opposite side—expected the end that night. Then the debate collapsed like eggshells. I and Hotchkiss were dining with his cousin at Brentford; we were both unpaired,* and we were called up by telephone, and set off at once in his cousin's motor. We got in barely in time, and on the way we passed my wall and door—livid in the moonlight, blotched with hot yellow as the glare of our lamps lit it, but unmistakable. "My God!" cried I. "What?" said Hotchkiss. "Nothing!" I answered, and the moment passed.

' "I've made a great sacrifice," I told the whip* as I got in. "They all have," he said, and hurried by.

'I do not see how I could have done otherwise then. And the next occasion was as I rushed to my father's bedside to bid that stern old man farewell. Then, too, the claims of life were imperative. But the third time was different; it happened a week ago. It fills me with hot remorse to recall it. I was with Gurker and Ralphs—it's no secret now, you know, that I've had my talk with Gurker.* We had been dining at Frobisher's, and the talk had become intimate between us. The question of my place in the reconstructed Ministry lay always just over the boundary of the discussion. Yes—yes. That's all settled. It needn't be talked about yet, but there's no reason to keep a secret from you. . . . Yes—thanks! thanks! But let me tell you my story.

'Then, on that night things were very much in the air. My position was a very delicate one. I was keenly anxious to get some definite word from Gurker, but was hampered by Ralphs' presence. I was using the best power of my brain to keep that light and careless talk not too obviously directed to the point that concerned me. I had to. Ralphs' behaviour since has more than justified my caution. . . . Ralphs, I knew, would leave us beyond the Kensington High Street, and then I could surprise Gurker by a sudden frankness. One has sometimes to resort to these little devices. . . . And then it was that in the margin of my field of vision I became aware once more of the white wall, the green door before us down the road.

'We passed it talking. I passed it. I can still see the shadow of Gurker's marked profile, his opera hat* tilted forward over his prominent nose, the many folds of his neck wrap going before my shadow and Ralphs' as we sauntered past.

'I passed within twenty inches of the door. "If I say good-night to them, and go in," I asked myself, "what will happen?" And I was all a-tingle for that word with Gurker.

'I could not answer that question in the tangle of my other problems. "They will think me mad," I thought. "And suppose I vanish now!—Amazing disappearance of a prominent politician!" That weighed with me. A thousand inconceivably petty worldlinesses weighed with me in that crisis.'

Then he turned on me with a sorrowful smile, and, speaking slowly, 'Here I am!' he said.

'Here I am!' he repeated, 'and my chance has gone from

me. Three times in one year the door has been offered me—
the door that goes into peace, into delight, into a beauty
beyond dreaming, a kindness no man on earth can know.
And I have rejected it, Redmond, and it has gone——'

'How do you know?'

'I know. I know. I am left now to work it out, to stick to
the tasks that held me so strongly when my moments came.
You say I have success—this vulgar, tawdry, irksome, envied
thing. I have it.' He had a walnut in his big hand. 'If that was
my success,' he said, and crushed it, and held it out for me
to see.

'Let me tell you something, Redmond. This loss is destroying me. For two months, for ten weeks nearly now, I
have done no work at all, except the most necessary and
urgent duties. My soul is full of inappeasable regrets. At
nights—when it is less likely I shall be recognised—I go out.
I wander. Yes. I wonder what people would think of that if
they knew. A Cabinet Minister, the responsible head of that
most vital of all departments, wandering alone—grieving—
sometimes near audibly lamenting—for a door, for a garden!'

IV

I CAN see now his rather pallid face, and the unfamiliar
sombre fire that had come into his eyes. I see him very
vividly to-night. I sit recalling his words, his tones, and last
evening's *Westminster Gazette* still lies on my sofa, containing
the notice of his death. At lunch to-day the club was busy
with his death. We talked of nothing else.

They found his body very early yesterday morning in a
deep excavation near East Kensington Station. It is one of
two shafts that have been made in connection with an
extension of the railway southward. It is protected from the
intrusion of the public by a hoarding upon the high road,
in which a small doorway has been cut for the convenience
of some of the workmen who live in that direction. The

doorway was left unfastened through a misunderstanding between two gangers,* and through it he made his way. . . .

My mind is darkened with questions and riddles.

It would seem he walked all the way from the House that night—he has frequently walked home during the past Session—and so it is I figure his dark form coming along the late and empty streets, wrapped up, intent. And then did the pale electric lights near the station cheat the rough planking into a semblance of white? Did that fatal unfastened door awaken some memory?

Was there, after all, ever any green door in the wall at all?

I do not know. I have told his story as he told it to me. There are times when I believe that Wallace was no more than the victim of the coincidence between a rare but not unprecedented type of hallucination and a careless trap, but that indeed is not my profoundest belief. You may think me superstitious, if you will, and foolish; but, indeed, I am more than half convinced that he had, in truth, an abnormal gift, and a sense, something—I know not what—that in the guise of wall and door offered him an outlet, a secret and peculiar passage of escape into another and altogether more beautiful world. At any rate, you will say, it betrayed him in the end. But did it betray him? There you touch the inmost mystery of these dreamers, these men of vision and the imagination. We see our world fair and common, the hoarding and the pit. By our daylight standard he walked out of security into darkness, danger, and death.

But did he see like that?

XXXII

THE COUNTRY OF THE BLIND

THREE hundred miles and more from Chimborazo, one hundred from the snows of Cotopaxi, in the wildest wastes of Ecuador's Andes, there lies that mysterious mountain valley, cut off from the world of men, the Country of the Blind. Long years ago that valley lay so far open to the world that men might come at last through frightful gorges and over an icy pass into its equable meadows; and thither indeed men came, a family or so of Peruvian half-breeds fleeing from the lust and tyranny of an evil Spanish ruler. Then came the stupendous outbreak of Mindobamba, when it was night in Quito for seventeen days, and the water was boiling at Yaguachi and all the fish floating dying even as far as Guayaquil; everywhere along the Pacific slopes there were land slips and swift thawings and sudden floods, and one whole side of the old Arauca crest slipped and came down in thunder, and cut off the Country of the Blind for ever from the exploring feet of men. But one of these early settlers had chanced to be on the hither side of the gorges when the world had so terribly shaken itself, and he perforce had to forget his wife and his child and all the friends and possessions he had left up there, and start life over again in the lower world. He started it again but ill, blindness overtook him, and he died of punishment in the mines; but the story he told begot a legend that lingers along the length of the Cordilleras* of the Andes to this day.

He told of his reason for venturing back from that fastness, into which he had first been carried lashed to a llama, beside a vast bale of gear, when he was a child. The valley, he said, had in it all that the heart of man could desire— sweet water, pasture, an even climate, slopes of rich brown soil with tangles of a shrub that bore an excellent fruit, and on one side great hanging forests of pine that held the avalanches high. Far overhead, on three sides, vast cliffs of grey-green rock were capped by cliffs of ice; but the glacier stream came not to them but flowed away by the farther slopes, and only now and then huge ice masses fell on the valley side. In this valley it neither rained nor snowed, but the abundant springs gave a rich green pasture, that irrigation would spread over all the valley space. The settlers did well indeed there. Their beasts did well and multiplied, and but one thing marred their happiness. Yet it was enough to mar it greatly. A strange disease had come upon them, and had made all the children born to them there—and indeed, several older children also—blind. It was to seek some charm or antidote against this plague of blindness that he had with fatigue and danger and difficulty returned down the gorge. In those days, in such cases, men did not think of germs and infections but of sins; and it seemed to him that the reason of this affliction must lie in the negligence of these priestless immigrants to set up a shrine so soon as they entered the valley. He wanted a shrine—a handsome, cheap, effectual shrine—to be erected in the valley; he wanted relics and such-like potent things of faith, blessed objects and mysterious medals and prayers. In his wallet he had a bar of native silver for which he would not account; he insisted there was none in the valley with something of the insistence of an inexpert liar. They had all clubbed their money and ornaments together, having little need for such treasure up there, he said, to buy them holy help against their ill. I figure this dim-eyed young mountaineer, sunburnt, gaunt, and anxious, hat-brim clutched feverishly, a man all unused to the ways of the lower world, telling this story to some keen-eyed, attentive priest before the great convulsion; I can picture him presently seeking to return with pious and infallible remedies against that trouble, and the infinite dismay with which he must have faced the tumbled vastness where the gorge had once come out. But the rest of his story of mischances is lost to me, save that I know of his evil death after several years. Poor stray from that remoteness! The stream that had once made the gorge now bursts from the mouth of a rocky cave, and the legend his poor, ill-told story set going developed into the legend of a race of blind men somewhere 'over there' one may still hear to-day.

And amidst the little population of that now isolated and forgotten valley the disease ran its course. The old became groping and purblind, the young saw but dimly, and the children that were born to them saw never at all. But life was very easy in that snow-rimmed basin, lost to all the world, with neither thorns nor briars, with no evil insects nor any beasts save the gentle breed of llamas they had lugged and thrust and followed up the beds of the shrunken rivers in the gorges up which they had come. The seeing had become purblind so gradually that they scarcely noted their loss. They guided the sightless youngsters hither and thither until they knew the whole valley marvellously, and when at last sight died out among them the race lived on. They had even time to adapt themselves to the blind control of fire, which they made carefully in stoves of stone. They were a simple strain of people at the first, unlettered, only slightly touched with the Spanish civilisation, but with something of a tradition of the arts of old Peru and of its lost philosophy. Generation followed generation. They forgot many things; they devised many things. Their tradition of the greater world they came from became mythical in colour and uncertain. In all things save sight they were strong and able, and presently the chance of birth and heredity sent one who had an original mind and who could talk and persuade among them, and then afterwards another. These two passed, leaving their effects, and the little community grew in numbers and in understanding, and met and settled social and economic problems that arose. Generation followed generation. Generation followed generation. There came a time when a child was born who was fifteen generations from that ancestor who went out of the valley with a bar of silver to seek God's aid, and who never returned. Thereabouts it chanced that a man came into this community from the outer world. And this is the story of that man.

He was a mountaineer from the country near Quito, a man who had been down to the sea and had seen the world, a reader of books in an original way, an acute and enterprising man, and he was taken on by a party of Englishmen who had come out to Ecuador to climb mountains, to replace one of their three Swiss guides who had fallen ill. He climbed here and he climbed there, and then came the attempt on Parascotopetl, the Matterhorn of the Andes, in which he was lost to the outer world. The story of the accident has been written a dozen times. Pointer's narrative is the best. He tells how the little party worked their difficult and almost vertical way up to the very foot of the last and greatest precipice, and how they built a night shelter amidst the snow upon a little shelf of rock, and, with a touch of real dramatic power, how presently they found Nunez had gone from them. They shouted, and there was no reply; shouted and whistled, and for the rest of that night they slept no more.

As the morning broke they saw the traces of his fall. It seems impossible he could have uttered a sound. He had slipped eastward towards the unknown side of the mountain; far below he had struck a steep slope of snow, and ploughed his way down it in the midst of a snow avalanche. His track went straight to the edge of a frightful precipice, and beyond that everything was hidden. Far, far below, and hazy with distance, they could see trees rising out of a narrow, shut-in valley—the lost Country of the Blind. But they did not know it was the lost Country of the Blind, nor distinguish it in any way from any other narrow streak of upland valley. Unnerved by this disaster, they abandoned their attempt in the afternoon, and Pointer was called away to the war* before he could make another attack. To this day Parascotopetl lifts an

442

unconquered crest, and Pointer's shelter crumbles unvisited amidst the snows.

And the man who fell survived.

At the end of the slope he fell a thousand feet, and came down in the midst of a cloud of snow upon a snow slope even steeper than the one above. Down this he was whirled, stunned and insensible, but without a bone broken in his body; and then at last came to gentler slopes, and at last rolled out and lay still, buried amidst a softening heap of the white masses that had accompanied and saved him. He came to himself with a dim fancy that he was ill in bed; then realised his position with a mountaineer's intelligence, and worked himself loose and, after a rest or so, out until he saw the stars. He rested flat upon his chest for a space, wondering where he was and what had happened to him. He explored his limbs, and discovered that several of his buttons were gone and his coat turned over his head. His knife had gone from his pocket and his hat was lost, though he had tied it under his chin. He recalled that he had been looking for loose stones to raise his piece of the shelter wall. His ice-axe had disappeared.

He decided he must have fallen, and looked up to see, exaggerated by the ghastly light of the rising moon, the tremendous flight he had taken. For a while he lay, gazing blankly at that vast pale cliff towering above, rising moment by moment out of a subsiding tide of darkness. Its phantasmal, mysterious beauty held him for a space, and then he was seized with a paroxysm of sobbing laughter. . . .

After a great interval of time he became aware that he was near the lower edge of the snow. Below, down what was now a moonlit and practicable slope, he saw the dark and broken appearance of rock-strewn turf. He struggled to his feet, aching in every joint and limb, got down painfully from the heaped loose snow about him, went downward until he was on the turf, and there dropped rather than lay beside a boulder, drank deep from the flask in his inner pocket, and instantly fell asleep. . . .

He was awakened by the singing of birds in the trees far below.

He sat up and perceived he was on a little alp* at the foot of a vast precipice, that was grooved by the gully down which he and his snow had come. Over against him another wall of rock reared itself against the sky. The gorge between these precipices ran east and west and was full of the morning sunlight, which lit to the westward the mass of fallen mountain that closed the descending gorge. Below him it seemed there was a precipice equally steep, but behind the snow in the gully he found a sort of chimney-cleft dripping with snow-water down which a desperate man might venture. He found it easier than it seemed, and came at last to another desolate alp, and then after a rock climb of no particular difficulty to a steep slope of trees. He took his bearings and turned his face up the gorge, for he saw it opened out above upon green meadows, among which he now glimpsed quite distinctly a cluster of stone huts of unfamiliar fashion. At times his progress was like clambering along the face of a wall, and after a time the rising sun ceased to strike along the gorge, the voices of the singing birds died away, and the air grew cold and dark about him. But the distant valley with its houses was all the brighter for that. He came presently to talus,* and among the rocks he noted—for he was an observant man—an unfamiliar fern that seemed to clutch out of the crevices with intense green hands. He picked a frond or so and gnawed its stalk and found it helpful.

About midday he came at last out of the throat of the gorge into the plain and the sunlight. He was stiff and weary; he sat down in the shadow of a rock, filled up his flask with water from a spring and drank it down, and remained for a time resting before he went on to the houses.

They were very strange to his eyes, and indeed the whole aspect of that valley became, as he regarded it, queerer and more unfamiliar. The greater part of its surface was lush green meadow, starred with many beautiful flowers, irrigated with extraordinary care, and bearing evidence of systematic cropping piece by piece. High up and ringing the valley about was a wall, and what appeared to be a circumferential water-channel, from which the little trickles of water that fed the meadow plants came, and on the higher slopes above this flocks of llamas cropped the scanty herbage. Sheds, apparently shelters or feeding-places for the llamas, stood against the boundary wall here and there. The irrigation streams ran together into a main channel down the centre of the valley, and this was enclosed on either side by a wall breast high. This gave a singularly urban quality to this secluded place, a quality that was greatly enhanced by the fact that a number of paths paved with black and white stones, and each with a curious little kerb at the side, ran hither and thither in an orderly manner. The houses of the central village were quite unlike the casual and higgledy-piggledy agglomeration of the mountain villages he knew; they stood in a continuous row on either side of a central street of astonishing cleanness; here and there their parti-coloured[*] façade was pierced by a door, and not a solitary window broke their even front-age. They were parti-coloured with extraordinary irregular-ity, smeared with a sort of plaster that was sometimes grey, sometimes drab,[*] sometimes slate-coloured or dark brown; and it was the sight of this wild plastering first brought the word 'blind' into the thoughts of the explorer. 'The good man who did that,' he thought, 'must have been as blind as a bat.'

He descended a steep place, and so came to the wall and channel that ran about the valley, near where the latter spouted out its surplus contents into the deeps of the gorge in a thin and wavering thread of cascade. He could now see a number of men and women resting on piled heaps of grass, as if taking a siesta, in the remoter part of the meadow, and nearer the village a number of recumbent children, and then nearer at hand three men carrying pails on yokes along a little path that ran from the encircling wall towards the houses.

These latter were clad in garments of llama cloth and boots and belts of leather, and they wore caps of cloth with back and ear flaps. They followed one another in single file, walking slowly and yawning as they walked, like men who have been up all night. There was something so reassuringly prosperous and respectable in their bearing that after a moment's hesitation Nunez stood forward as conspicuously as possible upon his rock, and gave vent to a mighty shout that echoed round the valley.

The three men stopped, and moved their heads as though they were looking about them. They turned their faces this way and that, and Nunez gesticulated with freedom. But they did not appear to see him for all his gestures, and after a time, directing themselves towards the mountains far away to the right, they shouted as if in answer. Nunez bawled again, and then once more, and as he gestured ineffectually the word 'blind' came up to the top of his thoughts. 'The fools must be blind,' he said.

When at last, after much shouting and wrath, Nunez crossed the stream by a little bridge, came through a gate in the wall, and approached them, he was sure that they were blind. He was sure that this was the Country of the Blind of which the legends told. Conviction had sprung upon him, and a sense of great and rather enviable adventure. The three stood side by side, not looking at him, but with their ears directed towards him, judging him by his unfamiliar steps. They stood close together like men a little afraid, and he could see their eyelids closed and sunken, as though the very balls beneath had shrunk away. There was an expression near awe on their faces.

'A man,' one said, in hardly recognisable Spanish—'a man it is—a man or a spirit—coming down from the rocks.'

But Nunez advanced with the confident steps of a youth who enters upon life. All the old stories of the lost valley and the Country of the Blind had come back to his mind, and through his thoughts ran this old proverb, as if it were a refrain—

'In the Country of the Blind the One-eyed Man is King.'

'In the Country of the Blind the One-eyed Man is King.'*

And very civilly he gave them greeting. He talked to them and used his eyes.

'Where does he come from, brother Pedro?' asked one.

'Down out of the rocks.'

'Over the mountains I come,' said Nunez, 'out of the country beyond there—where men can see. From near Bogota, where there are a hundred thousands of people, and where the city passes out of sight.'

'Sight?' muttered Pedro. 'Sight?'

'He comes,' said the second blind man, 'out of the rocks.'

The cloth of their coats Nunez saw was curiously fashioned, each with a different sort of stitching.

They startled him by a simultaneous movement towards him, each with a hand outstretched. He stepped back from the advance of these spread fingers.

'Come hither,' said the third blind man, following his motion and clutching him neatly.

And they held Nunez and felt him over, saying no word further until they had done so.

'Carefully,' he cried, with a finger in his eye, and found they thought that organ, with its fluttering lids, a queer thing in him. They went over it again.

'A strange creature, Correa,' said the one called Pedro. 'Feel the coarseness of his hair. Like a llama's hair.'

'Rough he is as the rocks that begot him,' said Correa, investigating Nunez's unshaven chin with a soft and slightly moist hand. 'Perhaps he will grow finer.' Nunez struggled a little under their examination, but they gripped him firm.

'Carefully,' he said again.

'He speaks,' said the third man. 'Certainly he is a man.'

'Ugh!' said Pedro, at the roughness of his coat.

'And you have come into the world?' asked Pedro.

'*Out* of the world. Over mountains and glaciers; right over above there, half-way to the sun. Out of the great big world that goes down, twelve days' journey to the sea.'

They scarcely seemed to heed him. 'Our fathers have told us men may be made by the forces of Nature,' said Correa. 'It is the warmth of things and moisture, and rottenness—rottenness.'

'Let us lead him to the elders,' said Pedro.

'Shout first,' said Correa, 'lest the children be afraid. This is a marvellous occasion.'

So they shouted, and Pedro went first and took Nunez by the hand to lead him to the houses.

He drew his hand away. 'I can see,' he said.

'See?' said Correa.

'Yes, see,' said Nunez, turning towards him, and stumbled against Pedro's pail.

'His senses are still imperfect,' said the third blind man. 'He stumbles, and talks unmeaning words. Lead him by the hand.'

'As you will,' said Nunez, and was led along, laughing.

It seemed they knew nothing of sight.

Well, all in good time he would teach them.

He heard people shouting, and saw a number of figures gathering together in the middle roadway of the village.

He found it tax his nerve and patience more than he had anticipated, that first encounter with the population of the Country of the Blind. The place seemed larger as he drew near to it, and the smeared plasterings queerer, and a crowd of children and men and women (the women and girls, he was pleased to note, had some of them quite sweet faces, for all that their eyes were shut and sunken) came about him, holding on to him, touching him with soft, sensitive hands, smelling at him, and listening at every word he spoke. Some of the maidens and children, however, kept aloof as if afraid, and indeed his voice seemed coarse and rude beside their softer notes. They mobbed him. His three guides kept close to him with an effect of proprietorship, and said again and again, 'A wild man out of the rocks.'

'Bogota,' he said. 'Bogota. Over the mountain crests.'

'A wild man—using wild words,' said Pedro. 'Did you hear that—*Bogota?* His mind is hardly formed yet. He has only the beginnings of speech.'

A little boy nipped his hand. 'Bogota!' he said mockingly.

'Ay! A city to your village. I come from the great world—where men have eyes and see.'

'His name's Bogota,' they said.

'He stumbled,' said Correa, 'stumbled twice as we came hither.'

'Bring him to the elders.'

And they thrust him suddenly through a doorway into a room as black as pitch, save at the end there faintly glowed a fire. The crowd closed in behind him and shut out all but the faintest glimmer of day, and before he could arrest himself he had fallen headlong over the feet of a seated man. His arm, outflung, struck the face of someone else as he went down; he felt the soft impact of features and heard a cry of anger, and for a moment he struggled against a number of hands that clutched him. It was a one-sided fight. An inkling of the situation came to him, and he lay quiet.

'I fell down,' he said; 'I couldn't see in this pitchy darkness.'

There was a pause as if the unseen persons about him tried to understand his words. Then the voice of Correa said: 'He is but newly formed. He stumbles as he walks and mingles words that mean nothing with his speech.'

Others also said things about him that he heard or understood imperfectly.

'May I sit up?' he asked, in a pause. 'I will not struggle against you again.'

They consulted and let him rise.

The voice of an older man began to question him, and Nunez found himself trying to explain the great world out of

449

which he had fallen, and the sky and mountains and sight and such-like marvels, to these elders who sat in darkness in the Country of the Blind. And they would believe and understand nothing whatever he told them, a thing quite outside his expectation. They would not even understand many of his words. For fourteen generations these people had been blind and cut off from all the seeing world; the names for all the things of sight had faded and changed; the story of the outer world was faded and changed to a child's story; and they had ceased to concern themselves with anything beyond the rocky slopes above their circling wall. Blind men of genius had arisen among them and questioned the shreds of belief and tradition they had brought with them from their seeing days, and had dismissed all these things as idle fancies, and replaced them with new and saner explanations. Much of their imagination had shrivelled with their eyes, and they had made for themselves new imaginations with their ever more sensitive ears and finger-tips. Slowly Nunez realised this; that his expectation of wonder and reverence at his origin and his gifts was not to be borne out; and after his poor attempt to explain sight to them had been set aside as the confused version of a new-made being describing the marvels of his incoherent sensations, he subsided, a little dashed, into listening to their instruction. And the eldest of the blind men explained to him life and philosophy and religion, how that the world (meaning their valley) had been first an empty hollow in the rocks, and then had come, first, inanimate things without the gift of touch, and llamas and a few other creatures that had little sense, and then men, and at last angels, whom one could hear singing and making fluttering sounds, but whom no one could touch at all, which puzzled Nunez greatly until he thought of the birds.

He went on to tell Nunez how this time had been divided into the warm and the cold, which are the blind equivalents of day and night, and how it was good to sleep in the warm and work during the cold, so that now, but for his advent, the whole town of the blind would have been asleep. He said Nunez must have been specially created to learn and serve the wisdom they had acquired, and that for all his mental incoherency and stumbling behaviour he must have courage, and do his best to learn, and at that all the people in the doorway murmured encouragingly. He said the night— for the blind call their day night—was now far gone, and it behoved every one to go back to sleep. He asked Nunez if he knew how to sleep, and Nunez said he did, but that before sleep he wanted food.

They brought him food—llama's milk in a bowl, and rough salted bread—and led him into a lonely place to eat out of their hearing, and afterwards to slumber until the chill of the mountain evening roused them to begin their day again. But Nunez slumbered not at all.

Instead, he sat up in the place where they had left him, resting his limbs and turning the unanticipated circumstances of his arrival over and over in his mind.

Every now and then he laughed, sometimes with amusement, and sometimes with indignation.

'Unformed mind!' he said. 'Got no senses yet! They little know they've been insulting their heaven-sent king and master. I see I must bring them to reason. Let me think—let me think.'

He was still thinking when the sun set.

Nunez had an eye for all beautiful things, and it seemed to him that the glow upon the snowfields and glaciers that rose about the valley on every side was the most beautiful thing he had ever seen. His eyes went from that inaccessible glory to the village and irrigated fields, fast sinking into the twilight, and suddenly a wave of emotion took him, and he thanked God from the bottom of his heart that the power of sight had been given him.

He heard a voice calling to him from out of the village. 'Ya ho there, Bogota! Come hither!'

At that he stood up smiling. He would show these people

once and for all what sight would do for a man. They would seek him, but not find him.

'You move not, Bogota,' said the voice.

He laughed noiselessly, and made two stealthy steps aside from the path.

'Trample not on the grass, Bogota; that is not allowed.'

Nunez had scarcely heard the sound he made himself. He stopped amazed.

The owner of the voice came running up the piebald path towards him.

He stepped back into the pathway. 'Here I am,' he said.

'Why did you not come when I called you?' said the blind man. 'Must you be led like a child? Cannot you hear the path as you walk?'

Nunez laughed. 'I can see it,' he said.

'There is no such word as *see*,' said the blind man, after a pause. 'Cease this folly, and follow the sound of my feet.'

Nunez followed, a little annoyed.

'My time will come,' he said.

'You'll learn,' the blind man answered. 'There is much to learn in the world.'

'Has no one told you, "In the Country of the Blind the One-eyed Man is King"?'

'What is blind?' asked the blind man carelessly over his shoulder.

Four days passed, and the fifth found the King of the Blind still incognito, as a clumsy and useless stranger among his subjects.

It was, he found, much more difficult to proclaim himself than he had supposed, and in the meantime, while he meditated his *coup d'état*, he did what he was told and learnt the manners and customs of the Country of the Blind. He found working and going about at night a particularly irksome thing, and he decided that that should be the first thing he would change.

They led a simple, laborious life, these people, with all

the elements of virtue and happiness, as these things can be understood by men. They toiled, but not oppressively; they had food and clothing sufficient for their needs; they had days and seasons of rest; they made much of music and singing, and there was love among them, and little children.

It was marvellous with what confidence and precision they went about their ordered world. Everything, you see, had been made to fit their needs; each of the radiating paths of the valley area had a constant angle to the others, and was distinguished by a special notch upon its kerbing; all obstacles and irregularities of path or meadow had long since been cleared away; all their methods and procedure arose naturally from their special needs. Their senses had become marvellously acute; they could hear and judge the slightest gesture of a man a dozen paces away—could hear the very beating of his heart. Intonation had long replaced expression with them, and touches gesture, and their work with hoe and spade and fork was as free and confident as garden work can be. Their sense of smell was extraordinarily fine; they could distinguish individual differences as readily as a dog can, and they went about the tending of the llamas, who lived among the rocks above and came to the wall for food and shelter, with ease and confidence. It was only when at last Nunez sought to assert himself that he found how easy and confident their movements could be.

He rebelled only after he had tried persuasion.

He tried at first on several occasions to tell them of sight. 'Look you here, you people,' he said, 'There are things you do not understand in me.'

Once or twice one or two of them attended to him; they sat with faces downcast and ears turned intelligently towards him, and he did his best to tell them what it was to see. Among his hearers was a girl, with eyelids less red and sunken than the others, so that one could almost fancy she was hiding eyes, whom especially he hoped to persuade. He spoke of the beauties of sight, of watching the mountains, of the sky and the sunrise, and they heard him with amused incredulity that presently became condemnatory. They told him there were indeed no mountains at all, but that the end of the rocks where the llamas grazed was indeed the end of the world; thence sprang a cavernous roof of the universe, from which the dew and the avalanches fell; and when he maintained stoutly the world had neither end nor roof such as they supposed, they said his thoughts were wicked. So far as he could describe sky and clouds and stars to them it seemed to them a hideous void, a terrible blankness in the place of the smooth roof to things in which they believed— it was an article of faith with them that the cavern roof was exquisitely smooth to the touch. He saw that in some manner he shocked them, and gave up that aspect of the matter altogether, and tried to show them the practical value of sight. One morning he saw Pedro in the path called Seventeen and coming towards the central houses, but still too far off for hearing or scent, and he told them as much. 'In a little while,' he prophesied, 'Pedro will be here.' An old man remarked that Pedro had no business on path Seventeen, and then, as if in confirmation, that individual as he drew near turned and went transversely into path Ten, and so back with nimble paces towards the outer wall. They mocked Nunez when Pedro did not arrive, and afterwards, when he asked Pedro questions to clear his character, Pedro denied and outfaced him, and was afterwards hostile to him.

Then he induced them to let him go a long way up the sloping meadows towards the wall with one complacent* individual, and to him he promised to describe all that happened among the houses. He noted certain goings and comings, but the things that really seemed to signify to these people happened inside of or behind the windowless houses— the only things they took note of to test him by—and of these he could see or tell nothing; and it was after the failure of this attempt, and the ridicule they could not repress, that he resorted to force. He thought of seizing a spade and suddenly smiting one or two of them to earth, and so in fair combat showing the advantage of eyes. He went so far with that resolution as to seize his spade, and then he discovered a new thing about himself, and that was that it was impossible for him to hit a blind man in cold blood.

He hesitated, and found them all aware that he had snatched up the spade. They stood alert, with their heads on one side, and bent ears towards him for what he would do next.

'Put that spade down,' said one, and he felt a sort of help-less horror. He came near obedience.

Then he thrust one backwards against a house wall, and fled past him and out of the village.

He went athwart one of their meadows, leaving a track of trampled grass behind his feet, and presently sat down by the side of one of their ways. He felt something of the buoy-ancy that comes to all men in the beginning of a fight, but more perplexity. He began to realise that you cannot even fight happily with creatures who stand upon a different men-tal basis to yourself. Far away he saw a number of men car-rying spades and sticks come out of the street of houses, and advance in a spreading line along the several paths towards him. They advanced slowly, speaking frequently to one another, and ever and again the whole cordon would halt and sniff the air and listen.

The first time they did this Nunez laughed. But after-wards he did not laugh.

One struck his trail in the meadow grass, and came stooping and feeling his way along it.

For five minutes he watched the slow extension of the cordon, and then his vague disposition to do something forthwith became frantic. He stood up, went a pace or so towards the circumferential wall, turned, and went back a little way. There they all stood in a crescent, still and listening.

He also stood still, gripping his spade very tightly in both hands. Should he charge them?

The pulse in his ears ran into the rhythm of 'In the Country of the Blind the One-eyed Man is King!'

Should he charge them?

He looked back at the high and unclimbable wall behind—unclimbable because of its smooth plastering, but withal pierced with many little doors, and at the approaching line of seekers. Behind these others were now coming out of the street of houses.

Should he charge them?

'Bogota!' called one. 'Bogota! where are you?'

He gripped his spade still tighter, and advanced down the meadows towards the place of habitations, and directly he moved they converged upon him. 'I'll hit them if they touch me,' he swore; 'by Heaven, I will. I'll hit.' He called aloud, 'Look here, I'm going to do what I like in this valley. Do you hear? I'm going to do what I like and go where I like!'

They were moving in upon him quickly, groping, yet moving rapidly. It was like playing blind man's buff, with everyone blindfolded except one. 'Get hold of him!' cried one. He found himself in the arc of a loose curve of pursuers. He felt suddenly he must be active and resolute.

'You don't understand,' he cried in a voice that was meant to be great and resolute, and which broke. 'You are blind, and I can see. Leave me alone!'

'Bogota! Put down that spade, and come off the grass!'

The last order, grotesque in its urban familiarity, produced a gust of anger.

'I'll hurt you,' he said, sobbing with emotion. 'By Heaven, I'll hurt you. Leave me alone!'

He began to run, not knowing clearly where to run. He ran from the nearest blind man, because it was a horror to hit him. He stopped, and then made a dash to escape from their closing ranks. He made for where a gap was wide, and the men on either side, with a quick perception of the approach of his paces, rushed in on one another. He sprang forward, and then saw he must be caught, and *swish!* the spade had struck. He felt the soft thud of hand and arm, and the man was down with a yell of pain, and he was through.

Through! And then he was close to the street of houses again, and blind men, whirling spades and stakes, were running with a sort of reasoned swiftness hither and thither.

He heard steps behind him just in time, and found a tall man rushing forward and swiping at the sound of him. He lost his nerve, hurled his spade a yard wide at his antagonist, and whirled about and fled, fairly yelling as he dodged another.

He was panic-stricken. He ran furiously to and fro, dodging when there was no need to dodge, and in his anxiety to see on every side of him at once, stumbling. For a moment he was down and they heard his fall. Far away in the circumferential wall a little doorway looked like heaven, and he set off in a wild rush for it. He did not even look round at his pursuers until it was gained, and he had stumbled across the bridge, clambered a little way among the rocks, to the surprise and dismay of a young llama, who went leaping out of sight, and lay down sobbing for breath.

And so his *coup d'état* came to an end.

He stayed outside the wall of the valley of the Blind for two nights and days without food or shelter, and meditated upon the unexpected. During these meditations he repeated very frequently and always with a profounder note of derision the exploded proverb: 'In the Country of the Blind the One-Eyed Man is King.' He thought chiefly of ways of fighting and conquering these people, and it grew clear that for him no practicable way was possible. He had no weapons, and now it would be hard to get one.

The canker of civilisation had got to him even in Bogota, and he could not find it in himself to go down and assassinate a blind man. Of course, if he did that, he might then dictate terms on the threat of assassinating them all. But—sooner or later he must sleep! . . .

He tried also to find food among the pine trees, to be comfortable under pine boughs while the frost fell at night, and—with less confidence—to catch a llama by artifice in order to try to kill it—perhaps by hammering it with a stone—and so finally, perhaps, to eat some of it. But the llamas had a doubt of him and regarded him with distrustful brown eyes, and spat when he drew near. Fear came on him the second day and fits of shivering. Finally he crawled down to the wall of the Country of the Blind and tried to make terms. He crawled along by the stream, shouting, until two blind men came out to the gate and talked to him.

'I was mad,' he said. 'But I was only newly made.'

They said that was better.

He told them he was wiser now, and repented of all he had done.

Then he wept without intention, for he was very weak and ill now, and they took that as a favourable sign.

They asked him if he still thought he could '*see.*'

'No,' he said. 'That was folly. The word means nothing—less than nothing!'

They asked him what was overhead.

'About ten times ten the height of a man there is a roof above the world—of rock—and very, very smooth.' . . . He burst again into hysterical tears. 'Before you ask me any more, give me some food or I shall die.'

He expected dire punishments, but these blind people were capable of toleration. They regarded his rebellion as but one more proof of his general idiocy and inferiority; and after they had whipped him they appointed him to do the simplest and heaviest work they had for anyone to do, and he, seeing no other way of living, did submissively what he was told.

He was ill for some days, and they nursed him kindly. That refined his submission. But they insisted on his lying in the dark, and that was a great misery. And blind philosophers came and talked to him of the wicked levity of his mind, and reproved him so impressively for his doubts about the lid of rock that covered their cosmic casserole that he almost doubted whether indeed he was not the victim of hallucination in not seeing it overhead.

So Nunez became a citizen of the Country of the Blind, and these people ceased to be a generalised people and became individualities and familiar to him, while the world beyond the mountains became more and more remote and unreal. There was Yacob, his master, a kindly man when not annoyed; there was Pedro, Yacob's nephew; and there was Medina-saroté, who was the youngest daughter of Yacob. She was little esteemed in the world of the blind, because she had a clear-cut face, and lacked that satisfying, glossy smoothness that is the blind man's ideal of feminine beauty; but Nunez thought her beautiful at first, and presently the most beautiful thing in the whole creation. Her closed eyelids were not sunken and red after the common way of the valley, but lay as though they might open again at any moment; and she had long eyelashes, which were considered a grave disfigurement. And her voice was strong, and did not satisfy the acute hearing of the valley swains. So that she had no lover.

There came a time when Nunez thought that, could he win her, he would be resigned to live in the valley for all the rest of his days.

He watched her; he sought opportunities of doing her little services, and presently he found that she observed him. Once at a rest-day gathering they sat side by side in the dim starlight, and the music was sweet. His hand came upon hers and he dared to clasp it. Then very tenderly she returned his pressure. And one day, as they were at their meal in the darkness, he felt her hand very softly seeking him, and as it chanced the fire leapt then and he saw the tenderness of her face.

He sought to speak to her.

He went to her one day when she was sitting in the summer moonlight spinning. The light made her a thing of silver and mystery. He sat down at her feet and told her he loved her, and told her how beautiful she seemed to him. He had a lover's voice, he spoke with a tender reverence that came near to awe, and she had never before been touched by adoration. She made him no definite answer, but it was clear his words pleased her.

After that he talked to her whenever he could take an opportunity. The valley became the world for him, and the world beyond the mountains where men lived in sunlight seemed no more than a fairy tale he would some day pour into her ears. Very tentatively and timidly he spoke to her of sight.

Sight seemed to her the most poetical of fancies, and she listened to his description of the stars and the mountains and her own sweet white-lit beauty as though it was a guilty indulgence. She did not believe, she could only half understand, but she was mysteriously delighted, and it seemed to him that she completely understood.

His love lost its awe and took courage. Presently he was for demanding her of Yacob and the elders in marriage, but she became fearful and delayed. And it was one of her elder sisters who first told Yacob that Medina-saroté and Nunez were in love.

There was from the first very great opposition to the marriage of Nunez and Medina-saroté; not so much because they valued her as because they held him as a being apart, an idiot, incompetent thing below the permissible level of a man. Her sisters opposed it bitterly as bringing discredit on them all; and old Yacob, though he had formed a sort of liking for his clumsy, obedient serf, shook his head and said the thing could not be. The young men were all angry at the idea of corrupting the race, and one went so far as to revile and strike Nunez. He struck back. Then for the first time he found an advantage in seeing, even by twilight, and after that fight was over no one was disposed to raise a hand against him. But they still found his marriage impossible.

Old Yacob had a tenderness for his last little daughter, and was grieved to have her weep upon his shoulder.

'You see, my dear, he's an idiot. He has delusions; he can't do anything right.'

'I know,' wept Medina-saroté. 'But he's better than he was. He's getting better. And he's strong, dear father, and kind—stronger and kinder than any other man in the world. And he loves me—and, father, I love him.'

Old Yacob was greatly distressed to find her inconsolable, and, besides—what made it more distressing—he liked Nunez for many things. So he went and sat in the windowless council-chamber with the other elders and watched the trend of the talk, and said, at the proper time, 'He's better than he was. Very likely, some day, we shall find him as sane as ourselves.'

Then afterwards one of the elders, who thought deeply, had an idea. He was the great doctor among these people, their medicine-man, and he had a very philosophical and inventive mind, and the idea of curing Nunez of his peculiarities appealed to him. One day when Yacob was present he returned to the topic of Nunez.

'I have examined Bogota,' he said, 'and the case is clearer to me. I think very probably he might be cured.'

'That is what I have always hoped,' said old Yacob.

'His brain is affected,' said the blind doctor.

The elders murmured assent.

'Now, *what* affects it?'

'Ah!' said old Yacob.

'*This*,' said the doctor, answering his own question. 'Those queer things that are called the eyes, and which exist to make an agreeable soft depression in the face, are diseased, in the case of Bogota, in such a way as to affect his brain. They are greatly distended, he has eyelashes, and his eyelids move,

461

and consequently his brain is in a state of constant irritation and distraction.'

'Yes?' said old Yacob. 'Yes?'

'And I think I may say with reasonable certainty that, in order to cure him completely, all that we need do is a simple and easy surgical operation—namely, to remove these irritant bodies.'

'And then he will be sane?'

'Then he will be perfectly sane, and a quite admirable citizen.'

'Thank Heaven for science!' said old Yacob, and went forth at once to tell Nunez of his happy hopes.

But Nunez's manner of receiving the good news struck him as being cold and disappointing.

'One might think,' he said, 'from the tone you take, that you did not care for my daughter.'

It was Medina-saroté who persuaded Nunez to face the blind surgeons.

'*You* do not want me,' he said, 'to lose my gift of sight?'

She shook her head.

'My world is sight.'

Her head drooped lower.

'There are the beautiful things, the beautiful little things—the flowers, the lichens among the rocks, the lightness and softness on a piece of fur, the far sky with its drifting down of clouds, the sunsets and the stars. And there is *you*. For you alone it is good to have sight, to see your sweet, serene face, your kindly lips, your dear, beautiful hands folded together. . . . It is these eyes of mine you won, these eyes that hold me to you, that these idiots seek. Instead, I must touch you, hear you, and never see you again. I must come under that roof of rock and stone and darkness, that horrible roof under which your imagination stoops. . . . No; you would not have me do that?'

A disagreeable doubt had arisen in him. He stopped, and left the thing a question.

'I wish,' she said, 'sometimes——' She paused.

'Yes,' said he, a little apprehensively.

'I wish sometimes—you would not talk like that.'

'Like what?'

'I know it's pretty—it's your imagination. I love it, but *now*——'

He felt cold. '*Now?*' he said faintly.

She sat quite still.

'You mean—you think—I should be better, better perhaps——'

He was realising things very swiftly. He felt anger, indeed, anger at the dull course of fate, but also sympathy for her lack of understanding—a sympathy near akin to pity.

'*Dear,*' he said, and he could see by her whiteness how intensely her spirit pressed against the things she could not say. He put his arms about her, he kissed her ear, and they sat for a time in silence.

'If I were to consent to this?' he said at last, in a voice that was very gentle.

She flung her arms about him, weeping wildly. 'Oh, if you would,' she sobbed, 'if only you would!'

For a week before the operation that was to raise him from his servitude and inferiority to the level of a blind citizen, Nunez knew nothing of sleep, and all through the warm sunlit hours, while the others slumbered happily, he sat brooding or wandered aimlessly, trying to bring his mind to bear on his dilemma. He had given his answer, he had given his consent, and still he was not sure. And at last work-time was over, the sun rose in splendour over the golden crests, and his last day of vision began for him. He had a few minutes with Medina-saroté before she went apart to sleep.

'To-morrow,' he said, 'I shall see no more.'

'Dear heart!' she answered, and pressed his hands with all her strength.

'They will hurt you but little,' she said; 'and you are going through this pain—you are going through it, dear lover, for *me*. . . . Dear, if a woman's heart and life can do it, I will repay you. My dearest one, my dearest with the tender voice, I will repay.'

He was drenched in pity for himself and her.

He held her in his arms, and pressed his lips to hers, and looked on her sweet face for the last time. 'Good-bye!' he whispered at that dear sight, 'good-bye!'

And then in silence he turned away from her.

She could hear his slow retreating footsteps, and something in the rhythm of them threw her into a passion of weeping.

He had fully meant to go to a lonely place where the meadows were beautiful with white narcissus, and there remain until the hour of his sacrifice should come, but as he went he lifted up his eyes and saw the morning, the morning like an angel in golden armour, marching down the steeps. . . .

It seemed to him that before this splendour he, and this blind world in the valley, and his love, and all, were no more than a pit of sin.

He did not turn aside as he had meant to do, but went on, and passed through the wall of the circumference and out upon the rocks, and his eyes were always upon the sunlit ice and snow.

He saw their infinite beauty, and his imagination soared over them to the things beyond he was now to resign for ever.

He thought of that great free world he was parted from, the world that was his own, and he had a vision of those further slopes, distance beyond distance, with Bogota, a place of multitudinous stirring beauty, a glory by day, a luminous mystery by night, a place of palaces and fountains and statues and white houses, lying beautifully in the middle distance. He thought how for a day or so one might come down through passes, drawing ever nearer and nearer to its busy streets and ways. He thought of the river journey, day by day, from great Bogota to the still vaster world beyond, through towns and villages, forest and desert places, the rushing river day by day, until its banks receded and the big steamers came splashing by, and one had reached the sea—the limitless sea, with its thousand islands, its thousands of islands, and its ships seen dimly far away in their incessant journeyings round and about that greater world. And there, unpent by mountains, one saw the sky—the sky, not such a disc as one saw it here, but an arch of immeasurable blue, a deep of deeps in which the circling stars were floating. . . .

His eyes scrutinised the great curtain of the mountains with a keener inquiry.

For example, if one went so, up that gully and to that chimney there, then one might come out high among those stunted pines that ran round in a sort of shelf and rose still higher and higher as it passed above the gorge. And then? That talus might be managed. Thence perhaps a climb might be found to take him up to the precipice that came below the snow; and if that chimney failed, then another farther to the east might serve his purpose better. And then? Then one would be out upon the amber-lit snow there, and half-way up to the crest of those beautiful desolations.

He glanced back at the village, then turned right round and regarded it steadfastly.

He thought of Medina-saroté, and she had become small and remote.

He turned again towards the mountain wall, down which the day had come to him.

Then very circumspectly he began to climb.

When sunset came he was no longer climbing, but he was far and high. He had been higher, but he was still very high. His clothes were torn, his limbs were blood-stained, he was bruised in many places, but he lay as if he were at his ease, and there was a smile on his face.

From where he rested the valley seemed as if it were in a pit and nearly a mile below. Already it was dim with haze and shadow, though the mountain summits around him were things of light and fire. The mountain summits around him were things of light and fire, and the little details of the rocks near at hand were drenched with subtle beauty—a vein of green mineral piercing the grey, the flash of crystal faces here and there, a minute, minutely-beautiful orange lichen close beside his face. There were deep mysterious shadows in the gorge, blue deepening into purple, and purple into a luminous darkness, and overhead was the illimitable vastness of the sky. But he heeded these things no longer, but lay quite inactive there, smiling as if he were satisfied merely to have escaped from the valley of the Blind in which he had thought to be King.

The glow of the sunset passed, and the night came, and still he lay peacefully contented under the cold clear stars.

XXXIII

THE BEAUTIFUL SUIT

THERE was once a little man whose mother made him a beautiful suit of clothes. It was green and gold, and woven so that I cannot describe how delicate and fine it was, and there was a tie of orange fluffiness that tied up under his chin. And the buttons in their newness shone like stars. He was proud and pleased by his suit beyond measure, and stood before the long looking-glass when first he put it on, so astonished and delighted with it that he could hardly turn himself away.

He wanted to wear it everywhere, and show it to all sorts of people. He thought over all the places he had ever visited, and all the scenes he had ever heard described, and tried to imagine what the feel of it would be if he were to go now to those scenes and places wearing his shining suit, and he wanted to go out forthwith into the long grass and the hot sunshine of the meadow wearing it. Just to wear it! But his mother told him 'No.' She told him he must take great care of his suit, for never would he have another nearly so fine; he must save it and save it, and only wear it on rare and great occasions. It was his wedding-suit, she said. And she took the buttons and twisted them up with tissue paper for fear their bright newness should be tarnished, and she tacked little guards over the cuffs and elbows, and wherever the suit was most likely to come to harm. He hated and resisted these things, but what could he do? And at last her warnings and persuasions had effect, and he consented to take off his beautiful suit and fold it into its proper creases, and put it away. It was almost as though he gave it up again. But he was always thinking of wearing it, and of the supreme occasions when some day it might be worn without the guards, without the tissue paper on the buttons, utterly and delightfully, never caring, beautiful beyond measure.

One night, when he was dreaming of it after his habit, he dreamt he took the tissue paper from one of the buttons, and found its brightness a little faded, and that distressed him mightily in his dream. He polished the poor faded button and polished it, and, if anything, it grew duller. He woke up and lay awake, thinking of the brightness a little dulled, and wondering how he would feel if perhaps when the great occasion (whatever it might be) should arrive, one button should chance to be ever so little short of its first glittering freshness, and for days and days that thought remained with him distressingly. And when next his mother let him wear his suit, he was tempted and nearly gave way to the temptation just to fumble off one little bit of tissue paper and see if indeed the buttons were keeping as bright as ever.

He went trimly along on his way to church, full of this wild desire. For you must know his mother did, with repeated and careful warnings, let him wear his suit at times, on Sundays, for example, to and fro from church, when there was no threatening of rain, no dust blowing, nor anything to injure it, with its buttons covered and its protections tacked upon it, and a sunshade in his hand to shadow it if there seemed too strong a sunlight for its colours. And always, after such occasions, he brushed it over and folded it exquisitely as she had taught him, and put it away again.

Now all these restrictions his mother set to the wearing of his suit he obeyed, always he obeyed them, until one strange night he woke up and saw the moonlight shining outside his window. It seemed to him the moonlight was not common moonlight, nor the night a common night, and for awhile he lay quite drowsily, with this odd persuasion in his mind. Thought joined on to thought like things that whisper warmly in the shadows. Then he sat up in his little bed suddenly very alert, with his heart beating very fast, and a quiver in his body from top to toe. He had made up his mind. He knew that now he was going to wear his suit as it should be worn. He had no doubt in the matter. He was afraid, terribly afraid, but glad, glad.

He got out of his bed and stood for a moment by the window looking at the moonshine-flooded garden, and trembling at the thing he meant to do. The air was full of a minute clamour of crickets and murmurings, of the infinitesimal shoutings of little living things. He went very gently across the creaking boards, for fear that he might wake the sleeping house, to the big dark clothes-press wherein his beautiful suit lay folded, and he took it out garment by garment, and softly and very eagerly tore off its tissue-paper covering and its tacked protections until there it was, perfect and delightful as he had seen it when first his mother had given it to him—a long time it seemed ago. Not a button had tarnished, not a thread had faded on this dear suit of his; he was glad enough for weeping as in a noiseless hurry he put it on. And then back he went, soft and quick, to the window that looked out upon the garden, and stood there for a minute, shining in the moonlight, with his buttons twinkling like stars, before he got out on the sill, and, making as little of a rustling as he could, clambered down to the garden path below. He stood before his mother's house, and it was white and nearly as plain as by day, with every window-blind but his own shut like an eye that sleeps. The trees cast still shadows like intricate black lace upon the wall.

The garden in the moonlight was very different from the garden by day; moonshine was tangled in the hedges and stretched in phantom cobwebs from spray to spray. Every flower was gleaming white or crimson black, and the air was a-quiver with the thridding of small crickets and nightingales singing unseen in the depths of the trees.

There was no darkness in the world, but only warm, mysterious shadows, and all the leaves and spikes were edged and lined with iridescent jewels of dew. The night was warmer than any night had ever been, the heavens by some miracle at once vaster and nearer, and, spite of the great ivory-tinted moon that ruled the world, the sky was full of stars.

The little man did not shout nor sing for all his infinite gladness. He stood for a time like one awestricken, and then, with a queer small cry and holding out his arms, he ran out as if he would embrace at once the whole round immensity of the world. He did not follow the neat set paths that cut the garden squarely, but thrust across the beds and through the wet, tall, scented herbs, through the night-stock and the nicotine and the clusters of phantom white mallow flowers and through the thickets of southernwood and lavender, and knee-deep across a wide space of mignonette. He came to the great hedge, and he thrust his way through it; and though the thorns of the brambles scored him deeply and tore threads from his wonderful suit, and though burrs and goose-grass and havers caught and clung to him, he did not care. He did not care, for he knew it was all part of the wearing for which he had longed. 'I am glad I put on my suit,' he said; 'I am glad I wore my suit.'

Beyond the hedge he came to the duck-pond, or at least to what was the duck-pond by day. But by night it was a great bowl of silver moonshine all noisy with singing frogs, of wonderful silver moonshine twisted and clotted with strange patternings, and the little man ran down into its waters between the thin black rushes, knee-deep and waist-deep and to his shoulders, smiting the water to black and shining wavelets with either hand, swaying and shivering wavelets, amidst which the stars were netted in the tangled reflections of the brooding trees upon the bank. He waded until he swam, and so he crossed the pond and came out upon the other side, trailing, as it seemed to him, not duckweed, but very silver in long, clinging, dripping masses. And up he went through the transfigured tangles of the willow-herb and the uncut seeding grasses of the farther bank. He came glad and breathless into the high-road. 'I am glad,' he said, 'beyond measure, that I had clothes that fitted this occasion.'

The high-road ran straight as an arrow flies, straight into the deep-blue pit of sky beneath the moon, a white and shining road between the singing nightingales, and along it he went, running now and leaping, and now walking and rejoicing, in the clothes his mother had made for him with tireless, loving hands. The road was deep in dust, but that for him was only soft whiteness; and as he went a great dim moth came fluttering round his wet and shimmering and hastening figure. At first he did not heed the moth, and then he waved his hands at it, and made a sort of dance with it as it circled round his head. 'Soft moth!' he cried, 'dear moth! And wonderful night, wonderful night of the world! Do you think my clothes are beautiful, dear moth? As beautiful as your scales and all this silver vesture of the earth and sky?'

And the moth circled closer and closer until at last its velvet wings just brushed his lips. . . .

And next morning they found him dead, with his neck broken, in the bottom of the stone pit, with his beautiful clothes a little bloody, and foul and stained with the duckweed from the pond. But his face was a face of such happiness that, had you seen it, you would have understood indeed how that he had died happy, never knowing that cool and streaming silver for the duckweed in the pond.

THE END

471

APPENDIX 1

Wells's Original Introduction to
The Country of the Blind, and Other Stories (1911)

THE enterprise of Messrs T. Nelson & Sons and the friendly accommodation of Messrs Macmillan render possible this collection in one cover of all the short stories by me that I care for any one to read again. Except for the two series of linked incidents that make up the bulk of the book called *Tales of Space and Time*, no short story of mine of the slightest merit is excluded from this volume. Many of very questionable merit find a place; it is an inclusive and not an exclusive gathering. And the task of selection and revision brings home to me with something of the effect of discovery that I was once an industrious writer of short stories, and that I am no longer anything of the kind. I have not written one now for quite a long time, and in the past five or six years I have made scarcely one a year. The bulk of the fifty or sixty tales from which this present three-and-thirty have been chosen dates from the last century. This edition is more definitive than I supposed when first I arranged for it. In the presence of so conclusive an ebb and cessation an almost obituary manner seems justifiable.

I find it a little difficult to disentangle the causes that have restricted the flow of these inventions. It has happened, I remark, to others as well as to myself, and in spite of the kindliest encouragement to continue from editors and readers. There was a time when life bubbled with short stories; they were always coming to the surface of my mind, and it is no deliberate change of will that has thus restricted my production. It is rather, I think, a diversion of attention to more sustained and more exacting forms. It was my friend Mr C. L. Hind who set that spring going. He urged me to write short stories for the *Pall Mall Budget*, and persuaded me by his simple and buoyant conviction that I could do what he desired. There existed at the time only the little sketch, 'The Jilting of Jane,' included in this volume—at least, that is the only tolerable fragment of fiction I find surviving from my pre-Lewis-Hind period.

472

But I set myself, so encouraged, to the experiment of inventing moving and interesting things that could be given vividly in the little space of eight or ten such pages as this, and for a time I found it a very entertaining pursuit indeed. Mr Hind's indicating finger had shown me an amusing possibility of the mind. I found that, taking almost anything as a starting-point and letting my thoughts play about it, there would presently come out of the darkness, in a manner quite inexplicable, some absurd or vivid little incident more or less relevant to that initial nucleus. Little men in canoes upon sunlit oceans would come floating out of nothingness, incubating the eggs of prehistoric monsters unawares; violent conflicts would break out amidst the flower-beds of suburban gardens; I would discover I was peering into remote and mysterious worlds ruled by an order logical indeed but other than our common sanity.

The 'nineties was a good and stimulating period for a short-story writer. Mr Kipling had made his astonishing advent with a series of little blue-grey books, whose covers opened like window-shutters to reveal the dusty sun-glare and blazing colours of the East; Mr Barrie had demonstrated what could be done in a little space through the panes of his *Window in Thrums*. The *National Observer* was at the climax of its career of heroic insistence upon lyrical brevity and a vivid finish, and Mr Frank Harris was not only printing good short stories by other people, but writing still better ones himself in the dignified pages of the *Fortnightly Review*. *Longman's Magazine*, too, represented a *clientèle* of appreciative short-story readers that is now scattered. Then came the generous opportunities of the *Yellow Book*, and the *National Observer* died only to give birth to the *New Review*. No short story of the slightest distinction went for long unrecognised. The sixpenny popular magazines had still to deaden down the conception of what a short story might be to the imaginative limitation of the common reader—and a maximum length of six thousand words. Short stories broke out everywhere. Kipling was writing short stories; Barrie, Stevenson, Frank Harris; Max Beerbohm wrote at least one perfect one, 'The Happy Hypocrite'; Henry James pursued his wonderful and inimitable bent; and among other names that occur to me, like a mixed handful of jewels drawn from a bag, are George Street, Morley Roberts, George Gissing, Ella d'Arcy, Murray Gilchrist, E. Nesbit, Stephen Crane, Joseph Conrad, Edwin Pugh, Jerome K. Jerome, Kenneth Graham, Arthur Morrison,

Marriott Watson, George Moore, Grant Allen, George Egerton, Henry Harland, Pett Ridge, W. W. Jacobs (who alone seems inexhaustible). I dare say I could recall as many more names with a little effort. I may be succumbing to the infirmities of middle age, but I do not think the present decade can produce any parallel to this list, or what is more remarkable, that the later achievements in this field of any of the survivors from that time, with the sole exception of Joseph Conrad, can compare with the work they did before 1900. It seems to me this outburst of short stories came not only as a phase in literary development, but also as a phase in the development of the individual writers concerned.

It is now quite unusual to see any adequate criticism of short stories in English. I do not know how far the decline in short-story writing may not be due to that. Every sort of artist demands human responses, and few men can contrive to write merely for a publisher's cheque and silence, however reassuring that cheque may be. A mad millionaire who commissioned masterpieces to burn would find it impossible to buy them. Scarcely any artist will hesitate in the choice between money and attention; and it was primarily for that last and better sort of pay that the short stories of the 'nineties were written. People talked about them tremendously, compared them, and ranked them. That was the thing that mattered.

It was not, of course, all good talk, and we suffered then, as now, from the *à priori* critic. Just as nowadays he goes about declaring that the work of such-and-such a dramatist is all very amusing and delightful, but 'it isn't a Play,' so we had a great deal of talk about *the* short story, and found ourselves measured by all kinds of arbitrary standards. There was a tendency to treat the short story as though it was as definable a form as the sonnet, instead of being just exactly what any one of courage and imagination can get told in twenty minutes' reading or so. It was either Mr Edward Garnett or Mr George Moore in a violently anti-Kipling mood who invented the distinction between the short story and the anecdote. The short story was Maupassant; the anecdote was damnable. It was a quite infernal comment in its way, because it permitted no defence. Fools caught it up and used it freely. Nothing is so destructive in a field of artistic effort as a stock term of abuse. Anyone could say of any short story, 'A mere anecdote,' just as anyone can say 'Incoherent!' of any novel or of any sonata that isn't studiously monotonous. The recession of enthusiasm for this compact, amusing form is closely associated in my mind with that discouraging imputation. One felt hopelessly open to a paralysing and unanswerable charge, and one's ease and happiness in the garden of one's fancies was more and more marred by the dread of it. It crept into one's mind, a distress as vague and inexpugnable as a sea fog on a spring morning, and presently one shivered and wanted to go indoors. . . . It is the absurd fate of the imaginative writer that he should be thus sensitive to atmospheric conditions.

But after one has died as a maker one may still live as a critic, and I will confess I am all for laxness and variety in this as in every field of art. Insistence upon rigid forms and austere unities seems to me the instinctive reaction of the sterile against the fecund. It is the tired man with a headache who values a work of art for what it does not contain. I suppose it is the lot of every critic nowadays to suffer from indigestion and a fatigued appreciation, and to develop a self-protective tendency towards rules that will reject, as it were, automatically the more abundant and irregular forms. But this world is not for the weary, and in the long-run it is the new and variant that matter. I refuse altogether to recognise any hard and fast type for the Short Story, any more than I admit any limitation upon the liberties of the Small Picture. The short story is a fiction that may be read in something under an hour, and so that it is moving and delightful, it does not matter whether it is as 'trivial' as a Japanese print of insects seen closely between grass stems, or as spacious as the prospect of the plain of Italy from Monte Mottarone. It does not matter whether it is human or inhuman, or whether it leaves you thinking deeply or radiantly but superficially pleased. Some things are more easily done as short stories than others and more abundantly done, but one of the many pleasures of short-story writing is to achieve the impossible.

At any rate, that is the present writer's conception of the art of the short story, as the jolly art of making something very bright and moving; it may be horrible or pathetic or funny or beautiful or profoundly illuminating, having only this essential, that it should take from fifteen to fifty minutes to read aloud. All the rest is just whatever invention and imagination and the mood can give—a vision of buttered slides on a busy day or of unprecedented worlds. In that spirit of miscellaneous expectation these stories should be received.

Each is intended to be a thing by itself; and if it is not too ungrateful to kindly and enterprising publishers, I would confess I would much prefer to see each printed expensively alone, and left in a little brown-paper cover to lie about a room against the needs of a quite casual curiosity. And I would rather this volume were found in the bedrooms of convalescents and in dentists' parlours and railway trains than in gentlemen's studies. I would rather have it dipped in and dipped in again than read severely through. Essentially it is a miscellany of inventions, many of which were very pleasant to write; and its end is more than attained if some of them are refreshing and agreeable to read. I have now re-read them all, and I am glad to think I wrote them. I like them, but I cannot tell how much the associations of old happinesses gives them a flavour for me. I make no claims for them and no apology; they will be read as long as people read them. Things written either live or die; unless it be for a place of judgment upon Academic impostors, there is no apologetic intermediate state.

I may add that I have tried to set a date to most of these stories, but that they are not arranged in strictly chronological order. Five of them, and these the latest—'The Country of the Blind,' 'The Door in the Wall,' 'A Vision of Judgment,' 'The Empire of the Ants,' and 'The Beautiful Suit'—are now reprinted for the first time.

H. G. WELLS

APPENDIX 2

The 1939 Version of 'The Country of the Blind'

*In 1939 this drastically revised version of 'The Country of the Blind'
was published in a limited edition of 280 copies by the Golden
Cockerel Press, London, together with an earlier text of the story
and a number of engravings by Clifford Webb.*

THREE hundred miles and more from Chimborazo, one hundred
from the snows of Cotopaxi, in the wildest wastes of Ecuador's
Andes, where the frost-and-sun-rotted rocks rise in vast pinnacles
and cliffs above the snows, there was once a mysterious mountain
valley, called the Country of the Blind. It was a legendary land, and
until quite recently people doubted if it was anything more than a
legend. Long years ago, ran the story, that valley lay so far open to
the world that men, daring the incessant avalanches, might clamber
at last through frightful gorges and over an icy pass into its equable
meadows; and thither indeed men went and settled, a family or so
of Peruvian half-breeds fleeing from the lust and tyranny of an evil
Spanish ruler. Then came the stupendous outbreak of Mindobamba,
when it was night in Quito for seventeen days, and the water was
boiling at Yaguachi and all the fish floating dying even as far as
Guayaquil; everywhere along the Pacific slopes there were landslips
and swift thawings and sudden floods, and one whole side of the old
Arauca crest slipped and came down in thunder, and cut off this
Country of the Blind, as it seemed, for ever from the exploring feet
of men.

But, said the story, one of these early settlers had chanced to be
on the hither side of the gorge when the world had so terribly
shaken itself, and perforce he had to forget his wife and his child
and all the friends and possessions he declared he had left up there,
and begin life again in the lower world.

He had a special reason to account for his return from that fastness, into which he had first been carried lashed to a llama, beside
a vast bale of gear, when he was a child. The valley, he said, had in

it all that the heart of man could desire—sweet water, pasture, an even climate, slopes of rich brown soil with tangles of a shrub that bore an excellent fruit, and on one side great hanging pine forests that held the avalanches high. Far overhead, a semi-circle of ice-capped precipices of grey-green rock brooded over that glowing garden; but the glacier stream flowed away by the farther slopes and only very rarely did an ice-fall reach the lower levels. In this valley it neither rained nor snowed, but the abundant springs gave a rich green pasture, that patient irrigation was spreading over all the valley space. The surplus water gathered at last in a little lake beneath the cirque and vanished with a roar into an unfathomable cavern. The settlers, he said, were doing very well indeed there. Their beasts did well and multiplied, and only one thing marred their happiness. Yet it was enough to mar it greatly; some sinister quality hidden in that sweet and bracing air. A strange disease had come upon them, and had made all the children born to them there—and indeed several older children also—blind. So that the whole valley seemed likely to become a valley of blind men.

It was, he said, to seek some charm or antidote against this plague of blindness that with infinite fatigue, danger and difficulty he had returned down the gorge. In those days, in such cases, men did not think of germs and infections but of sins; and it seemed to him that the reason of this affliction must lie in the negligence of these priestless immigrants to set up a shrine so soon as they entered the valley. He wanted a shrine—a handsome, cheap, effectual shrine—to be set up in the valley; he wanted relics and suchlike potent things of faith, blessed objects and mysterious medals and prayers. In his wallet he had a bar of native silver for which he would not account; he insisted there was none in the valley, with something of the insistence of an inexpert liar. The settlers had all clubbed their money and ornaments together, having little need for such treasure up there, he said, to buy them holy help against their ill. I figure this young mountaineer, sunburnt, gaunt and anxious, hat-brim clutched feverishly, a man all unused to the ways of the lower world, telling this story to some keen-eyed, attentive priest before the great convulsion; I can picture him presently seeking to return with pious and infallible remedies against that trouble, and the infinite dismay with which he must have faced the tumbled and still monstrously crumbling vastness where the gorge had once come out. But the rest of his tale of mischances is lost to me, save that I know he died of punishment in the mines. His offence I do not know.

But the idea of a valley of blind folk had just that appeal to the imagination that a legend requires if it is to live. It stimulates fantasy. It invents its own detail.

And recently this story has been most remarkably confirmed. We know now the whole history of this Country of the Blind from that beginning to its recent and tragic end.

We know now that amidst the little population of that now isolated and forgotten valley the contagion ran its course. Even the older children became groping and purblind, and the young saw but dimly, and the children that were born to them never saw at all. But life was very easy in that snow-rimmed basin, lost to all the world, with neither thorns nor briers, with food upon the bushes in its season, with no evil insects nor any beasts save the gentle breed of llamas they had lugged and thrust and followed up the beds of the shrunken rivers in the gorges by which they had come. The first generation had become purblind so gradually that they scarcely noted their loss. They guided the sightless youngsters who followed them hither and thither until they knew the whole valley marvellously, and when at last sight died out altogether among them the race lived on. They had even time to adapt themselves to the blind control of fire, which they made carefully in stoves of stone. They were a simple strain of people at the first, unlettered, only slightly touched with Spanish civilisation, but with something of a tradition of the arts of old Peru and its lost philosophy. Generation followed generation. They forgot many things; they devised many things. Their tradition of the greater world they came from became mythical in colour and uncertain. In all things save sight they were strong and able; and presently the chances of birth and heredity produced one who had an original mind and who could talk and persuade among them, and then afterwards another. These two passed, leaving their effects, and the little community grew in numbers and understanding, and met and settled all the social and economic problems that arose, sensibly and peaceably. There came a time when a child was born who was fifteen generations from that ancestor who went out of the valley with a bar of silver to seek God's aid, and who never returned. Then it chanced that a man came into this community from the outer world and troubled their minds very greatly. He lived with them for many months, and escaped very narrowly from their final disaster.

He was a mountaineer from the country near Quito, a man who had been down to the sea and had seen the world, and he was taken on by a party of Englishmen under Sir Charles Pointer, who had come out of Ecuador to climb mountains, to replace one of their three Swiss guides who had fallen ill. He climbed here and he climbed there, and then came the attempt on Parascotopetl, the 'rotten' mountain, the Matterhorn of the Andes, in which he was lost to the outer world so that he was given up for dead.

Everyone who knew anything of the mountain-craft had warned the little expedition against the treachery of the rocks in this range, but apparently it was not a rock-fall that caught this man Nunez but an exceptional snow-cornice. The party had worked its difficult and almost vertical way up to the very foot of the last and greatest precipice, and had already built itself a night shelter upon a little shelf of rock amidst the snow, when the accident occurred. Suddenly they found that Nunez had disappeared, without a sound. They shouted, and there was no reply; they shouted and whistled, they made a cramped search for him, but their range of movement was very limited. There was no moon, and their electric torches had only a limited range.

As the morning broke they saw the traces of his fall. It seems impossible he could have uttered a cry. The depths had snatched him down. He had slipped eastward towards the unknown side of the mountain; far below he had struck a steep slope of snow, and ploughed his way down it in the midst of a snow avalanche. His track went straight to the edge of a frightful precipice, and beyond that everything was hidden. Far, far below, and hazy with distance, they could see trees rising out of a narrow, shut-in valley—the lost Country of the Blind. But they did not know it was the lost Country of the Blind, nor distinguish it in any way from any other narrow streak of sheltered upland valley. Unnerved by this disaster, they abandoned their attempt in the afternoon, and Pointer, who was financing the attempt, was called away to urgent private business before he could make another attack. To this day Parascotopetl lists an unconquered crest, and Pointer's shelter crumbles unvisited somewhere amidst the snows.

And this man who fell survived.

At the end of the slope he fell a thousand feet, and came down in the midst of a cloud of snow upon a snow slope even steeper than the one above. Down this he was whirled, stunned and insensible, but miraculously without a bone broken in his body; and then the gradients diminished, and at last he rolled out and lay still, buried amidst a softening heap of the white masses that had accompanied him and saved him. He came to himself with a dim fancy that he was ill in bed; then realised his position, worked himself loose and, after a rest or so, out until he saw the stars. He rested flat upon his chest for a space, wondering where he was and what had happened to him. He explored his limbs, they ached exceedingly but they were unbroken. He discovered that several of his buttons were gone and his coat turned over his head. His knife had gone from his pocket and his cap was lost, though it had been tied under his chin. His face was grazed; he was scratched and contused all over. He recalled that he had been looking for loose stones to raise a piece of the shelter wall. His ice-axe had disappeared.

He looked up to see, exaggerated by the ghastly light of the rising moon, the tremendous flight he had taken. For a while he lay, gazing blankly at that vast pale cliff towering above, rising moment by moment out of a subsiding tide of darkness. Since the light struck it first above it seemed to be streaming upward out of nothing. Its phantasmal mysterious beauty held him for a space, and then he was seized with a paroxysm of sobbing laughter. . . .

After a great interval of time he became aware that he was near the lower edge of the snow. Below, down what was now a moonlit and practicable slope, he saw the dark and broken appearance of rock-strewn turf. He struggled to his feet, aching in every limb, got down painfully from the heaped loose snow about him, went downward until he was on the turf, and there dropped rather than lay beside a boulder, drank deep from the flask in his inner pocket, and instantly fell asleep. . . .

He was awakened by the singing of birds in trees far below.

He sat up stiffly and perceived he was on a little alp at the foot of a great precipice, grooved by the gulley down which he and his snow had come. Over against him another wall of jagged rock reared itself against the sky. The gorge between these precipices ran east and west and was full of the morning sunlight, which lit to the westward the mass of fallen mountain that had blocked the way to the world. Below him it seemed there was a precipice equally steep, but beyond the snow in the gulley he found a chimney dripping with snow-water down which a desperate man might venture. He found it easier than it looked, and came at last to another desolate alp, and then after a rock climb of no particular difficulty to a steep slope of trees. He took his bearings and turned his face eastward, for he saw it opened out above upon green meadows, among which he now glimpsed quite distinctly a cluster of stone huts of unfamiliar fashion. At times his progress was like clambering along the face of a wall, and after a time the rays of the rising sun were intercepted by a vast bastion, the voices of the singing birds died away, and the air grew cold and dark about him. But the distant valley with its houses seemed all the brighter for that. He presently came to talus, and among the rocks he noted—for he was an observant man— an unfamiliar fern that seemed to clutch out of the crevices with intense green hands. He picked a frond or so and gnawed its stalk and found it helpful. There were bushes but the fruit had not formed upon them.

About midday he emerged from the shadow of the great bluff into the sunlight again. And now he was only a few hundred yards from the valley meadows. He was weary and very stiff; he sat down in the shadow of a rock, filled up his nearly empty flask with water from a spring, drank it down, and rested for a time before he went on towards the houses.

They were very strange to his eyes, and indeed the whole aspect of that valley became, as he regarded it, queerer and more unfamiliar. The greater part of its surface was lush green meadow, starred with many beautiful flowers, irrigated with extraordinary care, and bearing evidence of systematic cropping piece by piece. High up and ringing the valley about was a wall, and what appeared to be a circumferential water-channel, which received the runlets from the snows above and from which little trickles of water had been led to feed the meadows. On the higher slopes above this wall, flocks of llamas cropped the scanty herbage amidst the tangled shrubs. Sheds, apparently shelters or feeding-places for the llamas, stood against the boundary wall here and there. The irrigation streams ran together into a main channel down the centre of the valley, that debouched into a little lake below a semi-circle of precipices, and this central canal was enclosed on either side by a wall breast-high. This wall gave a singularly urban quality to this secluded place, a quality that was greatly enhanced by the fact that a number of paths paved with green, grey, black and white stones, and each with a curious little kerb at the side, ran hither and thither in an orderly manner. The houses of the central village were quite unlike the casual and higgledy-piggledy agglomeration of the mountain villages he knew; they stood in a continuous row on either side of a central street of astonishing cleanness; here and there their parti-coloured façade was pierced by a door, and not a solitary window broke their even frontage. They were parti-coloured with extraordinary irregularity; smeared with a sort of plaster that was sometimes grey, sometimes drab, sometimes slate-coloured or dark-brown; and it was the sight of this wild plastering first brought the word 'blind' into the thoughts of the explorer. 'The good man who did that,' he thought, 'must have been as blind as a bat.'

He descended a steep place and so came to the wall and channel that ran about the valley, near where the latter spouted out its surplus contents into the lake. He could see now a number of men and women resting on piled heaps of grass, as if taking a siesta; in the remoter part of the meadow and nearer the village a number of recumbent children; and then nearer at hand three men carrying pails on yokes along a little path that ran from the encircling wall towards the houses. These latter were clad in garments of llama cloth and boots and belts of leather, and they wore caps of cloth with back and ear flaps. They followed one another in single file, walking slowly and yawning as they walked, like men who have been up all night. There was something so reassuringly prosperous and respectable in their bearing that after a moment's hesitation Nunez stood forward as conspicuously as possible upon his rock, and gave vent to a mighty shout that evoked a thousand echoes round and about the valley.

The three men stopped and moved their heads as if they were looking about them. They turned their faces this way and that, and Nunez gesticulated with freedom. But they did not appear to see him for all his gestures, and after a time, directing themselves towards the mountain far away to the right, they shouted as if in answer. Nunez bawled again and then once more, and as he gestured ineffectually the word 'blind' came once more to the front of his thought. 'The fools must be blind,' he said.

When at last, after much shouting and irritation, Nunez crossed the stream by a little bridge, came through a gate in the wall, and approached them, he realised that they were indeed blind. He knew already that this was the Country of the Blind of which the legends told. Conviction had sprung upon him, and a sense of great and rather enviable adventure. The three stood side by side, not looking at him, but with their ears directed towards him, judging him by his unfamiliar steps. They stood close together like men a little afraid, and he could see their eyelids closed and shrunken, as if the very balls beneath them had shrunk away. There was an expression near awe on their faces.

'A man,' one said, in hardly recognisable Spanish—'a man it is— a man or a beast that walks like a man—coming down from the rocks.'

But Nunez advanced with the confident steps of a youth who enters upon life. All the old stories of the lost valley and the Country of the Blind had come back to his mind, and through his thoughts ran this old proverb, as if it were a refrain—

'In the Country of the Blind the One-Eyed Man is King.'
'In the Country of the Blind the One-Eyed Man is King.'

And very civilly he gave them greeting. He talked to them and used his eyes.

'Where does he come from, brother Pedro?' asked one.

'Down out of the rocks.'

'Over the mountains I come,' said Nunez, 'out of the country beyond there—where men can see. From near Bogota, where there are a hundred thousands of people, and where the city passes out of sight.'

'Sight?' muttered Pedro. 'Sight?'

'He comes,' said the second blind man, 'out of the rocks.'

The cloth of their coats Nunez saw was curiously fashioned, each with a different sort of stitching.

They startled him by a simultaneous movement towards him, each with a hand outstretched. He stepped back from the advance of these spread fingers.

'Come hither,' said the third blind man, following his motion and clutching him neatly.

And they held Nunez and felt him over, saying no word further until they had done so.

'Carefully,' he cried, when a finger was poked in his eye, and he realised that they thought that organ, with its fluttering lids, a queer thing in him. They felt over it again.

'A strange creature, Correa,' said the one called Pedro. 'Feel the coarseness of his hair. Like a llama's hair.'

'Rough he is as the rocks that begot him,' said Correa, investigating Nunez's unshaven chin with a soft and slightly moist hand. 'Perhaps he will grow finer.' Nunez struggled a little under their examination, but they gripped him firm.

'Carefully,' he said again.

'He speaks,' said the third man. 'Certainly he is a man.'

'Ugh!' said Pedro, at the roughness of his coat.

'And you have come into the world?' asked Pedro.

'*Out* of the world. Over mountains and glaciers; right over above there, half-way to the sun. Out of the great big world that goes down from here, twelve days' journey to the sea.'

They scarcely seemed to heed him. 'The fathers have told us men may be made by the forces of Nature,' said Correa. 'It is the warmth of things and moisture, and rottenness— rottenness.'

'Let us lead him to the elders,' said Pedro.

'Shout first,' said Correa, 'lest the children be afraid. This is a marvellous occasion.'

So they shouted, and Pedro went first and took Nunez by the hand to lead him to the houses.

He drew his hand away. 'I can see,' he said.

'See?' said Correa.

'Yes, see,' said Nunez, turning towards him, and stumbled against Pedro's pail.

'His senses are still imperfect,' said the third blind man. 'He stumbles, and talks unmeaning words. Lead him by the hand.'

'As you will,' said Nunez, and was led along smiling.

It seemed they knew nothing of sight.

Well, all in good time, he would teach them.

He heard people shouting, and saw a number of figures gathered together in the middle roadway of the village.

He found it taxed his nerve and patience more than he had

anticipated, that first encounter with the population of the Country of the Blind. The place seemed larger as he drew near to it, and the smeared plasterings queerer, and a crowd of children and men and women (the women and girls, he was pleased to note, had some of them quite sweet faces, for all that their eyes were shut and sunken) came about him, and mobbed him, holding on to him, touching him with soft, sensitive hands, smelling at him, and listening for every word he spoke. Some of the maidens and children, however, kept aloof as if afraid, and indeed his voice seemed coarse and rude beside their softer notes. His three guides kept close to him with an effect of proprietorship, and said again and again, 'A wild man out of the rocks.'

'Bogota,' he said. 'Bogota. Over the mountain crests.'

'A wild man—using wild words,' said Pedro. 'Did you hear that—*Bogota?* His mind is hardly formed yet. He has only the beginnings of speech.'

A little boy nipped his hand. 'Bogota!' he said mockingly.

'Ay! A city to your village. I come from the great world—where men have eyes and see.'

'His name's Bogota,' they said.

'He stumbled,' said Correa, 'stumbled twice as we came hither.'

'Bring him to the elders.'

And they thrust him suddenly through a doorway into a room as black as pitch, save at the end there faintly glowed a fire. The crowd closed in behind him and shut out all but the faintest glimmer of day, and before he could arrest himself he had fallen headlong over the feet of a seated man. His arm, outflung, struck the face of someone else as he went down; he felt the soft impact of features and heard a cry of anger, and for a moment he struggled against a number of hands that clutched him. It was a one-sided fight. An inkling of the situation came to him, and he lay quiet.

'I fell down,' he said, 'I couldn't see in this pitchy darkness. Who could?'

There was a pause as if the unseen persons about him tried to understand his words. Then the voice of Correa said: 'He is but newly formed. He stumbles as he walks and mingles words that mean nothing with his speech.'

Others also said things about him that he heard or understood imperfectly.

'May I sit up?' he asked, in a pause. 'I will not struggle against you again.'

They consulted and let him rise.

The voice of an older man began to question him, and Nunez found himself trying to explain the great world out of which he had fallen, and the sky and mountains and sight and suchlike marvels, to these elders who sat in darkness in the Country of the Blind. And they would believe and understand nothing whatever he told them, a thing quite outside his expectation. They would not even understand many of his words. For fourteen generations these people had been blind and cut off from all the seeing world; the names for all the things of sight had faded and changed; the story of the outer world was faded and changed to a child's story; and they had ceased to concern themselves with anything beyond the rocky slopes above their circling wall. Blind men of genius had arisen among them and questioned the shreds of belief and tradition they had brought with them from their seeing days, and had dismissed all these things as idle fancies, and replaced them with new and saner explanations. Much of their imagination had shrivelled with their eyes, and they had made for themselves new imaginations with their ever more sensitive ears and finger-tips. Slowly Nunez realised this; that his expectation of wonder and reverence at his origin and his gifts was not to be borne out; and after his poor attempt to explain sight to them had been set aside as the confused version of a new-made being describing the marvels of his incoherent sensations, he subsided, a little dashed, into listening to their instruction.

The eldest of the blind men explained to him life and philosophy and religion, how that the world (meaning their valley) had been first an empty hollow in the rocks and then had come, first, inanimate things without the gift of touch, from these grass and bushes and after that llamas and a few other creatures that had little sense, and then men, and at last angels, whom one could hear singing and making fluttering sounds, but whom none could touch at all, which puzzled Nunez greatly until he thought of the birds.

The elder went on to tell Nunez how 'by the Wisdom above us' time had been divided into the warm and the cold, which are the blind equivalents of day and night, and how it was good to sleep in the warm, and work during the cold, so that now, but for his advent, the whole town of the blind would have been asleep. He said Nunez must have been specially created to learn and serve the wisdom they had acquired, and for all his mental incoherency and stumbling behaviour he must have courage, and do his best to learn; and at that all the people in the doorway murmured encouragingly. He said the night—for the blind call their day night—was now far gone, and it behoved everyone to go back to sleep. He asked Nunez if he knew how to sleep, and Nunez said he did, but that before sleep he wanted food.

They brought him food, llama's milk in a bowl, and rough salted bread, and led him into a lonely place to eat out of their hearing, and afterwards to slumber, until the chill of the mountain evening roused them to begin their day again. But Nunez slumbered not at all.

Instead, he sat up in the place where they had left him, resting his limbs and turning the unanticipated circumstances of his arrival over and over in his mind.

Every now and then he laughed, sometimes with amusement and sometimes with indignation.

'Unformed mind!' he said. 'Got no senses yet! They little know they've been insulting their heaven-sent king and master. I see I must bring them to reason. Let me think—let me think.'

He was still thinking when the sun set.

Nunez had an eye for all beautiful things, and it seemed to him that the glow upon the snowfields and glaciers that rose about the valley on every side was the most beautiful thing he had ever seen. His eyes went from that inaccessible glory to the village and irrigated fields, fast sinking into the twilight, and suddenly a wave of emotion took him, and he thanked God from the bottom of his heart that the power of sight had been given him.

He heard a voice calling to him from out of the house of the elders.

'Ya ho there, Bogota! Come hither!'

At that he stood up smiling. He would show these people once and for all what sight would do for a man. They would seek him but not find him.

'You move not, Bogota,' said the voice.

He laughed noiselessly, and made two stealthy steps aside from the path.

'Trample not on the grass, Bogota; that is not allowed.'

488

Nunez had scarcely heard the sound he made himself. He stopped amazed.

The owner of the voice came running up the piebald path towards him.

'Why did you not come when I called you?' said the blind man. 'Must you be led like a child? Cannot you hear the path as you walk?'

Nunez laughed. 'I can see it,' he said.

'There is no such word as *see*,' said the blind man after a pause. 'Cease this folly and follow the sound of my feet.'

Nunez followed, a little annoyed.

'My time will come,' he said.

'You'll learn,' the blind man answered. 'There is much to learn in the world.'

'Has no one told you, "In the Country of the Blind the One-eyed Man is King?"'

'What is blind?' asked the man carelessly over his shoulder.

Four days passed, and the fifth found the King of the Blind still incognito, as a clumsy and useless stranger among his subjects.

It was, he found, much more difficult to proclaim himself than he had supposed, and in the meantime, while he meditated his *coup d'état*, he did what he was told and learned the manners and customs of the Country of the Blind. He found working and going about at night a particularly irksome thing, and he decided that that should be the first thing he would change in his little kingdom.

They led a simple, laborious life, these people, with all the elements of virtue and happiness, as these things can be understood by men. They toiled, but not oppressively; they had food and clothing sufficient for their needs; they had days and seasons of rest; they made much of music and singing, and there was love among them, and little children.

It was marvellous with what confidence and precision they went about their ordered world. Everything, you see, had been made to fit their needs; each of the radiating paths of the valley area had a constant angle to the others, and was distinguished by a special notch upon its kerbing; all obstacles and irregularities of path and meadow had long since been cleared away; all their methods and procedure arose naturally from their special needs. Their senses had become marvellously acute; they could hear and judge the slightest gesture of a man a dozen paces away—could hear the very beating of his heart. Intonation had long replaced expression with them, and touches gesture, and their work with hoe and spade and fork was as free and confident as garden work can be. Their sense of smell was extraordinarily fine; they could distinguish individual differences as readily as a dog can, and they went about the tending of the llamas, who lived among the rocks above and came to the wall for food and shelter, with ease and confidence. It was only when at last Nunez sought to assert himself that he found how easy and confident their movements could be.

He rebelled only after he had tried persuasion.

At first on several occasions he sought to tell them of sight. 'Look you here, you people,' he said. 'There are things you do not understand in me.'

Once or twice one or two of them attended to him; they sat with faces downcast and ears turned intelligently towards him though with a faintly ironical smile on their lips, while he did his best to tell them what it was to see. Among his hearers was a girl, with eyes less red and sunken than the others, so that one could almost fancy she was hiding eyes, and she especially he hoped to persuade.

He spoke of the beauties of sight, of watching the mountains, of the sky and the sunrise, and they heard him with amused incredulity that presently became condemnatory. They told him that there were indeed no mountains at all, but that the end of the rocks where the llamas grazed was indeed the end of the world; the rocks became steeper and steeper, became pillars and thence sprang a cavernous roof of the universe, from which the dew and avalanches fell; and when he maintained stoutly the world had neither end nor roof such as they supposed, they were shocked and they said his thoughts were wicked. So far as he could describe sky and clouds and stars to them, his world seemed to them a hideous void, a terrible blankness in the place of the smooth roof to things in which they believed—it was an article of faith with them that above the rocks the cavern roof was exquisitely smooth to the touch. They called it the Wisdom Above.

He saw that in some manner he shocked them by his talk of clouds and stars, and so he gave up that aspect of the matter altogether, and tried to show them the practical value of sight. One morning he saw Pedro in the path called Seventeen and coming towards the central houses, but still too far off for hearing or scent, and he told them as much. 'In a little while,' he prophesied, 'Pedro will be here.' An old man remarked that Pedro had no business on Path Seventeen, and then, as if in confirmation, that individual as he drew near turned and went transversely into Path Ten, and so back with nimble paces to the outer wall. They mocked Nunez when Pedro did not arrive, and afterwards, when he asked Pedro questions to clear his character, Pedro denied and outfaced him, and was afterwards hostile to him.

Then he induced them to let him go a long way up the sloping meadows towards the wall with one complacent individual, and to him he promised to describe all that happened among the houses. He noted certain comings and goings, but the things that really seemed to signify to these people happened inside of or behind the windowless houses—the only thing they took note of to test him by—and of these he could see or tell nothing; and it was after the failure of that attempt, and the ridicule they could not repress, that he resorted to force. He thought of seizing a spade and suddenly smiting one or two of them to earth, and so in fair combat showing the advantage of eyes. He went so far with that resolution as to seize his spade, and then he discovered a new thing about himself, and that was that it was impossible for him to hit a blind man in cold blood.

He hesitated and found them all aware that he had snatched up the spade. They stood alert, with their heads on one side, and bent ears towards him for what he would do next.

'Put that spade down,' said one, and he felt a sort of helpless horror. He came near obedience.

Then he thrust one backwards against a house wall, and fled past him and out of the village.

He went athwart one of their meadows, leaving a track of trampled grass behind his feet, and presently sat down by the side of one of their ways. He felt something of the buoyancy that comes to all men in the beginning of a fight, but more perplexity. He began to realise that you cannot even fight happily with creatures that stand upon a different mental basis to yourself. Far away he saw a number of men carrying spades and sticks come out of the street of houses, and advance in a spreading line along the several paths towards him. They advanced slowly, speaking frequently to one another, and ever and again the whole cordon would halt and snuff the air and listen.

The first time they did this Nunez laughed. But afterwards he did not laugh.

One struck his trail in the meadow grass, and came stooping and feeling his way along it.

For five minutes he watched the slow extension of the cordon, and then his vague disposition to do something forthwith became frantic. He stood up, went a pace or so towards the circumferential wall, turned, and went back a little way. There they all stood in a crescent, still and listening.

He also stood still, gripping his spade very tightly in both hands. Should he charge them?

The pulse in his ears rang into the rhythm of 'In the Country of the Blind the One-eyed Man is King!'

Should he charge them?

He looked back at the high and unclimbable wall behind— unclimbable because of its smooth plastering, but withal pierced by many little doors, and at the approaching line of seekers. Behind these, others were now coming out of the street of houses.

Should he charge them?

'Bogota!' called one. 'Bogota! where are you!'

He gripped his spade still tighter and advanced down the meadows towards the place of habitations, and directly he moved they converged upon him. 'I'll hit them if they touch me,' he swore; 'by Heaven I will. I'll hit.' He called aloud, 'Look here, I'm going to do what I like in this valley. Do you hear? I'm going to do what I like and go where I like!'

They were moving in upon him quickly, groping, yet moving rapidly. It was like playing blind man's buff, with everyone blindfolded except one. 'Get hold of him!' cried one. He found himself in the arc of a loose curve of pursuers. He felt suddenly he must be active and resolute.

'You don't understand,' he cried in a voice that was meant to be great and resolute, and which broke. 'You are blind, and I can see. Leave me alone!'

'Bogota! Put down that spade, and come off the grass!'

The last order, grotesque in its urban familiarity, produced a gust of anger.

492

'I'll hurt you,' he said, sobbing with emotion. 'By Heaven, I'll hurt you. Leave me alone!'

He began to run, not knowing clearly where to run. He ran from the nearest blind man, because it was a horror to hit him. He stopped, and made a dash to escape from their closing ranks. He made for where a gap was wide, and the men on either side, with a quick perception of the approach of his paces, rushed in on one another. He sprang forward, and then saw he must be caught, and swish! the spade had struck. He felt the soft thud of hand and arm, and the man was down with a yell of pain, and he was through.

Through! And then he was close to the street of houses again, and blind men, whirling spades and stakes, were running with a sort of reasoned swiftness hither and thither.

He heard steps behind him just in time, and found a tall man rushing forward and swiping at the sound of him. He lost his nerve, hurled his spade a yard wide at his antagonist, and whirled about and fled, fairly yelling as he dodged another.

He was panic-stricken. He ran furiously to and fro, dodging when there was no need to dodge, and in his anxiety to see on every side of him at once, stumbling. For a moment he was down and they heard his fall. Far away in the circumferential wall a little doorway looked like Heaven, and he set off in a wild rush for it. He did not even look round at his pursuers until it was gained, and he had stumbled across the bridge, clambered a little way among the rocks, to the surprise and dismay of a young llama, who went leaping out of sight, and lay down sobbing for breath.

And so his *coup d'état* came to an end.

He stayed outside the wall of the Valley of the Blind for two nights and days without food or shelter, and meditated upon the unexpected. There were bushes, but the food on them was not ripe and hard and bitter. It weakened him to eat it. It lowered his courage. During these prowlings he repeated very frequently and always with a profounder note of derision that exploded proverb: 'In the Country of the Blind the One-eyed Man is King.' He thought chiefly of ways of fighting and conquering these people, and it grew clear that for him no practicable way was possible. He had no weapons, and now it would be hard to get one.

The canker of civilisation had got to him even in Bogota, and he could not find it in himself to go down and assassinate a blind man.

Of course, if he did that, he might then dictate terms on the threat of assassinating them all. If he could get near enough to them, that is. And—sooner or later he must sleep! . . .

He tried also to find food among the pine trees, to be comfortable under pine boughs while the frost fell at night and—with less confidence—to catch a llama by artifice in order to try to kill it—perhaps by hammering it with a stone—and so finally, perhaps, to eat some of it. But the llamas had their doubts of him and regarded him with distrustful brown eyes, and spat when he drew near. Fear came on him the second day, an intense fatigue, and fits of shivering. Finally he crawled down to the wall of the Country of the Blind and tried to make terms. He crawled along by the stream shouting, until two blind men came out to the gate and talked to him.

'I was mad,' he said. 'But I was only newly made.'

They said that was better.

He told them he was wiser now, and that he repented of all he had done.

Then he wept without intention, for he was very weak and ill, and they took that as a favourable sign.

They asked him if he still thought he could '*see.*'

'No,' he said, 'that was folly. The word means nothing—less than nothing!'

They asked him what was overhead.

'About ten times the height of a man there is a roof above the world—of rock and wisdom and very, very smooth.' . . .

He burst again into hysterical tears. 'Before you ask me any more, give me some food or I shall die.'

He expected dire punishments, but these blind people showed themselves capable of great toleration. They regarded his rebellion as but one more proof of his general idiocy and inferiority; and after they had whipped him they appointed him to do the simplest and heaviest work they had for anyone to do, and he, seeing no other way of living, did submissively what he was told.

He was ill for some days and they nursed him kindly. That refined his submission. But they insisted on his lying in the dark and that was a great misery. And the chief elders came and talked to him of the wicked levity of his mind, and reproved him so impressively for his doubts about the lid of rock that covered their cosmic casserole that he almost doubted whether indeed he was not the victim of hallucination in not seeing it overhead.

So Nunez humbled himself and became a common citizen of the Country of the Blind, and these people ceased to be a generalised people and became individualities and familiar to him, while the world beyond the mountains became more and more remote and unreal. There was Yacob, his master, a kindly man when not annoyed; there was Pedro, Yacob's nephew; and there was Medina-saroté, who was the youngest daughter of Yacob. She was little esteemed in the world of the blind, because she had a clear-cut face, and lacked the satisfying, glossy smoothness that is the blind man's ideal of feminine beauty; but Nunez thought her beautiful at first, and presently the most beautiful thing in the whole creation. Her closed eyelids were not sunken and red after the common way of the valley, but lay as though they might open again at any moment; and she had eyelashes, which were considered a grave disfigurement. And her voice was strong, and did not satisfy the acute hearing of the valley swains. So that she had no lover.

There came a time when Nunez thought that, could he win her, he would be resigned to live in the valley for all the rest of his days.

He watched her; he sought opportunities of doing her little services, and presently he found that she observed him. Once at a rest-day gathering they sat side by side in the dim starlight, and the music was sweet. His hand came upon hers and he dared to clasp it. Then very tenderly she returned his pressure. And one day, as they were at their meal in the darkness, he felt her hand very softly seeking him, and as it chanced the fire leaped then and he saw the tenderness of her face.

He sought to speak to her.

He went to her one day when she was sitting in the summer moonlight spinning. The light made her a thing of silver and mystery. He sat down at her feet and told her he loved her, and told her how beautiful she seemed to him. He had a lover's voice, he spoke with a tender reverence that came near to awe, and she had never before been touched by adoration. She made him no definite answer, but it was clear his words pleased her.

After that he talked to her whenever he could take an opportunity. The valley became the world for him, and the world beyond the mountains where men worked and went about in sunlight seemed no more than a fairy tale he would some day pour into her ears. Very tentatively and timidly he spoke to her of sight.

At first this sight seemed to her the most poetical of fancies, and she listened to his description of the stars and the mountains and her own sweet white-lit beauty as though it was a guilty indulgence. She did not believe, she could only half understand, but she was mysteriously delighted, and it seemed to him that she completely understood.

His love lost its awe and took courage. Presently he was for demanding her of Yacob and the elders in marriage, but she became fearful and delayed. And it was one of her sisters who first told Yacob that Medina-saroté and Nunez were in love.

From the first there was very great opposition to the marriage of Nunez and Medina-saroté; not so much because they valued her as because they held him as a being apart, an idiot, incompetent thing, below the permissible level of a man. Her sisters opposed it bitterly as bringing discredit on them all; and old Yacob, though he had formed a sort of liking for his clumsy, obedient serf, shook his head and said the thing could not be. The young men were all angry at the thought of corrupting the race, and one went so far as to revile and strike Nunez. He struck back. Then for the first time he found an advantage in seeing, even by twilight, and after that fight no one was disposed to lift a hand against him. But they still found his marriage impossible.

Old Yacob had a tenderness for his last little daughter, and was grieved to have her weep upon his shoulder.

'You see, my dear, he's an idiot! He has delusions; he can't do anything right.'

'I know,' wept Medina-saroté. 'But he's better than he was. He's getting better. And he's strong, dear father, and kind—stronger and kinder than any other man in the world. And he loves me—and, father, I love him.'

Old Yacob was greatly distressed to find her inconsolable, and, besides—what made it more distressing—he liked Nunez for many things. So he went and sat in the windowless council-chamber with the other elders, observing the trend of their talk, and said, at the proper time, 'He's better than he was. Very likely, some day, we shall find him as sane as ourselves.'

Then afterwards one of the elders, who thought deeply, had an idea. He was the great doctor among these people, their medicine man, and he had a very philosophical and inventive mind, and the idea of curing Nunez of his peculiarities appealed to him. One day when Yacob was present he turned to the topic of Nunez.

'I have examined Bogota,' he said, 'and the case is clearer to me. I think very probably he might be cured.'

'That is what I have always hoped,' said old Yacob.

'His brain is affected,' said the blind doctor.

The elders murmured assent.

'Now, *what* affects it?'

'Ah!' said old Yacob.

'This,' said the doctor, answering his own question. 'Those queer things that are called the eyes, and which exist to make an agreeable soft depression in the face, are diseased, in the case of Bogota, in such a way as to affect his brain. They are greatly distended, he has eyelashes, and his eyelids move, and consequently his brain is in a state of constant irritation and distraction.'

'Yes?' said old Yacob. 'Yes?'

'And I think I may say with reasonable certainty that, in order to cure him completely, all that we need to do is a simple and easy surgical operation—namely, to remove those irritating bodies.'

'And then he will be sane?'

'Then he will be perfectly sane, and a quite admirable citizen.'

'Thank Heaven for the Wisdom beneath it!' said old Yacob, and went forth at once to tell Nunez of his happy hopes.

But Nunez's manner of receiving the good news struck him as being cold and disappointing.

'One might think,' he said, 'from the tone you take, that you did not care for my daughter.'

It was Medina-saroté who persuaded Nunez to face the blind surgeons.

'You do not want me,' he said, 'to lose my gift of sight?'

She shook her head.

'My world is sight.'

Her head dropped lower.

'There are beautiful things, the beautiful little things—the flowers, the lichens among the rocks, the lightness and visible softness on a piece of fur, the far sky with its drifting down of clouds, the sunsets

and the stars. And there is *you*. For you alone it is good to have
sight, to see your sweet, serene face, your kindly lips, your dear,
dear, beautiful hands folded together. . . . It is these eyes of mine
you won, these eyes that hold me to you, that these idiots seek.
Instead, I must touch you, hear you, and never see you again. I
must come under that roof of rock and stone and darkness, that
horrible roof under which your imagination stoops. . . . No, you would
not have me do that?'

She shuddered to hear him speak of the Wisdom Above in such
terms. Her hands went to her ears.

A disagreeable doubt had arisen in him. He stopped, and left the
thing a question.

'I wish,' she said, 'sometimes—' She paused.

'Yes?' said he, a little apprehensively.

'I wish sometimes—you would not talk like that.'

'Like what?'

'It's your imagination. I love much of it, but not when you speak
of the Wisdom Above. When you talked of those flowers and stars
it was different. But now—'

He felt cold. '*Now?*' he said faintly.

She sat quite still.

'You mean—you think—I should be better, better, perhaps—'

He was realising things very swiftly. He felt anger, indeed, anger
at the dull course of fate, but also sympathy for her lack of understanding—a sympathy near akin to pity.

'*Dear,*' he said, and he could see by her whiteness how intensely
her spirit pressed against the things she could not say. He put his
arms about her, and kissed her ear, and they sat for a time in
silence.

'If I were to consent to this?' he whispered at last, in a voice that
was very gentle.

She flung her arms about him weeping wildly. 'Oh, if you would,'
she sobbed, 'if only you would!'

'And you have no doubt?'

'Dear heart!' she answered, and pressed his hands with all her
strength.

'They will hurt you but little,' she said; 'and you would be going
through this pain—you are going through it, dear lover, for
me. . . . Dear; if a woman's heart and life can do it, I will repay

you. My dearest one, my dearest with that rough, gentle voice, I will repay.'

'So be it,' he said.

And in silence he turned away from her. For the time he could sit by her no longer.

She could hear his slow retreating footsteps, and something in the rhythm of them threw her into a passion of weeping. . . .

He meant to go to a lonely place where the meadows were beautiful with white narcissus, but as he went he lifted up his eyes and saw the morning, the morning like an angel in golden armour, marching down the steeps. . . .

It seemed to him that before this splendour he, and this blind world in the valley, and his love, and all, were no better than the darkness of an anthill.

He did not turn aside to the narcissus fields as he had meant to do. Instead he went on, and passed through the wall of the circumference and out upon the rocks, and his eyes were always upon the sunlit ice and snow above.

He saw their infinite beauty, and his imagination soared over them to the things he would see no more.

He thought of that great free visible world he was to renounce for ever; the world that was his own, and beyond these encircling mountains; and he had a vision of those further slopes, distance beyond distance, with Bogota, a place of multitudinous stirring beauty, a glory by day, a luminous mystery by night, a place of palaces and fountains and statues and white houses, lying beautifully in the middle distance. He thought how for a day or so one might come down through passes, drawing ever nearer and nearer to its busy streets and ways. He thought of the river journey to follow, from great Bogota to the still vaster world beyond, through towns and villages, forest and desert places, the rushing river day by day, until its banks receded and the big steamers came splashing by, and one had reached the sea—the limitless sea, with its thousand islands, its thousands of islands, and its ships seen dimly far away in their incessant journeyings round and about the greater world. And there, unpent by mountains, one saw the sky—the sky, not such a disc as one saw it here, but a great arch of immeasurable blue, the blue of deeps in which the circling stars were floating.

His eyes scrutinised the imprisoning mountains with a keener enquiry.

It occurred to him that for many days now he had not looked at the cliffs and snow-slopes and gulleys by which he had slid and fallen and clambered down into the valley. He looked now; he looked but he could not find. Something had happened. Something had occurred to change and obliterate the familiar landmarks of his descent. He could not believe it; he rubbed his eyes and looked again. Perhaps he was forgetting. Some fresh fall of snow might have altered the lines and shapes of the exposed surfaces.

In another place too there had been slopes that he had studied very intently. For at times the thought of escape had been very urgent with him. Had they too changed? Had his memory begun to play tricks with him? In one place high up, five hundred feet or so, he had marked a great vein of green crystal that made a sort of slanting way upwards—but alas! died out to nothing. One might clamber to it, but above that there seemed no hope. That was still as it had been. But elsewhere?

Suddenly he stood up with a faint cry of horror in his throat.

'*No!*' he whispered crouching slightly. 'No. It was there before!'

But he knew it had not been there before.

It was a long narrow scar of newly exposed rock running obliquely across the face of the precipice at its vastest. Above it and below it was weathered rock. He still struggled against that conviction. But there it was plain and undeniable and *raw*. There could be little doubt of the significance of that fresh scar. An enormous mass of that stupendous mountain wall had slipped. It had shifted a few feet forward and it was being held up for a time, by some inequality of the sustaining rocks. Maybe that would hold it now, but of the shift there was no doubt whatever. Could it settle down again in its new position? He could not tell. He scanned the distant surfaces. Above he saw little white threads of water from the snowfields pouring into this new-made crack. Below, water was already spouting freshly at a dozen points from the lower edge of the loosened mass. And then he saw that other, lesser fissures had also appeared in the mountain wall.

The more he studied that vast rock face the more he realised the possible urgency of its menace. If this movement continued the valley was doomed. He forgot his personal distress in a huge solicitude for this little community of which he had become a citizen. What ought these people to do? What could they do? Abandon their threatened houses? Make new ones on the slopes behind him? And how could he induce them to do it?

Suppose that lap of rock upon which the mass now rested *gave*!

The mountain would fall—he traced the possible fall with his extended hands—so and so and so. It would fall into and beyond the lake. It would bury the lower houses. It might bury the whole village. It might spell destruction for every living thing in the valley. Something they ought to do. Prepare refuges? Organise a possible evacuation? Set him to watch the mountains day by day? But how to make them understand?

If he went down now, very simply, very meekly, without excitement, speaking in low tones and abasing himself before them. If he said: 'I am a foolish creature. I am a disgusting creature. I am unfit to touch the hem of the garment of the very least of your wise men. But for once, I pray you, believe in my vision! Believe in my vision! Sometimes such an idiot as I can *see*. Let me have some more tests about this seeing. Because indeed, indeed, I know of a great danger and I can help you to sustain it.' . . .

But how could he convince them? What proofs could he give them? After his earlier failures. Suppose he went down now, with his warning fresh in his mind. Suppose he *insisted*.

'Vision. Sight.' The mere words would be an outrage to them. They might not let him speak at all. And even then if he was permitted to speak, already it might be too late. At the best it would only set them discussing his case afresh. Almost certainly he would anger them, for how could he tell his tale and not question the Wisdom Above. They might take him and end the recurrent nuisance of him by putting out his eyes forthwith, and the only result of his intervention would be that he would be nursing his bloody eye sockets when the disaster fell. The mountain might hold for weeks and months yet, but again it might not wait at all. Even now it might be creeping. Even now the heat of the day must be expanding those sullen vast masses, thawing the night ice that held them together. Even now the trickling snow-water was lubricating the widening fissures.

Suddenly he saw, he saw plainly, a new crack leap across a

shining green mass, and then across the valley came the sound of it like the shot of a gun that starts a race. The mass was moving *now*! There was no more time to waste. No more time for pleas and plans. 'Stop!' he cried. 'Stop!' and put out his hands as if to thrust back that slow deliberate catastrophe. It is preposterous but he believes he said, 'Wait one minute!'

He ran headlong to the little bridge and the gate and rushed down towards the houses, waving his arms and shouting. 'The mountain is falling,' he screamed. 'The whole mountain is falling upon you all. Medina-saroté! Medina-saroté!'

He clattered to the house of old Yacob and burst in upon the sleepers. He shook them and shouted at them, going from one to the other.

'He's gone mad again,' they cried aghast at him and even Medina-saroté cowered away from his excitement.

'Come,' he said. 'Come. Even now it is falling. The mountain is falling.' And he seized her wrist in a grip of steel. 'Come!' he cried so masterfully that in terror she obeyed him.

But outside the house there was a crowd that his shouts and noise had awakened, and a score of men had run out already and assembled outside the house and stood in his way.

'Let me pass,' he cried. 'Let me pass. And come with me—up the further slopes there before it is too late.'

'This is too much. This is the last blasphemy,' shrieked one of the elders. 'Seize him. Hold him!'

'I tell you the mountain is falling. It is coming down upon you even now as you hold me here.'

'The Wisdom Above us that loves and protects us *cannot* fall.'

'Listen. That rumbling?'

'There has been rumbling like that before. The Wisdom is warning us. It is because of your blasphemies.'

'And the ground rocking?'

'Brothers, cast him out! Cast him out of the valley. We have been foolish to harbour him so long. His sin is more than our Providence can endure.'

'But I tell you the rocks are falling. The whole mountain is coming down. Listen and you can hear the crashing and the rending of them.'

He was aware of a loud hoarse voice intoning through the uproar and drowning his own. 'The Wisdom Above loves us. It protects us from all harm. No evil can touch us while the Wisdom is over us. Cast him forth! Cast him forth. Let him take our sins upon him and go!' 'Out you go, Bogota,' cried a chorus of voices. 'Out you go.'

'Medina-saroté! Come with me. Come out of this place!'

Pedro threw protective arms about his cousin.

'Medina-saroté!' cried Nunez. 'Medina-saroté!'

They pushed him, struggling fiercely, up the path towards the boundaries. They showed all the cruelty now of frightened men. For the gathering noise of the advancing rocks dismayed them all. They wanted to out-do each other in repudiating him. They beat at his face with their fists and kicked his shins and ankles and feet. One or two jabbed at him with knives. He could not see Medina-saroté any longer and he could not see the shifting cliffs because of the blows and because of the blood that poured from a cut in his forehead, but the voices about him seemed to fade as the rumbling clatter of falling fragments wove together and rose into a thunderous roar. He shouted weeping for Medina-saroté to escape as they drove him before them.

They thrust him through a little door and flung him out on to a stony slope with a deliberate violence that sent a flock of llamas helter-skelter. He lay like a cast clout. 'And there you stay—and starve,' said one. 'You and your—*seeing*.'

He lifted his head for a last reply.

'I tell you. You will be dead before I am.'

'You *fool*!' said the one he had fought, and came back to kick him again and again. 'Will you never learn reason?' But he turned hastily to join his fellows when Nunez struggled clumsily to his feet.

He stood swaying like a drunken man.

He had no strength in his limbs. He did his best to wipe the blood from his eyes. He looked at the impending mountain-fall, he looked for a high rocky ledge he had noted that morning and then he turned a despairful face to the encircling doom of the valley. But he did not attempt to climb any further away.

'What's the good of going alone?' he said. 'Even if I could. I shall only starve up there.'

And then suddenly he saw Medina-saroté seeking him. She emerged from the little door and she was calling his name. In some manner she had contrived to slip away and come to search for him.

'Bogota my darling!' she cried. 'What have they done to you? Oh *what* have they *done* to you?'

He staggered to meet her, calling her name over and over again.

In another moment her hands were upon his face and she was wiping away the blood and searching softly and skilfully for his cuts and bruises.

'You must stay here now,' she panted. 'You must stay here for a time. Until you repent. Until you learn to repent. Why did you behave so madly? Why did you say those horrible blasphemies? You don't know you say them, but how are they to tell that? If you come back now they will certainly kill you. I will bring you food. Stay here.'

'Neither of us can stay here. *Look!*'

She drew the air in sharply between her teeth at that horrible word 'look' which showed that his madness was still upon him.

'There! That thunder!'

'What is it?'

'A stream of rocks are pouring down by the meadows and it is only the beginning of them. *Look* at them. Listen anyhow to the drumming and beating of them! What do you think those sounds mean? *That* and that! Stones! They are bouncing and dancing across the lower meadows by the lake and the waters of the lake are brimming over and rising up to the further houses. Come my darling. Come! Do not question, but come!'

She stood hesitating for a moment. There was a frightful menace now in the storm of sounds that filled the air. Then she crept into his arms. 'I am afraid,' she said.

He drew her to him and with a renewal of strength began to climb, guiding her feet. His blood smeared her face but there was no time to remedy that. At first she dragged upon him and then, perceiving the strain she caused, she helped and supported him. She was sobbing but also she obeyed.

He concentrated himself now upon reaching that distant shelf, but presently he had to halt for breath, and then only was he free to look back across the valley.

He saw that the foot of the cliff was sliding now down into the lake, scooping its waters before it towards the remoter houses, and that the cascade of rocks was now swifter and greater. They drove over the ground in leaps and bounds with a frightful suggestion in their movements as though they were hunting victims. They were smashing down trees and bushes and demolishing walls and buildings, and still the main bulk of the creeping mountain, deprived now of its supports, had to gather momentum and fall. It was breaking up as it came down. And now little figures appeared from the houses and ran hither and thither. . . .

For the first time Nunez was glad that Medina-saroté was blind.

'Climb! my darling,' he said. 'Climb!'

'I do not understand.'

'Climb!'

A rush of terrified llamas came crowding up past them.

'It is so steep, so steep here. Why are these creatures coming with us?'

'Because they understand. Because they know we are with them. Push through them. Climb.'

With an effect of extreme deliberation that mountain-side hung over the doomed valley. For some tense instants Nunez did not hear a sound. His whole being was concentrated in his eyes. Then came the fall and then a stunning concussion that struck his chest a giant's blow. Medina-saroté was flung against the rocks and clung to them with clawing hands. Nunez had an instant's impression of a sea of rocks and earth and fragments of paths and walls and houses, pouring in a swift flood towards him. A spray of wind driven water bedewed him; they were pelted with mud and broken rock fragments, the wave of debris surged and receded a little and abruptly became still, and then colossal pillars of mist and dust rose up solemnly and deliberately and mounted towering overhead and unfolded and rolled together about them until they were in an impenetrable stinging fog. Silence fell again upon the world and the Valley of the Blind was hidden from him for evermore.

Pallid to the centres of their souls, these two survivors climbed slowly to the crystalline ridge and crouched upon it.

And when some hour or so later that swirling veil of mist and dust had grown thinner and they could venture to move and plan what they would do, Nunez saw through a rent in it far away across a wilderness of tumbled broken rock and in a V-shaped cleft of the broken mountains, the green rolling masses of the foothills, and far beyond them one shining glimpse of the ocean.

Two days later he and Medina-saroté were found by two hunters who had come to explore the scene of this disaster. They were trying to clamber down to the outer world and they were on the verge of exhaustion. They had lived upon water, fern roots and a few berries. They collapsed completely when the hunters hailed them.

They lived to tell their tale, and to settle in Quito among Nunez's people. There he is still living. He is a prosperous tradesman and plainly a very honest man. She is a sweet and gentle lady, her basketwork and her embroidery are marvellous, though of course she makes no use of colour, and she speaks Spanish with an old-fashioned accent very pleasant to the ear.

Greatly daring, I think, they have had four children and they are as stout and sturdy as their father and they can see.

He will talk about his experience when the mood is on him but she says very little. One day however when she was sitting with my wife while Nunez and I were away, she talked a little of her childhood in the valley and of the simple faith and happiness of her upbringing. She spoke of it with manifest regret. It had been a life of gentle routines, free from all complications.

It was plain she loved her children and it was plain she found them and much of the comings and goings about her difficult to understand. She had never been able to love and protect them as she had once loved and protected Nunez.

My wife ventured on a question she had long wanted to ask. 'You have never consulted oculists,' she began.

'Never,' said Medina-saroté. 'I have never wanted to *see*.'

'But colour—and form and distance!'

'I have no use for your colours and your stars,' said Medina-saroté. 'I do not want to lose my faith in the Wisdom Above.'

'But after all that has happened! Don't you want to see Nunez; see what he is like?'

'But I know what he is like and seeing him might put us apart. He would not be so near to me. The loveliness of *your* world is a complicated and fearful loveliness and mine is simple and near. I had rather Nunez saw for me—because he knows nothing of fear.'

'But the *beauty*!' cried my wife.

'It may be beautiful,' said Medina-saroté, 'but it must be very terrible to *see*.'

EXPLANATORY NOTES

EA   H. G. Wells, *Experiment in Autobiography* (London: Gollancz and Cresset, and New York, Macmillan, 1934)

THE JILTING OF JANE

First published in the *Pall Mall Gazette* (July 1894); first collected in *The Plattner Story, and Others*; included in *Thirty Strange Stories* and in vol. 1 of the Atlantic Edition. Wells wrote several early pieces arising from supposed domestic incidents. Most of these 'Euphemia papers' were collected in *Certain Personal Matters* (1897).

5   *'Daisy'*: the popular music-hall song 'Daisy Bell', or 'A Bicycle Built for Two', was written in 1892 by Harry Dacre (Frank Dean).

6   *gage*: a pledge: in this case, a love-token.

    Enquire Within and Mrs Motherly's Book of Household Management: the domestic reference book *Enquire Within upon Everything* first appeared in 1856. Among the most popular books of this kind was Mrs Beeton's *Book of Household Management*, which was first published in 1859.

7   *Plymouth Brother*: the Christian sect known as the Plymouth Brethren, founded in 1827, remains active to this day.

    "Smiles' 'Elp Yourself": Samuel Smiles's best-selling book *Self-Help*, advocating self-improvement and social reform, appeared in 1859.

11   *fly*: a light horse-drawn vehicle for hire.

THE CONE

First published in the *Unicorn* (September 1895); first collected in *The Plattner Story*; included in *Thirty Strange Stories, The Door in the Wall, and Other Stories*, and vol. 1 of the Atlantic Edition.

13   *Gehenna*: a synonym for 'hell', from the valley where the Israelites killed children, supposedly as offerings to the god Moloch. See Milton's *Paradise Lost*, i. 405.

17   *Hanley and Etruria*: Hanley and Burslem were among the six Staffordshire pottery towns which united in 1910 to form the present city of Stoke-on-Trent. Etruria, another town in the area, was home to Wells during March–June 1888 when, recuperating from illness,

he stayed with William Burton, a friend since his student days, who was employed at Wedgwood's pottery works in Etruria. According to *EA* ch. 6.2, 'The Cone' is all that survives of a melodramatic novel which Wells began during this stay with Burton. Another acquaintance of Wells's, a Frenchman and 'cuckold maker' with whom he had recently worked as a schoolteacher in Wales, supplied the name and possibly the character of Raut (Geoffrey West, *H. G. Wells: A Sketch for a Portrait* (London: Howe, 1930), ch. 3.1; *EA* ch. 6.1).

pot-bank: pottery.

ironworks: the description is based on the Shelton Bar Ironworks. See R. G. Hampson, 'H. G. Wells and the Staffordshire Potteries', *Wellsian*, 3 (1980), 1–5.

18 *Burslem*: see note to p. 17 above.

puddlers' furnaces: furnaces used for converting pig-iron into wrought iron.

19 *pillars of cloud by day ... pillars of fire by night*: according to Exodus 13, when the Israelites fled Egypt, God went before them in these two forms.

21 *clinker-heaps*: piles of cinders, or 'slag', from the furnaces.

Newcastle: i.e. Newcastle under Lyme, two miles west of Stoke-on-Trent.

22 *tuyères*: air-nozzles.

affluent: the inflowing stream of water.

Titans: in the mythology of ancient Greece, giant gods overthrown by Zeus.

THE STOLEN BACILLUS

First published in the *Pall Mall Budget* (June 1894); first collected in *The Stolen Bacillus, and Other Incidents*; included in *Thirty Strange Stories*.

27 *Go forth, increase and multiply*: cf. Genesis 1: 22.

29 *in the height of the season*: between May and July it was the custom of the 'fashionable world' to assemble in London.

screw: an old, unfit horse.

30 *Ravachol, Vaillant*: the anarchist Ravachol (François Koenigstein) caused at least two explosions in Paris in 1892, before being executed for a murder committed several years earlier. Auguste

Vaillant received the death penalty for bombing the Chamber of Deputies in 1893. Anarchist atrocities were much in the news at this time. In February 1894 a French anarchist, Martial Boudin, was killed by a bomb he had been carrying through Greenwich Park. This incident became the germ of Joseph Conrad's 1907 novel *The Secret Agent*, which he dedicated to Wells.

32 *Vive l'Anarchie!*: by his own account, it was with this cry that an Italian anarchist, Santo-Geronimo Caserio, stabbed to death the President of France in Lyons on 24 June 1894, three days *after* 'The Stolen Bacillus' was published. This seems a testimony less to Wells's prescience than to anarchist conformity.

THE FLOWERING OF THE STRANGE ORCHID

First published in the *Pall Mall Budget* (August 1894); first collected in *The Stolen Bacillus, and Other Incidents*; included in *Thirty Strange Stories* as 'The Strange Orchid'; also included in vol. 1 of the Atlantic Edition.

34 *labellum*: lower petal.

Horace: the many translators of the Roman poet have included W. E. Gladstone, who was British Prime Minister until five months before the story's publication.

diatoms: a type of microscopic algae. Their classification, Wells implies, was no easy matter.

35 *staggers*: a general name for a variety of animal diseases.

36 *Vandas . . . Dendrobe . . . Palæonophis*: all types of orchid.

rhizome: an underground stem which puts out roots and leafy shoots.

37 '*Men must work though women may weep*': the sentiment comes from Charles Kingsley's poem 'The Three Fishers' (1851): 'For men must work, and women must weep'.

chlorodyne and quinine: the former was a patent medicine containing chloroform. The latter is an alkaloid used against malarias and fevers.

39 *Darwin studied their fertilisation*: in *On the Various Contrivances by which British and Foreign Orchids are Fertilised by Insects* (1862). Darwin also wrote *Insectivorous Plants* (1875), which describes the carnivorous practices of the sundew.

Cypripediums: 'lady's slipper', a genus of orchids.

41 *inflorescence*: a mass of blossoms.

IN THE AVU OBSERVATORY

First published in the *Pall Mall Budget* (August 1894); first collected in *The Stolen Bacillus, and Other Incidents*; included in *Thirty Strange Stories*.

45 *ether*: there was a theory in the nineteenth century that, because space could carry electromagnetic waves, it must therefore be filled by some undetectable medium, to which the medieval name 'ether' was given.

50 *'There are more things in heaven and earth . . . our philosophies'*: cf. Shakespeare, *Hamlet*, I. v.

ÆPYORNIS ISLAND

First published in the *Pall Mall Budget* (December 1894); first collected in *The Stolen Bacillus, and Other Incidents*; included in *Thirty Strange Stories* and in vol. 1 of the Atlantic Edition.

51 *'Cypripediums'*: see note to p. 39.

52 *Æpyornis*: a gigantic winged bird of Madagascar, now extinct. Intact æpyornis eggs may still be found in sandy stream beds after exposure by heavy rains.

Sindbad's roc: a legendary giant bird which features in the Second Voyage of Sinbad in *The Arabian Nights' Entertainment*. See R. G. Hampson, 'H. G. Wells and *The Arabian Nights*', *Wellsian*, 6 (1983), 30–4.

ring: a business combination, the members of which try to control a market in their own interests.

Antananarivo: the capital of Madagascar.

rum: odd, peculiar.

54 *Jamrach's*: Charles Jamrach (1815–91) and his son Albert were London importers of wild animals for zoos.

58 *the waters above the firmament*: cf. Genesis 1: 6–8.

60 *wattle*: a fleshy outgrowth on a bird's neck or head.

cassowary: a bird related to the emu.

61 *heir of the ages and all that*: cf. Tennyson's poem 'Locksley Hall', l. 178.

THE REMARKABLE CASE OF DAVIDSON'S EYES

First published in the *Pall Mall Budget* (March 1895); first collected in *The Stolen Bacillus, and Other Incidents*; included in *Thirty Strange*

Stories as 'The Story of Davidson's Eyes'; also included in vol. 1 of the Atlantic Edition.

64 *intercalary*: inserted, intermediate.

65 *Bellows*: George Bellows is the narrator of several of Wells's early stories.

66 *cryohydrates*: mixtures of ice and another substance.

68 'Bishop Berkeley': in *An Essay Towards a New Theory of Vision* (1709) the philosopher George Berkeley argued that the connection between the objects which we see and those which we touch is purely a mental one founded on experience, unsupported by any abstract element common to both types of object.

71 *the special Pall Mall*: i.e. the magazine in which this story first appeared. The *Budget* was a weekly extension of the *Pall Mall Gazette*.

72 *changing views of a lantern*: in 'magic lantern' slide-shows, lights behind sliding plates of painted glass could be alternately brightened and dimmed to make one picture dissolve into the next.

73 *Antipodes Island*: located to the south of New Zealand.

74 *retinal elements*: the cells which make up the sensitive layer at the back of the eye.

THE LORD OF THE DYNAMOS

First published in the *Pall Mall Budget* (September 1894); first collected in *The Stolen Bacillus, and Other Incidents*; included in *Thirty Strange Stories*, in *The Door in the Wall, and Other Stories*, and in vol. 1 of the Atlantic Edition.

75 *Camberwell*: the world's first electric underground railway, the City and South London line, had been opened in 1890. The three dynamos which powered it were not, however, located in the south London suburb of Camberwell, but three-quarters of a mile to the west in Stockwell, where the line terminated

Carnot's cycle: an ideal heat-engine cycle of maximum thermal efficiency proposed by the French physicist Nicolas Carnot.

Pooh-bah: a character in Gilbert and Sullivan's comic opera *The Mikado*, first produced in 1885.

heraldic grotesqueness: forms as elaborately complex as a design on a coat of arms.

76 *Lord Clive*: aptly enough, in a story so sceptical about the achievements of imperial civilization, the ship is named after the general who helped lay the foundations of British power in India.

76 *Straits Settlements*: Penang, Malacca, and Singapore.

Shadwell: during the nineteenth century, a notorious waterfront slum district of London.

77 *blackleg*: strikebreaker.

Twelve per cent. on the ordinary shares: Holroyd's calculation of the dynamo's financial value to the company.

78 *Solomon*: in 'The City of Brass' in *The Arabian Nights' Entertainment*, Solomon kept genies imprisoned in bottles—a point noted by Hampson in 'H. G. Wells and the *Arabian Nights*' (see note to p. 52).

slop suit: loose garment.

Juggernaut: an avatar of the Hindu god Vishnu. While an idol of this deity was dragged through the crowd, worshippers, so it is said, flung themselves to their deaths beneath its wheels.

79 *peccant*: offending.

80 *Fetich*: an object worshipped because it is believed to contain a spirit.

armature: the part of a generator in which the electric force is produced.

THE MOTH

First published in the *Pall Mall Gazette* (March 1895) as 'A Moth, Genus Novo'; collected as such in *The Stolen Bacillus, and Other Incidents*; included in *Thirty Strange Stories* as 'A Moth (Genus Unknown)'; present title adopted for *The Country of the Blind, and Other Stories* and retained in vol. 1 of the Atlantic Edition and subsequent reprints. According to *EA* ch. 8.1, Wells had the initial idea for the story while he was working on *The Time Machine* and moths were fluttering through a nearby window.

85 *the great hate of the English and Scotch geologists*: a reference to the split between uniformitarians and catastrophists: those who thought that most geological changes were the result of gradual processes and those who pointed to sudden, short-lived events. The source of Wells's quotation is unknown.

odium theologicum: the hatred of theologians for each other's errors and/or for each other.

Professor Ray Lankester: at the time when this story was first published, the distinguished zoologist E. Ray Lankester held the

Linacre Chair of Comparative Anatomy at Oxford. He was later to become a staunch admirer and friend of Wells, and an adviser to him on scientific matters. The 'treatment of the Mollusca' appears in the ninth edition of the *Encyclopaedia Britannica*.

Smithfield: public executions took place on the site of this London meat market for over 400 years.

Cephalopods . . . Pteropods: types of mollusc.

Microlepidoptera: small moths of various kinds.

86 *the Chamber of Deputies*: the Lower House of the French parliament.

jobbing museum appointments: arranging placements in return for some form of bribe.

'mesoblast': the middle layer.

88 *Academy*: the Royal Academy of Arts holds its annual summer exhibition at Burlington House in Piccadilly, London.

'Island Nights' Entertainments': a collection of stories by Robert Louis Stevenson, published in 1893. 'The Bottle Imp' concerns a genie in a bottle which is able to grant its owner's wishes.

89 *'Inner House'*: a novel by Sir Walter Besant, published in 1888. The prologue, 'At the Royal Institution', is a melodramatic account of a scientist's announcement that he has discovered the secret of eternal life. (Although Wells admired the work of Stevenson and Kipling, he had little regard for that of Besant.)

diatoms: see note to p. 34.

THE TREASURE IN THE FOREST

First published in the *Pall Mall Budget* (August 1894); first collected in *The Stolen Bacillus, and Other Incidents*; included in *Thirty Strange Stories*.

99 *pigeon-English*: a pidgin is a simplified version of a language, used for purposes such as trade by people with no common tongue.

junk: a Chinese sailing-vessel.

THE STORY OF THE LATE MR ELVESHAM

First published in the *Idler* (May 1896); first collected in *The Plattner Story, and Others*; included in *Thirty Strange Stories* and in vol. 1 of the Atlantic Edition.

106 *Trentham*: Trentham Hall, outside Stoke-on-Trent, was a palatial mansion with one of the largest formal gardens in England. Wells's father had worked as a gardener there in 1853. Most of the house has since been demolished, and the gardens survive as an amusement park.

Shoolbred's premises: Shoolbred & Co. of Tottenham Court Road was a large firm which supplied and transported furniture.

111 *Kümmel . . . is Himmel*: kümmel is a liqueur flavoured with cumin and caraway seeds; *Himmel* (German) means 'heaven'.

112 *seidlitz-powder*: a laxative.

Futurus!: a toast to the future.

114 *dissolving views*: see note to p. 72.

115 *albumens*: nutritive materials in eggs and plants, a topic Eden had presumably been revising for his examination.

rouleau: cylindrical pile of coins.

116 *truckle-bed*: a low bed capable of being wheeled under a larger one for storage.

118 *the powers of three*: the numbers obtained by repeatedly multiplying three by itself.

UNDER THE KNIFE

First published in the *New Review* (January 1896); first collected in *The Plattner Story, and Others*; included in *Thirty Strange Stories* and in vol. 1 of the Atlantic Edition.

126 *a black barge advancing slowly, towed by a gaunt white horse*: probably an allusion to Revelation 6: 8—'And I looked, and behold a pale horse: and his name that sat on him was Death, and Hell followed with him.'

130 *portal vein*: the vein which carries blood from the intestines, spleen, and stomach to the liver.

134 *gibbous*: of a shape between half and full, unequally convex on two sides.

137 *jack-o'-lantern*: an alternative name for will-o'-the-wisp or *ignis fatuus*, a natural light liable to lead travellers astray, produced by burning marsh gas.

138 *a black rod*: possibly an allusion to Revelation 2: 27—'And he shall rule them with a rod of iron'.

139 *a noise of many waters*: cf. Revelation 19: 6—'And I heard as it were . . . the voice of many waters . . . saying, Alleluia: for the Lord God omnipotent reigneth.'

'There will be no more pain': cf. Revelation 21: 4—'and there shall be no more death, neither sorrow, nor crying, neither shall there be any more pain'.

THE SEA RAIDERS

First published in *The Weekly Sun Literary Supplement* (December 1896); first collected in *The Plattner Story, and Others*; included in *Thirty Strange Stories*.

140 *cephalapods*: a class of ocean molluscs which includes octopuses and squids. They have a ring of tentacles around the mouth and are carnivorous.

cachalot: sperm whale.

142 *skerry*: a reef of rock.

144 *laminaria*: tangled brown seaweed with large leathery fronds.

146 *standing in*: heading towards the shore.

148 *drab*: grey or dull brown.

151 *Newlyn*: a Cornish fishing-port favoured by late Victorian artists due to its mild climate.

THE OBLITERATED MAN

First published in the *New Budget* (August 1895) as 'The Sad Story of a Dramatic Critic', the title used in all editions except *The Country of the Blind, and Other Stories*; first collected in *The Plattner Story, and Others*; included in *Thirty Strange Stories*.

152 *Fiery Cross*: a left-wing journal in the novel *Demos* (1886) by George Gissing.

the beast in Revelation: the reference is to Revelation 4: 6–7.

G.R.S., G.B.S., G.A.S.: George Bernard Shaw (1856–1950), often known as 'G.B.S.', was one of Britain's foremost drama critics, music critics, and socialist intellectuals before going on to become Britain's most eminent playwright since Shakespeare. He and Wells were to be friends and rivals for half a century, and a characteristic mistrust of the older man's vanity and loquaciousness is visible even in this early comic 'aside'. Wells may also be glancing at G. S. Street, his own successor as drama critic of the *Pall Mall Gazette*.

152 *Fairly new, she was*: the 'New Women' of late Victorian Britain wanted the same rights and freedom of behaviour as men—in this case the freedom to smoke cigarettes in public.

Lamb: the essayist and poet Charles Lamb (1775–1834) was afflicted with a severe stutter.

153 *George Egerton and Justin Huntly M'Carthy and Gissing*: 'George Egerton' was the pen-name of the short-story writer Mary Chavelita Dunne (1859–1945). Wells probably had in mind her story 'A Psychological Moment: The Woman' in *Discords* (1894). Justin McCarthy (1830–1912) was an Irish journalist, novelist, historian, and politician. See ch. 1 of his *A London Legend* (1895). The novels of George Gissing (1875–1903) were much admired by Wells, and he was to befriend their author fifteen months after first publication of the present story. See Gissing's *New Grub Street* (1891), ch. 7.

Barnaby . . . made me . . . Dramatic Critic: Wells is drawing on his own experiences as a drama critic for the *Pall Mall Gazette* during the first half of 1895. See *EA* ch. 8.2, and Patrick Parrinder and Robert M. Philmus (eds.), *H. G. Wells's Literary Criticism* (Brighton: Harvester, and Totowa, NJ: Barnes & Noble, 1980), 19–47. The name Delia was probably suggested by the melodrama *Delia Harding* by J. W. Comyns Carr, which Wells reviewed on 18 April 1895. His review is especially critical of the style of acting employed, which he condemns in much the same terms as Craddock uses here.

Opera Comique . . . Surrey . . . Frivolity: the Opera Comique, in the East Strand, where Gilbert and Sullivan's first opera was staged, opened in 1870 and closed in 1899. The Surrey, in Blackfriars Road, had been in irregular use as a theatre from 1809. In Wells's day it was famed for sensational dramas and pantomimes. The building was later used for cinema and opera, and was demolished in 1934. 'Frivolity' may be Wells's humorous name for the Gaiety Theatre, in the Strand, which was a successful home for burlesque and musical comedy from 1868 to 1902.

155 *pari passu*: together.

156 *cheval glass*: a large mirror on a frame.

157 *Irving*: Sir Henry Irving (1838–1905) was the first actor to be knighted, in the year in which this story was first published. He was especially celebrated for his portrayal of Shakespearean villains.

159 *'Good-baye!'*: the affected pronunciation recalls George Alexander's performance in Henry James's play *Guy Domville*, a

theatrical disaster reviewed by Wells on 7 January 1895. See *EA* ch. 8.2.

160 *King John's abbot in his cope of lead*: according to the monk Roger of Wendover, in 1209 King John, as part of his dispute with the Church, had Geoffrey the Archdeacon of Norwich starved, imprisoned in chains, and crushed to death under a cope of lead. The story is completely untrue. Geoffrey survived to become Bishop of Ely in 1225.

'*to hold the mirror up to Nature*': cf. Shakespeare, *Hamlet*, III. ii.

THE PLATTNER STORY

First published in the *New Review* (April 1896); first collected in *The Plattner Story, and Others*; included in *Thirty Strange Stories* and in vol. 1 of the Atlantic Edition.

161 *Eusapia's patrons!*: it has been impossible to trace this reference. One suggestion is that Wells had in mind Eusebia, wife of the Roman emperor Constantius II.

163 *the Nordau standpoint*: *Degeneration*, Max Nordau's polemic on late nineteenth-century European culture (translated into English in 1895), criticizes the unhealthy, decadent mentality of the so-called *fin de siècle* era. Its relevance to Wells's own themes and subject-matter is discussed by Bernard Bergonzi in *The Early H. G. Wells* (Manchester: Manchester University Press, and Toronto: Toronto University Press, 1961), esp. 1–16.

164 *the Three Gases*: hydrogen, oxygen, and nitrogen.

166 *temerarious*: reckless, rash.

mumchance: fool. 'Mumchance' was an old card or dice game, played in silence.

167 *left not a wrack behind*: cf. Shakespeare, *The Tempest*, IV. i, though proverbial usage has changed Shakespeare's original 'rack' (wisp of cloud) to 'wrack' (piece of wreckage).

173 *Euclid riders*: propositions in the study of geometry, which pupils are required to deduce from previous propositions.

crib: a set of notes or answers.

177 *devil's dyke*: the Devil's Dyke is a V-shaped cleft in the South Downs, a chalk escarpment running along much of the south coast of England. Legend has it that, wishing to prevent the spread of Christianity through England, the Devil decided to flood this part of Sussex by digging a trench to the English Channel. When an

inquisitive local woman held up a candle, the Devil, mistaking the light for the rising sun, abandoned his digging and fled back to hell.

THE RED ROOM

First published in the *Idler* (March 1896); limited edition of twelve copies issued for copyright purposes in pamphlet form in the USA by Stone & Kimball, Chicago, in 1896; first collected in *The Plattner Story, and Others*; included in *Thirty Strange Stories* and in vol. 10 of the Atlantic Edition.

186 *Ganymede and Eagle*: the sculpture represents the abduction by an eagle of the Trojan youth Ganymede, whom Zeus wished to have for his cupbearer.

a buhl table: one that was decorated with inlays made from metal and tortoiseshell.

187 *apoplexy*: a haemorrhage or a clot in the brain.

188 *Ingoldsby*: the *Ingoldsby Legends* are humorous, mock-medieval ballads, written by R. H. Barham (1788–1845).

THE PURPLE PILEUS

First published in the *Black and White* (Christmas 1896); first collected in *The Plattner Story, and Others*; included in *Thirty Strange Stories* and in vol. 1 of the Atlantic Edition.

193 *dear, dead days beyond recall*: from the opening line of the popular song 'Love's Old Sweet Song', written by C. Clifford Bingham in 1882.

194 *flounces*: strips hanging from the skirt of a dress.

195 *drab*: thick, grey cloth.

connection: reputation with respectable society.

196 *Self-Help*: see note to p. 7.

Mephistopheles: the devil who, in legend, tempted Faust to go beyond the proper limits of human knowledge and action.

197 *pileus*: the cap of a mushroom or toadstool.

200 *slavey*: a domestic drudge, or maid-of-all-work.

201 *agaric*: a large family of fungi. Fly agaric is a poisonous, mushroom-like fungus, used by some to kill flies, but valued by others for its hallucinogenic properties.

203 *Good Templar*: a member of a temperance society modelled on the Freemasons.

divers: diverse, various.

204 *caravansery*: a caravanserai is a kind of inn or yard used as a stopping-place by desert caravans.

A SLIP UNDER THE MICROSCOPE

First published in *The Yellow Book* (January 1896); first collected in *The Plattner Story, and Others*; included in *Thirty Strange Stories* and in vol. 6 of the Atlantic Edition.

206 *the rocker microtome*: an instrument for cutting thin slices from plants, so that they may be examined under the microscope.

News from Nowhere: a Utopian romance by William Morris, published in 1890. The narrator wakes in the twenty-first century to find that England has become a pastoral communist society, without the heavy industries and social classes of the present.

the Oratory clock: the clock of Brompton Oratory, headquarters of the Roman Catholic Church in London, located in Brompton Road, close to the Royal College of Science.

207 *the Scotch universities*: university places were available for a greater proportion of the population in Scotland than in England.

holland: a coarse linen fabric.

208 *'From ovum to ovum is the goal of the higher vertebrata'*: i.e. from the biological point of view, individuals, including human beings, exist only to ensure the survival of the species by reproducing themselves.

211 *Landport*: a residential area of Portsmouth, on the English south coast.

blue paper: a form circulated to candidates who had done especially well in the science examinations of the Education Department, offering them scholarships to be 'teachers in training'. In 1884 such a blue form had brought Wells himself to the College of Science, known then as the Normal School of Science and Royal School of Mines.

the island of Portsea: a fortified island between Portsmouth and Langston harbours.

the seventh standard of the Board school: the 1870 Education Act set up local School Boards to bring elementary education to working-class children. In 1882, because some pupils were rising through the six standards of achievement faster and staying on at school longer than anticipated, a higher, seventh standard was added to the original six.

212 *attic visitors*: Hill lives in a cheap small room at the top of the building.

Carlyle: Thomas Carlyle (1795–1881), widely influential historian, philosopher, essayist, and social critic of the Victorian period.

mesoblastic somites: middle layers of body segments.

the blastopore: the orifice of an embryo at an early stage of its development.

a paying student: a student able to pay her own fees, as opposed to a 'paid student' like Hill, who receives a grant from the Education Department.

alisphenoid: a type of bone found in the skull of a vertebrate.

213 *Browning*: Robert Browning (1812–89), one of the major poets of the Victorian era.

214 *Longfellow . . . Tennyson . . . Shakespeare . . . Pope . . . Shelley . . . Eliza Cook and Mrs Hemans*: while many poems by Longfellow, Tennyson, Shakespeare, Pope, and Shelley are read and studied with pleasure to this day, the once-popular verses of Eliza Cook (1818–89) and Felicia Hemans (1793–1835) have shown less staying power. Some phrases from the latter ('the stately homes of England', 'the boy stood on the burning deck') have passed into ironic proverbial usage.

215 *'mugger'*: one who studies excessively, a 'swot'.

216 *Kew*: Bindon works most of the year at the Royal Botanic Gardens there.

217 *personalities*: derogatory remarks about particular people.

Bernard Shaw . . . William Morris . . . Walter Crane: well-known proponents of socialism. For Bernard Shaw see note to p. 152. William Morris (1834–96) was famous as an author of poetry and fiction, and as a highly influential designer, founder of the Morris & Co. design house and the Kelmscott Press. Morris's friend Walter Crane (1845–1915) was also an artist and designer, best remembered today for his illustrations for children's books. Wells first encountered Shaw and Morris when as a student he attended socialist meetings at the latter's house in Hammersmith. See *EA* ch. 5.4, where Wells criticizes these socialist 'poets and decorators' for their ignorance of 'scientific philosophy'. *EA* ch. 5 as a whole, an account of Wells's student days, supplies the autobiographical background to 'A Slip under the Microscope'.

218 *finger-bowl shibboleths*: judgements of social acceptability based on the skill with which fingers are washed when a finger-bowl is provided at the meal table, following the biblical use of the test-word 'shibboleth' (Judges 12).

epigrammatic cities of refuge: challenged in debate, such people would escape by using a witty saying to close the subject, as accidental murderers in biblical times could escape punishment by taking refuge in special cities designated by Jewish law.

cab-runner: someone employed to call cabs for passengers.

Ruskin and contemporary fiction: John Ruskin (1819–1900) was of enormous influence on Victorian thought, both as an art critic and as a social thinker. For his view on the role of women see *Sesame and Lilies* (1865), lecture 2, 'Of Queen's Gardens'.

aërated bread shop: the Aerated Bread Company's chain of inexpensive restaurants flourished in London from 1861 onwards.

219 *Bradlaugh and John Burns*: the radical journalist and politician Charles Bradlaugh (1833–91), advocate of birth control and atheism, was denied his seat in Parliament for over five years because he refused to take the customary religious oath. The socialist John Burns (1858–1943), an important figure in the London dock strike of 1889, was elected to Parliament in 1892.

a Hindoo god: an idol representing one of the many forms of God recognized by Hindus.

220 *staining re-agents*: substances with characteristic reactions used in chemical tests.

the Q. Jour. Mi. Sci.: the *Quarterly Journal of Mining Science*.

lenticel: a breathing-pore in bark.

222 *chop-house*: a restaurant specializing in mutton chop and beefsteak.

threepenny or ninepenny classics: cheap editions of famous works of literature.

strap and tongue: parts of shoes used by the cobbler as convenient implements with which to beat his son.

223 *liberal churchmen*: clergymen who remain in the Church although they cannot believe literally such doctrines as miracles and the resurrection.

225 *The Meistersingers*: *Die Meistersinger von Nürnberg*, an opera by Richard Wagner, first performed in 1868.

THE CRYSTAL EGG

First published in the *New Review* (May 1897); first collected in *Tales of Space and Time*; included in vol. 10 of the Atlantic Edition.

227 *Seven Dials*: an area of London between Shaftesbury Avenue and Covent Garden, named after a star-shaped road junction from which streets diverge in seven directions.

230 *so forth*: the alcoholic nature of the 'so forth' presumably accounts for Mrs Cave's headache and sleepiness the following day.

231 *bedabbled affidavit*: an affidavit is a declaration written under oath. Mr Cave's declaration is a verbal one, and he makes it in a sweat.

235 *pathetic*: tear-jerking; designed to arouse feelings of sorrow.

239 *holland*: see note to p. 207.

buff: light yellow, the colour of buffalo hide.

diurnal: daytime.

prehensile: capable of grasping.

240 *greensward*: grassy turf.

242 *St Martin's Church*: overlooking Trafalgar Square.

243 *Highgate*: i.e. Highgate Cemetery.

obsequies: funeral rites.

244 *Daily Chronicle and Nature*: the *Daily Chronicle* was a Liberal newspaper. *Nature* was and is one of the world's foremost scientific journals. From 1894 to 1939 it was edited by Wells's friend R. A. Gregory.

THE STAR

First published in the *Graphic* (Christmas 1897); first collected in *Tales of Space and Time*; included in *The Door in the Wall, and Other Stories* and in vol. 10 of the Atlantic Edition.

246 *outermost of all the planets*: it was not until 1930, thirty-three years after this story was first published, that an even more remote planet was discovered and given the name Pluto. Owing to its eccentric orbit there are times, such as the last two decades of the twentieth century, when Pluto is actually nearer to the sun than Neptune and the latter may still therefore be called the outermost planet.

Ogilvy: an astronomer of the same name appears in Wells's parallel story of cosmic destruction, *The War of the Worlds*, only to be incinerated by the Martians' heat-ray.

planetoids: the asteroids, to give them their more usual name, are small rocky bodies orbiting the sun in a belt between the orbits of Mars and Jupiter.

247 *quickening*: awakening.

248 *Boers . . . Hottentots*: inhabitants of southern Africa. The Boers, farmers of Dutch descent, have become today's Afrikaners. The separate identity of the Hottentots, a nomadic branch of the Khoisan people, has been severely eroded.

Gold Coast: a British colony in West Africa. Since 1957 it has been the independent nation of Ghana.

spectroscope: an instrument used to analyse light wavelengths.

far greater than our earth: Neptune is 17.2 times as massive as Earth, with a diameter of 48,600 km. to Earth's 12,756 km.

249 *compositors*: printers, making up newspapers by manually assembling the lettering or 'type'.

'Centrifugal, centripetal': a centripetal force is one which causes a moving body to travel in a curved path—here the gravitational pull of the sun. The centrifugal force is another name for the body's own inertia which, balancing the centripetal force, allows it to remain in a stable orbit.

250 *hectic*: flushed, feverish.

251 *refractive*: light-deflecting.

253 *the year 1000*: there was a widespread view in Europe, founded on Revelation 20, that the year 1000 might bring with it the end of the world.

the midnight zenith: the part of the sky directly overhead at midnight.

254 *Cotopaxi*: the world's highest active volcano, in Ecuador.

THE MAN WHO COULD WORK MIRACLES

First published in the *Illustrated London News* (July 1898); first collected in *Tales of Space and Time*; included in vol. 10 of the Atlantic Edition. A cinema adaptation by Wells was published by the Cresset Press, London, in 1936; the film was released by London Films the following year.

259 *pantoum*: a verse form of Malayan origin, in which the opening and the concluding rhyme are identical.

Torres Vedras tactics: the Duke of Wellington constructed a famous and successful defence system near this Portuguese town during the Peninsular War.

263 *shoppy*: slightly stale.

264 *studs*: i.e. shirt studs: double-headed buttons used to fasten shirt-sleeves at the wrist.

Moses' rod: in the biblical miracle it was actually Aaron who, at Moses' instruction, cast his rod down before Pharaoh, whereupon it turned into a serpent (Exodus 7).

'Tannhäuser': in the German ballad, made into an opera by Richard Wagner in 1845, the Pope tells the wandering singer Tannhäuser that he can no more expect God to forgive his sins than he can expect the papal sceptre to bring forth leaves. By the time the papal staff bursts into blossom three days later, Tannhäuser has already left Rome in despair.

Philharmonic: a society for the promotion of music.

Poona-Penang lawyer: a kind of walking-stick, made from the stem of a dwarf palm native to Penang and Singapore.

266 *manse*: residence of a church minister.

267 *Rhodian arch*: resembling the shadow which must have been cast by the Colossus of Rhodes, a gigantic statue of the sun-god Helios which stood by the harbour of this Greek island from about 280 to 230 BC. The statue, one of the Seven Wonders of the World, was destroyed by an earthquake.

thaumaturgist: miracle-worker.

269 *Mahomet . . . Yogi . . . Madame Blavatsky*: miraculous deeds have always been attributed to religious leaders, whether great (Muhammad, *c*.570–632, founder of Islam) or small (Helena Blavatsky, 1831–91, whose claims to supernatural powers were discredited by scientific investigation in the 1880s and 1890s). A yogi is a Hindu ascetic who withdraws from the world of the senses by mental and physical discipline. It is unclear which yogi in particular Wells has in mind.

the Duke of Argyll: the reference suggests that one of the Dukes of Argyll had published arguments defending the possibility of miracles or spiritualism, but at the time of writing this suggestion has not been confirmed.

270 *the black art*: magic derived from devil-worship.

Congregational: the Congregational Church, a Protestant sect which believed that each congregation should run its own affairs

independent of external authority, is now part of the United Reformed Church.

Sunday, Nov. 10, 1896: in his article 'A Theory of Errors: The
Altered Worlds of Fiction' (*Foundation*, 36 (summer 1986), 45–57)
David Lake has pointed out that 10 Nov. 1896 was actually a
Tuesday and has speculated that this might be a deliberate mistake
by Wells.

271 *Theosophists*: members of the Theosophical Society, a mystical
group founded by Madame Blavatsky and others in 1875.

272 *Welsh rarebit*: melted cheese (sometimes with ale) poured over
hot toast.

273 *post-prandial*: after dinner (usually, dinner with alcohol).

274 *'Joshua!'*: another reference to a biblical miracle. In order to allow
more time for the Israelites to massacre the Amorites, their leader
Joshua ordered the sun and moon to stand still (Joshua 10).

275 *leeward*: the direction towards which the wind is blowing.

276 *about nine miles per second*: David Lake (see note to p. 270) offers
nine miles per minute as closer to the actual figure, which he
calculates to be 10.882 miles per minute.

windward: the direction from which the wind blows.

A VISION OF JUDGMENT

First published in the *Butterfly* (September 1899); first collected in
The Country of the Blind, and Other Stories; included in vol. 10 of the
Atlantic Edition.

279 *the Last Trump*: cf. 1 Corinthians 15: 52.

Azrael . . . Michael: Azrael is the Angel of Death in Jewish and
Islamic mythology. The archangel Michael leads the fight against
the devil in Revelation 12: 7, and in Milton's *Paradise Lost*, Book
VI.

280 *Darwin*: Charles Darwin's theory of evolution, first put forward in
1859 in his *Origin of Species by Means of Natural Selection*, flatly
contradicted the biblical account of Creation. The resulting
controversy—in which the dean of Wells's college, T. H. Huxley,
had been a prominent spokesman for Darwinism—discredited
traditional religious belief and greatly undermined the authority of
the Church.

printers' overs: additional printing costs to allow for wastage.

280 *Henry the Eighth*: having taken England out of the Catholic Church, destroyed the nation's monasteries, married six times, and executed all who impeded his policies, including two of his wives and St Thomas More, Henry VIII might well be expected to face some serious questioning from the Lord God.

Paleolithic: belonging to the earliest part of the Stone Age, when *Homo sapiens* first appeared as a separate species.

282 *Milton's Satan*: see especially Book I of *Paradise Lost*, where Satan rallies his followers after their expulsion from Heaven.

Obelisk: a tapering, rectangular pillar of stone, often used as a monument.

285 *Sirius*: the brightest star in the skies of Earth.

JIMMY GOGGLES THE GOD

First published in the USA in *Cosmopolitan* (November 1898), then in Britain in the *Graphic* (Christmas 1898); first collected in *Twelve Stories and a Dream*; included in vol. 10 of the Atlantic Edition.

286 *put the kybosh on*: suppressed.

whist: a game which begins with the dealing of fifty-two cards.

287 *jolly-boat*: ship's boat.

brig: a two-masted sailing-vessel.

288 *mackintosheriness*: the smell of waterproof 'mackintosh' cloth.

sounding: lowering a line over the side to measure the depth of the water.

amby-theatre: mispronunciation of 'amphitheatre'.

289 *gunwale*: the upper edge of a ship's side, next to the bulwarks.

greenhorn: novice.

290 *forecastle*: the forward part of a ship, often in the form of a raised deck.

companion: way of access from the deck to the interior of the ship.

292 *blue funk*: great terror.

293 *a turned turtle*: once overturned, a turtle may be unable to right itself.

294 *tomtit*: name used for any small active bird, such as the blue tit.

a jobbing plumber: then as now, a plumber available for hire was greatly valued in emergencies, but subject to suspicion regarding workmanship and charges.

295 *joss*: an idol.

296 *wattle*: plaited twigs used as building material.

297 *pourra*: possibly a variant of 'puraka', a variety of the taro plant, widely cultivated in the Pacific for its edible rootstock.

lingo: foreign language.

like one o'clock: like a factory siren signalling lunch-time.

298 *Guy*: someone easily made a fool of or 'guyed'.

stocks and stones: cf. Milton's sonnet 'On the Late Massacre in Piedmont'.

Exeter Hall: a non-sectarian meeting place, in the Strand, London, originally used by a range of religious and philanthropic organizations. Since 1880 it had been in the possession of the Young Men's Christian Association.

sandy: with yellowish-red hair.

pith helmet: headgear designed to protect the wearer from the sun's rays and made of the inner tissue of the sola or 'hat plant'.

scissors: earlier texts refer to the trade in 'calico'. Perhaps by 1911 missionaries had found that manufactured goods were more attractive to their native audience.

299 *Banya*: possibly a misprint for Banka, an island off the south-east coast of Sumatra. But as is often the case when Wells uses exotic settings, many of the place-names in this story are either highly obscure or fictitious.

cut up rusty: became resentful and angry.

MISS WINCHELSEA'S HEART

First published in *Queen* (October 1898); first collected in *Twelve Stories and a Dream*; included in vol. 6 of the Atlantic Edition, in the preface to which Wells says that the story 'came into my head to tell my friend George Gissing on the Pincio one spring morning in 1898' during an Italian holiday.

300 *Horace and Benvenuto Cellini and Raphael and Shelley and Keats*: the classical poet Horace, the Renaissance artists Cellini and Raphael, and the expatriate English Romantic poets Shelley and Keats are a disparate group, suggesting an undiscriminatingly geographical basis to Miss Winchelsea's enthusiasm.

Shelley's widow: after Shelley had drowned in the Bay of Spezia, his body was cremated and his heart buried in the Protestant

Cemetery at Rome. His widow Mary, who edited the first author-itative edition of his poems, is best remembered today for her Gothic novel *Frankenstein* (1818), a forerunner of Wells's own science fiction.

Baedeker: the series of guidebooks produced by the German pub-lisher Baedeker was internationally famous, though sometimes regarded patronizingly owing to the facility with which it condensed cultural information into the space of a few lines.

301 *Mr Thomas Gunn's parties*: an allusion to the famous British travel agency Thomas Cook's, the first to organize such conducted excursions.

pepper-and-salt: mingled black and white.

302 *hostler*: more usually 'ostler': one who looks after horses at an inn.

Gladstone bag: a type of travelling-bag.

303 *Hare's Walks in Rome*: Augustus Hare's guide, originally published in 1871, was frequently reprinted and revised.

Chislehurst: exiled from France after the revolution of 1870, Empress Eugénie lived until 1881 in exile at Camden Place, Chislehurst, to the south-east of London.

pince-nez: a pair of spectacles with a spring for gripping the nose.

304 *Albion*: an ancient, poetical name for England, thought to derive from *albus*, Latin for 'white', and to refer to the white cliffs which face the Continent. The lines quoted from Shakespeare were prob-ably part of John of Gaunt's famous patriotic speech in Act II of *Richard II*.

306 *Soracte*: a mountain about twenty-five miles north of Rome. Horace's description of its appearance in winter comes at the beginning of Book 1, Ode 9.

matriculation: entrance examination of a university or college.

extension lecturer: one who lectures to those who are not full-time resident students.

Mr Ruskin's Florence: a reference to John Ruskin's *Mornings in Florence: Being Simple Studies of Christian Art for English Trav-ellers* (1875–7).

the Pitti Gallery: the left wing of the Pitti Palace contains on its upper floor around 500 masterpieces from the Medici collection.

307 *staccato*: musical term to describe notes played with distinct sep-aration. Fanny's 'admiration' takes the form of single exclamations, rather than the more elaborate, fluent response sought by Miss Winchelsea.

Tivoli: the Villa d'Este in Tivoli contains one of the great water-gardens of Europe, comprising more than 500 fountains.

308 *Bibulus . . . Balbus*: Bibulus, a colleague of Julius Caesar, was proverbial as a mere cipher in office. Balbus, another associate of Caesar's, was known to students of Latin from the sentence 'Balbus jumped over the wall', which many of them had to translate.

'70 buildings: buildings erected after Rome became the capital of modern Italy in 1870.

309 *Shelley's Beatrice Cenci!—in the Barberini Gallery*: Beatrice Cenci was executed in 1599 for helping to plot the murder of her own father. The famous portrait, sometimes attributed to Guido Reni, inspired Shelley's sympathetic portrayal of her in his tragedy *The Cenci* (1819).

the Palatine: one of the original seven hills of Rome, the place of residence of many famous Romans.

310 *autotypes*: photographic reproductions.

Rossetti and Burne Jones: the painter and poet D. G. Rossetti and the painter and designer Edward Burne-Jones were members of the influential group of Victorian artists, the Pre-Raphaelite Brotherhood. For their successor William Morris, see note to p. 217.

the Pincio: a terrace with public gardens, offering a panoramic view of Rome.

muro Torto: a fragment of Roman wall never rebuilt because it was believed to be defended by the Apostle Peter.

311 *badge sinister*: threatening sign—an image from heraldry.

312 *the Borghese*: it is unclear whether the reference is to the Villa Borghese, the most magnificent of Rome's parks, or the Palazzo Borghese.

316 *impositions ruled high*: many punishment-tasks were given.

317 *George Meredith*: the best-known book of verse by George Meredith, *Modern Love* (1862), depicts a disintegrating marriage. The husband takes a mistress; the wife subsequently dies.

enamelling: painting.

318 *octave*: the first eight of the fourteen lines which make up a sonnet.

A DREAM OF ARMAGEDDON

First published in *Black and White Budget* (May–June 1901); first collected in *Twelve Stories and a Dream*; included in *The Door in the Wall, and Other Stories* and in vol. 3 of the Atlantic Edition.

320 *Armageddon*: the great war between the forces of good and evil which will herald the end of the world—from Revelation 16: 16.

328 *Aurora*: coloured streamers of light in the polar skies, caused by solar particles charging the atoms in the upper atmosphere.

329 *Gresham*: this name is used in the present version of the story and in the Atlantic Edition. All other versions have 'Evesham'. Presumably Wells changed the name in 1911 in order to avoid confusion with another Evesham, a character (based on the Conservative Prime Minister Arthur Balfour) whom he had recently introduced in *The New Machiavelli* and who was to reappear in several later novels.

335 *ironclads*: ships with iron-plated hulls.

339 *the firing of a magazine*: the ignition of a store of arms and explosives.

342 *the peninsula*: i.e. Italy.

343 *impressed*: forcibly conscripted.

THE VALLEY OF SPIDERS

First published in *Pearson's Magazine* (March 1903); first collected in *Twelve Stories and a Dream*; included in vol. 10 of the Atlantic Edition.

350 *'Come up!'*: an expression used by a rider to urge on a horse.

353 *no foam*: a foaming muzzle would have indicated that the dog was rabid.

355 *comes about*: turns around, especially into a more favourable wind.

358 *lee*: shelter.

359 *spavined*: afflicted with a hard swelling on the inside of a hind-leg joint.

360 *reliquary*: a locket containing some religious relic.

THE NEW ACCELERATOR

First published in the *Strand Magazine* (December 1901); first collected in *Twelve Stories and a Dream*; included in vol. 10 of the Atlantic Edition.

362 *Folkestone*: Wells lived in Sandgate, near Folkestone, from 1898 to 1909. From 1900 his home was Spade House, built to his own specifications and, like Professor Gibberne's residence, located on the Upper Sandgate Road.

Mephistophelian: see note to p. 196.

363 *the ganglion cell and the axis fibre*: a ganglion is a collection of nerve-cells. The axis fibre, or axon, is the part of the cell body through which the nerve signal is transmitted.

the solar plexus: a network of nerves behind the stomach.

366 *char-à-banc*: an open coach for tourists, equipped with transverse rows of seats.

368 *Harley Street*: this London street has been renowned for its medical specialists since the middle of the nineteenth century.

rum: odd, peculiar.

retina: see note to p. 74.

369 *'gas'*: an anaesthetic, such as chloroform.

371 *capelline*: a light woollen hood, usually for evening wear.

372 *bath-chairs*: large-wheeled chairs for the disabled.

373 *we should . . . have burst into flames*: according to David Lake ('A Theory of Errors: The Altered Worlds of Fiction', *Foundation*, 36 (summer 1986), 45–57), the accelerated pair would not have survived long enough to ignite, since the human body could not endure the stress involved, and in any case the speed at which they were moving would have been sufficient to overcome gravity and hurl them into the stratosphere. The trajectory of the dog, too, follows the requirements of fiction rather than those of physics.

376 *that Time Garment of which Carlyle speaks*: cf. Carlyle's *Sartor Resartus*, bk. III, ch. 8.

THE TRUTH ABOUT PYECRAFT

First published in the *Strand Magazine* (April 1903); first collected in *Twelve Stories and a Dream*; included in vol. 10 of the Atlantic Edition.

378 *embedded*: i.e. in fat.

the truth, the whole truth, and nothing but the truth: from the oath taken by witnesses in English courts of law.

379 *'A priori'*: reasoning from general principles.

382 *Jamrach's*: see note to p. 54.

pariah dog: an ownerless stray dog, named from the lowest caste in southern Indian society.

383 *Trappistine*: a liqueur.

385 *apoplectic-looking*: see note to p. 187.

386 *Santos-Dumont*: Alberto Santos-Dumont was a pioneer aviator from Brazil. In 1901 he made a thirty-minute flight over France in an airship.

389 *niente, nefas*: 'nothing, monstrous' (Italian, Latin).

THE MAGIC SHOP

First published in the *Strand Magazine* (June 1903); first collected in *Twelve Stories and a Dream*; included in vol. 10 of the Atlantic Edition.

390 *Gip*: Wells's son, George Philip Wells (1901–85), grew up to be a marine biologist and, from 1954, Professor of Zoology at the University of London. In 1931 he collaborated with his father and Julian Huxley on their outline of biology, *The Science of Life*. After his father's death, G. P. Wells revised his *Short History of the World* in collaboration with Raymond Postgate, and edited for publication the memoir *H. G. Wells in Love*.

Regent Street . . . Oxford Street . . . Holborn: in 1903 the famous toy-shop Hamley's had branches in Regent Street, New Oxford Street, and High Holborn.

391 *Jessie*: possibly the wife of the novelist Joseph Conrad. Both families lived in Kent, and they were in contact at this time.

393 *over-sapid*: too heavily flavoured.

395 *whited sepulchres——*: cf. Matthew 23: 27.

rum: see note to p. 52.

panoplies: suits of armour.

398 *puss-in-the-corner*: a children's game in which one who is 'out' tries to catch one of the others.

400 *'Ansoms'*: a hansom was a two-wheeled, horse-drawn cab with a raised seat behind for the driver.

coram publico: in the presence of the public (Latin).

THE EMPIRE OF THE ANTS

First published in the *Strand Magazine* (December 1905); first collected in *The Country of the Blind, and Other Stories*; included in vol. 10 of the Atlantic Edition.

402 *Benjamin Constant*: the French politician and novelist gave his name to a Brazilian city, after which the boat is presumably named. Rather confusingly, this city is now called Remate de Males, while a town formerly known as Esperance has become Benjamin Constant.

Creole: a person born in Brazil, but of pure-blooded European descent.

Zambo: a person of mixed Negro and native descent.

404 *demi-john*: a large glass bottle encased in wickerwork.

406 *snags*: hidden obstacles in the river, such as embedded trees.

407 *monitor*: a low iron-clad vessel with revolving gun-turrets.

408 *casa*: building (Spanish).

409 *shipped sweeps*: long oars, fixed into position.

412 *mulatto*: a person born to one parent of black origin and one of European origin.

418 *British Guiana*: since 1966 the independent Republic of Guyana.

THE DOOR IN THE WALL

First published in the *Daily Chronicle* (July 1906); first collected in *The Country of the Blind, and Other Stories*; included in *The Door in the Wall, and Other Stories* and in vol. 10 of the Atlantic Edition.

420 *napery*: table linen.

425 *paroquets*: parakeets.

429 *North-West Passage*: Wallace's game is named after the quest for a short polar route from western Europe to Asia which was pursued by explorers between the sixteenth and eighteenth centuries.

431 *impositions*: see note to p. 316.

432 *wool-gathering*: day-dreaming.

433 *hansom*: see note to p. 400.

bulldog: a short pipe made of briar wood.

434 *like counting Stonehenge*: there is a superstition that the stones making up a prehistoric circle cannot be counted accurately.

435 *snatch division*: a sudden taking of a vote in the British House of Commons.

unpaired: Members of Parliament who are not going to be present when a vote is taken are, if possible, 'paired' with others who would have voted the opposite way.

whip: a Member who helps to organize his party's votes in Parliament.

436 *Gurker*: if Wallace was one of the 399 Liberal Members of Parliament elected in the 'landslide' victory of February 1906, 'Gurker' must stand for the Prime Minister Sir Henry Campbell-Bannerman.

436 *opera hat*: a tall collapsible hat.

438 *gangers*: foremen.

THE COUNTRY OF THE BLIND

First published in the *Strand Magazine* (April 1904); first collected in *The Country of the Blind, and Other Stories*; included in *The Door in the Wall, and Other Stories* and in vol. 10 of the Atlantic Edition. (For the revised version of 1939, see Appendix 2.)

439 *Cordilleras*: a chain of mountains.

442 *the war*: i.e. the Boer War (1899–1902).

444 *alp*: mountain pasture.

   talus: a sloping mass of debris at the foot of a cliff, also known as a scree.

445 *parti-coloured*: in patches of various colours.

   drab: see note to p. 148.

447 '*In the Country of the Blind the One-eyed Man is King*': the proverb dates back at least to the sixteenth century. In his poem 'Why Come Ye nat to Courte?' (1522) John Skelton writes,

> 'But have ye nat harde this,
> How an one-eyed man is
> Well-syghted when
> He is amonge blynde men?'

454 *complacent*: obliging.

THE BEAUTIFUL SUIT

First published as 'A Moonlight Fable' in *Collier's Weekly* (April 1909) and included as such in *The Door in the Wall, and Other Stories*; first collected in *The Country of the Blind, and Other Stories*; also included in vol. 10 of the Atlantic Edition.

THE WORLD'S CLASSICS

A Select List

HANS ANDERSEN: Fairy Tales
Translated by L. W. Kingsland
Introduction by Naomi Lewis
Illustrated by Vilhelm Pedersen and Lorenz Frølich

JANE AUSTEN: Emma
Edited by James Kinsley and David Lodge

Mansfield Park
Edited by James Kinsley and John Lucas

J. M. BARRIE: Peter Pan in Kensington Gardens & Peter and Wendy
Edited by Peter Hollindale

WILLIAM BECKFORD: Vathek
Edited by Roger Lonsdale

CHARLOTTE BRONTË: Jane Eyre
Edited by Margaret Smith

THOMAS CARLYLE: The French Revolution
Edited by K. J. Fielding and David Sorensen

LEWIS CARROLL: Alice's Adventures in Wonderland
and Through the Looking Glass
Edited by Roger Lancelyn Green
Illustrated by John Tenniel

MIGUEL DE CERVANTES: Don Quixote
Translated by Charles Jarvis
Edited by E. C. Riley

GEOFFREY CHAUCER: The Canterbury Tales
Translated by David Wright

ANTON CHEKHOV: The Russian Master and Other Stories
Translated by Ronald Hingley

JOSEPH CONRAD: Victory
Edited by John Batchelor
Introduction by Tony Tanner

DANTE ALIGHIERI: The Divine Comedy
Translated by C. H. Sisson
Edited by David Higgins

VIRGIL: The Aeneid
Translated by C. Day Lewis
Edited by Jasper Griffin

HORACE WALPOLE : The Castle of Otranto
Edited by W. S. Lewis

IZAAK WALTON and CHARLES COTTON:
The Compleat Angler
Edited by John Buxton
Introduction by John Buchan

OSCAR WILDE: Complete Shorter Fiction
Edited by Isobel Murray

The Picture of Dorian Gray
Edited by Isobel Murray

VIRGINIA WOOLF: Orlando
Edited by Rachel Bowlby

ÉMILE ZOLA:
The Attack on the Mill and other stories
Translated by Douglas Parmée

A complete list of Oxford Paperbacks, including The World's Classics, OPUS, Past Masters, Oxford Authors, Oxford Shakespeare, and Oxford Paperback Reference, is available in the UK from the Arts and Reference Publicity Department (BH), Oxford University Press, Walton Street, Oxford OX2 6DP.

In the USA, complete lists are available from the Paperbacks Marketing Manager, Oxford University Press, 200 Madison Avenue, New York, NY 10016.

Oxford Paperbacks are available from all good bookshops. In case of difficulty, customers in the UK can order direct from Oxford University Press Bookshop, Freepost, 116 High Street, Oxford, OX1 4BR, enclosing full payment. Please add 10 per cent of published price for postage and packing.